The Cartel Deluxe Edition:

Books 1-3

The Cartel Deluxe Edition:

Books 1-3

Ashley & JaQuavis

www.urbanbooks.net

Urban Books, LLC
300 Farmingdale Road, NY-Route 109
Farmingdale, NY 11735

ISBN 13: 978-1-62286-629-8
ISBN 10: 1-62286-629-0

First Trade Paperback Printing February 2018
Printed in the United States of America

10

This is a work of fiction. Any references or similarities to actual events, real people, living or dead, or to real locales are intended to give the novel a sense of reality. Any similarity in other names, characters, places, and incidents is entirely coincidental.

Distributed by Kensington Publishing Corp.
Submit Orders to:
Customer Service
400 Hahn Road
Westminster, MD 21157-4627
Phone: 1-800-733-3000
Fax: 1-800-659-2436

The Cartel Deluxe Edition:

Books 1-3

by

Ashley & JaQuavis

The Cartel

Prologue

"Diamonds are forever." —Carter Diamond

The packed courtroom was abuzz as the anticipation built, and the onlookers stared at the man who made it snow. Carter Diamond was the head of "The Cartel," an infamous crime organization, and the entire city of Miami knew it. Scattered throughout the courtroom, the entire Cartel was in attendance, all of them wearing black attire.

With a model's posture, he sat next to his defense lawyer, slowly rubbing his salt-and-pepper goatee, thinking about the weight of the verdict. Accused of racketeering and using his multimillion-dollar real estate company to launder drug money, Carter could potentially go to jail for the rest of his life. The case had drawn a lot of heat when key witnesses began to come up missing or dead, including a politician who turned informant to save his own behind.

A slight grin spread across Carter's face as he looked at the judge and realized that the chances of a guilty verdict were between slim and next to none. Just the night before, his accountant had wired the judge one million dollars to an offshore account. And just to ensure his freedom, eight of the twelve jurors had family members missing and in the custody of Carter's henchmen. At forty-three years old he was on top of the world. Fuck the mayor, Carter ran the city.

Carter glanced back at his family, his beautiful wife, daughter, and twin sons, who sat in the front row behind him. He winked at them and gave them his perfect smile.

It amazed Carter's family that he could be in the scariest of situations and still manage to make everything seem all right.

He stared into his wife's green eyes and admired her long, flowing, jet-black hair. Baby hair rested perfectly on her edges as her natural mocha skin glowed. Taryn, his wife, was a full-blooded Dominican and could have easily been mistaken for a top model. At age thirty-eight, she was just as beautiful as when she'd met Carter at sixteen.

Carter then glanced over to his daughter, Breeze, the spitting image of her mother and also his baby girl. At age nineteen, she was beautiful, intelligent, and being mixed with Black and Dominican gave her a goddess look. She had long, thick hair with green eyes, which made her every man's desire and every woman's envy. She smiled at her father, letting him know she was there to support him.

Carter looked at his two sons, Mecca and Monroe, AKA Money. They were the two oldest at twenty-one, and although they were twins, they were completely opposite. Mecca was the wilder of the two. He wore long braids and was a shade darker than Money. His body had twenty tattoos on it, including the two on his neck, enhancing his thuggish appearance. He was the more ruthless one. Mecca, wanting so badly to follow in the footsteps of his father and become the next kingpin of Miami, was notorious throughout Dade County for his trigger-happy ways.

Money was the humbler and more reserved of the two.

His Dominican features seemed to shine through more than his twin brother's. His light skin and curly hair made him look more like a pretty boy than a gangster, but his looks were deceiving. Unlike his brother, he wore a neat low-cut and had no tattoos. Focusing more on the money aspect of the game, Money was a born hustler, and if the streets gave out degrees he would've had a doctorate. Although he wasn't as coldhearted as his brother, he wasn't to be underestimated.

It was in their blood to be gangsters. In the early eighties their Dominican grandfather ran the most lucrative drug cartel Miami had ever seen, and their father was his predecessor. Their family was "street royalty" by all means.

The media had a field day with this trial, covering it since day one. CNN news cameras and several other stations had been broadcasting live footage of the spectacle for the last six months.

The sound of the gavel striking the sounding block echoed throughout the packed courtroom when the jurors filed into the courtroom after two hours of deliberation. The time had finally come for the verdict.

"Order in the court!" The judge looked over to the jury pool. "Has the jury come to a verdict?"

All eyes were on the juror as he paused before delivering the verdict, and all of the news cameras were pointed to Carter, trying to capture his reaction to his fate. The courtroom got so silent, you could hear a pin drop.

The head juror stood up with a small piece of paper in his hand. "Yes, Your Honor, we have. We the jury find Carter Diamond not guilty on all charges."

As the courtroom erupted with a mixture of victorious cheers and disappointing sighs, Carter nonchalantly loosened his tie and winked at the judge just before he firmly shook his lawyer's hand.

"Congratulations, Carter," the lawyer said as he gathered his files and placed them into his briefcase, the flashes from the cameras flickering nonstop.

"Thank you." Carter turned around to celebrate with his family.

When Taryn ran to him with open arms, he smoothly spun her around and kissed her passionately as if they were the only two in the room. He looked in her eyes and whispered, "I love you."

"I love you too, Carter Diamond," she replied as she hung from his neck.

Carter focused his attention on his kids. He kissed Breeze on the cheek, and she whispered in his ear, "Diamonds are forever."

"That's right, baby girl." Carter embraced her with one hand and grabbed Mecca's head with the other. He kissed him on top of the head and then did the same to Monroe.

Carter looked at all the reporters and photographers flocking in his direction and said, "Let's get out of here." With his wife and daughter under his arms, and his family around him, he made his way out of the courtroom.

News reporters tried to get a comment from him, but members of The Cartel stopped them before they could get close.

As soon as Carter exited the building, he embraced his right-hand man, Archie Pollard, AKA Polo, who was waiting outside of the courtroom, along with a wave of thugs wearing all black.

Polo leaned close to Carter's ear and whispered, "We did it, baby!"

"No doubt," Carter said. "This city is mine."

Carter stood at the top of the steps, feeling on top of the world. He pulled out a Cuban cigar and lit it, his diamond cufflinks blinging as he gave the world a view of his exclusive accessories. Looking out onto the streets, he noticed that the cops had sealed off the area to maintain traffic control. Everyone in the city was trying to get a glimpse of the "King of Miami."

Money noticed something wasn't right. As he looked at each officer and saw that they all had one thing in common. They all seemed to be of Haitian descent. By the time he realized what was happening, it was too late. One of the fake news reporters pulled out his 9 mm and pointed it at Breeze.

"Noooo!" Money screamed as he tried to warn his sister.

Polo became aware of what was about to happen and shoved the Haitian, causing him to tumble down the stairs before he could let off a shot.

All of a sudden, two dreadlocked Haitians popped out of the oversized dumpster, both with AR-15 assault rifles, and began letting off shots at The Cartel. It was complete pandemonium as shots rang out, hitting innocent bystanders, all in an effort to take out Carter Diamond.

Outnumbered, the members of The Cartel were defenseless. And Carter and his family were moving targets. As everyone scrambled for cover, Carter grabbed his daughter and wife and threw them to the ground, shielding them with his body.

A bullet ripped through Money's arm, and he fell to the ground. Mecca ran to his side, trying to protect his twin brother.

Meanwhile, Polo had pulled out his 9 mm and began to return fire. He had managed to keep the Haitians off long enough for the rest of The Cartel to come and help.

As the two crews traded bullets, many people got caught in the crossfire. The scene was a total bloodbath, with dead bodies sprawled out across the steps of the courthouse.

Carter, totally disregarding his own safety, tried his best to cover his two favorite girls from the raining bullets.

The police officer who had escorted Carter out of the courtroom shot at the Haitians. "Come on! Follow me," he yelled. He looked at Carter and waved his hand, signaling them to follow him.

Carter hated police, but at that moment he was happy to see one. He gathered up Taryn and Breeze and followed the officer back into the courthouse.

"I parked my police car in the back. Come on! They'll be coming in here after you any second now," the cop said as he closed the courthouse door.

"Let's go, y'all," Carter yelled in a panicked voice to his wife and daughter as they followed the policeman down the stairs and into the basement.

Carter thought about his sons outside, but he knew they could hold their own. His main concern was the women. They raced through the court halls and finally made it to the exit. Just as the cop said, he had his squad car parked in the back. Carter felt relieved. They all got in, and he frantically searched his wife's and daughter's body, making sure they were okay. "Are you hit? Are you guys okay?" he asked as he continued to search their bloodstained clothes. He realized that the blood was not from them, but from all the blood flying from the other people.

"No, I'm good, Poppa," Breeze answered, tears flowing down her face, her hands shaking uncontrollably.

"I'm okay," Taryn said.

Carter hugged and kissed them both and thanked God that they were okay. His concern now was for his sons. He looked up at the cop that sat in the front seat and said, "Thanks, bruh. Look, I need you to take them to safety while I go back and—"

Boom!

Before Carter could finish his sentence, the cop put a hollow-tip through his head, his blood and brains instantly splattering all over his wife's and daughter's face as he stared with dead eyes.

In total shock, both of the women yelled, "Noooo!"

The cop pulled off his hat, and his short dreadlocks fell loosely. He pointed the gun at Carter's body and filled him with four more bullets, ensuring that the job was done. The screams of the women didn't seem to bother him as he smiled through the whole process. The man wasn't a cop at all, but a full-blooded Haitian that could pass for a regular joe, his light skin disguising his heritage.

He pointed his gun at Taryn, and she looked directly in his eyes, unafraid of death, while Breeze gripped her father and cried hysterically. The Haitian couldn't bring himself to pull the trigger and hopped out the car.

This was the beginning of a war.

Welcome to The Cartel . . . first of a trilogy.

Chapter One

"Girl, females are going to hate, regardless. That's how you know you're that bitch." —Taryn Diamond

Seven Years Earlier

Carter sat at the head of the table with both of his hands folded into each other. He briefly stared at each of his ten head henchmen in the face as he looked around the table, then to his right-hand man Polo, who sat to his right. As he always did, Carter took his time before speaking. He always chose his words carefully and spoke very slowly with his deep baritone voice. He poured Dom into his oversized wine cup and took a sip.

"Family, today The Cartel has expanded. The days of hand-over-fist pay is over. It's a new day, a new world, a new era. For the last ten years I have flooded the streets of Miami with the finest coke and built a monopoly. I love all of you as if you were my own blood. That's why I'm giving you the opportunity to grow. You can't hustle forever. I've recently acquired a real estate company, and this way we can turn all of this dirty money into clean money. I want all my niggas to eat with me. So, if you want to be a part of this, here is your chance." Carter took another sip and passed the cup to Polo.

Without saying a word, Polo took a sip out of the same cup, signaling his response to Carter's proposition. He passed the cup to the next man, and he did the same. Real niggas did real things, and the cup got passed around the room, and all men drank from the same cup.

Mecca and Money peeked around the corner, listening in on their father's meeting. Although they were only fourteen, they wanted so bad to be a part of The Cartel. They both noticed at an early age how much respect their father received from everyone in the streets. They would get special treatment in school from teachers and students. Some of their friends' parents would go as far as giving them presents and hinting to them to mention it to their father. They loved how real their father was. He would talk to bums on the street as if they were the president of the U.S.A. He treated every man as his equal, as long as they respected him and his family. For lack of better words, Carter was a real nigga, and both of the twins admired him greatly and wanted to be just like him . . . but for different reasons.

Monroe loved the way his father stayed fresh at all times and was a great business and family man. He observed his father's style and immediately idolized him. Carter never wore the same shirt twice and only wore the finest threads. Money also took note of and admired his father's business savvy. Every move he made was a business move, a move that would benefit him in the future.

Mecca, on the other hand, admired his father's street fame. He loved the way the street respected and feared his father. He would hear stories about his father being the man that made it snow, in a city that had never seen a winter season, or cutting off fingers if workers stole. In Mecca's eyes, Scarface didn't have shit on his father.

While other kids were worried about candy and chasing skirts, Mecca was thinking about chasing money and being the next king of Miami.

As they eavesdropped on the conference, they watched as each man took a sip out of the cup.

"Mecca and Money, come in here." Carter calmly grabbed the cup that had rotated back to him.

Since Carter's back was toward them, when he called their name, it surprised them. It was as if he had eyes in the back of his head. They slowly walked into the room. The boys stood nervously next to him, knowing that they got caught spying on him and that their father was very strict when it came to handling business. They eased up when they saw a slight grin form on his face.

Carter passed Money the cup and looked around to make sure their mother wasn't around. "Take a sip of that," he said.

Money looked at the cup as if he was scared to take a sip.

Mecca noticed his brother's uneasiness and grabbed the cup from him. He took a gigantic gulp of the liquor, and a burning sensation rushed down his throat. It took all of his willpower not to spit it out. His face twisted up as he put one hand on his chest, hoping that the burn would go away.

Polo noticed his expression and laughed loudly. "That'll put some hair on ya chest, nephew!" he said in between laughs.

Carter joined him in laughter as he watched his other son take the cup and take a moderate sip. Money's face didn't change its expression. He took the gulp like a man.

Money handed the cup back to his father and stood there with his chest out, as if he was trying to prove that he was a man. Mecca followed suit.

"Why were you two eavesdropping on Poppa?" Carter playfully hit both of his sons in the chest.

Money shrugged his shoulders as if to say, "I don't know."

Mecca looked around the table, seeing nothing but hustlers and killers. He then looked at his father, who sat at the forefront of them, and a smile spread across his face. "Poppa, I want to be just like you. I wanna be a gangster," Mecca said as he stepped in front of his brother.

One of the hustlers at the table chuckled as he looked at Mecca. "Li'l man got hustle in him. That's a gangster in the making right there," the man said.

Carter shot a look at the man that said a thousand words. If looks could kill, the man would've been circled in chalk. "No, my son will never be that. Watch ya mouth, fam," Carter stated firmly as he focused his attention back on Mecca. "Look, sons, you are better than this. This game chose us, we didn't choose the game. You got the game twisted. I do this, so you don't have to," Carter said, as a somber feeling came over him. It hurt his heart to hear Mecca say that he wanted to be a gangster like him.

"Let me show you two something," Carter said before he looked at his henchmen that sat at the long red oak table. "How many of you have lost someone close to you because of this drug game?

Slowly everyone at the table raised their hands, to help Carter prove a point.

"How many of you go to bed with a pistol under your pillow?" Carter asked. "And how many of you want to get out of the game?"

Mecca and Money looked at everyone in the room holding up their hands, and Carter's point was proven.

"Do you two understand, this game . . . is not a game?"

Mecca and Money nodded their heads, understanding the lesson that their father had just sprinkled them with.

"Take another sip of this and head to bed." Carter smiled and handed Money the cup. After the boys took a small sip of the drink, he grabbed both of their heads at the same time and kissed them on top of it. "Don't tell your mother," he whispered to them just before they exited the conference room.

Although Carter had explained to them the cons of the street life, the allure of the game was too powerful, and Mecca and Money wanted in. They just had to wait their turn.

Breeze stood at her balcony, totally astounded by the view, and stared into the stars. Her balcony hovered over their small lake and faced their gigantic backyard. The Diamond residence was immaculate. They had just moved there, and it was a big jump from the dilapidated projects of Dade County. Breeze's twelve-year-old eyes were lost in the stars as her mother stood behind her and brushed her long hair. This was a ritual they did every night, and Taryn used this time to bond with her daughter.

"Breeze, what's wrong, baby? Lately you haven't been saying much," Taryn said as she continued to stroke her daughter's hair.

Breeze took her time before she spoke. Her father had taught her to always think about what to say before saying it. "I just miss back home. I don't like it out here. None of my friends are out here. I hate it in South Beach, Mommy." Breeze's eyes got teary.

"I know it's hard to cope with the sudden change, Breeze, but your father is a very important man, and it wasn't safe for us to stay in Dade. He did what was best for the family,"

Taryn answered, knowing exactly how Breeze felt. She herself had been a daughter of a kingpin, so she knew what it was like to be sheltered because of a father's notoriety.

"I just don't get it. Everybody loved Poppa in the old neighborhood. Why would we have to move?"

When it came to his baby girl, Carter held back nothing. He answered any question she asked him truthfully, wanting to give her the game, so another boy couldn't game her. She knew her father was a drug dealer, but in her eyes he was the greatest man to walk the earth. She saw how he treated her mother with respect at all times. She witnessed him put his family before himself countless times and admired that. She wanted her husband to be just like her daddy.

"I know exactly how you feel. You're too young to understand right now, Breeze. Just be grateful that you have all of this. Most women will go through their whole life and never have the things you already have."

I understand. I know what's going on. I know Daddy is the dopeman. I know more than you think I know. Breeze went into her room and flopped down on her canopy-style bed. Tears rolled down her cheek as she curled up on her pillow. She missed her old home so badly. She just wanted to be a regular around-the-way girl.

Taryn, her white silk Dolce and Gabbana nightgown dragging on the floor as she went to her daughter's side, slowly entered the room and saw that the sudden change really was bothering her only daughter. She sat on the bed and began to rub Breeze's back. "I know exactly how you feel, Breeze. I remember when I was your age and was going through the same dilemma. My father, your grandfather, was an important man also. I had it much worse. It took the murder of your uncle for my father to move out the hood. Your father is just being cautious. If anything ever happened to you or your brothers, our hearts would break. He's just protecting you." Taryn reminisced about her deceased brother, who died when she was only ten. He was only fifteen years old when he was kidnapped and killed while her father was in a drug war.

"I know that we have to live like this, but it's just not fair. I feel like I don't belong here. All the girls at school look at me funny because I'm mixed, and they whisper bad things about me. I try to ignore them, but it still hurts my feelings."

"Girl, females are going to hate, regardless. That's how you know you're *that* bitch." Taryn smiled and squinted her nose.

Breeze couldn't help smiling at her mother's comment. She looked at how beautiful her mother was, and her comment made her look at things differently. *Maybe they do look at me enviously,* she thought.

Before Breeze could say anything in response, Carter cleared his throat, startling them. He looked at how gorgeous the two main women in his life were. He suavely leaned against the doorway with his arms folded. "What are you guys smiling at?" He walked toward them.

"Nothing, baby." Taryn smiled and winked at Breeze. "Just girl stuff."

Carter bent over and kissed Taryn and then kissed Breeze on top of the head.

Taryn knew that Carter had come to tuck Breeze in, as he did every night, and decided to leave them alone. "I'll be in bed," she whispered to him. "Goodnight, baby," she said to Breeze as she tapped her leg. "I love you."

"I love you too, Mommy."

Taryn strolled out of the room, her stilettos clicking against the marble floor as she made her way out. Taryn would never get caught without her heels on. Nightgown and all, she always looked the part, playing her role as the queen of her husband's empire. She was wifey, there was no doubt about that.

Carter stared at his wife as she walked away and then turned his attention back to Breeze. "Hey, baby girl." He sat next to her.

"Hey, Poppa." Breeze sat up and focused on her father.

"How was school today?" Carter asked as he rubbed her hair.

"It was okay, I guess."

"Breeze, you know I know when you're lying. Tell Poppa what's going on."

"I just miss my friends. The people at my school are so funny-acting. I wish we could move back home." Breeze dropped her head.

Carter placed his finger under her chin and slowly raised her head. He looked into his daughter's green eyes and smiled. "Baby girl, don't worry about that. Everything takes time. They will come around eventually. I tell you what"—Carter stood up and smoothly put his hands in his $400 Armani slacks—"Why don't you call up some of your friends and tell them you're having a sleepover. You can invite as many of them as you want. I'll have a limo pick up each girl. Would you like that?"

Breeze's eyes lit up, and she gave him the biggest smile ever. "Yes! Thank you, Poppa," she said as she leapt into her arms.

Carter had promised himself that he wouldn't let outsiders enter his new home, but he had a weak spot for Breeze. She was his only daughter, and he spoiled her more than he did his twin boys.

"What about boys?" Breeze looked at her father. "Can I invite them too?"

His smile quickly turned into a frown as he looked at Breeze like she was insane.

"Gotcha!" she said as she broke out into laughter.

"Baby, don't do that," he said, joining her in laughter. "You almost gave this old man a heart attack." Although Breeze was joking around, he knew that the day when she would be serious was soon to come. A day that he would dread.

Chapter Two

"There is strength in numbers, and we will get through this as a family."
—Polo

Polo took a deep breath as he pulled into the South Beach, one of the many suburbs of Miami. As he looked around at the perfectly landscaped lawns and the children playing carelessly in the streets, he realized why Carter had moved his family so far away from the hood. With its gated community and million-dollar structures, it seemed as if it were a million miles away from the grit of the ghetto. Carter, positive that the upscale environment of South Beach would protect his household from the harsh reality that the street life had to offer, had told him that the move would be good for his family, but he was wrong. Now Polo was forced to bury his man.

Polo and Carter had known each other since they were young and hardheaded coming up in the trenches of Dade County. They quickly formed a brotherly bond as they took over the streets and inevitably entered the drug game. *The Cartel* was what they were labeled, a notorious, criminal-minded organization that was willing to stay on top by any means necessary. Carter and Polo had put in work for many years and worked hard to surround themselves with thoroughbreds that respected the hustle of the streets as much as they did. They earned money, power, and respect.

That is, until the Haitians from Little Haiti discovered the money that was being made and tried to muscle them out of town.

Carter's demise proved to Polo that the Haitians weren't to be taken lightly. He just hated that it took the death of their leader to figure that out. Nobody was untouchable. Now he had a nagging pain in his heart, and the stress of retaliation on his brain, but he knew that his hurt didn't compare to that of Carter's family.

When he pulled into the driveway to the ten-room, 7,000 square foot home, he prepared himself for the heartache that he was about to encounter. Polo personally made sure that Carter's wife and children were taken care of. He knew that they would be okay financially, but he was determined to ensure their safety. No expense was spared when it came to the security of their family. There were about ten armed henchmen stationed outside of the house, and he acknowledged them with a nod as he passed by and walked into the Diamond home.

"Unc Po." Mecca slapped hands with his father's best friend.

Polo could tell that Carter's death was weighing heavily on his heart by the sad look in Mecca's eyes. Polo then turned to Monroe and pulled him near as well. He held them close, his arms wrapped around their shoulders. All three men had their heads down.

Polo told them, "I know it doesn't feel like it right now, but it's gon' be all right, you hear me?"

Tears formed in Money's eyes. He nodded his head, praying that his Uncle Polo was right.

Polo whispered in their ears, "You both have to be strong for your mother and Breeze. This is gon' hit them the hardest. You know how protective your father was of them. It's time to step up to the plate, twins. You got to pull your family back together."

Both boys nodded in agreement as they quickly wiped the tears from the eyes. Having been trained by their father to never show emotion, they knew that to cry was to show weakness,

"Where are your mother and sister?"

"They're still upstairs," Money stated.

Polo ascended the steps two at a time. He approached the bodyguard that he had hired to stand by Taryn's side. "Fuck you doing?" he whispered harshly.

The bodyguard quickly snapped his cell phone shut, but before he could put it safely in his pocket, Polo slapped it out of his hands.

"Do I fucking pay you to talk on your cell phone?" Polo pointed his finger in the man's face. It didn't matter that he was only five foot eight, and that the bodyguard was 270 pounds of pure muscle. "How the fuck you supposed to protect anybody when you're focused on your fuckin' phone? As a matter of fact, get your ass out of here. Put somebody on this job that want to make this money, you pussy!"

The man didn't even protest as Polo lifted his Steve Madden and kicked him in the ass toward the staircase. He looked over the landing and yelled, "Mecca, show that mu'fucka the door and bring one of them niggas up that take this shit seriously." Polo fixed his clothes and wiped himself down before he knocked lightly on Taryn's door.

"Come in," she called out. "It's open."

Taryn looked as beautiful as ever standing in front of the full-length mirror in her white-on-white Dolce suit that fit nicely around her slim frame, the skirt stopping directly below her knee and hugging her womanly shape. Her neck was framed with rare black pearls that matched the pearl set that clung to her ears. Her long, layered hair was pulled back into a sophisticated bun. She spared herself of applying makeup because she knew that eventually her tears would ruin it anyway. Her natural beauty was enough to take Ms. America's crown, and her Dominican features made her look more like a mature model than a mother of three.

"Taryn, it's time to go," Polo stated as he stood in her doorway.

She nodded her head and closed her eyes as she said a silent prayer to God. *Please give me the strength to get through this for my children. They are all that I have left. Take my husband into grace and take care of him until we meet again.* "Okay, let's go," she said, trying to hide the shakiness in her voice.

She walked out of the room and down the hallway to her daughter's room. "Breeze," she said as she opened the door. "It's time."

"I don't think that I can do this," Breeze stated, tears running down her cheeks. It was obvious that she had been crying for hours, because her eyes were red and swollen. The distress from her father's murder was written all over her young face. It was almost as if her legs gave out from underneath her, because she fell onto the bed and put her head in her hands.

Taryn and Polo rushed to her side. Polo knew that Breeze would take her father's death the hardest. His only daughter, she was his pride and joy, and he had treated her like a princess since the day she was born. Breeze could do no wrong in his eyes, and they had shared a special connection all her life.

"I can't believe he's gone," Breeze stated. She felt as if the life was being squeezed out of her. "I can't do this, Uncle Po." She dreaded putting her father to rest. Never in her nineteen years had she felt a pain so great.

Taryn embraced her daughter as they sat side by side, cheek to cheek. "I know that you can't do this, but *we* can," she stated. "There is strength in numbers, and we will get through this as a family."

Polo was speechless as Taryn's words moved him. It was then that he realized that Carter was truly a lucky man to have a woman such as her by his side. He left the room and descended the steps. He waited in the foyer with Mecca and Monroe, and when the two women came down the steps, they all walked out of the house together.

The limo ride was silent as each member of the family tried to wrap their minds around the death of their patriarch. He was the one who protected them, fed them, clothed them, loved them, made all of their decisions. He was their educator and best friend, so without him, they all felt lost.

Dear Carter,

I know that you do not know me, but I know you very well. You are my husband's son. I have thought about you countless times. If you are anything like your father, I can picture your dark chocolate skin, strong jawbone, and wide, soul-searching eyes. I wish that I could have written you under better circumstances, but I am not contacting you to deliver good news. My husband, your father, has left this earth. He was killed, and although you do not know him, I wanted to give you the chance to say your good-byes. His funeral will be held Saturday June Third, 2008. I hope that you will join us in celebrating his life. Everyone is expected to dress in white attire. He would not want us to mourn his death, but to come together as a family and appreciate his life. I know that is how he would have wanted to go out.

Sincerely, Taryn Diamond

Carter folded the letter up and put it in the pocket of his Armani suit jacket. He had received the letter a week ago and was debating whether or not he should actually go to his father's funeral. He had never known his father, never even heard his voice.

Why am I here? he thought in confusion as he looked at his reflection in the mirror. His designer suit was tailored specifically to his six-foot frame, and his broad, strong shoulders held the material nicely. A small gold chain hung around his neck, displaying a small gold cross.

Checking his watch, he realized that he didn't have much time to get to the church. He reached underneath the hotel bed and pulled out a duffle bag that contained pure white cocaine and two handguns. He figured he may as well drop off some dope to some of his people in Atlanta while in the Dirty South. That way, if the funeral ended up being a waste of time, he wouldn't have wasted time and money coming to town.

He pulled out his chrome .45 and tucked it in his waist. He rubbed the waves on his freshly cut Caesar and took a deep breath. He had to prepare himself for what he was about to do. He had felt resentment toward his father ever since he was a young boy. He had never understood why he had grown up never knowing the man that helped create him. Although he harbored these feelings, he still felt obligated to show his respects.

A nervous energy filled his body as he headed for the door. It was time for him to say good-bye to a man he'd never met.

As the bulletproof limousine pulled up to the church, Carter's henchmen walked up and surrounded the vehicle.

"Leave your guns in the car," Polo instructed Money and Mecca. He opened the door and prepared to step out.

Mecca told him, "The heater staying on my hip, Unc. Them dreadhead mu'fuckas deaded my father. I'll be damned if they do the same thing to me." He popped the clip into the chamber.

"First, I'ma tell you to respect your mother, and watch your mu'fuckin' mouth, Mecca."

"Nah, Mecca's right, Uncle Po," Money said. "We need to be strapped at all times."

Polo put his foot back into the car and closed the door so that their conversation wouldn't be heard. "Okay, listen"—he looked around at the shaken Diamond family—"I know this is hard for you, but you have to trust me. Your father was like a brother to me. I love this family as if it is my own. I would never let anything happen to anyone of you. Now I promised the pastor that I wouldn't bring any weapons into his church. Your father's funeral is neither the time nor place for them. Everyone inside of that church is here to show love."

Mecca and Money reluctantly pulled their guns out of their pants and sat them on the seat in the limo.

"Everything will be fine," Polo assured them. He stepped out of the car first and held out his hand for Taryn, who graciously accepted. He put his hand on the small of her back and led her through the crowd of onlookers, and her children followed closely behind. They were all surrounded by so many bodyguards, one would have thought that Barack Obama was entering the building.

White on top of white was the only thing that could be seen when entering the sanctuary. Everyone attending the funeral was clad in their best white suits, and there were white bouquets of lilies and hydrangea flowers scattered throughout the room. The turnout was unbelievable.

Taryn immediately halted her footsteps when she saw the titanium and black casket that sat at the front of the church. She looked around the room and observed the extravagant funeral that she had put together, making sure to take care of each arrangement personally. No one knew her husband the way that she did, and she wanted to make sure that his funeral was comparable to none. Carter Diamond was the best at everything he ever attempted, so Taryn made sure that he went out in style.

She slowly walked down the aisle. The closer she got to her husband's casket, the weaker her knees became, but she had to be strong. She couldn't let the world see her break. *My children are depending on me,* she thought.

When she finally reached the casket, her heart broke into pieces at the sight of her lifeless soul mate lying before her. She reached down, grabbed his hand, and kissed his cheek. She whispered, "I will always love you, Carter, always." She then turned with the poise of royalty and took her position on the front pew as the first lady of the streets.

Mecca's heart beat wildly in his chest. He had never imagined what he would do if something ever happened to his father. He prided himself on being strong and fearless, but there was no way that he could be strong now. The sudden loss of Carter made him fear death.

He stepped down the aisle and gripped the sides of his father's casket when he saw his ashen face. The glow that his dark skin had once possessed was gone, and his eyes were sunk in. He felt the swell of water in his eyes cloud his vision. He closed his eyes to hinder them from falling. He picked the tiny cross necklace off his chest and kissed it. It was the chain that Carter had given all of his children the day that he'd brought them home from the hospital, fourteen-karat. gold crosses to hang around their necks. The chain had been changed over the years, but the cross was still the original. The children all valued their chains with their lives. Mecca walked over to his mother and sat beside her, trying to keep his emotions at bay.

Monroe stepped toward the casket next. He thought of all the times his father had spent with him. He knew that he needed to absorb all of Carter that he could, because this was the last time that he would ever see him again. He gripped his father's hand and leaned in close to his ear, as if he could still hear him, and said, "Thank you for everything, Poppa. I'll remember everything that you taught me. I'll never forget you." With those words, Money joined his brother and mother.

Breeze graced the church aisle as if it were a runway. All eyes were on her as she paused midstep. She knew that her life had been changed forever. Her Poppa, comparable to none, was the man of her dreams, and she didn't want to let him go. She stepped up to the casket as she fought to keep her pain under control. But as soon as she touched his cold skin, she lost it. Against her will, a small cry escaped her lips, and a fountain of tears cascaded down her precious face. She leaned over her father, gripping his hand, and silently prayed for God to take care of his soul. The sight of her so broken-down caused the attendees to break down as well. Her collapse signaled the collapse of the entire church, and wailing could be heard throughout.

Mecca went to her side, to get her to let go of Carter's hand. "Come on, *B*." He gently rubbed her hair and lifted her head. "Don't hold your head down. Poppa wouldn't have that." He smiled at her gorgeous face, and she gave him a weak nod of agreement as she finally left her father's casket and sat with the rest of her family.

Just as the pastor took his place at the podium, the church doors clanged open. Gasps rang out throughout the church as all eyes focused on the young man who stood in the doorway. Speculative whispers traveled throughout the pews as everyone watched the young man walk down the aisle. From his skin tone, to his confident stride and striking features, he was identical to the man they were there to bury, and one would be able to guess without reading the tattooed name on his neck that he was Carter Diamond's son. It was almost unnatural the resemblance that the two shared.

Mecca's eyes followed the man as he approached the front of the church. "Fuck is that?" he hissed.

"The nigga looks just like Poppa," Money commented in amazement.

"Mommy?" Breeze looked at her mother.

But Taryn needed no explanation. She knew exactly who the young man was. He was Carter Jones, her husband's illegitimate son.

Polo leaned into her and whispered, "Taryn, I have something to tell you. Carter didn't mean to—"

Without taking her eyes off the young man, she said, "Don't worry about it, Polo. No need for you to explain. I know who he is."

Carter felt the questioning glares of the people surrounding him. He stopped in the middle of the church and stared at the casket up front. His heartbeat was so rapid that he felt sick to his stomach. *I shouldn't be here,* he thought.

Just as he turned to leave, four men with long dreadlocks entered the room. They were the only ones wearing black. Carter frowned at their blatant disrespect. They bumped him violently as they walked past, but Carter let it ride as he turned his head and watched them continue down the aisle.

Mecca's temper immediately flared. He reached in his waistline for a pistol that wasn't there. "Fuck!" he whispered as he began to stand.

Polo grabbed his arm to halt him. "Wait a minute," he stated. "This is a part of the game." Polo didn't expect the Haitians to make their presence felt at the funeral. He had underestimated their coldness.

The church was silent as everyone waited to see how things would play out. It was no secret that the Haitians were responsible for Carter's death. The dreadheads walked up to the casket and stood silently with their heads down, as if they were in prayer.

Taryn gripped her sons' hands and let out a sigh of relief.

"See," Polo said, "they're only here to represent the Haitians. They're just showing respect for the deceased. We gon' handle that, just not here."

Before the words could reach Taryn's ears, she was in an uproar as she watched the Haitians hawk up huge gobs of spit and release them on her husband's body, defiling Carter's corpse.

"Hawk . . . twah!"

"Hawk . . . twah!"

Breeze watched in disbelief as the Haitians raised their feet and forcefully kicked the casket off the table, causing the body to roll out onto the floor. Carter's head hit the floor hard, causing a loud crack to pierce the air, and the attendees gasped in horror.

Polo, Mecca, and Monroe sprung into action, with the rest of The Cartel behind them.

"Poppa!" Breeze shouted as she rushed toward the front of the church to retrieve her father's corpse from the floor.

Taryn yelled in alarm, "Breeze!" as she watched her daughter head toward the mayhem.

Suddenly, bullets from an AK echoed throughout the church, *Tat, tat, tat, tat, tat, tat!*, little flashes of fire kissing the air, and was followed by the sound of people screaming and running for the exit.

Breeze didn't care about the gunfire. She just wanted to get to her father. But before she could reach him, one of the Haitian gunmen snatched her up.

Taryn yelled, "Breeze!"

Carter looked in horror at the front of the church. He recognized the young girl from pictures that he had been sent when he was younger. *She's my sister,* he thought as he pulled out his .45 without hesitation.

He stood up and scrambled to get between the screaming people as he aimed his gun and released one shot. His bullet hit its intended target, and the man holding Breeze dropped instantly.

Carter's clip was quickly emptied as the gun battle continued. He was clearly outnumbered, but that didn't stop him from reaching in his ankle holster and pulling out his 9 mm pistol as the three remaining Haitians shot recklessly, clearing a path to leave the church. Using his natural instinct for survival, he picked up the body of the dead Haitian and wrapped his arm around his neck, putting him in a chokehold from behind. The deadweight was heavy, but it was the only way for him to shield his body from the bullets being sent his way.

Carter yelled, "Y'all niggas wanna clap?" and shot his nine with one hand, while moving toward the Haitians, who were now headed for the door.

Carter's gun spit hollow-points toward the Haitians as the dead body in front of him absorbed his enemy's fire. *Pow! Pow!*

Just as he reached the exit door, one of the Haitians yelled, "Me going to kill you, muthafucka!" And the three remaining Haitians made a run for it.

Carter continued to shoot until he was sure they left the building. Once he was positive that everyone was safe, he dropped the dead Haitian to the floor and let off his last round into his skull. "Bitch nigga!" He hawked up a huge glob and spat directly in the dead man's face, returning the favor on behalf of his dead father.

He rushed over to Breeze's side. Rocking back and forth, she was holding on to her father's dead body and crying hysterically.

"Are you okay?" he asked.

"Get the fuck away from her. We don't know you, mu'fucka!" Mecca stated harshly as he pulled Breeze off the ground. Her head fell into his chest as he walked her away.

Polo looked around at the carnage inside of the sanctuary. A couple people had been injured, and the church was destroyed. "We've got to get the fuck out of here," Polo stated. "How did they get in?" Polo yelled in anger. He patted the Young Carter on the back. "Come on, let's go before the police show. Follow me back to your father's house."

A look of surprise crossed Carter's face.

"Yeah, I know you're his son, but right now that's the least of my worries. Just follow me back to the house. We need to talk." With those words, Polo escorted the family out of the church, and they darted inside of the limo.

The Haitians had sent a clear message—They were out for blood, and they weren't going to stop until The Cartel was out of commission.

Chapter Three

"Brother or not, next time homeboy step to me like that, I'ma rock his ass to sleep."
—Young Carter

The Diamond family sat in their living room along with Polo and Young Carter. The room was quiet; no one knew what to say. Taryn's and Breeze's eyes were puffy because of all the crying they had been doing, the horrific images of their loved one being kicked out of his casket haunting their thoughts.

Mecca's Armani shoes thumped the marble floor as he paced the room back and forth, totally enraged, twin Desert Eagle handguns in his hands. The Haitians had shown the ultimate sign of disrespect and were sending a clear message that they were trying to take over Miami. In fact, it was Carter's decision to not cut the Haitians in on his operation that ultimately led to his assassination.

Polo stood up and slowly walked to the window. He looked in the front and saw henchmen, all strapped, scattered around the house to ensure their safety. With the Haitians merciless tactics, he didn't underestimate them. He saw the fire in Mecca's eyes and tried to calm him.

"We have to keep our heads on straight. These niggas are going hard at us. The Cartel still runs Miami, remember that! We have to retaliate to get our backs out of the corner." Polo removed the suit jacket that rested on his black silk shirt.

"Fuck that! Let's get at they ass, guns blazin'! I don't give a fuck no more!" Mecca screamed, a single tear sliding down his cheek.

Money stared into space without blinking. He was in complete shock. The death of his father was very hard on him. He remained silent as his twin brother let out his frustrations. He couldn't come to grips with his father's death.

Money snapped out of his daze and looked over at Young Carter. It was obvious that he was his brother. He looked so much like Carter, it was unbelievable. Young Carter had thick, dark eyebrows just like his father, and he even shared his tall, lean frame. His mannerisms were even the same. He watched as Young Carter rested his index finger on his temple while in deep thought, just as his father used to do.

It hurt his heart that his father had an illegitimate child. The perfect image that he had of his father was somewhat tarnished by the news. *How could this nigga be my brother? Daddy wouldn't step out on Momma like that,* Money thought as he stared at Young Carter.

Taryn noticed Money staring and decided to address the issue. She knew that there were other things to worry about and wanted to explain the complex situation. With tears still streaming down her face, she stood up. "I want you guys to meet Carter Jones . . . your brother." Taryn rested her hand on Young Carter's shoulder.

Breeze lifted her head in confusion. She looked at her mother and then to Young Carter. "What?" she managed to murmur. She couldn't believe what her mother was telling them. The words were like daggers to her heart. She was so busy grieving, she didn't even notice how closely Young Carter resembled her Poppa.

As she looked at Young Carter, she couldn't believe her eyes. She just thought that he was one of The Cartel's henchmen. He looked like a younger version of her father. *Oh my God,* she thought as she placed her hand over her mouth.

Mecca came closer to Young Carter and stared him in the face while saying harshly, "This ain't my fuckin' brother. He ain't a mu'fuckin' Diamond!" Mecca gripped his pistols tighter, refusing to believe the obvious.

Young Carter returned the cold stare at Mecca, not backing down whatsoever, but he still remained silent. Young Carter was respectful because he was aware that his presence presented a conflict to the Diamond family, but he wasn't about to back down from anyone. And the way Mecca was gripping his pistols caused Young Carter's street senses to kick in. He slowly slid his hand to his waist, where his own banger rested. He stood up so that Mecca wouldn't be standing over him. Young Carter was a bit taller than Mecca, so he looked down on him, not saying a word.

"Mecca, he is your brother! Sit down and let me explain," Taryn yelled, trying to reason. She rushed over to Mecca as the two men stared at each other intensely. "Mecca!"

"Fall back, bro," Money said as he stood up.

Mecca jumped at Young Carter as if he was about to hit him, but Young Carter didn't budge. Not even a blink. Young Carter grinned, knowing that Mecca was trying to size him up.

"That's enough!" Polo made his way over to them.

Young Carter kissed Taryn on the cheek and whispered, "Sorry if I caused any more heartache. I didn't come here for this." And before Taryn could even respond, he was headed for the door.

"Yo, wait!" Polo said as he followed Young Carter out.

"Let that bitch-ass nigga go!" Mecca yelled as he continued to pace the room.

It took all of Young Carter's willpower not to get at Mecca, but he figured that he would give him a pass for now.

Polo caught up to Young Carter just before he exited the house. "Yo, youngblood, hold up a minute."

"There's no need for me to be here. I don't know why I even came to this mu'fucka anyway," Young Carter stated, an incredulous look on his face.

"Listen"—Polo placed his hand on Carter's shoulder, trying to convince him to stay—"Mecca has a lot on his mind right now. The family really needs you."

"Look, fam, I ain't got shit to do with them. I just came to pay my respects and keep it pushing, nah mean? Brother or not, next time homeboy step to me like that, I'ma rock his ass to sleep." Carter clenched his jaw.

Polo took a deep breath and saw that Carter was noticeably infuriated, but kept his composure out of respect. Young Carter reminded Polo of his late best friend in so many ways. Polo looked into Carter's eyes and said, "Just give me a minute to talk to—"

Carter cut him off mid-sentence, not wanting to hear any more. "Look, I'll be at the Marriott off South Beach until tomorrow night." With that, he left Polo standing there alone.

Chapter Four

"They were willing to murk women, children, hustlers, the good, the bad, and the ugly. It didn't matter, anybody could get it, if the price was right."
—Unknown

Carter flipped through the different denominations of bills as he diligently counted the cash that he had just acquired from his flip. After the drama he had experienced during his father's funeral, the business he handled in Atlanta made the trip better for him. He would now leave the Dirty South $180,000 richer. *This was definitely worth the trip,* he thought to himself as he admired the hood riches that lay scattered across the hotel bed.

He put the bills in ten-thousand-dollar stacks and wrapped rubber bands around each one, to keep the money organized. He counted the cash a second time to verify that his money was on point. He was thorough when it came to his paper. It was the one thing that he knew he could depend on. Money was his first and only love. Getting money came first in any situation, and he was determined to keep his pockets fed.

A knock at the door interrupted his thought process, and out of habit, he grabbed his pistol from the nightstand and approached the door.

He had been a bit paranoid from the events that had taken place the day before at the funeral, so he wanted to be as cautious as possible while he was in Miami. A nigga would never catch him slipping.

He looked through the peephole and eased up when he noticed the distorted image of his father's right-hand man. Sliding the chain from the hotel door, he unlocked it and allowed Polo to enter the room.

Polo shook his head as he looked at Young Carter. It was still hard for him to get over the resemblance. Young Carter looked so much like his father, it was uncanny. It was a shame that the two men never got the chance to know one another. "Can we talk?" Polo asked, both hands tucked inside of his pants pockets.

"Yeah, come on in." Carter set his pistol down. "You want a drink?"

Polo stepped inside. "Nah, I'm good." He noticed how on point Carter was and thought to himself, *like father, like son.*

Carter walked over to his bed and pulled the bedspread over the stacks of money to conceal his business. He then sat down and motioned for Polo to take a seat in the chair across from him.

"I just came to see how long you were in town for?" Polo knew that the Diamond family needed Young Carter now more than ever.

"I'm ghost tomorrow. Ain't nothing here for me."

Polo had predicted this reaction from Young Carter. He didn't expect him to feel any sense of responsibility to his family at first, but he knew that if he could convince Carter to stay around long enough, the attachment would eventually grow.

"I know this is a lot to put on your heart right now, but your family needs you."

Carter was quick in his response. "They don't even know me," he stated with disdain. "That's not my fam. I've only known one woman my whole life, and she the only family I need, nah mean?"

"Nah, I don't know what you mean, Young Carter. I saw the look in your eyes today when that Haitian mu'fucka had your baby sister at gunpoint. Only a man who had love in his heart would get at them niggas the way you did. It was instinct for you to protect her. Whether you want to admit it or not, that is your family, and they need you, especially Breeze."

"Ain't nobody tried to protect me my entire life. I've been out for self from the time I was old enough to understand the rules of the game. I don't have time to baby-sit. That's not my responsibility." Carter wanted to make it clear that he wasn't trying to get to know the Diamond family, didn't want to be around them.

Seeing their expensive house and luxury vehicles just made him resent his father even more. While he grew up in Flint, Michigan, a city that was known as the murder capital, the man that made him was taking care of the family that he had abandoned his first-born for. The pain of growing up without a father had left a bad taste in his mouth.

Polo stood and shook his head from side to side. "Everything isn't always as it seems, Young Carter. Your father had his reasons for leaving you and your mother, and it wasn't because he didn't love you."

"It really doesn't matter now. That man is in the ground, and it doesn't affect me. I just came to pay my respects. I didn't come here for nothing more or nothing less. That man has never done a damn thing for me, so I'm not gon' even hold you up and say that I feel obligated to step up and take care of his family. A better man might be able to, but that's not me."

"I understand you are frustrated Young Carter. You come here and see how happy your siblings are, and you feel cheated. I know you're asking yourself why you didn't have the same upbringing, but believe me, your father did the best he could under the circumstances," Polo stated, defending his best friend.

When Carter didn't reply he continued, "Your father—"

"I don't have a father. The nigga got my mother pregnant and then left us for dead to come play house with another bitch."

"Look, you need to watch your mouth." Polo, enraged by Young Carter's blasphemous statements, had to set the record straight. "I can't just sit here and allow you to disrespect my man like that. You don't know shit about nothing. If it wasn't for your father, you and your mother would have been dead a long time ago. He had to leave you in order to protect you."

"Fuck is you talking about?" Carter asked, hostility and anger in his tone.

Polo could see that the young man's temper was beginning to flare and then remembered that Young Carter had a valid reason to be upset. He took a deep breath and calmed himself down, to de-escalate the situation. "Look, Young Carter, I'm not here to bump heads with you. As your father's best friend, I've got nothing but respect for you. You have a misconception about the man that your pops was. I'm not saying that every decision he made regarding you and your mother was right, but he did the best that he could. Think about it, young'un. Your mother worked as a CNA since you were young. She's bringing home thirty stacks a year at the most, but you grew up in a two-hundred-thousand-dollar house in the suburbs of Flint. Who do you think purchased that house? Who paid those bills? Use your head, young fella. How many fourteen-year-old boys you know kept a thousand dollars a week in his pocket? When you graduated you were pushing a limited edition Mercedes. Who do you think copped that car for you? Let me tell you, it wasn't Mommy."

Polo's words were enough to silence Carter and make him think. His mother never told him about his father. She had never even talked about him and would explain their living situation by saying that she worked overtime, sometimes double-time, to allow them to live the way that they did. She often claimed to hit big at the casino or to have the winning lotto number. She had given her son every excuse in the book to explain the extra income. *All this time my father was sending money back home to take care of me?* Carter tried to wrap his mind around the fact that his father had never forgotten him.

"Your father never missed a beat in your life, son. You may not have gotten the chance to meet him, but he knew everything about you. It was nothing for him to fly in and out of Flint in the same day just so he could be at your Friday night football games. Remember that game you ran three hundred yards against Southwestern?"

Carter nodded his head as he placed it in his hands. "Yeah, I remember."

"Your father was there. I know he was there because he dragged my black ass with him every week. Every touchdown, every awards assembly, your graduation, he was there for all of that. When you got into that trouble with the law as a juvenile, he made sure that the case was thrown out. Fifty grand made that little mishap disappear from your record.

"Your father loved you very much, but he was a hustler too. He met your mother when she was fifteen and he was seventeen. They dated throughout his senior year in high school, and when it was time for him to go to college, he regretfully left her to better himself. Your mother was so upset with him that when he moved down here she stopped contacting him. He tried to call her, but she would never return his calls. A couple years later he met Taryn. She was beautiful, unlike any woman he had ever met, and they fell in love quickly. She is a full-blooded Dominican though, and they don't play that interracial dating shit. He had to prove himself time and time again just to be with her. If it weren't for his persistence and her refusal to leave him alone, they never would have been allowed to stay together. He knew that she was the daughter of Emilio Estes."

Carter lifted his head in surprise at the notorious drug lord's name. His eyebrows rose in speculation as he thought, *I know this nigga ain't talking bout—*

Before Carter could finish his thought, Polo said, "Yeah, I'm talking about *the* Emilio Estes."

"Damn!"

"Emilio took Carter under his wing. His coke connect allowed Carter to establish The Cartel as the most notorious and prosperous illegal enterprise Miami has ever seen. Emilio was clear in his concerns though. He told Carter that if he wanted to be with his daughter then he would have to keep up the lifestyle that she was accustomed to. Emilio told him that his family had to come first and that if he ever disgraced his daughter in any way then it would be the death of him."

"So he deserted me and my moms. He chose his family in Miami over me."

"Your father didn't even know about you until you were a young child. Your mother didn't even tell him that she was pregnant. When he found out, Taryn was pregnant with the twins, and if Emilio ever found out, you and your mother would have been put in direct danger. Knowing that he could trust his wife, he told her about you and your mother. Although she was upset at first, he explained that he had never cheated on her. She agreed to never tell her father, and they sent your mother money to support you from that day forth.

It pained him that he couldn't get to know you. He wanted to be a part of your life, but his connections with the Dominican Mafia prevented that from happening. You are his first-born. You look just like him. He loved you wholeheartedly."

Confusion and anger took over Carter's body. He didn't know if he should be relieved or enraged. "It still doesn't make up for the years I spent never knowing him. I don't give a fuck what I'm facing. When I have a shorty, my seed gon' know who I am. I'm gon' be a man and take care of my family, no matter what the circumstances are. Money can't make up for the times he wasn't there. My mother couldn't teach me how to be a man. I turned to the streets for guidance. My father came to my games, but he wasn't the one who showed me how to throw the football. He never showed me how to grip a pistol. He ain't show me shit. I had to learn all that shit off humbug on my own."

"Sending you money and supporting you from afar was the only thing he could do. That cash kept you fed and a roof over your head. Your mother didn't have to worry about shit. She chose to never spend the money on herself. She never had to work another day of her life if she didn't want to. He made sure of that." Polo looked in Young Carter's eyes, trying to read him.

Carter stood up to signal that he was done with the conversation. "It still doesn't matter. This ain't home, and first thing tomorrow I'm out."

Polo stood as well, He shook his head in contempt. "A'ight, I hear you, but now you hear me. There's a war going on. Your little brothers and your baby sister need you right now. They weren't raised the way you were. They're spoiled, and they underestimate the seriousness of what's going on. This family needs your leadership, your protection. There's a lot of unfinished business that needs to be handled. Your father's seat at The Cartel is waiting to be filled."

Carter's silence was enough to let Polo know that he was considering his options. He headed for the door. Before he left the room, he said, "There's a meeting tomorrow night at the Diamond house. Your presence should be felt. If you're still in town, you should drop in. I'll be in touch."

As the door closed behind him, Carter thought of all the times he had wondered about his father. He was going crazy as he tried to recount the endless gifts his mother had given when he was growing up. He remembered growing up in the inner city up until the age of ten. At that time, his mother had mysteriously packed up all their belongings and moved them to the suburbs of Grand Blanc. *That must be around the time that Carter found out about me,* he thought to himself.

A part of him wanted to leave town and never look back, but another part of him wanted to stay. The part that had seen the beautiful face of his baby sister, the part that had witnessed the arrogant swagger of his brother Mecca, and calculating discreetness of his brother Monroe. His emotions were at an all-time high, and for the first time in his life, he was indecisive.

Unable to stay cooped up in the hotel suite, he grabbed two stacks of money and headed for the door. He needed to clear his head. He figured that the best way to do that was to visit the floating casino that sat at the end of the pier on South Beach. He didn't know that gambling ran through his veins like blood. It was a habit his father also had. What he did know was that it relaxed him, which was just what he needed at the moment.

Carter stood at a lively crap table with nothing but hundred-dollar chips in his rack. The casino was unusually packed for a Sunday night, and every table was crowded with eager participants just waiting to be taken by the house. Carter was lax from the top-shelf Rémy he was sipping on. The liquor and the intense thrill of the game had calmed him down since his earlier encounter with Polo.

"All bets set!" the dice handler yelled before maneuvering the ivory across the table and placing them in front of Young Carter. "Dice out!"

With his drink still in one hand, Carter picked up the dice with the other and tossed them toward the other end of the table with a nonchalant swagger. The dice tickled the fabric as they danced before finally landing.

"Yo! Eleven, yo!" the dealer shouted, indicating that eleven had landed on the face of the dice.

Uproarious celebration erupted around the table as everyone collected their wins and anxiously awaited Carter's next roll. He had been on a hot streak all night, hitting point after point. His luck was unbelievable. He had held the dice for forty-five minutes, which was almost impossible to do in the game of craps. He schooled the dice against the table with his head down as he watched his hands work their magic. He concentrated heavily on his technique. Every hustler had his own rhythm with the dice, and Carter was no exception.

"Excuse me, can I get in here?"

Hearing the feminine voice amongst the crowd of boisterous men caused Carter to look up. A brown-skinned girl with shoulder-length, almond-colored layers and hazel eyes squeezed into the empty rack next to him. She was so close to him that her sweet perfume played games with his senses, and he felt his manhood acknowledge her presence. He put the dice down as he watched her reach into her skintight Seven jeans and pull out a small wad of money. He waited for her to throw her cash on the table before he continued his roll.

The dealer handed her a hundred dollars worth of chips, and she put them in her rack, arranging them by denomination. He smirked at her as she made a pattern with the different color chips. It was rare that he saw a woman at the crap tables, and the one beside him had his full attention.

The men around the table grew impatient, some of them clearing their throats to signal to Carter that he should pick up the dice.

The young woman squirmed beside Carter, trying to find her place between the big men surrounding her.

"My fault, baby," Carter stated. "Here, let's do it like this." He turned sideways and allowed her to ease in comfortably at the table, giving her more room to play.

"It's all right. You good," she responded with a New York accent that immediately told him that she wasn't from Miami. She looked up at him and smiled as he stared down onto her five foot five frame.

Captivated by her presence, he made mental notes as he admired her wide hips, thin waist, and perfectly manicured fingers and toes. His intense focus on her caused her to blush.

She lay her chips on the table. "Can I get a seventy-two dollar six?"

Carter noticed the small tattoo on the back side of her wrist that read Murder Mama. That immediately piqued his interest. She then pointed to the dice, reminding Carter that it was his roll. Carter tossed the dice at the end of the table. "Here go your six, ma."

"Hard six!" the dealer yelled.

The girl jumped up and down and squealed with joy as if she had just won a million dollars, and Carter couldn't help but chuckle at her enthusiasm.

The man next to her was so in awe of the woman that he dropped her a twenty-five-dollar chip and winked at her, saying, "Lady luck!"

The man was so busy taking a peek at Miamor's ass that he didn't notice her lift three of his five-hundred-dollar chips out of his rack. Miamor bent over and pretended to fix the strap on her stiletto, giving the man a nice view of her assets. She did all of this in less than ten seconds. While everyone was busy collecting their money from the dealers, Miamor used the distraction to her advantage. When she stood, she gave the old man a half-smile that seemed to light up the room.

Carter shook his head with a smirk on his face as he watched the young woman's game.

"What's so funny?" she asked with laughter in her voice as she looked up at him, one hand plastered to her hip, the other reaching onto the table to collect her cash.

"Nothing, ma. I'm just happy you won." Carter licked his full lips.

"Okay," she stated playfully, as she discreetly scanning his body from head to toe. "I see you clowning me, but you need to be minding your own business and hit that six again. I still got money on the table. Everybody ain't balling like you. I see you betting with your purple chips," she said, referring to his full rack of big bills.

"I got you," he said as he prepared for his next roll. "What you drinking on, ma?"

"Hpnotiq and Goose," she replied.

The two of them stayed at the crap tables all night. They joked and laughed, flirting openly with each other. Young Carter enjoyed her company and appreciated her presence because she took his mind off his deceased father. He noticed the size of her pockets as she tried to keep up with his bets and had calculated that she had lost at least two grand trying to hang in the game.

As the crowd began to disperse, they eventually were the only two left at the table. Drunk and feeling good, they made dumb bets, Carter not caring how much he spent, but the young lady watching every dollar that the dealers trapped up.

"Seven out!" the dealer called. The enthusiasm had left his voice, and it was apparent that everyone at the table was exhausted.

"Looks like your luck has run out." The girl leaned against the table. She faced him, her head cocked to the side, her eyes low and sexy from the effects of the liquor.

"I guess so," he replied as he stepped to her, closing the space between them. "You all right? You look a little tipsy."

The girl smiled seductively and answered, "Just a little bit, but I'm good. I didn't come here alone. My girls are around here somewhere. This was fun. Thanks for the drinks."

As she began to walk away, Carter gently grabbed her forearm. "Aye, hold up," he stated softly. He reached into his Prada pockets and pulled out a wad of money. He peeled off twenty hundred-dollar bills and opened the girl's hand to put them inside.

"What are you doing?" Her eyes opened wide in surprise. "I can't take this."

"Whenever you're in my presence, everything's on me. That should make up for what you lost, even though it wasn't yours to begin with." He rubbed her hand before letting it go.

"A'ight, I see you," she replied with a laugh. She threw the money onto the dice table.

"What you doing, ma?"

She put her hands to her lips as if to shush him and then told the dealers to put it all in the field. She picked up the dice, tossed them down the table.

"Two field bet two!" the dealer yelled in excitement, amazed at the young woman's luck. "Double the payout."

Carter shook his head in disbelief. He couldn't believe that the girl had just put two stacks on such a dumb bet. The payout was lovely.

She picked up six thousand dollars from the table and handed him back three thousand. "I make my own ends, but it's nice to know that there are gentlemen still out here."

Before she could walk away, Carter said to her, "I didn't get your name, shorty."

She brought her lips close to his ear. "That's because I didn't give it to you. If you're worth getting to know me, I'll see you again," she replied with a smile as she walked away from him.

"Miamor, who da fuck is da fine-ass nigga you were kicking game to?" Aries asked as she sat in the backseat of the Honda Civic.

"Aries, shut up. Wasn't nobody kicking game to nobody. I wasn't worried about that nigga. Y'all bitches just don't know how to tail a mu'fucka without being all obvious. Our mark was at the crap table in the upstairs VIP. I just chose the table that gave me a nice view to the stairway, so I'd know who was coming and going. Dude was just a prop to make it realistic. My eye never left the prize," Miamor replied, making sure that she kept her eye on the all-black Lamborghini that was three car lengths in front of her.

"I don't know, Mia. It looked to me like you were checking for him," Robyn teased.

Miamor smacked her lips, and a guilty smile spread across her face.

"Bitch, me knew it!" Aries shouted excitedly in her Barbadian accent.

"A'ight, a'ight, I'll admit it. The nigga was a little fly. He had an A game on him. But why the fuck is we discussing that nigga? This ain't playtime. Let's get focused on this business," Miamor stated, trying to get back to the task at hand.

"Now da bitch wanna be focused," Aries stated smartly.

"I know, right?" Robyn burst into laughter.

To the average person, the three girls were rare beauties out for a night on the town. One would have never guessed that these contract killers—they called themselves "the Murder Mamas"—were responsible for sixty percent of the drug-related murders in the Dade County area. If the paper was right, they were down for the job. Nobody was an exception. They were willing to murk women, children, hustlers, the good, the bad, and the ugly. It didn't matter, anybody could get it, if the price was right.

Come on, Mia, keep up with this fucking car, Anisa thought frantically as she watched her sister's car disappear in the side mirror. Her heart began to beat rapidly as she began to think of a way to buy her friends time to catch up.

"Mecca, can we stop at this gas station up here?" she said in her sweetest tone. "All those Long Islands are making me want to pee." She rubbed her left hand on his crotch.

Mecca's dick immediately responded to her touch and began to stiffen as he looked at her fat ass, which was melting into his leather seats. "Nah, we almost there. Just hold that shit. Come put those pretty lips to work," he said with a tone of authority that didn't leave her room to object.

Anisa looked in her mirror once again. *Fuck! Mia, where are you?* She unbuckled her seatbelt and leaned into Mecca's lap. She unzipped his pants and pulled out his throbbing dick. She was immediately aroused by the sight of his long thickness, which was a shade darker than his light skin, and was the prettiest thing she'd ever seen. Her mouth watered in anticipation. The fresh smell of Sean John cologne greeted her nostrils, and she licked her lips in delight. Anisa loved a big, clean dick and figured, since she was about to kill the nigga, she might as well give him the best head job of his life before sending him to meet his Maker.

She licked the head of his length and circled her tongue seductively around his hat, and his manhood jumped from excitement.

"Ohh shit," he uttered as he kept one hand on the steering wheel and put the other on the back of her head. He entangled his fingers in her hair and gently pushed her down onto him.

Anisa took all of him into her mouth, gagging a little from his size. Her mouth was wet and warm, and Mecca was in heaven as he glanced down at the beautiful woman. She slobbered on his dick as she deep-throated him. She knew she was nice with her tongue.

Not even five minutes had passed, and she felt the swell of his rod as he neared ejaculation. He closed his eyes and almost forgot he was driving as she slid her mouth down one last time, tickling the vein underneath his shaft on her way up. It was a wrap, as she sat up and watched Mecca come into an orgasm.

"Damn, baby, let's get you up to this room. A nigga need some of that." Mecca slipped one of his fingers up her skirt, pushing her thong to the side, and massaged her swollen clit.

"Hmm," Anisa moaned as Mecca fingered her dripping pussy. He was working his fingers in and out of her like a dick, and she began to work her hips as she felt the pressure building between her legs. *If this nigga can work his fingers like this, I know he can fuck good. I might have to fuck his sexy ass before I kill him.*

Anisa squirmed in her seat and continued to check her mirrors as she enjoyed the pleasure that Mecca was providing her.

Mecca pulled into the parking lot of the Holiday Inn and hopped out of the car, leaving his car with the valet. He pulled out a hundred-dollar bill and gave it to the valet. "Take care of my car," he said. "You fuck that up, I fuck you up. Understand?"

"Yes, sir," the valet answered immediately.

Mecca walked over to the passenger side and opened the door for Anisa.

"Thanks," she stated with a smile. She grabbed his hand and walked beside him.

When they entered the hotel, Mecca checked into a regular room, using one of his many aliases.

Butterflies circled in Anisa's stomach because she was sure that her girls had gotten lost in the sauce of Miami's nightlife traffic. *It doesn't even matter because, once I slip this nigga this GHB pill, this mu'fucka gon' be out for the count anyway.*

It'll give me enough time to let them know where I'm at, she thought as she reluctantly followed Mecca up to the tenth floor of the hotel.

"Where in the hell did they go?" Robyn asked in a panicked tone. "I don't see them! Can you see the car?"

"Nah, but you need to chill out. Now is not the time to start tripping. We've done this shit a thousand times. Let's just stick to the plan. Anisa knows how to handle herself. We fucked up by losing her, but she'll contact us when she can," Miamor stated confidently.

"Me don't know, Miamor. This job is on a whole 'nother level. What if she needs us?" Aries asked.

Miamor could feel the fear creeping into her team's heart. She knew that fear could easily manipulate any situation, and she was fighting to keep control. *Where are you, Nis? Let me know something,* she thought, as she too began to worry. She didn't like the fact that she had lost their mark, but she knew Anisa would be able to handle herself until they could get there.

"I just need to use the restroom. I'll be right out," Anisa said as she entered the hotel room. She quickly disappeared behind the safety of the bathroom door and locked it behind her. She sat on the toilet, her heart beating a mile a minute and pulled out her two-way. She sent the text to her crew—*I'm at the Holiday Inn on Biscayne Blvd. Room 1128*—then quickly put her phone in her purse and flushed the toilet for show. She washed her hands and walked out of the bathroom.

As soon as she opened the door, Mecca was standing there looking her in the face.

"Oh!" she exclaimed as she dropped her Chanel clutch purse onto the floor. "Shit!" she yelled out. The contents of her purse spilled out onto the floor, and she quickly squatted to retrieve the tiny packet of white powder before Mecca could see it.

"Why you so jumpy, ma?" Mecca asked, his stare penetrating her, his hand caressing the side of her face. Then he looked into the bathroom suspiciously. "I need to get in there." He walked inside and closed the door behind him.

"O—okay."

Anisa rushed over to the mini-bar and set up two glasses. She used Grey Goose because she didn't want to use dark liquor, afraid that the residue from the drug might float to the top. She used her finger to mix the powder into the glass and then removed her silver Chanel dress. She stood in her black Victoria's Secret bra and thong, and her four-inch Chanel stilettos.

When Mecca walked out, he saw her standing with two drinks in her hand. He admired the curves of her body. Her wide hips, flat stomach, and apple-shaped bottom gave him an instant hard-on. He could only imagine the treasure that she had between her thighs, and couldn't wait to taste her.

"Here, baby, I fixed us a drink. I want us to relax so that we can enjoy the night."

"I'm not drinking tonight."

Fuck you mean, you not drinking, nigga? You been drinking all fuckin' night, and now you want to change up?

Mecca could see the distress on her face. "That's a problem?"

"No, baby, I just want to make you feel good. How about we order some room service, have some drinks, and afterwards I'll let you put your dick in something warm?" She put the glass of Grey Goose in his hands and left a trail of kisses from his ear, to his chest, and continued to move south. She got to his pants and unbuckled his belt.

Just as she was about to go to work, he grabbed her hair forcefully, almost tearing it from the root. "You drink it," he stated in a menacing tone.

The look in her eyes confirmed his suspicions. When she didn't respond, he continued, "You got two choices. You can either drink it, or I'm gon' blow a hole through your top." He removed his gold-dipped Beretta 950 Jetfire and aimed it at her head.

"Mecca, what the hell is your problem?" Anisa stood to her feet. "I just want to make you feel good. You're pointing guns in my face and shit. We're supposed to be having a good time," she whined, trying to flip the situation in her favor.

"Save that shit. You think I didn't see the car that was following us, bitch? Drink up. If there's nothing going on, then you have nothing to worry about."

Anisa realized her plan wasn't working. *Where are you, Mia?* She slowly reached for the drugged drink. She knew that if she drank the liquor, she would be committing suicide. Mecca had peeped her shade, so she knew that she had to act fast. She grabbed the drink from his hands and tilted it toward her mouth.

Mecca watched intently, but just as her lips touched the glass, she violently threw the liquor in his face and darted for the door.

"Bitch!" he yelled as he cleared the wetness from his face and chased after her. She managed to open it slightly, but he was right on her ass and slammed his weight against her, causing the door to slam shut. Then he grabbed her neck and tossed her to the floor as if she were the size of a rag doll.

"Aww!"

"Bitch, you trying to poison me? You trying to set me up?" Mecca aimed his gun at her head, and before she could deny his accusation, he silenced her with two to the dome.

"There that nigga go!" Robyn pointed to Mecca as he rushed out of the parking lot.

Mia peered into his car, and immediately noticed that he was alone. It was at that instant that she felt something was horribly wrong. "Where's Nisa?" she asked, her tires screeching as she pulled up swiftly to the valet curb. She hopped out of the car and shouted to the valet, "Leave my car running. I'll be right out!"

Robyn and Aries were right behind her. They didn't wait for the elevator to make it down to the hotel lobby and darted straight for the staircase. Each girl was silent, all fearing the worst.

When they finally made it to the eleventh floor, Miamor took off for Room 1128. They were all out of breath but kept running as if their lives depended on it.

Mia noticed that the room door wasn't closed completely and pushed it open forcefully. "Nisa?" she called as she saw her sister lying in a small pool of blood. Tears immediately came to her eyes.

"Oh my God!" Robyn shouted when she saw her good friend's body on the floor.

Aries was speechless as she watched Miamor kneel by her sister's side.

"No! Nisa, wake up, baby. Don't do this, Anisa. Get up!" Mia shook her big sister's body as if she were only asleep. "Come on, help me get her up!" she yelled, looking back at Aries and Robyn for help. "Come on! She needs to get to a hospital. Help me please," she cried, her voice sounding like that of a small child.

"We've got to get out of here," Robyn whispered as she kneeled down beside Miamor.

"No! I can't leave her. Nisa, come on, get up."

"Mia, there's nothing that we can do for her now. It's too late. She's gone," Robyn said sadly. "She's gone."

Miamor nodded, her face frowned up in pain. "I know," she whispered in between sobs. She leaned over her sister's dead body and whispered in her ear, "I love you, Nis, and I'm going to kill him, I promise." She kissed her sister's cheek and then exited the room.

At first, killing the Diamond family was something that she had been paid to do. Now it was personal, something that she had to do, and no matter how long it took her, she would have her revenge.

Chapter Five

A nigga move a brick, and think he Gotti o' some-body.
—Young Carter

The conference room in the Diamond house was in complete silence. Every hustler in the room felt awkward. It was the first time that The Cartel had held a meeting without their boss, Carter, and everyone seemed to be just staring at his empty head seat. Carter usually started the meetings with a statement or a quote, and with him not there, things were odd.

Polo noticed the uneasiness of the henchmen and stood up. He looked at Money and Mecca, who sat to the right of him, and then back at the henchmen. He took a deep breath as he unbuttoned his Armani blazer.

He walked behind Carter's former chair and rested his hands on the back. "Family, we have suffered a great loss, but business must go on. Carter would've wanted it that way. The Haitians, them mu'fuckas have no respect for the game. These niggas playin' fo' keeps, but we won't bow down to anybody, believe that. We have to let them know that The Cartel still runs Miami, point-blank!" Polo slammed his fist on the glossed oak table.

The occupants of the room included all of the head block lieutenants from each district of Miami. They all seemed to see their paper begin to decrease and knew exactly what the reason behind it was.

Polo looked at Money, who had a law notebook in front of him. "Money, how much did we bring in this week?"

Money ran his finger down the pad and uttered reluctantly, "Two hundred fifty-three thousand."

This only added to Polo's frustrations. "What the fuck is going on, fam? Our operation does a million easy. That's barely enough to pay the runners. What the fuck!" Polo said as he focused back on the henchmen.

One of the henchmen rubbed his hand over his face and goatee. "Man, most of my workers are quitting or siding with the Haitians. They got niggas shook. Ma'tee and his crew are trying to take over the city."

"Got niggas shook? Fuck outta here. Y'all need to recruit more thoroughbreds then, real talk! We have to let the Haitians know that just because Carter is gone, it doesn't mean we're layin' down. We have to get back at them."

"That's all I been trying to hear." Mecca pulled out his twin pistols and laid them on the table. "And you know what? Them mu'fuckas tried to send some bitch at me the other day, like I wouldn't peep the shit."

"What happened?" Polo asked.

"What you mean, what happened? I left that bitch stankin' in the room." Mecca nonchalantly looked around the table.

"I told you about fuckin' with them hoodrats, Mecca. We in a war right now! You can't do that, bruh. You could have got yoself killed," Money said, obvious aggravation in his tone.

"Bitch ain't gon' catch Mecca slippin', believe that! I knew what the bitch was on from the jump. I just wanted to get the pussy before I off'd her ass." Mecca leaned back in his chair.

The henchmen laughed at how cold Mecca's attitude was.

Polo and Money were the only ones not amused by his overconfidence. They knew how wild and careless Mecca could be. They also knew eventually his rashness, if not controlled, would lead to their downfall.

Before Polo or Money could respond, the room grew quiet. Everyone's eyes shot to the door. Some of the henchmen thought they were seeing a ghost, but it wasn't a ghost. It was Young Carter.

Polo turned around to see Young Carter standing there with an all-black hoody, and a diamond cross that hung down to his belt buckle. Polo smiled, knowing that his talk with him paid off.

Mecca sucked his teeth, letting it be known he wasn't comfortable with Young Carter's presence.

Polo waved his hand over the table. "Come in and join us."

Young Carter scanned the room slowly and looked at each man present. He then walked over to the table full of hustlers.

"Everyone, this is Carter . . . Young Carter," Polo said, introducing him.

Everyone greeted him with a simple head nod or a "What up," and Carter returned the greeting with a nod.

Money pulled the chair out that was next to him. "Have a seat."

Carter accepted the gesture and took a seat.

Young Carter and Mecca traded mean stares as he walked over to the chair, but both of them knew that it couldn't escalate, seeing they were blood brothers.

Polo cleared his throat and picked up where he left off.

Carter peeped the surroundings and realized that his father was a powerful man. The man he went his entire life hating had boss status, the same thing he was trying to achieve. He looked at the henchmen and noticed that all of them wore luxury, expensive threads and didn't look like the hustlers he was used to back home. Miami had a whole different vibe.

Young Carter stuck out like a sore thumb amongst the others. Carter was from the street, he was hood, and he couldn't help it, so he wore street clothes, knowing nothing better. While he wore Sean Jean and Timberland, the men were rocking Roberto Cavalli and Ferragamo suede shoes, and everyone wore black.

He chuckled to himself. *These niggas really believe they on some Mafia shit, fo' real. Fuck outta here. A nigga move a brick, and think he Gotti o' somebody.* He couldn't understand why they had formed this organization. Where he was from, hustlers didn't come together at any point. It was a dog-eat-dog mentality, and everyone was out for self.

In the game since he was sixteen, Young Carter began moving bricks by age twenty-one. He was what you call a bona fide hustler. His mother died when he was twenty, and after that, he didn't look back. He went hard on the streets. He had Flint, Michigan's coke game on lock.

Now, at the age of twenty-five he ran the city, hooking up with a coke connect from Atlanta and completely taking over. Young Carter didn't know it, but he was following in the footsteps of his father.

He focused his attention on what was being said in the meeting.

"We have to get at the Haitians somehow. We have to be strategic," Polo said as he sat down and began to rub his hands together. He was in deep contemplation, and for the first time, he felt the burden of not having Carter's strategic mind. Times like these, Carter was a genius at playing mental chess with the enemies.

In the middle of the discussion, Money's cell phone rang. Normally he wouldn't pick up his phone in the middle of a meeting, but he had been waiting on that particular call. He flipped open his cell. "Yo," he said in his low, raspy tone.

He remained silent for a minute, while getting the information from the other end of the phone. Then he closed the phone without saying a word.

"One of my sources thinks he knows where Ma'tee resides," Money stated, referring to the leader of the Haitian crew that had them under fire. "Maybe we need to pay him a visit."

Oversized Chloe glasses covering her eyes and Foxy Brown pumping out of the speakers, Miamor cruised down the interstate pushing 100 mph in her rented GS coupe, her long hair blowing in the wind along with the chronic weed smoke she blew out. She could afford to buy her own car, but in her profession she had to switch up whips like she did panties, to be less noticeable. She took another long drag of the kush-filled blunt and inhaled it deeply.

Throughout the last two years, her and her crew put . . . their . . . murder . . . game. . . . down. I mean, you couldn't mention *Murder Mamas*, if *homicide* wasn't in the sentence. Murder for hire was the best way to sum it up. She had done numerous hits for Ma'tee; none of them resulted in these extreme measures. The recent loss of her older sister had Miamor's mind churning. She wanted to get revenge on the man that killed her blood. But first, she needed to see Ma'tee to get more information on this guy. Only thing she knew about him was that his name was Mecca and that Ma'tee had beef with his family. When they took a job, they usually didn't ask a lot of questions. The only question they needed answered was how much money was involved.

"I swear, that nigga is dead, word to my mutha," Miamor said to herself in her strong New York accent. She pulled off the freeway and entered the town of Little Haiti, where Ma'tee lived.

After taking several back streets and dirt roads, she made it to Ma'tee's residence. Miamor looked at the elegant mansion and the 15-foot steel gate that was the entryway. She pulled the luxury car up and stuck her hand out of the window to push the intercom button. A video surveillance camera faced directly toward her from the gate.

"Wan, state cha name?" a voice sounded in a Haitian accent.

Miamor yelled loud enough so she could be heard, "Yo, it's Mia!"

"Who?"

"Miamor, mu'fucka! Open up!" she spat out of frustration.

A brief moment of silence came about just before the sound of the metal clanked, opening up for her. Miamor maneuvered the vehicle through the gate onto the long driveway leading up to the palace. She noticed that Haitians were scattered throughout the property, all holding assault rifles.

It was only the second time she had been there, but the view amazed her once again. The grass was perfectly even and greener than fresh broccoli. The driveway was filled with luxury cars and lined with beautiful flowers.

As she got closer to the front of the house, she noticed that a birthday party was going on. It was about fifty children in the front yard with noise-makers and birthday cake on their faces and hands. She saw all of the children gathered around watching the clowns making balloon animals, the kids screaming loud in excitement, and all of them having a ball.

A beautiful dark-skinned girl with long, kinky hair was front and center. She had on a princess crown and was happily being entertained by the clown as she instructed him on what balloon animal to make.

That must be Ma'tee's daughter, Miamor thought, immediately noticing the resemblance. She felt bad for intruding on an obvious family event, but she needed to speak with Ma'tee. She also saw a couple of grown women amongst the crowd, obviously the mothers of some of the children. She thought about returning another day, but she had to find out more about Mecca. She was itching to slice his throat. It was only a matter of time.

Miamor made her way to the front door, where two dreadlocked men stood guard. "I'm here to see Ma'tee," she stated as she stood before them.

Without saying a word, the guards, both with pistol in hand, stepped aside and opened the door for her.

Miamor stepped in and admired the crystal chandelier that hung from the cathedral ceiling. The glass wraparound stairs stood in the middle of the room and sat on white marble floors. The all white walls and furniture gave the home an immaculate look. Miamor headed to the back for the sliding glass door.

Another man stood in front of it with a pistol in his holster. Unlike the other men, he didn't wear dreads; he had a neat low cut, but was darker than all of the other guards.

Miamor looked past him, trying to spot his boss. "Where can I find Ma'tee?"

"I need to check you before you approach Ma'-tee," he said, shifting his stance.

"I left the guns in the car," Miamor shot at him.

"Sorry, ma. I still have to search you." He shrugged his shoulders and crossed his arms.

Miamor let out a loud sigh, letting him know that she was irritated. She held out her hands and spread her legs. Her Seven skinny jeans hugged her large behind. Her stiletto heels made her assets seem even more enticing as she remained bent down and he began to search her from feet on up.

He felt her tiny ankles in search for a gun hostler.

"You know I can't fit a damn pistol in these tight-ass jeans."

"You never know," he said, continuing to feel her upper leg. He paused, his nose level with her crotch.

"Smells good, don't it?" Miamor said, hip to his game.

"Yeah, smells very good actually." He looked up at her and gave her a perfect smile.

"Too bad you'll never see her. I wouldn't even let you taste it. Hurry up. I ain't got all day." Miamor turned her eyes to the ceiling. She didn't even give him the respect of looking at him.

The man was obviously embarrassed as he hurried up and finished searching her. Once he was done, he opened the sliding door and pointed her toward Ma'tee, who was laid out in front of the pool, accompanied by beautiful women. There were beautiful women swimming completely nude in the pool while a shirtless Ma'tee watched in enjoyment as he sat on a beach chair, his feet crossed, and his hands behind his head. His dark skin glistened in the sun, and his muscular abs seemed to poke out of his stomach.

As Miamor slowly walked over to him, the clicking of her heels against the ground gained his attention.

He slowly sat up and looked at Miamor, admiring her shape and oversized behind. He loved the way her jeans hugged her hips, and the way she switched them when she walked. Her thighs seemed to stick out more than her waist. Ma'tee's fantasies were short-lived as he realized that Miamor was more than just a stunning woman—she was a cold-hearted killer too.

His dreads were much neater than his henchmen's, and the tips were bleached brown. He shook his head, letting them fall freely from its original ponytail. "Hello, Miamor," he said, greeting her with a smile.

"Hi, Ma'tee," she answered as she took a seat next to him. "Sorry I interrupted your daughter's birthday party, but I really needed to talk to you."

"Ey, mon, no problem. Miamor me girl, ya know," he said as he put on his shirt.

"Yeah, I know. But, listen, I need to know more about this nigga Mecca." Miamor stared in Ma'tee's eyes with deep sincerity.

Ma'tee saw the desperation in her eyes and stood up. "Why don't chu come to me office. We talk 'bout it."

Miamor nodded her head and got up to follow Ma'tee.

Just as they were about to reach the glass door, Ma'tee's daughter came running out. "Dadda, Dadda, the clown made me a giraffe, see?" She handed him the balloon animal.

"Yes, me see me baby girl's giraffe. Wonderful!" Ma'tee scooped her up in his arms.

"Dadda, when are you coming out to play with me?"

"Dadda gots to talk to me friend Miamor. Then me come back to you, okay," he said before he kissed her on the cheek.

"Okay. I have to use the bathroom now," his daughter said as she wiggled down and ran towards the wraparound stairs.

Ma'tee stared at his only child and smiled. He looked back at Miamor and said, "That's me baby girl, right dere."

Miamor smiled and continued to follow Ma'tee into his back office. She walked into the office, where Ma'tee had shelves of books. In fact with his extensive collection, the office sort of looked like a library. His shiny red oak table sat in the middle with a deluxe leather chair behind it.

Ma'tee made his way over to the chair and sat down. He waved his hand to the seat in front of him. "Sit, sit."

Miamor accepted his offer and sat down.

Ma'tee continued, "Me sorry to hear 'bout your sista. Me never meant for dat to happen, you know."

"Yeah, I know." Miamor dropped her head.

"Look, me still pay you, okay." Ma'tee pulled a briefcase from under his desk.

Miamor looked at the briefcase as Ma'tee popped it open. It was fifty stacks, ten percent of the agreed amount that they were to be paid after the job was completed. She knew that they didn't deserve the money, because they didn't finish the job, so she declined.

"No, Ma'tee, I'm good. I just want to know how to get at the mu'fucka that killed my—"

A loud scream came from upstairs. "Aghhh!" It was the voice of a little girl.

What the fuck? Miamor turned around and looked toward the door.

Ma'tee instantly recognized the voice to be his daughter's and grabbed his gun from his drawer and hurried to her aid.

Armed Haitians rushed upstairs where the girl was and what they saw devastated them. There were five bodies lying in their own blood, and Ma'tee's young daughter stood in the middle of them. She had discovered them when she went to use the restroom. The dead bodies were scattered throughout the hallway, each of them with double gunshot wounds through their heads.

Ma'tee's heart dropped when he saw his daughter screaming in the middle of the massacre scene. He hurried over to her and scooped her in his arms.

Miamor had followed him up the stairs and was completely flabbergasted when she saw the slaughter. "Oh my God," she whispered as she put her hand over her mouth.

Young Carter drove the van down the interstate while Jay-Z's Reasonable Doubt pumped out of the factory speakers. He looked in his rearview mirror and saw Money and Mecca, both dressed in baggy clown suits and size forty-four shoes, taking off their wigs and wiping off the clown face paint.

"Damn!" Mecca yelled as he forcefully snatched off his red wig. He was totally enraged that he didn't get a chance to kill Ma'tee. "I didn't see him. He was on the pool patio, and then when I snuck back in, he was gone. I should have popped him when I first saw him, but he had a guard by the door."

"He must've ducked off somewhere to smash that female that came in," Money added, noticeably discouraged also.

Carter got off on the highway and pulled into an empty parking lot, where Mecca's Lamborghini was waiting. "We'll get 'em next time," he said confidently, throwing the "clown" van in park.

Mecca peeled off the costume and jumped into his car. "If there is a next time. Because of what we just did, Ma'tee's security is going to be extra tight. We may never get that close to him again. Fuck!"

Carter and Money jumped in with him, and they pulled off on their way back home. They had just sent a clear message—The Cartel wasn't about to lie down.

Chapter Six

"In the middle of a war, there's no room for weakness."
—Young Carter

Miamor sat Indian-style next to her sister's grave, her spirit broken and feeling weak without her big sister in her life to guide her. Anisa was the reason why Miamor had been put on to the street life. She had taught her everything that she knew, and now she was lost forever at the hands of the game. Miamor had always known that the possibility of death was high, because of the lifestyle that she and her crew led. The same way that she was willing to murk a mu'fucka with no ifs, ands, or buts about it, she knew that somebody, somewhere, was willing to do the same thing to them. She just never thought that it would happen to Anisa at the tender age of twenty-five. If she could turn back the hands of time, she would have definitely done things differently that night. It wasn't her idea to use Anisa as a pawn, but she was outvoted by the rest of the Murder Mamas, and the majority always ruled. Things are always so much clearer in hindsight, and she wished that she had convinced them to come up with a better plan to get at the notorious Cartel.

It had been weeks, and it was the first time she had been to visit Anisa's resting place. *This is all my fault,* she thought as tears formed in her eyes. She tried to fan her face to stop her tears from falling. She hated to cry, but it was no use. The tears trickled out of her eyes and stained her cheeks as she put her face in her hands, allowing her soul to release the pain.

"I'm sorry, Nisa. If I had been on point like I was supposed to be, this never would have happened," Miamor uttered out loud. She knew that wherever her sister was she could hear her.

She hadn't told anyone how she felt. Not even Aries and Robyn knew the guilt that she felt over her sister's untimely demise. She knew that the moment she lost sight of Mecca's black Lamborghini that her sister's life had been put on a countdown.

How did I let this happen? She felt the coldness from the grass that was still wet from the morning dew creep into her body. She shivered as she closed her eyes and thought of her sister's face. She bowed her head and prayed to God, feeling a closeness to Anisa that she'd never known while her sister was alive. *I'm sorry, Nis.*

Young Carter pulled his black Range Rover up to the cemetery and sat in his car for a moment to gather his thoughts. He was about to face his father for the first time. His first attempt had been interrupted by the Haitians, but now he had no excuse. It was time to make peace with the man who had created him. He got out of the car and walked up to the large monument that was his father's tombstone. He put his hand on it and leaned into the large marble, his head down. A spectrum of emotions shot through his body as he read the engraved inscription.

Carter Diamond Beloved Husband, Leader, and Father of Four "Diamonds are Forever"

He ran his hand over his face as he tried to contain the sorrow that took him over. He didn't know why he suddenly felt love for his father, but there was an unexpected connection between father and son that transcended even death.

"I know that you know that I'm here. I don't even know why I decided to stick around. For so long I wondered about you and why you left, why I never knew you. I understand now. I can't say that I can forget the abandonment that I experienced, growing up without a father, but I do forgive you. I swear on everything that I love that the mu'fuckas that are responsible for your death will never hurt the family." Carter began to walk away. He didn't think that there was anything left to say.

As he made his way back to his car, he stopped in his tracks when he saw the beautiful woman leaning against the passenger door. She was dressed in black Donna Karan slacks that hugged her hips and loosened at the leg, a black Donna Karan sweater, and silver Jimmy Choo stilettos. The closer he got to her, the more he recognized her face.

"Hi," she greeted as she stood with her silver clutch bag in hand.

"Damn, ma, I didn't peg you as the stalking type," he commented with a sexy smile.

A tiny dimple formed on the left side of his mouth, and that feature immediately became her favorite part of him.

"I was about to say the same thing, seeing as how I was here first," she replied, returning his smile with one of her own. "I saw you pull up just as I was leaving, so I decided to wait here for you. Who are you here for?"

"Just a family member, no one I was real close to," he responded. "I just wanted to pay my respects." He noticed that her eyes were red and swollen and there were bags underneath them. She looked tired and weak. Although she was still beautiful, there was something different about her. "You all right?" he asked.

"I'm"—she paused to think of the best way to describe her current state of mind—"surviving. My sister passed away a couple weeks ago. That's why I'm here." The woman shuffled nervously in her stance and looked at her feet.

"I'm sorry to hear about that."

"Yeah, me too." She stared off into space, and the tears returned to her eyes. She willed them away and shook her head as she looked back at Carter. "I'm Miamor," she said, offering her hand to him.

"Oh, I'm worthy of a name this time?"

Carter chuckled as he took her hand into his and shook it gently. Her name, exotic enough to complement her around-the-way features, fit her perfectly. Her brown shoulder-length layers were curled loosely and shaped her almond-colored skin. Her white teeth composed the perfect smile, and her M•A•C cosmetics were applied just right, not too much, but enough to make her skin glow.

"I told you, if you were worth my time, I'd see you again." She tiptoed and peeked at the tattoo that displayed his name. "Carter," she said aloud.

He noticed how she never let go of his hand as she intertwined her fingers with his own. The sound of his name rolling off her pouty lips was enticing, and he couldn't help but to be intrigued by her.

"It was nice to meet you," she stated as she walked away. She didn't let go of his hand, until she was forced to, because of the widening distance between them.

As he watched her strut away, she waved one last time and got into a silver Nissan Maxima and pulled away. Carter shook his head from side to side, grateful for her departure. He knew that if he ever got to know Miamor, she would be his weakness. He smiled to himself as he watched her car disappear around the corner and then hopped into his own vehicle and departed. *In the middle of a war, there's no room for weakness. Love will get you killed,* he thought as he made his way back to the Diamond mansion.

Breeze stood over the kitchen table and argued as her mother, uncle, and twin brothers ate breakfast. "Uncle Polo, I'm not going out with this big, ugly bodyguard attached to my hip! How am I supposed to chill with my girls with him following me everywhere?"

Polo told her, "It's not negotiable, Breeze. You are not to leave this house alone. One of our men will escort you wherever you need to go. If you don't like that arrangement, you better ask one of your brothers to accompany you."

"I got plans." Mecca stated quickly.

Breeze rolled her eyes at Mecca and hoped that her other brother would come to her rescue. "Money, please?" she begged.

"Sorry *B*, no can do. Uncle Polo and Young Carter set up a meeting between me and the board of advisors at Diamond Realty. I'm going to be taking that over, and I need to sit down with the board to make sure that they understand that this is still a family business—"

"Yeah, yeah, whatever."

"Who said you were going to be the one to take over the real estate company?" Mecca inquired.

"Young Carter and I discussed it," Money replied. "We think it's best."

"And I didn't have a say in this decision?" Mecca asked in irritation.

Young Carter overheard the conversation as he walked into the room. "No, you didn't, Mecca." He gave both Breeze and Taryn kisses on the cheek, and then patted Polo on the back. "There is enough responsibility for all of us to get in on some part of the business. The real estate company is where Monroe needs to be. We need to keep one of us clean and legal, now that we are at war with the Haitians. We never know where this might lead, and the less Monroe is involved, the better." Carter slapped hands with Monroe and then sat down at the table.

Polo smiled at Young Carter's authoritative approach when dealing with his younger brothers. He knew that it was only a matter of time before the young man assumed a leadership position in The Cartel.

"Yeah, you're right," Mecca responded hesitantly as he slapped hands with his older brother. Mecca still didn't like the fact that Carter had appeared out of the blue claiming to be his father's son, but the more he got to know Young Carter, the more he respected him. There wasn't a doubt in anyone's mind regarding his bloodline, and he was slowly beginning to warm up to the idea.

"Have you eaten, Carter?" Taryn asked.

"No, I haven't."

Taryn stood to fixed him a plate and put it in front of him.

"Thank you."

Breeze whined as if she were still a child. "Uncle Polo?"

Polo sighed and pointed his fork at Young Carter. "Will you tell your sister that she doesn't need to leave the house without one of the men?"

Carter asked, "Where you need to go, Breeze? I'll take you,"

"Thank you. At least one of my brothers is willing to do something for me," she stated in playful exasperation. She grabbed Carter by the hand. "Come on, let's go. We'll get something to eat later."

Carter grabbed one last forkful of eggs and put it in his mouth before Breeze pulled him out of the kitchen.

Taryn laughed out loud at the sight. "Looks like Breeze has found one more man to spoil her. That child is rotten," she stated with a smile on her face.

Carter maneuvered the Range Rover in and out of the Miami traffic as his sister sat in the passenger side, the huge Ralph Lauren sunglasses covering most of her face.

"I haven't gotten a chance to kick it with you much, with everything that's going on." Carter wanted to know how his presence in Miami affected Breeze.

"I know it seems like the only thing everyone has been worried about is The Cartel. It feels like I'm living out some old gangster movie or something. I just want things to be normal again," she replied, looking out of the window.

"So what's your take on everything that's happened?"

"You really wanna know?" Breeze pulled her glasses from her face and rested them on top of her head.

Carter nodded his head and waited for her to answer the question.

"I feel cheated because I only got to know my father for nineteen years. I loved him, and I wanted him to be there when I got married, and when I had my first child. I wanted him to be here for me. I feel like, now that he's gone, everything is going downhill. My mom is afraid every single day that the Haitians are going to harm us. Since meeting you, Mecca has become extra hard. It's almost like he's trying to prove himself to you. It's like he wants to make sure that everyone knows he is Carter Diamond's son. Monroe is the same, Uncle Po is the same—"

"And what about you?"

"Me, I'm dealing with everything the best way I know how. I cry every morning when I think of my Poppa. It's like one minute I'm upset with God for Him taking my father away, and then the next minute, I'm thanking Him for bringing you into our lives when He did. You are my brother, and I am glad that you're here, Carter. I don't know how, but you make things seem like they'll be okay."

"I'm just here to help, Breeze. At first, I wanted to say, 'Fuck Miami,' and move on with my life as if none of you ever existed, but that would be selfish. I've never had a family, so I want to get to know you, Mecca, and Monroe."

"Well, I can tell you the way to win my heart," she said with a smile as bright as the summer Miami sun.

"How's that?"

"Everything today is on you."

"I got you, sis."

Breeze found out that she and Carter shared the same love for fashion. She took him from store to store as she shopped, picking up every designer she could find. He didn't complain or rush her in the same way her other brothers did, and he even gave honest opinions when she asked about an outfit she tried on.

"How's this?" she asked as she walked out of the dressing room in Saks Fifth with a skintight Seven jeans that fit low on her hips, almost revealing the crack of her ass, and a Fendi blouse that barely covered her breasts.

It was sexy, but definitely not something that he wanted his sister to wear. "I'm not buying that shit. As a matter of fact, you ain't wearing it even if you buy it yourself, so you might as well hang that back up." He flipped through his Apple iPhone, ignoring her.

"Come on, Carter, it's not that bad," she argued.

He didn't respond, and just continued to focus on his phone.

"You're just as strict as Poppa was," she stated with a little bit of attitude and a laugh. "I am a grown-ass woman, you know, big-head-ass."

"I heard that," he stated calmly as he leaned back in the leather chair, still flipping through his phone. He shook his head once she disappeared behind the dressing room curtain. As he waited for her to come out again, he mumbled to himself, "She gon' have me fucking these little niggas up in Miami."

They went through several outfits, and he had a comment for each one.

"Nah."

"That's whack, sis."

"That shit don't match."

Breeze went in and out of the dressing rooms until she finally grew tired of his disapproval. "Okay, Carter," she said, "out of all the stuff I've tried on, you've only liked three outfits. You tell me what's hot."

Carter put his phone on the clip of his belt buckle. "A'ight, let me show you how to do this. All that hooker shit you and your girlfriends be wearing is trash."

"Excuse me, everything in my closet cost a grip," she replied, one hand on her hip.

"That doesn't mean that it's classy. I'm a man, so I know what I'm talking about." He quickly located ten different items for Breeze to try on. "You want these niggas to respect you out here, especially you. You're the only daughter of Carter Diamond. You need to dress like the princess that you are and make men come at you correct when they checking for you."

"I hear you." Breeze took the items from his grasp. She tried on the first outfit, which was a pair of cropped white Ferragamo pants that hugged her shape as if it were tailor-made just for her body. Her white shirt had a sharp collar, dipped low in the cleavage area, and fit snugly around her slim waist, her sleeves stopping short just above her elbows, and a large black fashion belt adorned her waist. She slipped her feet into a pair of black stilettos. She had to admit, the outfit was nice and made her look like a kingpin's daughter.

She walked out of the dressing room and did a full spin for her brother.

"That's more you," he stated as he stood to his feet. He checked his presidential Rolex and noticed that they had been shopping for hours. He called one of the store associates over to them. "Can you have these items boxed and bagged for us?" he asked.

The woman grabbed the items from Breeze as she changed back into her clothes.

"Let's grab something to eat before we head back," he said as they walked out of the store.

"I know just the place. It's right up the street," Breeze responded as they walked out of the store. Breeze had at least five bags in each hand as they walked the distance to the restaurant.

Carter followed her across the street and into an elegant building that was made of marble and glass. He looked up at the sign that read *Breezes*. He looked at her in confusion.

She smiled. “Poppa bought it for me on my tenth birthday.”

Carter nodded, and they entered the restaurant to have a late lunch. There was a long line of patrons waiting to be served. The establishment was crowded, so they inched through the crowd until they reached the hostess.

“Hello, Ms. Diamond,” the hostess greeted, obviously recognizing Breeze. “Right this way.”

There were groans and complaints from the people who stood waiting, but Breeze and Carter eased right past them and into the lavish environment. The voice of Billie Holiday filled the darkened space, and all eyes seemed to be on Breeze.

As they passed the bar, Carter saw Miamor sitting on a stool with two other women and he winked at her as he passed by. When they arrived at their table, Carter pulled out the chair for his sister and then sat across from her.

Aries’ eyes followed Breeze and Carter to their table. “Miamor, isn’t that de guy from de Casino?”

“Yeah, that’s him.” Miamor’s arched eyebrows frowned at the sight of him. A twinge of jealousy crept through her heart, but she knew that she had no right to be upset. She didn’t even know Carter. Just because she was feeling him a little didn’t mean anything.

“Damn, is that his girl?” Robyn asked.

“Must be,” Miamor replied, her tone a bit more sarcastic than she intended.

“Me know you ain’t green?” Aries teased.

“Hell nah!” Miamor exclaimed. “Jealous for what? I don’t even know the nigga. Yo, for real, it ain’t even that serious. Since when have you ever known me to be that type?”

“Whoever that chick is, she’s rocking them Prada shoes.” Robyn nodded her head in approval.

Miamor rolled her eyes and sipped at her drink as she tried not to focus on Carter.

“What are you looking at?” Breeze asked.

"Just a friend," he replied.

Breeze turned around and stared toward the bar at the three young women that had so much of her brother's attention.

"You making friends like that already? You've only been here a couple weeks."

"It's not like that, so get your head out of the gutter."

Breeze laughed again. It was refreshing to see her smile. It was then that Carter realized that he had never seen his sister's smile, and it looked good on her. This was the first time that he'd ever seen her happy.

She peeked back at the girls one more time and then whispered, "Which one is she?"

"The one in all black," he replied as he watched Breeze look back. "Quit staring, Breeze."

"Shit, she's staring back," Breeze shot back. "She must think I'm your girlfriend or something, because her face is all twisted up." Breeze giggled. After she took a sip of water from her water goblet, she said, "You better go talk to her because she looks mad."

Carter looked past his sister's head and saw the look on Miamor's face. He stood from the table and looked down at Breeze. "I'll be right back."

Robyn turned on her bar stool. "Don't look now, but here come your boy. I think I need to use the bathroom. Come on, Aries."

"What you mean, come on? Me don't have to go with you," Aries stated with a devilish grin. She licked her lips at the sight of the dark man walking toward them.

"Aries!" Miamor whispered.

"Why me have to go with she?"

"Because she doesn't want you all in her face, bitch. Now, come on." Robyn laughed and pulled Aries away.

Miamor laughed for the first time since her sister died, and Robyn winked at her as they disappeared around the corner.

Carter slid into the seat next to Miamor. "Why is it that you're everywhere I seem to be?"

"I don't know, but if I had known that you and your girlfriend would be here, I would have gone somewhere else," she replied with an attitude.

Carter smiled at her jealousy. They barely knew each other, yet she was already staking her claim.

"Don't be like that." He scooted his stool closer to her and whispered in her ear, "I'm only interested in one woman in this room."

She smiled, but scooted her own stool away from him. "I don't want to have to fuck your girlfriend up, so don't start no shit," she said seriously.

"That flip lip you got don't suit you, ma. I'm gon' have to grow you up."

"Oh, really. I can't wait to see you try to do that because a man can't change anything that I don't want him to. I'ma do me, regardless. I most definitely ain't changing for a nigga that already got a chick." Miamor turned to see Breeze walking toward them. "Here comes your girlfriend. You better make sure she acts right." Miamor faced the bar and sipped her strawberry daiquiri.

Carter shook his head as he watched his sister approach. He definitely wasn't impressed by Miamor's feistiness, but he liked a challenge. He knew that it wouldn't take long for her to fall in line, so he let her smart mouth slide for the moment.

"I just got a phone call from Mommy. I told her that we'd do take-out and bring dinner home," Breeze stated when she walked up.

"That's fine with me, but first I want to introduce you to a friend of mine. Breeze, this is Miamor. Miamor, this is my *sister*, Breeze," he said with a wicked smile.

Miamor, an embarrassed expression on her face, cut her eyes at Carter. He had let her sweat and show her jealousy, when all along he was with his sister. She smiled and shook the girl's hand. "Nice to meet you, Breeze."

"You too," Breeze replied.

Carter stood to leave and didn't say a word as he walked away from Miamor and headed for the door.

No, this nigga didn't. Miamor watched his back as he made his way through the crowd.

Carter stopped at the hostess' desk and wrote a note to Miamor. He asked the hostess, "Can you hand this to the young lady at the bar?" He handed her a twenty-dollar tip, and then left out behind Breeze.

The hostess tapped Miamor's shoulder. "Excuse me, miss."

"Yes?"

"The gentleman that just left asked me to give you this." The hostess dropped the folded piece of paper on the bar.

"Thank you," she replied as she eagerly opened it.

Meet me at the end of the South Pier tonight at midnight. Don't front like you ain't coming, ma. Do yourself a favor and be there. I want to get to know you, Miamor.

Carter

PS: Dinner is on me

Miamor smiled as her friends reappeared at the table.

"What did he say?" Robyn asked.

"Nigga didn't say nothing," Miamor said. "He came over here to tell me that chick is his sister, that's all."

The friends resumed their conversation, and Miamor threw in an occasional comment to make them think that she was paying attention, but her mind was on Carter. She was definitely going to the pier that night. She checked her cell phone to see what time it was and immediately started counting down the minutes until she saw Carter again.

Chapter Seven

Only God can judge me.
—Miamor

Miamor stood nervously at the end of the pier. Goosebumps covered her arms as the mist from the turbulent ocean blew onto the pier and sprinkled her with light kisses. Looking out on the water, she watched the waves as they washed up onto the shore. The white foam that they created was the only color she saw as she stared out into the black night.

"What are you thinking about?" Carter asked.

The sound of his baritone voice caused her to jump slightly, and she turned around to greet him. "You," she replied as she looked up at him.

Carter took in her feminine essence as his eyes scanned her body. She wore a mocha-colored wrap dress that stopped mid-thigh. It fit snugly around her voluptuous frame, revealing one shoulder and her toned upper back. Her thick thighs and lean legs glistened under the moonlight, and her hair was swooped to the side in an elegant bun.

"You look nice."

"Thank you," she blushed as she wrapped her arm in his, and they began to walk toward his car. "So tell me where we are going tonight?" she asked.

"You'll see," he replied as he led her down the steps of the pier.

She followed him, but before stepping her feet into the sand, she removed her Louis Vuitton stilettos and placed them in her hands.

He chuckled at her as he watched her shrink before him.

"Shut up." She hit him softly on the arm. "These are a three-hundred-dollar pair of shoes. Where are we going anyway?"

"You'll see," he replied as he led her to a secluded area on the beach.

Miamor followed him behind a row of huge boulders that sectioned off a small piece of sand and smiled when she saw the intimate midnight picnic that Carter had set up.

"What is all this?" she asked in delight as she sat down on the blanket. There were fruits, champagne, melted chocolate, and white rose petals everywhere. Carter had even gotten jarred candles and set them up around the sight. No man had ever gone through so much trouble to impress her, and she was taken aback by Carter's effort. He was definitely a different type of man, and she looked forward to the night ahead.

"I want to get to know you. I don't want there to be people around, or for you to feel like you got to put up an act in front of me," he replied. "I see your tough-girl demeanor, but I'm not buying it."

Carter pulled the champagne out of the ice bucket and poured two flutes. He handed one to her, and she gratefully accepted the drink as she lifted the flute to her lips.

"Why is it so hard for you to believe that this is me?"

"Because I see through you," Carter replied. "I'm trying to get to know the real Miamor."

"Okay, so tell me what you want to know?" Miamor folded her legs behind her and grabbed some grapes.

"Whatever you want to tell me."

"There isn't a whole lot to tell. What you see is really what you get." Miamor didn't really know what Carter wanted to hear. How could she sum her entire existence up in a couple words?

"No offense, ma, but I don't see a whole lot," Carter stated.

Miamor cut her eyes at him and stood to her feet. *I don't know who the fuck this nigga think he is.* "Then what the fuck am I here for?"

She began to walk away. She didn't know why, but tears came to her eyes as she stormed off. It wasn't that she cared about what Carter thought of her. He wasn't the be-all and end-all, but she was offended by the fact that she appeared shallow at first glance.

This nigga don't know shit about me. He doesn't know that I caught my first body when I was just ten years old. It wasn't because I'm a killer or murderer, but because I mistakenly shot him while he was on top of my sister raping her. He doesn't know that after that Anisa and I were on our own because my mother was so enraged by the fact that we killed the man who kept a roof over our head. He sitting over there talking about he don't see much. Fuck him! She cursed him silently as she wiped her eyes and fled down the sandy beach.

Miamor was pissed off that Carter felt that he could pass judgment on her. *Only God can judge me,* she thought. She was so upset that her anger turned to sadness and regret as she thought about all of the negative things that she had been through. The average chick couldn't have survived her life's circumstances, but under pressure Miamor was forced to evolve into a woman who never wore her heart on her sleeve. She had become just as conniving, manipulative, and hardened as any man in the streets. *He really don't know who I am. He got me all the way fucked up.*

"Aye, hold up." Carter grabbed her arm.

"Let me go!" she yelled as she snatched her arm away from him and continued to walk away.

Carter could see that his words had hurt her, and he immediately regretted being so forward with her. He grabbed her again, and hugged her tightly from behind as she fought to free herself from his hold. She was crying and visibly upset.

Carter felt like an asshole, but he had no clue that her tears were from the many demons that she had battled throughout the years. Her sudden breakdown had nothing to do with him. She had learned to suppress her emotions well. In her area of expertise there was no room for feelings. Allowing herself to feel anything clouded her vision, and she always had to stay focused. Distraction meant death for her, and she'd learned that the hard way with Anisa. She hated herself for letting Carter see her so weak, which was why she fought so hard to get away from him.

"Whoa! Miamor, calm down," Carter stated.

"Get the fuck off of me!"

"I apologize. I was out of line," he said as he continued to hold her tightly.

Miamor's knees gave out underneath her as her sister's death hit her harder than ever before. It had been so long since she'd cried that, now that she had started, she couldn't stop herself. All the pain that she had suppressed over the past thirteen years was pouring out of her.

"Shh," Carter whispered in her ear as his arms comforted her. "Let it out, ma. This is what I was talking about. Now I see you. This is the girl I want to get to know," he told her.

Carter let her collapse onto the sand, but his arms never left her body. He sat with her as she cried her eyes out, and eventually she stopped fighting him and found a comfortable space within his embrace.

After the tears stopped, they sat there silently, yet content with the intimate moment that was unfolding, Carter holding her in his arms and Miamor listening to his strong heartbeat as she felt safe for the first time in her life.

"I'm sorry for popping off on you earlier," she finally whispered in a low tone.

"It's all right, Mia. I apologize for coming at you wrong. I didn't want to hurt your feelings. I just want to get to know the real you. The woman that I just saw break down is the one that I'm trying to know. You think you can make that happen?"

"Yeah, I can do that," she said with a half-smile.

"One day I want to know what made you cry like that. I want to learn everything about you. I want to know what makes you cry, what makes you laugh, what you want out of life, what your dreams are. I want to know you, ma."

Tears came to her eyes again as she stared into his brown, trusting eyes. She looked at the small scar that seemed to fit so perfectly with the features on his face. She was at a loss for words as she listened to him speak.

Miamor couldn't help herself as she looked at the handsome man before her. His words were getting to her. She didn't know if it was game or not, but if it was, she concluded that it was one that she would let herself believe. She felt compelled to kiss the lips that were saying all the right things.

She leaned in and kissed him softly. His lips were soft and big. His masculine hands lightly massaged the back of her neck, causing her heart rate to increase. The fresh scent of Issey Miyake filled her nose, and she inhaled deeply, enjoying the scent. She had the first-kiss jitters as butterflies fluttered in her stomach.

Carter picked her up without ever breaking their kiss and carried her back to their picnic site. Setting her down gently, he watched her as she leaned back on her elbows and looked up at him. The lust and passion that burned in her eyes signaled what time it was.

Miamor couldn't contain the fire that was ablaze between her legs. She had to have him, opening and closing her legs seductively while he gazed down at her.

Carter could see her neatly trimmed pussy hairs, and his excitement heightened when he noticed that she wasn't wearing any panties, her skin blending with the color of the sand perfectly. Her body exuded sexiness. Carter licked his lips as he pulled his shirt over his head.

Miamor put one finger in her mouth and sucked it erotically as she enjoyed the chiseled view in front of her. She took the moisture from her mouth and circled it on her clitoris. Her love button throbbed intensely as she rolled it between her fingers.

"You like what you see?" Miamor asked as she inserted two fingers inside herself. Miamor was so sure of herself. She wasn't shy and was comfortable in her own skin, so she continued to please herself for a minute or two. Her pussy was soaking wet, and she began to grind her hips to her own beat. She closed her eyes as her other hand massaged her now stiff nipples. The feeling caused a low moan to escape her lips.

Carter kept looking down at her and felt his dick get hard. His manhood was urging him to get in the game, but he contained himself, trying to savor the moment, not wanting to be too eager.

When Miamor took her finger out of her pussy to taste her own juices, Carter could no longer contain himself. The print of his eleven inches was bulging in his jeans, and he quickly stepped out of them and positioned himself on top of her. He grabbed one of the strawberries and put it in her mouth as she nibbled on it sexily. His mouth found hers, and their tongues intertwined. He could taste the sweet fruit on her tongue along with the sweet taste of pussy as his rock-hard erection rubbed against her thigh.

Carter stuck his finger in the melted chocolate and rubbed it on her nipples as he feasted on them, tugging at them gently with his lips and tongue.

"Mmm," Mia moaned, her back arched from the tingling pleasure that was shooting through her back.

Her body was like a buffet, Carter pouring champagne on top of her and licking it clean, never leaving a trace behind. He made his way down to her womanly opening and lifted one leg in the air, which she rested on his broad shoulders as her eyes rolled back in her head. Carter then introduced his tongue to her clitoris, licking it gently as if he were tongue-kissing her mouth instead of her pussy.

Miamor began to shake uncontrollably. No man had ever done her body so good. Carter definitely knew what he was doing. His head game was out of this world. Most men rushed and only went downtown to benefit themselves by getting the pussy more wet, but Carter took his time, inserting two fingers as she grinded on his face.

"Oh my God," she moaned as her hands found the back of his head. "Wait," she whined. Carter was eating her pussy so well that Miamor couldn't wait to return the favor.

She sat up on her elbows and attempted to get up, but Carter pulled her back underneath him as she lay back and watched his swell glisten in the moonlight, pre-cum resting on the tip. He rubbed her clit with his hat, and the warmth from his body temperature made her hot, sizzling against her honey pot.

It had been a long time since she had been intimate with someone, and it wasn't until now that she realized how much she missed a man's touch. "I want to feel you inside of me," she whispered as she wrapped her arms around his back and slid her hands down until they reached his toned behind.

"Wait, I don't have a condom," he whispered. He silently cursed himself for not being prepared.

Miamor looked him dead in his eyes. “Then don’t make a baby, if you don’t want one.” She pulled him into her, and he immediately filled the space between her legs, his thick hardness throbbing inside of her as her walls contracted around his large shaft.

“Shit, you feel so good,” he told her as he rocked in and out of her with a slow, passionate rhythm.

Miamor was silent as she stared into his eyes. She had never been with a man that looked at her the way Carter did at that moment. Their gaze expressed more than any words could ever do. They had a sexual chemistry that was out of this world, and he was making her body hurt in a pleasing way. A tear slipped from her eyes, and he kissed it away as it rolled down her cheek.

Miamor moved her wide hips in unison and matched him pump for pump, and Carter put his hands underneath her rear and lifted her hips, allowing him to dig deeper into her.

“Carter!” she called out in ecstasy as he explored depths in her that she didn’t even know existed. “Carter,” she repeated as he sped up and pounded into her a little harder.

She was about to cum, and from the low grunts that came out of his mouth, she could tell that he was about to nut at any moment. “Make me cum, Carter,” she whispered.

He pumped into her harder at the sound of her voice.

“Ohh shit, daddy, make me cum,” she begged.

He stroked her faster. “I’ma make you cum, Miamor. Oh shit, your pussy is so good, ma.”

She grabbed his ass and rotated her hips into him as she felt her body reach its peak. “Oh my . . . aww!” she screamed, as her toes curling and her body tensing up from the intensity of her orgasm.

“Damn, ma,” Carter said, pulling out and nutting against her flat stomach.

Miamor snuggled underneath Carter as they lay naked on the empty beach. He reached out and grabbed the blanket from their picnic and covered their bodies with it as they sat together and looked out on the ocean.

Carter was silent, and Miamor instantly began to regret having sex with him. *Damn, I know this nigga probably thinking I'm a ho. I shouldn't have fucked him this soon,* she thought. Miamor had only been with one other person in her entire life, and she didn't know why she had let Carter have her body so easily. There was something about him that she trusted, and he had her open.

"Carter, I don't want you to think—"

"I don't, so don't worry about it," he replied before she could even finish her sentence. He already knew what she was thinking, but he wasn't shallow enough to worry about anything that happened before him. They were both grown as hell, and he didn't want her to feel awkward for allowing him to enjoy her physically.

He turned her face toward his. "As long as you act like a lady, I'll never think anything less of you, understand?"

She nodded her head. "Will I get to see you again?"

"I want to spend some time with you, but I need to take care of some business back home first."

"Back home? You're not from Miami?" Miamor realized she didn't know a damn thing about this man.

"Naw, I'm from Michigan, from Flint." Carter played with her fingers. He brought her hand to his mouth and kissed it.

"How long will you be gone?"

Carter smiled. He could hear the disappointment in her voice. He knew he had to be careful with this woman. He could see that Miamor played tough on the outside, but on the inside, she was hurt and neglected from her past, which made her susceptible to heartbreak. Her vulnerability pleased him, and he was willing to become her protector, if she played her cards right.

"Not long. I just need to tie up some loose ends. It looks like I'm gon' be moving down here for a minute. Don't worry, Miamor, I'll make sure I check for you when I get back."

She sat with her back to his chest and turned her neck to kiss him on the lips. "I better get going," she said as she grabbed her dress and stepped into it.

Carter stood and slipped back into his clothing as well.

Miamor retrieved her clutch bag and pulled out a pen to write her number down. She grabbed his hand and wrote it on his skin and then wrote his number down as well.

"Call me when you come back in town," she said as she looked up at him with a smile.

Carter grabbed the back of her neck and brought her body close to his as he leaned down to kiss her lips. "Be safe."

Miamor stepped out of his arms and walked away. She smiled and waved before walking down the beach, toward the pier.

Carter shook his head as he watched her stroll away.

Her hair was a mess, and sand stuck to her legs as her hips swayed from side to side, but she had his attention. Her swagger was intriguing. He rubbed his goatee, and a sly smile graced his lips. "I'm gon' definitely check for you, Miamor, believe that," he said to himself as she disappeared into the darkness.

Chapter Eight

"Welcome home." —Unknown

Breeze hugged Carter good-bye. "Are you really coming back?"

"Yeah, *B*, I'll be back. I've got to get some things together in Flint, but as soon as that's taken care of, I'll be on the first flight down." Carter could see the doubt in his sister's eyes. "I promise."

Money and Carter slapped hands and embraced. "Be safe, fam," Money told him.

"No doubt, baby."

Mecca walked by and nodded his head, but didn't acknowledge Carter's departure with words, and Taryn hugged him gently.

"We better get out of here before you miss your flight." Polo patted Carter's shoulder, and they hopped into the black limousine and pulled away from the estate.

Ma'tee noticed the black limo pulling away from the Diamond estate and halted his driver. "Wait," Ma'tee instructed as he sat a block down from his intended destination, "me will sit here for a second and watch." He checked the 9 mm Desert Eagle that was holstered in his waistline to ensure that it was locked and loaded before he nodded his head at his driver. "Tell de guard dat Mr. Diamond forgot something," Ma'tee said, hoping that the guards would not want to check the inside of the car as they pulled up to the gated entrance. He wanted them to think that his limo was the same limo that had just left the estate fifteen minutes earlier.

His driver followed his instructions to the tee, and just as Ma'tee had expected, they were given access to the household without suspicion. The guards were clueless to the fact that their enemies were the true passengers behind the dark limo tint.

Ma'tee looked to his full-blooded Haitian soldiers that sat around him, all armed with semi-automatic pistols and ready for whatever. When the limo stopped in front of the house, he exited the limo calmly and rang the doorbell, his goons positioned behind him.

Breeze answered the door, and her smile quickly faded when she noticed the Haitian men at her doorstep. "Aghh!" she screamed.

"No need to scream, Diamond princess," Ma'tee stated calmly, realizing that he was standing in front of the only daughter of his sworn enemy, Carter Diamond. "Me come peacefully to talk with de head of de Cartel."

At that moment, Taryn came gliding into the room. "What are you screaming about, Breeze? Who is . . ." Her words trailed off, and her eyes turned cold as she stared into the eyes of Ma'tee, the man who had murdered her husband in cold blood.

"How dare you!" Taryn screamed as tears filled her eyes. She smacked Ma'tee across the face with all her might. Her rage was apparent, and she stood her ground, even though fear gripped her heart.

Ma'tee's soldiers tensed up at her reaction, but again Ma'tee instructed them to stand down.

"Go and get your brothers." Taryn spoke calmly but sternly, yet her eyes never left those of the enemy. She didn't want to give them the pleasure of seeing her intimidated.

Breeze ran out of the room to get her brothers.

"Me come in peace," Ma'tee repeated when Mecca and Monroe appeared.

"Fuck mu'fuckas coming to the estate!" Mecca screamed. He immediately pulled two .45s from his waistline and trained them on Ma'tee.

"We need to talk," Ma'tee stated. "As chu can see, chu family is not untouchable, young Mecca. If me wanted to bring malice to chu door, chu sista and mutha would be dead right now. Me come to call a truce."

"Only after you murdered my father and we put the heat on your ass. You're here because of what happened at your daughter's birthday party. *You* are not untouchable, Ma'tee. If we wanted to bring malice to your door, then you would've buried your fucking daughter last week," Monroe stated calmly. He pulled his own 9 mm from his waistline and rested it in his palm at his side.

"Me understand. Bloodshed came to close to me home wit' me baby girl. Me will stand down if de Cartel will."

Mecca yelled, "I'ma murder your fucking daughter, mu'fucka. Fuck a truce, bitch. You took my father, I take her—Fair exchange ain't no robbery!"

"Yuh kill me daughter, ah kill you sister, then what, young soldier? De Cartel has nothing to lose by calling a truce. Yuh keep yuh territory and we all gain peace of mind."

Monroe knew that a truce made sense, but was reluctant to make a deal with the devil. "How do we know you will keep up your end?"

"Me a man. Me will keep me word. Me word is all me have." Ma'tee held out his hand.

Monroe stared contemptuously at Ma'tee's hand, rage burning in his heart from the fresh wound of his dead father. He knew that the truce was a wise decision, at least for the time being. He shook Ma'tee's hand firmly, staring him in the eye. Monroe's gaze was nothing short of menacing, and it held an underlying message. One that said he had not forgotten what Ma'tee had done to his father.

"We have an understanding. Now see yourself off of our property," Monroe stated. He watched as the Haitians retreated and the limo disappeared beyond the security gates. Money turned to Mecca and said, "Go handle that stupid mu'fucka at the gates. Dead his ass. They should've never made it to the door."

Mecca stormed out of the house and walked across the large manicured lawn while Ma'tee and his limo approached the steel gate. They reached the exit at the same time, and Ma'tee rolled down his window.

The guard posted at the gate looked at Mecca approaching and then shifted his gaze back to Ma'tee.

"I just thought you should know why you're about to die," Ma'tee said as he lit a cigar and rolled his window back up.

At that exact moment Mecca reached the guard and removed his chrome 9 mm Ruger.

"Me-Mecca, I didn't know that was—"

Boom!

Mecca didn't hesitate to pull the trigger. The guard's life was ended instantly as the hollow-point bullet ripped through his skull. Mecca then hit the button to open the gate for Ma'tee's limo, and ice grilled the car as it rolled away toward safety.

Truce or no truce, I'm going to avenge Poppa's murder. Niggas got me fucked up.

Carter was finally home after being in Miami for the past couple of weeks. He walked into his spacious two-bedroom that sat in a suburban area just outside Flint, Michigan. Carter took a deep breath as he realized how good it felt to be there. His condo was small but comfortable. He had just purchased it a year earlier. He always said, when his money got right, he would move out of the hood, and that's exactly what he did.

The brick walls were ornamented with various Afrocentric paintings. A large picture of Bob Marley smoking a joint and playing his guitar hung above the fireplace. The place was definitely a bachelor's pad, but Carter had decorated it pretty well. He tossed the duffle bag full of money onto his brown sectional sofa and pulled his gun from his waist and placed it on the bar-style kitchen countertop.

Carter was getting money in Flint, and it wasn't a secret. For every getting-money dope man, there were a hundred broke niggas, so Carter knew that he was a target for the local stick-up kids in his old neighborhood. Moving out of the hood was not an option after Carter began to become a heavyweight in the streets.

Just as he was about to walk to the refrigerator and toss out some of the food he had left there, he heard a noise coming from the back. *What the fuck was that*? Carter scooped up his gun and listened closer. He heard commotion coming from his back room and knew that someone was trying to find his stash. His street instincts immediately kicked in. He switched his banger off safety and began to creep to the back.

As he got closer, he saw that his guest bedroom was where the noises were coming from. His door was closed, so he crept up and kicked it open, his gun drawn.

The big-butt Latino woman screamed, "Oh, daddy! Fuck me, *papi*!" as Ace beat it from the back.

The sounds of Ace's balls smacking against the woman's genitalia filled the air, and his chain jingled on his bare chest as he continued to sex the girl, while Carter pointed his gun at him. Carter smiled and lowered his gun as he chuckled to himself. He was laughing at how crazy his best friend was. He didn't even stop pumping when he saw Carter bust in. The girl was so busy getting her back blew out, she didn't even notice Carter come in.

Ace looked at his best friend and threw his head up, greeting him while still pleasing himself.

Carter walked out shaking his head from side to side. He knew it wasn't a good idea to leave an extra set of keys with Ace. He'd told Ace to come in and check on his spot periodically, not bring his jump-offs there. "That nigga is wildin'," Carter said in irritation as he walked to his living room and tossed his gun on the couch.

Ace and Carter had been best friends since third grade and were more like brothers than anything else. Carter didn't like the fact that Ace had a chick up in his spot, but didn't say anything. He didn't want to cock-block his man, but he was surely going to express his discomfort later.

Carter took a seat on his couch and felt his cell phone vibrate on his hip. He looked at the caller ID and smiled. It was Miamor calling. *I got to stay focused. I'm going to get at her later*, he thought to himself as a small grin spread across his face.

Carter wanted to pick up for her, but he wanted to stay focused on his brief return home. He was planning to move to Miami and get on his hustle. He figured Miami was a good place for him to take over and join the family business. He saw more money in the three weeks in Miami than in a year hustling in Flint. The move was a must for him.

Just as Carter finished his thought, Ace came from the back, buttoning up his Sean John jeans.

"Fam, what's good? I thought you weren't coming back for a week or so?" Ace walked over to the bar and rested his hands on the counter.

Carter remained silent and just looked at him with a piercing stare.

Ace knew that his right-hand man was upset with him, so he tried to make light of the situation. "Did you see that ass on that broad?" He nodded his head in the direction of the back room.

Just before Carter could tell Ace about himself, the naked Latino woman came walking out, and all eyes were on her. She walked out without a care in the world, as if she wasn't butt naked. Her behind was so big, you could literally sit a cup on top of it and it wouldn't move. The only thing she wore was red pumps, and her plump, voluptuous ass cheeks shifted sides with every stride. The nonstop jiggling had the two men in a trance.

"Hello, *papi*," she said as she looked over at Carter on the sofa. She then turned to Ace and gave him a passionate kiss before walking over to the refrigerator and grabbing some orange juice.

"Ace, you didn't tell me you were having company." She put her hand on her hip and cocked her head to the side.

Carter couldn't believe his ears. His man Ace was stunting for a ho, pretending that it was his condo, rather than Carter's.

Ace looked at him and read his mind. He grinned and shrugged his shoulders as if to say, "How could I not stunt for an ass like that?"

Carter shook his head and headed out the door. He motioned for Ace to follow him. Once they reached the door and out of earshot of the woman, Carter told him, "Have that trick out of my shit in an hour. You owe me a stack for fucking in my bed too, nigga. You buying me some new sheets and all." Carter's face was expressing his anger at that point. He peeked around the corner to get another look at the horse ass the woman was toting and then looked back at Ace. "Shorty got a fat ass, though," he said as he smiled and stuck out his hand.

Ace returned the smile and shook his man's hand. He was relieved and surprised by Carter's reaction. He was sure he was going to spazz out for him having a girl up in his house and pretending it was his own. He and Carter were like brothers and Carter wouldn't front his man out like that, but Ace surely was going to pay out of his pockets for his little fun.

"I got you, Carter. My fault about this little situation. You know my baby mama be popping up at my crib acting a fool. Anyway, I'm glad you back home, my nigga. Shit been crazy since you left. After I drop her off, I'll meet you at the spot. I need to pick up anyway."

"Look, I'll pick up the cash from the spot. You just get her out of here and meet me there when you finish up," Carter said as he opened the door and headed out. Just before he closed the door, he turned around and looked at Ace sternly. "Don't ever bring a bitch to my house, Ace. We got to stay smart, all right?"

"All right," Ace said just before he closed the door.

Carter drove his black-on-black 2008 Impala down I-75, bobbing his head to rapper T.I.'s CD. He was on his way to visit his candy shop. Having been away for weeks, he knew he had a nice piece of change waiting for him in the hood. Before he left, he had hit all his four head soldiers with a half kilo on consignment. That meant around $40,000 altogether was owed to him.

For years Carter had been dealing with straight blow—raw cocaine—but after he was exposed to Miami's heroin trade, he wanted in. Monroe and Polo had offered him a position in the business, and the offer was too good to refuse. He told them that he had to return home to handle some business and would return to join The Cartel.

Carter's soldiers didn't know, but he was going to refuse the consignment money and give it to them as a farewell gift. He was ready to leave the murder capital that he called home.

Carter pulled onto the block of North Saginaw and Harriet and saw his goons standing on the corner trying to make pay. He crept up the street behind his limo tint and parked on the curb in front of the candy shop.

As soon as Carter stepped out, he shut down the block. It was scorching hot at ninety-six degrees, and the sun seemed to bounce off his iced-out Jesus piece. Shirtless, his chain hung down to his belt buckle, and all of the tattoos on his ripped body were on display. He wore a Detroit fitted cap pulled low over his eyes, crisp jeans, and butter Timberland, to top it off.

Everyone had their eyes on him, and the hood threw him an onslaught of greetings. Even the small kids playing in the streets stopped and admired him.

Carter proceeded to walk into the candy shop.

"Carter! What's good?"

"Yo, Carter, glad you home."

"What up, boy."

Carter released a small smile and a peace sign as he headed into the apartment projects where the coke was manufactured. He walked up to the fifth floor of the projects. He knocked on the door in a pattern only he and his workers knew and gained entry. When he walked in, the smell of cooked dope filled his nostrils. It was business as usual with topless women cutting up the cooked coke on the round wood table, and naked women with a doctor's mask scattered over the room, doing their assigned job in the drug operation.

Carter smiled, knowing that his small operation was still running smoothly during his absence. He'd left Ace in charge while he was away, and just as he expected, everything was butter, making the offer that Polo had made him even more tempting.

Carter walked through the house and greeted his workers and henchmen as he made his way to the back where the money was held. He walked into the room and saw one of his head lieutenants, Zyir, a blunt hanging out of his mouth, running money through the money machine.

Zyir was a little nigga. Only eighteen, he was a smooth-faced, fast-talking hustler at the top of his game. He had been working for Carter since he was fourteen and was the one who ran that particular spot. Zyir reminded Carter of himself, and Carter knew that he was the future. He had a certain swagger about himself that typified gangster.

Zyir was so busy staring at the money, he didn't even see Carter enter the room.

"Family, family, what's good?" Carter asked as he walked toward the table.

"Oh shit! My nigga. What's good?" Zyir got up and embraced Carter. "When you get back?"

"I came in last night. How's business?"

"Up and down. Yo, I got that for you, plus interest," Zyir said, referring to the weight that Carter had hit him with before he left.

"Yeah, that's what I'm came to talk to you about." Carter took a seat. "That's on you, fam. You don't owe me anything."

"You serious?"

"Yeah, you good. I'm outta here for good this weekend. Take it as a gift, nah mean? From now on, you can get the coke from Ace. He got the same connect, and the prices are going to remain the same." Carter held out his hand.

Zyir shook Carter's hand. He was happy to hear that he didn't owe Carter any money, but sad to hear that his man was leaving the city for good. He knew that Flint was losing a thorough dude. Honestly, he didn't like the idea of buying coke from Ace because he knew how hotheaded he could be at times.

Zyir couldn't believe that Carter would give up his successful cocaine operation. "Yo, are you really leaving for good?"

"Yeah, fam, I'm done." Carter knew that the paper he was making in Flint was remedial, compared to the opportunity that awaited him in Miami with The Cartel. He was about to follow in his father's notorious footsteps. Carter turned to leave, but before he left, he took off his three-carat pinky ring and tossed it to Zyir.

Carter loaded his Range Rover with his luggage with the help of Ace and Zyir, as he prepared to leave for Miami. Once the car was loaded up, Carter slapped hands with his crew and told them that he would send for them, once he got comfortable in Miami. Anxious to get back to Miami, he got in the car and pulled off. He tried to convince himself that he was looking forward to getting money there, but seeing Miamor again was definitely a factor in his decision.

Chapter Nine

"We don't die, bitch!" —Mecca

When Monroe stepped into the conference room, he was shining like new money. The nervous energy in his stomach quickly subsided as he shook hands with the group of men who had invested in Diamond Realty. His Oleg Cassini designer suit and Steve Madden shoes solidified his position as the new head of his father's company. He walked, talked, and dressed the part, but he was aware of the skepticism and larceny in the hearts of his business peers. His father's business partners were not too keen at the thought of him heading the business.

Diamond Realty had been founded from drug money and private investments from the board members. In its seven years of being in business, the commercial and high-end residential real estate company had acquired some of the most sought-after properties in Florida and was worth well over a hundred million dollars in equity alone. The company's worth was growing by the day, and the board members felt that Carter's position should have been given to someone more qualified than his son.

"Monroe, it's good to have you on board," Harper Spokes greeted as he and Monroe shook hands.

"It's good to be on board, Harper," Monroe responded.

Harper took a seat at the head of the conference table, sat back comfortably in the chair, and loosened his necktie a bit. "I know that it's going to take some time for you to get used to the way we do things here. Getting into the swing of things is going to take some time, but I'm willing to teach you everything I know. A little training from me, and you'll be a pro," Harper stated confidently. He figured that if he played the role of mentor, it would be easy for him to call the shots from behind the scenes.

Monroe walked behind Harper and put his hands on his shoulders as he looked out at the rest of the board members. "That won't be necessary, Harper, although it was a gracious offer. The way we do things are about to change, indeed." Monroe patted the back of Harper's chair, signaling him to arise from his seat. He then tightened Harper's necktie and looked him sternly in the eye. "I'm the boss," he stressed. "The way that we do business will revolutionize so that I am familiar and comfortable with the daily operations and you all are the ones in training. You all will be the ones adjusting, because you have to learn the way that I conduct business."

Monroe pulled out a chair in the middle of the conference table. "Have a seat, Harper." He gave the man time to sit down before he continued. "Now I can assure you that it is very similar to the way that my father did things, but I will not allow myself to be at a disadvantage in my own company. New leadership brings about new policy. If any of you think that it is time for you to move on to new ventures, I completely understand. I will accommodate you with severance pay, but I can guarantee that if you stay on board we will all see a substantial rise in profits. The way that I am going to expand Diamond Realty is going to be nothing short of remarkable, and I would love to have each of you on my team. What do you say?"

Silence filled the room. Monroe wasn't naïve and was sure that there were members who doubted him and even some that wanted to get up and leave, but they were cowards and would never speak up. He took their silence for submission and was satisfied with their fear of him. It was the same type of respect that his father had demanded, and the torch had just been passed down. He nodded his head, hung his suit jacket on the back of his chair, and then took his seat. "Since there are no objections, let's get down to business."

"Are you almost done? This is taking all damn day."

Mecca looked over at the dark-skinned beauty sitting beside him. Her long legs glistened as she positioned them on his dashboard while painting her toe nails.

"Look, Leena, don't start popping that bullshit. I told you what I was doing today. You the one thought I was going to fuck with a bitch, so you tried to bring your happy ass with me. You know what time of the month it is, so just sit back and chill," Mecca stated with a smirk as he eyed the woman beside him.

Leena sucked her teeth and rolled her eyes, but remained quiet. She folded her arms across her chest and, out of habit, began to pout.

Mecca shook his head. He reached over to grab her hand. He knew that he was the one who had spoiled her, so he couldn't be too upset with her. He had been in an on-again, off-again relationship with Leena since they were young teenagers. She had witnessed his transformation from boy to man and knew of his involvement in his family's business.

"I'll take you shopping after this, a'ight."

"Yeah, okay," she replied as she tried to keep the smile from spreading across her face.

In truth he would do anything to keep a smile on her face. Leena was the only woman to capture his heart, and he loved her more than she knew.

Mecca drove up the avenue in his apple red F-150 pickup with chrome rims. He cruised slowly up the block so that his presence could be felt. It was the first of the month, which signified payday for The Cartel, and he was riding around like a landlord, collecting his rent. It was the first pickup since his father had died, and so far two of their many block lieutenants had come short, causing Mecca to have a short fuse.

These mu'fuckas coming short on my money. It's about to be a problem. Not a dime was missing when Poppa was alive. Now these fuck-ass niggas wanna step outta line. Mecca maneuvered his way to the two-story colonial-style house on the end of the block. He put his truck into park and pulled out his cell phone to call his worker inside the trap house.

"I'm outside. I'm about to send a bitch to the back door. Give my money to her."

Leena looked at Mecca like he was crazy and shook her head no. "Nigga, you got me fucked up. I ain't going up in there, and I don't know who the fuck you calling a bitch," she whispered more to herself than to him.

Mecca ignored her and continued to speak into the phone. "Is my money right?" he paused again to let his worker respond and then hung up. "It better be," he stated to himself. He then turned to Leena and said, "What the fuck I tell you about talking shit while I'm on the phone? Go get my shit, and don't look in the bag either, with your nosy ass."

"Whatever, Mecca. I'm not new to money. I don't have to take shit from you." Leena hopped out of the truck and walked across the lawn.

Mecca knew she wasn't lying. She had the type of beauty that made niggas want to wife her. She was sophisticated, and her superior attitude made her appealing to most men. If she wasn't on Mecca's arm, there would be many men willing to extend theirs, and she knew it. She turned many heads as her voluptuous behind shook with each step she took.

Out of respect for Mecca, the hustlers on the block didn't try to get at her, but Mecca shook his head and laughed to himself as he watched them drool at the mouth.

Thirsty-ass niggas, he thought as he watched Leena disappear down the long driveway. *They'll never get a taste of that. That's all me.*

"Hey, Mecca," a random hoodrat called out. She stepped close to his truck, while sucking on a red Blow Pop. In fact all of the groupie broads had come out of hiding as soon as they'd heard the beat from Mecca's subwoofers turn onto the block. The old saying, out of sight, out of mind, must have been true because as soon as Leena stepped out of sight, the hot girls on the block flocked to him.

Mecca looked up and down at the girl. She was attractive in a ghetto kind of way. Her skintight booty shorts left nothing to the imagination, and her sleeveless tube top hugged her ample breasts. What really got his attention was the way her tongue was pulling on that red sucker. It made his dick jump slightly. He scanned her quickly from top to bottom and was turned off by the re-washed Reebok classics that adorned her feet. Mecca knew his status and would never be caught dead entertaining a chick like the one before him. *Every nigga this side of Dade done probably dug this bitch out,* he thought in disgust. He even grew irritated that she had thought herself worthy of even stepping to him.

"Come here," he stated as he prepared to put the girl in her place.

Her lips spread into a seductive smile as she sashayed across the street. She stepped close to his window, but Mecca frowned at the fact that her focus seemed to be behind him. He instantly noticed that her eyes seemed to look past him to his passenger window. He could almost smell the .380-pistol that was creeping up on him.

Instinctively, Mecca's sixth sense kicked in, and he pulled his twin Desert Eagles from underneath his seats. With one gun in each hand he reached out on both sides of him and fired hollow-points—*Boom! Boom!*—dropping the girl and the gunman at his passenger window instantly.

Just then, a shotgun shell crashed through Mecca's rear windshield. Glass flew everywhere as the deafening sound vibrated through the vehicle.

Mecca ducked low as he reached for his door handle and scrambled out of the truck. *What the fuck?* He sent hollow-points flying across his truck hood in an attempt to keep the shooter on the other side at bay.

Mecca stayed low against his car door to avoid the gunfire of his attacker. He could hear people screaming as they ran to get out of the crossfire. He looked underneath the car and put bullets into the legs of the gunman.

"Aghh!"

Once Mecca saw the gunman go down, he sprang into action and rushed to the other side of the car. "Nigga trying to murk me!" he yelled furiously as he kicked the shotgun out of the fallen soldier's reach. He aimed his gun at the dude's head.

"Please, man, please don't kill me," the dude pleaded.

Mecca snatched the ski mask off the gunman's face. He had expected to see a dreadhead, due to The Cartel's ongoing beef with the Haitians. To his surprise, it was one of his very own soldiers lying at his feet. *What the fuck? My own camp plotting on me now?* Mecca was astounded and didn't know what to think.

"Don't bitch up now, mu'fucka! You had the balls to get at me!" Mecca screamed as he pistol-whipped the man. "Who sent you, huh?" Mecca brought the cold steel down across the man's face with brutal force, causing blood to splatter onto his white T-shirt. "You trying to kill me?" He hit the man once again, baffled that he had to prove that he was the king of Miami's concrete jungle.

Leena came running out of the house with a duffle bag full of money in her hands. "Mecca!" she screamed in fright at the sight before her.

"Go back in the house!" Mecca yelled at her without even looking her way.

The man groaned in pain as he bled on the hot pavement. Mecca pressed the gun to the middle of his forehead.

"Nah, man! Nobody sent us, I swear. We were just gon' rob you. My brother and his girlfriend, that's it, man. We just wanted the money. Please don't kill me."

"Niggas really think we slippin' out here!" Mecca yelled as he stood up and addressed the crowd of hustlers and courageous spectators. "Y'all niggas really think we touchable now, huh?" Mecca was like a pit bull as he stood above the dude and looked every hood nigga in his eye, while they watched on in horror. "We don't die, bitch! Diamonds are forever, mu'fuckas." Seething through a clenched jaw, Mecca unloaded the rest of his clip into the man's dome and then hopped into his truck, speeding away recklessly.

Mecca steadied his driving and eased off the gas pedal when he saw the Miami police cruisers coming his way. He hit the steering wheel repeatedly as he tried to gain composure of himself. His adrenaline was uncontrollable as he thought about what had just occurred. The song "Many Men" filled the interior of the truck as his cell phone continued to ring. He looked down at his caller ID and noticed that it was Leena. "Fuck!" he yelled aloud, realizing that he had left her there with a duffle bag full of drug money.

"Hello?" he answered.

"What the fuck you mean, hello? Mecca! You left me here! Why would you just pull off on me like that?" Leena screamed.

Mecca could tell that she was crying, and guilt immediately plagued him. He hadn't even thought to retrieve her from the house when he pulled off. The only thing that was on his mind was fleeing the scene before the cops arrived.

"Mecca!" Leena cried.

"Leena, listen to me, all right. Calm down. You know I wouldn't leave you for dead. You couldn't ride with me, baby girl. You saw how I left that nigga leaking. I didn't want you tied up in no murder, so I just pulled off. I'm gon' send somebody through to pick you up, a'ight."

"Mecca, oh my God, the police just pulled up. Please come and get me," Leena whispered, her tears flowing.

"Leena, I'ma send somebody through for you. Just sit tight. You didn't see shit, and you don't know shit, understand?"

"Yeah, baby, I understand."

Mecca told her, "Hurry up and put Sheed on the phone." When his block lieutenant came on, Mecca instructed him to hide the cash.

"What you want me to do about ol' girl?" Sheed asked.

"Just let her stay there for an hour or so. I'll send somebody to pick her and the money up when shit die down."

"Mr. Diamond, your brother Mecca is here to see you," the receptionist called out over the interoffice intercom.

Monroe hit the reply button on the intercom and picked up the phone so that the other members of the board couldn't hear both ends of the conversation. "Porscha, can you tell him that I'm in a meeting right now."

"I know, sir. I'm sorry for interrupting, but Mecca says it's an emergency."

"I'll be right out." Monroe turned to his business associates. "If you all will excuse me for a couple minutes . . . I have some business to tend to." Monroe quickly exited the room, and his eyes widened in shock when he saw his brother covered in blood.

"Umm, Porscha, can you tell the board members that this meeting is adjourned and find a time that works with them so that we can reschedule. Hold all calls too please." Monroe nodded for Mecca to follow him.

"Fuck happened to you?" Money asked as they entered another conference room.

"I just bodied a nigga in front of Sheed's spot."

"In front of Sheed's spot? What were you thinking, bro? You supposed to be handling the street business and you making shit hot on one of our most lucrative blocks?"

"I know but—"

At that moment Money's cell phone rang, interrupting Mecca. He checked his BlackBerry and noticed that it was Carter. He immediately picked up and put Young Carter on speakerphone.

"What's good, fam?" Carter greeted.

"Man, we got problems this way." Money knew that Carter could give them good advice on how to fix Mecca's mess.

"What up?" Carter asked.

"Mecca caught a body."

"What?"

"Man, Young Carter, it ain't even how Money making it sound. I wasn't on no hot shit or nothing. I send Leena into one of the spots to collect the cash, and these mu'fuckas run up with they pistols blazing and shit, trying to rob ya boy."

"You had your bitch with you while you were picking up the money?" Carter asked.

"I told yo ass about having Leena riding with you during business," Money stated sternly in disbelief. "You need to keep her out of harm's way, bro. Today is the perfect example."

"Look, the police came, so I hopped in the truck and sped off, but everything happened so fast, fam. I left Leena there with the money."

"You left her there?" Money askd.

"With the money?"

"Yeah, mu'fuckas, damn! I left her there with the money."

"That's your brother," Carter stated in amusement.

"That's *your* brother," Money told him.

"But on a serious note, Mecca, fall back for a couple days, just to let things settle, a'ight, fam."

"Yeah, I hear you," Mecca replied hesitantly. He hated taking orders from his older brother, and still wasn't used to there being more than Money, Breeze, and himself, but inside he knew that Carter was right.

"A'ight, fam, I'll be back in town in a couple days. I'll be in touch," Carter said before hanging up.

Mecca pulled his bloody T-shirt over his head and slapped hands with his twin brother.

"Go sit your ass down somewhere, bro. I'll go pick up the cash and drop Leena off at home." Money headed toward the door.

"Yo, Money!" Mecca shouted.

Money stopped and turned around to listen, raising his eyebrows to let his brother know that he had his attention.

"I love her, fam. Make sure she's okay for me, a'ight."

Money nodded and left the room.

Money pulled up to Sheed's spot. Sheed was one of their best workers, so he was positive that his street lieutenant would be able to handle the police. There were no squad cars in sight, but the block was live with residents sitting around discussing the events that had happened that day. Money stepped out of the car and all eyes seemed to be on him. He was slightly irritated at how much attention Mecca had brought to their block, but he understood that Mecca had to react. It was either kill or be killed, and Money knew that Mecca had made the best decision that he could have made under the circumstances.

He knocked on the front door, and it opened instantly.

"Fam, the police was asking everybody questions. I didn't see shit, nah mean?" Sheed allowed Monroe to enter his living room.

"You got that?" Money asked.

Sheed pulled the duffle bag out of his coat closet and tossed it to Money. Opening the bag to make sure it was all there, Money tried to inventory the cash quickly by sight.

"Come on, fam, don't insult me," Sheed said. "You know I'm one hunnid."

Money gave Sheed a look that spoke volumes. Sheed took the hint and shut up, while Money continued to thumb through the bag. Once he was satisfied, he took out five stacks and set it on Sheed's table. "Thanks for keeping things quiet and looking out for Mecca's chick. Where is she?"

"She's in the den. She's been tripping ever since she saw dude body on the lawn. She's spazzing, yo."

"Don't worry about it," Money said as he walked toward Sheed's den. "I'll take care of it." He walked into the room and saw Leena sitting on the couch, her face in her hands. "You all right?"

His voice startled her, and she looked up in surprise. "Money? Where's Mecca?" she asked, tears in her eyes. "He just left me here for dead. The least he could've done was come back for me."

"Come on, Lee, let's get out of here." Money reached for her arm and pulled her from the couch.

Money helped Leena into his 2009 pearl white Cadillac STS before getting into the car himself and speeding away. Leena was quiet, and it wasn't until they arrived at her luxury ocean view apartment that she did speak.

"There was blood everywhere," Leena whispered. "You didn't see it, Money. It was horrible." She walked over to her window and looked out onto the ocean below her. "How can a city so beautiful harbor so many secrets?"

Money didn't know how to respond, so he remained silent. He knew that she would be shook up after witnessing Mecca kill someone. It was natural.

"You know Mecca would never let anything happen to you, right?"

Leena laughed lightly and shook her head. "I don't even want to think about him right now," she stated, still upset with Mecca for leaving her at the murder scene.

Money walked toward her as she continued to stand in front of the window. He stood behind her, wrapping his arms around her waist and whispered in her ear. "You know I would never let anything happen to you, ma."

Money's touch sent shivers down her spine, and she closed her eyes and reveled in the moment.

"I love you, Monroe," she stated, guilt in her voice.

Leena had never meant to fall for both brothers, but over the years as she dated Mecca, she began to see that Monroe possessed everything he was lacking. Mecca had cheated on her, whereas Monroe was faithful, even though she wasn't rightfully his. Mecca had a temper, whereas Monroe was calm and always in control. Mecca loved the limelight, whereas

Monroe played the back. Mecca was a hothead, spur-of-the-moment type of man, whereas Monroe was strategic and calculating. They were completely opposite, but Leena loved them both. But Money was the one that she wanted to be with.

Leena turned around to face Money. "When are you going to tell Mecca about us?"

Money released her from his embrace and sat down on her oversized couch. "I don't know," he stated honestly.

"I can't keep doing this, Money. The more I'm around Mecca, the more I see that he's not the man for me. He isn't even ready to stop fucking around on me. I want to be with you. We shouldn't have to sneak around like this. Messing around with both of you has me feeling cheap and dirty. I'm not one of these little groupie chicks out here, Money. I feel like you want it to stay like this forever. What? You don't love me? You don't want to be with me? Is this thing we're doing just a game to you?"

"You know I care for you, Lee."

"But you don't love me?" she questioned with a slight attitude, nodding her head up and down as if she was starting to see things clearly.

"Yes, I love you, but he's my brother. He loves you too. You don't see it, but I hear the way he talks about you, Leena. He may not be ready to commit to you, but he loves you. No matter how much I try to justify this, he met you first. And I'm fucking you behind his back. You don't belong to me!" Monroe shouted vehemently as he stood and began to pace the room back and forth.

His words brought tears to Leena's eyes. "Oh, so is that all I am to you—a good fuck? A piece of property? Just to let you know, Money, I don't belong to anybody. I'm a grown-ass woman that deserves to be happy, and I'm not happy with Mecca." She shook her head at him in disgust. "I can't fuckin' believe you! Is that really all I am to you? Another bitch you fucking?"

"No!" Money yelled in frustration. He caught the volume of his voice and toned it down before he continued, "I love you, Leena. Don't act like you don't know, ma," he said as he wiped a tear from her face.

His lips touched hers gently, and the soft texture of her full mouth instantly aroused him. Monroe's hands moved with the experience of a Casanova as he slid her shirt smoothly over her head, revealing a purple satin bra. His kisses went from her lips, to her neck. He traced her collarbone with his tongue and moved south until his mouth met her large brown nipples. They were sensitive to the warm sensation of his tongue, and the more he licked and tugged at them with his lips, the harder they became.

"Hmm," she moaned as she inhaled deeply. Her fingers began to unbutton Money's designer shirt, and she ran her hands across his broad, well-defined chest.

Money paid attention to every single erotic spot on her body. He was in no rush to get between her legs. He knew that foreplay was the key to a woman's sexuality, and the more he explored Leena's body, the wetter she became. No spot on her body went untouched. He caressed, and his mouth became intimate with, some of her most delicate places.

He picked her up, scooping her into his arms and carried her into the lavish bathroom. He sat down on the edge of the large Jacuzzi-style bathtub while she sat in his lap. Their lips seemed to be glued together as Money reached for the brass knobs that turned on the water. He finished undressing Leena and then placed her inside of the water. She looked up at him seductively as she watched him remove the rest of his clothes.

His dick grew another two inches when he saw her fingers slip into her womanhood as her thumb massaged her clitoris. Joining her in the steaming water, he took her foot into his hands and rubbed them softly. A low moan escaped her lips as he kneaded her calf tenderly. Money kissed the bottom of her foot and then sucked on her big toe. The sensation that shot up her back caused her to cum instantly.

A sexy smirk crossed Monroe's face when he felt her body shudder. His hands moved up her leg, and he parted her thighs as he slid in between them, Leena reaching down and massaging his length.

He stood from the water, bubbles now dripping from his six pack. His eight inches were average, but the thickness of it was astounding. Leena's eyes beamed in anticipation because she knew that he would stretch her pussy walls to their limit, as he had done so many times before. Pre-cum began to ooze out of the tip, and it looked too tempting not to taste, so she got on her knees and took him into her mouth.

Monroe's jaw hit his chest as he looked down at the beauty beneath him, one of her hands wrapped around his pole, masturbating his length as she sucked it, the other hand tickling his balls. A grunt fell from his lips as he grabbed the top of Leena's head, tussling his fingers through her hair as he grinded slowly. He could feel his nut building, and he had to force himself to ease out of her mouth.

Her head game was superb, but her pussy was even better. It was wet, and warm, and tight. He pulled her to her feet and without words turned her around to bend her over. With the flexibility of a dancer, she bent over and clapped her ass cheeks together. Monroe slapped her big, dark behind and ran his dick up and down her dripping wet slit.

Damn, he thought to himself as he looked at the juices dripping down Leena's thigh.

Money inserted himself slowly and immediately went to work on her, his rhythm slow and his thrusts powerful, his light-skinned, muscular ass cheeks flexing as he moved in and out of her. Leena enjoyed the view as she admired his toned back and behind in the mirror that showed his reflection. The sight of him moving in and out of her, mixed with the fact that he had reached around her and was now fingering her clit, caused her body to shake.

She bucked her ass wildly. Each time she backed it up, their skin slapped together loudly. He was hitting it so good and making her so wet that her pussy began to fart.

Slap, slap, slap—fart . . . slap, slap, slap—fart . . .

The music that their bodies were making could be heard throughout her apartment.

"Money," she whined as she played with her own nipples, "I'm cumming."

"Tell me you love me," he whispered in her ear as he went into her as deep as he could go. Once he was all the way inside of her, he pulled her hips down quickly with force over and over.

"Aghh . . . I love you, daddy!" she screamed.

"Whose pussy is this? This my pussy?" he asked as he hit her with long, slow strokes, kissing the back of her neck each time he stroked her deep.

"Yes, baby, it's yours," she whispered as tears clouded her vision. "I'm cumming!"

She popped her pussy back so good that Money came with her, while he was deep inside her warmth, and they both collapsed back into the warm water in satisfaction.

They each washed and rinsed themselves quickly. They stepped out and Money wrapped a towel around his waist before wrapping her in a large red towel. He pulled her close and kissed her lips. "Never ever doubt my love for you, understand?" he said seriously as he stared Leena in the eyes.

Leena nodded her head. "Promise me that you'll tell Mecca soon. I can't continue to share myself with both of you. I love you too much. I only want to be yours." She reached up and took his face in her hands and kissed him lightly on the lips. "Promise me," she repeated.

Money sighed deeply. The last thing that he wanted to do was hurt his brother, but he couldn't share Leena with Mecca for too much longer. Every time Mecca and Leena were together, it ate him up inside. He knew that he couldn't put off the inevitable any longer. "I promise," he replied as he pulled her close and kissed her forehead. "I promise."

Chapter Ten

"Real bitches do real shit." —Miamor

Miamor, Aries, and Robyn sat at Applebee's dining and having drinks. They were there to discuss their new hit.

Miamor couldn't stop thinking about Carter. Their sexual episode lingered in her mind for days, and every time she thought about it, her clitoris tingled. It was hands down the best sex she'd ever experienced, and he had her mind blown. Her profession didn't allow her to fall for men, but the way Carter handled her and made love to her had her thinking about him in a different light than other men.

As she sat across from her girls, she thought, *I can't wait to see him again. It's something different about him, but I can't put my finger on it.*

"So how much is this nigga trying to pay?" Robyn asked Miamor as she took a sip of her Long Island Iced Tea.

"The job pays the usual eighty stacks. That's twenty"—Miamor stopped mid-sentence and remembered that the caper wasn't going to be split four ways anymore.

A brief moment of silence arose as the girls realized that this was their first hit since Anisa's death.

Miamor, wanting to be strong for her crew, continued. "Remember Black from South Beach?" she asked in a low voice as she clasped her hands and leaned into the table to be more discreet.

"Yeah, I remember him. He had us take care of that snitchin'-ass nigga a couple years back, right?" Robyn responded.

"Yeah, that's him. He wants us to take care of a nigga named Fabian. Black has a younger brother doing life in the pen for drug trafficking. From what he told me, his brother weighs like a buck twenty soaking wet. The story is that Fabian was violating Black's little brother in jail, doing him real dirty, you know, raping him and shit. Fabian got released from the joint about six months ago and 'posed to be moving major weight around his area. Black wants us to get at his ass. But there's a catch"—Miamor quickly glanced around to make sure no one was in her mouth.

"What's that?' Robyn asked.

"He wants us to cut off the nigga's dick off before we kill him." Miamor released a small smirk.

Aries and Robyn burst into laughter simultaneously. They knew Miamor had to be playing. The request was too outlandish to be taken seriously.

"Get da fuck out of here, bitch!" Aries said in between her laughter. But when she saw that Miamor's smirk had faded away, she knew that she was dead serious.

Robyn began to shake her head, not believing what was being asked of them. "You have to be fucking kidding me?"

"I know the shit sound crazy, but the nigga we supposed to hit was raping Black's brother in the joint. He wants him to feel violated the same way his brother did. He is offering us an extra twenty stacks if we do it his way."

"Twenty thousand?" Aries and Robyn asked at the same time.

"Twenty thousand dollars." Miamor nodded her head.

"Ooh, big daddy, you working with an anaconda," Robyn lied as she stroked Fabian's dick with her hand. As she prolonged her extended hand-job on Fabian, she thought, *Where the fuck are these bitches at? This dirty-dick nigga gon' want me to put my mouth on him in a minute.* Robyn had been getting in good with him for the past week and finally convinced him to go to a motel room without one of his goons tailing him for security.

"Show me what that head game like, ma." Fabian placed his hands behind his head and lay back on the bed.

Robyn was enraged on the inside. Miamor had told her that they would enter the room five minutes after they were in. Now fifteen minutes had gone by since they'd entered the motel room. *Where these bitches at? Fuck!*

She tried to figure out a way to buy a couple of minutes. Normally she would do whatever she had to do to get the job done, but in this case she had to reconsider. The thought of putting a homosexual's pipe in her mouth made her almost gag.

She stood up and improvised to stall time. "I'ma dance for you, daddy. Just sit back and watch," she said as she began to do the belly roll and move her mid-section in circles. She raised her skirt and exposed her neatly trimmed vagina. She put her finger in her mouth and then began to rub her clitoris slow and hard.

Fabian was going crazy thinking about going inside of her pretty, pink love box. He smiled while stroking his hard dick. He was so hard, veins were sticking out of his dick as the tip of his joint pulsated.

It wasn't Robyn's intention to get aroused, but the width of Fabian's big black rod made her dripping wet. *If the nigga wasn't a homo, I might've gave his fruity ass some. That's what wrong with these bitch-ass niggas now—All the brothers either down-low booty chasers or just don't got no act right.* She let her finger slide into her vagina. She was so wet, she felt her juices drip onto her inner thigh.

At that point Fabian couldn't take it any longer. He jumped up and swiftly grabbed Robyn under her butt cheeks, quickly lifting her so that she was face level. During his stint in the penitentiary, he had worked out extensively, and his bulky, muscular physique confirmed that. It was nothing for him to lift Robyn's entire body with ease.

"Oh, shit!" Robyn yelled, caught by the element of surprise. Her legs swung freely as her crotch sat dead in the middle of Fabian's face.

Fabian knew all the moves to get Robyn to nut. He began to work his tongue like a tornado on Robyn's clitoris. She couldn't believe the position that she was in and had only read about shit like that in books.

This nigga sho' can eat a pussy. Robyn gripped his bald head and ground her hips against his face. The top of her head kept hitting the ceiling, but she didn't mind, it was well worth it.

She kept looking at the door, expecting her girls to bust in at any moment. She had paid for the hotel suite earlier that day and gave Miamor the extra room key. Actually, she was hoping that they didn't come in at that moment because she didn't want Fabian to drop her while she was so high. She tried to get a couple more face thrusts in before it was over.

"Let me down!"

Fabian slowly let Robyn down and began to take off her clothes. He lay on the bed and sat up on his elbows as he stared at her drenched pussy.

Robyn knew that she had to think quickly because she wasn't about to give him a shot at her goods. *He ain't sticking that mu'fucka up in me, that's for damn sure.*

"Turn around on your stomach," she instructed as she sucked her own nipples.

"What?" Fabian asked in confusion.

"Turn around, nigga. I want to lick yo' ass," she lied seductively.

"What? Don't nothing go by my ass, ma. Come get on this dick and stop playing."

Robyn knew what the deal was. She knew that he liked what she was proposing, him being gay and all. She just had to play it right. "It will feel good, I promise."

Fabian lit up inside when Robyn first told him to turn around. He just didn't want her to know his little secret. Her request was music to his ears. He hadn't got a rim job since leaving prison. Fabian looked in Robyn's eyes and saw that she was serious and quickly flipped his muscular ass around.

Just then, Robyn saw Miamor and Aries slide through the door quietly, both with pistols in their hands. Fabian was so busy smiling and anticipating getting his back slurped, he didn't even see them coming.

"What took y'all bitches so long?" Robyn shouted as she began to put on her clothes.

"What?" Fabian asked as he turned around. But he didn't see what he was expecting to see. He was staring down the barrel of Miamor's 9 mm.

Before he could even react, Miamor went across his nose with her gun, causing it to split and swell up instantly. "Tie this mu'fucka up," she instructed calmly and reached into her bag to pull out the butcher knife.

Fabian instantly began to plead for his life as Aries tied him up to the bedposts. "Look, I will give y'all bitches anything you want," he pleaded as Aries finished tying him up.

Aries hit him in the eye with the butt of her pistol. "Watch chu mouth!" she said as she watched him grimace in agony.

"Let's hurry up and get this shit over with," Robyn said as she finished putting her clothes back on.

"Okay, here." Miamor handed Robyn the butcher knife.

Robyn shook her head from side to side. "I ain't cutting that nigga dick off!"

"Oh, shit! Oh fuck! Please don't cut my joint off. Please! What the fuck did I do to deserve this foul shit?" Fabian bucked against his restraints, and tears began to form in his eyes.

"Stop crying like a little bitch!" Miamor yelled. "Put a sock in that nigga's mouth."

Aries grabbed one of his socks off the floor and forced it down his throat.

Miamor handed Aries the knife. "Aries, you do it."

"You got Aries fucked up. Me ain't touching he dick, bitch." Aries stepped back from Miamor.

"Y'all bitches soft!" Miamor yelled. "I got to do everything myself! Real bitches do real shit." She grabbed Fabian's dick and gave it one good hack. The knife only went halfway through, so she whacked it again, this time cutting it clean off.

Fabian squirmed in pain, his muffled scream like a lion's roar, and his eyes flew open in excruciation, while his body writhed violently.

Miamor didn't know if it was more painful for Fabian to feel the knife or to see his soldier lying next to him, totally detached from his body. Blood began to cover the sheets and Miamor hopped off of him.

"I get the twenty stacks for that, straight up!" Miamor yelled as she grabbed a towel to clean her hands and the knife.

Robyn turned her head to avoid seeing the bloody scene and yelled, "Fuck that! We splitting that shit."

"Yeah. We split that!" Aries added.

"You bitches didn't wanna help, so why should I split it up?" Miamor contested.

"I . . ." Robyn paused. The stench in the air almost made her gag. She pulled Miamor into the bathroom, so she could tell her about herself.

Aries followed quickly, not wanting to miss anything, and the three girls huddled in the bathroom like sardines in a can.

"Yo, why you bugging, Mia? You know the rules. We always split the take evenly," Robyn said with attitude.

"Why do I have to do the dirty work and split it? Straight the fuck up! You two were scared to cut, but now you want a cut. Fuck that!" Miamor snapped her head to the side.

Robyn scowled. "Miamor, what's gotten into you? You are tripping. You ain't acting the same lately."

"It's de nigga she giving she pussy to. He got she head fucked up."

"Look, this ain't the right time to be talking about this, so step the fuck off."

"Yeah, she's right. Let's handle this nigga, and we will finish this later." Robyn opened the bathroom door and squeezed out.

"Oh, shit!" Robyn yelled as soon as she saw what had happened.

"What's wrong?" Miamor shouted as she hurried out of the bathroom. Miamor looked at the bloody bed and saw that it was empty and the door was wide open. "The nigga got away! Fuck!"

They all rushed to the door and saw the man running butt naked across the parking lot. Aries lifted her gun to shoot at him, but it was too late. He was already out of range.

"Fuck! Fuck!" Miamor yelled as she put both of her hands on her head. She knew that they had just fucked up big time, and now wasn't nobody getting paid.

Chapter Eleven

"Oooh, Carter, we got to stop, but this dick so good."
—Miamor

Miamor couldn't get Carter out of her head. Even while she was on a job, he was constantly entering her thoughts, and she hated herself for feeling him so much. It had been two weeks since their steamy encounter on the beach and she was open. *Why hasn't he called me?* she thought to herself. *I knew I shouldn't have fucked him so quick. He probably thinking I'm one of these sack-chasing busto bitches.*

Miamor shook the thought of Carter out of her mind as she reluctantly crawled out of her three-thousand-dollar cherry-wood canopy bed and stretched her arms high above her head. She tiptoed as her body extended in relaxation toward the sky, causing her to shriek in delight. She looked at herself in the mirror and wiped the sleep out of her eyes. She pulled her hair up in a raggedy ponytail and noticed the slight bags that were beginning to form under her eyes. *I've got to get some rest,* she thought. *I look like shit.*

Her eyes drifted down to the picture of her and her friends that sat on the dresser. She picked it up, and a smile slowly spread across her face as she looked at herself, Aries, Robyn, and, most importantly, Anisa. It had been taken over a year ago at a Fourth of July party. She reminisced how they used to step into the club. They were forever fly and were always led through the crowd by Anisa. Mad niggas lusted after their crew, and they got a lot of attention wherever they went. They were always the belles of the ball and the center of attention. Anisa had been the ringleader of their clique, the one to teach Miamor all of her murdering and hustling ways. Her big sister was truly her best friend, and now that she was gone, Miamor felt a strange hole in her heart.

A solitary tear leaked out of her eye, and she quickly brushed it off her face. She set the picture back on her dresser, turning it face down as she walked out of her bedroom. Every time she looked at something that reminded her of Anisa, she broke down. No matter how much Miamor's girls tried to convince her otherwise, she continued to blame herself for her sister's death.

She stopped in her hallway and looked down at her sister's bedroom door. It was closed. She hadn't stepped foot inside it since Anisa had been killed. She just couldn't bring herself to look at her sister's things. She quickly turned and made her way into her kitchen. She opened her cabinets and pulled out some pancake batter. Tears came to her eyes as she slammed the box of batter on the counter. She leaned onto the countertop and wept as she thought of her sister. Every Friday morning, she and Anisa would cook pancakes together. It was a silly tradition that they had shared since their pre-teen years, but it was something that she cherished. Miamor knew that she would never share another intimate moment with her sister, and it hurt her to the depths of her soul.

"Ughh!" she screamed in frustration. She hated feeling so weak. She had never been the emotional type, but her sister's death brought out years of harbored emotions.

Miamor looked around her condominium, and everything about it reminded her of Anisa. Anisa picked out the furniture, the scent of the candles, even the food in the refrigerator, all of which served as a constant reminder of her failure to protect the ones around her.

She poured the pancake mix out of the box and turned on the faucet to rinse it down the sink. "I can't stay here. This shit is gon' drive me crazy," she said out loud to herself. She opened up her kitchen drawers and searched until she found the card of the realtor that had sold her the condo. It was time for her to sell her place. *I have to find a new spot. I can't even breathe in here.* She grabbed her cell phone and quickly punched in the numbers.

"Harper Spokes, please."

Carter looked at all of the possessions he had brought back to Miami from Flint. There was no way he could continue to live out of a hotel. He had made the move South, now he needed to find his own spot. He picked up his cell and called Monroe.

"Money, this is Carter," he stated when his younger brother answered the phone.

"What's good, bro?"

"Aye, I just brought all of my stuff down here from Up Top. Now I need a place to put it," he replied, laughter in his voice. "Do you have time to show me a few properties today?"

"My schedule's pretty full today, fam, but I can get one of the board associates to take you around. You looking to rent or buy?"

Carter replied, "Come on, fam, do I look like one of these rent-a-center-ass niggas? You know I ain't living up in no shit I don't own."

"Yeah, I hear you. Well, come on down to the office when you're ready."

"A'ight, I'll be down there in about an hour."

Carter dressed simply in an all-white, short-sleeve Sean John button-up with a crisp, white T-shirt underneath, his light jeans and Prada sneakers completing his hookup. Then he put on a ten-carat necklace that had three tight rows of colorless diamonds.

After hanging his iPhone from his hip and tucking his .45 in his waistline, he was ready to go. Carter hopped in his Range, tucked his gun away in a hidden compartment behind his custom stereo, and then headed toward Diamond Realty.

When he walked into the office, he brought an instant smile to the face of the attractive receptionist sitting behind the desk.

"Hi, is there something that I can do for you?" Her eyes roamed suggestively over Carter's muscular build.

Her come-on was obvious, and he gave her a polite smirk in response. "I'm here to see my brother, Monroe Diamond."

The receptionist licked her lips and stated, "You can go right back to his office."

Carter nodded and then headed down the hall.

Before he was out of sight, the receptionist called out, "And if you need *anything*, don't hesitate to ask."

Carter smiled but didn't reply. He simply continued on his way until he came to an office that read *Diamond* on the door. He knocked lightly on the door.

"Come in," Monroe called out.

Carter entered the office and slapped hands with Monroe. They pulled each other close for a brief second before sitting down.

"Carter, this is Harper Spokes. Harper, this is my older brother, Carter."

Harper shook hands with the young man beside him and said, "You resemble your father."

"So I've heard," Carter answered.

"He was a good friend of mine. I'm sorry for your loss," Harper said.

"Thank you."

Money cleared his throat. "Harper tells me that we have a couple properties for you to view today."

Harper pulled out a portfolio with available properties inside, and Carter chose three that he was interested in purchasing.

"How quickly are you looking to move in?" Harper asked.

"As soon as possible."

"You *are* aware that Diamond Realty only deals in high-end properties. Do you need financing? How do you plan on paying for the property?" Harper asked, causing Money to look up from the stack of papers on his desk.

Money, a bit offended at Harper's question, replied bluntly before Carter could answer, "In cash."

Carter, offended as well, said, "What other way is there?"

"Just like your father . . . you work in cash. That's how I like it," Harper stated.

"I bet you do," said Carter in a sarcastic tone.

Although Miamor never kept a dirty house, she cleaned it from top to bottom to ensure that it was presentable for her prospective buyer. The only room that she hadn't touched was Anisa's.

She loved her realtor. As soon as she called him and told him she wanted to sell her place, he was on top of things. Within a few hours he had called her back and told her he had found a potential purchaser. The day slowly crept by as she waited for her realtor to arrive. It was five o'clock in the afternoon when she finally heard the knock on the door.

Miamor opened her door, and her jaw hit the floor when she saw Carter standing beside her realtor.

"Ms. Matthews, this is Carter Jones," Harper stated. "Carter Jones, Miamor Matthews."

Carter was just as surprised to see Miamor standing before him. She didn't seem too happy to see him but, for business purposes, held out her hand for him to shake it.

"Mr. Jones," she said.

Carter smirked at her act, but played along, giving off the perception that they had just met.

"Well, if you don't mind, we'll just take a look around," Harper stated.

Miamor shook her head in protest. "Oh no, Harper. Please allow me to show him around. You can make yourself comfortable here in the living room," she stated.

Miamor walked down the hallway, and Carter followed her into her bedroom. He closed the door behind him. Turning to face her, he noticed that she was standing with her arms folded across her chest. "Come here," he stated in a low voice.

Not one to hold her tongue, she asked, "Why didn't you call me?"

"I was out of town. You knew that." Carter stepped closer to Miamor and pulled her near him.

She rolled her eyes, but allowed herself to step into his personal space. "You still could have called. You had me here feeling all fucked-up about sleeping with you. Don't lie to me, Carter. You can tell me if you ain't checking for me like that."

Carter ran his finger across her breast until he felt her nipple swell under her silk dress.

Miamor's breaths became shallow as she reached up and pulled his head near hers. His tongue probed the inside of her mouth. It was thick, and his kiss was sensual. She immediately became wet as she thought of another place she would like him to lick with his juicy tongue.

There is something about this man that I can't resist, she thought as she reached down and gripped his throbbing manhood. She was so hot and bothered that she considered taking his tool out and fucking him on the spot, but she had a white man sitting in her living room.

"Wait!" she whispered as she continued to kiss him. "We can't do this right now." Miamor had spoken the words, but she made no effort to stop Carter from slipping his finger up her White House designer skirt. She wore no panties, so his fingers were instantly drenched in her feminine juices. "You didn't even call me," she moaned.

"I'm sorry, ma. It's all about you," he answered as she reached for his belt buckle.

"Don't lie to me," she whispered in lust.

"I don't lie, Miamor." He lifted her shirt and bent down to kiss her stomach gently.

The two were in pure lust for one another as they attacked each other.

"What do I got to do to get some of this, ma?" he asked charmingly. He'd wanted to call her and had every intention of doing so, but his mind had been preoccupied with business.

"Do what you feel," she stated frankly, staring at him in a challenging way, massaging his hardness through his Calvin Klein boxers.

Grunting lustfully, Carter picked her up by her waist as she wrapped her long legs around his body, grinding her hips into him with a fuck-me passion. The friction alone had her ready to climax. The heat between the two of them burned recklessly as Carter carried her to the oversized cherry wood dresser that sat against the wall, sweeping everything off of it in one motion, causing a loud crash to erupt through the condominium.

"Shh!" she whispered as she sucked on his neck. "Harper is going to hear us."

Carter ignored her and sat her onto the dresser. He opened her legs, while she unbuttoned his pants and slid them down. He entered her without hesitation, moving with a slow rhythm, holding both of her thighs open as wide as they would go. He looked down at his dick as it moved in and out of her. The sight of her massaging her swollen clitoris made his manhood swell even more, and he pounded into her relentlessly.

Knock, knock, knock!

"Is everything all right in there?"

Miamor's eyes grew wide in alarm at the sound of Harper's voice. Carter was fucking her so good that she couldn't stop the moans from slipping off her tongue. She looked at Carter.

"He heard us," she whispered.

Carter continued to fuck her as he whispered, "Then you better stop all of that moaning, ma."

In and out, in and out . . .

Miamor groaned in pleasure, "Uh-uh, I can't," as she thrust her hips at him in a slow grind. Until now she'd never had a nigga who had a big dick and knew exactly how to use it. She was losing her mind. "Oooh, Carter, we got to stop, but this dick so good," she moaned as she made the lower half of her body roll in circles.

"Excuse me, guys, is everything okay?" Harper asked again.

Miamor began to reply, "Everything is—ooh shit!"

But Carter hit her with the death stroke, hitting her G-spot and silencing her.

In and out, in and out, round and round.

"Oh, shit! Oh, shit!" she screamed as the mirror to her dresser began to hit the wall it was leaning against. "Carter! Oh my God, baby, yes!"

Knock, knock, knock!

"Harper, we're fine! Everything is—Yes, Carter, right there! Carter, don't stop!" she moaned.

Carter was making her body explode in ways she had never experienced, and her legs began to shake uncontrollably.

"I'm cumming!" she announced. "Oh my, oh!" she screamed one last time before her body went limp in Carter's arms.

Seconds later, Carter climaxed as well and kissed her sweaty forehead before releasing her.

"Get rid of Harper," she said as she pushed him gently off of her. "And when you do come back to me, I'll be waiting in my bed."

Miamor removed the rest of her clothing and then got underneath her luxury comforter as Carter pulled up his pants and backpedaled out of the room, eyeing every curve on her body. Harper stood checking his watch as Carter walked into the living room, adjusting his jeans.

When Harper looked up and saw Carter walking toward him with his shirt off, his mouth hit the floor in surprise. "Umm—I—I . . ." Harper didn't know what to say as he adjusted his glasses nervously. He had certainly heard what had taken place in the bedroom. The small hard-on that showed through his business slacks and the red embarrassing flush of his face indicated that he had heard everything.

"I'll take the first place we viewed. You'll have your money tomorrow." Carter opened the front door for Harper.

Astonished, Harper headed for the door. "Okay, I—I—"

Before he could say another word, Carter closed the door in his face.

He made his way back to Miamor and picked up where they had left off, pleasing her in every sexual way over and over again until she was so tired that she could no longer cum.

Miamor lay cuddled up to Carter. She was so comfortable in his embrace. *I could get used to this,* she thought.

"Why are you selling your spot?" he asked her out of the blue.

"I can't stay here. I shared this place with my sister, and ever since she died, it just doesn't feel like home. Everything in here reminds me of her. I miss her."

"There's nothing wrong with missing her, Miamor. Selling your crib won't erase that feeling."

"I don't want to talk about that," she whispered. "I just want to enjoy my time with you. Ain't no telling how long you'll be around. I have to appreciate you while you're here," she said half-jokingly.

"I'm here as long as you want me to be." Carter pulled her on top of his body. She lay directly on top of him and rested her head against his chest as he stroked the top of her head. Carter looked down at the beautiful young woman and felt connected to her.

Carter didn't know it yet, but she loved everything about him. She loved the way he was rubbing her head. She loved the way he dressed, the confident swagger that he possessed, and the dimple on the side of his face was an added plus. She definitely loved how he had put his thing down on her. Both times they had slept together she had been completely satisfied. She was checking for him in the worst way.

They lay there together for hours, and eventually Carter slipped into a comfortable sleep. Miamor heard his deep breathing and eased her body off of him. She made sure that he was undisturbed as she tiptoed away from the bed.

It had been so long since she had seen a man in her bed, and she couldn't believe that she had allowed Carter to seduce her once again. She didn't regret it though. Everything in her wanted to get to know the man that lay in her bed, and she was grateful for his presence. She picked up his button-up shirt and put in on. The shirt swallowed her, but she wore it anyway.

She went into the kitchen and opened her refrigerator to see what she had to cook. There wasn't much of anything. She and Anisa ate out most of the time, so besides breakfast food and bottled water, there wasn't much inside.

She grabbed the phone book and ordered a gourmet dinner from a five-star restaurant that was close to her home. She went out to pick up the food, and when she came back, she set up her dining room and arranged the table. She also brought out a bottle of vintage Merlot from her wine rack and lit two apricot-scented candles, setting the mood for the perfect evening.

Miamor didn't want to wake Carter before she showered, so she handled her business and then dressed in a seductive Victoria's Secret camisole and panty set. The gold fabric looked good on her brown skin. She then put soft curls in her hair and went into her room and climbed on top of Carter.

"Wake up," she called out.

Carter opened his eyes when he felt her nudge him. He pulled her down onto him playfully. He enjoyed the way she felt in his arms.

"I have a surprise for you."

"Oh yeah, show me what you got."

Miamor grabbed his hand and pulled him up. She dragged him into the dining room where a full-course dinner consisting of New York strip steak, steamed vegetables, garlic potatoes, and Caesar salad awaited him.

"You made all this?"

"Yeah, I can do a little something in the kitchen," she replied, telling a little white lie. She wanted to hook this man, and allowing him to think that she could cook was a part of her plan. *I'll buy this nigga breakfast, lunch, and dinner for the rest of his life if I have to.*

Carter looked at her with a "quit bullshitting" expression on his face, but was flattered by her attempt to impress him. He took a seat at the table, and they enjoyed the food and drank an entire bottle of champagne together.

They laughed and chatted like old friends, getting to know each other better, both of them hiding secrets that they couldn't tell if they wanted to.

After they ate, Carter removed her plate from in front of her and took it into the kitchen along with his own. "Yo, Mia, where your garbage?" he yelled.

"It's in the kitchen closet!" she yelled back. As soon as the words left her mouth, she hopped up out of her seat. "Wait!" As soon as she walked into her kitchen, she saw Carter standing with the food delivery bags in his hands and a smile on his face.

"Homemade, huh?"

"I never said *homemade*. Those were not my exact words," she defended playfully, knowing she had just been busted.

Carter put the bags down and wrapped his arms around her waist. "That's okay. You don't have to know how to cook, ma. We'll hire a chef."

Miamor laughed sweetly as she hid her face in his chest from embarrassment.

He lifted her face and kissed her lips gently. "I had a good time with you. I haven't been this comfortable with a woman in a long time."

"Good." She tiptoed and kissed his lips again. She could feel the night coming to an end and wished she could turn back the hands of time and relive the last few hours again.

"I've got to go," he stated. He noticed her eyes go from happy to sad in a split second.

Miamor nodded. "Don't make me wait another two weeks before you show your face again." She looked him in the eye seriously.

"Don't worry, ma, I won't," he replied as he walked into the room and gathered his clothes.

Miamor walked him to the door, and although she hated to see him go, she didn't protest. She didn't want to seem desperate, and she definitely didn't want to scare him off by being to clingy. She stood hugging her door as he walked out.

Carter kissed her forehead and said, "Close this door and lock it behind me."

"I will." Miamor waved one last time. She closed the door and locked it just as he had instructed then she leaned up against it, sighing deeply.

Carter. Carter Jones. He had a hood swagger, a gentlemen's finesse, and a businessman's savvy. He had her attention, and she couldn't wait to see him again.

The next morning, Miamor awoke to the sound of someone knocking at her door. No one beside her friends and now Carter knew where she lay her head, so she figured that it had to be one of those people. She looked at the clock on her bedroom wall. *Damn it! It's only nine in the morning. Who the fuck is this banging at my shit like they fucking crazy?*

She pulled herself out of her bed and went to answer it. Looking out of the peephole, she saw three people standing at her door. *What the fuck is going on?* She snatched the door open in irritation. "Can I help you?" she asked.

Miamor noticed that the woman before her held a white chef's hat in her hand, and she frowned in confusion.

"A Mr. Carter Jones has requested our services. He has contracted us to be at your service whenever you call," the woman explained.

Miamor couldn't help but smile. "So you are my personal chef?"

"Yes. We'll make you whatever you want at any time of the day. All you have to do is call," the woman stated with a friendly smile.

Miamor shook her head in disbelief and then stepped to the side as she let the woman and her two-man team into her place. *This nigga is too much,* she thought.

"I'm Rachel, by the way," the woman said as she extended her hand.

"Miamor," she responded as she shook the friendly woman's hand. As soon as she opened her mouth to speak, her cell phone rang. She rummaged through her Hermes bag until she located it. "Hello."

"I just wanted to see if I could stop by for breakfast."

The sound of Carter's baritone brought a smile to her face. "I don't know. I'm not that great of a cook."

"I thought I took care of that problem."

"Well, I'm not really dressed. I don't like to have company over when I'm looking a mess," she replied, playing hard-to-get. Miamor heard her doorbell ring again and rolled her eyes to the ceiling because of the interruption.

"You see, considering how you got up out the bed last night to shower and do your hair before you woke me up, I figured you were high maintenance."

Miamor smiled and replied, "Just a little bit," as she made her way to the door. She was so into her conversation that she opened her door without looking out of the peephole.

Carter stood before her leaning against her doorframe, his cell phone in one hand and a black designer garment bag in the other. "Now you don't have an excuse." He handed her the bag and hung up his cell phone. "Go get dressed. I'll be waiting for you when you get out."

Miamor was ecstatic. She had never been courted in such an upscale manner. Half the time she didn't even have time to seriously entertain a man, but she was going to make time for Carter. She took the bag from his hand with a bashful smile and unzipped it, revealing a Marc Jacobs original. She had heard that the popular designer was coming out with a new high-end line of clothing, but it wasn't due out until early 2010. Here Carter was standing in front of her with a dress that hadn't even hit stores yet.

How the hell did he get his hands on this dress? Bitches about to hate. "Make yourself comfortable. I'll be out in about an hour," she said, blushing graciously.

Miamor hopped into the shower and applied her M•A•C cosmetics before attempting to put on the dress. She wore her hair in a bone-straight wrap, with Chinese bangs cut in a slant across her forehead. Spraying Donna Karan's latest fragrance all over her body, she found herself hoping that Carter would like the scent. It was odd for her to care about what a nigga thought of her, but she had to admit that she wanted Carter to feel her as much as she was feeling him.

Miamor admired her strapless pale yellow dress that fit her body loosely and ended just below her knee. The silk fabric wrapped around her slim waist and lay seductively around the curves of her body, giving the ensemble an edgy look, while the simplicity of the rest of the dress had an old Hollywood glamor. It was sophisticated and much different than her normal style, but she liked the change. And she had the perfect Manolo stilettos to go with it.

Looking at herself in the full-length mirror, she had to smile. She was the shit and she knew it. She emerged from the bathroom an hour later and walked back into the living room, where Carter sat waiting patiently for her.

He looked up at her, and the look on his face told her all that she needed to know. He was pleased with her appearance. She had accomplished her goal.

"Thank you for the dress," she said. "I love it."

"Thank you for wearing it. I love it too." Carter grabbed her hand and led her over to her dining room, where Rachel, her chef, presented them with breakfast.

"You are too much. You know that, right? I've never met a nigga like you." Miamor laughed. Carter was on point in every way.

"There ain't another nigga like me," Carter replied with a smirk.

Normally conceit appalled Miamor. There was nothing worse than a stunting-ass nigga who couldn't back up all the shit that he talked, but Carter's confidence was attractive, and he had already proved that he didn't make empty promises. She knew that he was an entirely new breed. His game was different than the Down South men she had encountered, and she appreciated his refreshing Flint swagger.

"You got a passport?" he asked out of the blue.

"Yeah, I got one. Why?"

"I want you to come away with me this weekend to Costa Rica." Carter said it in a nonchalant manner, as if he was merely asking her to go out on a casual date.

"I can do that," she replied with a breathtaking smile.

Carter knew that she was trying to keep her cool, because the infectious smile she displayed gave away her excitement.

They ate their breakfast together, chatting like old friends, and then spent the entire day together. They shopped arm in arm as they hit the designer stores, and although she was prepared to pay for her own items, Carter covered every expense. She couldn't believe how perfect he seemed to be. He was the one thing that her life had been missing.

For so long, everything had been negative in her life. She was all about her business—murder, murder, murder, kill, kill, kill—and had forgotten how good it felt to just live. She had cut off her emotions, because allowing herself to feel anything was a sure way to get herself killed. Carter, however, was becoming the exception to her rule, and she only hoped and prayed that he was worth the risk.

Chapter Twelve

"All I need in this life of sin is me and my girlfriend." —Tupac Shakur

Miamor and Carter, both with an oversized martini cup in their hand, sat on the secluded shores of Costa Rica, enjoying the scenery. The sun began to set, illuminating an orange hue onto the ocean as they sat at the edge of the water.

Miamor glanced over at Carter and smiled. She was definitely impressed. Carter's body was intact, and she loved it when a man took care of his body by being in shape. She glanced at his six-pack, and then she looked at the noticeable bulge in his white linen shorts. She smirked, remembering how he'd laid the pipe down the previous night. Carter's sex game was on point. He never left her disappointed and made sure that she got hers every time.

Carter noticed her staring and playfully asked, "What you looking at, ma?"

"You," Miamor answered sexily, leaning over to kiss his lips.

Carter examined Miamor's body and loved the way her one-piece Chanel swimsuit hugged her frame. The fabric could barely hold in her voluptuous ass cheeks, and Carter loved every minute of it. He watched as Miamor reached into her matching Chanel bag and pulled out a Dutch and a bag of Miami's finest. She licked and split the Dutch like a pro and filled it with the goods.

"You on this wit' me?" she asked, knowing Carter didn't smoke.

Carter shook his head no and watched as she lit up the "la." Carter loved the fact that Miamor was so street, so hood, but yet so classy all at the same time. Her Brooklyn accent turned him on. When he was with her, he felt like he was with his partner, because they could relate on so many levels. He knew that either, one, Miamor's father was a real street cat, or two, she had a serious relationship with a street nigga. Either way, he knew that she had been taught well.

What Carter didn't know was that neither Miamor's father nor any of her exes had been in the streets. She was a street bitch in her own right.

Carter decided that he wanted to know all about Miamor and thought now would be the perfect time to ask. "So what's your story?" he asked as he took a sip of his drink.

Miamor slowly blew the smoke out. "What do you mean?"

"What do you do? I noticed that you wear the best clothes, and that expensive condo you trying to sell ain't cheap. How do you get your money? You got a nigga back home cashing you out?"

"No, ain't no nigga breaking me off. I make my own money."

Miamor hit the la, to buy herself more time to think of her lie. *I can't tell him that I kill niggas for a living, and that my crew and I have caught over forty bodies over the years. What am I supposed to say—'Yo, I'm a Murda Mama?'* "My father left me a nice piece of change before he died." She looked into Carter's eyes, trying to sense if he bought the lie or not. "And he had a lot of properties back home in New York that I own now."

Carter looked in Miamor's pretty hazel eyes and instantly knew that she wasn't telling him something, but he was determined to find out more about his beautiful mystery woman. His stare was so deep that he made Miamor nervous.

"Thank you for bringing me here," she said, desperately trying to change the subject.

"I enjoy your company. No need to thank me. I needed to get away."

"From what?"

Carter sat up in his chair and looked her directly in her eyes. He had encountered many women in his life, but none compared to the one before him. She seemed to have the complete package. He had seen prettier chicks, even some with better bodies, but Miamor was different. A bit rough around the edges, he was confident that she could be trained.

While every other woman he had ever courted tried to become wifey, Miamor just went with the flow and was comfortable with her status in his life, whatever it may be. There was no pressure with her, and he appreciated the fact that she didn't sweat him.

"Take a walk with me," he said as he stood and reached down to help her up from her seat.

Miamor lifted her designer shades off her face and placed them on top of her head as she looked up at Carter. "Where we going? You know I'm tipsy, nigga. We've been sipping on mai tais all day." She laughed. "I probably can't even stand."

"I got you." Carter licked his lips.

Miamor stood and held his hand, clinging to his arm as she steadied herself. It felt so good for her to just be able to relax.

They walked through the sand of the darkening beach, the horizon a phenomenal mixture of exotic oranges and reds, setting the perfect atmosphere for an intimate walk on the beach.

In the States, she could never let her guard down, so to be so far from home was like heaven to her. *Me and Nis used to always dream of traveling,* she thought. She looked down at her feet as thoughts of her murdered sibling crossed her mind.

Carter noticed the sad expression take over her striking features. "What's wrong?"

"Nothing. I was just thinking about my sister. I'm sorry. I didn't mean to ruin the mood," she said with a weak smile.

"You didn't. Tell me about her."

"She was the most perfect person ever," she whispered.

A wind gusted up to shore from the ocean, and Miamor wrapped her arms around herself. "She always wanted to travel. She would be so jealous that I'm here right now if she was alive." She laughed, thinking of how Anisa would've cussed her out if she hadn't invited her. "She taught me everything I know, and she saved me from living my life in fear and in pain."

"In fear of what?"

Miamor stopped walking and put her head down as memories of her childhood came rushing back to her. Carter lifted her chin with the tip of his finger and noticed the look of rage going through her eyes.

A single tear trailed her cheek. "My mother abandoned us for a boyfriend who liked to molest little girls. One night he came into my room to touch me, and my sister told him to take her instead. I remember the first time it happened. I heard her screaming for him to stop, and I laid in my bed the entire night listening to him violate her. He threatened to kill us if we ever told our mother." Miamor had tears streaming out of her face as she stared out into the ocean, the dark arms of the night enveloping her and Carter on the deserted beach. "Anisa got pregnant. She was only twelve and was walking around with a baby in her stomach because of him. We were afraid to tell our mother, so she came up with a plan to lose the baby. She purposefully started a fight with these girls in our neighborhood and told me not to jump in, no matter what. They beat her until her body miscarried the baby. There was so much blood, and she was in so much pain, but we got through it . . . together. I remember being so scared. I thought my sister was dying. That same night, our mother's boyfriend was back in our room. He pulled Anisa into his bed. She was crying and screaming, and I couldn't take it anymore. I knew that she was in pain. I grabbed a gun that my mother used to keep hidden in the coat closet and I killed him. I shot him in the head. I saved her then, but I wasn't around to save her this time. I was supposed to be, but I wasn't, and now she's gone. The one time that she needed me most, I let her down."

Carter didn't know what to say. He knew that no words would heal the old wounds that she'd just reopened. He pulled her close, and she wrapped her arms around him as she wept in his arms. No words were spoken, but a bond was established between the two of them.

"I'm scared, Carter. I didn't use to fear shit, because I had Anisa behind me. Now it's just me, you know?" Miamor exhaled.

"You don't have to be afraid of nothing, ma, not with me. I got you. Understand? All I ask is that you keep it real with me."

Now that he knew her history, he had a much better understanding of the woman she was today. He knew what made her tick. He felt the walls that she had built around her heart, but he was willing to be patient as he knocked them down one by one. She had let him in. That was the first step.

Carter and Miamor stood on the beach for what seemed like hours just engrossed in each other's embrace. It wasn't until the tropical rain began to fall that they retreated to their five-star resort room.

When they showered together, Miamor ran her hand all over Carter's soapy physique as her honey pot heated up.

"Uh-uh." He removed her hands before she caused him to get an erection.

After learning of Miamor's past, he was even more intrigued by her. She wasn't just another chick that he wanted to fuck. He knew that she played tough on the outside, but was really a fragile soul on the inside. Carter told himself that he would be careful with her heart. He didn't want to be the one responsible for breaking it.

"I already know your body, Miamor. On this trip I want to get to know your mind and your heart." He kissed the nape of her neck, rinsed his body, and stepped out of the shower while she followed close behind.

His words touched her, and she realized that she had never been treated with as much respect as Carter had just given her. The way he was spending money, wining and dining her on this trip, she planned on paying him back as soon as they hit the sheets.

Carter read her thoughts and said, "You don't owe me shit. I'm feeling you, ma, but if you gon' be my bitch, you got to be my nigga too. I have to trust you with everything I am. There are some things that you don't know about me."

Miamor's eyebrows rose in disapproval.

"It ain't about no other chick or nothing. But there are some things that I just can't trust with everybody, nah mean? I'm trying to build a friendship with you so that *if* we decide to take this to a serious level, the relationship will have legs to stand on."

Carter didn't know it, but his logic and the way that he spoke it made Miamor trust him more than anyone she had ever known. He was literally blowing her mind. Miamor kissed his neck and nibbled on his ear as she whispered. "I hear you, Carter, but I already trust you." She took his fingers and placed them between her slit. "And I don't want you for a friend. I have enough friends. I want you as my man." She kissed a trail down to his rising manhood and took him into her mouth.

"Ooh, shit," he moaned as he grabbed the back of her head.

Miamor looked Carter directly in his eyes as she gave him the best head he'd ever received in his life.

The club was jammed packed as Rick Ross blared out of the speakers, and the entire Cartel was in attendance at Club Moon, a club that Polo was a silent partner in. It had been months since they went out and partied because of the war with the Haitians, but Polo thought it would be a good tool to get everybody's mind off the current turmoil.

Mecca, Money, Breeze, and Leena were in the middle VIP section popping bottles of Rosé, celebrating Breeze's birthday, while other members of The Cartel were scattered over the room, their hands close to their bangers, ready for whatever if something popped off.

Mecca had two bottles of champagne in his hand. He said to Breeze, "It's jumping in this mu'fucka!"

Money held a single wineglass in his hand and had been sipping on the same glass all night. He wanted to be on point at all times, and by the way Mecca was downing the drinks, he knew that he had to be extra cautious. "Yeah, it's popping tonight, bro." Money took a small sip. He looked over at Breeze who was dancing with Leena and waving her hands in the air and yelled, while holding his glass in the air, "Happy birthday, *B*!"

"Thanks, baby!" she yelled as she began to dance on two guys that approached her.

One of the guys turned around and began to dance with Leena as the DJ switched to a slow R. Kelly song. Money smiled as he saw that everyone was having a good time and laughing. It had been so long since he had seen Breeze smile and she looked like her old self again.

Mecca walked over to Money, almost tripping over himself. It was obvious that he was drunk. "Bro, I need another bottle of"—he paused mid-sentence as he noticed the man dancing on his woman. His anger began to set in when he saw the man rubbing all over Leena's ass while she danced seductively on him. Mecca's eyes were glued on them as the liquor made the innocent dancing rendezvous seem more sexual than it actually was.

Money knew his brother too well and saw that he was getting ready to flip. "Yo, Mecca, fall back. They're just dancing, nigga. Goddamn!" Money laughed lightly and nodded his head to the song.

Mecca took another gulp of the champagne, menacingly staring at the guy who was feeling up his woman. "Do he know who the fuck I am?" Mecca asked himself as he continued to down the drink.

Money brought his ear closer to Mecca. "What?"

Before Money could stop him, Mecca jumped up and walked over to Leena and the guy. Without warning, he broke the champagne bottle over the guy's head, causing him to drop instantly.

The guy's friend, who was dancing with Breeze, ran up on Mecca, but before he could touch Mecca, he was staring down the barrel of a pearl-handled 9 mm handgun.

"What, nigga? What!" Mecca screamed as the DJ stopped the music.

"Mecca! Stop!" Leena yelled as she grabbed his arm. "We were just dancing, baby!" She looked at the man holding the back of his bloody head.

Mecca wasn't trying to hear that. "Bitch, you my woman! This nigga was grabbing yo' ass like y'all was fuckin' or something!" he yelled.

The vision of another man groping his woman was too much to bear, and jealousy took over. Mecca pointed the gun to the man's leg and let off a round, causing a loud thud to echo throughout the spacious VIP room.

"Aghhh!" the man yelled in agony as he gripped his bloody leg. The entire room was in complete pandemonium as people ran for cover, afraid of getting hit by a stray bullet.

Money got up and grabbed his drunken brother. "Yo, Mecca, that's enough!" He signaled for one of his henchmen to come over to them. Money leaned in the henchman's ear and told him to call their family doctor to fix the man up and instructed him to give the man twenty-five thousand dollars as hush money.

Money was noticeably frustrated with his Mecca's recklessness, since it wasn't the first time he had to clean up his mess. He forcefully grabbed him and took him out the back exit, where their cars were parked.

Leena and Breeze followed them out, not believing what had just happened.

"Mecca, you always fuckin' shit up. Damn!" Breeze shook her head from side to side.

As Money, Mecca, Breeze, and Leena exited the club through the back, all you could hear was Breeze arguing with Mecca. "You always go and do some crazy shit. Damn, Mecca! We can't even have a good time without you popping off! You're nothing like Poppa. You need to learn how to control your emotions!"

"Breeze, I'm sorry, sis, but the nigga was tryin' to disrespect me. You know I ain't having that shit. This city is mine," he said in a drunken slur as he stumbled to his car.

"Whatever!" Breeze said before she got into Money's Escalade.

Money was giving Mecca a look of disappointment and shaking his head from side to side. He knew his brother was getting out of hand and that his rashness could eventually lead to his own demise. "Bro, you can't move like that. That shit was straight-up stupid. Shooting a nigga don't make you no gangster. That ain't what we about, family. Now, if the nigga went against the grain, I would've been right there with you, but what you did was wrong and simple-minded. You have to think first and then react," Money said, quoting his deceased father. Carter Sr. had always told hotheaded Mecca, "Think first and then react."

Guilt began to set in with Mecca, so naturally he began to put it off on someone else. He didn't respond to Money and looked over to Leena, who was leaning on his car and crying in her palms.

He stormed over to her and grabbed her by the shoulders forcefully. "It's all yo' mu'fuckin' fault! If yo' ass wasn't flirtin' with the nigga, this wouldn't have happened. You were inviting that nigga to touch all on you."

Leena yelled, "Mecca, stop! You're drunk, and you're hurting me!" She tried to break loose from his grasp.

Mecca's mixture of intoxication and anger caused him to backhand Leena, and she fell to the ground. Mecca quickly grew remorseful as he saw his woman hit the concrete.

Money rushed over and pulled Mecca away. "What the fuck is wrong with you?" he yelled. "Hitting a female?" He helped Leena up and examined her face and bloody lip. "Are you okay?" Money whispered, as he wiped the blood away from her lip.

Leena looked in the eyes of the man she was desperately in love with. "Yeah, I'm okay." She wanted to be with Money rather than Mecca so badly. Even though Mecca and Money were twins, they were the exact opposite, and Leena felt like she was with the wrong sibling.

"Get in the car, okay. I'll take you home." Money focused back on his drunken brother. "What the fuck is yo problem, Mecca? You are getting out of hand." He gripped Mecca up by his collar, pulling him close to him so that he could be the only one about to hear what he had to say. "If you ever hit a woman again, I'll"—Money was so enraged by his brother's actions, he couldn't finish his sentence. He just pushed Mecca toward his car and pointed his finger at him and shook his head in disappointment.

Mecca remained silent, knowing he was dead wrong.

Money looked at Breeze, who was in the passenger side of his car, and yelled to her, "Take this drunken fool home! I'll take Leena home and meet you at the house." He walked over to Mecca's car and opened the passenger door for Leena.

Mecca was overwhelmed with guilt as he tried repeatedly to apologize to Leena, but the pleas fell on deaf ears.

"Come on, Mecca." Breeze grabbed his hand and helped him into the car.

Mecca dropped his head in shame as he realized that he had overreacted, and the guilt began to sink in.

Carter drove Mecca's Lamborghini down the highway toward Leena's home.

Money hated driving Mecca's cars. In his eyes, they were way too flashy and drew too much attention. He glanced over at Leena, who was crying quietly, wishing she had never come out that night.

Money wanted so badly to be with Leena, but he couldn't betray his brother in that way. He gently ran his hand over her cheek and wiped away her teary eyes, trying to comfort her. "Mecca doesn't mean any harm. He does love you. He just has a fucked-up temper, nah mean?"

"He sure has a fucked-up way of showing me he loves me," Leena said, tears streaming down her face. She kissed Money's hand as he rubbed her cheek.

Money thought Leena was crying because of what Mecca had just done to her, but that was the farthest thing from her mind at that point. The tears were coming from the thought of her knowing that she and Money could never be.

Leena placed her hand on her stomach as she melted in Money's hand. She had found out that morning that she was three weeks pregnant with his child. She knew it was Money's, because she hadn't been intimate with Mecca in months. He had been too busy to satisfy her lately. She decided to have an abortion and take her secret to her grave, but the pressure was too much to handle by herself. She had to tell Money.

"Money, I'm pregnant," Leena said almost in a whisper.

"What?" Money asked as he swerved in traffic, not believing what he had just heard.

"I said I'm pregnant, Money. It's your baby."

"What are you talking about? How do you know it's mine? It ain't mine. I strapped up every time."

"I know it's yours because you are the only person I have been with. Mecca and I haven't done anything in months. I know it's yours. Remember that night, after them niggas tried to rob Mecca?" Leena asked, referring to the last time they'd made love without using protection.

Money kicked himself inside, knowing the time she was talking about. He was so caught up in the moment, he'd slid up in her raw. "Fuck!" He hit the steering wheel out of frustration. The guilt began to set in as Money thought about how he had betrayed his best friend and twin brother.

"I love you, Leena," Mecca whispered just before he lowered his face to his table to inhale the line of cocaine.

As soon as Breeze had dropped him off, his conscience began eating at him. He felt bad for putting his hands on the only woman he'd ever truly loved. His long hair was wild and unbraided, which made him look like a mad man as he used his nose as a suction vacuum for his preferred drug. Mecca threw his head back and held it up to prevent his nose from running. Mecca was high out of his mind. He had snorted five grams of coke within twenty minutes, and the effects of the drugs were kicking in.

He grabbed the bottle of Rémy Martin and took a large swallow of it. He distantly heard a Tupac song pump out of his home stereo and recognized the tunes. He stood up almost stumbling and went over to turn the music up.

All I need in this life of sin is me and my girlfriend.

Down to ride to the very end, just me and my girlfriend.

Mecca held the bottle of Rémy in his grasp and drunkenly rapped along, thinking about his love, Leena. He couldn't take it anymore. He had to go over to her and make things right. Although he treated her bad at times, he really was in love with her, and she was the only woman he had truly ever loved.

Mecca staggered over to the keys to his Benz and snatched them off the counter. He was about to confess his love for Leena. "Leena, I love you, baby. I'm sorry," he said as he stumbled out the door and into his Benz to go see his woman.

"I don't know what to do, Money. I'm in love with a man I can't have," Leena said as tears streamed from her eyes. She sat on her sofa across from Money expressing how she felt about him.

Money was speechless as he looked into Leena's eyes and realized the feeling was mutual. He began to slowly shake his head, knowing that what they had done was wrong. His father had taught him that family always came first and that loyalty was the single most important thing a man can have for his family. Money's father's teachings were embedded in his brain as his heart and mind played tug of war. On one hand, he knew that betraying his brother was wrong, but on the flip side, not taking responsibility for what he had created would eat at him. His father had also told him that abortion was wrong and that a real man takes care of his family by any means necessary. Money was lost.

"Leena, this ain't right. This ain't right," Money mumbled as he buried his face in his palms. All he could think about was his twin brother.

Money had no other choice but to force an abortion upon Leena. He wasn't willing to let a woman come between him and his sibling. *That's my flesh and blood, my brother. Blood in, blood out, I can't let her have that baby,* Money thought as he looked at Leena crying her eyes out.

He sat next to her so that he could console her. He ran his fingers through her hair and gently put his finger under her chin and made her look at him in the eyes. "Leena, we are going to get through this . . . together." He returned the deep stare at Leena. "We can't have this baby, though. It's wrong."

"I never wanted it to be like this," Leena told him, heartbroken.

"Everything is going to be okay. But this between us has to stop." Money gently kissed Leena on the lips. Money's lips were magic to Leena. Just by his touch, he drove Leena wild. She felt her friend in between her legs begin to thump, and before she knew it, her hands were in his pants looking for his rod. She gently began to stroke it, to make it grow.

Money promised himself this would be the last time he would have sex with his forbidden love.

"*All I need in this world of sin . . .*" Mecca sung drunkenly as he approached Leena's house. He was going to apologize to his woman and make things right.

When he pulled up, he noticed his Lamborghini parked in her driveway. "Money still here?" he asked himself as he pulled two houses down from Leena's house. He threw the car in park, grabbed the half-empty bottle of Rémy, and hopped out.

Mecca staggered to Leena's house and noticed that the front light was on. He walked in front of the house, and what he saw through the front glass made his heart drop. Mecca dropped the Rémy bottle, causing it to shatter into pieces on the sidewalk. He saw his twin brother passionately kissing his woman. He watched as Money pulled out one of Leena's big brown breasts and began to suck on it. Mecca was in complete shock as he watched Leena straddle his brother. His eyes bugged out as he saw his brother rub on Leena's behind with one hand, while removing her thong with the other.

"What da fuck!" Mecca walked closer to the front glass and witnessed the treachery happening.

Money and Leena were so into one another that they didn't notice Mecca staring at them through the large front glass. And Leena's moans could be heard from the outside as she rode Monroe with more passion than she had ever ridden Mecca.

Mecca's sadness instantly turned into rage as he reached for his gun and headed for the front door. Seconds later, bullets from his .40-caliber pistol was ripping through the wood of the front door.

Leena scrambled to the corner of the room out of fear. She didn't know what was going on, and Money grabbed his pistol from his waist and pointed it at the door. Then he saw Mecca burst through the front door, tears in his eyes.

"Mecca!" Leena yelled as she saw the look in his eyes. She knew that their secret was out of the bag.

Mecca pointed his gun at Leena. He screamed, "I can't believe you, bitch!"

Money put away his gun and tried to calm down his brother. "Mecca, put the gun down. It's not what it looked like," he tried to explain.

"It's not what it looked like? Nigga, fuck you!" Mecca pointed his gun at his brother. The two people he thought he could trust were the very ones deceiving him. He pulled the hammer back on his gun and aimed it at his brother's head.

Money put both of his hands up and tried to reason with him. He knew his brother very well, and when he looked in Mecca's eyes, it was obvious that he was high as a kite. "Bro, listen, put the mu'fuckin' gun down. You high. Now stop, before you do something you gon' regret."

"The only thing I regret is fuckin' with this stankin' ho!" Mecca pointed his gun back at Leena. The thought of her being intimate with his brother sent him over the edge. "I hate you!" Mecca screamed as he put both of his hands on his head, and his tears began to fall freely. "I loved you," Mecca whispered just before he pointed the gun at Leena and let off two rounds. He watched as the bullets ripped through her chest, and she fought for air.

"Noooo!" Money yelled as he rushed over to Leena and cradled her in his arms. "Breathe, Leena, breathe!" he instructed her as blood oozed out of her mouth.

Leena fought for her dear life as she gripped Money's hands and looked into his eyes.

"Breathe, Leena!" Money screamed as he tried to keep her from slipping away. "Call an ambulance!" He looked back at Mecca, who was pacing the room with both of his hands on his head.

Mecca whispered, "Oh my God! What have I done?" He frantically continued to pace the room. He looked over at his brother and Leena, and what he saw and heard broke his heart.

Leena was taking her last breath, but before she slipped away, she looked Money in the eyes and whispered, "I love you, Monroe Carter," just before she stared into space, leaving this earth.

A single tear slid down Money's face, and he felt Leena's grip suddenly loosen. He knew that she was gone.

A tear fell from Mecca's eye also, but it wasn't one of sorrow, but a tear of rage. He'd just witnessed the woman he loved tell his brother that she loved him. "Her last words were that she loved you, not me," he whispered as he slowly raised his gun and pointed at Money.

Money ran his hand over Leena's eyelids to close them, and then he gently kissed her forehead before he turned his attention on his brother. "Mecca, put the gun down." Money put his hands in front of him. He knew his brother was unstable.

"You always thought you were better than me, nigga. You could've had any woman you wanted, but you had to take mines. Now look at you. Look what you made me do."

"Look! Poppa and Ma always favored you over me." Mecca's tears fell freely down his face, and his hand began to shake. He remembered what his parents used to say when he would get in trouble and began to mimic them. "You need to be more like Monroe. Monroe wouldn't act like that," he said, his voice shaky.

As all of his emotions boiled over, Mecca looked Money in the eyes and let off a single shot that entered the left side of his chest where his heart resided.

Monroe heard the gunshot, but didn't believe his own flesh and blood had shot him. As the burning sensation in his chest settled in, he fell to the ground, and his life slowly slipped away.

High out of his mind, Mecca watched as his brother lay dying in a puddle of his own blood.

"Unc Po!" Mecca yelled into the phone as he held his twin brother's corpse in his arms, "They killed Money. Oh my God! They killed my brother!" He instantly regretted what he had done, and remorse quickly brought his cocaine high down.

"Mecca, what are you talking about? Calm down! What's going on?" Polo didn't want to believe what he'd just heard.

"Them Haitian mu'fuckas, they killed Money!" Mecca responded as he cried like a baby.

"No, no, no." Polo dropped to his knees. The news of his godson's death was too much for him to bear.

"They killed Leena too. Come and get me, Unc. They killed Money. They killed my brother," Mecca stated as he wept uncontrollably. He hung up the phone and put his own gun to his head. "I love you, bro. I'm sorry. I'm so sorry," Mecca whispered right before he pulled the trigger, but fortunately for him, the gun jammed.

A knock at the door awakened Carter and Miamor, and he sleepily arose to answer it.

"Mr. Jones, I have an urgent message from your uncle." The concierge held out the piece of folded paper.

Carter opened it and read the words:

Money was killed last night. Come home immediately. It's an emergency. Polo

"Fuck!" Carter screamed as he punched the wall nearest him and balled the tiny note up in his palm. He rested his head against the doorframe and let out a roar of pain that caused a shiver to run down the concierge's spine.

Miamor rushed to his side. "Oh my God! Carter, what's wrong?"

"We've got to go. Pack your things. I have an emergency back home," he said through tear-filled eyes.

Chapter Thirteen

"Bitch, you's a Murder Mama! . . . We don't give a fuck where the coroner bag 'em."
—Robyn

"Bitch, are you paying attention to me?" Robyn threw a pillow in Miamor's face, snapping her out of her trance. "Yeah, I'm listening. I hear you, damn," Miamor replied with a slight attitude as she tossed the pillow back.

"Whatever. You didn't hear nothing me just said," Aries teased. "Bring your head out de clouds, Miamor. We got a chance to get back at The Cartel and get at that mu'fucka that killed your sister. This is important."

The three girls sat comfortably on Miamor's bed while they plotted their revenge. Miamor was trying her hardest to concentrate, but she couldn't. Every time she closed her eyes, Carter crept into her thoughts. Her time in Costa Rica was like a fantasy. He had showed her a side of life that she had never experienced before and had opened up the heart that she thought had been forever closed by lock and key.

Miamor shook her head, sat up against her headboard, and looked at both of her friends. They were her sisters, her partners in crimes, and she knew that her distraction could put them in jeopardy. *I have to get focused,* she thought.

"What did that nigga do to you over on that island?" Robyn asked with an insinuating tone. "I know you ain't stressing him like that. Not Miamor, not the one who said niggas ain't good for shit, but a broken heart."

"He's not like that," Miamor stated in Carter's defense.

"I know I did not just hear she say that." Aries put her hand on Miamor's forehead. "Are you sick or something? 'Cuz this ain't de same bitch I sent over to that island."

Miamor had to laugh as she knocked Aries' hand away. "I'm serious. Yo, he's not like that. I don't know, there's something about him that has me stuck. He's . . . he's . . ."

"You fucked him, didn't you?" Robyn asked.

The smile that spread across Miamor's face revealed the answer before she could even speak.

"Ohh. She fucked him! Was he good? 'Cuz he could get it any day from me." Aries stood up and bounced her voluptuous behind up and down doing a freaky dance. "I would put it on him."

Miamor laughed as she pulled a .45 from the shoulder holster she was wearing. She removed the clip and popped the single bullet from the chamber then pointed the pistol at her friend. "Bitch, I'ma put this on you if you keep talking like that."

Aries ignored Miamor's idle threats as she continued to pop her ass and hips. "Whatever. I would have that fine mu'fucka all up in me. Them bullets don't stop no show."

Miamor and Robyn were laughing so hard that tears were coming to their eyes.

"Okay, okay, can ya'll bitches concentrate for a hot little minute while we discuss this business?" Robyn asked.

Aries stopped dancing and sat back down on the bed, while Robyn pulled the daily newspaper from her Hermes bag and spread it across the bed.

"You think Ma'tee still want the Cartel job done?" Robyn asked.

"I don't know. There was a truce or something established between them, so now I'm not so sure." Miamor shook her head.

"Well, you need to call and see, because we gon' get at the boy Mecca, regardless. We might as well get paid in the process. You feel me?" Robyn asked.

Miamor nodded and flipped up her cell phone to dial Mat'ee.

Ma'tee greeted her as soon as he answered the phone, "Miamor? Me ain't hear from yuh? How yuh doin'?"

He knew exactly who was calling him due to his high-tech security. When he received a call, he knew your first and last name along with your current location, so she wasn't surprised. He was always on point.

"I'm well. Thanks for asking," she hesitated but was urged on when she noticed Aries waiting in anticipation. "Look, I'm calling regarding that unfinished business we had with each other. You still need that job done?" she asked, getting straight to the point.

"Unfortunately, me have to put that on hold. After what happened at me little angel's party, me hand was forced to call a truce. Me a man of honor. Me word is all me have. Me will not break de truce. The only way me will put the contract back up is if de Cartel break de agreement first. Then and only then will me pay yuh for de bounty."

"I hear you. Look, if you change your mind, we're ready. Just say the word, and we'll make it happen. Is the ticket still the same on that?" she asked.

Ma'tee let out a small chuckle. "If they do not hold up their end, then me will pay one point five for it."

"Well, like I said, Ma'tee, I'm trying to see that, so let me know," she said before hanging up.

"What did he say?" Robyn asked eagerly.

"Bounty's not good unless The Cartel breaks the truce first. Otherwise, he is going to keep his word. He's willing to pay a mill five, if they do show shade."

"Then we have to make sure The Cartel breaks de truce, so we can see that cash and kill de kid Mecca," Aries replied.

"I don't know, y'all. Y'all talking about initiating a war between two sides that have agreed to lay low. With everything that happened with Nis, my head is all over the place. Emotions throw my judgment off. Everything I've been going through with her death has me all fucked up. I don't know if I'm ready to get at them again."

"It's hard on all of us, Mia. We loved Anisa too, and it's not just about the money anymore. They made it personal when the nigga Mecca killed her," Robyn said.

"I haven't forgotten, Robyn. He's gon' get it, believe that," Miamor said, venom in her voice and tears in her eyes.

"Well, we think we found a way to get at him and bring down the Cartel too." Robyn pointed her finger at the newspaper on the bed, causing Miamor to pay attention to it.

"Is this Mecca's obituary?" Miamor picked up the paper and studied the face closely. Confusion swept over her face, and her forehead dropped in a deep frown. "Somebody got to him before we did?"

"Not Mecca, his twin brother Monroe," Aries stated smugly.

Robyn added, "The funeral's tomorrow, Mia. You know Mecca and the rest of The Cartel will be there. It's our chance to catch 'em while they're weak,"

Miamor lifted her eyes from the newspaper to meet Robyn's gaze. "At his brother's funeral?" she said with doubt. "I don't know."

"Bitch, you's a Murder Mama! Ain't nothing to think about. We don't give a fuck where the coroner bag 'em. The nigga disrespected—" Robyn yelled.

"So he got to get it," Aries chimed in, finishing her friend's sentence. "Fuck them, Mia. Let's get at these niggas."

Miamor nodded her head in agreement, and in an instant the coldness in her heart settled back in. Fuck The Cartel. Fuck Mecca, his world, and everyone in it. Miamor was about to avenge her sister's death and make Mecca's mother feel what she had felt when she buried her sister. "I'm in."

Mecca sat in the family room of the Diamond house. His insides were hollow, and he cried to himself, tears falling uncontrollably from his eyes. *What did I do? Money, my baby, my blood, what the fuck did I do?* he thought silently. His conscience was eating him alive. He had murdered his twin brother. They had come out of the womb together, and now that Money was gone, Mecca didn't feel whole. He couldn't believe that his rage had blinded him to this point, and he knew that if he hadn't been so intoxicated from the drugs and booze that his temper would've never taken him so far. *I'm so sorry, bro. I love you, baby. I love you, man.* His mind was spinning, and his heart ached. "This is all my fault," he cried.

"Mecca, this is not on you. Those Haitians are to blame for this, not you. Nobody saw this coming," Polo stated as he paced back and forth.

Mecca knew that the lie he'd told would hold up. It was a convenient story that pointed the blame toward their beef with Ma'tee, but seeing the anguish that he had caused his family was more than he could take.

"Why is this happening to us?" Breeze asked. "First Poppa, now Money. They are tearing our family apart." Her eyes were red and swollen as if she hadn't gotten sleep for days. She looked to her mother for answers.

But Taryn was stricken beyond belief and could not open her mouth to answer. She knew that if she spoke then, her tears would leak from their confinement. She couldn't allow that to happen. Just as she had been the foundation that held her family up during her husband's funeral, she had to be strong now and perform what was once her husband's role and be the glue that held her family together.

The sound of the doorbell interrupted them, and Mecca went to answer it. When he opened the door, Carter stood before him. They slapped hands, and when Carter pulled him close, they fell into a hug as Mecca cried. Young Carter was the only brother he had left. The only other male in the Diamond family he could call on. He was family, and all they had was each other. "I'm sorry, fam," Mecca sobbed.

Holding his brother and hearing him break down caused tears to come to Carter's eyes. "It's all right, fam. Let it out, baby, let it out," Carter whispered as he pulled Mecca's head into his chest as if he was his li'l nigga.

Mecca was always so boisterous, so hard; now his spirit was half gone. He was getting ready to bury a part of himself, and he knew that when Money's casket hit the dirt, his heart would too. His twin brother was gone, and Carter had no idea that Monroe's death had been at the hands of Mecca himself.

Polo stepped into the foyer, but when he witnessed the two men united as brothers he paused. He didn't want to interrupt their moment.

"He was my brother, man. My baby," Mecca sobbed.

Carter and Mecca released one another. They stood there face to face, and for the first time there wasn't even the slightest bit of animosity between them.

When Polo cleared his throat, they turned around to face him. “We need to talk. In the kitchen,” he said.

They followed Polo to the kitchen and took a seat at the table.

Carter stared at Polo. “How the fuck did this happen?”

“It’s my fault, man. Money took Leena home because of me. We had a fight, and he was doing me a favor. Once I cooled down, I decided to go over there to check on her. When I got there, I saw two dread mu’fuckas running out of her crib. I rushed in to see about Leena, and they both were laid out in there, fam.” Mecca dropped his head, unable to hold his brother’s stare. He couldn’t tell them what he had done. It was something that he would take to his grave.

“We’ve got to get a handle on this,” Polo stated.

“What the fuck happened to the truce? We kept our end up. What triggered this?” Carter asked.

“We don’t know, but we’ve got to retaliate,” Polo replied.

“Right now we just need to make it through today. I don’t think it’s too smart for us to keep fanning the flames. It’s obvious that we’re touchable right now. They’ve killed two of our soldiers, our leaders, and we’ve only knocked out their henchmen. We need to think before we attack,” Carter said.

“I agree,” Polo stated.

Taryn walked into the room. “The limo is here,” she announced, her voice barely audible.

Carter arose from his seat and hugged her tightly. “I’m sorry,” he told her as they embraced.

“You have to fix this, Carter,” Taryn told him. “I need you to save my family . . . our family. Keep Breeze and Mecca safe. I don’t know how much more of this I can take.”

Carter nodded. “I will, I promise.”

Polo escorted Taryn to the car, and Breeze held onto Carter’s arm for dear life as they followed behind. She cried softly. It was almost time for the funeral to begin.

“Look, when we walk in this mu’fucka, we go straight to the front of the church. Mecca will be sitting on the front pew, so that’s the easiest way to hit him. Act like we’re going to view the body and then start blazing on ’em. There will be members of their entourage all over the church, so make sure you spray anybody that's standing in the way. There are three of us going in here, so I want there to be three of us leaving out," Miamor stated.

The girls wore knee-length H&M raincoats with knee-high boots. Inside their coats they held "street sweepers." They weren't fools. They knew that they were outnumbered in bodies, but in bullets and ammunition, they were equal to anything that The Cartel could throw at them.

They exited their vehicle and walked into the church. There were hundreds of people inside the place as the girls made their way down the aisle, but they noticed that security was on point.

Miamor's hand gripped the steel inside her coat, and she could hear her heartbeat in her ears. She could see the backs of the family's heads as she walked. Mecca sat on the end. She knew it was him because of his long braids, and a slight smirk crossed her face. She could already taste his blood in her mouth as she bit down on the inside of her cheek, something she always did when she saw her unsuspecting prey. She was indeed a calculating killer.

Miamor stepped to the casket and looked down at Monroe. Robyn and Aries stood by her side. They all waited for her signal.

Miamor stood silently, and a single tear slid down her cheek. Monroe looked so peaceful, so gentle. He looked to be the exact opposite of his murderous twin brother Mecca. She exhaled and jumped slightly when she felt someone grip her arm. She turned around, ready to bust off on the first face she saw, but the man before her caused her to take a step back.

"Oh my God," she whispered.

Her girls looked at her in confusion.

"What are you doing here?" Carter asked her.

Miamor's eyes gazed over at Mecca. His face was in his hands. She scanned the entire pew and took in the faces of the Diamond family. Her eyes stopped when she noticed Breeze. *Breeze is Carter's sister. Breeze is Mecca's sister. Carter is Mecca's brother. He's a part of The Cartel,* she thought. The room felt like it was spinning as she looked up at Carter. *This was the emergency,* she thought, putting two and two together slowly in her head.

"I didn't know you knew my brother."

"I—I—" Miamor was at a loss for words, and her mind was unable to formulate a lie.

Robyn stepped up and said, "She doesn't, I do. We were friends, and I'm just coming to pay my respects. I'm sorry for your loss."

"Thank you." Carter peered at Miamor. "You okay?"

She nodded, still unable to speak.

"Look, I've got to get back to my family, but I'll call you, ma." He leaned in and kissed her on the cheek before walking away.

Miamor turned to her friends. "I have to get out of here," she whispered.

"Mia, what about the plan?" Robyn asked.

"Fall back. I can't do this right now."

"But, Miamor—" Aries interjected.

"I said fall the fuck back." Miamor walked out of the church and almost ran to her car. When she got inside, her head fell to the steering wheel in defeat. "He's his brother," she said aloud. "He's a part of The Cartel."

Robyn and Aries exchanged glances. They knew that Miamor was feeling Carter. She had broken her number one rule and gotten emotionally involved.

"Miamor, fuck him. He's one of them. Let's go back in there and do what we came here to do," Robyn stated.

Aries looked sympathetically at her friend, but kept quiet.

"I can't, Robyn. It's not that simple."

"It is that simple. You gon' choose him over Anisa? Somebody has to pay for what Mecca did to her."

"Robyn, shut de fuck up, okay. That's she sister you're talking about," Aries said in Miamor's defense.

"I thought she forgot," Robyn said smartly, her arms folded across her chest.

"Bitch, shut the fuck up talking! That's your fucking problem—you talk too fucking much. I can't even hear myself think. I know what the fuck I have to do. I was there, Robyn. I know, okay. I just can't do this right now," Miamor said as she started her car and drove away.

She dropped her girls off at the apartment that they shared. The car ride there was filled with silence and tension.

"We're going to make that money, so don't think this is over. It's us versus them, Mia. He's the enemy," Robyn stated before she got out of the car, slamming the door behind her.

Aries looked back at her friend, who was staring straight ahead, looking at the road. "Do you love him, Mia?"

"No," she quickly answered. Her heart fluttered when the word left her lips, letting her know that her body knew better. She closed her eyes, and Anisa's face popped into her mind. She slowly opened them and breathed deep. "I'm gonna kill him and everybody he loves."

Aries stepped out of the car and watched Miamor as she drove away. She looked up at Robyn, who was standing on the stairs to their building.

"Did you have to be so fucking rude? Give she a break, Robyn. Damn! You know she's in a fucked-up situation," Aries stated. "You lucky I not she, 'cuz I woulda beat your ass first and made up with you later."

Aries and Robyn walked into their building arguing, both knowing that there would never be any real beef between them.

Miamor drove around the city for two hours trying to make sense out of her dilemma. Instinctively she found herself driving toward the cemetery. She had to talk to her sister. When she made it there, she saw the same crowd of people that she had seen at Money's funeral. She knew that they were there to bury his body next to his father's, the infamous Carter Diamond, founder of The Cartel. She didn't care though. She still parked her car and walked over to her sister's grave. She knelt down and cried.

"Anisa, he's Mecca's brother," she said as she touched her sister's headstone. She closed her eyes. "He's the brother of the man who killed you. I miss you so much. I promise you that I'm not going to forget what he did to you. I'm gonna kill him. I swear on everything I love." Thoughts of Carter filled her head, but she quickly replaced them with her sister's face. "Why is this so hard?"

"It just is," a voice behind her said.

Startled, she stood to her feet and turned around.

Carter stood there in a black Sean John suit, his hands tucked away in his pockets, and his muscular physique hung his linens well. His eyes were red as they gazed down at her tear-stained face. "It's always hard when you lose someone you love," he said.

Miamor didn't respond. She had so much hate for him and his family in her heart. Her sister was underneath her feet at this very moment because of what Carter stood for.

He reached for her, but she pulled away slightly. "Don't," she whispered.

He didn't listen and stepped closer to her.

She wanted to run from him. He was the only person she had ever encountered who intimidated her, and she despised him because of it. *He's a part of The Cartel. I slept with this man. I kissed him and let him explore me. I opened up my mind and body to him. I was willing to give him my heart, and he's Mecca's brother,* she thought painfully.

He put his arms around her waist and pulled her near, even though she still tried to resist. "I wish I could've met her," he said as he pulled out a handkerchief and wiped away her tears.

His touch was so gentle, so loving. He was so perfect.

"You love her so much. I can see it in your eyes that you're hurting."

"Don't talk about her," she replied in a whisper. She didn't want him to speak Anisa's name. He had no right to.

"I want to be here for you, Mia. I want you to be here for me. I didn't know how I was going to make it through today, until I saw you at the church. Seeing your face did more for me than you know."

Miamor looked up at him, and his words played funny tricks with her heart. Loving him would be wrong. Being with him would be wrong, but playing on his feelings toward her to inflict her revenge would be so right. *Can I be around this man and not love him though? Can I do this?* she asked herself. *Yes, I'll do it. It's never been hard for me to murk a nigga before. I'm going to finish what I started.*

"I'm sorry about your family," she said sincerely as she reached up and wrapped her arms around his neck. "I'm so sorry, Carter."

Carter thought that she was apologizing out of respect for Monroe. What he didn't know was that she was apologizing for the death and pain that she was about to cause his family. She was going to become his only weakness and then use it against him. He didn't know it yet, but he was going to contribute to his family's demise.

Chapter Fourteen

"God, please forgive me for I have sinned. Money, Poppa, I'm coming to join you."
—Mecca Diamond

Leena's eyes shifted back and forth frantically as her blurred vision became clearer by the second. She didn't recognize where she was. Tubes were coming from her nose, and the steady beep of the heart monitor echoed through the room. The last thing she remembered was Mecca pointing the gun at her and hearing a loud blast.

Instinctively, she began calling for her man. "Mon—Monroe," she whispered as she blinked her eyes rapidly, trying to regain clear vision. She tried to sit up, but an excruciating pain shot through her body. She felt the tenderness in her arm and then realized that was where the bullet struck her.

She immediately began to think about the unborn child that she was carrying. She nervously began to feel on her belly and wondered, was her child okay. That was when she heard the unfamiliar sound of a man's voice, and she instantly grew terrified.

She saw a tall, older man with a beer belly. He had on an expensive silk shirt with the first three buttons unbuttoned, typical gangster attire for older Florida natives. An unlit cigar hung from his mouth as he stood up and walked toward her. The man was of Dominican descent and had slick hair that was neatly brushed to the back.

Leena tried to scream, but she was too weak to project her voice. She immediately tried to reach for the emergency call button next to her bed, but she was unable to move her arm.

The man loomed over her and gently tapped her, whispering, "It's okay, it's okay."

Leena quickly smacked his hand off her, and tears formed in her eyes. She knew one of Mecca's goons was there to finish what he had started.

"Don't worry. I'm not going to hurt you, Leena," the man said as he sat at the edge of her bed.

"Who are you, and how do you know my name?" Leena scooted to the opposite side of the bed, trying to get as far away from him as she could. She grimaced as she felt the pain in her arm. She clenched her stomach, all the while keeping her eyes on the man in front of her.

"My name is Emilio Estes. Monroe was my grandson," he said as he dropped his head, noticeably saddened.

"Was? What do you mean, was? Where is Money?!" Leena's face frowned up.

"He didn't make it. He's gone."

Estes stood up and wiped the tear that threatened to fall. The thought of Monroe's death made him weak. He quickly regained his composure and stared into the eyes of the woman who would birth his great grandchild. He had been with her throughout the whole time she was in a coma.

When he got to Leena's house on the night of shooting, he was the first to discover that the Haitians had left Leena alive and that she was carrying a child. He'd arranged for Leena's status to be kept a secret and got her moved to the top floor of the hospital, where they usually admitted celebrities and people of prestige. The doctor told him that the baby would be fine, and he was determined to make sure Leena would be taken care of until she delivered his first great grandchild.

Leena stared aimlessly in complete shock. The words that left Estes' mouth sent a dart straight to her heart.

"He's gone? No, he can't be," Leena said as her voice began to shake. Her whole world had just crumbled, knowing that the only man she ever loved was gone.

"His funeral was a couple of days ago. Sorry, sweetheart," Estes said as he stepped closer to the bed.

Heartbroken, Leena broke down in tears and cried like a child.

Estes put his hand on her hair, slowly stroking it to comfort her.

She gripped her stomach, remembering that she was carrying Monroe's child. Fear sunk in as she wondered if her baby was okay; it was the only piece of Monroe she had left.

Estes noticed the sudden look of worry in her face. "The baby is fine, Leena," he said.

Leena took a deep breath and buried her face into her hands. "Thank God. Thank God, my child is safe," she whispered as she continued to cry a river.

Estes wanted to be supportive of Leena, but revenge was the main thing on his mind. He wanted to affirm that Ma'tee's Haitian mob was responsible for the killing.

"I know you are going through a lot right now, but I have to ask you a question. Who killed my grandson?"

"Your grandson," she repeated as she briefly stared him in his eyes.

Estes took the cigar out of his mouth and slightly frowned, "What did you say?' he asked in a heavy Dominican accent.

"Mecca killed Monroe. Mecca did it."

Estes was at a loss for words as he clenched his teeth and involuntarily balled up his fist. He was hurt by her words, and his anger got the better of him. He angrily grabbed Leena by her hand and squeezed it tightly. "Don't fuckin' lie to me!" he yelled.

"I'm not lying, I swear to you. Mecca shot both of us. He went crazy. Monroe and I were fooling around and he walked in. But I wasn't serious with Mecca. Monroe was the one I loved."

Estes caught himself and released Leena's hand. He shook his head from side to side and remembered the look in Mecca's eyes at the funeral. He knew something wasn't right with his only living grandson. Estes was a firm believer in family morals and loyalty.

What Mecca had done was the ultimate betrayal, and Estes quickly disowned him. Estes was from the old school and played by the rules. If you went against the family, you weren't considered family anymore. The thought of vengeance was the only thing he could fathom. He motioned to the man that was in the corner of the room to come to him.

Leena was startled. She didn't even realize that they weren't alone.

A Dominican man emerged from the shadows of the darkened room, and Estes whispered something in his ear. The man quickly exited the room, and Estes sat next to Leena and instructed her that he would look after her, and everything would be okay. Unbeknownst to Leena, Estes had ordered the death of his only remaining grandson, Mecca.

Mecca sniffed the long line of cocaine, using his nostrils like a Hoover vacuum. His hair was unbraided and wild all over his head, giving him the look of a crazed man. He quickly jerked his head back so that his nose wouldn't run. He stared at the items on the table—a bottle of Rémy Martin, two Desert Eagle handguns, and a bowl of pure coke. He had already sniffed two grams and was high out of his mind.

He reached over to his end table to grab the picture of himself, Money, and their father. It was a picture that was taken when they were little boys, both of them sitting shirtless on their father's lap. He remembered that day and smiled. That smile quickly turned into a saddened expression, which was then followed by tears. He was deeply remorseful for his actions and continued to shed silent tears as he picked up the bottle and took a big gulp of liquor then another line of blow.

"I'm sorry, Money, I am so sorry, bro," he said as he broke down crying hysterically. "I love you, man," he whispered as he stood up, almost falling back down. He looked around his tri-level condominium that overlooked the sands of Miami's coastline. He staggered over to his balcony with the bottle in one hand and the picture in the other. He forcefully pushed open the door and stumbled out. He looked into the sky as the moonlight shined down on him. He felt worthless, like he was the scum of the earth.

He took another swig of the drink and threw the bottle off the balcony and watched it land in the Olympic-sized swimming pool below. His condo was three stories above ground, and as he glanced down, the mixture of liquor, height, and cocaine caused him to become disoriented. He looked at the picture again and kissed it. He remembered back when he was innocent and untainted by life's ills. He wished he could start back over and have his life back with his father and brother. But now both of them were gone.

Mecca took off his Timberland boots and carefully climbed on top of the railing. He took off his shirt, exposing his definitive tattoo that covered chest and arms. He closed his eyes and spread his arms out like an eagle soaring in free air.

"God, please forgive me for I have sinned. Money, Poppa, I'm coming to join you," he said as he prepared to jump to his death.

Before he took the leap, he heard a stampede of feet coming from beneath him. He opened his eyes and glanced down and couldn't believe his eyes. *Am I drunk*? he asked himself as he saw at least fifteen men of Dominican descent creeping into his first floor patio door, all of them carrying assault rifles or handguns.

Mecca knew who'd sent them, his own grandfather. He had seen those same goons wipe out other crews while growing up. Mecca instantly grew enraged. His pride was still intact, and he figured, if he was going out, it would be with a bang.

Mecca hopped off the rails and stepped back into the house. He walked over to the table and grabbed both of his guns. He then dipped his entire face into the cocaine bowl and took a deep sniff. Cocaine was all over his face as he rose up with bloodshot-red eyes. He walked over to the radio, and the sounds of Tupac blared out of the speakers. He turned the volume up as high as he could, so the intruders didn't have to guess what part of the house he was in.

"Come on, mu'fuckas!" Mecca yelled. He pounded his chest just before breaking the bulbs in the big lamp that lit the room up. He wanted to kill every single man who came for him. He was about to set that mu'fucka off.

Mecca ran to the corner of the spacious room and kneeled behind the couch and cocked both of his guns. "Y'all trying to come in my home and get me? Do y'all know who the fuck I am? Huh!" he yelled over the couch, as four men ran into the room and positioned themselves.

Mecca's body was sweating profusely because of the drugs and his anxiousness. He was ready to get it popping. He rose up blasting, shooting anything that was moving.

The sound of Estes' henchmen's assault rifles filled the air as they tried their best to take Mecca's head off.

Mecca, even though he was high as a kite, aimed with a marksman's precision, picking them off one by one. He ducked behind the couch briefly for cover and then emerged blasting. Busting his gun was like second nature to him, and he began to kill the men in the room. Before he knew it, he was the only one left standing.

When he heard the sounds of feet coming up the stairs, he realized that he had no chance against the army. A man ran through the door, and Mecca rolled across the floor and fired his gun at him, but nothing came out. He was out of bullets.

Mecca rushed for him, but the man popped him in the shoulder. But that didn't stop Mecca. He ran and struck the man across the face, causing him to drop his gun. Mecca then began to beat the man to a pulp. Swollen to twice its normal size, the man's face became like a bloody stew as Mecca pounded the man with his gun. That's when the others came up the stairs, and Mecca caught another bullet to the mid-section.

"Ahhh!" he screamed as the burning-hot bullet ripped through his torso. Mecca fell on his back in pain and saw another man coming for him.

The room was dim, so the man couldn't see Mecca clearly and began firing aimlessly.

Mecca grabbed the dead man's gun and fired a bullet through the man's head, dropping him on contact, and the rest of the goons came in blasting.

Mecca then struggled to his feet and ran full speed toward the balcony. With bullets whizzing by his head and body he thought he had no choice, so he leaped.

"Everything is going to be okay," Young Carter said as he consoled Taryn. "I'm going to find him."

Taryn had been worried all night about her only remaining son. She had gotten the news from her father that he would be killed. She knew the rules to the game, but as a mother, there was no way she could accept the contract on her son. She tried her best to convince her father to call it off, but he wasn't budging.

She had been calling Mecca all night to tell him to flee. She just couldn't believe what Estes was telling her. She didn't want to believe that Mecca had killed Monroe.

Estes had decided not to tell Taryn about the baby, and he moved Leena in with him, so he could protect her. Potentially she could have been carrying a boy, and that would be another opportunity for a male heir to bear his last name. By Taryn being past her biological time frame to have babies, he wanted to shield Leena until the baby was born.

“I know Mecca didn’t do what they saying he did. I went over there this morning, and his place was empty and riddled with bullet holes. I have to find my baby.” Taryn cried hysterically on her stepson’s shoulder.

“I will find him for you. Mecca is a soldier. I know he is still alive, okay. You know Mecca. He’s probably laid up somewhere with a female right now. Them goons just came over and trashed the place, trying to intimidate him.” Carter was selling Taryn a dream. He knew in his heart that if Estes put a contract on Mecca then most likely he wouldn’t half-step. “Look, I’m going to check around and see what I come up with, okay.”

“Okay, Carter. Thank you so much. Please bring my baby home. I can’t lose another son.” Taryn grabbed his face gently. She looked into his eyes and was amazed at the resemblance he held with his father. At that moment, she had faith that he would make things right.

She then looked over at Breeze, who was on the couch crying, and went to soothe her.

“I will. I’m going to find him. Just don’t worry,” Carter said just before he exited the house. He hopped into his car and grabbed his phone from his waist so he could call Ace and Zyir to roll with him. He picked up his phone, but dropped it when he felt someone grab him from his backseat.

“Yo, Carter, it’s me!” Mecca said as he released Carter.

“Man, what the fuck are you doing?” Carter asked as he turned around to look at Mecca. He saw that he was shirtless and bloody. The atrocious smell of liquor and blood invaded Carter’s nostrils.

“Don’t look! Stay turned around! They watching,” he said as he lowered his voice and stayed crouched down out of sight. “Yo, fam, pull off so we can talk.”

Carter pulled off, and once they were clear of the house, Mecca sat up and looked around nervously. "Man, they trying to kill me."

"I know. Taryn told me what was going on. Man, tell me you didn't do what they say you did."

"Hell nah, I didn't kill Money. I told you I saw them mu'-fuckin' dreads running out when I came. I didn't have my banger on me, so I couldn't get at them." Mecca kept his eyes moving.

Carter immediately had skepticism, because as long as he knew Mecca, he was always strapped. It didn't sound right, but he was going to give him the benefit of the doubt. "I knew it couldn't be true, man. You know we have to get at them niggas, right? We have to go to war."

"Most definitely, but I can't, with my grandfather on my ass. I have to lay low for a minute." Mecca's voice began to break as he explained to Carter how he jumped off his balcony to get away from Estes' goons and landed in his pool. He needed medical attention for his wounds and was losing blood rapidly.

Carter looked at Mecca's bloody shoulder. "We have to get you to the hospital, man."

"Nah, I can't go to the hospital. Estes will find out. He has the whole city in his pocket. I need to holler at Doc," Mecca said, referring to one of his father's old friends that happened to be a surgeon. "Then after that I am going to have to lay low, feel me?"

"I got you. I'm gon' hold you down. I have an idea," Carter said as he jumped on the highway. He had to make Mecca disappear for a while and only knew one place where Estes would never look for him.

Chapter Fifteen

"This ain't Flint town, baby. Money flows like water in Miami, and I got a crazy connect. I'm getting the birds straight off the boat . . ."
—Carter Jones

Taryn looked directly into Mecca's eyes. A part of her was relieved that he was safe and sound, but another part of her ached at the fact that he could possibly be responsible for Money's demise. She could never imagine him committing such an act of sin. Certainly the hands that had shed her son's blood were not those of his brother. It couldn't be.

"Mecca, I need to ask you a question. I will only ask you once, and I need to you to be honest," she stated. Her voice cracked from emotion. She was losing everything that she and Carter had worked so hard to maintain. She composed herself, and once Mecca's eyes met hers, she asked, "Is it true? Did you harm Monroe?"

Mecca fixed his lips to answer honestly. He wanted to be truthful with his mother, but the look in her eyes revealed her inability to forgive. Killing Monroe wasn't a trespass that she could dismiss, and he loved his mother too much to give her a reason to hate him. He couldn't change the fact Money was gone, but he was still breathing and needed his mother's love like a newborn that hadn't yet been removed from the womb, so he lied.

"No."

The lie ripped through his heart like a hollow-point, and he couldn't contain his emotions. He held onto his mother, trying to feel her heartbeat through their embrace while he wept on her shoulder, mourning the death of his brother and the loss of his sanity. Ever since he had killed Monroe, his head wasn't the same.

"Everything is going to be all right, son. I love you. No matter what your grandfather says, I know in my heart that you would never do what you've been accused of. Monroe was your other half, and you are too selfish to hurt a part of yourself." Taryn held Mecca's face in both hands. The sight of him so weak and exposed reminded her of his childhood years, and she wished that she could turn back the hands of time. She wanted to go back to the days when her husband was their protector, but those days were lost, and now it was up to her to salvage what was left of her family.

Mecca had tears in his eyes as he sniffed loudly. He knew that his mother was unaware that he was responsible for Monroe's murder, and the secret was eating out his insides.

"Now you are the only son I have left. Walk through these doors and you man the fuck up, do you hear me?"

Mecca knew that she was serious because swearing was something that his mother rarely did. He nodded his head in understanding.

"Your father isn't here, Mecca. My baby Money is gone. I'm not losing you too."

He hugged his mother tightly, and Breeze stepped up and wrapped her arms around him as well.

"Mecca, I love you," Breeze whispered as they all embraced tenderly.

"I love you too, *B*," he answered, holding on to her as if it were the last time he'd ever see her. He looked up at Carter, who stood next to his Uncle Polo, both hands tucked away in his Cavalli slacks. "Take care of them for me, man," Mecca said in an almost pleading tone.

"You know it, fam. Get your head right, baby boy. I don't know what's going on inside you, fam, but we need you healthy, nah mean? Don't worry about anything. I'ma take care of everything," Carter told him.

Mecca embraced Carter briefly and gave his Uncle Polo a nod before he turned around to walk through the double glass doors and into the therapeutic mental institution.

Breeze fell into Carter's arms as soon as Mecca disappeared from sight, and her tears flowed freely down her golden face.

"I don't want to lose you, Carter. Everyone's leaving me. All of my brothers are gone except you," she whispered in a broken voice.

Polo and Taryn stood silently as they watched the youngest member of the Diamond family break down. They knew it had been a long time coming. Breeze was by far the most vulnerable member of their dynasty, and with nothing but misery around her, they were all waiting for her to crack.

"Shh," Carter whispered. "That's not happening, Breeze. I'm not going anywhere, and neither is Mecca. He's going to get better, I promise you that. We're going to rebuild this family, you hear me?"

She nodded and rested her head against his shoulder as he walked her to Polo's Bentley.

"Get some rest, *B*. I'll be by to check on you later, a'ight."

"Okay," she said as she stepped into the open car door. "Be careful, Carter. I don't want to bury you too."

"You won't have to," Carter replied as he closed the door. He turned to Taryn and Polo then said, "Taryn, can I speak with Polo for a second?" He rubbed his hands over his neatly trimmed goatee in frustration, the stress evident on his face.

Taryn nodded and then excused herself to the passenger seat of the car.

"Yo, what the fuck, fam? Shit is getting wild. Mecca got these mu'fuckas after him, got his mental all fucked up. My baby sis is breaking down, and Money . . ." His words broke off in his throat as he thought of his current circumstances. He had just become acquainted with his siblings, and he was already losing them. "I swear to God, fam, I'm ready to murder Ma'tee."

Polo could see Carter was hurting, and he felt his pain. He had been a part of the Diamond family from the conception of the very first seed, and he too was feeling the burdens of the war with the Haitains. "Listen, son, we've got to stay smart . . . strategic. You said it yourself. We've got to think before we move. Right now, The Cartel's taking a lot of losses. We need to be about the business, get our money up and our soldiers strong before we get back at Ma'tee. We need to sit down and promote some of our street lieutenants—"

Carter interrupted Polo, "Nah, fam, I can't rock with them mu'fuckas, man. No offense, fam, I respect what The Cartel is and all that it stands for, but I don't trust them niggas. I haven't bled with them, fam. They don't know my hustle. I need my own people down here. These Haitains is playing for keeps, and I'm gambling with my life, nah mean? I need niggas around me that I can trust."

Polo nodded. "A'ight. Put your peoples on the first flight out, and let's get this money so we can dead this beef and get back on track." Polo walked toward his car and got in, leaving Carter standing on the curb alone.

Flipping up his cell phone, Carter called his right-hand man. "Yo, Ace, what's good, baby? It's about that time. I need you, fam."

It was all that needed to be said. Ace knew what time it was. He agreed to gather Zyir and be on the next flight out to chop it up with his best friend.

The next night Carter waited patiently as he watched Ace and Zyir emerge through the airport doors. A sense of relief instantly washed over him when he saw the faces of his two most trusted associates. With his own squad in town, he could lay niggas down with no reservations because he had his right and left hand beside him. He greeted Ace first, slapping hands with the one person he had come up in the game with. They were thick as thieves and had taken over their hometown of Flint with relative ease. They were seasoned and thorough. They had been putting in work together for years, and he knew that the transition to Miami would be a smooth one.

"You good, fam? You had me worried on the phone. You ain't sound right," Ace commented as they embraced.

Carter nodded his head and greeted his protégé, "Li'l Zyir, what's good, baby? I'm glad you came down, fam."

"My nigga call, I come running, fam. That's how we do, nah mean? Besides, it's warm than a mu'fucka down here. It'll do ya boy some good getting away from that Arctic shit up north."

Carter walked toward his Range, and they all packed their bags inside before pulling away from the curb, Jay-Z's *American Gangster* CD immediately filling the leather interior.

Out of habit Ace punched in the code to Carter's hidden compartment, revealing three chrome pistols. He removed two, tossing one in the backseat to Zyir.

Carter, Ace, and Zyir were the last of a dying breed and would never be caught without their heaters. Zyir and Ace had the exact hidden compartments in their own whips. The compartments always held three guns, one for each of them in case of emergencies.

"So what's so important that we had to come all the way down here?" Ace asked, admiring the change of scenery that Miami offered. The palm trees and busy streets seemed worlds away from the dilapidated houses and potholes of his hometown. "It's nice down here, fam," he commented as he waited for Carter to reply.

"It's the same game with a different face, fam. Don't let this glamorous shit fool you. I'ma be real honest about the shit that's going on here. My father—"

"Your father?" Ace asked in astonishment, knowing that his best friend had never known his dad.

"Yeah. That's how all this started. My father was the leader of a criminal enterprise called The Cartel. Basically they run all this shit down here. Drugs, real estate, politics, anything that happens here, The Cartel makes happen or is a part of in some way."

"Yo, so these Cartel mu'fuckas on some real organized crime type shit, huh?" Zyir asked.

"Yeah, and business was good, up until my father was murdered by Ma'tee. Ma'tee runs little Haiti, and this nigga ain't holding no punches. Since killing my father, he's murdered one of my little brothers and sparked a war that is fucking with my money."

"Your money?" Ace asked. "You a part of this Cartel shit?"

"I run The Cartel. It's mine now, which is why I need the two of you here. Y'all know how I move. I trust both of you with my life," Carter said seriously.

"You know we're with you, fam, but how is the money down here? We were making at least a hunnid thou a month in Flint. You know how lovely the hustle was there. We had our blocks on smash," Zyir said proudly.

"A hunnid thou?" Carter raised his eyebrows and looked at Zyir in the rearview mirror.

"Each," Zyir bragged. "That's good money, nah mean? Ya boy was eating."

"Don't worry about the cash, fam. You gon' eat. You will make a hunnid thou easy," Carter guaranteed.

Zyir nodded in approval, but he lost his mind when Carter added, "A week."

"Nigga, you bullshitting!" Ace exclaimed.

Carter remained silent.

Ace looked back at Zyir and said, "Yo, this mu'fucka is really serious."

"This ain't Flint town, baby. Money flows like water in Miami, and I got a crazy connect. I'm getting the birds straight off the boat, ninety percent pure, but these Haitains is plugging up my leak, nah mean? They are taking out my soldiers, which is slowing up my money. We about to rebuild, and when we're where we need to be, we'll get rid of them mu'fuckas."

Ace and Zyir trusted Carter and was with him before he even finished what he was saying.

Carter drove them to a luxury apartment community near the Diamond household. It was a 2,500 square foot space with three bedrooms for them to share. They walked in through the attached two-car garage, a Hummer for each of them resting inside.

Carter removed two sets of keys and tossed one to each of his friends. "Y'all are all set up. This place is close to my family's home. They live a few miles from here. I'll take you through tomorrow to meet them and introduce you to your new workers."

"A'ight, a'ight, fam. I know we down here on business and everything, but, nigga, this is Miami, and ya boy trying to see the city tonight. Let's do it big tonight for ol' times' sake, and tomorrow we can be all about the business." Zyir anxiously unlocked his new truck and hopped inside.

Ace and Carter laughed at Zyir's excitement, but they knew that he was young. At 18 he still had the world to experience. They had seen and done so much more than him, and they both knew that he was only trying to follow in their footsteps.

"A'ight, fam. We can do it right. I'll show y'all around town."

Miamor pulled out her cell phone in the middle of the crowded club to see if Carter had called. He hadn't tried to contact her in two days, and his sudden absence from her life was starting to bother her. She usually spoke with him at least twice a day, and he always made it a point to come and check for her. Now that he was doing disappearing acts, she didn't know what to think.

Aries could see the discouraged look on her friend's face. "You okay?" she shouted over the loud music.

Miamor looked up and realized that her two friends were staring at her, so she put her emotions at bay and replied, "Yeah, I'm good. I was just wondering what time it was."

"Why hasn't he called you?" Robyn asked, not buying Miamor's lie.

"He's going through a lot right now. His brother just died, and his family is having—"

"Do you hear yourself right now?" Robyn said to her. "Miamor, he is a mark. The Cartel is our mark. He runs The Cartel now. They killed Anisa."

With each day that passed, it was becoming more difficult for Miamor to keep up the charade. Yes, it was true that she harbored ill feelings toward The Cartel and wanted to murder Mecca. But it was also true that she was falling in love with Carter. She knew it, and in a way she hated herself for it. She felt like a traitor. She wanted to be wifey, wanted to be a part of Carter's life, but she knew that what she was building with him would eventually be torn down by a plot that she herself had devised. When the time came, she was going to kill him. She didn't have a choice.

"Miamor, you have to get he to break de truce with Ma'tee. That is the only way we can get de bounty on de Cartel. Push him, Mia. Make he react," Aries urged.

Miamor nodded.

"Are you sure you can handle this?" Aries asked.

"Yes," she answered simply as she took a sip from her Long Island Iced Tea.

"Then handle it," Robyn told her.

"Look, this is going to take some time. The Cartel is not like any of the other jobs. I have to be careful. Carter isn't dumb. He'll see straight through me if I'm too pushy. I have to do this my way. I have to play wifey so that he'll trust me, but don't worry, it's gonna get done. I'm good, just trust me."

"Fuck it. That's not what we here for anyway. Let's just have a good time," Aries said.

The girls agreed, and Miamor leaned with her back against the bar as she swayed sexily to the music. She made sure that she could see every angle of the club, a habit that she had acquired over the years. She was always aware of her surroundings.

Miamor held the attention of many of the men in the club. Her black spaghetti strap Prada dress dipped low in the front, revealing her C-cup cleavage and her flat stomach, and silver Choo stilettos accented her shapely, athletic legs. Her healthy hair glistened under the strobe light and was cut in a long bob with Chinese bangs, while her M•A•C cosmetics complemented her almond-colored skin. The term "Shorty is the shit," had to be meant for her, because her features always outshined every other chick in her vicinity, and that night was no different.

Miamor watched as most of the women in the club flocked toward the door. She squinted to see who had entered the club that deserved so much attention.

"Speak of the devil," Robyn commented as she saw what the commotion was all about.

Carter and two other men walked into the club clad in Cavalli jeans and fresh kicks. Carter simply wore a gray Lacoste sweater with a white collared shirt underneath. He was simple, but his jewels stood apart from every other nigga in the club. He was wearing so many carats that he was almost hypnotic as the strobe lights played hide-and-seek with the diamonds around his neck.

Miamor watched as Carter and his friends selected three girls to take up to the VIP section with them.

"That's why we can't get shit poppin', Mia?" Robyn continued as if Carter didn't impress her. "The nigga is playing you, Miamor. He has your fucking head gone. You sitting up in here turning down mad niggas, waiting on him to call, and he out courting these busted-ass bitches."

Miamor could feel her temperature rising. She was hot as she watched Carter place his hand on the small of the girl's back and guided her through the crowd. *Is he for real?*

"Just say the word and I all over that bitch," Aries stated.

The sight before Miamor had her tight. She was so upset that she was seeing red, which usually meant blood was about to be shed, but she controlled herself and saved face in front of her girls. "Fuck him. He ain't my man. The nigga is a job, nothing more and nothing less," she stated coldly. *I can't believe I was feeling his lying ass,* she thought to herself. She wanted to leave the club, because deep inside she knew that her heart was broken, but she stayed. She knew that if she left, she would be admitting that she was falling for him.

She couldn't believe what she was seeing. Carter was hers. At least, he was supposed to be, and she was jealous that his attention was focused on another woman. Carter was popping bottle after bottle of champagne and had his arm draped around the young woman as if he were proud to have her on his hip. *This is bullshit,* she thought silently as she inventoried her competition. The girl with Carter was pretty in the face, but her twice-borrowed dress and Claire's jewels were a disgrace. *This shit is unfucking-believable,* she thought.

Her girls looked on in shock. They could tell that Miamor was beyond upset.

Carter was having a good time. His head had been fucked up since arriving in Miami, and it felt good to have his niggas by his side again. For a long time, Ace and Zyir had been the only "brothers" he'd known, and he trusted them whole-heartedly. His love for them ran deep, and they shared an unbreakable bond.

He looked around at the random chicks that Zyir had picked out of the crowd and had to admit he hadn't been so carefree in a long time. Carter was what some women would call arrogant. He was very selective when it came to who he shared his time with, and it was very rare that he dealt with a lot of women at one time.

It was even rarer to see him in a nightclub, but Zyir and Ace had talked him into it, so he decided to let loose. He told himself that he deserved to relax after all that he had been through in the past couple of months.

Carter noticed that their drinks were getting low, so he leaned over and whispered for Zyir to go to the bar to get some more Moët. Zyir arose and made his way over to the bar. He slid into the empty space next to Robyn and placed his order.

Robyn automatically clocked his pockets when he pulled out a wad of cash. She had to admit, she was impressed, because he was working with all big faces. *I should rob his young ass,* she thought playfully to herself.

Zyir noticed her watching and smiled as he licked his full lips. "Ay, ma, why don't you and your girls come and join me in VIP?" he stated.

His boyish charm was cute, and Robyn could tell that he was young from his approach. "What's your name?" she asked.

"Zyir," he replied.

When the bartender brought his drinks, he grabbed the three bottles. "You coming, or you gon' hug the bar and wait for one of these broke-ass niggas to come over and waste your time?"

Robyn leaned over and whispered in Miamor's ear, "You wanna go?"

Miamor shrugged nonchalantly. "It's whatever."

"We don't have to stay. Just let that nigga see that you see him. Maybe his guilt will get shit moving a little faster." Robyn turned to Zyir and said, "Lead the way."

Miamor took a deep breath and followed behind her girls as they approached Carter's table. Her stomach was in knots as she continued to watch him closely. It seemed like the closer she got to him, the more her eyes began to fail her. Tears built up, and she was forced to blink them away before they could fall.

"Yo, my friend and her girls are going to join us," Zyir stated as he sat the bottles of Moët down on the table.

The girl had Carter's face turned toward hers, and she had his full attention as she whispered something in his ear, so he didn't even notice Miamor.

"Yo, I didn't get y'all names," Zyir stated.

"I'm Robyn."

"Aries."

"Miamor."

As soon as her voice blessed Carter's ears, he turned his face and looked up at her in surprise. He could tell from the hurtful expression on her face that she had been there for a while, and he instantly knew that he had fucked up. He withdrew his arm from around the groupie and stood up.

"No, please don't let us break up y'all little thing," Robyn protested sarcastically to Carter.

Carter tried to make eye contact with Miamor, but she refused to look at him. She just shook her head in disgust before beginning to walk away.

Robyn turned to Zyir. "Thanks for inviting us over, but it looks like you all have enough company as it is. It's a shame too, 'cuz you had potential, young'un," she said sweetly as she lightly kissed his cheek, and they walked away from the table.

Carter excused himself and followed behind Miamor. Grabbing her arm gently, he stopped her from leaving as he tried to explain. "Miamor, it's not what it looks like," he began.

Miamor snatched her arm from his grasp and shook her head in disbelief. She was pissed and hurt. She hated herself for caring so much when the man before her was simply supposed to be a means to an end. *What is it about him?* she asked herself silently.

"Come on, ma, say something."

Miamor wanted to forget what she had just witnessed. A part of her wanted to leave the club with him, but she had never been a silly broad who believed lame excuses, and she wasn't about to become one that night. *I know what the fuck I saw. He was all in the bitch face a minute ago. If I hadn't walked up, he would probably be taking the bitch home tonight. Fuck him.*

"You know what, Carter? It doesn't even matter. Now I know who you really are. You are just like every other nigga—a liar."

Her words hit him like darts to the heart. When she turned to walk away, he reached for her hand. "Miamor."

Just then the girl he had been with in VIP eased up behind him and wrapped her arms around him as she stared Miamor down. It was obvious she was trying to make her presence felt and stake her claim. Miamor shook her head and backpedaled toward the door.

Carter removed the girl's arms from his body.

"You just made this so much easier for me. He's all yours," she said as she stormed away, her stilettos stabbing the floor to death with each step before she disappeared through the exit of the club.

The pain that was etched on her face was the last thing that Carter saw before she left. "Fuck," he whispered.

"What's wrong, daddy?" the girl asked.

Carter looked down at the girl, and all of a sudden she had become a nuisance. "Look, ma, I need some air," he said. "I'm not trying to play you or nothing, but ain't shit poppin' off tonight, a'ight." Then he walked away, leaving her dumbfounded in the middle of the dance floor.

Chapter Sixteen

"Just do your job and be my fucking bulletproof. That's what being a rich, spoiled, dumb little bitch gets you—a mu'fucka like you to take bullets for me."
—Breeze

"Hi, you've reached Miamor. Unfortunately I'm unavailable right now. Leave me a message, and I'll return your call."

Carter hung up his phone and sighed deeply from frustration. Miamor refused to take any of his calls. Each time he attempted to contact her, she gave him the fuck-you button and sent him straight to voice mail. He knew that his mind needed to be on his paper chase, but the feelings that he had begun to develop for her were unlike anything he'd ever experienced with a woman. He had never found any one who held his interest in the way that she did, and now he was kicking himself for being so stupid. He knew what it must have looked like, but he never intended on taking the girl from the club home with him. She was just someone to entertain him and his boys for the time being. He knew that it didn't make his actions any less hurtful in Miamor's eyes, and he hoped that she gave him the chance to make things right with her before she decided to write him off completely.

Carter maneuvered his car in front of Ace and Zyir's building then called upstairs to let them know he was outside. It was time for him to get focused. With his own team in town, money was sure to flow. The sooner he got paid, the sooner he could avenge his brother's murder and move on with his life. He was on a three-year hustle plan for Miami. He wanted to flip and re-flip his money into the hundred-million-dollar range, and he knew that it was entirely possible, considering Miami's lucrative drug trade, and his father's real estate company, to which he was now the acting CEO.

Ace and Zyir hopped into Carter's truck, and he pulled away from the curb.

"Yo, fam, what was that shit that happened with you and that chick in the club last night?" Ace asked. He had noticed his friend's demeanor change drastically, but was too wrapped up in his female acquaintance to address it.

"Man, some ol' crazy shit. The chick Miamor that Zyir brought over to the table, I been kicking it with her since I've been down here. I didn't know she was in the building. My actions would've been a whole lot different, nah mean?" he stated with a smirk.

Zyir laughed from the backseat. "Shorty was tight. I could see that shit all on her face. I ain't mean to throw salt in your game, fam."

"It's all good," Carter said. "I'm about to introduce the two of you to my family. This is serious, and all jokes aside, whenever they are around, it has to be about protecting them. I'm not trying to see anything else happen to them. They've been through enough, and I'm all they have left right now, at least until Mecca comes home."

Carter pulled up to the gated home and greeted some of the security he had hired to post up around the premises. He parked his truck directly in front of the magnificent house.

"Damn, yo people's paid, fam." Zyir got out and admired the massive estate.

Carter walked into the house and was immediately greeted by Taryn.

"Carter, it's so good to see you, sweetheart," she said as she hugged him. "Have you eaten? I can fix you something if you'd like."

"No, I'm fine, Taryn. Thanks. I came by to introduce you to my friends from Up Top. They are in town because of everything that's been going on with this war."

"Well, if they can help, then I am certainly pleased to meet them."

Ace stepped up first and held out his hand. “Hello, ma’am. I’m Ace,” he said politely.

Taryn smiled graciously and accepted his hand. “It’s very nice to meet you, Ace, but please call me Taryn.”

“And this is Zyir,” Carter said, making the introduction for his second partner.

“I’m glad to have you both here,” Taryn said with a grateful smile.

Carter detected the melancholy tone in her voice and knew that she was at her breaking point.

Breeze glided into the room with the accurate style of a supermodel. Her long hair was in its natural curly state and was held back by a silver headband. She wore black leggings with an H & M silver mini dress and silver Hollister flats. Her face lit up when she saw her brother.

“Carter! I didn’t know you were here,” she stated as she ran to hug him.

“Breeze, I want you to meet my best friend, Ace, and my little nigga, Zyir. They are like brothers to me. They are the only people besides me and Polo that are allowed to enter this house. No one else has my permission. They are the only ones I trust with your lives. We have to keep you both safe, okay.” He spoke sternly but gently as he tried to stress the importance of his rule to his hardheaded little sister.

“Okay, I understand. I’m about to go, but I’ll call you later on.”

“Hold up. Where you going?” Carter asked.

“To the beach and out to meet with an event planner. Poppa used to always throw a white party for the Fourth of July, so I’m throwing my own this year, you know, to get my mind off of everything.”

“That’s cool, *B*, but I want you to do me a favor and take Zyir with you,” he said.

Breeze looked past Carter toward Zyir. His chocolate skin and medium build attracted her slightly. The tattoos that adorned his arms and neck appealed to her. *He may not be too bad,* she thought.

Carter smirked at his sister’s blatant interest in his friend, but knew that Zyir would never be interested in a girl like Breeze. They were from two different worlds.

"Okay, I'll take him," she answered as she walked out of the door.

Zyir didn't know that he was going to be babysitting, but he agreed just because his man asked him to.

Breeze pulled her two-seater BMW-Z series from the garage and pulled up in front of Zyir.

"You coming or not?" she asked sweetly as she put on oversized Chloe glasses.

As Zyir reached for her door, she pressed her gas slightly, making the car move forward without him.

"You playing, shorty? I ain't gon' chase you, ma," he said, his vernacular smooth and low.

Breeze laughed. "I'm sorry. Come on, get in."

Zyir shook his head as he entered the car, and they rolled off.

Breeze was silent as she cruised through the Miami streets. She didn't know what to say to Zyir and felt awkward around him. It was clear to see that they were extremely different, but he was sexy, and she loved his dark skin. His serious demeanor reminded her of her father.

"You don't talk?" Breeze asked innocently, once she had grown uncomfortable with the silence between them.

Zyir smirked as he let his seat back and sat down low in the car.

"What, you don't want to be seen with me or something?" she asked, frowning.

Zyir looked at her. "Breeze? Is that your name?"

She nodded.

"Breeze, I talk. I just don't like to talk when there ain't nothing to talk about. I don't talk about shopping or gossip or gay shit like that. My conversations revolve around one thing."

"Oh yeah, and what's that?"

"Money."

"Money ain't everything."

"What you know about getting money, girl? You've been spoon-fed your whole life." Zyir wasn't trying to be rude, but he wasn't one to hold his tongue.

"So what? You judging me? Yeah, I grew up with money, but don't act like you're the only one who's struggled. My father died trying to give me the best of everything, so you damn right, I'm gon' take advantage of everything that he left me. Ain't that what you trying to do? Provide for your family? Or are you only worried about pushing new whips and bullshit like that?"

"I'm just doing me, shorty, that's it. I don't got no kids to think about, and bitches ain't worth the headache. So, right now, I'm about stacking my chips, nah mean?"

When she didn't reply, he answered for her, "Nah, you don't know what I mean."

"Why are you so rude? Is that how you niggas in Flint get down? You act just like Carter."

"Carter basically raised me. He's the only father figure I know. I met him four years ago when I was only fourteen. He took me in and taught me everything I know. And I'm not trying to be rude, ma, so if I offended you, I apologize. You're just a little spoiled, that's all."

"You don't even know me." Breeze couldn't believe his nerve. No one had ever talked to her that way. Most were afraid to overstep their boundaries because of her affiliation with The Cartel, but Zyir didn't care. He said what he wanted to say, and she found it attractive.

"I don't have to know you. I know your type."

"So what? Because you came from the bottom, you hate everybody that's at the top? I guess you like them ol' raggedy Reebok-wearing bitches, huh? If a chick ain't from the ghetto, then you ain't interested."

"I like smart chicks. It doesn't matter where they're from." Zyir turned to face her.

"And I'm not that?"

"I don't know. You tell me. I mean, I'll admit I don't really know you, but it seems to me that you are a little naïve, self-centered." Zyir smiled. He could see that his words were bothering her. He had to admit, she was a gorgeous young woman, but her head wasn't in the right place.

"Self-centered?" Breeze repeated, her face frowned in disagreement.

"Check it, ma—After everything your family has been through, you out here trying to throw parties and shit. Trying to keep up your perception and be the center of attention while mu'fuckas is running up in your people's funerals and killing the ones you love. You're in the middle of a war and you making yourself accessible. You're the type of target a nigga would love to touch. If I was working for the other side, you would be the first one I would gun for. You're easy to get to." Zyir looked toward her and noticed the solemn expression that crossed her face. The girl was fighting back tears, and he instantly regretted bringing up the death of her loved ones.

"Yo, ma, I'm sorry—"

"You know what? Just don't say shit to me. I get it. You think I'm stupid and spoiled, so there ain't no need for us to be social, but don't ever say anything about my family. You just got here. You don't know us. Just do your job and be my fucking bulletproof. That's what being a rich, spoiled, dumb little bitch gets you—a mu'fucka like you to take bullets for me," she said arrogantly.

Breeze pulled in front of the event planner's office and slammed her door as she got out of the car. She stopped on the sidewalk in front of the building and thought about what Zyir had said to her. She couldn't help it that she was spoiled. Her father had always provided for her, but she had never been called selfish before. Zyir's words had been like a mirror that showed Breeze her true reflection. She was her family's weak spot, and it hurt.

"Damn it!" she yelled as she kept walking past the party planning spot and onto the sandy beach across the street.

Zyir watched her from the car and put his hand over his face when he saw her storm off. "Fuck, man! I should've just shut the fuck up. All this dramatic shit ain't for the kid," he mumbled to himself. He reluctantly climbed out of the car and walked down the street behind her. "Getting my mu'fuckin' kicks dirty and shit," he complained as he walked through the sand near the edge of the water in his crispy white Force One's.

He walked up behind her. "Breeze."

"You're right," she said.

"Nah, ma, I was out of line. You're right. I haven't been here. I don't know shit, just forget about it, a'ight," he said attempting to make her feel better. He wasn't used to being sentimental, and he had never apologized for anything in his life, so he felt awkward changing his persona for her.

"I remember my father used to bring me here when I was little. We would come to the beach, and he would let me run around all day. I would shop up and down these boulevards for hours. I was the only little girl rocking Chanel and Ferragamo." She laughed at the distant memory and then looked Zyir in his eyes. "You see, I've always had everything I've ever wanted, ever since I can remember. Every year he threw a white party for all of our friends and family. Everybody came out to show The Cartel love. I miss him so much. I just want things to be how they were before all this happened. They are taking everything from me. My father, Money, Mecca's half-crazy. All I have left are my memories and the money that my father left me. I'm not trying to put my family in jeopardy, but I don't want to stop living my life while I wait around to die. Eventually they are going to get me too," Breeze whispered, as tears burned her eyes.

"No, they not, ma," Zyir said confidently. Seeing her so weak hit a soft spot with him.

"How can you be so sure?"

"I'm your bulletproof, remember?" He nudged her shoulder gently, trying to make her smile.

She wiped her face and smirked slightly. "Sorry about that comment."

"It's nothing, shorty, but for real, if you want to make it through this war, you got to be just as smart as the mu'fuckas gunnin' for you. Don't be the weak link, ma. If you wanna go somewhere, all you got to do is call. I'll take you, 'cuz, believe me, a nigga ain't murking me."

"Thank you, Zyir," she said graciously as her curly hair blew with the ocean-misted wind.

"You're welcome, beautiful."

"Oh, so you think I'm beautiful?" Breeze grinned as she put her sunglasses back over her eyes.

Zyir shook his head and grabbed her hand to lead her back to the car. "You still trying to throw this party, or you gon' be smart and play it safe?"

"I trust you. I don't want to put my family in danger."

"Well, let me put you up on some new shit, something that will occupy your time." He hopped into the passenger seat and said, "Take me to the nearest bookstore."

Breeze and Zyir spent the entire day together. He took her to Borders and introduced her to reading, which was a pastime that she never had.

The most that Breeze ever did was flip through the pages of fashion magazines, but Zyir spoke about African American literature as if she were missing out on something. His obvious passion for reading was intriguing. He piqued her interest as he spoke fervently about authors such as James Baldwin, Langston Hughes, and Alice Walker. He even put her up on street fiction, starting her out on Donald Goines and then suggesting street writers like Ashley & JaQuavis, Keisha Ervin, and Sister Souljah. Breeze had never met anyone like Zyir. He was intelligent, honest, and most importantly, she felt safe when they were together. She trusted him with her life, and she had just met him.

"What am I going to do with all these books? I can't read them all today. Maybe I should come back for some later," Breeze said, almost intimidated by the stack of books that were piling up in her hands.

"I'ma tell you like Carter told me. Start at the beginning and work your way through until you've read them all. You've got to feed your brain, ma. Don't let these crackers hide shit from you within these pages. That's how they keep our minds imprisoned. That's why I said there is nothing more unattractive than a dumb chick," he said. "I'm surprised Carter ain't gave you that speech yet. The nigga stay grilling me and I ain't even his family."

Breeze laughed. "Well, that's a conversation that I can avoid having because you've already taught me. I guess I'll take them all then."

Zyir purchased all of the books for Breeze, and when it was time for her to go, she was reluctant to go back home. "I had a good time today," she said.

"Me too, ma, me too."

"I just feel like I finally have someone I can talk to, you know? My brothers are all about this war, and I sort of get lost in the sauce. This was nice."

"I better get you back."

Breeze shook her head in protest and smiled. "You bought me all these books and now you gon' leave me hanging? You know I might need you there to help me get through some of these big words, you know, since you think I'm dumb and all."

"First impressions are sometimes wrong. I misjudged you."

"So tonight is not over yet?" she asked as she stepped into her car.

"Nah, shorty, it ain't over. We can kick it at my place."

Zyir told her his address, and twenty minutes later, they were pulling up in front of the building.

Carter pulled up to Miamor's place and saw her as she walked across the parking lot with ten shopping bags in her hands. He smirked when he noticed that the bags were all from high-end designers. *She is definitely high-class. She can hurt a nigga's pockets for real.*

He admired her runway strut before approaching her. "You need some help?"

"What are you doing here?" she asked quietly as she stopped dead in her tracks.

"We need to talk."

"There's nothing to say," she answered quickly and sternly.

Her tone was short, and he knew that she was still upset. The way her jaw clinched was an indication as to how mad she really was. Her jealousy told him more than her words could ever say. He knew that she had feelings for him that ran deeper than she wanted to admit, and that she was stubborn, and it would take some effort for him to get back in her good graces.

He pulled the bags from her hands and motioned his head for her to walk ahead of him. She hesitated, but didn't protest as she began to walk into her building. The natural sway of her hips commanded his attention as he followed behind her.

The smell of vanilla filled Carter's senses as soon as he stepped foot inside her home. Her place was spotless, and that was one of the things he loved most about her. She was clean. She was sensitive. She was a real woman.

"Thank you for carrying my bags up. You can leave now," she said as she opened the door for him and folded her arms across her chest.

"Can we talk?"

"I told you ain't nothing to talk about," Miamor stated. "Go talk to your little girlfriend from the other night." She knew that she was being childish, but she didn't care.

"She was nobody," Carter stated as he stepped into her. He put one hand on the side of her face and swept her hair from in front of her eyes. "She was just some little bitch I met at the club. You don't have to worry."

Miamor laughed arrogantly. "Worry? Look at me, Carter—Do I look like the type of bitch that needs to worry over a nigga? No! I have a million in line that were waiting for you to fuck up. They didn't have to wait very long now, did they?"

Carter nodded his head, and for the first time she saw him get angry. His nose flared slightly, but he kept his composure.

"Okay. I'ma let that slick shit you popping slide, because I fucked up. I hurt you."

"Whatever. Please do not give yourself that much credit," Miamor replied quickly. She knew that she had to keep the smart comments rolling off her tongue to stop herself from crying. "You know what? I don't even know why you are here. You don't have to explain anything to me. I'm not your girl, and I don't really give a fuck about what you do. I'm just glad that I found out how you are before I . . ." She stopped speaking abruptly before she said too much. *Don't let this nigga control the situation. Keep your emotions in check and use them to your advantage.*

"Before you what?"

She was silent as she tried to keep her composure.

"Tell me," he demanded.

"Before I gave you a chance to break my heart."

Carter closed his eyes and rested his forehead against hers as he released a deep sigh. She could see the regret on his face, and it was then that she knew he never meant to hurt her.

It was too late for her to care though. She had let him into her heart, and he had showed her shade, no matter how small it may have been. He was her enemy. *Yep, nigga fall right into my trap, lying-ass mu'fucka. You should feel bad,* she thought angrily.

"I'm sorry, ma. I was stupid. I shouldn't have even been in a club, especially with a bitch. I've got a lot on me right now. She didn't mean shit, and she ain't shit to me. I don't even know the girl's name. I apologize for hurting you," he whispered.

"You didn't," she said, her words stubborn and cold.

"I did. I can see it in your eyes, Miamor, and I am sincerely sorry, ma. I'm caught up in some shit with my family right now, and I wasn't thinking. I don't want you to doubt the way that I feel about you."

His words were making her weak, and she felt a single tear escape her eyes. "Just leave me alone," she whispered. Miamor wanted to kill Carter so badly that she could taste his blood in her mouth. *I hate this nigga, but I love his ass too,* she thought.

How could she love a man whose organization took her sister away from her? She was so torn and confused that she didn't know what to do. Her girls were wrong, Carter didn't have her head, but he was slowly capturing her heart.

It's too bad, I'ma have to murder this nigga, she thought sadly.

Carter pulled her away from the front door and closed it. With her back against the wall, he kissed her neck gently. Her nipples hardened, and he removed her shirt and unclasped her bra in one motion. His hands were experienced, and he'd perfected the art of seduction like a ball player perfected his jump shot.

His full lips found their way to her breasts, sucking them gently before making his way further south. He removed her jeans, slipped her panties to the side, and licked her pussy so good that she automatically forgave him. His warm tongue wiggled in and out of her honey slit with skill. She felt the throbbing sensation in her swollen clitoris, and his lips circled around the tender spot as he sucked on it slowly, gently, passionately, French-kissing it with skill.

He slipped two of his thick fingers inside of her as his tongue continued to work its magic on her clit. His fingers felt like a hard dick as he caused her to squirm from his touch.

"You forgive me?"

"No," she moaned as she rotated her pussy in his face. She looked down, and the sight of her juices all over his face aroused her even more. She grinded furiously on his fingers as her pussy squirted multiple orgasms. She never knew getting her pussy ate could feel so good. Either the niggas she was fucking with before were amateurs, or Carter was blessed, but either way she was in heaven.

He stood back to his feet, leaving his jeans on the floor beneath him. His dick already rock-hard from the pleasing sounds erupting from Miamor. His fingers were still inside her, and she was pleading for him to continue. His manhood grew another inch, just from the seductive look on Miamor's face.

"Please put it in," she moaned. "Carter, I need you. My pussy needs you."

Carter lifted one of her legs around his waist and rubbed the head of his dick up and down her wetness. His head resembled a flower in bloom, and the width of it was mesmerizing. The heat radiating from him caused her to tremble as he teased her by rubbing it slowly against her puddle of wetness.

"Please, baby, put it in!"

He pressed the tip against her clitoris repeatedly, causing her to hump nothing but air. She was fiending for the dick, she wanted him so badly.

"You forgive me?"

"I can't," she said.

"Yes, you can," he replied as he filled her tight space.

"Oh my God! I can't, Carter," she moaned, tears slipping down her face. "I want to kill you," she admitted through her moans.

Carter was oblivious to the fact that she meant every word.

"I hate you," she moaned over and over again.

Carter lifted her other leg and balanced her against the wall as he dug into her, going in as deep as he could go.

"Ooh shit," she called out. "Right there, daddy! Yes, right there!"

"You forgive me?" he asked as his fingertips melted into her voluptuous ass.

"Yes! Yes! Oh . . . what are you doing to me?"

"I'm fucking you, ma. Them other niggas can't do this pussy like this. You fucking with another nigga?" he asked as he clenched his ass muscles.

"No! Only you. This is your pussy, Carter. I hate you! This is yours, daddy. Oh my . . . oh shit," she moaned. "I'm about to nut, Carter. I'm cumming . . . aaah!"

Carter felt her body tense up, and when her walls contracted on his dick, he released his seed inside her, with no condom and no regrets.

Her legs gave out when he set her back on the floor, so he picked her up and carried her into her bedroom. He lay down with his arms wrapped snugly around her.

Miamor felt so right in his arms, and she hated what she was doing. She knew that she would eventually have to destroy him, but being with him right now at that very moment was the only thing that she wanted to think about.

"I'll never hurt you again, ever. On everything I love, I'ma make you mine. I love you, Miamor."

She couldn't stop herself from responding, "I love you too."

Ring, ring!

Ring, ring!

The shrill sound of Carter's cell phone woke him and Miamor out of their peaceful sleep. He looked at her digital alarm clock, which read 3:42 A.M. He groggily reached for his phone. "Hello?" he answered as he sat up in bed.

"Carter! Thank God! It's Breeze," Taryn stated in a panic. "She hasn't come home yet."

"What?"

Miamor sat up when she heard Carter's tone of voice. "What's wrong?" she asked.

Carter held up a finger for her to hold on and returned his attention back to his phone call. "Look, if she was with Zyir, I'm sure she's fine. I'll call you when I catch up with them. Give me about an hour," he said.

Carter knew that Breeze should have been safe with Zyir, but when he called his phone and didn't receive an answer, he began to worry.

"I got to go, ma," he said as he jumped up and began slipping into his clothes.

Miamor's face expressed her disappointment, and under normal circumstances, he would've handled her later, but he had just gotten back into her good graces.

"Slip on some clothes. You're coming with me," he said.

She jumped up, and in five minutes flat they were out the door.

Carter pulled up to Ace and Zyir's apartment at 4:15 A.M. and was relieved to see Breeze's car sitting out front. He still needed to see her face to make sure she was okay. *What in the fuck is she doing over here anyway?* he thought to himself. He rushed up to apartment 8B and rang the bell.

Ace answered it. "Damn, fam! Whatever it is, it can't wait until the morning?" he asked sleepily.

"Where's Zy?"

"Fam is in his room. He's been in there all night with the door closed. Why? What up?" Miamor stood silently as she watched anger cross Carter's face.

"Is Breeze in there with him?"

"I don't know, fam."

Carter walked to the back of the apartment and opened Zyir's room door without knocking. He took a deep breath when he saw his baby sister sleeping soundly in Zyir's bed, with Zyir sleeping in the chair next to the bed, his feet propped up. They both had *Dope Fiend*, by Donald Goines, in their hands and had fallen asleep with the book still open.

Carter laughed at himself for thinking the worst. Zyir would never put his sister in danger or disrespect him by hitting and running on her. If Breeze was interested in Zyir, it was a bridge that he would cross when they all got there, but for now, she was safe and he was satisfied.

"Everything good?" Ace asked.

Carter nodded. "Yeah, fam, everything's good. I'm tripping. We gon' crash on your couch out here until morning, a'ight."

"Yeah, bro, make yourself at home. You know where everything at."

Carter placed a call to Taryn and informed her that Breeze was just fine.

"Are you all right?" Miamor asked.

"Yeah, I'm good. Let's get some sleep," he said as he pulled her near and closed his eyes.

Chapter Seventeen

"The coke connect died with my grandson. . . . Now get the fuck out."
—Emilio Estes

"I got you, young'un. I'm about to go and talk to Estes and try to plug you in. The game is all yours now," Polo said just before hanging up the phone with Young Carter. He was just about to have a meeting with Estes. He wanted to see if he could set up a meeting with him and Carter, so he could retire and move to LA. He was done with the seesaw game that treated him both good and bad.

He pulled up to the loading dock's parking lot and smoothly got out, wearing a straw sun hat, and a toothpick sticking from his mouth. He saw that Estes and his henchmen had already arrived before him, just like he expected. He slowly approached the Dominican men, who stood on the boardwalk that led to Estes' speedboat. He raised both of his arms without them having to instruct him. He knew the drill only too well.

After getting searched, he boarded the boat and saw Estes at the head of the bow, his back turned, smoking a Cuban cigar.

"Good evening, Estes," Polo said loudly as he stuck his hands in his white linen pants.

Estes signaled for his henchmen to pick up the anchor so that he could take off.

"Polo," Estes said, not even giving him the respect of looking him in the eyes. Estes started the boat and pulled off.

Polo sat in the seat uncomfortably and wondered where Estes was taking him. He slightly moved his hat off his head, but not all the way off. He didn't want the small .22-caliber pistol he had under the hat to fall.

After a ten-minute ride, Estes finally stopped the boat, and all they could see was water. There was no sign of anything else but the royal blue Atlantic Ocean.

Estes turned to Polo and took a deep puff of his cigar. "You wanted to talk, right? Talk," he said coldly.

"First, we need to get at the—"

"That's already taken care of. The entire Haitian mob is dead. There will be no more bloodshed. The only one left is Ma'tee, but we cut his legs from under him. He has no money or no army, and most likely Miami won't see him again."

Polo was surprised at how quickly Estes moved. Estes was two steps ahead of him, managing to wipe out the whole Haitian mob with ease. He knew that Estes was the boss of all bosses, and it was another day at the job for him.

Polo continued, "Yeah, I wanted to discuss a few things. You know, since Carter died, I've been the one you've supplied. The way I see it, I'm not getting any younger, and the game has changed. I'm trying to make an exit and give this game up for good."

"You're a smart man."

"I really have faith in Young Carter, and I was wondering—"

Estes raised his hand to stop him from talking. "Let me tell you something. I never liked you. Hell, I never liked Carter, but I gave him the connect because my daughter was in love with him, and I wanted him to be able to provide for her. So, you see, this is where it all stops. No more product for The Cartel. I want nothing to do with you people. The connect died with my grandson," Estes said as he looked past Polo.

Naturally Polo followed his eyes and saw that two boats were approaching. "Oh, so that's how you gon' play it, huh?" Polo asked in disbelief as he nodded his head repeatedly. He was ready to go for his gun, but he saw the two boats pull up, one on either side.

Estes stood up and began to unzip his pants. He unleashed his small tanned penis and began to urinate on Polo's shoes.

Polo quickly moved his feet, and it took all of his willpower for him not to go for his gun and shoot Estes in the face. He felt totally disrespected, but he knew that he would only be committing suicide if he did that.

One of the men picked up a small one-person rowboat and tossed it in the water.

"Now get the fuck out," Estes said calmly as he turned his back to Polo.

Polo clenched his jaws so tightly, it began to hurt as he realized that Estes was going to make him row all the way back to shore. Swallowing his pride, Polo stepped onto the small boat, staring a hole through Estes the whole way down.

One of the henchmen tossed Polo a paddle, and they all pulled off, leaving Polo alone in the middle of nowhere. Polo, his ego bruised beyond repair, knew at that moment it was time to leave the game alone. He was tired of everything that came with it. If that would have been five years ago, he would have gone out guns blazing for the stunt that Estes pulled. But Polo had matured and knew that he would've started a fight he could never win.

Carter would have to find his own connect and start from the ground up. In the meantime, Polo had some serious paddling to do.

Chapter Eighteen

"Ain't shit changed! You know the deal, so stop playing yourself."
—Miamor

Miamor's hands shook uncontrollably as she chopped the peppers and onions on the cutting board. She took a deep breath. *Why am I so fucking nervous?* she questioned silently as she worked swiftly, following the recipe book to a tee, trying to complete the meal she was preparing for Carter before he arrived at her house. Her eyes darted towards the clock. She didn't have much time. She needed to be dressed and finished before he knocked on her door.

She stuffed the smoked salmon with a lobster, portobello, and spice bake then put it into the oven. She prepared a special lemon sauce to drizzle over the top of it once it was done baking.

Miamor didn't know how she had gotten so deeply involved with Carter, but she was ready for it all to end. She wasn't acting like herself, and the pressure that her girls were putting on her was becoming overwhelming. She knew that she had to make a move and do it quickly, but everything was so uncertain now. Miamor's head was spinning.

Carter had thrown shit in the game by going hard at Ma'tee. The entire Haitian operation had been disabled, and, Ma'tee, a man who she had thought was so untouchable, was now on the run for his life. She was frustrated and confused all at the same time. She felt like a trader. She wanted to kill Mecca for bringing the Grim Reaper to her sister's door, but there were too many doubts. Too many variables had been added to the equation. An eye for eye did not seem as simple as it did before she met Carter. He was making her weak. With three little words, he'd changed who she was.

Ding-dong! The ringing of her doorbell startled her.

He can't be here yet. It's only eight o'clock. He's not supposed to be here until nine.

She quickly went to the mirror that was hanging near her entryway and scanned herself. She wasn't even dressed. Carter had never seen her dressed so casually. She wore a wife-beater with baggy sweatpants, and her hair was pulled up in a raggedy ponytail. She tried to run her French tips through her hair to make herself look a little decent, but that was useless.

She sighed deeply then opened the door slightly. "What are you doing here so early? I'm not even dressed yet, Carter."

"You look fine," he replied as he leaned down to kiss her on her forehead. "You don't have to dress all up. We're staying in anyway. This is your house, so be comfortable."

"Comfortable is not the same as tore down," she joked as she went back to the mirror.

Carter walked up behind her and kissed the nape of her neck as he slid his strong arms around her waist. He looked at their reflection in the mirror. "You're beautiful, ma. Stop tripping."

She smiled. Carter was considerate and always made her feel like she was worth more than she was, because in actuality, she felt like she wasn't shit. He was caring, and she wasn't. If she was, there would be no way that she could have put thallium sulfate in his dinner. She had made sure to put the odorless, tasteless powder in the lemon sauce that she planned on drizzling over his lobster. She was done bullshitting with The Cartel. She concluded that the timing would never be right for her to get at them, so tonight was just as good as any.

Unfortunately for Carter, he would be the first to go. She really needed to kill him first because then she wouldn't have him around all the time, making it difficult for her to stay focused.

"Are you hungry?" she asked sweetly as she pulled out one of her dining room chairs and motioned for him to have a seat.

"I don't know. Is the food safe to eat?" he asked.

His statement threw her off slightly.

Does he know? "W—what?" she asked, her eyes penetrating his.

"I mean, you know you ain't the world's best chef." A smile appeared on his face.

Miamor gave him a playful left jab to the chest. "You ain't funny, nigga," she said, breathing a sigh of relief. *Relax. He doesn't know anything is up. Stop acting so damn guilty.*

Her silent demands caused her nerves to settle some, and she went to the oven and pulled out the lobster then fixed two plates of food.

Her heart began to beat so loudly in her ears that she was sure that even Carter could hear it as she placed his dinner in front of him. She lit the candles on the table, poured them both a glass of wine, and then grabbed the lemon sauce. She poured it all over Carter's lobster then took a seat.

"This looks good, ma. Thank you for cooking for me. I know you said you didn't like to cook. I appreciate you going through all of this trouble."

Miamor smiled and watched him intently as he took a sip out of his wine goblet.

"I want to talk to you about something important," Carter stated. He didn't wait for Miamor to respond. "I'm into you, Miamor, but there are some things that you don't know about me, or about my family."

I know all I need to know about your family. Miamor tried to conceal her hatred behind her eyes.

"Tomorrow is not promised to me right now, ma. My family is at war with some very dangerous people, and I don't ever want to put you in jeopardy. My father and little brother have already been murdered behind this beef. I'm willing to accept the fact that I could be next, but I would never forgive myself if something happened to you because of me. It's not safe for me to be with you, and believe me, it's so hard for me to say this to you, but right now is not a good time for this, Miamor. I can't bring you into my world right now. I would kill a nigga if he ever tried to hurt you. I love you, ma, but I'm no good for you. I have to let you go in order to keep you safe."

Miamor couldn't stop the tears from forming in her eyes. It was like his words were medicine to her ailing heart. Her conscience immediately began to turn on her. How could she hurt a man who cared so much about her? She was more than capable of taking care of herself.

Carter didn't know it, but she was the safest bitch in the city because she would pop a nigga without regret for running up, but just the simple fact that he wanted to take the burden off of her shoulders and protect her himself touched her.

Carter picked up his fork and brought it to his mouth. All she had to do was let him eat the food.

I can't, Miamor thought painfully. She stood and swept all of the food off the table in one dramatic motion. "Aghh!" she screamed in agony as she picked up a glass and threw it at the wall in frustration. The glass shattered into tiny pieces, reminding her of how her heart felt the day that she'd held her dead sister in her arms.

"Whoa! Ma, what the fuck you doing, yo?" Carter moved toward her to restrain her temper tantrum.

"I can't do this." She shook her head from side to side. The emotional levees in her gave way, and tears built in her eyes.

"Miamor, calm down," Carter said as he took her into his arms.

"I can't do it," she cried as she breathed deeply, trying to contain herself.

Miamor wanted to get back at The Cartel for taking her sister away, but how could she, when her heart and her mind was pulling her in two different directions?

Why in the fuck did he have to tell me he loved me? Why did he have to make it so real?

Her brain felt like it was going to explode. She was playing mental chess with herself. She wanted Carter to be her opponent so desperately so that she could follow the rules of the game and defeat him. She wanted to bag his queen, not be it. She yearned to kill his family, but her heart wouldn't let her, and she was quickly beginning to realize that her only opponent, the only person standing in her way of her revenge, was herself. Her heart was following a completely different set of rules, rules that were unfamiliar to her. Her heart was begging her to open up and allow herself to feel happiness with a man. To trust a man, to believe in a man . . . her man, Carter Jones.

The emotions that she felt for him were so foreign to Miamor that they scared her and caused her to question her loyalty. In her world, hesitation never existed. There was no room for it. That was something that could get you murked in her profession. Murdering a nigga had always been simple. Some people were good at math, others good at sports, many good at singing or painting, but Miamor was good at death. When she declared war, she brought it to a nigga's doorstep without fear, without doubt, but with swagger and expertise. Now her job seemed so complex, and she didn't know what to do.

How did I let him get this close? she asked herself.

With her back to the wall, she used it for support and slid down until she felt the floor catch her. She pulled her knees into her chest, put her head down, and held herself as she cried.

Carter hadn't expected for her to take it this hard and was amazed at her reaction. He hated to see her in pain, but was oblivious to the real reason behind her outrage. *She doesn't know what the fuck she's getting herself into,* Carter thought, when in actuality he was the one in unknown territory. He was dancing with the devil by allowing himself to love her.

Carter picked her up and cradled her in his arms as she continued to cry. "Shh, it's all right, ma. I'm not going anywhere," he said.

As soon as he spoke the words he knew that he meant them. Dangerous or not, he could not stay away from Miamor. He had never felt a connection like the one he shared with the beautiful woman in his embrace. There was something about her, something that was so forbidden, it made him want her even more.

Miamor knocked on Robyn's and Aries' door early the next day. She wore Rock & Republic denims with a Lela Rose top and Christian Louboutin peep-toe pumps. Everything on her body was designer, and worth more than most people's monthly rent, yet she still felt worthless. Her usually M•A•C-designed face was as bare as her soul, and her hair was pulled up into a sophisticated bun. She tried to appear as if she was in control, but her red, puffy eyes revealed the truth and gave away the fact that she had cried herself to sleep in Carter's arms the night before.

Knock! Knock! Knock! Knock!

Aries opened the door.

"We need to talk," Miamor stated gravely without even offering a hello. "Is Robyn here?"

"Yeah, I think she in she room. What's wrong? You crying?" Aries asked in astonishment.

Miamor stormed past Aries and took a seat on their love seat. She placed her Gucci clutch next to her. Her cell phone rang. It was Carter calling her. She knew that he was calling to make sure she was okay. He had stayed the night at her place the night before, but as soon as daylight crept through her curtains, she got up and rushed to see her friends.

She sent him to voice mail and then looked up at Aries. "I can't do this anymore, Aries. It's over. This entire plan is done."

"What?" Aries shouted. "What do you mean, over? Why? What happened?"

"That nigga done got up in her head, that's what happened." Robyn suddenly emerged from her bedroom and leaned against the wall. "Am I right, Miamor? That is why you want to quit, ain't it?"

"I just can't do this anymore, Robyn. I can't do Carter dirty like that."

"What you mean, you can't do him like that? Oh, but you don't have a problem doing us dirty?"

"You're not the one in his face every day, Robyn. I'm fucking him! I know him, and he doesn't deserve this. I won't make him pay for his family's mistakes. I don't want to see him hurt. When does it end? I kill him or somebody in his family then they retaliate and kill another one of us. What happens after that? Huh? It doesn't bring Anisa back!"

"Miamor, he stole your sister from you."

"Don't even waste your breath, Aries. She had her mind made up who she was picking as soon as she walked through the door. We don't need her. We'll do it ourselves."

"Shut the fuck up, Robyn! You don't know shit! It's over, plain and fucking simple. Don't nothing move unless I say so! Ain't shit changed! You know the deal, so stop playing yourself. And don't pretend that you are all about the crew. You're in this for the money. This has nothing to do with my sister. Carter has already gotten to Ma'tee. There is no more beef. It's squashed. The bounty probably ain't even good anymore, so you ain't losing nothing. I'm out," Miamor yelled as she walked toward the door. She knew that she had taken it a little too far by accusing Robyn of not caring for Anisa. It was a low blow, and she knew that it wasn't entirely true, but her anger had spoken for her.

Miamor was resentful because it was always herself and Anisa that acted as the leaders. Robyn and Aries just followed suit, which meant they always played the back, while Miamor and her sister put themselves in harm's way. She wasn't trying to end up in the dirt anytime soon, so she was going to walk away . . . breathing.

"So that's it? You gon' choose him over us after all we've been through?"

"What do you want me to do, Robyn? This is it! This shit is a wrap! Aries, if you want to take it the same way, you can. It is what it is. I love you guys. You're my sisters, but I'm in love with him, Aries. I didn't mean for it to happen, and I didn't want to give him my heart, but I did. Yes, his family is responsible for Anisa's death, but how many people have we brought the same fate? We have to take responsibility for the role we played in this. We all knew it was possible. We just got caught slipping. That is something that I will regret for the rest of my life, but I won't make him pay for it."

Miamor stormed out of the house with a heavy heart. She knew that Aries would eventually forgive her, but Robyn would take it as a personal slap in the face. It was possible that their friendship may never be repaired, but it was a chance she was willing to take.

Miamor walked into her home and heard her shower running. She was glad that Carter was still there. After the morning she'd had, she needed him to prove to her that he was worth it. She walked into the bathroom. She pulled back the shower curtain and admired Carter's toned body as he washed himself. She stepped inside of the shower in her clothes and all then held on to him tightly. She hoped that he wouldn't make her regret her decision. She was taking a chance on him, trusting someone other than her immediate circle for the first time in her adult life.

"Hey, what's wrong? You're getting yourself soaked, ma," he whispered in protest, yet he never let her go.

Miamor had no regrets. She knew that he was worth the risk. She could feel his love for her even in the way that he held her. Deep inside her heart she knew that he would never hurt her. She just hoped and prayed that she could keep herself from hurting him.

"I could fucking kill her!" Robyn yelled as she paced back and forth for the twentieth time, practically burning a hole in the floor.

"What has gotten into her?" Aries asked. "Love? She's killed so many people, me didn't even know she had a heart."

"Fuck this! I'm about to call this bitch because she is not about to just bail out on the plan. I don't care if I have to murder her little boyfriend myself—We are finishing this job! She can thank me later for getting rid of her distraction."

Robyn grabbed the cordless phone off the wall and dialed Miamor's number. The humming of a cell phone filled the room.

Aries walked over to the couch and picked up Miamor's purse. She checked inside, retrieved the phone, and threw her hands up in exasperation. "So much for that. She left she damn bag here. We have to get it together because I was depending on the money from the bounty."

A smirk came across Robyn's face as she took Miamor's phone from Aries' hand. She flipped it open and searched her address book.

"What are you doing?" Aries questioned.

"Finding Ma'tee's number. If Miamor wants out, that's fine, but we are going to get this money. It doesn't matter to me if she's with it or not. We don't need her."

Robyn located Ma'tee's number and pressed dial. She was determined to finish what they had started. By any means necessary, she was going to get paid and then get out of town.

Chapter Nineteen

"Why are you always acting like I don't matter to you?"
—Breeze

Breeze walked beside Zyir as they headed to the bodega where a black-owned bookstore was located. They had grown quite fond of each other. Zyir was the only person that Breeze really talked to. Everybody only took her at face value, but Zyir saw through her. He knew her and took the time to actually listen when she talked.

Zyir slowly felt himself growing closer to Breeze. He didn't want to because he knew that it could possibly cause conflict between him and Carter, but the more time he spent with Breeze, the more important she became to him. They were together twenty-four seven. Carter demanded that Zyir keep her safe, so they stayed side by side.

At first Zyir found her annoying and immature, but once he got to know her, he realized she was inexperienced in the aspects of the street because her family had kept her sheltered. She had never had to think about protecting herself because her father and brothers had always done it for her. Now it was Zyir's responsibility to ensure her safety, and it was a job he took very seriously, partly because of his duty to Carter, but mostly because of his feelings for Breeze Diamond.

Day in and day out, they rocked with each other, building a solid friendship, even though they both knew they would take it to the next level if and when the time was right. They agreed to keep their friendship under wraps until they could figure out a way to tell Carter.

Since losing Monroe and sending Mecca away, Carter had been extra strict with and overprotective of Breeze. Zyir kept one hand near his waistline, the other wrapped around Breeze's shoulder, as he leaned into her.

Breeze whispered in his ear, "You need to quit fronting, acting like you don't want me to be your girl." She kissed the side of Zyir's face lightly.

Zyir smiled and rubbed his chin. Breeze wasn't as innocent as she looked, and he enjoyed her mystique. "I told you, ma, I like things like they are right now. We're cool as is. I'm not tryin'-a disrespect my man Carter by coming at you. You're his baby sister. You already know how he feels about that."

Breeze grabbed his hand that was draped around her and kissed it lightly. "I don't care how Carter feels about us. And how do you know he will trip? He will probably be glad I'm messing around with you instead of one of these other dudes out here."

"I just know, a'ight. I know Carter. I can see it in his eyes when the nigga see us together. It wouldn't be a good look for us right now," he said seriously. "You know how I feel about you, ma, but unfortunately for us, it ain't in the cards."

Breeze stopped walking and put her hands on her model-thin waist. "Zyir . . ."

"What up, *B*?" Zyir stopped walking, preparing himself to be sucked in by her charm. Zyir was usually so focused on his money, but Breeze was a constant and pleasant distraction from his everyday grind. He was constantly molding her, transforming her from a shallow little rich girl to an intelligent young woman. The beauty had always been present, and if it was up to him, he would have definitely made her wifey. If only it were up to him.

"Why are you always acting like I don't matter to you? Do you really just want us to be friends?"

That was one characteristic that Zyir couldn't change about her. She was spoiled through and through. He smiled and shook his head as he rubbed his fresh Caesar cut. "Come on, *B*, you know you matter. Stop being like that, a'ight. I'm gon' figure it out, but there's too much going on right now. We don't need to put another problem on Carter's mind. Let's wait until things die down first, a'ight."

Robyn, Aries, and Ma'tee watched closely as they sat in the BMW with tinted windows, following the young couple's every move. They had been stalking Breeze for three days straight. They needed to know when and how she moved, so constant surveillance was necessary.

Miamor had left them on stuck when she decided to grow a conscience and play wifey to their enemy, but the Murder Mamas wasn't having it. After contacting Ma'tee, they decided to kidnap the weakest member of the Diamond family and hold her for ransom. Once the ransom was paid, they planned to kill Breeze in retaliation for Anisa's murder, and then they would leave town. They hoped by then that Miamor would come to her senses. They had all been together for too long to break apart now, but with or without her, they were doing this so they could relocate to L.A. The West Coast was the only place they hadn't been yet, and they wanted to go some place where their reputation didn't precede them.

"How de fuck we suppose to grab de bitch if that nigga always with she?" Aries screwed the silencer on her .357-Magnum. "Ah should blast he right now for being such a fucking punk, lover boy-ass nigga. How are we supposed to catch she alone if he constantly with she?"

"No," Ma'tee said. "We will stay in de shadows until de time is right, and we will get her when they least expect it. Just continue to watch. Her routine is de same each day. They come to dis same bookstore at the same time. He is her only barrier of protection, but we still have to be smart. We will get her soon enough." Ma'tee leaned back in the plush leather seat. "Soon enough."

Chapter Twenty

". . . The Murder Mamas. They're ruthless. Bitches will kill they own fucking mothers without thinking twice."
—Fabian

Miamor awoke to the feel of Carter's lips on her neck. She smiled and adjusted her neck so that she could kiss him. For three days straight she had been laid up with Carter in his beachside condo. They had seen no one but each other, and being wrapped up in him kept her mind off her girls. She felt bad for switching up on them, but they didn't understand. They could never understand why she couldn't kill Carter. He was the only man who had gotten inside of her heart and made her give regard to human life. Miamor's body was exhausted from the "sexual Olympics" that Carter had taken her through. She was spent, but it was all worth it because she had pleased her man.

"What time is it?" she asked, stretching her arms above her head.

"Three o'clock. Get up and put on some clothes. I'm taking you out tonight."

No man had ever spoken to Miamor with such authority in his voice, and surprisingly she respected Carter, doing anything he asked of her.

Miamor arose, showered, and was dressed in Dolce in less than twenty minutes.

As they drove through the busy streets, Miamor's fingers intertwined with Carter's. She was silent as she watched the city fly by in a blur. *I need to contact Aries and make sure they are straight. They've been my girls for too long for me to turn my back on them now. I can help them come up on some money with a different job, but I can't go through with this one. I have to get them to understand where I'm coming from.*

Miamor was so engrossed with her thoughts that she didn't see the detour that Carter had taken until the car was parked. She frowned as she looked up at the Mercy Mental Health Hospital. She looked at Carter in confusion. "What are we doing here? I thought we were going to dinner."

Carter rubbed her hair as if she were his child. The way he soothed her made her smile. "Don't worry about it, ma, we're just making a quick stop. I need to see somebody here," he explained as he opened the car door. He walked around to her side and opened the door for her. "Come on, I don't know how long I'll be. I don't want you sitting in the car twiddling your thumbs."

Miamor got out of the car and followed him inside.

When they entered, Carter signed in and then put his hand on the small of Miamor's back as he led her down a narrow hallway into a waiting room where patients were visiting with their family and friends.

Miamor stopped walking when she saw who Carter was going to see. *So this is where the fuck this nigga been hiding,* she thought. She began to scratch the palm of her hand. Most people's hand itched when they were about to come into money, but Miamor's hand itched when she was about to commit a murder.

"Let me go holla at my brother, ma. Have a seat. I won't be long," Carter whispered then pecked her quickly on the cheek.

It took all of her self-control not to run up on Mecca, and she stared cruelly at her sister's killer.

Carter snapped her out of her daze. "Ay, you good?"

Miamor nodded and forced herself to look away. "Yeah, I'm good. Go ahead. I'll be right over here."

Carter approached Mecca and slapped hands with him.

"What's good, fam?" Mecca eyed Miamor. "That's you?"

Carter laughed. "That one's off-limit, fam. How's everything with you? You good? You need anything?"

"Nah, I'm good, bro. Have you heard anything from Estes?" Mecca asked. "I'm tired of hiding out in this mu'fucka like a bitch. This shit in here is too calm, fam. I'm ready to come out busting at whoever standing in the way."

Carter shook his head. "That wouldn't be smart, Mecca. You barely survived the first time. I know your record. You ain't got to prove shit to me, fam, but your grandfather is operating on an entirely different level. If he wants you touched, then you will be touched. Just give things some time to settle down. You talking to the therapists about Money?"

Carter knew that Mecca didn't want to talk about Monroe's murder, but he was worried about his brother. He'd noticed the change in Mecca after Money's demise and thought it might be wise if Mecca could get whatever was bothering him off his chest.

"Fuck these crackers, man, they will never understand," Mecca replied.

Fabian emerged from his room and into the visiting room. He was eager to see his mother. She had traveled from Virginia just to come and see her only son. He sauntered out of his room with his piss bag taped to his stomach. Walking past Mecca's table, he stopped mid-step and stared in shock at Miamor. His yellow skin turned pale white as if he had seen a ghost. "Oh shit, man, oh shit!" he stated as he began to cry. He ducked down directly behind Mecca's chair.

Carter noticed the strange man and frowned. "Fuck is this crazy nigga behind your chair, fam?"

Mecca turned around and looked down at his crouching roommate. "Fuck is you doing, nigga? Is there a problem?"

"Please, man, please, man, just hide me. I don't want to die, man. Please just hide me," Fabian begged.

Mecca and Carter looked around the room. There wasn't one person in the room that seemed to be paying attention to Fabian. They didn't know that Miamor, who was calmly sitting in the corner, flipping through a magazine, had chopped off his most precious jewels.

Carter shook his head from side to side and stood from the table. All of a sudden, being inside of the hospital was becoming unbearable. *These mu'fuckas in here are loony as hell,* he thought.

Fabian was so deathly afraid of Miamor noticing him that he stayed crouched to the floor as if he were in the army, and maneuvered his way back to his room. He even missed his visit with his mother because he was afraid that Miamor would see him.

Mecca extended his hand and slapped hands with Carter.

"Stay sane in this mu'fucka, fam. Call me if you need anything, and be careful. Estes got eyes everywhere, nah mean?"

"Yeah, I hear you. Be easy, duke."

Mecca pulled up his sagging pants and strolled back to his room, where his roommate was hiding out. He looked at the nigga in disgust. He had never even held one conversation with the man. Mecca wasn't in the hospital to make friends. He simply needed to lay low for a while, so conversing and entertaining niggas that weren't on his level was pointless. He knew that, once they found out who he was, they would try to get on and would hassle him about being down with The Cartel.

"Is that bitch still out there?" Fabian asked.

"What the fuck? You running from a chick?" Mecca asked. "What, the bitch trying to stick you with child support or something?" Mecca laughed at the sight of the grown man crying before him.

Fabian shuffled to their bedroom and peeked outside in the hallway. Once he saw the coast was clear, he closed the door. "It's not just any chick," Fabian explained. "She's a Murder Mama."

"Say what?" Mecca had never heard of the group, so he wasn't impressed.

Fabian went underneath his bed and pulled out a box. Inside of it were newspaper clippings and one photo of the four girls together. "Man, I'm not in here because I'm crazy. I'm hiding from these bitches called the Murder Mamas. They're some killers, family." "Some bitches?"

Fabian nodded as his eyes continued to roam nervously.

"Yeah, nigga! I'm telling you that bitch was here to finish me off. Look, man"—Fabian unzipped his pants and pulled them down, revealing his chopped off genitals.

Mecca turned his head and frowned. "Whoa, fam! Pull up your fucking pants, yo. You bullshitting on that faggoty shit, mu'fucka."

"I ain't on no homo shit, fam. Just look at my dick, nigga. These bitches did this to me," Fabian stated. "That bitch that was here with your visitor chopped me up."

Mecca's looked at Fabian in shock. "With my visitor?"

"Yeah, man. How did that bitch find me?"

"She did that to you?"

"Yeah, man, her and these two bitches—The Murder Mamas. They're ruthless. Bitches will kill they own fucking mothers without thinking twice." Panic-stricken, Fabian began throwing the little clothing he owned in a plastic garbage bag.

"Stop bullshitting, nigga."

Fabian shoved the pictures in Mecca's hands. "Look, nigga, that's a news article on them. They almost got caught up in some bullshit in New York. Needless to say, somebody produced some big money and made the case disappear."

Mecca's nostrils flared when he stared at the news photo. He saw four girls—Miamor, his brother's new chick, two girls he didn't recognize, and Anisa, the girl he had killed in the hotel room. He knew that Ma'tee had tried to have him hit that night and had sent the girl at him. He put two and two together. He knew that Miamor had to be sent by Ma'tee to get at Carter.

"Who do they work for?" Mecca asked, to confirm his suspicions.

"Nigga, anybody who can afford their services. I heard that this boss nigga from St. Louis paid them to do a job against some hustler he was beefing with. They fucked around and killed that same nigga two months later because somebody put that cake up to have it done. They don't have no loyalty, man. Anything is game. You see what they did with a nigga love stick, man. I got to get the fuck up out of here." Fabian peeked out in the hall once more then rushed out of the room.

Mecca's head was spinning. If it were under any other circumstances, he would have fucked Miamor. The fact that she had the balls to cut a nigga dick off amused him.

He had never seen any shit like that in real life, only in the movies.

Carter couldn't have known that this chick was affiliated with Ma'tee. From what Mecca knew, Miamor had been fucking with Carter for a little while now, so he silently wondered why she hadn't made her move yet. He didn't want to jump to conclusions. He needed to get out and back on the streets so that he could keep a watchful eye over his brother's new girlfriend, and find out more information, but he knew that if he left anytime soon, then Estes would put the dogs on his heels. Mecca decided that he would fix his problems with his grandfather first, and as soon as it was safe, he would find out more about The Murder Mamas . . . before it was too late.

Chapter Twenty-one

"I am Miami, nigga!" —Mecca

"Zyir . . ." Breeze mumbled as she held both of her legs open for him, giving Zyir a clear pathway to her clitoris. The sand on her back and the waves washing up on the shore heightened Breeze's first sexual encounter. She had never felt the type of pleasure she was experiencing at that moment, staring into the stars and moaning constantly.

It was around midnight that Zyir had convinced Breeze to sneak out and talk with him, and what started off as a conversation ended up becoming a night of passion.

Breeze had masturbated plenty of times, but she was a virgin to a man's touch. Zyir operated on her love box like a skilled surgeon would on a patient on the sands of the small, secluded beach just five miles away from the Diamond estate. She moaned loudly as she gripped his head tightly and moved her buttocks in a circular motion, gyrating in his face.

Zyir arose from Breeze's warmth and looked into her green eyes. Never had he seen a woman so pure, so beautiful. "You are very special, ma," he said in a low tone. "I want to be inside you." He let his rock-hard pole exit his boxers.

Breeze's body squirmed as she was soaked with her own juices. She gently grabbed Zyir's face, and they began to kiss passionately.

As Zyir attempted to enter Breeze's tight virgin wound, she grabbed him by the shoulders, stopping him. "Zyir, you got a condom on?" she asked.

Damn! Zyir thought as his world came crumbling down. He wanted to feel her virgin walls without any latex. That was a dope boy's dream, and she was ruining it for him. "Come on, ma, I want you so bad right now." Zyir rubbed his tip against her clitoris, trying to persuade her to finish what they'd already started.

"No, Zyir. No glove, no love. Let's just run to that 7-Eleven around the way." Breeze moved his pole and sat up.

Zyir took a deep breath and gave in. "All right. Let's go. You drive a hard bargain, ma," Zyir said.

They both broke out into laughter and put their clothes back on.

Zyir pushed his black tinted Benz through the Miami streets like a madman. He was anxious to feel the inside of Breeze Diamond. As they approached the store, he swerved into the parking lot, almost hitting another car. "I'll be right back," he said as he threw the car in park and jumped out. His manhood was erect and pulsating, showing in his baggy jeans.

He walked into the store and headed straight to the front counter and grabbed a three-pack of Magnum condoms. "Let me get this and a box of lemon heads," he said as he tossed them on the counter to the pimple-faced Asian clerk.

That's when the bell rang, indicating someone was entering the store. Zyir's eyes immediately shot toward the door, and he saw a beautiful woman walk through. He didn't want to stare, but the Daisy Duke shorts she was wearing, not to mention her pumps, demanded his undivided attention. His soldier stood even straighter in his jeans as she strutted behind him to get in line.

"Looks like someting's happy to see me," she said in a thick accent.

Zyir looked down and saw his rod pitching a tent in his pants. He smiled as he looked back up at the girl, but he got a big surprise—A .22-semi-automatic pistol was pointed to his head.

"Getcha bitch-ass hands up," Aries said as she gripped the gun. She looked over at the clerk, who looked like he shitted on himself. "And turn your Jackie Chan ass around before ah smoke yuh."

Instantly the clerk put his hands up and turned around as ordered.

Zyir kicked himself for not having his gun on him. He was so worried about pussy, he didn't even think to grab his gun out of his glove compartment before getting out of the car.

He glanced out of the store's front glass window and saw a woman stuffing Breeze into the trunk of a Dodge Charger. He immediately yelled, "Damn!" while keeping both of his hands up. He knew that the Haitians had sent for her, and watched the girl walk backwards toward the door, the gun still pointed at him.

Once she exited the door, she lowered her weapon, jumped into the Dodge, and they screeched off.

Zyir quickly ran out and went to his car, but he noticed that all four tires had been slashed. "Shit!" he yelled as he rushed to the passenger side and grabbed his gun out of the glove box. He ran to the middle of the street, busting his gun wildly, trying to hit their tires, but they were too far away. Zyir dropped to his knees in the middle of the street with both hands on his head. He had failed to protect Breeze, and guilt consumed him. He screamed, "Nooo!"

Ma'tee smiled as he peeked through the safe house's blind and saw the Dodge Charger pull in. He knew that their payday was soon to come, and the thought of his murdered daughter came into play. He promised himself he would make the Cartel family feel the same pain that he had just experienced.

Aries and Robyn had been tailing Breeze and Zyir for days and were waiting for the right moment to put their plan into play. They noticed that they were getting careless, and Ma'tee wanted to pounce on the opportunity. As the girls brought Breeze, a pillowcase covering her head, Ma'tee sinisterly smiled.

Ma'tee was in dire need of money since Estes' goons had robbed all of his safes and took all of his drugs. He had nothing left. Not even one of his former workers made it; they were all dead. He was lucky he wasn't at the house when they ambushed him. Actually he wished he was, so he could have died with his baby's mother and only child.

Ma'tee instructed the girls to take her to the back room, where only a mattress on the floor occupied the room. When they got to the room, Robyn aggressively tossed Breeze onto the floor by the mattress and locked the door shut.

Breeze had duct tape across her mouth under the pillowcase, so she was unable to scream. Her arms were also duct taped behind her back. Fear took over Breeze's body as she cried and used her legs to scramble to the corner. *Oh my God, they are going to kill me,* she thought as she tried her hardest to escape from the duct tape.

Breeze was unlike the other members in her family and hadn't been exposed to the drugs or hands-on violence. Not built for a situation like this, panic overwhelmed her. She heard someone come in the door, and that's when her nerves got the best of her, and she vomited. The tape caused the vomit to stay in her mouth, choking her.

I can't breathe, I can't breathe, she thought as she choked on herself.

Suddenly she felt a strong hand snatch the pillowcase from her head and then the duct tape. Her throw-up flowed out of her mouth as she began to cough harshly.

Ma'tee stared at Breeze and was amazed on how beautiful she was. He was in total awe of her. Her silky black hair and olive skin tone were marvelous to Ma'tee's eyes. *Too bad I have to kill she,* he thought as he paced the room, staring at her.

After Breeze caught her breath, she looked up at Ma'tee. "What do you want from me?" she yelled.

"Ah want revenge!' Ma'tee said through his clenched teeth.

When Breeze heard the accent and saw Ma'tee's dreadlocks, she knew who he was. At that point, she knew her life was on a countdown. She began to cry her eyes out.

Ma'tee just stared at her as if she was a work of art, no remorse in his heart. He walked out of the room and couldn't wait until he could get the fiasco over with so he could return to his homeland, where he would stay for good.

Taryn was on the floor praying and crying, a scene that was becoming too familiar. She had been through more than any woman could handle the past year.

Carter pounded his fist against the wall as Zyir, Ace, Polo, and Mecca stood in the Diamond kitchen. "Fuck!!" he yelled as he read the ransom note that was left on the doorstep the previous night.

They had been out all night looking for Breeze after Zyir rushed and told everyone what had happened, leaving out the part about them about to have sex. He told them that she wanted to go for a midnight stroll to clear her head and that he forgot to bring his gun. Zyir was dying inside from guilt.

"I'ma kill that nigga!" Mecca roared as tears fell down his cheek. He looked at Zyir, who was across the counter from him, with deadly eyes, not comfortable with the fact that he was with her when she got grabbed and didn't protect her. "And yo bitch ass probably working for the dreads!" Mecca made his way around the counter to put his hands on Zyir.

Zyir smoothly slid his hand down to his pistol. He'd already told himself that he would put a hollow-tip through Mecca's forehead if he ran up on him.

Carter quickly put his hand on Mecca's chest and almost in a whisper said, "Mecca, you don't want to do that." Carter knew his young'un would not hesitate to rock Mecca to sleep if he ran up. He'd taught Zyir himself to shoot first, ask questions last.

Mecca stopped dead in his tracks and looked Carter directly in the eye.

Carter prepared for Mecca to spazz out, but he did the complete opposite. Then there was a brief moment of silence before Mecca broke down in tears and lost his balance, falling into Carter's arms.

Carter embraced his half-brother. "It's okay, fam. We're going to get her back," he tried to assure him, even though he didn't know that for a fact.

"They want a million. We have to give it to them." Polo shook his head, knowing that his goddaughter was somewhere suffering.

"Yeah, I will go to the safe deposit box now," Carter affirmed.

"No, fuck that!" Mecca straightened up and wiped his teary eyes. "I'ma beat whoever picks up the money until he tell me where Breeze is at. I'm tired of mu'fuckas underestimating our family. We're still strong. We still run Miami! I am Miami, nigga!"

"No, Mecca, we have to give them what they want if we want to see Breeze again." Polo looked at the note that told them the time for the drop-off and the location.

"He's right, bruh. We have to play their game and see if they give her up first. But you have to stay levelheaded and chill with that wild shit. You have to think and play chess with that Haitian mu'fucka. If we outthink him, we will always win, trust me," Carter said, sounding just like his father.

Mecca could do nothing but respect it. He just wanted his sister back.

Zyir and Carter sat in his Range Rover and waited for the man that was supposed to pick up the ransom money to arrive. They were behind a closed-down steel factory and seemed to be alone, but that wasn't the case. Carter had arranged for his goons to circle the building, and Ace and Polo were on top of the factory with telescoped semiautomatic rifles, to make sure everything ran smooth.

Carter's plan was to do the switch and have one of his henchmen tail the money, hoping that it would lead them to Breeze. He decided to make Mecca stay home with Taryn. He told him that his mother needed him, but the reality was, Carter didn't want Mecca to do anything hotheaded and stupid.

"Yo, you ready, Zyir?" Carter pulled the duffle bag from the backseat.

"Yeah, I'm good," Zyir said without enthusiasm, still feeling badly for falling off his square.

Carter could sense that Zyir was taking it hard, because he knew Zyir loved to bust his gun and lived for moments like this one.

"Listen, that could've happened to any one of us, young'un. We're going to get her back though. Watch what I tell you," Carter said as he saw a tinted Hummer pull up. He watched as the man rolled down the window, exposing himself.

A dreadhead who didn't look over a day over sixteen years old appeared. He was dark as tar, with wild, nappy dreadlocks all over his head. "Yuh got de money?" he asked as he looked down into Carter's car.

"Where's Breeze, li'l nigga?" Carter yelled as he gripped the gun that was placed on his left.

"Yuh will get de girl after we get money, after I make call to me boss, feel me?"

Before Carter could even answer, he saw Mecca swiftly come out of nowhere on a motorcycle and pull up next to the driver. Before the young dread could even react, Mecca had him by his collar, and put a shiny chrome .380 to his head. "Where is my fucking sister? Huh?" he yelled while getting off his bike. Mecca pulled the boy out of the window and had him on ground.

"What the fuck is this nigga doing?" Carter said in frustration as he got out of the car.

He rushed over to Mecca and screamed for him to fall back, but Mecca was zoned out. He only wanted to know where Breeze was at.

"I'ma ask you one more time—Where . . . is . . . my . . . sister?" Mecca gripped the gun even tighter and dug it into the boy's neck.

The boy remained silent.

Mecca, tired of playing, pointed the gun at the boy's thigh and let off a round.

"Aghhh!" the boy yelled as he squirmed like a fish out of the water.

"Where is she?" Mecca yelled again.

The young dread was full of loyalty and honor, and he knew that if he told Mecca where the safe house was, he was going to die. He also knew that if he didn't, he was still going to die. So he did what would make Ma'tee proud. He spat in Mecca's face. Blood splattered over Mecca's bottom half of his face. The young dread followed by these words, "Bitch, she's dead. Chu' sister is dead bitch. Me see you in hell!"

Mecca lost it. He put five bullets into the boy's head at close range, rocking him to sleep forever, and sealing his own sister's fate.

Carter screamed, "Noooo!"

Robyn and Aries had already packed up their things. Word got back that Ma'tee's worker got killed, and they knew at that point that they had to kill Breeze. They were finished with Miami. Finished with Miamor. In their eyes, she had gone soft, which was against their creed.

As they boarded the plane, Aries asked Robyn, "Yuh ready to leave Miami for good?"

"Fuck Miami. L.A. is our next playground. They never saw bitches like us. Murder Mamas 'bout to takeover a new city, that's for damn sure. We could never eat in Miami. We've done too much dirt here. It's time to go," Robyn said as they got on the plane, leaving Ma'tee to kill Breeze. They were leaving and never looking back.

Ma'tee stared at Breeze with a shotgun in his hand. He hated that he had to kill someone so beautiful, but they didn't play the game fair. He would settle the score with The Cartel forever. As Breeze cried and pleaded for her life, he blocked the remorse in his heart. He pointed the shotgun at her head and whispered, "Say goodnight."

Chapter Twenty-two

"You my lady forever." —Carter Jones
Six Months Later

A giant projector screen covered the back wall as old home-videos of Breeze as a little girl played, while people held wine glasses and mingled amongst each other, and the ballroom was decorated with balloons of Breeze's favorite colors, turquoise and cream. A live band serenaded the small crowd and created a soothing ambience.

Of course, Taryn, personal friends of the family, and "The New Cartel" were in attendance. One hour before, they'd held a memorial service in honor of Breeze's life. They'd all put personal notes and gifts from Breeze in a casket before it was buried.

Mecca didn't even show up. In fact, no one had seen him since the day they were supposed to drop off the ransom money for Breeze, and he hadn't surfaced since. After hearing the man say that his sister was dead, something inside of him snapped.

Taryn sat at the front table along with Carter, Miamor, and Polo, trying her best to keep from breaking down and crying.

Carter noticed her agony and placed his hand on top of hers and gently gave it a squeeze. He leaned over and whispered to Taryn, "Are you sure that you can do this?"

A tear slid down Taryn's face as she returned the squeeze and looked into Carter's eyes. She was grateful for his presence. Even though he was her husband's illegitimate child, she loved him for being there in such trying times. She had planned a celebration for Breeze after grasping the fact that her only daughter was dead.

Taryn waited every day for Breeze to walk through the front door. False hopes and worry were driving her insane. It hurt her every day, knowing that Breeze's body was somewhere in a river or rotting somewhere. As a matter of fact, it took months before Taryn was willing to accept Breeze's fate, and for the family to come to the realization that the youngest member of the Diamond family wasn't coming home.

Taryn had lost a husband, a son, and now a daughter to drug wars and revenge. She was done. She had decided to move West with Polo to start a new life. She hadn't seen Mecca, her only living son, since everything had gone down, which was months ago, and she missed him tremendously. She knew it was time to leave Miami for good.

"Yes, I'm sure. I can't have any more funerals. I'm tired of burying the people I love. That's why I wanted to celebrate Breeze's life," she said as she broke down crying. She looked at the video of her husband pushing a five-year-old Breeze. She would trade anything to go back to that time.

"I understand." Carter nodded his head slowly. He looked at the video along with her and felt the pain of losing Breeze. He felt that he was partially to blame for her getting kidnapped.

He looked across the room and noticed Zyir in the middle, being very solitaire and observant. Carter could tell Zyir was taking it hard also and wondered why he was feeling so much grief when he barely knew Breeze. Little did Carter know that Zyir knew Breeze very well and was the last one to be with her before she was abducted.

Zyir felt so guilty and felt it was his fault that Breeze was dead. He'd never told Carter that he was about to have sex with her and left her side to pick up condoms, which was how she got kidnapped.

Carter looked over at Miamor, who sat beside him, and leaned over to kiss her on the cheek. "Hey, baby. I have something very important to tell you later on." He grinned slightly.

Miamor smiled back and nodded her head. She couldn't help but feel guilty at the celebration. She was sitting in the midst of Breeze's family, when she knew her two best friends were responsible for the murder. She hadn't talked to Robyn and Aries in months, and the only thing she knew was that they'd moved West, and to her knowledge, they were still up to their same ways.

I can't wait for this shit to be over, she thought as she tried her best not to look at the projection on the wall.

She was itching to see Mecca as she scanned the room. No one knew where he was. She was ready to leave her past life alone and spend the rest of her life with Carter, but not before she got even with Mecca. That was one itch that she just had to scratch. She couldn't let go of the fact that he had taken her sister from her. Revenge was still fresh in her heart, and she wanted him dead.

"Excuse me, ladies." Carter stood up so that he could go and talk to Ace, who was standing guard by the door, making sure only invited guests entered. Carter approached Ace and slapped hands with him.

"Yo, what's good? How you holding up?" Ace asked.

"I'm good. Just can't wait until this shit is over. I can't look at Breeze's pictures without wanting to break down, feel me?" Carter shook his head from side to side.

"Yeah, it was fucked up how everything went down. Zyir taking the shit hard too. I think he was feeling shorty," Ace said, talking too much.

"Is that right?' Carter didn't like what he heard, but he didn't want to ask Zyir about it, not now at least. "Yo, how is that money in Liberty City? Did they come to see you yet?" he asked, referring to Liberty City's hustlers. He wanted to know if they had re-upped yet.

"Yeah, they got ten yesterday. Them Overtown niggas, they copping heavy too. We're going to need another shipment in soon."

Carter began to rub his hands together and nodded slowly, knowing that Ace was talking big money. Ever since Carter had put his coke on the streets, he'd been making a killing. He saw more money in six months in Miami than he had seen his entire life back home. Carter had expanded his operation outside of Florida, hitting major cities like Atlanta, Houston, and New Orleans as well, and labeled his organization "The New Cartel."

The New Cartel was run completely differently from The Cartel. Carter recruited young hungry cats from all over

Dade County and pushed out the old heads. He had a clique of goons trying to make a name for themselves, which made them ruthless. Miami was definitely treating him good.

"Cool, I will put in an order later this week. The way shit going, we're going to be able to retire in a couple of months, feel me?" Carter said.

"No doubt," Ace added.

Carter walked over to Zyir, who seemed like he was in a daze. He had to nudge him to snap him out of his mental hiatus. "Zyir, you good?"

"Yeah, I'm okay. Just got a lot of shit on my mind."

"We all do right now. You holding down them blocks I gave you, right?"

"Yeah, everything gravy. But yo man been acting kind of funny lately. I don't know what's up with the nigga."

"Who you talking about, Ace?"

"Yeah. He be taking all day when I call him so I can re-up. My young'uns be running through that shit. So when he takes all day to call me back, we losing money. He never picks up my call. Shit gets frustrating, feel me? Nigga acting like a fed o' something," Zyir stated seriously, as he ice-grilled Ace.

Although he and Ace lived together, Zyir had noticed a lot of things that didn't sit right with him. Since being in Miami, Ace had changed, and it definitely wasn't for the better.

"I'll talk to him about it. Don't worry about Ace. I've known him since we were in the sandbox, fam. He ain't no mu'fuckin fed, believe that."

Carter smiled, admiring Zyir's boldness. He reminded Carter of himself at his age. Zyir was only eighteen, but moved through life like it was a big chess game. *That nigga don't trust anybody.*

Carter felt a hand on his back. It was Miamor.

"Hey, can I have this dance?" she asked sexily as the reggae band began to play a number.

Carter smiled as he took Miamor's hand and slowly began to dance with her. He pulled her slowly to him, and the delightful scent of her perfume made him smile. Though the mood in the dancehall was sad, Carter planned to brighten it up later that night by asking Miamor to marry him.

"You my lady forever," Carter whispered in Miamor's ear as he smoothly spun her around. *I love this woman with all my heart, and I want her to be my wife.* He closed his eyes and swayed back and forth to a rendition of Bob Marley's "No Woman, No Cry."

Miamor closed her eyes and enjoyed her man's embrace, swaying back and forth with him as she rested her head on his chest. "I love this song," she whispered, snapping her fingers that rested on Carter's upper back.

Just as Miamor opened her eyes, her heart nearly skipped a beat as she saw the crazed eyes of Mecca staring at her from across the room. The way he was looking at her would've sent chills through the toughest man's body. She regained her composure and stopped dancing.

Carter felt her body tense up. "What's wrong?"

"Your brother just walked in," Miamor said, trying to not seem startled. She immediately thought about her deceased sister and instantaneously wanted to get at Mecca. *When the time is right, when the time is right*, she repeated in her head as she imagined herself putting a hole through Mecca's neck.

Mecca viewed the whole room. He rubbed his neatly cut hair, trying to get used to not having his natural long-flowing mane. He had been dead to the world for six long months for three reasons: to stay away from Estes, to grieve his sister's death, and also to plot. He walked in and noticed that all eyes were on him. He ignored the staring and made his way to his mother, who was so busy sobbing into a handkerchief at the front table, she didn't see her son approaching.

"Hello, mama," he said as he stood before her.

She didn't respond, so he reached over the table to try to hug and comfort her.

"It's okay, mama. I'm here now," Mecca said in a soft voice. The guilt of killing the man that picked up the ransom for Breeze burdened him. Every day he regretted that he let his anger get the better of him.

Taryn looked up and saw that her baby boy was holding her; she hugged him tightly and placed her hands on his cheeks. "Baby, I was worried about you. I didn't know where you were," she said as she hugged him again tightly, squeezing him as if he might disappear before her eyes.

"I know, I know, but I'm home now, mama, and I'm not going nowhere," Mecca assured his mother as he rubbed her back.

Mecca then looked over at Carter and Miamor and decided to go have a chat with Carter. He wanted to tell him about his woman. He was about to put Miamor on blast. He knew that Carter didn't know who she really was.

During his brief absence, he began to do research on the Murder Mamas and confirmed that they were allies with Ma'tee. Fabian had known a lot of people that the Murder Mamas had done jobs for. That immediately threw up a red flag with Mecca. Miamor was a cold-blooded killer, and he knew she had an ulterior motive with Carter, who was sleeping with the enemy.

Mecca poured a glass of wine and headed across the room to talk to Carter.

Carter continued to dance with Miamor, but he knew that her mood had suddenly changed since Mecca entered the building. "Is everything all right?" he asked concerned and confused.

"Yeah, I'm good. Just got a light headache, that's all," Miamor responded distractedly.

As soon as she finished her sentence, Mecca came over with a wine glass in his hand. He came over with a smile and greeted his half-brother with a light hug. "What's up, bro?" Mecca yelled.

"What's good, Mecca? Glad to you could make it," Carter answered.

Mecca looked at Miamor and put on a fake smile. "Hello. It's Miamor, right?"

"Yes, it is. Hello to you," she answered coldly as she stared into his eyes.

Mecca quickly picked up Miamor's hand and kissed it like a gentleman would do. He then gave her the glass of wine and said, "May I borrow your fella for a minute? We have to discuss business."

"Sure." Miamor grabbed the wine and walked over to talk to Taryn. Her blood boiled as she itched to kill Mecca. She had to just wait for the perfect timing to do it. *He's going to get his,* she thought as she sat next to Taryn to comfort her.

In the meantime, Carter and Mecca began to converse.

"It's good to see you, Mecca. How is that place that I set you up in?" Carter asked, referring to the low-key apartment that he had for Mecca in Atlanta, far out of the reach of Estes and his goons.

"It's cool. But, look, I have to tell you some shit about your girl. She's not who she seems to be." Mecca rubbed his goatee.

"What?" Carter asked, totally taken aback by Mecca's comment.

"Look, man, the bitch is foul!" Mecca said under his breath as he looked in Carter's eyes.

"Watch yo' mouth, fam," Carter said through clenched teeth. He put one hand in his pocket and raised a wine glass to his lips with the other. He eyed Mecca and could see the larceny in his heart. It took everything in him not to smack the shit out of him for even having Miamor's name in his mouth.

Before Mecca could respond, Miamor walked up to them. She had watched their entire conversation and couldn't tell what they were saying, but Carter's body language told her that he was upset. She gently kissed him on the cheek, calming him down, and then she grabbed Mecca's hand.

"I never got a chance to get acquainted with you. Can I have this dance?" she asked sweetly.

Carter looked at her like she was crazy and thought about what Mecca had just told him. He was totally confused. *What the fuck is she doing?* He stepped back and watched them begin to dance. Miamor wasn't being disrespectful since there was distance between them while dancing, but Carter was still heated.

"So I guess we finally get to talk, huh?" Miamor asked as she danced with Mecca.

They both squeezed one another's hand tightly, obviously both of them trying to hurt the other.

"Yeah, bitch! Finally!" Mecca said as he kept a fake smile on his face as a front.

At that moment Miamor knew that Mecca knew her past and her connection with Ma'tee and the women that killed Breeze.

"You knew about Breeze getting kidnapped, didn't you? You were how they got so close and told them how to get her, didn't you?" Mecca asked.

Miamor's nails were dug so deep into Mecca's hand, blood began to trickle. "No, I had nothing to do with that, but I am going to have something to do with your murder. You killed my sister, and you're going to pay," she said between clenched teeth.

They continued to dance as if they weren't having a murderous conversation.

"Let me tell you something—You won't get the chance to kill me. I'm a mu'fuckin' Diamond, and Diamonds are forever. I got a surprise for you, Murder Mama," Mecca said sarcastically with a scowl on his face.

"And what's that?" Miamor never showed an ounce of intimidation. She was indeed a bad bitch and had tangoed with the best in her field, always coming out victoriously.

This dance she was doing with Mecca was nothing new. She was going to kill him, even if it meant she had to die in the process.

"You know, that glass of wine you just drank, it was full of sodium hydroxide, a poison that first invades your respiratory system and makes you feel like you're drowning right before your heart bursts and kills you. That shit is killing you right now. I say you have about thirty more seconds until you drop dead. You're dying, bitch," Mecca said smugly.

"Is that it?" Miamor asked. "Now, I have a surprise for you, Mecca Diamond." Miamor stopped dancing and then leaned over to whisper in Mecca's ear, "I would never drink anything you give me. I'm a Murder Mama for a reason, nigga. I gave the drink to your mama. She's dying, bitch," she muttered just before gently kissing Mecca on the cheek.

Mecca instantly looked over at Taryn, who grabbed her neck as if she was choking, her face turned bloodshot red. A small crowd began to form around her. He took off to try to help his dying mother, but just before he reached her, dozens of FBI agents burst through the door with guns drawn.

Mecca crawled over to his mother as she fell on the floor. Tears were in his eyes as he witnessed his mother struggle for air. She clawed at Mecca, as her body shook rapidly. Her eyes began to roll in the back of her head, and Mecca tried to shake his mother out of it, but nothing could save her. He saw the empty wine glass next to her and knew that there was no saving her. He had put enough poison in the glass to kill ten people, but it wasn't meant for his mother.

"Help!!" Mecca cried like a baby as tears flowed down his eyes. He watched as Taryn took her last breath and fell limply into his arms. He closed his mother's eyelids and kissed her on the forehead. Murder was the only thing on his mind.

"Everybody on the ground now!" the sergeant yelled. He went straight for Carter and handcuffed him. He began to read Carter his rights.

Miamor was in shock. "Carter, what's going on? What's going? Why are they arresting you?" Miamor watched them escort her man out.

"Don't worry about it. Come bond me out!" Carter yelled as he got guided out with his hands handcuffed behind his back. He glanced across the room at Mecca, who was lying on the floor with Taryn, and he didn't know what had happened. Carter watched as Zyir and Ace were also handcuffed, and at that point he knew that someone had been snitching. They went straight for the heads of his operation, so they knew about The Cartel and its chain of command.

Mecca went for his gun on his waist but stopped himself, because he knew that he could not retaliate at that moment with all the feds in the room. With shaking hands and a broken heart he snuck out of the back without being seen.

Carter's leather Mezlan shoes clicked and echoed through the cell as he paced back and forth. He kept wondering what they were arresting him for exactly. He figured it was in connection with his drug empire, but he was hoping otherwise. But when he saw the federal agents bring some of his workers out of Overtown in, along with bags and bags of cocaine, he knew the deal. They had seized the drugs from his stash spot.

"Damn!" He knew he was in deep shit. *How the fuck did they find out where my spots were*? Carter thought as he continued to pace the room. He ran his business very precisely, and his operation was built for perfection. They only thing that could bring turmoil was snitching. That's how he knew there was a snake amongst him. He wished he could talk to Ace and Zyir, but they were all put in different cells. The Cartel was about to go down, and the police had enough coke to put Carter away forever.

Ace sat in the interrogation room sweating bullets. He hated himself for what he had done. Two months back, he had gotten pulled over with two kilos in his trunk. The cops found it and immediately cut him a deal. As soon as he mentioned The Cartel, they knew that they had snagged the big fish. He had ratted on his own team and their leader, and for the past month, they had been putting Zyir and Carter on wiretaps, recording their conversations.

Miamor's hands shook as she guided Carter's Range Rover out of the parking lot as she headed for the police station. She had already contacted Carter's lawyer, instructing him to meet her at the precinct.

After the feds searched everyone and took everyone's names, they let the people at the party go. Miamor kept visualizing the look in Mecca's face when she told him that he'd poisoned his own flesh and blood.

As she pulled up to a red light, without warning, a strong hand covered her mouth. She could smell an intoxicant on the rag that was suffocating her, and knew it was only a matter of time before her body lost its strength. She got a glimpse of the man's face when she looked in her rearview. It was Mecca.

She was getting weaker by the second. The smell of the strong substance burned her nostrils as she began to slip in and out of consciousness. Trying to struggle against Mecca, she mistakenly put her feet on the gas, and the car began to swerve wildly.

"Aghh!" she screamed as she scratched at his arms, forgetting she was driving.

Miamor's eyes widened when she felt the car go out of control, spinning wildly and crashing violently against the brick wall on the side of the street. She couldn't help but think that this was the day she was going to die.

Chapter Twenty-three

"Yuh a long way from Miami." —Ma'tee

Ma'tee moved around the kitchen swiftly as he prepared a meal for his new companion. He looked at the security monitors that he had installed in each room of his immaculate home in his native land of Haiti. He had become extra cautious, some would even say paranoid, since the invasion of his home at the hands of Estes. It was the same day that fate had robbed him of his beautiful little girl.

The fresh Caribbean wind tickled Ma'tee's neck and his paranoia kicked in full throttle, causing him to turn around with a butcher knife clasped tightly in his hand. He sliced at an imaginary enemy, and his breathing was labored as his eyes bucked wide open. He looked around in panic, but calmed himself down when he realized that there was no one else in the room.

Although he loved his homeland and its majestic tropical setting, he hated being forced out of the States by The Cartel. His entire organization had been dismantled. His most loyal soldiers were now casualties of a drug war that he himself had initiated. He was like a pariah on the streets of Miami, and to show his face right then would've been like committing suicide. So he didn't have a choice but to stay low.

No one knew Haiti like Ma'tee knew it, and in order to stay alive, he needed to be in his own neck of the woods.

In fear of his life, he retreated to the Black Mountains. No one knew of his home there, and he was confident that he would be safe and could live without the intrusion of his adversaries. There were no neighbors. His 5,000 square foot home sat atop a plateau that went on for miles and miles. It was 4,000 feet above the town below, too high for sight or sound to be captured by the townspeople. He was in complete seclusion and planned to stay there until he could rebuild his empire.

He would get his revenge for the undeserving murder of his daughter. His daughter had been innocent, but she was forced to pay with her life when the Dominican mob annihilated his men. The Dominicans had taken no prisoners and felt sympathy for no one, not even his only child. When she was murdered in cold blood, Ma'tee's world came crashing down around him because he knew that he only had himself to blame. *If they can do this to me beautiful princess, what do they have planned for me?* His body shuddered at the thought and he knew that he didn't want to find out what cruelty lie in store for him.

The only time he intended to leave his fortress was when he planned to make the trip to the market for food and supplies, and his only human contact would be that of his new queen. The woman that he knew was meant for him. The voyeur in him watched her in the monitors as she slept, and a wicked smile crept across his face. He couldn't tear his eyes away from the monitor.

Since the death of his daughter, he hadn't been the same. Something in his head, or rather his heart, was broken, and he no longer respected the social limits of right and wrong. He was no longer the composed, self-respecting man that he once was. He was now a predator, and he was staring at his prey on the monitor. His dick hardened at the sight of her. She was beautiful, and he was well aware of his growing obsession.

He was supposed to kill her, that was the plan, but once their kidnapping scheme had gone wrong, he and the Murder Mamas decided it was time for Breeze to go. When it was time to pull the trigger, he couldn't will himself to complete the task. He was drawn to her beauty, which was just as addictive as the cocaine he sold. So instead of killing her, he drugged her and then retreated with her, taking her across the U.S. border on a private boat.

Ma'tee fixated and fantasized over his new island beauty. He admired her slim frame, her long flexible legs, and her naturally curly hair. He was positive that he loved her, or maybe he needed someone to love him, since his daughter no longer could, but either way, he needed her and was determined to keep her.

Her body curled up in a fetal position, and her hands tucked between her legs, she hadn't awakened since they'd made the trip across the seas. The vicious beating that the Murder Mamas had inflicted upon her had left her badly injured, and right at death's doorstep.

For six long months Ma'tee had taken great care of his young princess, nursing her back to health. Now he anxiously awaited her arousal. Her body was ripe, and ready to be plucked. He knew she was made just for him from the first moment he saw her.

He finished squeezing the juice from the fresh oranges and placed a glassful onto the tray then made his way downstairs to awaken his sleeping beauty.

She heard the heavy thud of footsteps as they descended the stairs. She played possum, not wanting to wake up and face her captors. She didn't know how long it had been since she had been taken. The last thing she remembered was taking blows to her head with a gun.

"Diamond Princess, my princess, wake up." Ma'tee placed the tray of food on the nightstand beside the luxury queen-sized bed.

Startled, Breeze jumped up and scrambled away from him. Her body shook as she put as much distance as possible between herself and Ma'tee. Her arms and legs were weak from being in bed for so long, but she was determined to get away. Her back hit the wall and she pulled her knees close to her body as she huddled on the bed. She surveyed her surroundings. There were no windows, only a pale light bulb illuminated the room.

It was far from a dungeon, however. Ma'tee had made sure that anything she could ever need was inside the room. The plush red carpet, imported French furniture, and marble bathroom made the space look like a studio apartment.

Breeze was instantly confused. She remembered being kidnapped, and she had heard the girls that had taken her say that they were going to kill her. *What happened? Why am I here?* Quivering and crying, she looked around frantically. "W—where am I?" she asked. "You can't keep me here. My family will come for me," she stated, her words breaking in her throat.

Ma'tee sat on the bed and crawled over toward Breeze. He felt his manhood harden. She was so beautiful, so young, and her body so tight, and now she was his and his alone. He ran his fingers through her hair, his eyes focusing on her as if he were staring at a piece of historical art.

She cringed as his fingertips touched her face and she smacked his hand away. "Don't," she whispered weakly.

"You don't have to be afraid of me, princess. I won't hurt you. Just let me touch you," he whispered lustfully.

"No! Help me! Please, somebody help!" Breeze screamed at the top of her lungs as she fought Ma'tee off.

Ma'tee was relentless in his pursuit. He was like a dog in heat. He just had to discover the treasure that Breeze was hiding between her legs. He didn't care that she screamed in protest. No one could hear her. And even if she did run, there was nowhere for her to go. She would never be able to navigate her way through the Black Mountains and the Noire Forest that accompanied them.

He groped her and ripped at her clothes, as he forced his tongue into her mouth.

Breeze did the only thing she could think of and bit down as hard as she could on his tongue.

"Aghh!" Ma'tee screamed. He smacked Breeze across the face, causing her to hit her head against the nightstand hard enough to leave her disoriented.

A river the color of crimson flowed onto the white sheets, and she felt the pressure of Ma'tee's weight as he climbed on top of her.

"Ah didn't mean to hurt you. Ah just want to love you. Stop fighting me, my princess. Yuh belong to me now."

Those were the last words she heard before her vision became blurry, and her entire world went black.

When Breeze awoke, her entire body ached, and Ma'tee was by her bedside, watching her. She could see insanity in his eyes. *What does he want from me?* She felt a pounding underneath her skull and reached up to find a bandage across her forehead.

"So yuh finally decided to awaken?" he asked. "I tasted you while you were asleep. Me never tasted pussy as sweet as yours. Me will be with you forever."

The way he said the word *forever* caused a shiver to travel down Breeze's spine. Forever wouldn't be very long, if she had anything to do with it. She refused to live as his prisoner, even if the cell she'd been confined to was a luxury one. She'd die first. *At least then, I'd be with Poppa and Money.*

Tears came to Breeze's eyes, and her hands shakily found their way to the space between her legs. It was wet, and when she examined her fingers, she noticed the blood on her fingertips. She immediately knew that Ma'tee had been inside of her. He had touched her, invaded her, and taken her against her will. Her once virgin pussy no longer existed, thanks to Ma'tee.

"Why the fuck are you doing this to me?!" she screamed, her hatred and fear evident in each word. "My family is going to come for me, and when they find me, they are going to kill you!"

Ma'tee remained calm, because he didn't entertain idle threats. "Yuh dead to yuh family. Yuh been missing for six months. They haven't come for yuh yet, and they will never come for yuh. Nobody knows yuh alive," Ma'tee said, a smug expression on his face. "Me brought yuh hear to make yuh me princess. The longer yuh resist me, the harder it will be on yuh. Yuh can scream, fight, yell all yuh want, no one will hear. There are no windows for yuh to escape from. The doors are double bolted and chained. Yuh a long way from Miami. This is yuh new home. Welcome to Haiti."

Breeze's hopes began to die as Ma'tee's words penetrated her brain. She knew that no one would be coming for her, if what he was speaking was indeed true. She jumped up from the bed and ran up the flight of steps. "Help! Please somebody help me!" she yelled. She looked back at Ma'tee in fear as he approached her. Her screams became frantic. "Please!" Tears burned her eyes, and her hands hit the wooden door so hard that her skin began to bleed.

In her heart she knew that it was true. She had felt the sway of the boat and heard the waves of the ocean as she was being brought over to the island. She thought that it was just a dream, a hallucination of some sort, but it was her reality. She felt like a slave and that Ma'tee was her master, the man who killed her father and brother.

"Right now yuh fear me, but yuh will grow to love me with time," Ma'tee stated with a crazed look in his eyes. "Ah will never let yuh go. Haiti is yuh new home. When yuh ready, me will let yuh out of this dungeon, but not until yuh ready to accept your new life here as my queen. Forget who yuh were, and accept who yuh are now. No one is coming, ever. Me will kill yuh before me let yuh go."

Breeze fell to her knees and sobbed desperately at the feet of Ma'tee. "Please don't do this," she begged. "I just want to go home."

"This is home."

Breeze reverted to her childhood ways as anger began to simmer inside of her heart. She began to demolish the room. "This is not my home!" she screamed forcefully as she threw lamps and overturned tables and chairs. "This is not my home! Let me go!"

She broke any and everything in her path as Ma'tee watched her without giving her a reaction. Once she ran out of energy and things to break, she collapsed on the floor and bawled in defeat.

"Yuh can destroy as much as yuh want and scream all day and night. It won't change the fact that yuh here. Nothing can change that. Yuh belong to me."

Ma'tee walked over and removed the tray of food that he'd brought her. He walked past her and made his exit. Before he left, he said, "Yuh will see food when yuh show me yuh deserve to eat. The longer yuh deny me, the longer yuh will starve."

When he closed the door, Breeze heard the clicking of multiple locks, and all of a sudden, the entire room went black. She thought of the ones that she loved. Her mother's face flashed before her eyes. Then she saw her brothers, Carter and Mecca. Last but not least, Zyir's face appeared.

Please help me, Zyir. Please don't stop looking for me, she thought as she tried to send a message from her heart, hoping that she was as connected to him as she thought she was. Even though their love was new, she hoped that it was strong enough for him to feel her presence. She needed him to believe she was alive. She needed him to get her family to come for her.

After she wrecked her body with exhaustion from crying, Breeze did the only thing that she could do. She prayed.

Chapter Twenty-four

"Who you praying to, bitch? I am God." —Mecca

"Hmm," Miamor moaned as she drowsily opened her eyes and became aware of what was going on around her. "Hmm." She tried to speak, but something muffled her sounds. She jerked against the chair that she was sitting in but couldn't move. She shook the fuzzy haze from her mind and forced herself to become focused. *Okay, Mia, okay, stay calm. You can get out of this,* she thought.

Gagged and bound to a chair, her head was pounding from the impact of the crash, and she had no idea where Mecca had taken her. The odds were against her, no doubt, and she feared for her life. She knew that she was dealing with a man whose murderous abilities matched her own. Her senses were heightened, causing her anxiety to skyrocket.

She bucked against the chair quietly, trying to keep her noise to a minimum. She didn't want Mecca to realize she was awake. She needed to level the playing field and free herself from her constraints before facing him. She tried to see through the darkness that had enveloped the room.

Where the fuck am I?

Her body ached all over, and she shook uncontrollably as the cold crept through her skin. She smelled the scent of weed burning somewhere in the room and realized she wasn't alone. She froze instantly. Unable to see, her other senses worked overtime as they helped her locate who she assumed to be Mecca. She forced the towel out of her lips with her tongue and coughed uncontrollably as the pressure eased from her choking chest.

"What the fuck you hiding for, you bitch mu'-fucka?" she asked, her teeth chattering. *Why the fuck am I so cold?* She couldn't get control of her reflexes, as her body shivered involuntarily.

"You talk a lot of shit for a bitch that's tied to a fucking chair," Mecca stated as he stood. He had sat silently in the dark for hours, waiting patiently for her to wake up. He was itching to kill her since she was responsible for the murder of both his mother and sister.

As Mecca flipped the light switch, he appeared before Miamor's eyes. Her vision was blurry, and all she saw was a shadow standing in front of her. "What the fuck? I can't see," she whispered, shaking her head from side to side, trying to clear her vision.

"That's the bleach eating at your eyes, bitch. I'm gon' love killing you. I'ma torture you slow, so get comfortable."

Miamor's eyes fell to her thighs. She was naked. Her clothes had been stripped, and she had a lot of tiny cuts all over her body. "What the fuck did you do to me?" she yelled.

Mecca didn't respond but instead circled her as if he was preparing to attack. He carried a long, thick chain in his hands. It scratched the floor as he walked, making Miamor's skin crawl from the eerie sound. He brought the chain up and swung it with as much force as he could over Miamor's body, cutting her skin almost to the bone.

Miamor cringed in agony as her eyes ran with continuous tears. She was in tremendous pain. She could see the blurry hue of blood on her legs.

Mecca brought the chain down on her again, this time using more force.

"Aghh! Fuck!! You!!" she screamed. She refused to give Mecca the pleasure of crying or begging for her life.

For years she had dished out the same cruel and unusual death sentences, so if it was her time, she wasn't going to cry like a little bitch, but be a woman about her shit and go out like the killer she was.

The chain whipped her again, this time hitting her bare breasts and stomach.

"Aghh!"

"You're not gon' beg like your sister, bitch? Huh?" Mecca asked through clenched teeth as he hit Miamor repeatedly. And he found pleasure in bringing so much pain to the person responsible for his sister's and mother's death.

"Fuck you, pussy! Faggot-ass nigga! Fuck—Aghhh!— you!" Miamor yelled. Her mind told her to stay strong, but her body rebelled against her.

"Suck my dick, you dirty bitch," Mecca stated. "I'ma put your ass in the dirt just like I did your sister."

Mecca had beaten Miamor for so long that he was out of breath and sweating profusely. He threw the chain to the ground and retrieved the bottle of ammonia from the corner. He knew that the liquid fire would eat through her skin like acid as soon as it doused her open wounds. He unscrewed the top and splashed the poisonous liquid all over Miamor's bloody body, which now resembled that of a runaway slave.

"Aghhhhhhh!"

Her blood-curdling scream was enough to make the average man cringe in regret, but Mecca continued his relentless assault on her without mercy.

Miamor felt like she was burning alive. Her eyes, legs, arms, hell, even her hair hurt. She knew that she would never make it out of the basement alive. Mecca had too much to prove.

"Our Father, who art in Heaven, hallowed be Thy name—"

"Who you praying to, bitch?" Mecca asked, taunting her, as he slapped the words from Miamor's mouth. "I *am* God."

Miamor could hear the insanity and hate in his voice. She knew that he wasn't going to stop beating her until there was nothing left to beat. She couldn't change that fact. This was her fate. She felt herself growing faint and continued, "Thy kingdom come, thy will be done, on Earth as it is in Heaven."

The chain seared through her skin once more, but this time she didn't scream. She was past the point of pain. She was near death. She felt the walls closing in on her. She could see the shadow of the devil standing behind Mecca. She knew she wasn't destined for Heaven. She had too much blood on her hands. She had sinned beyond reproach, and the devil was waiting to snatch her soul and damn her to hell. She knew it. She embraced it. She was a bad bitch, and she was going to die like one.

As Mecca's fist collided with her face one more time, she slowly turned her head toward him. She spat blood. "Fuck you, Mecca! I hope you enjoy watching me die just like I enjoyed watching your mother and sister die, mu'fucka!"

"Shut the fuck up!" Mecca grabbed the ammonia, pinched the sides of her mouth harshly, and poured the chemical down her throat and on her face.

Miamor struggled against his grasp, desperately trying to close her eyes and mouth. It burnt her lips and nose. She saw the Grim Reaper stepping closer to her.

"I got something for you, bitch. I'm not gon' kill you. I'ma let my man handle you."

Miamor watched as Mecca walked out of the room and the devil stepped closer to her, her heart jumping with every step the devil took. His face came into view, and when it became fully visible, her eyes grew wide in shock. *Fabian!*

The shadow in her peripheral vision wasn't the devil, but a part of her wished that it was. Surely, death would have been better than what Fabian had in store for her. He had a score to settle. She closed her eyes to finish talking with God. "Give us this day, our daily bread and forgive us our trespasses as we forgive those who trespass against us." Her voice broke, and tears filled her eyes.

Fabian leaned into her, his hot breath blowing against her burning skin. "It's too late for prayers, bitch. You're gonna die tonight," he stated with no emotion.

Miamor couldn't believe that her past had come back to haunt her. This scary mu'fucka was the same one begging her for his life just months ago. Now he was standing before her getting ready to take her own.

"I should have cut off your fucking balls when I took your dick, mu'fucka. Do what you got to do, nigga. Fuck you!"

Fabian punched Miamor with so much force that her jaw collapsed on the right side.

Miamor felt the weight of her face as her jaw caved in. She cringed, absorbed the pain, recited the Lord's Prayer in her mind, and then spat teeth and blood onto the floor. She sat up straight and prepared herself for what was in store. She hoped for a quick death, but she knew that it wasn't going to happen, so she breathed deep, squared her shoulders, and forced herself to open her eyes, ignoring the agonizing pain from the chemicals in her eyes. She stared Fabian directly in the eyes and smirked.

This nigga ain't a killer. He'll never be like me. Fuck it, if I'ma go out, it ain't gon' be on my knees. "Fuck you!"

The Cartel 2:

Tale of the Murda Mamas

Prologue

"I'm going to kill you, bitch!" Fabian threatened as he prepared to finish the job that Mecca had started.

Miamor's body was giving up on her. She shook violently from the cold that was settling in. *It's so cold . . . so cold!* she thought as her teeth chattered. Death loomed in the air like an elephant in the room. She could feel death coming. She didn't fear it—unlike the bitch nigga in front of her—she embraced her fate. She smiled slightly, because she knew that she would see Fabian in hell and wouldn't hesitate to get it popping. Even in death, she would be sure she had the last laugh.

She couldn't fight Fabian off of her. She was too weak, and on this day, she felt it in her soul that she was going to die. She knew that she was at a disadvantage. For the first time in her life, she was the weak one. She was at the mercy of the man in front of her, and to make matters worse, she was personally responsible for his strife, so he had something to prove. Miamor knew how niggas thought, and by cutting off his dick, she had robbed him of his manhood. His pride was wounded, and because of that, he would show her no mercy.

The fact that she was a female didn't mean shit to Fabian. He had seen firsthand what she was capable of. He had been her victim, and now she was his. Fate had tipped in his favor, and karma is a bitch . . . a big bitch. He was determined to get his revenge, and it would be sweet . . . slow and sweet.

Miamor was confined to the chair. The ties dug into her skin, rendering her helpless while Fabian attacked her. She felt each blow as he struck her repeatedly. The impact of his fists invaded her brain, terrorizing her existence. Oddly enough, she was grateful for Fabian's attack, because it was much less vicious than the tyranny Mecca had bestowed upon her. Miamor began to laugh slightly because she realized that even at her weakest state she was still stronger than Fabian.

Mecca's blows had left her helpless, and made her respect his ruthlessness. Mecca was her equal. His murder game matched her own, but Fabian was beneath her. At this moment, he was physically stronger than she was, but mentally he was pathetic, and she could still sense that he feared her, which is why he hadn't hit her with all his might.

"What the fuck are you laughing at, bitch?" Fabian asked in frustration as he struck her again, enraged that he wasn't making her feel pain like Mecca had.

Miamor had begun to cough up blood, but that didn't stop her from laughing. Her bloodstained teeth agitated Fabian even more as he watched her spit out a glob of blood. She knew that the only way to get out alive was to get inside of Fabian's head. She had to tip the scales in her favor again. She was going to make him fear her without even laying hands on him. He had no heart and she sensed it. She, on the other hand, had the heart of a lion and was about to eat him alive.

Fabian eventually stopped hitting Miamor and staggered away from her. Sweat dripped from his forehead as he looked at her in confusion. His chest was heaving in exhaustion. *This bitch is crazy!* he thought as the dismay he felt spread across his face.

"I let you keep your life last time," Miamor said as she spit blood from her mouth. She was dizzy and she knew that she didn't have much time. Her life was on a countdown. She was slipping away. Her energy was low, and she could feel her life fading. Her body urged her to succumb to the pain, but her mind and strong will pushed her forward. If this was her day to die, then so be it, but she had never given up anything without a fight. She was going to fight for her life, and her weapon of choice was her mind.

"What?" Fabian asked. He was in disbelief at how resistant Miamor was to pain. He didn't know that she was suffering in agony, because she would never allow him to see it.

Miamor was fucking up his mental, playing a game of mental chess where she devised the rules. She could see the hesitation in his eyes. All she had to do was keep talking. "You think my girls don't know where I am right now, Fabian?

Even if you do kill me, there are two bitches just like me that are still out there, and they are going to come for you, my nigga," she said.

"Bitch, you can't threaten me," Fabian said nervously as he slapped her once more, the force behind it fading even more.

"I don't make threats, sweetie. I make promises. What? You think they won't know who did this to me? Your fingerprints and DNA are all over this fucking basement, dummy! They're all over *me*, Fabian. We do this for a living. It's not a game with us. We *let* you live last time. You can kill me, but you better know that my girls are gon' come for you, and next time, they are going to do a lot more than leave you dickless. They're coming, Fabian . . ."

Fabian's eyes shifted around the room as if he was the one who was there against his will, as if he was looking for an escape.

Miamor coughed violently and her breathing became labored as she struggled to keep her strength. *Keep talking, Mia. Talk yourself right out of this shit,* she thought. "They're coming, Fabian. Now, you just got to decide. Are they coming to rescue me? Or are they coming to murder you? Killing me won't make you a bigger man. You're stepping into the big leagues by fucking with me, Fabian. Are you ready? Do you think you have what it takes to kill someone like me? Every action has a reaction. Even in death, I can touch you, Fabian. Trust!" she spat.

"Fuck!" Fabian shouted as he began to pace back and forth in the room. He was torn. He didn't want to see the wrath of the Murder Mamas, but at this point, he felt like he was in too deep. He couldn't turn back now. He pointed his gun at Miamor, deciding to just kill her and get it over with. His finger wrapped around the trigger, but when his eyes met hers, he saw the devil in them. His lip began to quiver. He lowered his weapon. "I know you're not just going to let me get away with this. Even if I don't kill you, you're going to come for me."

"Maybe, maybe not," Miamor said. "The point is that you have a chance to live if you *don't* kill me. You show me favor, I might show you mercy. But if you kill me, then you might as well set your watch, nigga, because within the week, you'll be eating hollow points."

Fabian fidgeted, his hand began to shake, and he put his hands over his ears to drown out her words. "*Set your watch, nigga! You'll be eating hollow points within the week.*" Miamor's words echoed through his brain, and what had started out as a planned murder was becoming a game of survival of the fittest.

Fabian didn't know it, but he had just transferred the power right back into Miamor's hands by letting her fuck with his psyche. If he had been smart, he would have killed her quick, but he had given her time to think. He had given her the opportunity to bring it to his ass, without even knowing that she had just conquered him mentally. No doubt about it, if Miamor was a nigga, she would have been an American Gangster. She was just that crucial. Even while teetering at the edge of death, she refused to lose.

"I want your word," Fabian said as he pointed the gun back at Miamor. His aim was so shaky that even if he pulled the trigger he would miss his shot. His nerves were shot, and he truly feared the woman in front of him. He knew that whoever made her the way she was had to be ruthless. He hated her, but he didn't want to be the one to bring her death in fear of the repercussions. "If I let you go, you won't come for me. Say it!"

Miamor bit her tongue, because she knew that it wasn't a promise that she could keep, but she extended it anyway in order to save herself. She swallowed what felt like a lump in her throat, but the salty taste of blood let her know that even if Fabian let her go, she could still die. Time was of the essence, and her body was letting her know that if she didn't get help soon, she would be going to meet her maker. She and her sister would be reunited sooner than she thought if she didn't get out of there. "Let me go. You have my word."

Fabian approached her slowly and kept his shaky aim on her as he removed one of her hands from the duct tape. He then backpedaled toward the stairs. Miamor's eyes never left him. They were like a constant threat as he took the stairs upward one by one, until finally he reached the top. Miamor nodded and watched him rush out of the door.

As soon as he disappeared from her sight, she let out a scream of excruciating pain. “Aghh!” she yelled as tears filled her eyes. She used her free hand to try and remove the rest of the tape from her body. Her grip was so weak, which made the effort of freedom so much harder to attain. She was hurt, badly. She could barely breathe, and no matter how hard she tried, she just couldn’t free herself from the chair. The world around her spun wildly as if she was on a merry-go-round. In frustration, she rocked the chair back and forth as she struggled to loosen her arms. *Come on! Get the fuck up! Get out of this! You cannot die down here!* she cried silently, forcing herself to move.

Miamor put two hands on the ground and attempted to stand again. She resembled a child who was learning to walk for the first time as she put her arms out to steady her balance. She closed her eyes to stop the spinning and stumbled as quickly as she could up the stairs. She fell repeatedly as blood poured from every opening on her body. Her eyes burned from the chemicals Mecca had doused her with. She could barely see; the world through her eyes was one big blur, making the steps almost impossible to climb. Her bleeding legs, back and arms were unbearable. She didn’t care that she was naked; all she wanted to do was get out of there. She needed to get to a hospital quickly. She burst from out of the basement with a desperation she had never known. Panic set in, and her legs threatened to give out. She stumbled out of the abandoned house and onto the city street. She saw people and urged her body to carry her in their direction.

“What the fuck?” she heard someone say. “Oh my God!” another voice called out.

Her vision blurred, and the merry-go-round in her head spun faster and faster as she grasped at the air for support that wasn’t there. “H . . . h . . . help me!” she whispered. These were the last words that left her mouth before she collapsed face first. Her head hit the pavement with a sickening thud, causing her entire world to go black as blood flowed onto the streets.

***

"Help! Somebody help me!" Breeze yelled. She felt the branches and leaves hitting her face and arms like whips as she ran full speed through the thick jungle. She felt the dirt and rocks underneath her bare feet, cutting them and nicking them as she ran, but her only concern was getting away from a crazed Ma'tee. She scrambled desperately, crying to herself as she made her way. She didn't know where she was going. She just wanted to get as far away from Ma'tee as she could. She was going to run as long as her legs allowed her to. She could hear his voice yelling her name, and it only encouraged her to run faster. His voice echoed through the jungles that sat in the secluded Black Mountains, and sent chills through Breezes spine.

She had been locked in his basement for the past eight months, and finally got a chance to escape when Ma'tee had gotten comfortable and let her upstairs. The warm rays of the sun felt unfamiliar to her, because her body had become adjusted to the confinement of the luxury basement that she had been trapped in.

Breeze couldn't see anything but tall, green exotic plants and leaves as she brushed past them with both hands in front of her, pushing them aside to protect her face. She ran and ran until the sound of Matee's voice faded in the distance behind her. She stopped to catch her breath and sat at the base of a tree while looking around in fear. She breathed heavily as tears streamed down her face and her lungs worked in overdrive, desperately searching for more oxygen. The air was thin and muggy, which made it hard to breathe due to the high altitude of the tall mountains.

"Where the fuck am I?" Breeze asked herself as she rested her hand on her chest and felt her heart beating rapidly. Her eyes scanned her surroundings anxiously . . . desperately as she stood back up to continue her escape. Little did she know, she was just wasting her time. The jungle's shape was a gigantic circle, that lead right back to Ma'tee's palace.

While Breeze breathed heavily in attempt to catch her breath, she felt a painful pinch near her ankle. She quickly jerked her leg back and began to examine it, but she didn't see anything. She directed her eyes directly on where the pain was coming from, and noticed a small blood puddle on her ankle that resembled a bite. The sting instantly became an excoriating hurt, and she began to grimace while rubbing the small bite. She tried to stand up, but she quickly was knocked back to her bottom because of her dizziness. Her sight began to blur and sweat beads began to form, eventually trickling down her forehead as she began to experience hot flashes. Before she knew it, she had passed out at the result of all of the pain.

Hours later Ma'tee found Breeze passed out against that same tree, defeat written all over her face. He smiled as he whispered, "Sleeping Beauty," as he approached her. He took his time before going after her after she had escaped, knowing that it was impossible for her to navigate her way out of the jungles. It was nearly impossible for someone to exit the Black Mountains if they didn't know them like the back of their hand. Ma'tee approached Breeze and ran his finger through her hair, hoping she would wake up. He noticed that she didn't move and was sweating profusely. She was still breathing, but something wasn't right. He shook her with force, but still didn't get a response.

Ma'tee then looked at the exotic tree that she was lying underneath, and noticed that it was a black oak tree. He quickly became nervous and scooped up Breeze into his arms. Her body was limp, and she wasn't responding to his touch whatsoever. "See what chu un done to chu self?" Ma'tee said in his heavy Haitian accent. Ma'tee noticed the thin red streaks going up Breeze's legs, an indication of a spider bite. He instantly knew that she had been bitten by a black widow, one of the most poisonous spiders found in the Black Mountains. The black oak was known for housing their nests. He knew that he had to get her back to the house before it spread any further. He had antivenom back home, and knew it was only a matter of time before the bite would kill Breeze. He held Breeze securely in his arms and headed back to his place to administer the medicine to his beauty queen.

Zyir sat in front of the thick glass that separated him and his mentor, Carter. He watched as the guard escorted Carter to the seat. Carter wore an orange jumpsuit, and Zyir noticed that being incarcerated hadn't changed a thing about him. He still had the same confident swagger he possessed the day he went in. He had grown a small beard, but besides that, Carter looked the same.

Carter sat down and looked across at the young man that he had molded into his likeness. Zyir picked up the phone and placed it to his ear. Before picking up the phone, Carter paused and smirked as he looked at Zyir.

"Good to see you, my nigga," Carter said after he finally picked up the phone.

"Good to see you too, Carter. How you holding up?" Zyir asked with sincerity all in his voice.

"I'm good. Ready to see that outside, feel me?" Carter said with intensity in his eyes.

Zyir nodded his head, already knowing what Carter was getting at. "I feel you. I just been waiting for the word, fam," he replied as his adrenaline began to pump.

Their former comrade had turned snitch, and was set to testify against Carter in the upcoming trial, which was set to start a week later. The authorities let Zyir go in aspirations of catching the big fish, which was Carter. The judge had let Zyir out on bail, but held Carter after the DA had informed him of Carter's kingpin status. They saw him as a potential flight risk because of his international drug ties and his unlimited finances, so he was forced to remain behind bars.

"I want you to start putting everything in motion. We un' let them have their time to shine. Now it's my turn," Carter said, referring to the media and the District Attorney's Office. They had made it a big deal in the local and national media that they had captured the head of one of the most treacherous drug rings in the south: The Cartel. They had news conferences displaying the drugs recovered from the bust, and acted as if they had Carter's conviction in the bag, but little did they know.

Carter was just holding his cards for the right time, and since the trial was approaching, it was his turn to make his move. The only thing linking Carter to the drugs was the testimony of Ace. Ace was once Carter's right hand man, but folded under pressure and cooperated with the law; wrong move.

"Everything's taken care of. Mecca is on it now," Zyir said as he slightly grinned.

Mecca looked down and watched as his shaft disappeared and reappeared at the expense of Sheila's head game. He placed his hand on the back of her head as he tried his best to stay hard as she pleased him. He was in no way attracted to the girl that was going down on him, but it was all business, and he had to do what he had to do to get his brother, Carter free. He was back in Flint, Michigan, Carter's old hometown, and also the hometown of Ace's snitching ass. Ace was in the custody of the FBI, under the witness protection program, so he had to lure Ace to him, rather than go after a federally protected man.

"I can't believe this shit!" Mecca mumbled under his breath as he looked at the rolls that hung out of Sheila's halter-top. He didn't mind being with a girl with a little meat on her bones, but Sheila was straight up sloppy. She let herself go after Ace got her pregnant, and a couple months after she got knocked up, Ace left for Miami with Carter and Zyir.

Mecca had been dealing with Sheila for over a month and played the role of a man who was falling in love, but in actuality, he couldn't wait until Ace slipped up and contacted her. His time was running out because of the upcoming trial, at which Ace was scheduled to take the stand. Carter was sure to get life on the drug trafficking charges if convicted.

"I want some of this dick," Sheila seductively said as she rose up and began to slowly take off her clothes.

Mecca stood up with his tool in his hand and watched attentively. He wasn't at all fascinated by her body, but when he saw juices dripping from her pulsating womanhood, he got hard as a missile. His pole grew two inches longer as he stepped out of his pants and slowly stroked himself as she got completely naked. The veins in his rod began to show, and his blood began to flow to his tip. Mecca reached for a condom out of his pants pocket and gave it to her so she could do her trick, which was putting on the rubber without using her hands. He watched and threw his head back and prepared for the ride Sheila was about to take him on. Once Mecca was protected, Sheila straddled him and let him ease into her wetness.

"You like that, Chris?" Sheila asked as she called Mecca by the wrong name.

Mecca almost didn't answer, forgetting that he told her a fake name to conceal his true identity. "Yeah, I like that, ma," Mecca answered just before he took her left breast into his mouth and palmed both of her big cheeks.

Sheila rotated her hips in slow circles while moaning loudly and throwing her head back in pleasure. The sounds of skin smacking echoed throughout the small apartment, which must have awakened the baby, because crying erupted from the next room over, interrupting their sexual flow.

"Ooh shit!" Sheila said as she tried to get as many strokes in as possible before she had to go check on her infant baby boy. "Let me check on my baby," she said as she stopped moving and hopped off of Mecca, leaving him with a stiff one.

Mecca watched as she walked away, and stared at the tattoo that was on her lower back that read "Ace." The thought of Ace made Mecca furious, as he held his rod in his hand.

Just as Sheila got the baby to stop crying and laid him back into his crib, her house phone rang. Mecca looked at the caller ID while alone in the bedroom, and saw that the call was from a blocked number. He quickly sat up and called to Sheila, "Want me to get your phone?" he asked, knowing that Sheila wasn't going to allow that.

Sheila hurried back into the bedroom so that she could pick up the phone. She didn't want Ace to call and find out that she had another nigga in her house. She knew that the money would stop if he knew her little secret. "I got it!" Sheila replied anxiously as she picked up the phone. "Hello."

"Hey, baby," Ace said on the other line in a low calm voice. He was at a payphone in Wyoming right outside of the motel where he was being held until the upcoming trial. He looked around to make sure that the federal agents didn't see him at the pay phone. They weren't supposed to allow him to use the phone at all, but he snuck out while they were asleep to talk to his baby mother. "I miss you," he added.

"I miss you too, baby," Sheila said as she walked out of the room and gave Mecca a signal to be quiet by putting her finger on her full lips. "Where are you at, Ace? I have been worried about you. I haven't heard from you in months," she said as she stood in the kitchen with one hand on her hip.

"I can't tell you that right now, Sheila. But anyway, how my shorty doing?" he asked in concern as he kept looking over his shoulder to check and see if the coast was clear.

"He's fine. He's in there sleep right now. He misses his daddy though. I have been worried sick about you. I can't get a phone call or anything, huh?" Sheila asked with obvious irritation in her voice.

"I'm in some heavy shit right now, but everything is going to be okay in a couple of weeks," Ace said, thinking about how he would start a new life in Wyoming under the witness protection program. He planned on taking his 'hood rat baby mama and settling down so they could raise their son together. He thought that neither Carter nor Zyir knew about his son, but the streets were talking, and it didn't take much for Zyir to find out Ace's little secret. When Zyir found out about the baby, he quickly put Mecca on Sheila.

"I hope so, because we need you here with us," Sheila responded as she smiled at the sound of Ace's voice. She almost forgot that "Chris" was in the back waiting for her to have sex, and she peeked back toward the back of the apartment and saw him opening the refrigerator. She slightly tensed up. She didn't even hear him creeping up behind her while on the phone. She placed her finger on her lips once again to remind him to remain silent. She looked away from him and continued to listen closely to Ace.

"Have you been getting that money I've been sending you?" Ace asked.

"Yeah, I—" Before Sheila could finish her sentence, a loud blast erupted and her brains were all over the kitchen wall. Mecca stood behind her with a smoking gun as he watched her body collapse and the bloody phone fall to the floor.

"Sheila!" Ace yelled as he jumped at the sound of the blast through the phone. "Sheila! What was that?" he yelled into the phone as his eyes began to shift nervously while he gripping the phone tightly.

Mecca let off another round in Sheila's twitching body for good measure, and reached down to pick up the phone. He had been waiting for Ace to call for weeks, and his wish had just been granted. "What's going on, playboy?" Mecca said with enthusiasm as if he was greeting a friend.

"Fuck!" Ace scoffed as he took the phone from his ear and put it on his chest. He already recognized Mecca's voice and his heart rate sped up. He hoped to God that the second gunshot wasn't for his son. He slowly put the phone back to his ear.

"Listen real close, okay? Your bitch is already gone to meet her Maker. Now it's your choice if you want me to send li'l Ace right behind her," Mecca said as he went to the back, set his gun on the dresser and picked up Ace's baby boy. "Hey, li'l man!" Mecca said in a playful voice while still holding the cordless phone to his own ear so Ace could hear him clearly.

Ace sat and listened to the giggles of his own son, and regretted not taking his own flesh and blood out of harm's way. "Don't touch my mu'fuckin son!" he seethed in between his clenched teeth.

"Whoa, whoa! Hold up! You are not in the position to be barking orders, homeboy. You listen to me, and I'ma tell you what *you* are going to do," Mecca commanded as he held li'l Ace in his arm and rocked him gently. "You aren't going to testify against my man. You are going to get up there on that stand and catch amnesia, feel me?"

"Yeah, I hear you. Just leave my kid out of it, man," Ace said in a pleading tone.

"Should of thought about that before you got to singing like a mu'fuckin' bitch. Snitch-ass nigga!" Mecca yelled, getting upset just at the thought of Ace being a rat.

Ace remained silent, knowing that he couldn't possibly snitch on Carter and The Cartel anymore. Too much was on the line. He would rather face federal charges himself than leave his newborn son at the mercy of a nigga like Mecca.

"If Carter gets convicted, say good-bye to your son. It's all on you," Mecca threatened just before he hung up the phone and dropped it. He held Ace's baby up and blew on his stomach playfully, making li'l Ace laugh and squirm.

Mecca smiled and hoped that he wouldn't have to send the baby to the same place he had just sent Sheila. He didn't want to be a killer, but snake niggas like Ace left him no choice. He stared down at the baby in his arms and whispered, "It's all up to your daddy, li'l man. It's all up to your snitching-ass pops."

Chapter One

Miamor

I'm trapped . . . stuck in between my past and my future, and I don't know which one to choose or which way to go. I remember everything that happened to me. It's so vivid in my mind. I can still feel my heart beat rapidly for the love I have for Carter, and at the same time I can feel my temperature rise at the thought of his brother, Mecca. I remember Mecca fucking me up. I can still feel the whip of his chain as it ripped through the flesh on my legs. I can still hear the menacing sound of his voice. How in the fuck he caught me slipping, I don't know, but I can't let him beat me. He can't win, but there's nothing I can do when I can't even open my eyes. No matter how hard I try, I can't seem to wake up. I can't speak, I can't move, I can't do anything, and everything around me is black. I know how I got here, but how the fuck do I get out? For the first time in a long time I'm afraid.

I wish I had my girls with me, because with them, nothing is impossible. With them, we run through niggas like Mecca, collect our paper, and keep it pushing to the next job. But our difference of opinion on The Cartel broke us apart. I did what I thought I would never do. I chose a nigga, Carter, over The Murder Mamas.

I can see the light that so many people talk about before dying, but in my case, it is more like a fire that is waiting to consume me. I'm standing between the gates of hell and my childhood, but they are equal to one another. Either way I go, the pain will be too much for me to handle. My past is something that I don't want to remember. I forgot about it for a reason. I gave myself amnesia so that I wouldn't have to relive it, and I left it behind a long time ago. I don't want to have to repeat it, but I don't want to die either. I have a choice: I can walk into the light right now and let it all end here. I can submit myself to God's mercy and face my judgment in that light, or I can face my past and figure out how my childhood affected me and made me into the woman, the killer, the bitch that I am today. Those are my options; face death or face life. That's a hell of a choice, but I guess it's my destiny. I'm not ready to meet my Maker. I still have too much to do, and there are so many things left in my life unsettled. There are so many debts that I still have to collect on, and so many that I still owe.

So, I'm going to introduce you to my past. I'm going to let you meet the innocent little girl I used to be before the corruption, the money, the bodies, and the bullshit. Don't judge me, just rock with my story as I tell it all . . . the 'hood, the bad and the ugly. This is me, Miamor, the life of a Murder Mama.

Chapter Two

Miamor
1995

Sitting in the bottom of my closet, I shook uncontrollably. The stench of piss was strong in the air, and my hands covered my ears trying to block out the screams. I was terrified. My heart beat uncontrollably and I closed my eyes from fear. I wished I could disappear and avoid the tragedy that was my life, but I couldn't. I relived this nightmare every night.

As soon as my mother left the house, I knew what would take place: The molestation; the screams; the feelings of helplessness. It always happened at the same time. Like clockwork at 1:00 a.m., he came like a thief in the night. No matter how much we avoided it, no matter how many times we begged our mother not to stay the night away from home, nothing ever saved us. She always said no. The bitch made us stay there with him, and even though we cried and pleaded, her answer was always no. If she did not know what was going on, she should have. The shit was happening under her own roof, so I could never give her the benefit of the doubt. Fuck her too! She invited him into her home and unknowingly into her daughters' bed. He was always there, with a fucking grin on his face. We were trapped, and our fates were inevitable.

My sister, Anisa was the victim, and our step-father, Perry was the bastard who shattered our childhoods. Lollipops and daisies were never a part of our world. All we knew was pain and corruption. It seemed as though abuse and neglect were the only constants in our lives. All we had was each other, and whenever he snatched Anisa from her bed, I always felt her pain.

"Please stop . . . please, it hurts!" Anisa screamed.

Tears stained my cheeks. I could hear my sister crying, but I couldn't do anything. I wished that we could switch places; that was how much I loved her. I knew the pain that she went through, and would take it all for her if I could, but I couldn't. He never chose me. It was always her. She was fourteen, and budding into womanhood early, while I was only twelve and still composed of all elbows and knees. There wasn't a curve to my body, so he ignored me mostly, but he violated Anisa, which meant he violated me.

I could hear the bed creaking from the other room, the headboard banging against the wall as a constant reminder of the atrocity that was happening behind closed doors. We wanted to tell someone, but who would believe us? Perry was smart. He made sure that he never hit Anisa. He never even left a mark. The sucking he did on her premature breasts was done lightly as to not leave any sign of trespass. We were scared, always walking around on eggshells and feeling like strangers in our own house.

The knocking of the headboard against the wall stopped, and I knew that it was finally over.

I waited in the bottom of the closet just as Anisa instructed me to. She always told me to hide and not come out until she came for me. The closet door creaked open and there stood my big sister. Her hair was wild and her eyes were red from crying. I took her hand and led her into the hallway bathroom. I was used to this routine. She never liked to talk afterwards, and she never looked me in the eye. I knew she was ashamed, but what she didn't know was that I was ashamed too, because I just sat there and let it happen to her. I locked the bathroom door and ran a tub full of steaming bathwater. Anisa got right in, ignoring the sting of hot water against her bare skin. She hugged her legs to her chest, and I rubbed her hair gently while we both cried silently as she scrubbed her sins away.

The next day when I awoke, Anisa was already out of her bed. I knew our mother was home because I could hear the sounds of Teena Marie blaring throughout the house. Walking into the bathroom, I saw Anisa leaned over the toilet, gasping for air. "What's wrong, Nis?" I asked.

"Nothing, Miamor. Get out . . . go and get ready for school," she said. She barely got the words out before she was throwing up again.

"I'm going to get Mama," I said. I had never been one of those tattle-telling little kids, but I didn't know what else to do. I could tell from the way Anisa was sprawled all over the toilet that she needed more help than I could offer.

"No!" she yelled, grabbing my arm to stop me from leaving the bathroom. She wiped her mouth with the back of her sleeve and began to cry.

"Anisa, what's wrong?" I asked.

Anisa couldn't stop crying. The deep sob that escaped her lips was a cry that was too mature for such a young girl. The cry signified what she had endured and the things her young eyes had seen before their time. She lifted up her shirt, and I noticed a slight bulge in her belly. It wasn't big at all, but my sister was naturally skinny. Her stomach had always been pancake flat, so the bump seemed out of place on her. I wondered how I could've missed it. I had seen Anisa naked plenty of times, and I had even noticed that she had gained a little bit of weight, but the thought of pregnancy never ever crossed my young mind. I was naïve and green to the game. For months, Perry had been raping my sister, and neither of us ever thought of the possibility of a baby.

"I'm pregnant, Mia!" she cried. "I don't know what to do! I tried to tell him no. He wouldn't stop."

"We have to tell," I said.

"Miamor, no! I don't want anybody to know!" Anisa whispered as she grasped my arm, her teary eyes desperately searching mine as if I could solve this problem. "I have to get rid of it. You have to promise me you won't say a word."

I nodded my head, but tears filled my eyes as I watched Anisa lower her shirt. She was pregnant at fourteen by our mother's husband.

Bam! Bam! Bam! My mother knocked on the door. "I hope y'all ready for school! You better get your asses dressed so you can catch this bus!"

I wanted to open the door and tell my mother everything that we had been through, but Anisa was still gripping my hand. "Don't say anything, okay?"

As badly as I wanted to tell, I couldn't. I trusted my sister and was loyal to her. If she wanted me to keep this secret, then I would. I wiped my eyes, flushed the toilet, and sprayed air freshener in the air before opening the door.

We dressed in silence and headed off to school, our souls heavy and our minds on problems that we were both too young to truly comprehend.

Brooklyn born and raised, we kept to ourselves. It was only Anisa and I. We weren't cliqued up like some of the other bitches in our borough. We had already been jumped on twice behind some beef that Anisa had caught with some girls from her high school, so I learned quickly to stay bladed up. I had seen Anisa put a razor blade in her mouth and carry it around all day without taking it out. I had cut my shit up a couple times trying to be like her, and when they caught us both slipping, she finally taught me how to tuck a blade away in my mouth just in case I ever needed it.

We knew the spots that these girls hung around, and we usually avoided those paths at all costs just to stay out of unnecessary conflict. So when Anisa hit a left and headed up toward their block, I stopped mid-step, not knowing why she would walk right into an ass whooping.

"Nisa, what are you doing? You know if we go that way we're going to have to fight. You're pregnant, Nis. We can't fight them girls off right now," I said.

"I know. I don't want to win the fight, I just want to fight," Anisa said with a determined look in her eyes.

I didn't understand at that moment what she was getting at, but I soon found out. "What?" I asked in confusion, looking at her like she was half stupid.

"Look, I've got to get this baby out of me, Miamor, and I can't tell Mama. I'm too young to go to a doctor and get an abortion by myself. I know this girl who was pregnant, but she got her ass beat and lost her baby. I got to do this, Miamor. This is the only way. You go the safe way. Get on the bus and go to school. I'll see you when you get home," she said. She hugged me and pushed me in the other direction.

Reluctantly, I walked away, confused. My heart kept telling me to go back, but I always listened to Anisa no matter what. I had to roll with her plan. We were both so naïve to think that this homemade method of abortion was the way to go. We had no idea how dangerous it was or the damage that Anisa was doing to her body.

I headed to school, but the thought of my sister fighting alone ate me up inside. After walking four blocks toward the bus stop, I turned around and ran full speed back toward Anisa. It was the first time I had ever disobeyed her. I knew she would be mad, but I couldn't stand the thought of her fighting without me by her side. That's how we were. Where one went, the other one followed, and no matter what she said, I couldn't let her go through this alone. I ran as fast as I could, nearly out of breath when I reached the crowd of girls. I saw the group of girls jumping on Anisa, and surprisingly, she wasn't even trying to fight back. They were stomping her out under the overpass of the train, and my heart ached as I saw them kicking her repeatedly in her stomach and back.

I pulled my blade without thinking twice. They were so focused on Anisa, that they didn't even see me coming. "Bitch!" I brought my blade up and sliced one of the girls across her face, then started throwing mad punches to anybody within arm's reach. Those bitches were twice my size. My little fists didn't do much damage, but with my sneak surprise I had the advantage. As soon as they realized I was there, it was a wrap. It was one of the worst ass whoppings I'd ever taken, but it didn't matter. I was there with Anisa. We took that ass whooping together.

The sound of police sirens blaring caused the group of girls to scatter, leaving Anisa lying on the ground and me kneeling beside her with a bloody lip.

"I told you to go the other way," Anisa groaned as I helped her up. She was lumped up and bruised.

The police officer approached us and hopped into his car. He escorted us home, where our mother threw a fit and sent us to our room. We both sat impatiently looking at each other, waiting naïvely for something to happen.

Hours passed before Anisa doubled over in pain. "I think it's happening, Mia!" she whispered, her face contorted in pain.

"What? What do I do?" I asked.

"Aghh! Miamor, I think something's wrong!" Anisa agonized as she held her lower stomach and crouched down at the side of the bed. A small spot of blood showed through her jeans, but slowly grew to a large stain in between her legs.

"Anisa, what do I do?" I asked. I was panicked. It was the most blood I'd ever seen. It was like her period, but ten times worse, and she was sweating profusely. Her hands were shaking in trepidation.

"I need to go to the bathroom," she said as she took her jeans off and put them in a plastic bag.

I helped her across the hall and locked the door. As soon as she sat down she opened her mouth in pain, but no sound came out. She stood, and blood was dripping between her legs, her thighs stained in crimson. The toilet was filled with it, and it looked like blood clots had fallen out of Anisa.

"What do I do? What do I do?" I asked, my voice cracking from concern and my eyes filling with tears. I knew I was in over my head and I wanted to go run for our mother, but I had promised, and even at such a young age, my word was all I had. I never broke it for anybody.

"I don't know!" she said as she was wracked with more pain. Anisa sat on the toilet as her premature body violently miscarried her baby.

I held her hand tightly as if she was bringing life into the world instead of flushing one down the toilet. I couldn't say anything. It wasn't my decision to make and it was already done, so all I could do was be there for my sister. She didn't ask to be in that situation. Perry had put her in it before her time, so I didn't judge her for wanting to get rid of it secretly.

Anisa was weak and could barely stand, so I helped her to our room and cleaned up the mess. I gave her two of our mother's pain prescriptions and washed her up before she fell asleep. This was the first time that I was grateful for my mother's ignorance. I didn't want her to come in and find out what we had done.

Just as I went to throw away the bloody towel, my mother was coming up the steps. "Where did all that blood come from?" she asked.

"I . . . um . . . I . . . it was from the fight. I got cut and I had to clean it," I lied.

"Oh, well, that serves you right for fighting in the first place," she said. "I was coming to tell you and your sister that I'm off to work. Perry will be home in about an hour. Come lock the door behind me."

I followed her to the door, and once she was gone, I raced back up to Anisa. She was still asleep. I lay beside her and we wrapped our arms around each other. I knew that we had to get out of that house. Even at such a young age, I was aware of danger. I just felt it in the pit of my stomach that things were never going to get better. With Perry around we would never feel safe, and Anisa had just gone through hell just to hide what he was doing to her. I wanted out. I wanted something better for both me and Anisa, and I promised myself that once we broke free, we would never look back.

I awoke when I felt the bed sink down on Anisa's side, but I didn't open my eyes. I already knew it was Perry. I recognized the familiar scent. It made me gag, and I felt a burning at the back of my throat. I hated him for what he had done to Anisa. I knew what he wanted, and I froze out of fear. I lay there stiff as a board, playing possum. I prayed that this night wouldn't be like all the others. It was this night that made me lose faith in God, because if there truly was one, He would have surely intervened. God would have protected us . . . saved us.

"No, stop!" I heard Anisa say. "Please, just not tonight! I can't!" she cried.

I had never heard her sound so weak, and I squeezed my eyes tightly as my heart beat out of my chest. *Please God, help her,* I pleaded. But just like all the other times, God never came.

Perry pulled Anisa by the arm, but I got up and pulled her other arm. "She said no!" I screamed.

Perry stopped and looked at Anisa with a menacing smirk. "It's either you or her." That was the choice he gave her.

I trembled, and Anisa looked back at me while gripping her stomach. I could tell she was still in pain. Tears fell down her face. She hugged me and whispered, "Everything will be all right, Mia. Go to the closet and wait for me to come and get you."

"No!" I said defiantly, my tears no longer willing to hide. "I'll do it, Anisa. He can take me this time." Snot dripped down my nose as Perry forcefully grabbed me from the bed, carrying me out of the room by my waist kicking, and screaming.

"No! Let her go!" Anisa screamed as she fought him. "Please! Stop it . . . she's too young!"

Perry turned around and backhanded Anisa into the wall and threw me to the ground. "Bitch, get your ass up and let's go!" he yelled at her. I crawled over to Anisa and we huddled in the corner.

"Anisa, don't go!" I whispered.

Perry loomed over us as he unbuckled his pants and pulled out his oversized penis.

"Miamor, go get in the closet," Anisa whispered.

I shook my head no.

"Just do it!" she yelled in between her tears.

Anisa left with Perry, and I climbed into the closet, covering my ears while crying uncontrollably. This had to stop. I couldn't understand why this was happening to my sister. It all seemed so unfair.

"Agghhh!"

The scream sent shivers up and down my spine. I had never heard my sister scream like that. Something was different this time. She needed me.

"Aghh. No! It hurts! Please!"

I thought of all the blood I had seen earlier. All of it had come out of Anisa. I never wanted her to go through that again. I couldn't just sit there and do nothing. I ran out of the closet and into my mother's room.

Anisa was lying there with a pool of blood underneath her while Perry was on top, humping furiously like a dog in heat. It was a sight that petrified me. I thought he was killing her. "Get off of her!" I yelled as I rushed at him and began hitting him. I felt his hand cross my face as he backhanded me to the floor, his wedding ring leaving an imprint in my face.

"Miamor, help me!" Anisa cried.

I ran as fast as I could to the downstairs closet. I knew it was where my mother kept her shotgun. She didn't know that I knew, but I did, and I needed it more than she ever would.

"Mia!"

I closed my eyes at the blood curdling cry. Anisa needed me. I pulled out the double barrel shotgun, but couldn't find the shells as I looked frantically, hands shaking, as I could barely hold up the big gun. Tears clouded my vision as I ran into the kitchen. The headboard was banging loudly against the wall, creating a sickening scene in my head as I pictured Perry molesting Anisa. I tore every drawer out of the cabinets before I sent a box of shells scattering across the floor. My shaky hands barely allowed me to load them into the chamber. I had played with the gun enough to know how to use it with expertise. I was only able to load one shell in. I couldn't waste any more time trying any more than that.

I raced up the stairs and burst into the room. Anisa's hand was outstretched for me as Perry was on top of her. She needed me. Without hesitation, I lifted the shotgun and fired. The blast sent me flying back against the wall.

Perry grabbed his chest as the buckshot filled him. His chest looked like Swiss cheese and he tried to gasp for air.

Anisa jumped out of the bed, blood dripping from her womb down her legs, but before she could reach me, she collapsed. My heart felt as if it was going to burst. I had never been so afraid in my entire life.

I picked up the telephone and dialed 911.

"Hello, nine-one-one Operator. What is your emergency?"

I was out of breath, and I breathed into the phone as I watched Perry's life slip away before my eyes. "He . . . he raped my sister! I shot him! Please, we need help!"

I then crawled over to Anisa and put her head in my lap. "It's going to be okay, Nis. They're coming," I sat in the room with my sister until help arrived. I wouldn't leave her side until she opened her eyes. "I got him, Anisa. He won't hurt us anymore," I said when she finally looked at me. Anisa didn't respond, but from the look in her eyes, I knew that she had heard me.

Once the police arrived and I told them what happened, they handcuffed me and put me in the back of a police car.

I knew that I was in trouble and would probably be going away for a while, but Anisa was safe, and that's all that mattered. I would have done the same thing if I had to do it over again. Nobody could hurt us anymore, and I felt that it was worth it. So, when I went before a judge and told him that I would do the same thing, he said I had no remorse, and was a menace to society. He remanded me to a juvenile facility until my eighteenth birthday. Bitch-ass nigga! After getting the news, I looked at my mother, and she had tears in her eyes, but I knew they were for Perry and not for me. I rolled my eyes at her and then I turned to Anisa and smiled. "I love you Nis!" I mouthed.

"I love you too, Miamor! Thank you!" she mouthed back as sincere tears streamed down her face.

Chapter Three

Miamor

Six years of lockup in juvie was too much to even recall. The loneliness, the abandonment, every day spent there took a little bit more of my sanity away. It was bullshit. Day in and day out it was the exact same. The only thing that kept me going was the fact that Anisa was waiting for me on the outside.

My mother tried to come and see me, but I never accepted her visits. I didn't have shit to say to her because I felt there was no excuse. She wasn't there for Anisa and me when we needed her most, and as a result, I got locked up and Anisa had skeletons in her closet that she would harbor for the rest of her life. I didn't fuck with my mother, and I probably never would. All Anisa and I had was each other. That was enough, and she did my time right along with me, keeping my account full as well as visiting me weekly.

I never regretted my actions . . . not once. That's part of the reason why they made me do all six years. They had me going to therapy as if I needed rehabilitating. All I had to do was show remorse, and they would have let me go early, but remorse for a mu'fucka like Perry was something I couldn't even fake. I hated him. He deserved to die, and the older I got, the more I truly understood that I had done the right thing. Nobody knew the connection I had with my sister. Everyone kept saying that my actions weren't justified because *I* was never actually raped, but fuck everybody who thought that, and fuck you too if you're thinking that! Eventually, my turn would have come, and before it did, I erased that nigga from the map. I did what was necessary, and if the tables were turned, I know Anisa would have done the exact same thing for me.

The day I said good-bye to lockup, I promised myself I would never go back. Doing that much time as a child had turned my heart cold. I had changed, but it wasn't for the better.

Anisa was waiting at the gates. She had really grown up. As I admired her True Religion jeans, matching top and Zanotti pumps, I knew she was doing well. Her hair was cut short in a bob. Her light skin was radiant, and she had the smile of a woman who had seen no struggles. She looked truly happy, as if she was able to let go of what had happened to her. My big sister was beautiful. She was a grown-ass woman now, and I hoped to leave the past behind and be just like her.

I was eighteen, not yet a woman, but definitely not a little girl. I was on my own, and the world was at my feet. All I had to do was conquer it.

"Miamor!" she yelled as we ran toward each other with open arms.

"Hey, bitch!" I replied as we embraced. We hugged and cried in excitement.

"I'm so glad you're out! I missed you, Mia!" Anisa got teary eyed and put her hands on my shoulders so that she could look me in the eye. I already knew what she was about to say. It was something that had been in the air for a long time.

"I'm so sorry, Miamor. I love you. You're my sister. I'm so happy that you did what you did. You saved my life. I'm just so sorry that you had to go through all of this behind my bullshit," Anisa said. "Anything you need, I got you. First thing we got to do is get you out of this bullshit ass jail gear."

I nodded, and we hugged once more before hopping into the car, leaving skid marks behind us as we sped off. She was whipping a nice little Chrysler 300 with leather seats and tinted windows. It wasn't a Benz, but the shit was fly and more expensive than the average whip.

We rode into Brooklyn, and the first place we went was to the salon. My hair was long as hell because I kept it braided while I was locked up. When my shit was freshly permed and wrapped, it was down my back, all natural, no weave. My skin was flawless, and my figure was on point. I made sure to work out daily, keeping myself lean and feminine in the process with curves all in the right places.

After shopping and getting me a completely new wardrobe, we headed to the apartment that Anisa shared with her man, Murder. I was tripping at how freely she spent money. She was cashing out on me like it grew on trees, even giving me five stacks to keep in my pocket until I got on my feet. Her carefree attitude regarding money had me wondering what she did, because I knew her ass wasn't working.

"I can't wait for you to meet Murder. He's really good to me . . . that's my baby!" Anisa bragged as she smiled and batted her eyelashes.

I looked at her in high regard. At first glance, no one would have ever been able to tell what she'd been through. She was the shit, and I admired her for being so strong. I would have thought she would have never been able to trust a nigga. I sure as hell never would. A man who had watched us grow for years had betrayed us without a thought. If *he* could fuck us over, then I didn't put shit past any other nigga out there. Love wasn't in the cards for me.

"What kind of name is Murder?" I asked.

Anisa laughed and replied, "It fits him . . . trust. That's the perfect name for that nigga."

I shrugged as we parked in her building. "You live here?" I asked as we got out of the car. I looked up at the tall sky rise building.

Anisa answered, "Only the high life, babe. I'll put you up on game later. Right now, let's get you settled."

Walking into Anisa's crib, weed smoke invaded my nostrils, lifting me into a contact high almost immediately.

"Babe, come out here!" Anisa yelled.

Murder walked into the room with a blunt hanging from his lips, his aura commanding my attention and respect instantly. Anisa had definitely done well. The nigga was fly. His chocolate complexion and lean figure was attractive. He had a ball player's height, but was a bit on the skinny side. It looked like Anisa weighed more than he did. His face was average, maybe even a little below average, but when I inventoried a man, I considered more than his looks. The jewels that were hanging around his neck indicated his status, and the fact that he had my sister plushed out in a luxury condo was all the evidence

I needed to know that he was getting money. How? I didn't know, but he was definitely papered up. He walked over to Anisa and kissed her cheek with casual nonchalance. He grabbed a couple Heinekens out of the refrigerator and tossed one to me, then handed one to Anisa.

"You must be Miamor. I've heard a lot about you," he said, his strong New Yitty accent complementing his words.

"It's nice to meet you," I replied. "Thanks for letting me stay here."

"Not a problem. You're family. Anisa put me up on everything that happened, and I respect it. You can set yourself up in the extra room." Murder sat down on the couch across from me and passed me the blunt.

Although I had never smoked weed, I accepted it. I had a lot of adjusting to do and a lot to think about as far as my life was concerned, but I didn't want to stress it. I embraced the temporary relief and put the blunt to my lips. I inhaled deeply. Big mistake! My virgin lungs rejected the weed instantly, and I coughed uncontrollably as I put my hand over my mouth trying to hold the cough in. My shit was on fire, but I was mostly embarrassed, because both Anisa and Murder were cracking up, having a big laugh at my expense.

"You never smoked before?" Anisa asked as the burning finally eased in my chest.

I cut my eyes at her and shook my head no. Her ass knew damn well I hadn't done shit before—fuck, smoke, drive, even flirt with the opposite sex. Hell, I just had gotten out of lockup! I was a virgin to everything . . . green to the game. Everything that the average 'hood chick had experienced by the age of fourteen, I had never been able to do.

"We about to break you in then," Murder stated with a small grin.

Anisa and I sat up all night, catching up on each other's lives, filling Murder in on our childhood and the few good times we had experienced. He didn't interrupt, but instead passed the weed back and forth while letting us do our thing. He just sat back and observed like a gangster would. The weed had me so relaxed and I knew that I had found my new favorite pastime.

By the time daylight crept through the curtains, we were all fucked up. The time had flown by, our reunion making up for the time we were separated. Smoking and drinking all night had me done, but it was the first time that I had felt comfortable in a long time. I was home, and it felt good . . . real good.

The ringing of the phone the next morning was like tiny bombs going off inside my head, and when it didn't stop, I figured that Anisa and Murder were just as hungover as I was. Forcing myself to get out of bed, I got up and made my way to the living room. "Hello?" I answered.

Before the caller could respond, Murder appeared behind me and snatched the phone from my hand. He hung it up quickly without even seeing who was calling. "Don't answer the phone, and don't use this phone. I handle business, and business only on this line," he said. His tone was stern, and I wanted to ask him who the fuck he thought he was talking to, but I held my tongue. He was letting me stay at his house and had welcomed me with open arms, so I didn't want to create conflict over something petty. I frowned, but before I could say a word, he went into his pocket and pulled out a wad of money. He peeled off five hundred dollars and held them out for me. "Take this and get a cell phone today. Nobody uses this phone, a'ight?" he said as he softened up his tone. I guess he realized that he had been kind of harsh.

"Yeah, okay," I said reluctantly. *What the fuck is up with that?* I thought as I made my way back to my room. *I know this nigga don't got bitches calling here. What else could be so important?* I made a mental note to discuss it with Anisa, and went back to sleep.

I decided to not even bring the phone thing up the next day. Anisa seemed happy, and I wasn't trying to be the one to break up her happy home. Murder hadn't really shown me shade. I was just making assumptions, so I swallowed it.

"Hey, sleepy head," Anisa greeted as I walked into the kitchen. She set a plate of pancakes and eggs in front of me and kissed the top of my head as if I was her child, before taking a seat herself.

"Hey, Nis. I'm so fucked up right now," I said with a half-smile.

"The food will make you feel a little bit better," she replied.

"Did Mommy ever try to contact you?" I asked.

"She tried," Anisa said vaguely. She sighed deeply. "Look, it's like this. I don't have any family. Family is there for you. They protect you, and Mommy never did none of that. The only family I got is you."

"What about Murder?" I questioned curiously. I wanted to know how deep their bond was. I never wanted to see Anisa hurt again . . . not by Murder or anyone else.

"He's good to me. I care about him. He makes sure I have everything I need. I'm glad he's a part of my life, but with him, you can't really plan ahead. I have to take it as it is today, because one day he's not going to make it through that door. We both have a clear understanding about where we stand. It works between us because neither of us is looking for love. He doesn't disrespect me with other chicks or nothing, but if it ever came to that, I'm not tripping. He's security, and I need that right now, nothing more, nothing less."

I couldn't really understand why she had Murder on a short term relationship plan, but I didn't question her. She knew him better than I did. In any relationship there is baggage, and she knew what Murder was carrying.

"Can I borrow your car?" I asked.

"You know it, babe," she replied without question.

That was one of the reasons why I loved her so. She wasn't on no fake shit. What she had, she was more than willing to share with me. It had always been that way. If there was only two pieces of bread left, we split it and made ghetto-oneslice sandwiches. If she came across a dollar, then she changed it out and we both had fifty cents. I knew that she would give me her last, and it made me love her even more.

"Where you going?"

"I've got to stop by the mall and pick up a phone. I answered the phone earlier this morning, and Murder kind of flipped," I said.

"Oh, that ain't shit. He only gives that number to people he does business with. Don't worry about it. Even he takes his personal calls on a cell phone. Did he come at you wrong?" she asked, getting defensive.

"No, it wasn't like that. He just let me know not to answer it. He's good. I like him. I think he's cool people," I said, calming her down.

"Well, I'm chilling today. You can call me if you need me. My keys are on the table. Don't crash my shit, Miamor! Your ass probably can't even drive!" she said jokingly.

"Bitch, I got my L's. I took the class in lockup for having good behavior," I answered as I went to dress.

"You? Good behavior? I know you're lying now," Anisa said. "Not one scratch. Mia! I'm not playing!" she warned, her voice following me out of the room.

She knew me all too well, because there wasn't a damn thing legal about me behind a wheel, but I was anxious to spin the block. I just wanted to get out and spread my wings.

Putting on brand new Seven jeans, red stilettos, and a white Ralph Lauren top, I dressed and applied M•A•C cosmetics. I admired myself in the mirror. Everything about me screamed fly, and I knew it. I was only eighteen, so yes, I was arrogant as hell and itching to get into something.

Before I could even hit the door, Anisa stopped me.

"Run them L's, Miamor. I want to see your license before you hop in my car," she said seriously as she sat on the floor in front of the coffee table, rolling a spliff. Murder was stretched out on the couch behind her, his hat dipped low, pistol on his waistline, and flipping the channels on the seventy-two-inch plasma TV.

"Anisa, ain't nobody gon' crash your car. Stop tripping. I'm just going to the mall," I pleaded.

"I'll take her. I'm going that way anyway. I got to pick up a new joint for that job I'm into tonight," Murder said as he stood.

"Fine by me, long as my shit come back in one piece," Anisa said. "I'll teach you how to drive later this week, and take you to handle the official paperwork. The last thing you need is to run into Jake out there with no license. You just got out. I'm just trying to keep you out, sis."

I rolled my eyes. She could tell I had an attitude. Anisa knew she was wrong for sticking me with a babysitter, but I obliged and followed Murder out of the condo. We didn't talk until we got to the parking lot. He tossed me her keys and gave me a smile.

"I'm driving?" I asked in surprise.

"Fuck I look like, your chauffer?" he asked smoothly as he stepped into the car. "Anisa's your big sister. She's overprotective. I'ma teach you how to drive."

I was geeked and all smiles as I got into Anisa's car. Murder leaned his seat back and put one foot on the dash. "Do you!" he said with a grin.

I turned the ignition and adjusted the seat. Anisa was a little bit taller than me. Once I was comfortable, I put the car in reverse and backed out slowly. My heart was beating out of my chest, only because Anisa's ass had made me nervous.

"Relax, you're good, ma. You control the car, not the other way around," Murder reassured.

I nodded my head, took a deep breath and switched gears to drive before pulling out of the parking lot. Murder was silent as I crept down the streets of New York. Impatient drivers flew past me and I stuck up my middle finger as they drove by, causing Murder to laugh. "What?" I asked as I laughed too.

"Nothing, ma . . . nothing at all. Concentrate on the road. Fuck whoever's behind you," he said.

I put in a CD, and the sounds of R&B filled the car. The music eased some of my apprehension, and I relaxed behind the wheel, as my foot became heavier on the gas pedal. Before you knew it, I was cruising, snapping my fingers to the beat, while Murder rode shotgun, never interrupting my flow. The fact that he trusted my driving made me trust myself, and all of my fears went out of the window. I was whipping through the 'hood like I had been doing it for years. I was on cloud nine as I listened to Keyshia Cole's latest joint. I had never been in a relationship before, so I couldn't relate to the lyrics in the song, but it didn't stop my head from spinning from the feelings homegirl was screaming through the speakers. I couldn't see myself giving my heart to anybody, but I was feeling the song as if my heart had been broken a thousand times. Before I knew it, I was pulling into the mall.

"See, it's easy," Murder stated. He had to be the coolest nigga I'd ever met. He was so laid back, yet his demeanor was so 'hood. "Come on, don't have me in this mu'fucka all day. You can hit up all the shoe shops and shit with Nis. But me and you, we in and out. Cool?"

"Okay," I responded, but in and out became a day full of me tearing up the mall and Murder carrying my bags. I couldn't help it. The little shopping spree that Anisa had given me the day before hadn't quenched my thirst.

Murder wanted to complain, but he didn't. I could tell from the look on his face that shopping wasn't really his thing. He allowed me to shop until I grew tired, and I felt like I had a personal bodyguard with me the way he was mean mugging niggas who were trying to get at me.

"You ready to leave?" I asked. "We've been here all day and you haven't bought one thing."

He sighed and gave me a half smile. "Nah, go ahead. Get whatever you want, ma," he said. "It's on me."

I was like a kid in a candy store, picking up everything that I had neglected to get when I had gone shopping with Anisa. By the time I was done, it was dark outside, and as we walked to the car, Murder asked, "You hungry?"

"I could eat," I responded.

Murder put the bags in the trunk and walked around to the driver's side.

"I'm not driving?" I asked.

He put his hand up and I tossed him the keys. "Nah, I don't got time to coach you through it right now, sis. I got to get to my man before his spot close. Then we'll go grab some food. Call Anisa and see if she's hungry."

I called Anisa, and she declined our invitation to dinner. "I don't feel like getting dressed. Y'all go ahead. Just bring me back something," she said.

I agreed, and then disconnected the call with her. "She said bring her something back," I told Murder.

I reached for the radio to turn it up, but Murder popped my CD out and tossed it in the back seat. "Driver picks the music," he said smugly as he ruffled my hair. I slapped his hand away and laughed as he turned the radio all the way up.

". . . While I'm watching every nigga watching me closely, My shit is butter . . ."

Jay-Z's lyrics filled the interior, and no words were spoken, but it was a comfortable vibe between us, and the more I became acquainted with Murder, the more questions I had.

He drove until he pulled up to a pawnshop way out in Queens. I looked around the dark alley we were parked in. A chill went up and down my spine, but I shook the feeling of fear. "Get out," he instructed. He popped the trunk and pulled out a pillowcase, then entered the building from the rear.

When we got inside, an older white man with wire rimmed glasses sat behind a counter. "Who's the girl?" he asked immediately, causing my heart to flutter. The old man shot me a look of suspicion that had me feeling out of place.

"She's good. I vouch for her. She's my li'l sister. Don't worry about her. Let's just handle this business, just like every other time," Murder stated with authority.

"You always come alone," the man insisted, still eyeing me.

I pretended as if I wasn't paying attention, but I was picking up on it all. I was so aware of my surroundings, that the sound of the seconds ticking by on the clock made the hairs on the back of my neck stand up.

"Come on, Schultz, you know me. This ain't a new routine. I don't do bad business, and I'd never bring heat to your establishment. She's with me. She's cool," Murder stated, never showing an ounce of intimidation. He put the pillowcase on the countertop, removed three pistols and then placed two thick wads of money next to them. "I need to make these disappear, and I need another one. An automatic."

The man rose, then locked the front door, flipping the sign to closed. "Follow me," he said.

Murder grabbed my hand and I reluctantly followed him down a long hallway, then down a flight of steps. It was so dark that I couldn't see in front of me, and there was a strong pungent smell in the air. I wanted to cough, but I didn't. My breathing was labored, and I held onto Murder's hand a little tighter for reassurance. *Where the fuck is this nigga taking me? What type of shit he into? Has Anisa ever been here?*

I asked myself as a thousand and one questions plagued my mind. I didn't know what I was about to see and when the old man turned on the dim light, and I sighed in relief and released Murder's hand. I felt foolish for letting my imagination run wild. The old basement walls were filled with guns; all types, sizes, and calibers, along with three large barrels that contained some type of liquid.

The man gently placed the three pistols Murder had given him into a metal crate, then slowly lowered them into the barrel. The liquid bubbled and sizzled for a couple minutes before making the guns disappear. He then pointed to the arsenal of weapons behind him and said, "Take your pick. What would you like this time?"

Murder quickly wrapped up his business and led me back out to the alley. Once we were safely back in the car, I turned to him and said, "What was that all about?"

"Don't worry about it, ma. That's not for you. The only reason I let you come inside is because it was dark and I didn't want you in the car for that long. That's the last thing I need is to fuck a nigga up over you in the middle of Queens. You still hungry?"

"Nah, I'm all right. I'm tired now anyway," I lied. I just wanted to get back to Anisa and find out what the fuck was up. She knew exactly what Murder was into, and now I was curious too, but before we got out of the car, Murder grabbed my arm.

"Yo, Miamor," he said.

"Yeah?" I looked back at him and noticed the serious expression he had on his face.

"I know you and Anisa are close and I would never come between that, but I need you to keep what you saw tonight to yourself, a'ight?"

The way he looked at me wasn't menacing or intimidating, but sincere, as if I held his life in my hands. I knew that it was important to him. I had never kept a secret from my sister in my life. She was my other half, and I owed her everything, whereas I owed Murder nothing. But for some strange reason, I nodded my head in agreement.

Chapter Four

Miamor

Months passed, and as Anisa and I grew closer, so did Murder and me. Anisa and I spent day in and day out together. She was my love, and although I wasn't a little girl who followed everything that she did, I still admired her greatly.

Most days we were shopping or taking day trips to the spa. The notion of getting a job was never an option, because Murder made it clear that his lady didn't need a job, and said that since I was just like Anisa, he was claiming me too. So I wasn't to lift a finger. The only thing I did was count his money. The average chick would have been jealous of how close Murder and I had become. I rode shotgun in his car more than Anisa did, but she wasn't tripping because it wasn't like that. Anisa never planned on being with Murder long term. She was just 'riding the wave', she would say. When the ride was over, she was getting off. She would always say that there was no room for love in the life he was living, and since he always said he was never giving it up, they maintained a relationship. They pledged that they would never get too serious. He looked out for her though, and I knew he would do anything for her, because in the short amount of time he'd known me, he gave me his all. He called me his "li'l mama" and kept me grounded, because he said fucking around with Anisa, I was becoming a diva.

All in all, life was good, but I still had no idea exactly what Murder did to fund the lifestyle. All I knew is that when that phone rang, it meant money. Sometimes after answering it, he would be gone for days, but when he'd come back, I'd have a whole lot of new faces to count—big faces—Ben Franklins.

Before I knew it, I had been out for a year, and my birthday was rolling around. Anisa had spoken to Murder about throwing me a party, and although he wasn't really feeling the idea, he consented anyway. I was turning nineteen and feeling myself more than ever. The past year of my life had been amazing, and I couldn't wait to celebrate.

Murder rented out a tri-level loft in Brooklyn and invited the entire 'hood out to the affair. He even paid Young Jeezy to perform.

As I dressed for my big night, I oiled my body down and applied body shimmer before putting on a chocolate Fendi dress with gold braided straps that crisscrossed in the rear, revealing my toned back. My wide hips, flat stomach, and shapely behind had the dress hugging me precisely. My gold stiletto Zanotti's and gold matching clutch were the perfect accessories. The dress was short, and completely opposite of my normal attire. I was usually geared, always fresh with skinny jeans and a cute blouse or top with heels, but that night, I was getting my grown woman on from head to toe, leaving very little to the imagination. My hair was curled and hung down my back, while my makeup was professionally done and gave me a dramatic smoky look.

As I sat on the bed and fastened the ankle strap on my shoe, Anisa walked in. Her strut was runway flawless and her dress effortlessly sexy. "You look like a grown-ass woman, Mia," she complimented with a smile.

"I've been that, you didn't know?" I asked with a smile to match.

Anisa pulled a Tiffany box from behind her back and handed it to me. "Happy birthday, Miamor! I love you!"

I opened it and gasped at the diamond necklace and matching tennis bracelet. "Thank you, Anisa!" I said with a big hug.

Anisa laughed and replied, "I had to give you my gift first. Murder's gift to you is shitting all over mine."

"I highly doubt that." I put the necklace and bracelet on just as Murder knocked on the door. I didn't show it, but I was excited to see what my big bro, Murder had gotten me. I couldn't imagine that anything topping Anisa's gift though.

"It's time to—" he stopped mid-sentence and nodded his head in approval when he saw me, as if my appearance had taken him by surprise. "You look beautiful, sis. Happy birthday!"

"Thanks," I blushed. "Is it time to go?"

He nodded and held out his arm for me. I grabbed it and walked out with him, with Anisa trailing behind us. We were almost out the door when Murder's business line began to ring. He stopped mid-step.

"Murder, come on! Not tonight!" Anisa said, raising her eyebrows in annoyance.

"You're right," he said. He kissed her on the side of the cheek. "It's about Miamor tonight."

I let Anisa walk ahead and I whispered to Murder, "Go 'head and get it. I'll keep her on ice for you," I said, knowing that if Murder didn't answer the call, he would be thinking about the money he had missed for the whole night.

"Cool," he said almost as if he was relieved, and he rushed to the phone and picked it up.

I talked to Anisa on the way down to the car, and told her that he had to go use the restroom to distract her. Moments later, Murder came rushing down the stairs and caught up with us. He winked his eye at me to say thanks, and we got in his car and headed to the party.

We arrived at the club, and the line was out the door. It was ridiculous the amount of people who had come out. Undoubtedly, they weren't all there for me. I didn't fuck with anybody, and I had no friends besides my sister and Murder, but just the fact that the place was packed in my honor pleased me. We stepped out of the limo with a million eyes fixed on us. We bypassed the line and walked straight in, making our way to V.I.P. I felt like a celebrity, and I was all smiles, and so was Anisa.

Murder had an uncomfortable look on his face as he escorted us in. I could tell he was uncomfortable around all the people. His head was on a swivel, and his arm stayed tucked in his hoody, palming his pistol as we entered. That nigga never took a day off! He was always on his toes, and I had to respect it.

The entire place was decorated in turquoise and white. There were already bottles of Cris, Remy Louis XII Grand Cognac, and bottles of Mo spread out in ice buckets around my spot. The music was already at screaming level, and the party was going at full blast.

"If you need anything, let me know. I'ma watch the niggas handling my money at the door and make sure everything goes smoothly. You have a good time. This is all for you," Murder whispered in my ear.

I nodded, and we all sat down to get it cracking.

Murder frequently peeked into the main room and checked on us, and then he would head back to the front door. He didn't mingle at all. Instead, he sat back and watched me and Anisa do our thing.

I was walking through the party, the DJ plugging my name every few minutes making it known that I was the guest of honor. After that, I was shown mad love. Niggas were pinning money to my dress and buying me drinks, regardless of the fact that I had $500 bottles sitting on ice back at the table.

Anisa and I were doing it big, dancing and getting fucked up. I was nineteen and still a virgin, and the slew on fine niggas in the building had my hormones on fire. If I was a different type of chick, I would have had one picked out for the after party, but Anisa had already groomed me. Niggas treated you how you allowed them to, and I was never going to be anybody's a.m. jump off, so I kept my raging emotions at bay.

After circulating the building a couple times, I was about $3,000 richer from all of the birthday money niggas had given me. They were all trying to put their bids in to see who I was going to choose, but little did they know, I was going home alone. I didn't fuck with niggas who paid to play, because a bitch like me wasn't for sale.

I was tipsy, but Anisa was loaded. Niggas was really on her because she had the body of a goddess, and her dress was barely covering her ass. Her dress looked like it was sprayed on, and the bottom of her ass cheeks kept showing as she constantly had to pull down her dress to cover herself. It was all fun and games, until Anisa broke her own rule and became one of the drunken bitches in the club who ended up getting carried out. I noticed her stumble a little.

"Nis, are you okay?" I yelled, trying to be heard over the music.

She shook her head. "I need some air," she admitted.

I grabbed her hand and led her to the front entrance where Murder was. He saw me trying to keep Anisa balanced and rushed over to help me.

"What happened?" he asked.

"She had too much to drink," I explained, while trying to keep her steady. "Maybe we should just go. It's getting late anyway."

Anisa shook her head. "No, Miamor, it's your party. I just need to sleep this off. You stay and have a good time. I can take the limo back home. I'll be fine."

"Are you sure, Anisa? I don't mind coming with you," I replied.

"No, stay. The night isn't over yet," she said.

Murder helped her into the limo and tipped the driver to take her home and make sure she got into the condo safely, then turned his attention back to me. "You good?" he asked.

"I know how to handle my liquor," I said with a smile. "I learned from the best." I was referring to him, because he and I had gotten fucked up together plenty of times since I'd been home.

"Go have a good time. I'll be in shortly. We're closing the doors in a half an hour," he said.

I went back into the club and made my way to my table, but was detoured when I felt someone grab my hand. I turned around to the sexiest nigga I had ever seen in my life. No bullshit. His gray eyes penetrated mine and I smiled. "You're grabbing me like you know me or something," I said with an attitude as I snatched away flirtatiously.

He held my hand up, and I did a sexy half spin so he could admire what I had on.

Drake's latest hit came on, and we began to dance. The dude's hands felt good on my body, and I was beyond intoxicated. Any other day I probably would have smacked the shit out of him, but when my song came on, the liquor told me to make an exception. I was rocking my hips and grinding on him sexily, having a good time, until I felt somebody snatch me up. I looked up to see Murder glaring at the nigga.

"Is there a problem, my nigga?" the dude asked.

"I don't know. Is there?" Murder asked. The look of rage behind Murder's eyes surprised me, and told a story all their own.

The dude stepped back with his hands raised in surrender. "No disrespect, fam. I ain't know she was with you," he muttered. If he did have a chance with me, after seeing him bitch up so easily, he for damn sure didn't have one after that.

Murder snatched my ass all the way across the dance floor and into the back of the loft until we were in a quiet room.

"What the fuck? Murder, why are you tripping?" I asked.

"Don't make me fuck one of these niggas up, Miamor!" he said in an overprotective tone. "Nigga got his hands all over you!" He was yelling, and I had never ever seen him lose his temper. I was speechless. For the first time, I saw a look in his eyes that I had never seen before. I guess I *had* seen it before. It had been there all along, but this was the first time that I had acknowledged it. There was something in the air between us.

"We were dancing, that's it," I whispered. "It wasn't a big deal." We had spent so much time together before, yet this was the first time it felt awkward. My heart was racing and my palms were sweaty. I was nervous around him, not because I was afraid of him, but because I was afraid of the way he had me feeling. I didn't want him to be mad at me or to be disappointed in me. I cared a lot about what Murder thought of me. I left the room and chilled at my table, while Murder hugged the bar until the party was over.

After the entire place cleared out, Murder approached me with the last bottle of champagne in his hands. It had a red ribbon tied around it. "You have a good time?" he asked.

I nodded. "I did. You're too good to me," I said aloud. "I didn't mean to upset you earlier. It was innocent. You acted like I was fucking dude or something."

"I know, Miamor. I over reacted. I don't like the idea of a nigga disrespecting you. I will murder a nigga over you," Murder said sincerely as he looked me in my eyes. "Pop one last bottle with me?" he asked.

I nodded and gave him a half smile as he filled two champagne flutes. He popped the cork, causing champagne to spill over the top. “Happy birthday, Miamor!” he said. “To you!”

“To me!” I agreed as we raised our flutes.

One bottle turned into three as we laughed and conversed with one another. We were both toasted by the time we decided to leave. In my mind, I went over all of the times I had been around Murder. We had formed a bond with one another and it started out innocent, but as I sat across from him, I felt my heart beating furiously inside my chest. The feelings and thoughts I was having were far from right. They were not the feelings that one has for her big brother, but ones that a bitch had for a nigga she was trying to make her man. I was slowly admitting to myself that I was feeling him in a deeper way, and that fact was tearing me up on the inside.

He held out his hand and I followed him out of the loft. My heels echoed off of the concrete floor, and when I got outside, my mouth dropped open at the sight of a silver SL 550 Benz sitting there with a red bow wrapped around it. I turned around and looked at Murder. “This is my car?” I asked.

He smiled charmingly, and I already knew the answer.

“Oh my fucking God!” I yelled as I ran around to the driver’s side. The keys were already in the ignition, and I admired the custom leather seats and the wood grain dash. He stood outside, leaning on the back door as I explored every aspect of the car. I jumped out and hugged him tightly.

“Thank you . . . thank you . . . *thank you!*” I screamed excitedly. “This is too much!”

Murder grabbed my hands and intertwined his fingers with mine. Feelings of guilt instantly came back, because we were both letting the liquor cloud our judgment. He kissed my forehead, something that he had done many times before, but my body had never reacted like this. Butterflies fluttered in my stomach, and I felt like I had to throw up, while tiny darts of electricity awakened my southern lips. “Murder!” I whispered as I wrapped my hands around his neck.

“What up?” he asked in a low, raspy slur.

I stood on my tip toes and kissed his lips. I couldn’t help it. The voice in the back of my head that was telling me to stop was overpowered by my growing attraction to him.

Murder was my brother . . . literally. He was Anisa's man. Even the thought of he and I was wrong, but everything about his touch felt right, like his fingers were made exclusively for me. I was so lost in his embrace. He lifted me, his hands supporting my bottom as I wrapped my virgin legs around his back. I had an itch that I desperately needed scratched. I could smell the alcohol in the air, and I moaned as my head fell back in ecstasy as his tongue molested my neck.

Anisa's face popped into my mind, and almost simultaneously, Murder pulled away from me as if she had invaded his thoughts too. "Wait! Miamor, we can't," he said out of breath. "We can't do this, ma."

I could hear the disappointment in his voice. If we had met in another time or another place, then we would have been so right for each other, but we had not. He belonged to Anisa, and I loved her more than I loved myself. *How could I do this to her?* I thought as I instantly sobered up, the sting of betrayal causing my eyes to burn with tears as I wiped my lips in embarrassment. "I'm sorry," I said with a hint of sadness in my voice. "It should have never gone this far."

"I know," he agreed as he rubbed the top of his head. We both knew that we had just fucked up. "I know," he repeated.

"How do I tell my sister something like this? She will never forgive me," I whispered. "I'm so stupid."

Murder pulled me close and kissed the top of my head. "Don't worry about it, Mia."

I could not stop the tears from coming down my face. "She's going to hate me!" I cried hysterically.

"Shh! Miamor, Shh! Don't cry, ma. Your sister loves you. I heard about you every day before I ever laid eyes on you. You are all she talks about. She made me love you, Miamor, before I even knew who you were. We both made a big mistake. That's it. She doesn't have to know. I would never break her heart like that. We cannot let this happen again though. It's not meant to be."

It was the first time I had let anyone penetrate my heart, besides Anisa, and I did not like the sacrifice it took to love another person. Love costs too much. I learned on that day that it was sacrificial. In order to obtain it, I would have had to hurt someone else—more specifically Anisa—and that was something that I refused to do. My sister had endured enough pain in her lifetime. We both had. And although I yearned to know what happiness felt like, I refused to do it at her expense.

As we got into the car, I cried on the inside. This was one more emotional scar that I would have to deal with.

"Miamor?" Murder called as he ruffled my hair playfully. I knew that he was trying to switch the mood back to what it used to be—playful, brotherly and pure—but I moved my head away from him and didn't respond as I stared out of the window the entire ride home. I already told myself that any unnecessary interaction between us would have to stop. I had never been naïve. I knew that things would never go back to the way they used to be.

Chapter Five

Miamor

After my birthday, I avoided Murder at all costs. It wasn't "fuck you" between me and him. I could never hate him, It was more like, out of sight out of mind. As long as I wasn't in his presence, I would never have to deal with what we had done. So, when he was home, I made sure that I was gone, and it seemed like he was avoiding me too. While I used to see him every day, now I was lucky to see him once a week.

Anisa noticed the change in his presence, but she wasn't tripping. He was bringing in more money than a little bit, taking any and all business calls that came through for him, and as long as the paper trail didn't stop, Anisa did not give a damn if he laid next to her at night or not.

Despite our strained relationship, business did not stop, and he still had me count up his paper. He would drop it off on the inside of my door at night while I was asleep. In the morning, I would count it, write the total on a slip of paper and put it all in his safe. It was ridiculous how we were acting, but it was our reality at the time.

Lying in bed, I had not been able to sleep since my birthday. I felt so guilty over what had almost occurred between me and Murder. As I tossed and turned, I knew sleep would not come easy. I threw the covers off of my body and got out of the bed. My head was pounding, so I didn't bother to turn on the lights. I went into the kitchen and poured myself a glass of water.

On my way back to my room, I saw a silhouette sitting in the darkness on the couch. "Anisa?" I called out. I flipped on a light switch and saw her sitting there, anger written all over her face. "Why are you sitting in the dark? It's three o'clock in the morning."

"I'm waiting for Murder to get home," she replied coldly. "That mu'fucka cleared out his safe, and I want to know why. He's barely been here for the past three weeks, and now he moved his money. Ever since I've known him, I've always had access to his paper. He must have met some bitch who got him open, and I'm trying to find out what's up."

I was in shock. It wasn't even like Anisa to be talking like this. "So you think he's cheating? Anisa, his ass is not cheating on you," I defended him.

"I don't give a fuck about that nigga cheating. He can fuck the entire borough for all I care, but he's not about to be bank-rolling the lifestyle of these busted-ass hoes out here. I get the dough. Me, and only me. So when his ass comes through the door, he gon' have to explain to me why I opened up his shit today and the mu'fucka was on E," she said adamantly.

Anisa was livid, and before I could respond, Murder entered the condo.

"Where you been?" Anisa asked him. She got straight to the point, and from the look on Murder's face, I could tell she had caught him off guard.

"Fuck you mean, where I been?" he shot back. "You know what's up."

"Yeah, I do know what's up, and how you been acting lately ain't it. I went into your safe today, and guess what I found?" she asked. Anisa was on a roll because she didn't even give him a chance to answer. Her hands were on her hip and her neck was rolling while her mouth spouted words out like they were on fire. "Nothing, that's what I found. It was empty. Are you fucking with another bitch?"

"Anisa, you're wildin', ma. I don't got time for this shit," he dismissed casually. "I've got business I need to finish taking care of tonight."

"You always got business lately! You never used to hit the streets like this before, and when you were out, the safe was full, not empty! So, you cashing out the next chick now?" she asked.

I could see Murder getting upset, but he was trying to keep his composure. But like every woman does so well, Anisa knew how to push her man's buttons. "Look. I'm not fucking with another bitch, and you know better than to question how I move. I tried to wife you, Anisa. You said you didn't want that. You didn't want to take the risk, talking all that shit about me not being dependable and about you needing a nigga to change before you could commit. Now you in here making a scene in front of li'l mama? What you want me to tell you, Anisa? You know how I get down. Ain't shit changed. It's never been about another bitch. It's about business!" Murder reached into the duffel bag he was carrying and pulled out a thick wad of rubber banded money. "And since it's all about the money, here!" He tossed that shit in Anisa's face, then looked at her in disgust before walking out the door. "I'm out!" The door hit the hinges so hard that it shook the walls.

Anisa threw her hands in the air and screamed in frustration. "Fuck that! I know his ass is up to something!" She grabbed her keys off of the table and looked at me. "Put on your shoes and ride with me for a minute."

"What? Anisa, I'm not even dressed! Where are we going?" I asked, astonished at how far she was taking this.

"We're about to follow his ass," she declared.

I wanted to tell her no, because I knew that Murder was faithful to Anisa. He was never home because of me, but of course I couldn't tell her that. Anisa was tripping over money, making herself look like a real gold digger, and that wasn't even her personality. Murder always took care of home. Whatever reason he had for clearing the safe, I knew it was a good one.

"Come on, Miamor!"

I slipped a hoody on over my camisole and slipped into some skinny jeans. I stepped into my flip flops and was out the door. I had never seen my sister and Murder even disagree, so this full-fledged argument was so out of character for them both. I felt like I was the cause of it. Everything was fine before I made the stupid mistake of kissing Murder.

We slid into Anisa's Chrysler, and just as Murder pulled out of the parking lot, we tailed him, making sure we stayed at least a half block behind him at all times.

"Anisa, are you sure you want to do this?" I asked when I noticed us getting onto the bridge headed out of New York and into Jersey. The look she shot me told me to shut the fuck up and ride, so that's what I did, even though in my gut I knew that something about the entire situation did not feel right.

"You don't know Murder like you think you do, Miamor," Anisa said. "The nigga ain't the saint that he be trying to make himself out to be. You wanna know why you can't answer the phone in the house? The type of business he's into? The nigga is grimy, Miamor."

"He's a hustler, Anisa. He's never done you dirty. How can you say that?" I asked.

"Baby sister, open your eyes. He ain't a hustler. He's the one the hustlers call when they got a problem or when they need to make a problem disappear. He's a killer, Miamor. He would murk yo' ass if the money was good. Why the fuck you think his name is Murder?" Anisa stated harshly as she floored the gas pedal, trying to keep up with Murder.

A killer? I thought incredulously. *I'm around him all the time. How could I have not known? Why didn't he just tell me? I'm a big girl. I could've handled it.*

I was lost in my thoughts and couldn't picture the attentive man I had come to know killing anybody, but then the look of rage that I had witnessed in his eyes the night of my party flashed through my mind. *"I will murder a nigga over you!"* he had said. I could hear his words as if he was in my ear whispering them at that very moment. Syllable by syllable, the phrase replayed in my mind. At the time I thought he was being overprotective, but now I knew that he had meant every word he had spoken. It was something flattering about the fact that he would take a risk like that over me. Instead of feeling fear, I smiled, but quickly wiped it off my face so Anisa wouldn't take notice.

I felt the car jerk as she hit her breaks suddenly, and cut off her headlights. "There that nigga go right there. What the fuck is he doing way out here? He gone make me beat a bitch ass!" Anisa threatened. She was so blind with rage that she was not making sense.

As I looked around, I frowned. We were pulling onto a dead end street. There was nothing around us but old, abandoned buildings. "Anisa, I think you're taking this too far," I finally spoke up.

"I'm not trying to hear all that. All I know is if he's meeting a bitch here, I'm gon' fuck some shit up," she said.

I sighed and noticed lights approaching from behind

"Get down. Here comes somebody," she said.

We inched down in our seats until the car had passed us, and noticed that it was stopping directly next to Murder's vehicle. The brake lights came on, and somebody stepped out of the car. It was hard to see because all of the street lights were busted out in this part of town.

"I can't see shit," Anisa whispered. "Can you see who just got out of the car?"

"I can only see Murder," I replied.

"Fuck this!" Anisa said. She got out of the car and shouted, "Murder, what the fuck is going on?"

"Nigga, you trying to set me up?" I heard a man's voice yell out angrily.

I scrambled to turn on the headlights because I still couldn't see what was going on. Finally, I turned the lights on, illuminating the dead end.

Murder reached for his pistol, but before he could pull it from his waistline, the guy Murder had been meeting withdrew first, pointing a chrome .45 in Murder's face.

"No!" I heard Anisa scream as she ran toward the scene.

"Anisa!" I yelled after her as I got out of the car.

Murder rushed the dude who had to be twice his size, and his sneak attack caused the guy's gun to slide across the concrete.

"Murder!" Anisa cried out as she watched the two men tussle on the ground

Murder finally pulled his gun, but the dude wasn't giving up easily. He grabbed Murder's wrists and used his weight to his advantage as they struggled for power, both knowing that whoever ended up with the steel in their hands at the end was the only one leaving the scene alive.

Anisa ran straight into the confrontation, grabbing the guy by the shirt. He flung her to the ground and muscled the gun away from Murder.

I ran as fast as I could toward them. My flip flops came off halfway there and the gravel dug into the bottom of my feet as

I sprinted toward my sister. He had the gun pointed their way, but never saw me coming. I picked up a brick and smashed it against the side of his face with all my might. It was like an ant going against a giant, because although it dazed him, it didn't stop him from firing the gun. He slapped the shit out of me, sending me flying to the ground. I landed on my stomach, something hard digging into my side as I heard the gun shots ring out.

Boom! Boom!

"No!" I screamed. I felt Murder's gun directly underneath me and I grabbed it without thinking, and still lying on the ground, I scrambled backwards and fired.

Boom! Boom! Boom! Boom!

The dude dropped instantly and in the blink of an eye, and behind some beef that I did not even own, I'd caught my second body.

Flashes of Perry came back to me. I started to relive that nightmare all over again . . . Anisa's screams in my ear, the baby she had killed because of him . . . all of the sudden the man lying before me dying was Perry. The dude was scrambling, holding his stomach and choking on his own blood. Shakily, I stood to my feet, walked over to him, and put the gun to his head. I pulled the trigger again and again and again, until the click of an empty chamber forced me to stop, and his blood splatter covered my shirt.

"Oh my God! Oh my God!" Anisa yelled out. "I'm so sorry, Murder! I'm so sorry!"

I could hear sirens in my ears, but I couldn't force myself to move. My feet felt like they were made of cement.

"Miamor, help me . . . he's shot!"

I was in a daze. I heard Anisa calling my name, but it wasn't until I heard Murder call me that I snapped out of it. "Miamor!" he called out sternly. I turned my head, my chest heaving, tears in my eyes, and distress in my heart. "I need you, ma!"

His shirt was soaked in blood, and Anisa helped him to his feet. He cringed in pain as her hands searched his body. "Where are you hit?" she asked, the sirens getting clearer.

Murder lifted his shirt to reveal the vest he wore underneath. "It's just a shoulder wound," he stated. "Come on, we've got to get out of here," he said with urgency.

He led Anisa back to her car and put her in the passenger side. She was crying and kept apologizing over and over. "Get in the car, Anisa!" he yelled as he stuffed her inside and closed the door. He then came over to me. The sounds of the police were right around the corner now. I knew they would be here at any minute.

I looked up at Murder. "I shot him!" I whispered. My hands were shaking. The second murder of my life had not been as easy to commit as the first. This one shook me to the bottom of my soul. *Did he have kids? A wife? He was somebody's son. Did he deserve to die?* All of these things ran through my mind in a split second.

Murder put his hand on the side of my face. "I know what you're feeling, ma."

I couldn't look him in the face.

"Look at me," he said. "You did what you had to do. Now, I need you to get your head together and fast. I need you to get out of here. Take this gun and take care of it for me. Listen to me, Miamor, it's important." He grabbed my shoulders and stared at me intensely. "No weapons, no body, no murder. I need you to make that happen. I'm trusting you, li'l mama. I'll distract the police away from you."

"You're hurt! What about you? He's dead. They'll arrest you," I said as I shook my head.

"Just do it!" He pushed me inside the car and hit the top of the roof. "Drive, Miamor. Go now!"

I skirted out of the dead end and took off down the road as I watched him run back and get into his car. I made a right off of the dead end street just as a police car was pulling onto it. Then, Murder turned recklessly to the left and sideswiped the police car purposefully to get them to follow him.

"Oh my God! Miamor, they're going after him! Why did I do this? This is all my fault! That's not even me, Mia. I don't even do shit like this!" Anisa cried hysterically.

"Shut up, Anisa!" I yelled. "What's done is done. You have to calm down. I have to get rid of this gun, and we need to lay low. I can't think with you in my ear with all that crying."

Anisa sat back in her seat and muffled her cries, while I found myself driving back into the city. I worried about going across the bridge and paying the toll. I was paranoid. If by some chance the police had gotten the plate number on Anisa's car, then they would be waiting for us for sure. If the car got searched, then it would be a wrap, because the murder weapon was under my seat with my prints all over it.

When I came to the toll, I felt like my heart was going to explode. I was sweating, my face was swollen from being slapped to the ground, and I knew I looked a mess. The worker didn't even look my way as she took my money and allowed me to enter New York.

"Where are we going?" Anisa asked.

"I have to do something," I replied quietly. "It's important." I found myself driving to Queens, to the pawnshop that Murder had taken me to when I first got out. I was surprised that I remembered where it was, but instinct led me there. He had told me to get rid of the gun. This is the only way I knew how to.

It was too early for the pawnshop to be open, so we waited. Anisa eventually fell asleep, but I couldn't. Not after everything that had gone down. I was wide awake and more afraid than I had ever been. The moon disappeared as the sun kissed the city streets and welcomed a new day. Hours had passed, and when I finally saw the owner approach the pawnshop, I jumped out of the car and met him at the front door.

"I need your help," I said frantically.

He looked at me curiously, probably wondering what hell I'd been through since my face was bruised and there was still blood all over me. "Murder sent me. I need to get rid of a gun."

The older man nodded and ushered me inside, then locked the door behind us. I put the gun on the counter the same way I had seen Murder do months before.

"It's five hundred each gun," he said.

"I don't have any money," I admitted.

"I'm not running a charity, girl. Five hundred is my price," he stated.

I held the car key to Anisa's whip in my hand. I held it up for him. "Take the car."

"For a five hundred dollar debt you are giving me a brand new car?" the man asked suspiciously.

"Look!" I yelled in desperation. "I need to get rid of this gun. I don't give a fuck about the car. How much is the car worth?"

"I'll give you ten grand for it," the man stated.

"Fine. Give me nine thousand, five hundred dollars and make this gun disappear," I settled.

He nodded, and I followed him to the basement where the barrels of acid were located. After watching the gun dissolve in the acid, I felt relieved.

"You need anything else?" he asked, and motioned toward the wall of guns and weapons.

I nodded. After what I had just done, I didn't want to be caught slipping. I had no idea what type of repercussions would come from my actions, and I wanted to be prepared. "Give me something small."

The old man pulled a small black .25 from the wall. "How does that feel in your hands?" he asked.

I gripped the tiny handgun and nodded my head in approval. "I'll take it."

I rushed out of the shop to find Anisa waiting anxiously in the car.

"Get out," I instructed.

"What do you mean, get out? What's happening?" she looked terrible. Her eyes were bloodshot from crying and she had bags full of worry.

"I sold your car," I said.

"What?" she exclaimed.

"Nis, this car can be traced back to that murder scene. It's not worth it." I split the money I had left with her. "We'll take the subway back home. We need to wait to hear from Murder."

"How did you know where to go to get rid of the gun?" she asked.

I stopped walking and turned toward her. "Murder taught me," I replied.

Chapter Six

Back to the Cartel

Carter sat inside the Diamond Estate . . . his father's home . . . now his home, and sighed in angst from his current circumstance. He had been released from jail just weeks before because the prosecutor's star witness, Ace, suddenly had a change of heart. Carter smiled, knowing that Mecca and Zyir had came through for him and got him off the hook. Now that he was out, he had more important things on his mind instead of prison. Mecca sat across from him, cautiously watching Carter.

Both men were silent, each with a different pain in his heart. The war with the Haitians had been won, but at what cost? They both felt like they had given up too much in order to win. Yes, they still had control of the city, but everything that really mattered in life had been destroyed. Their family had been dismantled all for the sake of power.

"Where is she, fam?" Carter asked aloud as he opened and closed the black velvet ring box that contained the engagement ring that he had planned to give to Miamor. It had been months and he hadn't heard from her. As soon as he was arrested, Miamor had disappeared, and although he could deal with the thought of incarceration and he could handle all of the risks that came with the game, he could not fathom the idea of never seeing her again. He could see her face, her smile, her eyes, as if she had been by his side just yesterday. She was on his brain constantly, and as long as he was unaware of her whereabouts, he would not be able to concentrate on anything else. She was important to him . . . the only thing he had left to keep him sane. She was the woman who was supposed to be his wife and bear his children. *How could she just walk away?* He thought grimly. The thought angered and saddened him at the same time.

Mecca stopped himself from smirking. *Look at this love-sick ass nigga!* he fumed. He was tired of Carter sulking over Miamor. He didn't feel a need to tell Carter of Miamor's deception. He had handled that beef personally, and now that she was out of the picture, he was completely satisfied. He had avenged the deaths of his mother and sister. Although vengeance had come at the expense of Carter's heart, he knew that in time Carter would move on with his life.

"Nigga, you need to take them blinders off when it comes to that bitch," Mecca stated harshly. "She left you stinking. You haven't seen or heard from her since the day you were knocked. She was probably a Fed or something. Forget about her. Grimy-ass bitch was playing a role to get you caught up. You took the bait. It happens to the best of us."

Mecca's words made Carter's heart throb in agonizing pain. The thought of Miamor's betrayal was too heavy a burden for him to carry. "Maybe you're right, bro," he said with doubt.

"Nigga, I am right. That bitch got you around here fucked up. You a clean nigga. She got you growing beards and shit," Mecca joked, making light of the situation. "You need to be thinking about keeping the Feds off your doorstep. Just because that snitch nigga, Ace is in the wind don't mean you're in the clear. The government doesn't lose often. You walking free is an embarrassment to them. They're not done with you yet, so we need to be prepared for whatever they have planned. After your freedom's guaranteed, the rest will fall into place."

Carter nodded, knowing that Mecca was speaking the truth. He was focused on all the wrong things. His life was hanging in the wings, and he needed to be at his best in order to overcome the odds that were stacked against him.

Mecca stood. "I'm outta here, fam. I'll get with you later. I won't be making too many more trips to this side of town coming to check on you. I still got issues left unsettled," he said, reminding Carter of his unfinished business with Emilio Estes.

"Keep a body with you at all times," Carter said with authority. "Don't be on that Superman shit, Mecca. You can't go against the Dominican mafia alone."

Mecca lifted his shirt with one hand, revealing a .380 snub chrome 9 mm, and a .45 tucked against his rock hard abdomen. "Fuck another nigga! I got my bitches lined up right here," Mecca replied arrogantly. "They won't catch me slipping again."

Carter nodded. "I hear you. Be smart and be careful," he said.

Carter arose and walked around the immaculate mansion. The gray sweats and white T-shirt he wore were very uncharacteristic of him. The fear of the unknown had him out of his element, and he spent his days confined to the house, his thoughts of Miamor driving him insane. He had everything in the world that a man could want—power, money, luxury, but without her, it all held no value. He would easily give it all up to be with her, and had thought that her love for him ran just as deep.

Pouring himself a glass of Remy VSOP, he made his way over to the picturesque window that overlooked the front of the estate. A cable van sat on the street, undoubtedly filled with federal agents who were monitoring his home, trying to build a new case on him. He wouldn't give them the ammunition they needed to send him away. Prison wasn't for him. He'd send them to their graves before they shipped him back to prison. He opened the door and walked outside. He acknowledged his armed workers with head nods as he carried the glass of cognac in his hand. Fifty men surrounded the estate, all fully aware of everything and everyone around them, but no one was allowed to enter his home, with the exception of Mecca and Zyir. Carter made his way to the gate and nodded for his keeper to open it. He walked to the edge of the street to retrieve his daily newspaper. A huge picture of his face covered the front page:

Drug Kingpin Carter Jones Walks Free.

The cable truck was not even five feet away from him. He smirked and held up the paper for the Feds to see, then he approached the van. "Good morning, gentlemen," he greeted when he finally reached the driver's side.

"We've been made," he heard an agent whisper from the back. The driver of the van watched him with cold eyes.

"Of course you've been made. Look up and down this street," Carter said. "Cable vans don't quite fit in with hundred thousand dollar cars."

His arrogance and power intimidated even the highest of the law. He could see that he made them nervous. It takes a wolf to catch a wolf. Carter was one man who would not be easy to get to. They were playing out of their league, and their amateur tactics of surveillance proved that.

"Step away from the vehicle, Mr. Jones," the driver commanded.

Carter smiled at the officer's attempt to be dominant, but the tremble in his voice revealed his cowardice. "Not a problem, but I would like to see your badge. Since it's obvious that you'll be guests in front of my home, I need to be sure you are who you say you are . . . you understand," Carter answered sarcastically.

The federal agent removed his badge and handed it to Carter. Carter inspected it with the same hand he held his drink in, then passed it back. He tapped the inside of the driver door. "Agent Marshall," he said as he smiled and walked away. Carter had slyly slipped a transparent audio device, no larger than a small piece of tape, onto the back of the agent's badge, and also one on the inside of the van. *Idiot mu'fuckas!* he thought to himself as he entered back onto his property and disappeared inside his home. They thought that they were watching him, but now he would know exactly what they were saying. He would always be one step ahead of them now that he had infiltrated their operation. The listening device had a radius of 100 miles, and wherever that badge went, Carter's ears would follow. *I'll even hear you fucking your wife at night,* he thought.

Carter rubbed the abundance of hair on his face and thought, *Mecca is right. I need to get my shit together and stay focused.*

***

Breeze whimpered weakly as a cold sweat drenched her body and chills stiffened her spine. Her light skin was a sickly bluish tint, and she was barely strong enough to lift her head. Ma'tee had tried to stop the poison from spreading, but his home remedies were useless, and the medicine he had given her had no effect on her condition. Breeze's foot was swollen and the skin directly around the spider bite was black. The red streaks going up her leg was a clear indication that the poison was spreading. If she didn't get medical treatment in a matter of days, she would be dead. "Water!" she whispered desperately as Ma'tee jumped at her every beck and call. The tender way in which he touched her revealed his growing obsession. He was crazy over her. In his mind, no one loved her more than him. He would die before he gave her back. Breeze was the only thing he had left in this world, and he imprisoned her so that she would only be his. She was too beautiful for anyone else to see, too delicate for anyone else to touch. She belonged to him.

He could not see it, but his possession over her was slowly causing her sanity to abandon her. She did not have the strong Diamond will that the rest of her family possessed. Her eyes were empty as if her soul was now gone. She had lost all hope, and as she looked up at the man who had taken her away from everyone she loved, she cried. She didn't have the strength to fight anymore. She was his slave in every sense of the word. He had taken her body, her mind, and her spirit, and trapped them in Haiti. Even if she did ever make it out alive, she would never be the same. Things could never go back to the way they used to be. She had endured too much. Psychologically, she was ruined. Emotionally, she was drained. Physically, she was raped. The lovely young woman that Breeze used to be did not exist anymore. Only Ma'tee had the key to set her free, and she knew that would never happen.

Breeze began to cough violently and bile flew from her mouth, her body desperately trying to get rid of some of the venom that was slowly killing her.

Ma'tee sat near her bedside and applied ice to her wound and a cold wet towel to her forehead to try and lower her fever. Her temperature was dangerously high, yet she felt so cold that she shivered. He desperately tried to bring Breeze's health back up to par, but the more days that passed, the worse she became. He wasn't ready to let her go. He refused to lose her, even to death, so his only alternative was to take her to the only doctor in town. Ma'tee knew that he was taking a big risk by taking Breeze to town, but if he wanted her to live, then he had to.

He stood to his feet and looked around at all of the Polaroid pictures he had taken of Breeze. They covered the walls, almost entirely constructing his very own wallpaper of lunacy. They were his masterpiece. "So beautiful!" he whispered. The photos chronicled her time in Haiti. Her smileless face and hateful expressions went unnoticed by him. He was delirious to think that he loved her. The misery and fear that he was causing her was evident on her face in every photograph. He went upstairs to retrieve his gun, rummaging through his kitchen drawers until he found bullets to load it with. He was unsure about taking her to town, but his hand was forced. He did not have a choice.

Ma'tee returned to her side. "Me princess," he said as he stroked her face with the nose of his gun.

Breeze turned her head in disgust, causing her to vomit even more.

"Me am going to take you to town to see de medical doctor, but chu have to promise not to run. Me run de entire city. If chu say one word to anybody, me will kill chu, young Breeze. Chu understand?"

Breeze did not respond. Hot tears had dried on her ashen face.

"Do chu understand?" Ma'tee asked again.

Breeze nodded her head and felt Ma'tee lift her from the bed. The feel of his hands on her body made her cringe as he carried her to the back of his mansion and into the thick of the jungle. The average person would become lost in the jungle-filled mountain terrain, but Ma'tee had grown up here. He navigated the area well, and knew the dangers that lay underneath the deceiving appearance of the land. Even the most beautiful flower could be deadly.

Breeze tried her hardest to remember the path that Ma'tee took, so that she would know the way to town, but she was so weak and everything looked the same.

"Chu will never remember de way," he said as if he was reading her mind. "So stop trying."

They came to a clearing where a green Hummer sat covered in a tarp that was disguised by brush and leaves. Ma'tee sat Breeze down on the ground and removed the large tarp, then placed her in the passenger seat.

There's a car here, she thought. *I have to remember how to get back to this spot,* she told herself.

Ma'tee started the Hummer and rode the rough terrain the rest of the way down the mountain, navigating the deadly path like an expert, until he reached the town below.

For the first time in months, Breeze saw other faces besides Ma'tee's as they passed some of the townspeople, but her health was fading. Everything appeared blurry, and the pain radiating through her body was becoming unbearable.

Ma'tee drove with one hand on his gun and the other on his steering wheel. "Remember what me told chu," he instructed as the car finally stopped moving.

He attempted to carry her out of the car, but she fought him, pushing him off of her. "Don't touch me! I'll walk!" she screamed in frustration. She shook like a leaf in a strong wind as she stepped out of the car, but she was determined to not have his hands on her in public. However, when she put weight onto her poisoned foot, her body came crashing down like a house of cards.

"Stop fighting me and let me help chu," Ma'tee whispered the words, but it sounded more like a demand as he bent down and scooped her up in his arms.

She had lost a considerable amount of weight and was light as a feather. Against her will, her head fell onto his chest and she looked up at her captor. It was the first time she had ever looked directly at Ma'tee, and his heart melted into her grey eyes. "Please, let me go!" she pleaded.

"I can never do that, my princess. Once you learn to love me, your life will be filled with riches," he promised. He carried her into the doctor's office and rushed over to the receptionist's desk. "Please, help me! Me daughter was bitten by a black widow and is extremely sick!"

The receptionist took one look at Breeze and stood to her feet in a panic. "Doctor!"

The most beautiful woman Breeze had ever seen came rushing out of the back. "Oh my!" she exclaimed at Breeze's condition. "Please, put her over here . . . hurry!" Ma'tee rushed and placed Breeze on a stretcher. The doctor began to wheel her to the back of the office while Ma'tee followed closely behind.

"No, please sir, chu need to wait up front and let me do me job. Me will take care of she," the doctor reassured. "Me receptionist has paperwork for chu to fill out. Me will keep chu updated."

Ma'tee's eyes shifted from the doctor to Breeze as he became nervous. He had not planned on leaving Breeze's side. He nodded and said, "Can I just speak to me daughter for one moment?"

The doctor nodded and Ma'tee walked over to Breeze. "Me will kill chu!" he said as he wrapped his hands around her tiny neck. He applied pressure and leaned over her so that the doctor could not see what he was doing. He had killed many men in his lifetime, and he knew that there was a delicate balance between death and unconsciousness.

Breeze felt her oxygen being cut off, and she wanted to struggle, but her body felt so heavy. The poison was rendering her helpless.

"If chu say a word, me will kill chu."

Those were the last words she heard before she went unconscious. Ma'tee had cut off her air supply long enough to knock her out without killing her. He hoped she would stay that way until the doctor would allow him to be by her side again. He turned to the doctor in panic. "She's passed out! Please help she!" he whispered as he wiped tears from his eyes.

"It's de poison. It's shutting down her nervous system. Why didn't chu get help sooner?" the doctor asked.

Ma'tee played the grieving father well. He acted as if he was so choked up that he couldn't respond.

"Me will do all me can," the doctor said before taking Breeze and disappearing behind two double doors.

Ma'tee paced back and forth in the waiting area for two hours. He kept watching the clock, each minute taunting him and threatening to expose him. Finally, the doctor emerged through the double doors.

"How is she?" Ma'tee asked.

"She will be fine, with medicine and rest," the doctor replied.

"Can me see her?" he asked.

The doctor shook her head. "Not right now. She is still asleep. We have her in a sterile recovery room. Me cannot allow chu back there and risk infection. When she awakens, me will come get chu."

Ma'tee sat down impatiently, his leg bouncing in anticipation as he watched the doctor disappear into the back once more.

Breeze's eyes were so heavy that she could barely open them. Flashes of white light sneaked through her closed lids as she slowly came out of the anesthesia. Her head was groggy, and she could barely remember where she was, but when she closed her eyes, it all came rushing back to her like a bad dream: The jungle; the spider bite; the doctor. Every detail was fuzzy, but it was all slowly coming back to her. *I'm at the doctor's office. I have to get out of here before Ma'tee comes for me,* she thought. It took all of her might to roll onto her side. Her neck felt as if she were a newborn baby. She couldn't support her head and her vision was blurry. *Get up!* she urged herself. *Get up!* There was an IV in her arm. She snatched at it. She was so weak that she could barely get the needle out of her arm. Forcing herself to sit up, she stood on wobbly legs which caused excruciating pain to shoot up the right side of her body. She shook her head from side to side trying to clear her vision, and saw that she had an incision that ran down the length of her leg, and that her foot was bandaged. The anesthetic hadn't completely worn, off and it was hard for her to stay focused. Her limbs were so lazy, every move she made exhausted her, but she fought the urge to lie back down.

The ringing of a phone snapped her to attention. *I have to get to that phone,* she thought. Breeze was in a state of emergency. This was her only shot to reach out to her family. She knew that if she didn't make it to that phone, she could kiss everything she ever knew good-bye.

She forced herself to stand on her injured foot. She wanted to scream at the pain that she felt when she was fully standing, but instead, she closed her eyes and took deep breaths until the blinding ache died down and she was able to move. The excruciation kept her alert as she used the objects in the room to help her toward the door. "Where is the phone?" she whispered to herself. She stuck her head into the hallway. She could see the double doors that led to the lobby. Behind them was Ma'tee, lurking, preying on her. Her heart rate increased from the fear of seeing his face again.

Desperation and adrenaline filled her as she put her back against the wall and crept to the next room. She opened the door and frantically scanned for a phone. "Thank you, God!" she cried as she rushed toward it. Moving too quickly, she fell. "Aghh!" she accidentally cried out as her leg hit the floor. She covered her mouth to stop herself from making too much noise. Tears flooded her face as she reached for the phone. The dial tone she heard was like music to her ears. Her fingers trembled as she tried to dial out, causing her to call the wrong number, 810. *Shit! What is his number?* Her mind was so frantic that she could barely recall the correct sequence, 1-810-625-1816.

She could hear footsteps coming down the hallway, and she cradled the phone for dear life. *Please answer! Come on, please pick up!*

Ring! Ring!

Answer! she begged as the footsteps drew closer.

Please, I need you . . .

Ring! Ring!

Zyir bobbed his head to the Rick Ross that was blaring from his speakers, when he felt his cell phone vibrate on his hip. He was on his way back from Opa-locka, and he had a quarter million dollars in his trunk and rode with a pistol in his lap for extra security. He turned down the stereo and looked at the unknown call coming in on his BlackBerry. "Yo?" he answered.

All he heard was crying in the phone, and he started to end the call thinking that someone had the wrong number.

"Zy . . . Zyir!" the shaky voice said.

He recognized her voice instantly. Emotions came rushing over him. "Breeze?" he whispered in disbelief as his heart sank into his stomach.

Breeze was so hysterical when she heard him answer the phone that she couldn't get her words together. Every time she tried to speak, only sobs came out.

"Breeze, talk to me, ma! Calm down! Where are you? You've got to tell me where you are!" she heard him yell.

Just the sound of his voice caused her to fall apart. "Zyir!" she whispered frantically. "Zyir, please . . ." were the only words she was able to get out before the footsteps were at the door. She hurried and pushed the telephone underneath the bed, but didn't disconnect the call.

The door opened, and a confused doctor rushed inside. "What are chu doing in here? Chu should still be in recovery," she said.

"Please, Zyir . . . I have to talk to Zyir!" Breeze pleaded with the doctor, but she was quickly silenced when she heard Ma'tee demanding to see her. The heavy impact from his boots echoed against the hospital floor, announcing his presence. "Don't let him take me!" Breeze cried as she looked the doctor in her eyes.

The doctor could see the frightened look on Breeze's face, and she instantly knew that something was not right.

When Ma'tee appeared in the doorway, the doctor looked from Breeze to Ma'tee.

"Is everything okay back here?" he asked.

His voice was eerie and threatening. Breeze's fear of him was so great that she felt like she was having a heart attack.

She couldn't stop herself from crying. Zyir was so close. She had heard his voice. *I just needed a few more minutes to tell him where I am,* she thought as she sobbed.

"Everything is fine," the doctor answered nervously. She helped Breeze into the bed and lifted her leg. "She is in a lot of pain, and I haven't administered her any pain medications yet. This type of pain will make a grown man cry. It is not unusual."

"Me need to get her back home. She can recover there," Ma'tee asserted. His tone did not leave room for protest, and he came into the room and sat next to Breeze who trembled timidly from his presence. Ma'tee examined her closely, intimidating her.

The doctor could sense tension in the air. She rubbed Breeze's shoulders. "The anesthesia has she temperature low," the doctor said, covering for Breeze.

Breeze wasn't shaking because she was cold. She was angry. She was terrified. She was praying that Zyir had not hung up his phone and that he could somehow save her.

The doctor looked Breeze directly in the eyes and said, "Everything will be fine. "I'm going to get discharge papers for you to sign, young lady. Me will be right back," she said.

The doctor disappeared, and Ma'tee sat down directly on the bed with her. The smell of him nauseated her and made her skin crawl. He didn't say a word to her, but instead stared at her intensely, trying to determine whether or not she had told anyone anything.

Breeze closed her eyes and thought of Zyir. She recalled his face in her mind, and forced herself to calm down.

The doctor reentered the room. "Oh, please sir. You can wait in the hallway while she dresses. Me will help she, and then get chu de medicine she needs. She will be fine," the doctor said.

Ma'tee reluctantly left the room, but he made sure to watch through the peephole at the top of the door.

The doctor handed Breeze a clipboard. Her hands shook, because something told her that this young girl was in grave danger. She knew who Ma'tee was. Everyone in Haiti knew who he was and what he was capable of. The doctor did not want to get involved out of fear of being hurt herself.

Breeze cried as she took the pen. She wrote her first and last name on the clipboard, and then jotted a quick note.

> *Please help me! Call this number, 1-810-625-1816. Tell him I am alive. I'm trapped somewhere in the mountains. Please!*

Breeze dressed slowly, and then Ma'tee whisked her away from the doctor's office and back up to captivity.

Chapter Seven

The Cartel

"Breeze!" Zyir screamed into the phone as he strained to hear the conversation on the other end of the line. He could barely hear what was going on, but he knew that it was her. He felt it in his gut. She had only said his name, but she was the only person who had the ability to say it so sweetly. "Breeze! Pick up the phone!" he yelled. Tears came to his eyes when the call was disconnected. His heart was beating so rapidly that he had to pull the car over. He hit his steering wheel in frustration. She had called him. He didn't know where she was or why it had taken her so long to reach out to him, but she was alive, and he had to find her. He picked up his phone and speed-dialed Young Carter.

"Zy, how that money looking out in—" Carter started to speak, but Zyir interrupted him.

"She's alive, fam! Breeze is alive, man!" Zyir stated, getting choked up. After months of her death haunting him, his faith was restored. Breeze had been the only chick who had been able to steal Zyir's focus away from his hustle. He had nightmares about her death every night. He felt responsible for what had happened to her, but now he was sure that she was out there somewhere, and out of all the people she could have called, she chose him.

His statement took Carter by surprise. "Zyir, fam, Breeze is . . ."

"Carter, she called me! She called my fucking phone! She's alive! I'm on my way to you!" he screamed urgently.

"I'm not at home. I'm leaving my barber now. We don't need to meet at the house. Feds are crawling all over the place.

Meet me at Mecca's money house. I'll give him a call," Carter answered.

Zyir's stomach was hollow as he raced toward Liberty City where Mecca stashed the drugs and money that he distributed and collected from the Lib City hustlers. He beat both Mecca and Carter there. He scoped the entire block, removed the money he was transporting, and with the duffel bag in one hand and his pistol in the other, he entered the home. He quickly opened the safe and stuffed the money inside. Carter's rule was to count the cash before putting it away, but Zyir's head was all over the place. He didn't give a fuck about anything or anyone but Breeze.

He paced the living room floor, trying to play back the pieces of conversation he had heard on the phone. "Where is she?" he mumbled to himself. "Think. What did you hear?" he said over and over.

Zyir was driving himself crazy. He was so deep in thought that he didn't even hear Carter come in. Mecca walked in directly behind Carter and they watched as Zyir talked to himself. Carter noticed the worried look on Zyir's face. He had seen Zyir sell crack to his own mother and not bat an eye. He knew his li'l nigga through and through. The look of concern that Zyir held was the same one that Carter felt inside for Miamor. It was then that he knew Zyir's love for Breeze ran deeper than anyone knew.

"Zyir," Carter called out, startling him.

"Fuck is up with you, fam?" Mecca asked.

"Breeze . . . she's still alive," Zyir stated.

A look of anger flickered in Mecca's eyes, and he pointed his finger sternly toward Zyir. "Don't speak her name, nigga. You didn't even know her like that. After eight months, you talking about she's alive!" Mecca said, becoming emotional over his baby sister.

"Fuck you! Bitch-ass nigga!" Zyir yelled back. He didn't give a fuck. He knew Mecca was a killer, but Zyir had been taught to only fear a nigga who didn't bleed. "I just told you your sister is alive! Whether you want to believe it or not, she's out there, and I'm gon' find her!"

Mecca's hands automatically rested on his waistline for easy access to his burner, but he had to remember that Zyir was family now. That fact alone kept Zyir breathing after disrespecting Mecca, but he was skeptical, and his doubt showed on his face. "She's been gone eight months," Mecca stated sadly.

"She called me!" Zyir yelled.

"She called you?" Mecca answered. "How the fuck you know it ain't one of these lurking-ass mu'fuckas trying to throw you off and set you up? Huh? Why the fuck would she call *you?*"

Carter watched the exchange back and forth as he attempted to figure out where Zyir's logic was coming from. Zyir had never given him a reason to doubt him before, and he was slowly beginning to recall all the time that Zyir and Breeze had spent together.

"It wasn't nobody else. I know her voice, mu'fucka. She called me. She was crying and she said my name. I'm her man, and she needs me! I have to find her, and I'll murk any nigga who tries to stop me!" Zyir said through clenched teeth as he looked Mecca directly in the eyes. Zyir was an emotional wreck. Breeze was still alive, he would put his life on it, and he was willing to go against a thousand armies to get her back. She had been out there alone and vulnerable for eight months, while The Cartel had buried her and moved on.

Seeing Zyir's conviction brought tears to Mecca's eyes, which he quickly brushed away as he felt his anger rise. He wanted to shoot Zyir's ass in the foot for fucking around with his little sister in the first place, but he was glad that she had chose a nigga who was built right, one who was willing to go to the ends of the earth because of a phone call. Breeze had chosen a li'l nigga who Mecca thought their father would have approved of. Mecca nodded his head and looked at Carter, who sat there calmly, grinding his jaw, a clear indication that he was angry.

"We buried her. We counted her out, and she's been out there all this time," Zyir said.

"What did you hear?" Carter asked.

"It was muffled, but it sounded like she was talking to a doctor," Zyir replied.

"Check the hospitals . . . every hospital in the state if you have to," Carter instructed to Zyir. "Mecca, you too, but stay out of Florida. Estes is still on your ass. He's lying low, but that don't mean he's gone. You check hospitals in Georgia and Alabama, and even go as far as Mississippi if nothing shakes. If she's out there, we won't stop until we bring her home. If anyone hears anything, let me be the first to know."

Mecca left in search of his baby sister. It had been a long time since he'd prayed, but for this, he closed his eyes and asked God for help. When he was gone Carter turned to Zyir.

"Why did she call you?" Carter asked. He already knew the answer, but he wanted to see if Zyir would keep it one hundred with him.

Zyir rubbed the top of his head, his eyebrows raised in distress. "I was fucking with her, fam," Zyir admitted.

Carter stood sternly. "And the day she was taken?" Carter asked.

"She was with me," Zyir admitted.

Carter nodded his head.

Zyir could see the fire blazing in his demeanor, but out of respect, he held his tongue.

Carter began to walk out of the house and stopped at the doorway. "Find her," he said simply, then left Zyir to his thoughts.

Zyir searched high and low, visiting hospitals, spending every minute of his day looking for Breeze. He doubted that she was still in the city. He couldn't imagine her being so close for this long without word getting back to The Cartel. He started in the surrounding cities. From Palm Beach to Tampa to Orlando and Ft. Lauderdale, he drove for hours, fighting fatigue on a desperate mission to find her. He had a list of over 100 hospitals in Florida. He called some to see if they had any patients who fit Breeze's description. If there was even a possibility that a patient could be her, then Zyir hit the highway.

After ten hours of disappointments, he had exhausted every hospital on the list, except for the local Miami institutions. He decided to visit Baptist Hospital first.

A tight knot filled his stomach as he whipped his Lexus through the city streets. He was tired, but he couldn't call it a night. He didn't have time to sleep. The thought of Breeze suffering somewhere would not allow him to stop his hunt. He had heard the fear in her voice. Wherever she was, she was in danger and she was defenseless. Every time he closed his eyes, he imagined the terror she may be going through.

Little did he know, he could not fathom what she was being forced to endure. Her fate was worse than death. Her torture was unimaginable.

Zyir pulled into the emergency room parking lot and jumped out. He walked into the hospital. Doubt and apprehension ate away at him as he approached the nurse's station.

"Can I help you, sir?" a young black girl asked without looking up from the paperwork in front of her.

"I'm looking for a girl who may have been treated here. Her name is Breeze Diamond," Zyir stated.

At the mention of the last name "Diamond", the girl looked up. Her eyes scanned Zyir from head to toe. She instantly knew he was a part of The Cartel. Everything about Zyir screamed power, and his swagger made her wet instantly. The young nurse had never had the pleasure of being this close to one of The Cartel's members. She had only heard about their prestige because their reputation rang loudly in every 'hood in Florida. The last name Diamond was associated with money in the city of Miami, but it was an exclusive club, and not everyone had access to them. *Today must be my lucky day,* she thought as she ogled him from head to toe. She put the tip of a pen in her mouth seductively, obviously vying for his attention.

Zyir's patience was non-existent at this point. He was immune to her flirtation. "Look, bitch, I don't got time for all that extra shit. Type in the name and see if she's here," he said crudely without ever raising his voice.

An embarrassed expression appeared on the girl's face as she turned toward the computer. "Breeze Diamond," the girl repeated as she typed the name. She shook her head. "She wasn't treated here. There is no record of a Diamond being admitted."

Zyir massaged his jaw line and hit the desk in frustration, causing the girl to jump. His red eyes were filled with worry. "Look, I need to find her. She's young, light skinned, long curly hair . . . she has a small mole on the side of her neck and a scar on her collarbone. She may not be here under her name. I just need you to check to see if there's anybody here that fits her description. Please!" Zyir said desperately. "It's important!"

The nurse could sense his agony and nodded her head. "Okay. You can have a seat. I'll check."

Zyir sat down with his head in his hands. Minutes passed, but it felt like time was frozen still.

"Sir?" the nurse called to him.

He rushed over to the desk.

"We have a Jane Doe here. She came in a few months ago with no ID, and no one has been here to claim her yet. You can take a look to see if it's who you're looking for," the nurse stated with sympathy.

"Thank you, ma," Zyir stated as he followed her to the elevator and down a long hallway. Zyir breathed deeply. *Please, let this be her!* he said in his mind.

The nurse stopped in front of a room. "I just want to warn you, she's in pretty bad shape. There are injuries to her face and body," the nurse warned.

Zyir wiped his nose and nodded his head to prepare himself for what he was about to see. The nurse opened the door. The room was dark, and the sound of machines beeping was all that could be heard. He stepped closer to the bed, and when the lights turned on, he gasped in shock.

"Is this her?" the nurse asked.

Zyir was at a loss for words as he stared at the woman before him. She was barely recognizable. She looked as if she was hanging onto her life by a thread. He shook his head and backpedaled out of the room. "No, it's not her," he said. He rushed out of the hospital and immediately dialed Carter's number. It was two o'clock in the morning, but it was a phone call that could not wait.

"Hello?" Carter answered groggily.

"Fam, it's me," Zyir said.

"Did you find her?" Carter asked.

"Carter, I found your girl. I found Miamor!"

Carter entered the hospital with an entourage of twenty men behind him. Members of The Cartel guarded all entrance and exit points of the building, shutting it down. No one was allowed to enter or exit the premises. Zyir and a select few of Carter's most efficient workers followed him up to the fifth floor where Miamor was located. The same nurse who had assisted Zyir jumped up from her post when she saw the men enter the building. "Excuse me. It's past visiting hours. There are too many of you. You all can't just roam through the hospital," she protested. Carter brushed past her, never even acknowledging her. Zyir put his fingers to his lips and told her, "Sit back down and do your job." He slipped her a stack of money and kept his stride alongside young Carter. "Text Mecca, and tell him to get here quickly," Carter ordered. His Mauri alligator's echoed against the tile floor. His black Armani sweater, white collar shirt and black tie gave him a distinguished look. As he stepped onto the elevator, he was silent, eerily silent, and Zyir knew that once Carter saw Miamor's condition, the entire city of Miami would rain bullets. Zyir hadn't prepared Carter for what he was about to see. He did not want to be the messenger that delivered the bad news. He thought it would be best if Carter saw it for himself. He led Carter to Miamor's room and stopped at the door. The five men who had come up with them dispersed themselves throughout the fifth floor. Zyir posted up outside of the door. "I think you need to go in alone, fam," Zyir said.

Carter entered the room. The smell of death lingered in the air. He walked over to the bed and flipped on the lamp that sat on the stand beside it. When he saw her face, the strong visage he had put on crumbled, and he lowered his head to his chest and squeezed her bed rails in agony. It felt as if someone had knocked the air out of his lungs, and he balled his fist and bit his knuckles to stop his dam of emotions from giving way.

He stared down at his lady . . . the woman he loved. Her face was black and blue, her left eye seemed caved in, and her skin was puffy and swollen with infection. There were parts of her body that were cut deeply, and medical stitches were everywhere. Carter took in every laceration, every cut, every imperfection, and absorbed the pain as his own. He instantly felt guilty, because he could only assume that whoever had done this to her had done so to get to him.

How did I let this happen? He asked himself. He grabbed her hand and noticed how ice cold she was. Her lips were dry and cracked, and her hair was breaking off onto the pillow. *She's been here for three months. I left her here alone, fighting for her life,* Carter thought sadly. He wanted to climb into the bed beside her, but he was afraid that he would hurt her. She looked so fragile, and the many machines and tubes connected to her body prevented him from getting that close.

He pulled a chair near her bedside and sat down. "I'm here, Miamor," he whispered. "I'm right here with you, ma." He brought her hand up and kissed it over and over again as he closed his eyes in defeat. "I'm going to murder the niggas that did this to you. Don't worry about it, ma. I'ma take care of you. I'ma take care of everything!"

Mecca pulled recklessly up to the hospital doors. When he'd gotten the text to come straight to Baptist Hospital, a wave of relief washed over him. He too had been searching all day and night for Breeze. *They found her!* he thought gratefully. He couldn't wait to see her face. He promised himself that now that he had her back, he would never allow anything to happen to her ever again. He left his car at the entrance, causing the security guard to approach him.

"Sir, you need to move your car. You can't park it there."

Mecca noticed some members of The Cartel standing near the entrance, and tossed them his keys. "Take care of it," he instructed as he rushed inside.

When Mecca stepped off of the elevator, he saw Zyir pacing back and forth. He rushed toward him. "Where is she?" Mecca asked.

Zyir nodded his head toward the room door and said, "Carter's inside with her now, but Mecca, it's not—"

Before Zyir could finish his sentence, Mecca rushed inside the room. "Breeze!" he yelled as he rushed over to Carter.

Carter stood suddenly. *He thinks it's Breeze,* he thought as he stood and pushed Mecca backwards. "Mecca, wait . . . it's not her. It's not Breeze."

Mecca pushed past Carter and stopped dead in his tracks when he saw Miamor lying in the bed. Hate filled his heart when he realized who it was, and that his attempts to kill her had failed. "This dirty-ass bitch!" he yelled as he lunged for the bed.

Seeing Mecca's rage toward Miamor sent Carter over the edge. Brother against brother, Carter grabbed Mecca by his neck and slammed him against the wall. Mecca struggled against Carter, but the forearm that was pressed against his throat had him off balance, giving Carter the upper hand.

Carter put his finger in Mecca's face. "Fuck is wrong wit' you, fam?" he seethed, his eyes deadly as he hemmed Mecca up.

Mecca pushed Carter off of him, breathing hard from anger. "I thought she was Breeze!" Mecca yelled as he punched a hole through the hospital wall. "Fuck!" he screamed as he glared at Miamor and shook his hand in pain. The only thing standing between him bringing her the death that she deserved was his brother, Carter. "You in here worried about this bitch, and my sister is out there somewhere!"

Their confrontation was interrupted when a man entered the room, wearing a lab coat and carrying a chart. "Gentlemen, I'm Doctor Shaw," the white man introduced. "We've been waiting for someone to claim this young woman. You are?"

Mecca glared at Miamor with a hatred that Carter had never seen. Carter contained himself and approached Mecca. He could understand how Miamor had taken Mecca by surprise, but he did not appreciate the disrespect. He took a deep breath, and walked up on him then whispered in his ear. "Now isn't the time or the place for this. Now, I don't know what the fuck you got against her, but whatever it is, you settle that shit. Now that I found her, she's gon' be around, so get used to it. If you ever come out your mouth again about her, I'ma handle you, my nigga. Believe that. Now, you need to go for a walk. Use all of that energy you got and use it to find Breeze, and put the word out to find the nigga who is responsible for doing this to Miamor." Under normal conditions, Carter would never threaten his brother, but seeing the larceny in Mecca toward Miamor had forced him into a protective rage over his woman.

Mecca stormed out of the room, startling Zyir. "I'ma murder that bitch!" he heard Mecca mumble as he passed by.

Zyir looked back in the room to see what had gone down, but Carter closed the door, then turned to focus his attention on the doctor. He took a deep breath to calm himself before he spoke.

"I apologize for my brother's behavior, Dr. Shaw, I'm Carter Jones," he said as he extended his hand.

"How do you know the patient?" the doctor inquired.

"She's my fiancée," Carter explained. "Can you tell me how this happened? How is she?"

The doctor sighed and checked Miamor's vitals as he began to explain her condition. "No one knows exactly what happened to her, Mr. Jones. She was found like this outside of an abandoned house. She's in a coma. She has severe head trauma, and she's had numerous blood transfusions. She has three broken ribs, and her jawbone is shattered. If she ever wakes up, she may want to consider reconstructive surgery to correct the jaw. She also has chemical poisoning. There were high levels of toxins found in her blood. Whoever did this to her never intended for her to survive. She's strong. I have never seen someone hold on for this long after everything she's been through."

Carter found the news extremely hard to hear, and his stomach was in knots as he stared at Miamor. "Will she ever wake up?"

The doctor sighed. "That I cannot answer for you. The good news is we ran a CT scan on her, which revealed high levels of brain activity. She's thinking, and still has the capacity to function mentally. She may even be able to hear you, but for some reason right now she can't come into a conscious state. Only time will tell."

Carter found the news extremely hard to bear. He put his hand on his head, rubbing the waves on his freshly cut Caesar, and took a deep breath. "The machines?" he asked, his voice cracking from emotion. He cleared his throat and continued, "Why is she hooked up to so many machines?"

"One of her lungs isn't functioning properly. We have her on a ventilator to ensure that she is getting enough oxygen. Once the lung heals and kicks back in, she should be able to breathe on her own. Until then, I will do all that I can to make her comfortable," the doctor said with sympathy.

Carter shook his head. "Thank you, Dr. Shaw, but I'm taking her home where I know she will be safe." Carter walked out of the room to where Zyir was waiting in the hallway with a briefcase in his hands. Carter took the case and popped it open. Inside, $100,000 lay in neat bundles. "I'm sure this will take care of any resources that your hospital has used to treat her."

Despite the doctor's protests, Carter took Miamor back to the Diamond Estate. He had a room set up for her where all of her medical needs would be met. He sat down next to Miamor's bed. The night had been long, and the sunrise crept over the horizon and illuminated the room as he gripped her hand, his emotions running wild. A 9 mm sat in his lap. The hum of the medical machines was torture to his ears.

First Breeze, now this, Carter thought, overwhelmed. He hadn't found peace since he had come to Miami. He did not know how his father had ever handled the massive empire that he had built with such ease. Carter felt like everything and everyone he loved was slipping through his fingers. *Maybe this is why my father walked away from my mother, so that he would not have to watch her suffer at the hands of the game. I should have followed my first mind and kept Miamor at a distance. If I had walked away from her, this would have never happened,* he thought miserably. His father's logic made much more sense to him now as he watched Miamor fight for her life.

He lowered his head and rested his face in the palm of his hands. He picked up his cell and dialed Mecca's number. He needed his brother. He couldn't handle all of the chaos alone, and he was not trying to lose the only family he had left.

Carter did not know that in order to keep Miamor, he was going to have to let Mecca go. He would eventually have to choose one or the other, because there was no way that Mecca and Miamor could ever co-exist.

Mecca sent Carter to voice mail as he pushed his Lamborghini through the streets. His foot was like lead on the gas pedal. There was only one thing on his mind . . . murder. He called Fabian repeatedly, but never got an answer.

Bitch-ass nigga couldn't handle one fucking job. Kill the bitch! That's all I asked him to do, he thought.

His luxury whip left rubber on the ground beneath him as he made his way to his destination. He pulled up to an apartment community and slammed his car door furiously as he made his way inside. Too impatient to wait for the elevator, he stormed up the stairway all the way to the seventh floor. He found apartment 7B.

Knock! Knock!

Fabian opened the door, keeping the security chain in place, but when he saw Mecca's face, he tried to close it quickly.

Mecca pushed his way into the apartment, causing the door to hit Fabian in the face.

"Oww, shit!" Fabian grimaced as he held his nose and backed up into the apartment. M-M-M-Mecca! What's good, homeboy? Fuck is all this for?" Fabian stuttered nervously while blood leaked from his busted nose.

Mecca didn't say a word. He removed his .38 and then began to screw the silencer on as his eyes burned a hole through Fabian, daring him to move.

"Mecca, man! Please, man!" Fabian begged.

Mecca aimed his pistol at Fabian's head and fired two shots. The only sound that could be heard was Fabian's body hitting the floor, and just as quickly as Mecca had come, he left. He had no regrets and no remorse. All he wanted was revenge. He knew that talking to Carter was useless. Miamor had him blinded. Carter had placed Miamor on a pedestal so high that he refused to see the truth, but Mecca was determined to get to her. *As soon as the nigga turns his back, I'ma murder his bitch.*

***

Dr. Nataya Azor walked into her practice and sighed. She knew that today would be a long and dreadful day. She hadn't gotten much sleep last night, thinking about the young girl she had treated the day before. She knew for a fact that Ma'tee was not the girl's father, but she wanted to stay out of it. She wanted no part of whatever was going on. To get into the business of a man as ruthless as Ma'tee could put her in a bad position. She could easily come up missing if she chose to intervene. She tried her best to ignore the situation, but then she thought of her own beautiful children. *If they were in trouble, I would not want another mother to turn a blind eye to dem,* she thought with indecision. Dr. Azor had gotten the message that Breeze had written her, but fear had stopped her from making the call on the girl's behalf. She had tried to put the note in the back of her mind and remain professional, but all night she tossed and turned, thinking of the look of terror she had witnessed in Breeze's eyes. She looked at the clock. She still had an hour before her office opened. She put her things down and walked over to the file cabinet where she kept her patients' files. She flipped through them until she retrieved what she was looking for. "Breeze Diamond," she whispered aloud. Her mind told her to put the file away and go about her day, but the motherly instinct in her forced her to find Breeze's note. She took a deep breath and picked up the phone, but quickly changed her mind and slammed it back down. Her foot tapped nervously against the floor as she contemplated on what to do. She read the note again: *Please help me! Call this number. 1- 810-625-1816. Tell him I am alive. I'm trapped somewhere in the mountains. Please!*

"One phone call will not hurt," she said. She picked up the phone and slowly dialed the number, silently hoping that no one would answer.

"Hello?"

"Please listen carefully. A girl by the name of Breeze was treated in me doctor's office yesterday. She asked me to call this number. She's in danger. She's is in Haiti. Ma'tee has her trapped in de mountains," Dr. Azor said.

***

"Who is this?" Zyir shouted as he sat straight up in his bed, but all he got in response was a dial tone. He immediately threw on some jeans and his kicks and grabbed his keys. *Haiti!* he thought in despair. *What the fuck? Ma'tee?* Zyir knew that if what the caller said was true, then Breeze was in much more danger than anyone could have ever imagined, and he had to get to her . . . before it was too late.

Chapter Eight

The Cartel

Breeze began to feel better, and Ma'tee had allowed her to roam free in the secluded basement without being bound to the bed. It had been a week since she was at the hospital, and she couldn't stop thinking about Zyir's voice. She knew that she had blown the only chance that she had to be saved. She paced the room back and forth as she tried to think of a way out of the clutches of Ma'tee, but she was beginning to realize that she would never escape. He was in complete control, and had become obsessed with her. She broke down into tears as she began to accept her reality. "I would rather die!" she whispered as she felt like giving up on life. She was a Diamond, and she took pride in that name. She would rather die on her feet rather than live on her knees. She, at that moment, gave up on life.

The sound of the door unlocking startled her, and she stared at the steps until she saw the feet of Ma'tee emerging. He walked down, smiling as if he was a husband coming home to his wife.

"I hate you!" Breeze whispered as she backed into a corner, watching him walking toward her. She saw the look in his eyes, and already knew what his intentions were. He came down there for sex. "No, Ma'tee! Don't do this!" she begged as she held her hands out in front of her.

"Relax, beautiful gal," Ma'tee said as he licked his lips and thought about how good it felt to be inside of Breeze's tight wound. He had broken her virginity months ago, but every time seemed like the first time to him.

Breeze learned that fighting back only made it worse for her, so she reluctantly got up and walked toward the bed. Ma'tee followed closely behind her and began to rub her behind. He relieved her of her gown and looked at her naked, slender body as she lay on the bed. Tears were running down her face, but he paid them no mind as he prepared to have his way with her. He dropped his pants and began to degrade her.

Ma'tee went down on her and performed oral sex on her as she laid there not responding to him at all. Her legs shook, not in pleasure but in fear as he ate her out sloppily. Tears ran down her face as she had no choice but to submit to Ma'tee.

Zyir's heart raced as he waited patiently for Mecca to return. He had been blowing his phone up, trying to let him know that Breeze was alive and somewhere in Haiti. Zyir looked at Carter, who was coming down the stairs while talking on a cell phone. Carter was scheduling a helicopter to drop them off in Haiti. Zyir had never come clean about everything that happened on the night that Breeze was kidnapped. Carter and Mecca knew that he was the last one with Breeze that night, but what Zyir didn't tell them was that he was in the process of taking Breeze's virginity. Their sexual act had caused his distraction, and his sloppiness had led to her being taken. *How would he take it?* Zyir asked himself as he buried his face in his hands. He quickly shook off the feeling of overwhelming guilt and focused on the positive; Breeze was alive.

"Did you get in touch with Mecca?" Carter asked as he flipped down his phone and grabbed a phone book.

"I can't reach him. I've been trying to call him all morning, but he's not answering the phone," Zyir said as he stood up and began to pace the floor. He picked up the phone and tried to reach Mecca once again, but he just got the voice mail like before. "Damn! We are just going to have to go without him," Zyir said as he pulled his gun out, ready to kill whatever and whoever to get Breeze back.

Carter ran his finger down the phonebook's page, searching for a home health aide. He didn't want to leave Miamor there alone without help. He wanted her to see a friendly face if she awoke from her coma, rather than one of his goons that he had guarding her room.

He glanced over at Zyir, who was pacing the floor, looking nervous and anxious. Carter stopped what he was doing and walked over to him. He put his hand on Zyir's shoulder and stopped him in his tracks. "You got to calm down. I want you to relax and take a step back. We don't know what we are about to walk into when we get to Haiti, so we have to be ready for whatever. But we will most definitely be at a disadvantage if you're all riled up. Fall back, fam," Carter said as he watched Zyir letting his emotions get the best of him. "You really cared for her, huh?" Carter asked as he looked at Zyir and saw the flame in his eyes.

"Yeah, we were getting close, ya know. This shit ain't for her, man. I'm ready to go get her," Zyir said seriously, looking his mentor in the eyes.

Before Carter could respond, the door opened and in came Mecca.

"Yo, Mecca! We got her. We know where she's at," Carter said.

Mecca smiled as his trigger finger began to itch. He would deal with Miamor when he got back. Now it was time for him to get his sister back. "Let's go get my baby sister," he said in a low raspy tone as he pulled out his gun and cocked it back. He felt his heart flutter at the sound of Carter's words. She was the only remaining full-blooded sibling he had left, and he was determined to bring her back home where she belonged.

Carter, Zyir, and Mecca rode in the aircraft that flew 1,500 feet above land, all of them wearing headphones to drown out the overwhelming loud noise of the helicopter's propeller. Carter had rented a private helicopter to make this trip to Haiti in the hope of finding Breeze. Everyone remained silent as they watched the pilot maneuver the aircraft over the ocean. The light blue water beneath seemed so beautiful, but none of them had beautiful thoughts on their minds; only murderous ones. The helicopter finally cleared the water, and the beautiful island of Haiti was now visible. The tall exotic trees and dirt trails took up most of the land, and the pilot spotted a safe landing spot in the middle of the town of Saint-Marcs, a city in the middle of the island. It was also the same place that

Breeze was treated. With their connections, they found the exact location where the call was from. They all were anxious as the helicopter swayed back and forth as it prepared to land. As the helicopter hovered over the open field, the grass blew wildly because of the velocity of the chopper's propellers. Carter cocked his gun back, making sure he was locked and loaded. He didn't know if they were walking into a trap, so he was getting himself prepared for whatever. Zyir and Mecca followed suit and did the same thing. Once the helicopter landed, they all hopped out, and Carter instructed the pilot to wait there for them to return, and left him with a rubberband roll full of money; ten thousand dollars to be exact. Zyir grabbed the duffle bag that was full of extra ammunition and automatic guns, preparing for whatever Ma'tee would have in store for them.

The hot, muggy climate and Haiti's air felt different from Miami's air as the sweat began to drip from their brows. They made their way toward the dirt roads that led to the buildings that were just a mile down.

Carter spotted a tall building that resembled a small, rundown hospital, and pointed. "Is that the place right there?" He asked Zyir, and he used his other hand to block the sun from his eyes.

"I think so. The nurse said there is only one doctor's office in the entire town," Zyir said as he looked toward the building and pulling out a small piece of paper.

Just as they were making their way to the building, a young boy ran across the road while kicking a soccer ball.

"Ayo, li'l man!" Carter yelled, trying to get the young boy's attention.

The boy didn't seem any older than ten years old. He was very skinny and had nappy, small beads on his head that was his hair. He stopped kicking the ball and looked at Carter. "Me?' he asked as he looked around and pointed at himself.

"Yeah, you," Carter said as he unleashed a smile. The boy, without fear, picked up his ball and walked toward them.

"What up, mon?" the boy said in his heavy Haitian accent.

"You want to make some money, baby boy?" Carter asked as he reached into his pocket.

The young boy's eyes followed Carter's hands. Carter pulled out a roll of money, and the young boy's eyes grew as large as golf balls. He had never seen a man carry so much money in his entire life. Wealth was not something common in Haiti, and the boy was astonished. "Wow!" he said as he snatched the money from Carter. "Yeah, mon, I want to make dis money!" His eyes were glued on the big-faced bills that were in his hands.

"Okay, well I need your help," Carter said as he placed his hand on the boy's shoulder.

"Anyt'ing, mon! Chu' just name it!" he said energetically.

"I need you to take me to . . ." Carter started to say just before he looked at Zyir for the name of the hospital.

"Hondas Hospital," Zyir said, reading the piece of paper that he had pulled from his pocket.

"Hondas is down the road," he said as he pointed north, in the opposite direction where they thought the hospital was.

"Show us," Carter said as they followed the boy's finger." What's your name, li'l man?" Carter asked.

"Ziggy," he said with his rabbit-like two front teeth.

"All right, Ziggy. We following you," Carter said as he urged Mecca and Zyir to follow him.

Mecca frowned up his face and pulled Carter close as he began to whisper. "How we know this li'l nigga ain't taking us into a trap?" he asked as he kept his eyes open.

"You don't trust anybody, do you?" Carter asked smiling. "Let's just follow him. How else are we going to find our way around?" Carter said, giving Mecca reason to see things his way.

"All right, Carter. But if this li'l nigga on any bullshit, I won't hesitate to blow his shit back," Mecca said as he patted the gun that was on his waist.

Carter shook his head and continued to follow the young boy up the path. *That nigga doesn't have a conscience*, Carter thought. *I'm glad he is on my team, rather than against me.*

After about fifteen minutes of walking, they reached the small hospital. It was a rundown building that resembled a plantation style house more than an actual hospital.

"Here it goes," Ziggy said, pointing at the front door.

"Let's go," Carter said as he hurried into the building, looking for the nurse that called them. He told Ziggy to wait for them on the outside, and whistle if anybody comes in. He slipped him another hundred dollar bill for good measure.

Ziggy proudly accepted the responsibility as the watchman, and smiled proudly as he stuck out his chest and answered, "Yes sir!"

Carter, Zyir, and Mecca rushed through the hospital, all of them with gun in hand.

Mecca called the doctor's name loudly, and his voice echoed throughout the halls. "Where is the nurse that called us?" he yelled as loud and clear as he could.

Nurses and patients gasped at the sight of the men mobbing through the place like they owned it. A woman emerged from one of the rooms, and Mecca immediately knew that she was the person that they were looking for.

"May I help you?" she asked, frowning in confusion.

"Are you the nurse that called?" Mecca asked as he gripped his pistol and pointed it directly at her. Carter quickly placed his hand on Mecca's gun and lowered it for him.

"Yes, I'm Azor," she answered with fear all over her face and shaking limbs.

"Relax!" Carter said under his breath, as he knew Mecca was at his boiling point, ready to shoot whomever. "Let me handle this," he said, just before he focused his attention on the doctor. "Azor?" Carter asked the lady as he stared at her with kind eyes.

"Yes, that's me. Let's talk in here," Azor said, and she opened up an empty room. They all followed her in, and the doctor closed the door after she looked around to make sure that the coast was clear.

"You called my man right here, and said that a young lady was in this place, right?" Carter asked as he placed his hand on her shoulder to calm her. She was noticeably shaken up.

"Yes, I did," she said.

"Is this the young lady you saw?" Carter asked, wanting to make sure that it was Breeze. He pulled a picture out of his pocket of Breeze. It was one of her senior picture she had taken years before. The doctor stared at the picture for a minute and nodded her head to verify that it was her.

"Where is she?" Mecca interrupted, as he quickly grabbed the nurse by her hair and put the gun to her temple. The nurse instantly put her hands up and began to cry out of pure fear.

"What the fuck you doing?" Zyir asked in confusion as he saw the murderous look in Mecca's eyes.

"Fall back, Mecca!" Carter yelled as he put his hand up to signal Mecca to stop.

"No, fuck that! My sister is alive, and this bitch is going to take me to her!" Mecca screamed as the veins in his neck and forehead began to slightly bulge out.

The doctor's words got caught in her throat as she tried to give Mecca the best answer she knew. "She is with Ma'tee. That' all I know. Ma'tee is a very powerful man in this town, and all that I know is that he lives somewhere in the Black Mountains. You have to go up the mountain and through the jungle to get to his place," she said quickly.

"Where's that at?" Carter asked as he listened closely while Mecca still had a tight grip on her.

"It's five miles down the road and up the mountain. It's barricaded, so no cars can get through. You will have to hike the trail and climb the mountain to get there," she said as tears streamed down her face. Her hands shook nervously, and she flinched at every little movement that Mecca made.

Carter heard enough, and headed out. "Come on, Mecca," he said as he opened the door.

"If you are lying, I will come back and kill you and your whole family," Mecca said, meaning every word that came out of his mouth. He unleashed the doctor and headed outside.

Carter rushed outside and went directly to Ziggy, who was waiting for him on the steps of the hospital. "Ziggy, I need you, li'l man," Carter said.

"Anything. What chu want?" he asked.

"Do you know how to get to the Black Mountains?" he asked.

"You mean Ma'tee's place?" Ziggy asked as he scratched his head.

His statement was music to their ears. They knew that they were about find Breeze and bring her home at that point.

Zyir was beaming on the inside. He knew that it was a chance for him to reunite with the woman he loved; Breeze. "Yeah, you know where it's at?" Zyir asked.

"I know exactly how to get there," Ziggy said as he headed north toward the Black Mountains.

Chapter Nine

The Cartel

Breeze cried as she watched Ma'tee pull up his pants and look down at her. There was no remorse on his face. The fact that he was killing her slowly on the inside meant nothing to him. The sweat from his brow dripped down his dark face, causing Breeze's stomach to turn in disgust. The sick smile that he wore terrified her. He was so sure of himself . . . so proud of the sexual acts he had forced upon her. Ma'tee had even gone as far as to ejaculate inside of young Breeze, in a twisted attempt to impregnate her. He knew that a child would join them together forever, and that was his ultimate goal. Without saying a word, he walked away and up the stairs. Breeze heard the sounds of Ma'tee locking the deadbolts that trapped her in the basement.

Breeze sat up and began to cry. She felt so violated and dirty. Ma'tee had degraded her on many occasions, and she was forced to give her virginity to a man that she hated; the same man that was responsible for her father's death. She got on her knees and began to pray to God, hoping that her father also heard her prayers. She was at a point where she didn't want to live anymore. Her regard for life was slowly fading.

The longer she stared at the four walls of her imprisonment, the more her mind abandoned her. Breeze knew that if she didn't find a way out, then she would go insane.

She finished her prayer and got up to walk to the bathroom that was connected to the basement. She stood over the sink and looked at her reflection in the mirror. Her eyes were bloodshot and swollen from her endless crying, and as she stared at the woman in the mirror, she couldn't even recognize herself. She was not the same girl. The young woman staring back at her was not Breeze Diamond. At that point, she realized that she had not looked at herself in almost a year. Every time she used the bathroom, she would just avoid eye contact with the mirror, almost as if she were ashamed. Ma'tee had stripped her of her innocence a long time ago, and she was not who she once was. The naïveté of a young little rich girl had disappeared. She now knew pain. She now knew what war really was. She now knew loneliness.

"Diamonds are forever!" she whispered as she wiped away her tears and repeated a motto that her father would always say to her as a young girl. She knew that she had the blood of a king, and at that moment, refused to let Ma'tee hurt her anymore.

She glanced over at the corner of the room and saw something that could possibly help her escape Ma'tee grasp. She took a deep breath and walked toward it. She had just gotten an idea.

Sweat dripped off of each of the men as they tried to keep up with little Ziggy as he walked up the rocky trail. The trail wrapped around the tall mountain, and the sun was just setting. "Come on, guys. We have to beat the sun," Ziggy emphasized as he led the way, while holding a big stick in his hand.

Carter took off his shirt as the sweat cascaded down his body. They had been climbing the mountain for nearly two hours, and the air was getting thinner as they got higher up in altitude.

"You sure this is the way, li'l man," Zyir asked as his legs grew tired.

"Yeah, I'm sure. Me and me friends used to come and play in this jungle every day. We snooped around here last summer when Ma'tee was away in Miami. We're almost there," Ziggy said, showing no sign of being winded.

On the other hand, the rest of them were exhausted, but their love for Breeze kept them going. Zyir couldn't wait to hold Breeze in his arms and tell her that he loved her. He was going to be her knight in shining armor and save her.

That thought alone made him put some pep in his step as he sped up, trying to reach their destination.

Mecca's mind was on shooting Ma'tee right in between the eyes. Breeze was his only full-blooded sibling that was still alive, and he would die if that was the cost of getting her back. "*Here I come, Breeze*, he thought as he climbed the trail.

Carter swatted the unfamiliar flying insects away from his face as he looked up and saw the abundance of tropical trees.

"Here is de' jungle," Ziggy said as he stopped and pointed to the woods. "Ma'tee's house is straight ahead. Just stay north."

Carter stopped and caught his breath, along with Zyir and Mecca. He then looked at Ziggy and rubbed the top of his head. "Thanks, Ziggy. You are real li'l nigga," he said as he smiled. Carter reached around his wrist and pulled off his designer watch and handed it to Ziggy. "That's yours," he said as he watched Ziggy admire it like it was a masterpiece. "Now, you have to take off," he told him, and stepped to the side so that Ziggy could go back down the mountain.

"Thanks Ca'ter!" Ziggy said, mispronouncing his name because of his accent. Then Ziggy smiled and ran up and hugged him. "But remember, you have to follow de dirt path or chu will get lost. De jungle is a big circle, mon," he reminded him as he headed back down.

Carter watched as Ziggy disappeared down the trail, then focused back on Mecca and Zyir. "Let's go get Breeze," he said, and they ran through the jungle, following the trail.

After fifteen minutes of running full speed down the trail through the jungle, they saw the house. They all stopped in their tracks when they saw the gigantic house that was before them. They had expected Ma'tee's house to be guarded and surrounded by gates, but to their surprise, it was wide open and unguarded.

Zyir dropped the bag on the ground that he was carrying, which was full of the automatic guns and bullets. He opened the bag, giving a variety of choices to Carter and Mecca. Mecca opted for the 12 gauge, and Carter got the AK 47 assault rifle, also known as a "chopper" because of its ability to spit bullet after bullet, chopping up whatever is in its path. They all strapped up and headed to the house. They were about to go in with guns blazing.

***

Breeze smiled as she thought about escaping Ma'tee's wrath. It would soon be over, and she would be a free woman. She looked down from the chair she was standing on and wrapped the belt around her neck. Ma'tee had left this leather belt down there after he had sex with her. Little did he know that he had provided Breeze an exit by doing so. Breeze tugged on the belt to make sure that it was wrapped around the pipes above her head securely. Tears began to fall down her face as she shook nervously. The only thing she would have to do was kick the chair out from under her feet, and the nightmare would finally end.

Carter put three fingers up, signaling the countdown. Mecca stood at the front door with a 12 gauge shotgun, aiming it at the lock. Zyir held two pistols in his hands, ready to rush in right after Mecca blew the door open. "Three, two, one!" Carter whispered.

Boom!

Mecca blew through the lock and they all rushed in.

Ma'tee heard the blast while he was in the shower washing the smell of sex off of his body. He quickly turned off the shower and ran into his room that was attached to the bathroom. He reached for the tech-nine automatic handgun he kept under his pillow. He looked at the monitors that were on his wall and gasped. He had his entire house under surveillance, and saw three men running through the downstairs of his home with guns.

"What de blood clot!' he yelled as he held his gun in his hand while dripping wet, and still completely naked. He looked at the security monitor that was watching the basement where he kept Breeze. Ma'tee's heart skipped a beat and he gasped at what he was witnessing. He gripped the sides of the monitor in anguish at the sight of Breeze's feet swinging from the ceiling. He was witnessing her committing suicide. "Nooo!" he yelled as he rushed downstairs to save her. He didn't care that he was going up against three guns, he just wanted to save his love before she died. "Breeze!" he yelled as he ran down the stairs, gun in hand.

Mecca was the first to spot Ma'tee, and reacted without thought or hesitation. He cocked the shotgun back and let off a round, just barely missing Ma'tee. Ma'tee returned fire, spraying anything he saw moving as he made his way down the stairs. Zyir also opened fire as he came from the opposite corner of the room. He hit Ma'tee in the arm, sending him flying down the stairs violently. Carter was toward the back of the house, and came running when he heard the gunshots.

Ma'tee dropped his gun as tumbled down the stairs, leaving a bloody trail behind him. He landed at the bottom of the stairs awkwardly. "Hmm!" he grunted as he tried to sit up and gather his bearings. When he looked up, Mecca was standing over him with a shotgun to his face.

"Where is Breeze?" Mecca screamed as he dug the barrel into on one of Ma'tee's eyes. Before Ma'tee could say anything Mecca kicked him forcefully in his temple out of anger. His emotions got the best of him, and he could not contain himself. Ma'tee was the man who had caused his family grief like no other, and his rage emerged like a bolt of lightning, striking hard and swift. "Where is she?" he yelled as he looked at Ma'tee, who seemed to be losing consciousness.

Ma'tee was dizzy because of the blows Mecca had just given him. He could barely speak. "Breeze!" he whispered as he thought about her hanging in the basement.

"Fuck that! Breeze!" he yelled as he ran up the stairs, skipping two at a time in a desperate race to find his girl. Carter headed to the back of the gigantic house screaming her name also.

"Breeze!" Zyir yelled as he invaded every room of the house. His heart pounded furiously in his chest, and his instincts told him that something was wrong. *If she's here, why isn't she answering?* He thought. "She's not up here! I can't find her!" he screamed as he descended the steps in worry.

Mecca saw the look in Zyir's eyes, and knew that something was wrong. "Where is she?" Mecca shouted as he looked down at Ma'tee, gripping him by his dreadlocks.

"In . . . the . . . basement," Ma'tee mumbled as blood dripped from his head.

"She's in the basement!" Mecca yelled just before he sent a shotgun blast through Ma'tee's chest, killing him on contact.

Carter rushed to the front, and Mecca told him that she was in the basement. They all rushed to the back of the house and tried to open the basement door, but it was secured with five dead bolts.

"Stand back!" Carter said as he pointed his gun at the lock. He let of five rounds, breaking each lock with each bullet he fired.

"I love you, Poppa. I love you, Mama. I love you, Mecca. I love you, Monroe. I love you, Uncle Polo. I love you, Carter," Breeze whispered, giving each one of her loved ones a personal and final good-bye. She put her hand over her heart and wished that Zyir would've come and saved her. She wished that when she called, she could have gotten the chance to let him know exactly where she was, but she didn't, and now she was about to make her grand exit from her hell on earth. "I love you, Zyir," she added just before she prepared to take her own life. She heard gunshots coming from upstairs, but she was so focused on what she was about to do that she paid them no mind. Breeze kicked the chair from underneath her and her body immediately dropped and dangled from the pipes. She began to squirm and hold her neck. The kiss of death gripped at her body. The pain was so great that she almost regretted her decision, but she would rather face a few moments of it then a lifetime of grief in the shackles of Ma'tee. The pressure building in her head was so great that she began to see stars. Each second was agonizingly slow as her lungs begged her to inhale. The strength of human will caused her to grab at the belt to avoid the suffocation. Her nails broke from grabbing at the leather, and she kicked wildly as the pulse in her head became audible in her own ears. She could hear her heartbeat fading, and just as she was on the brink of unconsciousness, she heard Zyir calling her name. "Breeze! I'm coming!" Zyir's voice came from upstairs.

Zyir! That's Zyir! she thought as she continued to struggle for air. She heard someone trying to get to the basement, but the locks were stopping them.

"Breeze!" Zyir yelled again as he tried to kick the door down. She jerked and contorted her body, trying to release herself, but it didn't work. Frantic and out of air, she grabbed at the belt around her neck, scratching her skin as she attempted to create some slack in the belt. Her world became gray, and her eyes felt like they would pop out of her skull as she put the last bit of strength she had into freeing herself. Her efforts were in vain. It was too late. She was already in the Grim Reaper's hands, and there was nothing she could do. She tried to yell for Zyir, but her airway was cut off. She only could let out small grunts. Her grunts were too low for anyone to hear, and she felt herself slipping away. She couldn't take it anymore, and she finally stopped struggling as life left her body.

Zyir pushed the door open and was the first to head down the stairs. He held his gun in front of him as he crept down the stairs, not knowing who was down there. Carter and Mecca followed closely behind him. Zyir got to the bottom step and his heart broke in two at the sight before him. Breeze was swinging from a ceiling pipe, swinging slowly from left to right. He quickly dropped his gun and ran over to her lifeless body.

"Breeze! Nooo!" he yelled as he held her up by her legs trying to stop her from choking, but it was far too late; she was already gone.

Carter saw Zyir holding Breeze and quickly ran over and picked up the chair so he could stand on it and untie her. His hands shook as he looked at Breeze's limp body.

Mecca was still by the stairs, frozen in heartache. He dropped to his knees and silently cried as he watched his sister's body drop into Zyir's arms. Zyir had never mourned anything or anyone in his life, but as he sat with Breeze in his arms, he rubbed her face as tears flowed down his cheeks. He kissed the top of her head over and over again as he rocked her back and forth while whispering her name again and again. "It wasn't supposed to go down like this!" he whispered into her ear. "Not like this!" he repeated as he wept over her. He looked down at the only girl who had ever stolen his heart and regretted the day he had ever met her. He had never felt a pain so great before she had entered his life. "I'm so sorry,

Breeze. This is all my fault," he whispered as he closed his eyes tightly and tried to get the image of her suicide out of his brain.

"Zy," Carter began. He inched closer to Zyir. "Let her go, fam. This ain't on you. Just hand her to me," Carter instructed, seeing that his protégé's grief was as great as his own.

"Don't take her from me, man, not yet. Just don't touch her!" Zyir spoke in a low tone. "She needed me. She was hopeless and she killed herself because I wasn't there." Zyir sat with Breeze for an hour before Carter could convince him that it was time for them to depart. Zyir even tried to give Breeze CPR. They all knew that it was useless, but Zyir wouldn't stop until he tried everything to bring her back. She held the key to his heart, and now that she was gone, it would be locked forever. The beautiful Breeze Diamond was dead.

Chapter Ten

The Cartel

All with tears in their eyes, Mecca, Carter and Zyir walked down the dirt path that led to their awaiting helicopter. They had just climbed down the mountain, none of them saying anything to each other on their way down. Breeze's limp, lifeless body was in Zyir's arms as he carried her with strength, determined to hold her upright and comfortable, even though it was in vain.

The town's patrons followed as they saw Zyir carrying the dead body. It looked as if a parade was going on, with Carter, Zyir, and Mecca leading the pack.

Mecca held his gun out in the open as he walked in broad daylight, with onlookers looking at them in disbelief. With tears flowing, he promised himself that anyone he saw that resembled a Haitian would die in honor of his hatred for Ma'tee. Mecca was at a point where he didn't give a fuck about human life anymore. He was already ruthless, but he had crossed the line, graduating to psychotic. He just wanted somebody to pay for all the grief that Ma'tee and his Haitian mob had caused his family. It seemed as if every Haitian resembled Ma'tee, and Mecca wanted vengeance.

He saw a spectator with a head full of dreads on the side of the road, along with the crowd. Mecca was going all out in tribute to Breeze.

He glanced at her body, and the sight of the red belt marks around her neck made him sick to his stomach. That sight was the most hurtful thing he had ever seen. He knew that Breeze loved herself too much to kill herself. For her to commit suicide, life had to be unbearable. This thought infuriated

Mecca and pushed him to his boiling point. He looked back at the dread head and let him have it. Mecca pointed and fired, catching him in the chest. Although the man had no association with Ma'tee and posed no harm, Mecca didn't care. He was borderline insane at that point. As the thunderous sound of the gunshot echoed through the air, people began to scream in horror and run for cover as Mecca looked for any other Haitian that even resembled Ma'tee.

The gunshots didn't bother Carter or Zyir. Usually they would try to tame Mecca, but this time they let his rage flow uninhibited. Neither of them even flinched as Mecca let off round after round, while never stopping his slow pace as they walked. They knew that Mecca was creating therapy for himself in some sort of sick way. Who were they to tell him how to grieve? They were both heartbroken, and the only thing on their minds was getting Breeze back to the States for a proper burial.

Zyir cried silently and kissed Breeze on the forehead while she was in his arms. "I love you," he repeatedly whispered to her as he continued down the trail.

Mecca continued to shoot calmly, with no expression on his face. People were yelling in terror and scattered like roaches as Mecca continued his therapy session.

They reached the helicopter, and the driver was waiting, just as Carter had told him to.

"I can't do this anymore," Carter whispered to himself, referring to burying loved ones. It was as if a healed wound was reopened when they saw Breeze's body hanging from that belt. They had to suffer her death twice, and it was taking a toll on what was left of The Cartel.

They entered the helicopter and the pilot carried them back to the States. The chopper ride remained silent and painful, as tears fell down all of their cheeks.

Carter, Mecca and Zyir stood over the hole in the graveyard. Two of the graveyard's workers began to dump dirt on the cherry oak casket that contained Breeze's body. Breeze's headstone was next to the rest of the Diamond family. Mecca looked at all the tombstones, and noticed that he was the last one left alive with the Diamond bloodline, besides Carter. Zyir stared, as the dirt getting dumped on top of the casket and the flowers that he laid on top of it, slowly disappeared with each scoop. Nothing was said. Each of them were entertaining their own thoughts and grieving within themselves. They all had stonecold stares with heavy hearts. They were all cried out, and at that moment, they knew that The Cartel was over. All of the heartache and anguish wasn't worth it. "I'm done," Mecca said as he stared at the hole in the ground. "Me too . . . me too," Carter whispered as he threw his arm around his brother. "This game is so cold. It wasn't supposed to be like this. We supposed to pop champagne and live the life; but not this. The game has no loyalty," Zyir added as he fought back a single tear for Breeze. Carter began to think about Miamor, and how he had left her there alone for the past couple of days when they had gone to Haiti, and then took care of Breeze's burial. He was fed up and ready to move on and start a life with Miamor.

He looked over at Zyir, the only real nigga he had besides Mecca. He didn't want Zyir to fall victim to the game, and promised himself at that moment that he would not let Zyir fall into the pitfalls of this game.

They stayed there for hours and mourned her death before they headed back to the Diamond residence. Carter knew he would have to start making plans for his exit out of the drug game.

Carter pulled into the Diamond Estate, and the gates were opened by one of his many henchmen that he had guarding the house. Carter gave him a nod and pulled up the long, curvy driveway. He had just dropped Zyir off at his condo, and Mecca decided to stay over at Zyir's. Mecca was acting strange in Carter's eyes. Carter chalked Mecca's awkwardness up to him mourning his sister's suicide. But little did Carter know, Mecca wanted to stay away from Miamor, because he knew that he would eventually kill her if he stayed under the same roof as her. Mecca wanted to wait until she woke from her coma before he killed her. He wanted Miamor to see his eyes as he sent her to her Maker. He was determined to finish the job Fabian had failed to do. Carter got out of his car and entered the house. When he walked in, his henchmen were all on the couch, playing a video game. They were so busy ranting and raving that they didn't notice him come in. "What the fuck is going on here?" he asked loudly, startling all five of the henchmen. They quickly jumped up, sensing the hostility in Carter's voice. "We were just—" the henchmen said, just before Carter threw up his hand, dismissing whatever he had to say. He began to walk over to the crowd of men with both hands behind his back. His body gestures didn't display anger, but the veins that were forming in his neck and forehead was a sure giveaway. "Who is watching Miamor?" he asked calmly, as he looked each one of them in their face.

"Carter, it wasn't—" one of the men said, trying to explain why they were on the east wing, and no one was guarding the front door or Miamor's room as Carter had ordered.

Carter grabbed the man and pulled out his own gun, putting it in the man's mouth. "Open up, nigga!" Carter yelled as he harshly rubbed the barrel of the gun on the man's lips.

The man opened his mouth and put both of his hands up, not believing what was happening. The other henchmen just looked on in fear. They had never seen Carter lose his composure whatsoever, so to see him so irate was terrifying.

"I pay you niggas good to watch and protect my fortress, and look what you do. You niggas don't know how to make money. The only thing you have to do is stay on your post. I don't pay you niggas to stand around and play games. What the fuck? Anybody could have come in here and hurt my lady!" Carter yelled as he thought about how he could've crept past them without anyone knowing. "Who was supposed to be at the door?" he asked as he continued to grip the man by his collar. He glanced around looking for an answer, but no one said anything. "Who!" he asked again as he dug the gun deeper in the man's mouth.

The man he was holding raised his hand, unable to talk because the gun was in his mouth. Carter had found out all that he needed. He pulled the trigger, rocking him to sleep. Blood and noodles shot out the back of the man's head, and Carter released his grip, letting his body fall to the floor. He didn't even look at him fall. He just turned around and headed to check on Miamor. "Clean that shit up!" he yelled as he put his smoking gun on his hip. He had to send a message that he wasn't playing, and that's exactly what he did. Maybe if so much wasn't going on, he would not have gone that far. He wasn't the one for making regrets, so he whispered, "Don't fucking play with me!" to himself, as he climbed the stairs to get to Miamor.

When Carter walked in the room, he saw the nurse that he had hired sitting next to Miamor, half-asleep. She was an older black woman who seemed to be in her early fifties. He had hired her from a health care service just before he went to Haiti. Carter walked over to the nurse and placed his hand on her shoulder. "Hello, Mrs. Smith. You can leave now," he said as he greeted her with a smile and pulled out a wad of cash.

She smiled back and got up to retrieve her things.

Carter looked at Miamor, who was still in a comatose state. She never looked more beautiful in Carter's eyes. He bent over and kissed her on the head. "Hey, baby," he said as he smiled.

The nurse headed out of the door, and Carter remembered what he had just done downstairs, so he told her to exit out of the west wing's door. He didn't want her to see the gory scene that was downstairs by the main door.

She nodded her head in agreement, and exited the room, leaving him alone in the room with Miamor.

Carter sat at the edge of the bed and placed his hand on top of Miamor's. He would give anything for her to just open her eyes. He would pay for her to tell him that she loved him. He still didn't know who could do such a heinous act to such a beautiful girl. But when he found out who had done it, he would make them pay.

Never in his wildest dreams could he have guessed that her injuries were at the hands of his own flesh and blood, Mecca.

Carter was exhausted, and he was ready to go to sleep. He pulled up a chair so that he could fall asleep right next to Miamor, hoping that she would awaken. He grabbed a small blanket from the foot of the bed and positioned himself comfortably. He prepared to call it a night and closed his eyes. So much had been going on over the past week, and it had him drained. He said a quick prayer for his sister, Breeze, and whispered, “I love you.”

Out of nowhere, Miamor, with a cracked and low voice, whispered, “I love you too,” as she opened her eyes and let out a small grunt.

Carter quickly jumped up and looked into her eyes. He smiled. It felt so good to see her eyes after so long. “Oh my God, baby! You’re up! I’m here. I got you,” he said as he bent down and kissed her repeatedly on the forehead.

Miamor was so weak that she could barely keep her eyes open. They were so heavy that it felt like someone was pulling her eyelids down. She tried to move, but her body wasn’t responding. It took all of her energy to whisper those three little words, “I love you,” but those words were music to Carter’s ears. He was so grateful, so happy.

“I thought I lost you, Miamor. I would have waited forever for you to wake up,” Carter said as he felt his hands shaking. His nerves were getting the best of him because he was overwhelmed with joy. His queen was back.

Chapter Eleven

Miamor

"What are we going to do?" Anisa asked as she paced back and forth and stared at Murder's arrest on the TV.

"I don't know," I replied, clueless.

The police had Murder in handcuffs, and had confiscated the money he had on him; all the money he had to his name. His head hung low, and he tried to avoid the flash of the media cameras.

My stomach was doing somersaults as I watched in disbelief, and my foot tapped anxiously against the floor. I was pissed at Anisa, but I would never tell her. If she had not gone off on her ridiculous tangent, then none of this would have ever happened. No words needed to be spoken to establish guilt. We were both there, we knew how it had gone down, and she knew that it was her fault. In a zombie like state I walked past her. I was still covered in blood and needed to take a shower.

The eyes of the man that I had killed haunted me. I put the soiled clothing in a plastic bag and stepped under the hot stream of water. It was almost too hot to bear, but I needed it to cleanse myself. I was desperate for the shower to wash away the sins that I had committed that night. The blood ran down my body and turned pink as it swirled down the drain.

Why did this have to happen? I asked myself as my tears kicked in. I cried silently for all that I had lost. After everything that I had been through when I came out of lockup, my life finally felt normal. I had felt like I found a family in Murder and Anisa, but my disillusioned view of safety had come crashing down around me the moment I pulled my second trigger. Two lives had gone extinct behind my actions, and although I would never regret killing Perry, my second murder was weighing heavily on my heart. It was then that I realized I was not normal. I never had been, and after tonight, I never would be.

Scrubbing my skin until it was raw, I washed my body until the water ran cold. I was grateful for the film of steam that covered the bathroom mirror. I wasn't ready to face myself. I didn't want to look into my eyes, because I was sure that I would not recognize the girl who stared back at me.

Knock! Knock!

"Miamor, are you okay?" Anisa called through the door.

My hands shook as I picked up the plastic bag filled with my blood-soaked clothes, and I opened the door to let her in. "I'm fine," I answered. "I need to take these clothes to the incinerator."

She took my hand, reminding me of how she used to take care of me when we were little, then led me out of the apartment. We entered the room where the incinerator was and I tossed the bag inside. Anisa rubbed my hair and put her arms around me as we both watched it burn.

"Everything is going to be okay, Miamor. We have to move on, and you have to forget that tonight ever happened," Anisa said.

I looked at her with a blank expression. "What about Murder?"

Anisa didn't look at me. Instead, she stared into the fire. "Murder knew the risks of the game he was playing. I knew one day something would go down and he wouldn't come home. Today is that day."

I wanted to tell her that today would not have been "the day" if it hadn't been for her, but I had to take responsibility in the situation too, because I could have stopped it. "We have to help him get out of this, Nis," I protested.

"There is no getting out of this, Miamor. He got caught. I'm not going to risk you going away again. I can let him go, but I will never forgive myself if I have to see them take you away again. Murder is gone . . . it is what it is," she said coldly.

***

Murder ended up taking a plea. He got five to seven years on a weapons and tax evasion charge. They couldn't connect the body to him, because I had disposed of the gun, so that case went unsolved. I wanted to visit Murder, but Anisa thought it was best if we cut our ties and start fresh. Living life without Murder was easier said than done, however. Gone were the days of shopping sprees and lounging. Without him bringing in the paper, things got real tight for us. Anisa and I used up the money we'd gotten for her car in a matter of a couple months. Rent, groceries and bills ate that cash up quick. Murder's absence was felt almost immediately, because we realized all that he did for us, and now that he was gone. The ringing of the house phone was our only reminder that he was ever really there. We resulted to petty hustles; boosting clothes and petty credit card schemes just to get by, but still at the end of the month, dollars was short and we were on the verge of being thrown out on our asses.

"I'm not for being broke," Anisa stated seriously. "You might have to sell your car, Miamor."

I raised my eyebrows and looked at her like she was crazy. "Bitch, I'm not selling my whip. I'll sell some ass before I get rid of my car," I said adamantly.

Anisa burst into laughter as the ringing of the phone interrupted our conversation. "Well, we are going to have to think of something, because rent is due in a few days," she reminded me, the stress written all over her face.

The phone stopped ringing, and we sat in silence as we each searched for resolutions to our problems, but it wasn't long before it started again blaring in our ears.

"Fuck! I can't even think from that mu'fucka ringing all the damn time!" Anisa shouted.

"Why don't they just stop calling? I know they saw Murder's arrest in the papers and shit," I replied.

Anisa shook her head. "Nobody knew who Murder really was. To the rest of the world, he's just another nigga lost to the system. I'm the only person who knew about what he did. To everybody else, he was just a voice on the phone."

"How'd he collect his money?" I asked curiously.

"They'd wire the money to a Cayman account. Half up front, half after the job is done. Murder didn't trust anybody though. He always cleared the account after every job and stashed his dough in the safe."

Ring! Ring!

"Do you have access to the account?" I asked curiously.

"I had access to all of Murder's money, whether he knew it or not," Anisa smirked.

I shook my head and smirked. "Yo' slick ass!" I commented.

Ring! Ring!

My mind was spinning. My pockets were on empty and I was in desperate need of a dollar. My sister and I were three days off of being put out in the street. "Why don't we just answer it?" I asked.

"What?" Anisa said skeptically. She lowered her voice to a whisper as if we weren't in the apartment alone. "Miamor, I told you what type of business Murder was into . . ." Anisa said, but she stopped mid-sentence when she saw the look on my face. "Miamor, what the fuck are you thinking?" she asked, reading my mind.

"I'm just saying; we need money, and there is cash money on the other end of that receiver. All we got to do is pick it up," I said unsurely as I stood up and walked over to the phone.

Ring! Ring! Ring! Ring!

Anisa and I stared intensely at one another. We both knew that once I answered that line, there would be no turning back. She looked back at the table full of bills and then up at me. She nodded her head, and I lifted the phone to my ear. It was the day we accepted our first job, and the day the Murder Mamas was born.

Chapter Twelve

Miamor

Benjamin Wilkes aka Benny Dough was our first hit. I could never forget his name, because he was getting paper, and being flashy was what he lived to do. All of Brooklyn knew who he was. A big time party promoter in the city, he wasn't hard to find. We couldn't have asked for an easier mark. Like clockwork, on Sunday nights he frequented Tenders, a local strip joint. It was ballers' night, which attracted all the get-money niggas in the 'hood.

Anisa and I came out shining that night, whipping my Benz up to the club's valet as if we belonged amongst the 'hood's rich and infamous list. Rocking Gucci, diamonds, and Prada, to the naked eye we fit right in with Brooklyn's elite, but we knew the deal. We were fronting and dead broke, but we were about to put in work. Legs greased, body right, and hair and makeup on point, we slid into the club. Weed smoke was in the air and liquor flowed freely as we found a booth in the corner of the room. The small burner I had purchased from Murder's gun connect was underneath my dress, strapped to my inner thigh. We didn't have time to purchase another one, so we rolled with a single pistol, figuring that it would be all the muscle we would need to take care of the job.

Benny Dough was in the VIP section, popping bottles as he and his entourage made the club rain. They were being entertained by three strippers, and even I had to admit that they were some bad bitches. They each looked like they had been ripped straight from the pages of *King Magazine*. They were the type of bitches that regular chicks loved to hate, and they had his full attention as they danced seductively in front of him.

"We might have some competition," Anisa whispered in my ear.

I shook my head. "We're not trying to juice the nigga's pockets. We're here for a completely different reason. He's drunk, and they are the perfect distraction. Let them do what they do, and we'll do what we do," I replied. "Let's go to the bar. We can see better from over there."

Anisa and I made our way through the darkened club. Our hips commanding the attention of the patrons, the two of us together gained more interest than some of the dancers, but we kept it pushing. It was our first job, and neither of us wanted to fuck it up. Fifty thousand dollars was at stake, and we were about nothing but our paper that night.

"Can I get an apple martini?" I asked the bartender. I never took a sip from the drink, but I held it for good measure. I didn't want to be the only person at the bar without a glass in my hand. I wanted to blend in while I discreetly watched every move that Benny made. I watched Anisa kill her drink, and I could see that she was nervous, but the liquid courage she'd just consumed would be more than enough to get her through the night. We both prayed that everything went perfectly. We were a far cry from the seasoned killer that Murder was, but we were stepping into his shoes. I crossed my fingers and hoped that things played out right.

I was so focused that I didn't even notice the dude that had slid into the seat next to me. He turned the swivel stool I was sitting in around so that I was facing him. I frowned, and was about to say something until he leaned into my ear.

"You and yo' girl about to rob that nigga or something?" he asked.

His question caught me completely off guard, and my heartbeat began to speed up. *Are we that obvious?* I thought as I gave him the evil eye and stood to leave.

Dude grabbed my arm gently and pulled me near him. "I respect your hustle, ma. It's sexy as long as I don't come into your crosshairs, nah mean?" his BK accent was strong, and his Usher cologne invaded my space while his dark bedroom eyes scanned me from head to toe.

"I don't know what you're talking about," I responded shortly as I titled my head to the side and looked up at him. He smiled; I didn't.

Any other day I might have listened to what he was kicking. The presidential on his wrist indicated that he was worth my time, but I wasn't there for all that. I really wished the nigga would get out of my space so that I could re-focus, but he wasn't moving. I looked over at Anisa, who was still on point. Benny Dough had never left her eyesight. I turned back around to the man in front of me. "Did you want something?" I asked him.

"What's your name?" he asked.

"Nigga, what's your name?" I countered.

He laughed and rubbed the hairs of his full beard. "Joell," he responded. "I own this club."

I clapped my hands sarcastically and said, "Congratulations! That must impress a lot of women." I rolled my eyes, hoping that the nigga would take a hint and get lost, but again, he didn't.

"I just thought I'd tip your hand a little bit and let you know that all eyes are on you. You walk into my strip joint looking good, smelling good . . . got these niggas watching you more than they watching my dancers, but you got your sights on one nigga. He looks like a mark to me. Somebody like you shouldn't have to rob and steal to eat, Ms. Lady. You could be very well taken care of," he said.

"I'm not putting on no show, and I don't know nothing about all that you talking. We're just here for the entertainment," I replied without looking at him. My eyes found Benny Dough, and noticed that he was preparing to leave. He wasn't sloppy drunk, but I could tell that he was tipsy. I nudged Anisa and grabbed my clutch. "It was nice to meet you, Joell. You have a good evening," I said with a curt smile.

He leaned back against the bar and watched me walk away. I put an extra switch in my hips just to show him something that he would never get, and walked right past Benny Dough out of the club.

As soon as Anisa and I claimed our car from valet parking, we changed clothes inside, removed our makeup and put on jeans and sneakers. Arab scarves were tied around our necks. We waited patiently, and minutes later, Benny Dough came out of the club with the stripper chicks and two other men following behind him. We were silent and breathing hard in anticipation as we followed him and his entourage to a cheap motel. They were two cars deep, so we made sure that we didn't tail them too closely. The last thing we needed was for them to get suspicious.

"There are six of them and two of us. You know all of them niggas is strapped. How are we gon' pull this off now?" Anisa asked.

"We wait," I said. I wasn't exactly sure how we would pull it off either. We were outnumbered and outgunned, but we really didn't have a choice. We were already paid half up front. We had to come through on our end, so it was all or nothing. We watched the room for a half an hour, and suddenly the door opened. One of the guys came out. Anisa went to get out of the car.

"What are you doing?" I whispered harshly as she got out and waved the dude over.

"Hey! I'm sorry to bother you," she said as she walked toward the guy. "Me and my girl are having some car trouble. It won't start. Can you help us please?" she asked.

This was not a part of the plan, and butterflies fluttered in my stomach. *What is she doing? Now this nigga done seen her face and everything!* I thought heatedly.

The nigga was a sucker for a pretty face, because he came right over without question and tapped the front of the car. "Open the hood," he instructed. I did as I was told and then hit the release button for the trunk as well. I saw him lean over to check out the engine, so I grabbed the gun, and got out of the car.

"Show me your hands," I said as I raised the gun to his head. Surprise swept over his face and he opened his mouth to speak. "If you want to live to see tomorrow, then you'll shut the fuck up," I said calmly. The look on his face told me that he was fuming. "Yeah, you fell for the okey doke," I commented, further pissing him off.

Anisa reached into his waistline and relieved him of his cell phone, the hotel room key, and a black .45. "Thank you," she sang as she released the safety and cocked it back.

With steel pressed to both sides of his head, the dude became much more humble. "I got a daughter, man!" he pleaded. "I don't know what y'all bitches want, but you can have it. My whip, money, whatever."

We didn't respond, but we took that nigga for a walk to the back of the car. I lifted the trunk. We were moving in sync as if we had been doing this for years. She was the Thelma to my Louise. "Get in," Anisa ordered.

The dude reluctantly climbed inside, and we closed the trunk. After making sure that he was locked inside, I turned to her with big eyes and whispered, "What the fuck was that, Nis? You've got to warn me before you make a play like that! The nigga saw our faces and everything," I fussed.

"So, we'll pop his ass so that he ain't telling nothing," she responded as she pulled her scarf over her face. I did the same. The only thing that could be seen was our hair and our eyes as we made our way to the door. I put my finger to my lips and then put my ear to the door. The sounds of music could be heard.

Anisa inserted the key slowly, and when the locked released, I rushed inside. "Everybody on the floor! If I have to say it more than once, I'ma leave you stinkin' in this bitch!" I yelled as Anisa and I pointed our guns around the room.

"What the fuck? Do you bitches know who the fuck you're fucking with?" one of the guys asked.

Boom!

He fell dead where he stood. I was surprised that Anisa had shot him, but I didn't show it. I barely even flinched, because I knew in order to stay in control, I'd have to keep my composure. "Now, does anybody else have any more questions?" I asked. "Sit on your hands!" I demanded.

"There's a nigga—" one of the girls began to speak, but I smacked the shit out of her with the gun.

"Didn't I tell you to shut the fuck up?" I asked. I could see the larceny in her eyes, but I didn't come there for her, so I kept it moving.

We took the zip ties out of our pockets and began to bind everybody by their hands and feet, but before we could get to the last girl, a nigga came bursting out of the bathroom. He rushed me and at the exact same moment Benny Dough tackled Anisa.

Boom! Boom!

I heard two gunshots go off, and then heard Anisa groaning as I struggled against the dude as we both tried to get a good hold on the gun. He was using his weight as an advantage and had me pinned to the floor, but I was holding on to the gun for dear life. I couldn't get to the trigger. He smacked fire from my ass, causing the entire right side of my face to burn and stars to appear before my eyes. I knew it was over when I found myself looking down the barrel of the gun.

"Yeah, bitch! Where's all that mouth now?" he asked.

I closed my eyes and prepared for the worst. I didn't want to see the bullets that ended my life. I inhaled deeply, gulping in the last bit of air that my lungs would ever taste.

Boom! Boom! Boom!

The gunshots deafened my ears, but when I didn't feel any pain, I opened my eyes. I scrambled backwards until my back hit the wall as I watched the dude fall to his knees as three bloodstains began to spread through the front of his shirt. I expected to see Anisa holding the smoking gun, but instead, one of the strippers had shot him.

"Anisa!" I yelled as I crawled over to her. Her neck was raw from being choked, and she was covered in blood. "Anisa . . . where are you hit?" I asked as my hands roamed her body.

She coughed and gulped in air. "It's not mine, Miamor . . . I'm good."

I helped her to her feet and retrieved our guns.

The girl who had saved me was cutting the ties from her friends' hands.

"Thanks," I said as I looked her in the eye. I had every intention of killing them when I came into the room, but after what she had done, I knew that I couldn't go through with it.

"I hope you bitches don't think that y'all are getting what's in they pockets. This was our lick in the first place," the girl I had smacked spoke up. "I tried to tell your ass there was a nigga in the bathroom," she said as she rubbed the side of her face and ice-grilled me. "Now you mu'fuckas done fucked up our money. We won't be able to get back to the nigga house to hit the safe. It was a hundred thousand in that bitch."

"One-hundred-thousand dollars?" Anisa asked.

"Yeah, bitch, a hunnid stacks," the girl shot back.

"If we can take you to the safe, we split the money five ways," Anisa said.

"Bitch, you killed everybody who knew the combo! Crazy ass bitches!" the same girl yelled.

"Bitch, I ain't gone be too many more of your bitches," I said seriously. "Now, can we discuss this somewhere else, before the police come in here and arrest all of us?"

I took a pillowcase off of the bed and tossed my gun inside. I then held it out for the three girls. I knew they were strapped, because the one who had helped me had pulled her gun from nowhere. "We don't know y'all like that. As long as we talking about getting this money, ain't nobody carrying burners," I said. Each of the three girls put their guns inside, and then Anisa followed suit. They reluctantly followed us to our car.

The guy in the trunk kicked and screamed when he heard us start the car. The three girls were in the backseat.

"What the fuck type of shit is y'all into? Y'all got niggas in the trunk?" one of them asked. I looked at them in the rearview, but didn't respond. We were all silent as we drove to a twenty-four-hour diner, where we came to some type of agreement regarding the money in the safe. Anisa and I didn't say anything about what we had been paid to do. They didn't need to know all of that. We just wanted our piece of their pie.

Robyn was the leader of their clique it seemed, and also the one I had smacked. Beatrice was a dark-skinned, weave wearing ghetto chick. I couldn't read the two of them very well at first, but I was instantly endeared to the third girl, Aries. She was the one who had saved my life that night.

After getting to know one another, we led the girls back out to the deserted parking lot. It was the middle of the night and there was no one around, so we popped the trunk. We all burst out laughing when we saw the dude curled up like a bitch. He was so scared that he had pissed on himself.

"Damn! Me can't believe me was actually going to give chu some," Aries stated.

We all pulled our guns back out of the pillowcase since a low level of trust had been established. Aries pointed her gun at the dude. "Get chu bitch ass out de trunk," she said. The dude climbed out and stared at the five of us standing around him with pistols in our hand. "Chu going to lead us to Benny Dough's house, and chu going to help us crack de safe," Aries instructed.

The guy didn't respond, so Anisa cocked her gun, putting one in the chamber and pointed it at him. "Get in the car."

Twenty minutes later, we were pulling up to a two story suburban home. "Who else lives here?" I asked.

"Nobody," the dude responded wearily.

I turned around to look him in the eye. I knew he was afraid. I could hear the fear in his voice. "Remember that daughter you were talking about earlier. Don't be stupid. We just want the money," I explained.

He nodded his head and then led us into the house. The guy reached under a flowerpot and grabbed the spare key, then opened the door. He had five bitches with attitudes on his ass, so he knew not to make a bad move. He led the way up the stairs to one of the bedrooms, then removed a painting from the wall.

"What's the combo?" Beatrice asked.

"I don't know the combination to that man's safe," the guy protested.

I knew he was lying when he said it, so I shot him without hesitation. I was tired of playing games.

"Aghh!" he screamed in agony as he dropped to the floor and held onto his bleeding foot.

"If you want to keep the other one, start talking," I instructed.

"Ha! Bitch, you really are crazy as hell!" Beatrice laughed out in amusement as she watched the dude hold his foot and cry in excruciation. "I'd fuck with her all day! That bitch ain't scared to do shit!" she said, meaning it as a compliment.

"Thirty-four, twenty-three, ten!" he yelled. "Fuck!" His screams of pain echoed throughout the house.

Anisa tried the set of numbers and smiled as she opened the safe. "Oh shit!" she exclaimed. "This looks like more than a hundred thou."

As soon as I saw the money stacks sitting in the safe, I pulled the trigger on that nigga. He had seen my face, and there was no way I could send him home to his daughter in any other way except for in a box. To my surprise, he got hit with three more bullets as well, because as soon as I withdrew, so did Aries, Beatrice, and Robyn. We filled him with lead, filled our pockets with paper, and disappeared into the night.

We all headed back to my apartment, where we decided we wouldn't spend any money until we heard what the streets would say about the murders. Since we didn't know one another, we all wanted to be in each other's presence to make sure nobody fucked up and got loose lips.

Chapter Thirteen

Miamor

I woke up early the next day and maneuvered silently throughout the apartment. I didn't want to wake Anisa or the new tagalong bitches we had picked up the night before. I didn't know Robyn, Aries, and Beatrice, but I was grateful that they were there. *Things could have gone real bad for us last night,* I thought as I shuddered at the thought of how close I had come to death. If it had not been for them, Anisa and I would have both been taking dirt naps, despite that fact I still did not trust them. Respect them, yes . . . trust them, hell no!

I thought that my heart would be full of dread, but strangely, my conscience wasn't phased by what I had done the night before. It was like the higher my body count rose, the less it affected me. I was choosing to become a killer. I had made the decision to pick up where Murder left off, all in the pursuit of the American dream, and there was no turning back. *It's just business,* I told myself as I made my way to my car.

My black skinny jeans looked as if they were painted on, and the white Marc Jacobs blouse revealed my cleavage and jewels. The white peep-toe Prada heels I wore completed my outfit as I climbed into my car and peeled out of the parking lot. I didn't tell anyone where I was going, not even Anisa. I knew she'd hit the roof if I told her I was going to see Murder, but I had to check on him. Plus, I thought he deserved a cut of the money we'd made last night. I promised myself that I would keep money on his commissary and put the rest of his cut aside until he got out.

I couldn't understand how it was so easy for Anisa to move on and just forget about all that Murder had done for her, because in the short year that I had known him, he would always be a part of me. I had feelings for him. If it wasn't for him, I would have been locked up. Instead, he took the heat, and I felt fucked up because I was just getting around to visiting him. My bone-straight wrap and Chinese bangs ruffled as the wind whipped through my hair. I hoped I wasn't making the trip for nothing. I didn't even know if I was listed on his visitor's log, but it was a chance I was willing to take.

I hit a department store first and picked up items that I thought Murder might need; a small care package that could hold him over for a while. Then taking the BQE toward Queens, I exited at Astoria Boulevard, then followed the city blocks until I hit Hazen Street. When I arrived at Riker's parking lot, I stepped out of the car with the box of personal items in my hands as I made my way to the bus that was traveling over the bridge to the facility.

As soon as I stepped foot on the bus, I knew it was going to be a miserable trip. There were babies crying, ghetto baby mamas arguing and talking cash shit, and tired wives who had done this routine time and time again. I shook my head, knowing that I could never be one of the chicks waiting on the outside. I had done years of lockup on my own as a child. I wasn't trying to do five more waiting on Murder or anybody else. It was then that I knew that I could not ride out Murder's sentence with him. When a loved one is locked up, that time affects the inmate and everyone around him.

As I looked at an older woman with a wedding band on her finger, I couldn't help but ask, "Are you here to see your husband?"

My question caught her off guard, but she shook her head and answered, "No, baby. I'm here for that knucklehead son of mine. He grew up watching me make this same trip to come and see his father, and now he's landed himself in the same predicament . . . behind the white man's walls. Like father like son, I guess."

The sadness in her eyes scared me, and I fidgeted uncomfortably in my seat as I noticed the lifelessness in the woman. She had no hope, no light in her eye. *That'll never be me,* I thought as uneasiness filled my stomach. As much as I cared for Murder, I knew that after today I would not come back. *The best I can do is letters and make sure his money is right,* I thought. I knew it was selfish, but it was real. The truth of the matter was, Murder was not my man, even though somewhere deep inside I wished that he had been.

After practically being molested by the guards and storing my personal items in a locker, I was finally escorted into a waiting room. I sat at the small table, growing more nervous as each minute ticked by. My manicured hand tapped impatiently, as butterflies filled my stomach. I was in the middle of a prison, but I felt as if I was going on a blind date. I rubbed my sweaty hands on my jeans, and then finally Murder came waltzing into view. His swagger was still so on point. Even in the jail hookup he had on he possessed an aura of respect. I smiled as he came near me.

"Hey, Murder!" I greeted as I stood to hug him.

He held me extra tight and extra close.

"My li'l mama!" he whispered, "Thanks for coming."

"I'm sorry it took me so long. It's been rough. I had to let things die down, you know?"

Murder nodded his head, then motioned for me to take a seat. "I know," he answered. "Where's your sister?" His eyebrows dipped low when he mentioned Anisa, as if he already knew the answer to his own question.

"Um, she couldn't make it, Murder. She told me to tell you—" I was about to make up an excuse on her behalf, but Murder waved his hand in dismissal.

"Don't do that, ma. You've never lied to me before. Don't start now because of your sister. I know Anisa. A nigga can't keep her when he's down; only when he at the top. I don't want to talk about her," he said with a hint of sadness in his voice. He touched my chin, making me smile. "You're here. Let's talk about that. Why did *you* come?"

His question had me stuck. *Why did I come?* I asked myself. I looked him directly in the eyes. The chemistry between our gaze was magnetic. "I owe you," I said.

"That's it?" he countered with a boyish charm.

"I was worried about you."

"Uh-huh," he responded. "You sure that's it?"

I hesitated before I continued, but knew that I wasn't being honest with myself. "I care about you, Murder."

"It's a little bit deeper than that, li'l mama, but I'll play by your rules. I care about you too, ma. Always have . . . always will," he said as he grabbed my hand.

My heart was beating out of my chest. "I'm sorry. I feel like it's my fault you're in here."

"This ain't on you. These walls ain't shit to me. In five years, I'ma walk out the same mu'fucka," he said as he kissed the inside of my wrist.

Seeing him in good spirits felt good. The interaction between us felt so natural . . . so right. He was my nigga, first and foremost. Murder and I were friends, but the fact that my attraction to him was growing by the second had me thinking about waiting for him; had me wanting to be there for him for those long five years.

"Murder, Anisa will never understand this. She's my sister, and I can't pick you over her, no matter how much I'm feeling you," I told him.

He nodded his head in understanding. "I know, Miamor. I would never ask you to. I know the type of woman you are. You're loyal, and that's one of the reasons why I feel the way I do about you. Like I told you before, it's not meant to be for us, but it don't stop me from wanting you. In five years, I'ma look you up, believe that, ma. You're my li'l mama always. Life moves on, and I would never ask you to wait or to hurt your sister. I'ma come check for you when I'm free though."

I smiled and pulled my hand away from Murder's. "I have one more thing to tell you," I said. He was silent as he waited for me to continue. "I answered your phone," I said. My words hit him like a ton of bricks, and his face collapsed into a mixture of sorrow and anger. "I'm on that now. Every time, I'll have your paper put aside for you and I'll keep your books on full in here. When you get out, you'll have money waiting on you."

Murder put his face in his hands and shook his head from side to side. "I didn't want that for you, Miamor. That's not for you. You deserve better than that."

I stood to my feet and wiped the tears from my eyes. "I don't think a better life is in the cards for me," I whispered.

Murder stood and pulled me close, putting his hands in my back jean pockets as we hugged. He pulled a picture out of my pocket. "What's this?" he asked.

I had meant to give it to him when I first arrived. It was a picture of us together on my birthday, holding up bottles of champagne.

He pulled me near him one more time and whispered in my ear. "Be careful. Never think twice about pulling a trigger. Turn your heart cold, Miamor. Think like a nigga, because acting like a bitch will get you killed. It's the only way you'll make it. Slump a nigga before he can slump you. No body, no weapon—"

"No murder," I whispered, finishing his sentence, our lips so close together that they touched when I spoke the words.

He pulled back and looked me in the eye. "You've already done your first job," he said in surprise.

I nodded my head, stood on my tip toes and kissed his cheek. "Good bye, Murder."

He held onto my hand as I walked away, until the distance finally separated us. "Holla at me, Miamor . . . at least once a month to let me know you're okay!" he yelled after me.

I nodded my head in agreement, and then walked out of his life.

When I returned to the apartment, the atmosphere was tense. Everyone was silent and staring at me in suspicion as soon as I set foot inside the door.

"Where the fuck have you been?" Robyn asked.

I looked at her like she was crazy, and bypassed her without responding as I went into my room. The silly bitch obviously didn't know about me, because if she did, she would have known that I would smack fire from her ass for talking to me out the side of her neck.

She followed behind me. "Look, you're the one who said we should lay low and let the streets cool down before we get to spending money, then when we wake, up you're ghost," she said. "What are we supposed to think?"

"I don't really give a damn what you think. I had to handle something, that's all you need to know," I replied.

The girls made their way into my room, and Anisa stood by the door. I could feel her staring at me. I knew she wanted to know where I had disappeared to so early in the morning, but I wasn't telling. Nobody needed to know. Where I went was my business. Fuck all them hoes!

"Well, I've been thinking," Beatrice stated as she sat on my bed and looked around at everyone in the room. "Y'all didn't even know about the money in the safe before we told you, so that means y'all were there for something else. We want in."

"Want in?" Anisa repeated.

"Yeah, whatever y'all got going on, we want in. There is only two of y'all. Without us, things could have turned out different for y'all last night. I don't know what exactly y'all do, but I know this plush condo and that Benzo you driving don't come cheap. We want in," Beatrice asserted.

Anisa and I looked at each other with raised eyebrows, and as if on cue, the phone began to ring.

Ring! Ring!

I was skeptical at first, but I knew that having more chicks on our team could be a good thing. Our chances of being caught slipping would decrease drastically if we hooked up with Robyn, Aries, and Beatrice.

Ring! Ring!

"A'ight," I said. "We're not into the petty robbery game though."

"We don't give a fuck what you into it. If it's about money, then we're with it," Robyn spoke up confidently.

Ring! Ring!

"We'll see," I replied as I stood up and rushed to pick up the phone, with them hot on my trail. I took down the details of the call and turned around to face the group.

"You want in?" I asked.

"We want in," Aries reiterated impatiently.

I handed her a piece of paper that had the name of our next hit on it. "Murder that nigga. It needs to be done quickly and quietly," I instructed, and then walked away, leaving them to their thoughts.

Anisa followed behind me, and once we were in my room alone, she closed the door. "Are you crazy!" she asked.

"They want in, so let them prove that they can handle it. If they fuck up, we will handle them," I responded. "Just relax."

The next day, I received a text message from a number I didn't recognize: WATCH THE NEWS! I frowned when I read the words, but went into Anisa's room and told her to turn the channel:

> *". . . This is Allison Fisher, reporting for WWOR. Gun violence has once again taken a hold of the Bronx. Thaddeus Johnson was gunned down in his vehicle today on East 142nd Street. Witnesses say that two unidentified females were riding a red motorcycle, when they pulled up to a traffic light next to Mr. Johnson's car and opened fire. This young woman was the passenger in Mr. Johnson's car when the shooting took place. "Can you tell us what you saw?" the reporter asked.*

The girl's voice shook as she replied, "It all just happened so fast. All I remember is listening to the music one second, and hearing loud gunshots the next. I was ducked down in my seat. I was too afraid to look up. There was so much blood. I thought that I would die. I can't believe this happened . . ."

Anisa and I watched the newscast in shock. The girl who was being interviewed was Robyn, and the guy that had been killed was the hit I had given them. Anisa chuckled and said, "She deserves an Oscar for that performance."

"They pulled it off!" I whispered in disbelief as I sat back against the headboard on Anisa's bed. Anisa looked at me and shook her head from side to side. My cell phone rang, and an unknown number popped up. "Hello?" I answered.

"So, we're in?" I instantly recognized Aries' distinctive accent.

"You're in," I replied with a smile. The average type of chick would not have been able to pull off what the three of them had. They were ruthless and conniving. They were just like me, and now they were on my team.

Chapter Fourteen

Miamor

A year passed, and life was good! Anisa, Beatrice, Robyn, Aries and I were lying in the sun on a cruise ship just off the coast of Miami. We had planned that particular trip to celebrate our success. After Anisa and I got to know the other girls, we knew that they could be very helpful in our newfound profession. Before I even knew it, we established the Murder Mamas. At first it was a little joke, but the name was fitting and sort of stuck. We all even got "Murder Mama" tattooed on ourselves to show our allegiance.

It did not take long for niggas to catch wind of us. We had expanded and took jobs from Jersey, Philly, and even D.C. The word spread quickly in the streets, because our phone constantly rang for new jobs. We only took jobs by referral, meaning you would have to know someone that hired us before to even have a conversation with us about our services. We had a secret society, and the only thing we asked for was trust. We sometimes set up clowns that were stunting too hard and robbed them, but we only did that when we traveled out of town. Our main hustle was murder-for-hire. That's what paid the bills.

The one thing about killing is; just like everything else you do, the more you do it, the better you get. I believe my heart had grown the coldest of our whole crew. I never thought twice about a murder once it was done. The only thing I thought about was the payoff. Some might call it cold-blooded, but I call it just being Miamor.

We all sat, sipping our exotic drinks and enjoying the sun. I looked over at Beatrice, who lay out on the deck with her big Gucci shades on and smiled. "Bitch, you know you don't need any more sun," I joked, referring to her dark ebony skin tone. We all burst into laughter, knowing she was the darkest of the crew.

Beatrice held up her middle finger without saying a word as she smiled and continued to sip her Long Island iced tea. She is what you called "ghetto fabulous." She originally was from BX, and I loved her style. She always told it how it was, and had a tendency to be loud at the wrong times. But it was what it was; she was my girl . . . real bitch.

Robyn was kind of sneaky in my eyes, but I dealt with her because she was resourceful. Her ass was like the sibling that you loved because you had to. She was my sister, but I could not stand her ass sometimes. She was a little older than me, about Anisa's age, and she knew every hustler in every borough. Don't ask me how, but she always knew who was coming up on the streets and who was next in line to be "the man." That was useful for us when we occasionally robbed niggas. But we did have one golden rule—never rob or take a hit on anyone we encountered before. It would be too much of a risk for us.

Aries was a sweetheart. She had a heavy Barbados accent, and it was hard to understand her at times, but I managed. She was petite, with beautiful shoulder-length twists in her hair that fit her exotic personality perfectly. She was one year younger than me, and kind of quiet. But don't let that fool you. Aries was a killer. I noticed that she didn't hesitate to kill if the money was right. She was the closest person to me, besides Anisa, because we were just alike. She was an asset to the squad for sure.

We all enjoyed the sunrays and sounds of the churning waves as we relaxed and conversed. In the midst of our conversation, the phone rang. We all sat up, recognizing that particular ring. I had all the calls from Murder's line forwarded to a cell phone used only for our hits. I put my finger over my lips to signal the girls to be quiet before I picked up. They all stared at me as I flipped up the phone and placed it to my ear. I remained silent and just listened.

"I have a job that requires your services. I want you to listen, and listen very closely," a man said with a deep Russian accent. He continued, “I have a problem that needs to be resolved. I want this done within thirty days. The contract is worth one-hundred-thousand-dollars. Half will be given up front, and the rest will be paid upon completion. You can find the information on the target in locker number 1356 at the Grand Central train terminal, and you can find the key under the station’s bench, eight rows down.”

I quickly reached into my purse and grabbed a pen and a small piece of paper to jot down the information. I just listened and wondered what type of job this was. I never had someone come so organized, and also we mainly only dealt with ’hood niggas. This was far from a ’hood guy” that we were used to handling business with. He paused, and there was a brief moment of silence on the phone before he continued.

“I take it that you want the job, since you haven’t hung up,” the Russian said before he let out a small chuckle. “Very well then. The money will be placed in a bag in the locker along with the information. Good day,” he said before he left me with the dial tone.

I slowly closed down the phone and looked at my girls, who were all staring at me, anxiously waiting to see who had called.

“Well what did he say?” Anisa asked as she threw her hands up.

I took my time before I spoke, almost too excited to let the words come out of my mouth. “One . . . hundred . . . stacks!” I said as I jumped up and watched as my girls cheered and slapped hands. This was the payday we were looking for. That was about $20,000 apiece. Usually we would have to split $50,000 for one hit. Twenty to ourselves sounded real good. It was the last day of the cruise, and we were all eager to get back to NY to get that money . . . the Murder Mama way.

We sat in our condo in midtown Manhattan. We all moved in with each other a couple of months back. We didn’t want to live in the ’hood, now that our operation was booming. Everyone sat and waited patiently for Anisa to return. She went to the station to retrieve the money and information. She told us that she wanted to go alone, just in case it was a setup by police, considering that we had never done business with this mysterious Russian guy before. She said there was no reason for all of us to do down. “Do you think it’s legit?” Beatrice asked as she split open a blunt and began to fill it with kush weed. That girl knew she loved her weed. She was a bigger weed head then me, and I had learned from the best, being that Murder and I had shared at least three blunts a day before he was arrested. “I don’t know. I hope so,” I responded as I looked down at my watch. “Where is she? She should be back by now,” I said, noticing that she had been gone longer than expected. Just as the negative feelings began to invade my thoughts, Anisa came through the door with a duffel bag and a big manila folder. “What took you so damn long?” I asked as I stood up. “I had to think about if I should take the money or not,” she answered. All of us grew confused looks on our face.

“What chu mean?” Aries asked as she put her hands on her hips. Obviously, she already had plans for her share of the money, as we all did.

“Look at this,” Anisa said as she threw the folder on the coffee table.

I picked up the folder, and when I saw the face of the man in the pictures, I quickly understood what Anisa meant.

“Fuck!’ Beatrice said as she looked at the picture along with me. It was Joell, the owner of the club, Tenders, and also Robyn, Aries, and Beatrice’s former boss. Taking this job would be breaking our golden rule: never hit someone we know or had ever encountered before.

“Me no believe dis’ shit!” Aries exclaimed as she flopped down on the couch and put her hands on her head.

“He used to be our boss! He knows us!” Beatrice exclaimed. “We can’t hit anybody we know, remember!” she said in total frustration.

“Fuck that! I’m about to get this money, with or without y’all. Me and Miamor don’t know this nigga,” Anisa exclaimed.

I remembered encountering Joell back at the strip club a while ago, but I remained silent, because I wasn’t ready to give up on that money just yet. “Just hold up a minute. We are talking about one-hundred-thousand-dollars, ladies,” I said, trying to weigh our options.

"You said it was a Russian guy on the phone, right?" Beatrice asked as she squinted her eyes, letting us know she was thinking hard about the task at hand.

"Yeah," I responded.

"I remember one time at the club, two Russian men burst in and put a gun to Joell's head in front of the whole club. Remember that, Robyn?" Beatrice asked.

"Yeah, I remember that shit. They were yelling about him owing them some money. You know Joell got that gambling bug bad," Robyn stated.

"That's the reason why they are at his ass," I added, as things started to make more sense. "I know we said we can't hit anybody that we know, but think about it. This is a lot of money. It is enough to move out of this grimy city. Miami looked real good this past weekend, ladies. Think about living near an ocean and not having to worry about karma catching up with us. If we stay in New York, we will always have to look over our shoulders. This is our way out," I said as I grabbed the duffel bag from Anisa's shoulder and dumped the stacks of money on the coffee table. Everyone's eyes were glued to the money, and it provided a sort of adrenaline rush for everyone. We were all paper chasers, and at that moment, I knew they would be down to kill Joell. The looks in their eyes told it all.

Anisa and I looked at each other and smiled, knowing that they were game. If they weren't, then Anisa and I would have done it by our damn selves, I'm sure of that.

It seemed as if all the tension left the room and everyone had small smirks on their faces. We were about to put a plan in motion.

Three weeks passed, and we were in the perfect position to take care of Joell. Everything was going as planned. Come to find out, Joell was sweet on Beatrice, but she never gave him any play. I told her to approach him as if she had a change of heart, so we could get close to him. I told her she would have to give up the pussy, and it was all in the game. Beatrice was smart, and she always lived by money over everything, so she wasn't hard to convince. Her deep chocolate skin, slim waist and extraordinarily large ass was eye candy to any man, so when she presented that to a sex fiend like Joell, he took the bait with no problem. Joell was a hard man to hit, I must admit. He knew there was a contract on his head, so he moved accordingly. He never went anywhere without his goons. Even when he met Beatrice at a hotel, he had two goons standing outside waiting for him. This hit was far more difficult than any of us imagined, but we were not called the best for nothing.

Beatrice spent every day with him for weeks, softening him up for the inevitable. She eventually convinced him to take her to Connecticut for a weekend at the world famous Clearwater Hotel and Spa, without his goons. I don't know how she did it, but she got him to do it. I guess she was putting it on him in the bedroom to get him to step out of his square. However, she did it, I didn't care. The only thing I knew was that we were about to be one-hundred-thousand-dollars richer.

I pulled into the luxurious spa parking lot alone. I arrived there six hours before Beatrice and Joell were scheduled to get there. I wanted to get there early and scope the scene, preparing myself for the hit. I got out and checked myself into the hotel. I carried my Gucci luggage to the front entrance and walked with a model's precision across the immaculate marble floor that made up the hotel's lobby. I wore a blonde wig and big shades, trying to avoid the chances of me being identified on camera. I checked in under an alias with the help of my fake ID and credit card. I told the other girls to stay home and let me do this one on my own. I didn't want all of them to come to the spa. It would only draw more attention to us. Too many black mu'fuckas in Connecticut was sure to raise somebody's red flag. Only Beatrice and I were going to complete this job, and would return to them once it was over.

Anisa and I argued over who would be the one to actually go with B to do the hit. She didn't want me to go without her, but we all agreed that I was the most ruthless of the crew, and she had to fall back. I assured her that Beatrice and I could handle it. B was going to ride up there with Joell, and I would kill him later that night while he was naked on a masseuse table.

***

Make it quick. In five minutes, come in. The door will be unlocked.

I looked at Beatrice's text on my cell phone and took a deep breath as I prepared myself mentally, focusing on the goal at the end of it all . . . money. Beatrice and I had gone over this plan the previous night at least fifty times, and we both knew the drill. First, she was going to get him drunk and relaxed. Then, she was going to offer an erotic massage on a masseuse table, naked of course, so he wouldn't have access to his gun that he kept on him at all times. I would sneak in and hit him with two hollow points to the back of the head. "In and out, like a robbery," as we would say. He would never see it coming; rock his ass to sleep . . . *Cha-ching*!

I looked at the clock, and it was a couple of strokes past ten p.m. My heart no longer beat rapidly before I killed someone. Repetition had taken away all of my insecurities when it came to my murder game. I looked at murder as if it was a job, not a sin. I went about killing just as a doctor would go about performing surgery, with expertise and precision. I was meticulous about every detail and never allowed my nerves to rattle me.

I carefully placed the bullets in the clip of my small .25 caliber pistol. I wore gloves to avoid the possibility of leaving any prints on the bullets. I had music playing in the background to get me in my mood, and bobbed my head to the rhythm while loading the gun. After I was locked and loaded, I removed my gloves and put them, along with the gun inside my purse. I had on a black business suit, the blond wig, and my stilettos on. My life wasn't a damn movie. You couldn't wear all black—mask and gloves—when you went to murk someone. You have to blend in, so people wouldn't look at you twice when you're leaving the scene. So I looked into the mirror and gave myself a once over before I exited the room. I had already put my bags in the car, and Beatrice and I were planning to make a quick getaway after the dirt was done.

I slowly walked out of the room and closed the door on my way to the top floor where Beatrice and Joell were. I then removed my gloves from my purse and stuffed them into my pocket as I headed toward the elevator. While on the elevator, I avoided facing the camera, turning my back to it as I pulled out my phone. First, I texted Beatrice and confirmed that I was on my way up, and then I dialed Anisa's number. I surprisingly had service on the elevator.

"Hello," Anisa said as she picked up the phone.

"Okay, I'm about to take care of it now. I love you," I said to her just as I always did before we took care of business.

"I love you too," she said back to me.

With that, the bell rang, signaling that I had reached my floor. I hung up the phone and walked out of the elevator. I reached the room, and just as promised, the door was slightly open and ready for me to sneak in. When I stepped in, I heard smooth jazz playing and the sounds of running water as I crossed the threshold of the door. The aroma of lavender scented candles danced in the air as the flickering candle lights illuminated the spacious presidential suite. My girl had set it up so nice for me. Beatrice was always on point like that. The lights were low, just like I anticipated. He would never see it coming. The room was so dark that I could barely see anything. The steam from the hot tub had it all foggy inside. I stepped a couple of feet in and I pulled out my gun, expecting to see Beatrice rubbing down Joell, but before I could even react, I felt a strong arm grab me from behind, and then I felt the cold steel of a gun pressed to my head.

The lights came on, and what I saw would be sketched in my mind forever. Beatrice was tied to the chair with blood running down her neck. She had been cut from ear to ear, and her eyes were staring aimlessly. She was dead. I then saw Joell smiling as he held a bloody knife, alongside three of his goons. The goon that had me at gunpoint quickly relieved me of my weapon and gripped me tightly from behind, placing me in a tight chokehold.

"Well, well, well! We have been waiting on you," Joell said as he reached into his pocket and pulled out Beatrice's cell phone and looked at it. He obviously saw the texts that I had sent her the whole time.

I had walked straight into a trap. I was speechless. The sight of Beatrice's bloody body was devastating. I felt my knees getting weak, and my heart seemed as if it was about to beat out of my chest.

The goon walked me over to the bed and forcefully pushed me down on it. “Beatrice!” I yelled as I crawled to her and hugged her tightly. Her lips were purple and her body was ice-cold. She was long gone, and somewhere in the plan, we had failed, and this was the end result. I couldn’t believe she was dead.

They watched me and laughed as I cried my eyes out in agony. Joell had seen enough, and pulled me off of her. He grabbed me by my neck and stood me up against the wall. I was on my tip toes as I felt his strong hand wrap around my neck.

“You think you can touch me?” Joell asked rhetorically. “You can’t kill me, bitch! You came barking up the wrong tree. I sniffed y’all out from day one. Since the day Beatrice approached me, I have been watching all of you. This game isn’t for rookies, and I am far from a rookie, Sunshine!” he said with passion as he squeezed my neck so hard I was unable to breathe. I stared into his bloodshot red eyes with no fear, even though inside I was terrified. I wouldn’t give him the satisfaction of knowing that he had achieved such a feat.

“Oh, okay. I see you are a tough one, huh?” Joell said as he unleashed his grip on me, letting me fall to the floor, panting for air. I held my neck as I tried to catch my breath, and I felt someone pick me up and toss me on the bed.

“I’ma break you down. I’m going to show you not to fuck with me,” Joell said with a sinister look in his eyes.

“Kill me and get it over with,” I said as I breathed heavily and sat up on the bed.

“I’m not going to kill you. But you are going to wish you were dead when I am done with you.

Joell’s goons grabbed me and pinned me down while ripping my clothes off, leaving me completely nude. I tried to stop them, but they were much more powerful than I was, and I couldn’t fight them off. I saw one goon pull down his pants, exposing his rock hard tool. I saw about twelve inches of nightmare. He straddled me while the other men held me down, and forcefully penetrated me, causing me to arch my back in complete anguish. No man had ever been inside of me, and my virginity was now being stripped from me in the worst way. I could feel my pussy being ripped open. It was so painful and so degrading, causing me to let out screams that were muffled by a hand. He went in and out of me violently. I could feel myself splitting, and the pain shot through my entire body. He was much too large for my rather small opening. I cried and yelled, but it was to no avail, as no one could hear me through the soundproofed rooms, and Joell and his crew had no intentions of stopping.

Once he was finished, he squirted semen all over my upper torso and face. Just when I thought the chaos was over, he switched positions with another goon, and then he began to have his way with me. Joell just sat and watched in pleasure as he got his sweet revenge. Tears continued to run down my face, but the yelling stopped as I quit fighting back.

The rape lasted for an entire hour, as his four goons took turns on me, leaving me bloody and sore. It reminded me of the torture that my stepfather used to put Anisa through, and I wished that my big sister was there to save me from this pain. They violated both holes, and left me in agonizing pain, curled up on the bed.

Once they were finished, Joell put a gun to my head and whispered sternly, "Go tell whoever sent you that they shouldn't have sent a woman to do a man's job. If I ever see you or any of them other bitches, you're going to end up like this bitch," he said as he threw his head in the direction of Beatrice dead body. With that, he left me in the room alone and traumatized.

I weakly looked over at Beatrice and whispered, "Sorry B! I am so sorry!" as the tears flowed.

Things were never the same after Beatrice died. We all were shaken. It felt like everything was falling down around us. We didn't feel safe in the Yitty anymore, so we all packed our shit and relocated to Miami. We all had aspirations of leaving the foul game alone. With Beatrice gone, we had a piece of us missing. Getting out of New York was mandatory.

We had to worry about Joell retaliating even more, and also we had to worry about the Russians. We took their money without completing the job, so we knew that we had created another enemy; an enemy that we couldn't stand up against. That botched hit taught us that we were not invincible, and at any time we could be gone. I hate that it took me being raped and Beatrice's death to teach us that hard lesson, but nevertheless, it was taken in heed. We moved with precision and intelligence from that day forward. We buried our girl in the Bronx, her hometown, and never looked back.

When we moved down to Miami, we tried our best to stay straight, but the allure of the game called for us, and when the money was low, we went back into business. We hooked up with a Haitian named Ma'tee, a powerful drug trafficker in Miami, and the rest is history. We never had any problems, except for the day we took on our biggest hit . . . The Cartel.

Chapter Fifteen

The Cartel

"Have chu heard from Miamor?" Aries asked as she handed Robyn a moving box to carry into their new apartment. They were in L.A., living the life, and after months of functioning out of hotels, they finally decided to move into their first West Coast spot. Their apartment overlooked Santa Monica Beach. They had made sure to get a three bedroom, just in case Miamor decided to join them one day.

"Nah, I haven't heard from her since we left. She's too wrapped up in that mu'fucka, Carter. I can't believe she chose him over us. That's been our rule since the very beginning; Fuck a nigga! Get your paper! I guess she forgot about all of that," Robyn stated with a shoulder shrug as they made their way inside.

Aries placed the box she held in her hands on the floor and sat down to go through its contents. She frowned when she opened it to find it full of envelopes that were addressed to Miamor. "Me think chu made a mistake and took some of Miamor's stuff out of storage. This box is full of old letters to she," she stated.

"It's probably just old letters from Murder," Robyn said. "I probably grabbed them by mistake. She stayed writing that nigga back in the day. You would have thought *he* was her man instead of Anisa's."

Aries had never met Murder, but she had heard a lot about him. "Miamor used to talk about he all de time," she recalled.

Robyn nodded her head as she continued to unpack boxes and rearrange their place. "Uh-huh. Between me and you, I think they had a little thing for each other. It was like after that shit happened to her and Beatrice, she wasn't really worried about no dudes. I think that rape fucked her head up more than anything. Then, when she met that nigga, Carter, she was on some other shit; talking that love bullshit."

"Me don't trust de' nigga, Carter. Me think Miamor is in over she head," Aries stated. "She might need us."

Robyn waved her hand in dismissal. "I ain't worried about Miamor. She made her decision. Nobody forced her to stay back in Miami. She can take care of herself."

Aries opened up one of the letters and read the intimate words that Murder had written Miamor. It was obvious to her that Miamor and Murder had been close. In his letter, he expressed his concern for her, and also expressed how he wished he could take care of both Miamor and Anisa. It seemed like he was the only other male attachment Miamor had ever had.

Aries went into her room and pulled out a piece of paper. Robyn appeared in her doorway and asked, "What are you doing, girl? We still have so much stuff to unpack out of the car," she came in and flopped down on Aries' bed.

"Don't chu think it's strange that she hasn't even called us? We haven't gone one day without talking since de' day we met. Now all of a sudden, Mia just falls off the map. Me gut tells me something is wrong," Aries said.

"You're right," Robyn stated.

"Me think me's going to write Murder and let he know what's up with she," Aries said.

"What is he going to do? He's locked up," Robyn replied.

Aries showed Robyn the letter she had just read from

Murder. "According to this, he will be out soon. Maybe he can talk some sense into she." "A'ight, girl, go for what you know," Robyn stated. She hugged Aries and left her to write her letter.

Murder walked on the platform of his tier, his khaki jail pants hanging slightly off of his behind as he strolled toward his cell. He received much love from the other inmates, but he didn't deal with many. His business was still popping in prison. He survived in the joint by murking niggas who stepped out of line. He was paid with cigarettes, drugs, shoes, clothes, books, and basically whatever else an inmate had to offer. It was far less than what he had killed for while he was on the outside, but behind the walls was a completely different world. Something as simple as a pack of cigarettes could be as worthy as gold in prison. He entered his cell just as the bars began to close.

A CO walked by. "Brown, you've got some mail," the fat white guard said as he stuck a single envelope through the bars of his cell.

A look of surprise crossed Murder's face. He only received mail from one person, but he hadn't heard from her in years. Miamor was the only person who had ever contacted him while he was locked up. He opened the letter and read:

Hey Murder:

Chu' don't know me, but I'm a friend of Miamor's. Me know chu know all about the Murder Mamas and what we are about. Anisa used to tell us stories about chu, so me know what chu about and how chu get down.

Anisa was killed down in Miami, and me think de' same people who killed she may have hurt Miamor too. She started fucking with one of our marks, and me thinks she is in trouble. Chu' are de only person who she might listen to. Please call me so that me can put her on three-way. Maybe chu can talk some sense into she. 852-444-9683. Me put some money on de' commissary for chu. Call soon.

Aries

Murder knew exactly who Aries and Robyn were. Miamor had told him all about them in some of her letters. He was now worried about Miamor. He didn't know what was going on, but he fully intended on finding out. He was up for parole, and would be out the joint in a couple of weeks. He wrote Aries back and asked her and Robyn to meet him in Miami.

He had done five years easily, but now that he knew Miamor was in danger, the next two weeks were going to creep by torturously slow. *I know li'l mama better be a'ight, or niggas in Miami gon' bleed!*

Chapter Sixteen

The Cartel

Mecca stood over Miamor and looked at her with pure hatred. He had finally gotten a chance to be alone with her without any supervision, and he was going to make the most out of that opportunity. It was in between the nurse's shift, and his heart was racing as he looked down at his worst enemy. He wanted to tell Carter about Miamor, but he didn't want to take the chance of Carter siding with her. He saw how much Carter loved Miamor, and it enraged him, knowing that Carter loved the same woman that he hated so much. The last thing he wanted was to be in a beef with his only remaining blood brother over a female. He figured that what Carter didn't know, couldn't hurt him. *This bitch got his head gone, but I'm about to end this game and send her to her Maker,* he thought as he stared at her, clenching his jaws.

Mecca looked over his shoulder and made sure no one was coming just before he focused his attention back on his worst enemy. He bent down and began to whisper in Miamor's ear, hoping to God that she could hear him. He was unaware that she had come out of her coma earlier that day, so when she opened her eyes, it startled him. He saw the lazy look in her eyes and knew that she was weak. He was glad that she was conscious. Now she would know who was taking her life. Mecca was about to gain his sweet revenge.

"I hate you, bitch!" Mecca whispered as he began to pinch her oxygen supply. "I want you to die a slow death. I'ma finish what Fabian couldn't do," he whispered and he smirked as he heard her heart monitor begin to beep faster.

Miamor wanted to return the gesture by saying, "Fuck you!" but she was too weak to even open her mouth. The only thing she could move was her fingers.

Mecca looked down at her hand and noticed that she managed to stick her middle finger out. He chuckled as he pulled the pillow from under her head. Stopping her oxygen flow wasn't quick enough for him. He wanted her dead. He held the pillow up and prepared to suffocate her to death.

Miamor tried again to say something, tried to call for Carter, but only a low raspy grunt came out.

"Nobody can save you now, bitch!" Mecca whispered.

"What's going on?" Carter asked as he walked into the room.

"I was just fluffing her pillow, bro. Your sleeping beauty looked uncomfortable," Mecca said as he began to fluff the pillow, hoping that Carter didn't see what he was really trying to do.

Carter smiled and walked over to Mecca and put his hand on his shoulder. "I'll take it from here," he said, not knowing that Mecca was just about to murder his only true love. "I have to talk to you and Zyir when I finish up in here," Carter added, thinking about the plan that he was putting together for their relocation.

"Cool. I'll be downstairs," Mecca said just before he shot Miamor a cold stare.

Miamor matched his stare, and she wished that she could say something. Mecca and Miamor both despised each other with equal passion, and it was obvious that neither of them wanted to tell Carter the truth. Both of them wanted to kill one another and still keep a bond with an unknowing Carter.

Mecca exited, and Carter focused his attention on Miamor. He pulled up a chair to her bed and began to stroke her hair and look into her eyes. "Hey, beautiful," he said just before he leaned over and kissed her cheeks. He heard Miamor grunt while moving her lips, trying to talk.

"Shhh. Save your energy, baby," he said as he put his finger over her lips. "The nurse said it will take a couple of days before you will be able to talk or sit up. You just have to rest," he explained.

Miamor looked into Carter's brown eyes and knew that he was the man that she wanted to spend her life with. However, she knew that Mecca was trying to kill her. *I wish I could just tell him. Come on, Miamor, move your lips. Talk!* she thought as she tried to say something. But it was to no avail. I have to tell him the truth. Will he still love me? Will he understand and pick me over Mecca.

Carter picked up Miamor's hand and kissed it softly. "I am going to kill whoever did this to you, I swear. I know it's all my fault. I was in the middle of a war and never thought about my enemy coming for you," he said, feeling guiltier with every word.

Your brother is the one trying to kill me! Miamor thought as she heard the sincerity in his voice. She promised herself that if Mecca didn't kill her, she would tell Carter the truth as soon as she was able to. She was tired of running from herself. She was looking into the eyes of the future. Her future was in Carter Jones.

"Just listen," Carter said slowly and sternly. "After you get well, we are moving from Miami. No more wars no more of the fast life. We can work on us and become one," he said, meaning every word of what he was saying. He wanted to spend the rest of his life with Miamor, and he was willing to give up the dope game for good just to make that happen.

Carter couldn't take Miami's ills anymore. Breeze's death was the last straw. It was as if Breeze had died twice, because just when they were coming to terms that she was gone, she reappeared, but only to commit suicide when they were only seconds away from saving her. Carter was tired of everything . . . everything except for Miamor. *She is the only thing good in my life,* he thought as he clenched his jaw, thinking about his deep love for her. Just to see her lying in that bed helpless almost brought a tear to his eye. He was ready to make her a happy woman, and eventually, his wife.

A tear slipped down Miamor's cheek, and Carter believed it was tears of joy. But in actuality, it was a tear of pain. It pained Miamor to think about how she would have to tell him that she was connected to the man that killed most of his family, that she gave the drink to Taryn that killed her, and that she was a killer—a cold killer.

The nurse had just arrived, and Carter looked back, greeted her with a smile and stood up. "Get some rest. I will be back to check on you in a while," he said as he pecked her on the forehead and exited the room gracefully.

"Man, what the fuck is wrong with you?" Zyir asked half jokingly as he watched Mecca take a shot of Patrón.

Mecca was noticeably angry and irritated. "Nothing. I'm good, Zy," he said, thinking about how he couldn't get to Miamor. *I'ma kill that bitch tonight. I don't give a fuck. She's got to die,* he thought as he tried to conceal his feelings from Zyir, who was staring at him like he was crazy.

"You sweating and shit. I'm just saying, you look like you got something on your mind," Zyir said as he sat on the couch.

Before Mecca could respond, Carter entered the room. "Yo fam, I need to talk to y'all for a minute," Carter said as he sat on the Italian leather couch next to Zyir. Mecca sat across from them and wanted to hear what Carter had to say.

"Our time has passed with this organization. We have to clean our money and get out of the game. I have been talking to a couple of business associates, and I'm putting something together for us in Phoenix. We can wash our money and get into the casino business."

"A casino?" Zyir asked as he sat up, not expecting to hear what was coming out of Carter's mouth.

"That's right, Zy. We have to get out of the dope game and go legit. Some business partners of mine are willing to sell us a small share of a new casino that's being built there. It's the only way that we are going to ever prosper. The Feds are on me, and the connect ain't fucking with me because of the indictment. We are in a lose-lose situation. It's only a matter of time before The Cartel goes under, feel me?"

"What you talking about? Diamonds move dope! We run these streets, and I'm going to run these mu'fuckas until I die. Just like Poppa did," Mecca said, sounding more ignorant with every word.

"That's the mentality that's going to land us all in jail. Think about it, Mecca," Carter said as he emphasized his words with subtle hand gestures. "If snitch-ass Ace would not have had a baby mama, I would be serving a life sentence right now. We just barely got out of that situation, Mecca. We are under a microscope, and next time, I might not be so lucky!" Carter said, breaking down the truth to his younger brother.

"Maybe Carter is right," Zyir added as he began rubbing his hands together. "We have to get out of this 'hood mentality and expand. Think about not having to worry about, 'are we going to get caught' or 'whose next to die'. We're losing those we love behind this shit," he said as he thought of Breeze. "I'm with it," Zyir conceded as he held out his hand and slapped hands with Carter.

"Mecca, you in?" Carter asked as he and Zyir looked at him.

Yeah, I'm in, but first I got to kill your girl, Mecca thought as a small smirk appeared on his face. He was going to have fun killing Miamor. The fact that he was doing it right under Carter's nose added more enjoyment for him. "I'm in, bro," he said as he reached over and slapped Carter's hand.

"Good, good," Carter said as he stood up. "Look, but first we need to finish off the last shipment. We have to get our money out of the streets. Anybody that owes us money from consignment needs to pay up. We are out of the game officially today. I know that the business slowed down while I was locked up, but now I'm home, and it's time to collect. Zyir, I want you to collect from them Liberty City niggas, and Mecca, you need to collect from the Overtown crew. We hit them each with fifty joints, right?" Carter asked, not sure of the amounts that they had spotted the crew with on the previous shipment.

"Yeah, that's about right. I haven't heard from any of them either," Zyir added as he thought about the money that they had in the streets.

"Niggas thought that they wouldn't have to pay up since you got locked up. They think The Cartel is over. It's time for them niggas to pay," Mecca added as Carter refreshed his memory. "I almost forgot about that debt they owe us."

"I didn't," Carter added as he stood up to walk out of the room. "It's time for The Cartel to collect," he added just before he disappeared in the darkness of the hallway.

Zyir grabbed his keys, and so did Mecca. "I'm going to head out and take care of that," Zyir said, planning to head to Liberty City.

"Me too," Mecca said as his trigger finger began to itch.

He wanted to go and put a bullet in Miamor's head so badly, but he decided to wait until he came back. He wanted Miamor to be in fear. She didn't need to know when he would kill her, but she knew he was lurking, and that was enough to plant his seed of fear. He wanted to make her miserable before taking her life. Mecca smiled and headed out of the door, followed closely by Zyir.

Miamor watched as the nurse dipped the towel in the soapy wash pan. It pained Miamor to know that she was helpless and couldn't move on her own. *I feel so weak*, she thought as she felt the warm towel on her skin. Mecca constantly stayed on her mind. She didn't know when he would return to kill her, and she knew that he would succeed, because she was too weak to defend herself. She saw a man's silhouette in the door and her heart began to speed up, hoping that it wasn't Mecca.

Before she could play the guessing game, Carter appeared, leaning in the doorway. "How is she doing?" he asked as he slowly walked in.

"She is going to be fine. She just needs a lot of rest and love," the nurse said as she continued to wipe Miamor's arms and neck, cleaning her.

"Great," Carter said as he leaned over and kissed Miamor's forehead. He stared at Miamor, and couldn't wait until he took her away from the chaos. He had already decided that he would ask her to marry him and be his forever. But first, he would have to nurse her back to health.

"Yeah, that's the nigga right there," Robyn said as she watched Mecca and Zyir leave the house. "The Dominican on the right, that's Mecca Diamond, and the other one is Carter's li'l nigga, Zyir." Murder clenched his jaw and breathed heavily through his nose as they camped in a truck outside of the Diamond's estate. They had been eyeing the place for hours, because Murder wanted to check out what he was going up against. He wanted to find Miamor, but first, he would have to find Carter.

"He's the one that killed Anisa?" he asked as he grinded his teeth together, feeling the anger building up inside of himself.

"Yeah, that's him," Aries added as she remembered when Anisa was murdered.

Murder didn't get the name "Murder" for nothing, and he was good at what he did. That's why he always checked out the competition before just jumping into the situation blindly. He knew he would kill Mecca in due time, but he would have to be patient. His main concern was finding Miamor.

Zyir and Mecca got into two different cars, and they pulled out. Murder decided to follow Zyir, hoping he would lead him to Carter or Miamor.

Zyir slowly nodded his head to Nas as he maneuvered his car through the streets of Liberty City. He smiled as thoughts of Breeze invaded his mind, and just as quickly as the thought lit up his world, it brought him down. He blinked away tears as he thought about how their relationship never got the chance to grow. She had been taken away from him before they could build their love, and he missed her in a new way as each day passed. He looked at the picture he had of her on his dashboard, and gripped the steering wheel tightly as visions of her hanging crossed his mind. He checked his rearview, and noticed a white truck that had been behind him for a minute. *What the fuck?* He thought to himself as he switched lanes, and just as he expected, the truck switched lanes also. He then knew he was being followed. Just to be sure, he made two rights hitting each block with speed, and the truck followed him. Zyir reached under his seat and pulled out his Tech-nine. He set it on his lap and glanced at the truck once again. He wasn't about to play the "cat and mouse" game, so he decided to see what was happening. He approached a red light, and the white truck was behind him about two car lengths. He tried to look and see who the driver was, but the black tint kept him or her a mystery.

Zyir threw his gear into park and hopped out with his gun in hand. He pointed at the truck as he walked toward it. "What's good, my nigga?" he yelled as his jaw tightened and he was ready for whatever. He couldn't see who was behind the glass, so he hesitated to squeeze. The truck burned rubber and sped past him, as Zyir kept his gun on the vehicle. He pointed the

Tech at the truck until it was out of sight. He didn't know who was following him, but they were about to get aired out by his little friend.

Zyir hopped back in his car and headed to Liberty City to pick up the rest of The Cartel's money. "Whew!" he huffed as he turned up the music and proceeded. "Maybe, I'm tripping," he said, pulling off.

Chapter Seventeen

The Cartel

Six Weeks Later

Carter's eyes were bloodshot red as he sat near Miamor's bedside. His worry for her had taken a toll on his body. He hadn't gotten a good night's sleep since finding her, because he sat in the rocking chair in her room all day and night to make sure that she was okay. He was grateful that she had come out of her coma, but she was still so weak, and he felt that he needed to be strong for her. He wanted to keep her spirits up until she was fully recovered. He leaned forward in his chair and rested his elbows on his knees as he sighed. He watched her stir in her sleep slightly.

"No . . . no . . . !" she groaned while still asleep. She began to struggle and lash out as if she were fighting someone.

Carter stood and approached her bedside. "Miamor," he said. "Wake up, ma."

"No!" she screamed as she sat straight up in bed and fought against Carter. It was dark in the room, and Miamor had been dreaming of Mecca killing her. When she awoke and found a man by her bed, she thought that he had come for her again. She was sweating and her breathing was labored. She was shaking, the terror in her heart paralyzing her while her eyes darted wildly around the room.

"Miamor, it's me, baby . . . it's just me!" Carter said soothingly as he held on to her tightly.

When Miamor heard Carter's voice she broke down in his arms. "He's going to kill me!" she sobbed as she held on to him like a frightened little girl clinging to her father.

Concern was written all over Carter's face. He grabbed her by the shoulders and forced her to look into his eyes. "Who, Miamor? You have to tell me who you're afraid of," Carter said. He was determined that when he found out the identity of Miamor's attacker, he was going to kill him.

Miamor saw the sincerity in his eyes, which only made her cry harder.

He sighed and pulled her to his chest. "Shh. It's okay, ma. I'm not going to let anything happen to you. I almost lost you once. I won't lose you again," he promised.

He scooped Miamor into his arms and carried her to the rocking chair. He sat down with her and stroked her hair while he rocked back and forth.

"I can't stay here, Carter," she whispered. She gripped the collar of shirt in fear. She was holding on to him for dear life.

"Shh . . . I got you, ma. I promise you—"

"Carter, no!" Miamor yelled as she sat up shakily and looked at him with sad eyes. She wanted to be a part of this charade. She wanted to live here with him, but with Mecca around, her life would always be at risk. "I can't live in this house. I don't feel safe here. I won't stay here, Carter. If you try to make me, I'll run. I'm like a sitting fucking duck in this bitch!" she cried. She had never been this emotional, but since coming out of her coma, her fear had rendered her helpless and feeble. All she did lately was cry. "He can touch me here. I have to go to a place where he can't find me."

"*Who,* Miamor? Who the fuck is after you? I can't help you if you don't talk to me," Carter said in frustration. "I'll handle that nigga. You don't have to run. You don't have to worry about it if you just trust me. Give me your burdens, ma," he whispered as he put his hand gently behind her head and pressed his forehead against hers.

Miamor desperately wanted to give her all to him. She wanted to put her life in his hands, but how could she, when the one man she feared on this earth was Carter's flesh and blood? She hated Mecca just as much as she loved Carter. *If I show him who I really am, I'm going to lose him,* she thought as she shook her head and kissed his lips. "I can't Carter. You would never understand. Just please get me out of here. Right now. I need to feel safe," Miamor pleaded.

It hurt Carter that after all they had been through, Miamor still didn't trust him enough to feel secure in his home. He tried to understand where she was coming from. He figured that she was just paranoid from her attack. She was afraid, and he was determined to give her a sense of security. "All right, ma. Let me get you dressed then we'll go. We'll go wherever you want to go," he assured her. He placed her back in the bed and put a pair of sweat pants on her.

He touched her with such gentleness that it made Miamor yearn for him, not in a sexual way, but in an emotional way. He was so stable. He was always so focused and in control. Every move that he made was calculated concisely. Miamor wanted to depend on him and take his lead, but it could never happen. In the grand scheme of things, they would always be adversaries. Like Romeo and Juliet, their allegiances lay on different sides, while their hearts were in each other's hands.

"Let me get your pain medication. It's in the master bedroom. I'll be right back," Carter said before kissing the top of her head.

She nodded and watched him disappear into the hallway. *This man is my soul mate, but we can never be together,* she thought grimly.

She looked over to the nightstand that was beside the rocking chair. A gun lay on top of it. She swung her legs over the edge of the bed, wincing in pain as she stood to her feet. Her legs felt like Jell-O, but she used all her energy to make it over to the stand. She leaned against it and took deep breaths as she grabbed the gun. Holding the pistol in her hand caused a wave of relief to wash over her. She gripped it as her head hung on her chest, and she inhaled deeply.

Miamor had been through hell, and she would never be the same woman that she was before. Her body was scarred for life. She would never be able to forget what had happened, because the war wounds would be a constant reminder of her plight. Like a Jew who had been terrorized by Hitler or a slave that had been victimized by their master, Miamor would always remember. She would always feel the pain; she would always harbor fear, resentment, and insecurity . . . she would never forget. Mecca had changed her life for the worst, and now she had to refocus. She had to retrain her body, and she had to regain composure over her emotions, because she was determined to get back at Mecca. But, she didn't have a choice but to wait. She had to give herself time to heal.

Carter came back into the room and frowned when he saw Miamor standing. He rushed over to her. "What are you doing? You shouldn't be on your feet," he said. His eyes went to the gun in her hands. He tried to take it from her, but she shook her head.

"Don't, Carter. I need it," she whispered seriously.

Carter picked her up, and with the gun in her hand he carried her out of the room.

All of the luxury inside of the house meant nothing to Miamor. By being there, she was in Mecca's territory, and she refused to stay. She clung to her man and kept her finger on the trigger of the gun as he carried her outside to his car. After making sure that she was secure in the passenger seat, he hurried around to the driver's side, and they pulled away.

Murder sat up in his seat when he saw Carter carrying Miamor out of his house. It was the first time he had seen her in five long years, and it was evident that she was badly injured. His blood boiled at the thought of someone putting their hands on her, and the intimate way that Carter handled her enraged Murder even more. *I'ma handle that nigga personally,* he thought as he palmed his pistol and leaned low in his seat as he watched Carter drive by. Murder pulled out into traffic and followed. This was the opportunity he had been waiting patiently for. There were no bodyguards surrounding Carter. *It's just me and him. This mu'fucka riding around with my shorty like she's his bitch,* Murder thought angrily. *I'ma bout to claim that, and wipe him and his people off the map.*

Murder made sure that he kept Carter's car in sight. Now that he had seen Miamor, he was more determined than ever to bring her home.

***

Anger pulsed through Carter as he drove in silence. He was livid, not with Miamor, but with whoever had instilled so much fear in her heart. He stroked her hand reassuringly as he sped through the city streets, headed toward the Four Seasons Hotel. Miamor didn't ask him where he was taking her. She trusted that he would take her to a place where she couldn't be touched.

When they arrived, Carter didn't let Miamor's feet touch the ground. Seeing her so broken was tearing him up inside. All he wanted to do was treat her like his queen, and if tucking her away inside a fortress was what she wanted, then he would give it to her. He picked her up, and she nestled her head into his chest. He tucked the gun inside of his jacket so that it wouldn't be visible as he took her inside.

"I need your Presidential Suite," Carter said to the front desk clerk. The young man behind the desk looked awkwardly at Carter, who was still holding his woman in his arms. "Now!" Carter reinforced with authority.

When Carter entered the room, he lay Miamor down on the bed. "Close your eyes, ma. You're safe here. Nobody knows where you are but me," he said as he pulled the duvet up to cover her battered body.

Tears accumulated in her eyes until they were so full that they had nowhere else to go but down her face. "Will you hold me?" she asked.

Carter removed his clothes as Miamor's eyes took him in. Her love button began to throb as she admired his chiseled abdomen and chest. He stood before her in nothing, but his boxers. He was exquisite . . . the ideal specimen of a man in every way. He was the Adam to her Eve, but seeing his perfection brought about her insecurity as she reached up to touch her face. She had yet to look at herself in a mirror, but she knew that she didn't look the same. Her face felt differently, as if Mecca's fists and torturous beating had rearranged her features in the worst possible composition.

Carter climbed into the bed and spooned Miamor from the back.

"I can't keep you," she whispered. "I'm all fucked up. I can feel it. My face isn't the same. Everything about me is fucked up. My body, my face, my heart, my soul." She spoke so low that Carter could barely hear her.

"You can't keep me away from you, ma," Carter said, his lips gracing her ear. He stood up and retrieved a mirror from the vanity. He brought it over to Miamor.

Her hands shook as she reached for the antique handle. When her face came into view, she had to put her hand over her mouth to stop herself from crying too loudly. She could not bear to look at herself. Her face was almost unrecognizable. The left side of her face suffered a broken jaw, and was healing, but remained swollen and bruised. The blood vessels near her left eye were permanently damaged, and a green bruise would always remain near her temple, not to mention the many cuts that marred her once smooth skin. Everything that she loved about herself was non-existent. All of her perfect features were destroyed. "How can you even stand to look at me?" she asked as she tossed the mirror aside. "I'm not even the same woman you used to know." Now, her face reflected the way she had always felt inside . . . ugly, scarred, and bruised. She had always felt like damaged goods.

"Miamor, you're beautiful, ma. Everything about you is beautiful," Carter whispered as he climbed back in bed with her, holding her tight. "Do you know how fucked up I was when I thought I'd never see you again?" Miamor didn't answer, so he continued. "I was lost, ma. You were made for me. These scars show you're a fighter. You're supposed to be dead right now, but you're not. Your body will heal, Miamor. You just have to give it time. But I love you for what's inside you. You're my lady, forever," he whispered as he took her hand and held it up for her to see. He knew that she had been in so much pain lately that she never even realized that he had slipped a diamond ring onto her finger. She gasped when she finally noticed it. "Be my wife."

Miamor was sobbing so hard that she could not form the words to respond. Carter kissed the back of her neck. "I don't want to see you cry, ma," he whispered. "I know you love me, Miamor, but you refuse to let me all the way in. Trust me. Let me protect you. Let me see all of you."

"You won't like what you see," Miamor admitted with sorrow in her tone.

Carter's lips made their way south as he kissed from the back of her neck to her shoulders, to her back, and further on. He parted her legs and slipped his tongue between her thighs.

The intense pleasure temporarily erased her pain as a sigh escaped from her lips. "You don't really know me," Miamor moaned as she allowed him to kiss her inner thigh. She could see the top of his head as he slowly traced the creases of her vagina with his tongue.

"Teach me," he responded. He pulled her southern lips apart, revealing her pearl. "Trust me," he said as he took it into his mouth, causing Miamor to squirm underneath him. "Marry me," he whispered as his tongue made love to her clit, plucking it like a delicate flower.

The heat from his mouth drove her crazy, and her eyelids closed in ecstasy. Her love for this man was so deep, that from the very first time she saw him, she knew he was her Achilles heel. He was one of the few people who had actually ever gotten her to feel. She experienced emotions with him that she never knew existed. He had found her and nursed her back to health. He loved her despite her appearance, but she was not sure that he would accept her once he found out who she really was. Her soul rained as teardrops graced her cheeks. Her cry was inaudible, but her heart was bleeding for the love that she needed, but she knew that it was one she could never have.

Carter worked her over until she came in his mouth. Her love came down like a waterfall, and Carter licked her clean, sucking her clit until her legs shook in satisfaction. He arose silently and walked into the bathroom and drew her a bath.

The feelings he had for Miamor made him weak, but it was a weakness that he embraced. She made him a better man, and no matter what she said, she would always belong to him. He wasn't taking "no" for an answer. He was so torn up about what had happened to her. He blamed himself every day. He just wanted to make her happy. After everything he had lost in the war with the Haitians, she was all he had left. As he sat on the side of the tub and watched it fill with water, he felt himself becoming emotional. *I let this happen to her,* he thought.

He felt her arms envelop him, and he looked up to see her standing there. Her health had come a long way since the day he had found her close to dead in the hospital, but she still needed to rest. He knew that it had taken a lot out of her to come and check on him. As he looked up into her eyes, he saw the woman his heart was meant for. She was a fighter, but he didn't want her to have to endure anymore anguish. He had to be strong for her. He quickly restored his composure and pulled her down onto his lap.

"I'm sorry I wasn't there to protect you," he whispered, his words stopping in his throat.

Hearing the stress in his voice caused Miamor to close her eyes in torment. *I have to tell him. I can't let him think that he did this to me. I can't hurt him like this. He thinks he loves me, but he doesn't even know the real me. I'm the reason why everyone he loves is dead. I can't marry him. There is no way that we can ever be together,* she thought dismally. Even if she agreed to marry Carter, in her heart of hearts, she knew that it would never happen. Their wedding would turn into somebody's funeral, because he was sure to find out about her affiliation with the Murder Mamas and her role in Taryn and Breeze's misfortunes. She also did not trust herself, because as soon as she crossed Mecca's path, she knew that she would get it popping.

I am not the housewife type. If you really love him, then you will let him go, she told herself over and over. Miamor had to convince herself that their love affair was over just to stop herself from yearning for his touch. Carter was like a drug to her. She had become addicted to his swagger; the way he walked; the way he talked; the unspoken boss status that he possessed' the way he smiled . . . all of it endeared her to him. She was willing to settle down, willing to be faithful, willing to trust him. She was ready, but she had to walk away. Out of everything she had been through, leaving Carter would undoubtedly be the hardest thing she ever had to do. *I don't have a choice,* she told herself. She hoped that Carter would remember them for what they were to each other before all of the shit had been thrown into the game. He would always hold a special place in her heart. Miamor wiped away a tear as she closed her eyes.

"Carter, I have to tell you something," she uttered as she massaged the back of his head gently. Knowing that it would be the last time she would ever touch him, she took her time and stared him in his eyes. "I'm not who you—"

Before Miamor could get the words out of her mouth, Carter's lips covered hers. He kissed her passionately as he removed the hotel robe she was wearing. He didn't want to make love to her. She was still too weak for that. He just wanted to take care of his queen, to nurture his woman, to sit back and spend time with his future wife. He removed his Calvin Klein boxers and pulled her gently into the tub.

"Carter, I really need to tell you this—"

"Shh!" his lips never left hers as he silenced her. "If you're not saying "yes", then I don't want to hear it. Will you marry me?" he asked.

A lump formed in Miamor's throat. How could she tell him no? She nodded her head and gave him a weak smile. "Yes," she answered, but as soon the words left her mouth, she knew that she had made a mistake. *In the morning . . . I'll tell him tomorrow,* she told herself.

The next morning, Carter awoke to find Miamor staring at him. Her eyes were swollen and red from crying all night as she watched him sleep.

"What's wrong, ma? Everything a'ight?" he asked as the palm of his hand graced her face. "Are you in pain?"

"More than you can even understand," she admitted.

"I'ma take all of that away, Mia," he said. "We're moving to Phoenix. I've already begun making the arrangements. In a week, we'll be miles away from Miami."

Miamor put her finger to his lips. "Carter, I need to tell you something. There is something that I need to get off my chest. It's important."

Carter frowned. He could see the worried look in her eyes. There was something heavy on her mind, and he wanted her to know that she could tell him anything. "Just say it, Miamor. You can talk to me."

"First, I want you to know that everything I feel for you is real. It's more real than anything I've ever known. I love you more than I've ever loved anyone in the world. You mean everything to me, Carter, but I can't accept this ring," she said as she removed it from her finger.

"Don't do this, Miamor," he said. "Don't shut me out."

Miamor stood up and paced the room, her wobbly legs barely able to keep her up. *Just tell him,* she urged herself. "Carter, there's a lot about me that you don't know. I've been lying to you—never about how I feel—but all along, you never knew who I really was. Ma'tee paid me and my girls to get at The Cartel!"

Carter sat up in the bed and his eyes instantly turned cold. He stood and put his hands on the wall as he lowered his head and absorbed her words.

"I belong to a group called the Murder Mamas. We've hit niggas from New York to the South. Ma'tee paid us to come at Mecca, but he ended up killing my sister, Anisa. I've been at him ever since, but he got to me first. He beat the shit out of me. All these cuts and bruises came from him, all because he knew who I was. He gave me a poisoned drink at your sister's memorial, but I gave it to Taryn. I knew the drink Mecca had given me had something in it, and I gave it to her anyway. I was willing to do anything to get back at Mecca for taking my sister away. When I first met you, I didn't know you were a part of The Cartel!" Miamor cried.

Carter was calm, as he used the wall for support. He was too calm for what she was telling him, and she had a bad feeling in the pit of her stomach, but she still continued her confession.

"Carter, you have to believe me. If I had known that you were a part of it, I would have never fucked with you. I came to your brother's funeral to kill Mecca. That's when I found out who you were, but by then, it was too late. I had already fallen for you. I love you Carter, but there is something wrong with me inside. Killing is all I know. I've been doing it since

I was twelve years old. You don't know me! I'm a bitch! I'm a Murder Mama! I'm heartless and cold! I'm all of these things, except when I'm with you. You are the only person in my entire life who has ever taken my pain away!"

Carter clenched his teeth as he listened to Miamor's story. The realization of who she really was hit him like a ton of bricks. The thousand lies that she had told him were a slap in the face. It was all too much for him to even comprehend. He could feel his anger rising as he thought of how he had trusted her. He had made the mistake of letting her get close. All this time, he had been sleeping with the enemy. She had been plotting on him while he had been investing his time and commitment into her. She had played him. He thought of the day he had seen her at Monroe's funeral, and then the faces of his deceased loved ones popped into his mind. She had contributed to the madness, and he had allowed her to. Everything had gone down right underneath his nose. Mecca had tried to warn him about her treachery, but Carter had refused to see. *That's why he hates her so much!* he thought.

Miamor walked over to Young Carter. His silence was killing her. "Please, say something!" she begged.

Carter didn't even feel himself react until it was too late.

Smack!

His rage took over, and he slapped her with such force that it sent her flying to the ground. She instantly tasted the salty blood that oozed from her busted lip.

Carter stormed over to the nightstand where he had stored his gun. Miamor's eyes grew large when she saw him approach her with it in his hands. He loaded the clip and cocked it back, then knelt down over her. With tears in his eyes, he grabbed her hand forcefully. "Take the gun, bitch!" he mumbled through clenched teeth as he held the barrel up to his chest while she gripped the handle. "You wanted to get back at The Cartel that bad? Do you know how many innocent people you've hurt? Pull the trigger, Miamor. I *am* The Cartel! Now is your chance!"

Miamor lay beneath Carter with the gun in her shaky hands. "Carter, don't do this!" she beseeched.

"Kill me, you grimy bitch! This is what you wanted. I told you I'd give you anything. You wanted this, so I'm giving it to you." Carter was so livid that he was foaming at the mouth, and his grip was so tight on her hand that it felt like her bones would crush from the pressure.

Miamor had never let anybody test her or even speak to her in such a way. Carter was pulling her card, and her murderous instincts clicked back in slightly as she glared into his eyes. He was challenging her, calling her bluff, daring her to shoot him. *This mu'fucka must not know,* she thought as her nostrils flared. Miamor was like a pit bull. When she was docile, she was one of the most loyal and gentle creatures in the world. But when provoked, something inside of her snapped, and once she clicked on, it was very hard to turn her off.

Miamor's finger wrapped around the trigger, but when she looked into the eyes of the man she loved, she could not bring herself to finish what she had started. Too many things had changed. Her heart wasn't as cold as it used to be. "I can't!" she wept. "I can't!"

Carter snatched the gun from her and put it to her head, pressing it point blank range as his finger danced on the hair trigger. Hatred and betrayal was in the air as he contemplated ending her life. She had peeled away at his outer layers, the same way that he had done to her. They had penetrated each other's souls, which is why her treachery stung so much. He knew that he should kill her. She deserved to die, but not at his hands. He threw the gun across the room as he arose to his feet. "Get the fuck out," he said calmly, but Miamor didn't move. Instead, she rolled onto her side as she cried. She was paralyzed in her grief.

"I'm sorry!" she screamed.

"Bitch, get out!" Carter repeated. His voice roared throughout the suite, and he showed no mercy as he dragged Miamor across the hotel room floor, disregarding her already injured body.

"Carter, no! Please!" she yelled as she fought him. She was fighting to stay in his life. With all of the energy she had left, she was clinging to him because she knew that once she let go he would no longer be hers.

By the time he got her out of the suite, he was sweating and out of breath and she was curled up in the hallway. "What am I going to do?" she cried while looking up into his face.

He showed no emotion, no sympathy, no love as he turned on his heels and re-entered the room. He snatched her phone up then tossed it into the hallway beside her. "I don't give a fuck what you do, Miamor," he said, the tone of his voice revealing his disappointment. "I'm done. You have got five minutes to call a cab. If you're not gone by then, I'm going to finish this, and unlike you, I *will* be able to pull the trigger," he threatened. He took one last look at her and shook his head in disgust.

She could see the hatred in his eyes. There was nothing left to say. It was over, and he had tossed her out with nothing. He slammed the door in her face, closing the best chapter of her life.

Chapter Eighteen

The Cartel

Miamor had never felt so low as she sat in the hallway of the luxury hotel, pleading with Carter to forgive her. Her ego and principles were thrown out of the window. When it came to matters of the heart, she was willing to look foolish and willing to swallow her pride if it meant that Carter would be with her. She cried her heart out to him through the closed door, but it never opened. He had shut her out of his life, and she had to accept it. She was physically and emotionally spent as she stood to her feet. Using the wall to hold her up, she made her way to the elevator. Her hair was wild, her face stained with dried tears, and she wore nothing but a bathrobe as she made her way out of the hotel. Stares and whispers surrounded her as her bare feet carried her through the lobby.

"Excuse me, Miss," the maître d'hôtel of the establishment rushed over to her with two security guards in tow. "I received a call from the Presidential Suite. I'm going to have to escort you off of the premises."

The security guards grabbed her arms and she snatched them away. "Don't touch me!" she screamed, making an even bigger scene. She made it outside and walked as far as her feet would take her, but every step felt like a thousand. She was too fragile to make it on her own. She had exhausted all of her energy, and gave up as she fell to the ground to catch her breath, the hot pavement burning her skin. At this point, she felt hopeless. She had given up everything and had betrayed her girls trying to chase a dream. At least before she had them as her family. Now, all she had was herself.

Murder had sat in the car all night watching the hotel, waiting to see Miamor and Carter emerge. He was so close to her, and he wasn't going anywhere until he brought her home, back to New York where she belonged. He cringed at the way Carter touched Miamor, and jealousy loomed over him like a dark cloud.

When he finally saw Miamor emerge from the hotel alone, struggling, and barefoot, he grabbed his gun and jumped out of the car and ran toward her. His baggy khaki shorts, white T-shirt and red fitted cap represented the complete opposite of what Carter's poised demeanor did, but the two men had one thing in common. They both loved Miamor.

"Miamor!" he yelled, grabbing her attention.

Miamor didn't even look in his direction. She heard a man screaming her name and instantly thought of Mecca. She looked around for something to defend herself with, but she could barely scrape herself off of the ground. She frantically tried to hide, but there was nowhere to go. Traumatized and too tired to put up a fight, she screamed when Murder finally reached her. It wasn't until he picked her up off the ground did she realize that she wasn't in danger.

"It's okay, ma. Murder's back. I'm gonna handle that nigga and anybody associated with him," he sneered. "Word to my mutha', ma. I'ma cook that beef personally!

Miamor thought that her eyes were deceiving her. "Murder?" she called out as she touched his face.

"It's me, shorty. I got you."

Relief washed over Miamor and she gave into her body's urge to rest. She closed her eyes, knowing that she was in the arms of family, and that nothing would happen to her while he was around. It had been five long years since she had felt that safe. It seemed like a lifetime ago since she had felt the secure connection with Murder. But now that she had seen his face again, she realized he was still so prevalent in her life. Even with Carter, there was the constant threat of danger, but with Murder, there were no secrets. No lies dwelled between them. There was only trust.

Murder took Miamor back to the motel room where Robyn and Aries were waiting. It was a far cry from the Four Seasons, but it was how he got down. Murder was not into the glamorous life. He wasn't a flashy type a nigga. He was a 'hood nigga and a goon who had established his track record in the 'hood from the sandbox up. He didn't need all the extras. He actually found the entire Cartel establishment to be a joke. *Those clown-ass niggas on that Hollywood Godfather shit,* he thought as he put Miamor down and stared at her. *That Rico Suave-ass nigga don't know how to keep a bitch like Miamor. Shorty a gangsta, not some high society broad.*

"What happened to she?" Aries asked as she and Robyn rushed to Miamor's side and observed their dear friend.

"That bitch-ass nigga, Mecca happened to her," Robyn stated as she shook her head and wiped away a tear. She and Miamor hadn't always seen eye to eye. They butted heads more than a little bit, but that's what family does. Miamor was her sister. They had been through the fire together, and to see her so beat up enraged her.

"That nigga, Carter let the shit happen to her. Mecca's his brother. He wanted to be her man, so he should have been her man and made sure she wasn't touched, nah mean?" Murder said. "He gonna feel it too."

Miamor heard the voices around her and slowly opened her eyes.

"How are you feeling, mama?" Robyn asked.

Miamor smiled slightly and shook her head from side to side. "I lost him!" she whispered.

Aries and Robyn looked at one another, and then back down to Miamor. They couldn't understand her love for Young Carter, and they were past the point of trying. They were just glad that they had gotten their friend out while she was still alive. They knew that Miamor no longer had the malice it took to kill, so they would handle it for her.

She doesn't even have to know, Robyn thought. *Once Carter and Mecca are out of the picture, she will be able to move on with her life. She'll be back to her old self in no time.*

"Chu have us, Mia," Aries stated. "That's all chu need."

"I'm so sorry for turning my back on y'all. You guys are all I have," Miamor said.

Robyn knew that Miamor wasn't herself, because she had never apologized for anything. The new, emotional woman in front of her was not the same girl she had met years ago.

She wasn't the same chick who had cut off a nigga's dick for money, or the same one who had taught her to shoot a gun properly. Miamor had changed. She was vulnerable. *Love has really made her ass go soft,* Robyn thought.

"It's okay, honey. We're sisters. We're always here for you. Me and Aries are going to let you get some rest, but there's somebody else here for you," Robyn said as she stood. She grabbed Aries' hand and they exited the room.

Miamor turned her head and smiled when she saw Murder posted by the door, with one foot resting against the wall. He scanned her from head to toe. Neither of them said a word, but they stared intently at each other. They were both surveying the changes they saw in one another.

He finally walked over to Miamor and knelt beside the bed. He grabbed her hand and turned it over to see the tattoo on her wrist. "You still my li'l mama, huh?" he asked as he kissed the tattoo. He knew what the phrase "Murder Mama" meant. It meant that she was his, and she knew it too.

"Always," she replied as she touched his face, remembering the bond that they had once shared.

"I missed you, Miamor. I thought about you every day while I was on the island," he said.

She wiped a lone tear away and gave him a half smile. She used to think about Murder all the time, before she met Carter. "I missed you too," she responded.

Murder looked at her, and the anger inside of him was evident. It radiated off of him, and because she knew him so well, she was able to read him like a book. His presence was exactly as she remembered it. He was still strong and commanding as he had always been. Prison had done him good. He was solid and strong, his swagger still the same . . . low key and mysterious.

"I didn't want this for you, Miamor. This wasn't supposed to be your life," Murder stated as he kissed her hand.

"This is all I've ever known. Every time I find someone that I love, I realize that fate is playing a sick game with me. I can never have someone to call my own. You belonged to Anisa. Carter belongs to The Cartel. I wanted you both, but neither of you were meant for me," she said miserably, the sorrow of her broken heart affecting her words.

"I came to take you home," Murder stated.

"Ha!" Miamor laughed obnoxiously as she shook her head. "Home? I don't think I've ever had one of those. I've never been in one place long enough to consider it home. I've never felt safe enough to be 'at home'," she said. "Where's home for me, Murder?"

"With me," he stated simply.

Miamor knew that because Anisa wasn't around, things could be different between them. He loved her. He always had, but she wasn't an eighteen-year-old girl anymore. She was a grown-ass woman who had evolved. With her emotions for Carter all over the place, she didn't know how she felt. When she had come to Miami, she had put Murder out of her mind, but it was obvious to her that he had never forgotten about her. He had come for her after five long years, just as he had promised he would. He never broke his word to her. He would give her the world if he could. *Can I offer him the same loyalty in return?* she asked herself.

"I don't know if I can give you what you want from me right now, Murder. I've never lied to you, so I do not want to start now. My heart is with someone else," she admitted sadly. It was something that she did not want to say, but something that he had to hear.

Murder winced and released her hand. He hated Carter for locking down Miamor's heart. The look in her eye when she spoke of Carter was the same look that used to be reserved for him years ago. "That nigga almost cost you your life, Mia," he reminded.

"He didn't know what I was into . . ."

Murder heard her as she tried to defend him, but he interrupted. "Aw, ma, don't give me that. The nigga knew what *he* was into! That's all that matters. If he's a boss, then he protects those around him, especially his bitch. You know the game, ma. I know you know, cuz I taught you. You should have murked him, Miamor. Quick, and without a second thought, because that was the job you were paid to do. That was what you signed up for when you picked up that phone years ago. You're my li'l mama. You're Murder's mama baby, girl. You know what it is between me and you. That's why you got my name tatted on you."

Miamor turned up her lips and rolled her eyes as she sneered at him in denial. "We all got the same tattoo," she defended.

"Yeah, but it was your idea, and it meant the most to you," he said, knowingly. He smiled and lifted her chin, forcing her to reveal the truth in a smile of her own. After all this time, he still knew her all too well. "Forget about him, Miamor. I'm back now. I cared for your sister, but she's gone. Everything that stopped us before does not matter now. Nothing is in the way now. I came here for you, and another nigga will never hurt you while I'm around. Get some rest. We are leaving for New York in a couple days."

Chapter Nineteen

The Cartel

"We got to dead these niggas," Murder whispered as he looked over his shoulder to make sure Miamor was still asleep. He, Robyn and Aries were huddled up, putting their game plan in motion. Murder wanted what was left of The Cartel dead. He planned on killing Carter first, and then making Mecca come to them. He was about to set a trap for The Cartel.

Miamor was dead to the world, as she lightly snored in the bed just a couple of feet away from them. The painkillers that she had been taking had her drowsy, and for the past two days she had done nothing but sleep. She was still recovering from a coma, and also from a broken heart. It pained Murder to see her heartbroken over another man. He felt like Carter had stolen what was his. The Miamor he remembered was feisty and was never pressed over a dude. *This Carter guy really has her heart*, Murder thought as a small streak of resentment ran through his body. He glanced over at Miamor and admired her beauty. Even with the marks and scars on her face, she was beautiful to him. He focused back on Aries and Robyn and spoke.

"We got to handle this dude," Murder said as his trigger finger began to itch.

"I know, but I cannot get to the nigga. Miamor is not going to help us murk him. She's in love with him," Robyn said, trying to explain to Murder how Miamor had changed.

"It's okay. We are going to make him come to us," Murder said as he put his plan together in his mind. He felt obligated to kill Mecca and Carter because of all the pain they had caused the only women who he had ever let into his life, Anisa and Miamor. He took the trespass against them personally, and he wasn't leaving Miami until all scores were settled.

"Grab Miamor's phone," he instructed Aries, as he had it all mapped out. Carter was about to die, and then Mecca soon after. He planned on using Miamor as bait.

Robyn walked over to the night stand and sneakily removed Miamor's cell phone. She walked back over to Murder and handed the phone to him. Murder quickly went into Miamor's contact list and began to scroll down, looking for Carter's name. He located it and quickly began to text him in hopes that Carter would think Miamor was texting him.

"I'ma make this nigga come straight to us," Murder said as he pushed the send button and began to patiently wait for Carter to take the bait. "Now, we just sit back and wait," he said just before he got up and walked over to Miamor. He stood over her and bent down to kiss her on her forehead. "I'm taking you back home, Miamor. Everything's going to be all right," he whispered in her ear as she slept comfortably. "I love you." Murder had never said that to anyone, besides Miamor. He had never trusted anyone enough to extend something so great, but as he looked down at her, he knew that he meant every word.

"I love you too Carter," Miamor whispered back, while still in her sleep. It was obvious that Murder was not the man in her dreams. Hearing those words were like daggers through his heart, but he understood. He was just ready to end The Cartel and move Miamor back to Brooklyn, where she belonged.

Carter watched as the movers moved all of the expensive décor and statues from the Diamond Estate. The immaculate mansion didn't even look the same now that it was half empty. Carter's Phoenix venture was all in place. His partners were just waiting on his arrival to get the ball rolling. The Cartel was about to go legit and leave the entire street business behind. Carter possessed all of the business savvy his father once had, but never knew how much he was like him. He felt his BlackBerry vibrate and quickly pulled it off of his waist and looked at it. It was a text from Miamor, asking him to meet her somewhere so they could make things right between them. He quickly dismissed it and shook his head. He missed her dearly, but he hated her at the same time. She had betrayed him to the fullest extent, and in the process she broke his heart, making him feel like a fool. He knew that he should have killed her on behalf of The Cartel, but he could not pull the trigger. There was a small part in him that still loved her, even though she was responsible for the fall of his family. *Why can't I let her go?* Carter asked himself as he slowly paced the room with his hands behind his back. The clicking sounds of his Mauri gators echoed throughout the house as he thought deeply about Miamor. Zyir walked in, interrupting his thoughts. "I'm all packed up and ready to leave this mu'fucka for good," he said and his Jordan sneaks scuffed the marble floor. "Phoenix is a good look," he said as he approached Carter and slapped hands while embracing him. "About that," Carter said as he stepped back. "I want you to fall back for a month or two. Go back to Flint and I'll send for you," he said as he looked into Zyir's eyes.

"Wha . . . What? Why you want me to go back home, Carter?" Zyir asked, totally confused about Carter's sudden change of heart.

"Zyir, it's not what you're thinking. I am doing this to protect you. You are the only one that I fully trust on this earth. Mecca's my brother, but his head isn't always in the right place. He's impulsive, while you are a thinker. You plan every move before you make it. You are like a little brother to me, and I just want you to be safe. I want to check out the new turf first, and then I'll send for you. I need you out of harm's way for a while, just in case something happens to me. If that day comes, you will know what to do. I've already made arrangements just in case you have to step into my shoes," Carter said, thinking two steps ahead.

"I don't get it, fam," Zyir said with a confused look on his face.

"I'm taking a lot of money up there to get washed, feel me? I don't know if I am dealing with undercover agents or what. If anything goes down, I want you to be safe and I want to leave my business in the hands of someone I trust. You all I got left, Zy," Carter said as he put his hand on the back of Zyir's neck. Carter knew that Zyir would not like the news, but it was something that he had to do. Zyir was exactly like him. He had the same swagger, same morals, and same thought process as he did. Carter practically built Zyir from the ground up to be a real nigga. He would never be able to forgive himself if Zyir got caught up in some bullshit on his account. Carter kissed the top of Zyir's head and pulled him close. That was his li'l man, and he had much love for him. He knew that Zyir was a boss in the making, but that was not the path he wanted for him. He had big plans for his little man that would introduce him to an entirely new world . . . the business world. All Zyir had to do was be patient. "Just trust me, family. Just trust me," Carter said as he released Zyir.

Zyir felt like his world had come crashing down. To not be with Carter was like taking his other half. Carter was his nigga, his father figure, and his only family. He wanted to protest, but Carter had yet to tell him anything wrong, so he nodded his head in agreement. "Okay," he answered in reluctant agreement.

"Cool. I got your plane tickets on the table in there. Your stuff will be sent to you when you get up there. You got your paper up, right?" Carter asked, referring to Zyir's cash.

"No doubt," Zyir confirmed as he thought about the half million dollars he had stashed away in a foreign account. The proceeds from the Miami drug game had done him lovely, and he had enough to be comfortable at that point. He walked into the room to retrieve his one-way ticket to the murder capital of Flint, Michigan. He knew something was wrong with Carter, but could not place his finger on it. In Zyir's eyes it was as if Carter was telling him good bye.

Carter's flight was scheduled for that next morning, and he was ready to leave everything behind. No matter what he did, he couldn't get his mind off of Miamor. He felt his phone buzz again and he looked at the screen. It was Miamor again. "Just leave me alone, Mia! You're killing me!" he said in a low whisper as he dismissed the text.

Zyir returned back to the front with his plane ticket in his hand. He saw the look in Carter's eyes, and there was no mistaking that something was wrong.

The Final Chapter

The Cartel

Carter, please respond. I miss you. I know you're upset, but I need to see you. Love Always, Miamor.

Young Carter read the words twice before deleting the message, just as he had done all the others. It had been seven days since he'd put Miamor out of his hotel room, and she was constantly on his mind. Every message she sent reminded him of what they both had lost. He hoped the relocation would help give him a fresh start.

The Cartel no longer ran Miami. They were out of the drug business and moving on to new heights in a new environment. All of the death, destruction, and deception would be left behind. Miamor would be left behind. He wished that things could be different, but the truth of the matter was she was untrustworthy. He had done her one last favor by keeping Mecca off of her ass. He felt that he owed her that much. Although she had lied to him, everything that he had told her was the truth. He had indeed fallen in love with her, and because of that, he allowed her to live. Now he could skip town and forget that he ever knew her.

The sound of a door opening and closing indicated Mecca's arrival. He walked into the house. His long hair was pulled back into a ponytail, and he wore a sad expression on his face. Carter had never seen Mecca so humble and serene.

Melancholy filled the room as Mecca looked around at the nearly empty mansion. "I came up in this house," he said. "I watched Poppa run his meetings out of this house. Me, Breeze and Money used to play in that backyard." Mecca's eyes had tears in them as he recalled the fond memories of his family, but he let none fall and kept his head held high, just as his father had taught him to do. He wished that he could rewind the clock to happier times, but nothing could erase the hollow feeling he felt. "I'm the last one standing."

Carter didn't respond. He had never known the infamous man who had fathered him, but he respected him all the same. He had grown to love Taryn as much as his own mother, and the deaths of his siblings had destroyed him because he had been robbed of his time with his newfound family.

"It doesn't feel right leaving all this behind," Mecca stated.

"We have to," Carter stated. He extended his hand to Mecca, and they embraced briefly. Carter picked up his Louis luggage, and they both headed toward the door. All of the other contents of the house had already been shipped to Arizona. A new house would be set up and waiting when they arrived.

"Where is Zyir?" Mecca asked.

"He has a couple stops to make, but he'll be flying back to Flint tonight. The arrangements are already made for him," Carter explained.

Carter's BlackBerry rang out loud, and he saw that Miamor had text him again.

Carter, if you ever really loved me, please text me back. I'm sorry for everything. I don't want to lose you.

Mecca watched Carter as he typed into his phone. *I know this mu'fucka ain't still in contact with that bitch,* he thought. Mecca had a gut feeling that Carter was responding to Miamor, and although he had given his word to Carter that he wouldn't touch her, he had lied. That was an itch that he was determined to scratch. He just couldn't let his hatred for her go. He had a score to settle, and he had a good feeling that he was going to get a chance to do it before he left Miami. His brother was going to lead him right to her.

Sorry's not enough. I'm leaving town tonight. Good luck with your life, ma, Carter typed back.

Within seconds, his phone was going off again with another message from Miamor.

Carter, please do not leave me like this. At least give me a chance to say good-bye. Meet with me, Carter. Please. I won't take up too much of your time. I just want to see you.

"What's up, fam?" Mecca inquired, trying to sound casual.

Carter looked up at him. "Oh, ain't shit. Just a little something I forgot to take care of. What time does the private jet take off?"

"Six o'clock," Mecca replied.

Carter looked at his watch. It was only three p.m. That left him with three hours to spare. He thought about never seeing Miamor again, and his stomach turned over. She was right. They did need to see each other face to face before he left. They needed closure.

There's a warehouse in Opa-locka on Twenty-seventh Ave. Meet me there in an hour.

Carter instructed Mecca to meet him at the landing strip, and the two parted ways.

"It's about fucking time!" Robyn yelled out as she flipped Miamor's Sidekick closed. She looked at Aries and Murder. "He responded. He thinks he's meeting her in Opa-locka in an hour."

Murder was about to put his game down like only he could do, and a devilish leer spread across his face. He went into the closet and put on black gloves and grabbed a black .45. He tucked it into his waistline.

"We should come with chu," Aries stated as she stood.

Murder shook his head. "Aries, you stay here with Miamor. Robyn, you come with me. I'ma personally rock this nigga to sleep. When Miamor comes out of the shower, get her ready to go. Pack up all our shit and wipe the room down. We I get back, we're out," he explained.

Miamor closed her eyes as the stream of shower water licked her wounds. She was still not at full health, but was grateful for the little bit of strength that was returning to her limbs. *At least I can stand up and walk around without passing out,* she thought as she washed her body. A part of her was happy to be getting out of Miami. She had too many bad memories here. It was where her sister had been killed, where she had almost been killed, and where she had lost the man she loved. *Fuck Miami!* she thought bitterly. She was trying to rebuild her callous attitude. Being tough had stopped her from being hurt in the past. She had built walls around herself that only Carter had been able to scale. *Forget about him. He doesn't want you. It's over,* she said to herself.

She got out of the shower and wrapped a towel around her body. Green bruises covered her everywhere, but her body was healing and she was grateful for that. If only her heart would heal as well.

She walked out into the room and saw Aries packing up their things. "What's going on?" she asked.

"Nothing, Mia. Get dressed. When Murder and Robyn come back, we're leaving," Aries stated.

"For New York?" Miamor asked.

"Yeah."

"Tonight?"

"Yeah, Mia, we are leaving tonight," Aries said as she looked on in sympathy. She knew that Miamor was mourning over losing Carter.

When all of their bags were by the door, Aries turned and said, "Me will go fill up the tank at the station on the corner. Mia, chu need anything while I'm out?"

Miamor shook her head no as she stepped into a pair of Robyn's Juicy Couture sweat pants and put on a wife beater and sneakers. "Nah, go ahead. I'm good."

Aries shrugged. "All right. Me will be right back. By the time they get back, we'll be ready to dip."

Aries left out, and Miamor locked the door behind her. She lay down on the bed and closed her eyes, when her phone began to ring. She walked over to the dresser where her phone lay. She hadn't checked it since she had been there. She had forgotten that she even had it. The name "Carter Jones" appeared on her screen, and butterflies instantly appeared in her stomach. She flipped open her PDA and saw that she had an unread text message:

I'm on my way

She frowned when she read the message. "On your way where?" she asked aloud. Miamor searched the outbox of her phone, and her eyes widened in shock. *I didn't send these,* she thought as she read through every one. *They are going to set him up! Carter's going to walk right into a trap!* She put her hands over her mouth and speed dialed his number. Her anxious heart felt as if it would explode. She tapped her fingers impatiently against the desk as the phone rang in her ear. The voice mail popped on and she hung up to dial him again.

"Pick up the phone!" she urged nervously, knowing that Carter's life rested in her hands. *If Carter arrives at that warehouse, he's dead,* she thought. It wasn't that she thought Carter was a punk, but she knew Murder would expire Carter on sight. When she received his voice mail again, she screamed in frustration. "Answer the fucking phone!" She tried to reach him once more, but to no avail. Either he wasn't taking her calls, or Murder's job was already complete.

She looked to see what time he had texted her last. *I still have a half an hour,* she thought. She was so overwhelmed that she wanted to cry, but now was not the time for her to bitch up. *I have to get to him,* she thought. *I'm the only person who can stop Murder. I'm the only person who he won't kill.* It had been a long time since she had prayed, or since she had even believed in God, but for this, she raised her head to the sky and closed her eyes. *Please don't let Carter die. I need him.*

She paced back and forth until finally Aries came back. Aries instantly recognized the fire in Miamor's eyes. Miamor tossed the phone at Aries.

"How could you do this?" Miamor asked.

The look on Aries' face established her guilt, but she responded, "We've done this a thousand times."

"I love him!" Miamor yelled. "This time is different!" She took a deep breath, not wanting to overexert herself. She could feel the room start to spin. "Give me the keys," she demanded.

Aries hesitated, but then handed them over without contest. She removed a chrome .45 from her waistline and passed it to Miamor as well.

Miamor brushed past her, and just before she exited the room, Aries called her name. "Mia!"

Miamor turned around and stared at her friend.

"I'm sorry."

Miamor didn't respond. She knew that if something happened to Carter, that her relationship with her girls would never be the same. She stormed out of the room, hopped into the rental car and sped off recklessly, praying that she was able to stop the madness before it was too late.

Carter pulled up to the vacant warehouse. It was one of the many stash spots that he had used to store guns and drugs. He sat in the car for a few minutes, trying to gain his composure. *No matter what she says, it's over. I can't trust her,* he told himself. He knew that once he saw her face, his emotions would try and override his intellect. He could not allow that to happen. A beautiful woman had been the downfall of many men. He refused to allow Miamor to lead him to a premature demise. She had showed shade. There was larceny in her heart, and because of that, he had to make a clean break. He exited his vehicle and activated his car alarm, then proceeded into the building. He stopped walking in mid-step and turned around to return to his car. He popped the trunk and hit a button that caused the floor of the trunk to slide back, revealing an arsenal of weapons. He had to remember that he was no longer dealing with the woman he loved. He was dealing with a Murder Mama, and although he did not truly believe that Miamor would harm him, he was not about to walk in unstrapped and chance it. After Miamor's confession, he had done his research on the Murder Mamas, and found out they were more treacherous than he could have imagined. Their work was exquisite, precise, and professional. Carter couldn't imagine Miamor doing some of the jobs that he had heard she had pulled off, and a part of him was intrigued by the mystique of it all. The other part of him was enraged, because she had been hired to take down his family, including him. That put them at odds in a territory where love couldn't exist. He had gone over all the possibilities in his head. There was no way under any circumstances that he would ever be with her.

***

"He's here," Robyn whispered down to Murder from the second floor. She had a perfect view of the parking lot, and from where she stood, she could easily shoot anything moving on the floor below. She would let Murder handle his business, but if things went awry, she would kill Carter. Robyn watched Carter walk up to the building, then all of the sudden he disappeared. Murder waited behind the front entrance to sneak him from behind. After five minutes passed, Carter still hadn't walked through the door. "Yo, what the fuck the nigga doing?" Murder asked, trying to keep his voice low so that his presence wouldn't be known in the warehouse. "I don't know. I can't see him. He walked right up to the front door, then I lost sight—" Robyn stopped speaking abruptly when she felt the cold kiss of death. Carter was standing behind her with his pistol to her neck. He wasn't a fool, and he didn't run the largest drug operation in Florida for nothing. He didn't trust Miamor, and he was glad he had followed his gut instincts and entered the building through the secret entrance on the side of the building. Carter peered over the ledge to see what he was going up against. He couldn't believe that Miamor had tried to set him up. He could see Murder waiting for him, lurking with his gun already aimed, and he realized that if he had walked through the front door, he would have been shot at point-blank range.

"Murder?" Robyn called out loudly as she struggled against Carter.

Murder looked up to where Robyn hid and saw Carter walk out of the shadows with his gun drawn. Carter had an advantage over him. From where he stood, he could have easily shot him.

"Fuck is you?" Carter asked as he began to descend the steps, with Robyn in a chokehold. He surveyed the room looking for Miamor.

Murder smirked and aimed his gun at Carter.

"I wouldn't do that if I was you. Unless you want me to splatter this bitch's brains all over the floor," Carter threatened.

Murder laughed as if Carter had told a joke, and then without hesitation, he turned his gun toward Robyn.

Boom!

With a marksman's aim, Murder hit Robyn with a hollow tip in the center of her forehead. She folded in Carter's arms, then dropped lifelessly to the concrete floor. She never saw her end coming.

Carter glanced down at Robyn's dead body in disbelief, and in that split second Murder capitalized on the opportunity.

Boom!

Murder let off a shot, hitting Carter in the leg, causing him to drop his gun. Carter didn't even have time to react as he grabbed his leg in pain. "Aghh!" he screamed as a burning flash of heat terrorized him as a bullet ripped through his leg.

Murder wanted to kill Carter slowly. He hated the fact that Miamor had fallen for another man, and he was going to enjoy snuffing his lights out.

Miamor hit 100 mph as she drove and ran through red lights, frantically trying to make it in time. When she was four blocks away, a traffic jam slowed her car down to a crawl. "Damn it!" she yelled as she hit the steering wheel in frustration. "I can't wait this out! He'll die if don't get there!" she whispered urgently. An emotional lump formed in her throat. *Calm down, Miamor,* she told herself. *You can do this . . . you have to do this if you want to save the man you love.*

She grabbed the gun off of the passenger seat and pulled the car over to get out. She could see the tall warehouse about a quarter mile up the street. *I have to run,* she thought wearily. She was doubtful that she could, because she could barely stand on her feet for too long without feeling weak. She knew that her body wasn't ready for what she was about to put it through, but she had no choice. Carter was worth the pain.

Miamor took off running full speed, ignoring the ache of her limbs and the excruciating beat of her heart as she pushed her body to the limit. Her broken ribs screamed in protest with every step that she took. Each time her feet pounded the pavement, she felt as if she would pass out. Her lungs burned, but she refused to stop. "Aghh!" she screamed as she continued on.

No longer able to endure the pain, she stopped and placed her hands on her knees to balance herself. She gulped in air as if she was suffocating, and could no longer stop the tears from coming. "I can't do this!" she whispered. "Murder's going to kill him!"

Carter grabbed his piece off of his ankle holster, and returned fire, sending bullets sailing past Murder's head, and then stood to his feet. "Fuck!" he grimaced as blood soaked through his Evisu jeans. Murder took cover behind a stack of steel barrels and spit bullets until his clip was empty. He immediately put a fresh clip in his gun and ducked for cover, his brief pause giving Carter the chance to gain a slight advantage.

"Fuck you hiding for, you bitch-ass nigga?" Carter screamed as he fired more shots.

Murder couldn't get a shot off. Every time he rounded the corner of the barrels, Carter popped off. He was relentless with his weapons, and he wasn't going to stop until Murder stopped breathing.

Damn! This nigga shooting like his clip don't expire, Murder thought in irritation as he waited for Carter to run out of ammunition. What he didn't know was that Young Carter stayed strapped. He had one in his waistline, one on his ankle, and two in a shoulder holster, so the bullets would be coming for days.

Carter stopped firing and waited, so that Murder would think he had run out of bullets. But as soon as Murder jumped on the opportunity, Carter came up blasting, hitting Murder in the shoulder. The power from the .9mm blew him back, almost knocking him off his feet.

"Aghh! Fuck!" Murder shouted. He was livid. In all the years he had been pulling jobs, he had never been hit. The pain radiated through his shoulder and traveled down his entire body as sweat dripped from his forehead.

Murder stepped from behind the barrels and faced his adversary. Both men extended their guns, standing within five feet of each other, and looking down the barrel of one another's guns. The malice in their eyes displayed their hatred for one another. Carter and Murder wrapped their fingers around their triggers at the same time. They were both prepared to go out in a blaze of glory.

Miamor staggered up to the front door of the warehouse. Her body was so beat up that she practically collapsed into the entrance from fatigue. "Murder, no!" she screamed when she saw the two men that she loved preparing to kill each other. She pulled her gun and pointed it in their direction.

"You sent this nigga here to kill me!" Carter yelled, never taking his eyes off of Murder.

"No! Just please, stop!" she pleaded. "Murder . . . Carter don't do this!"

Miamor's voice fell on deaf ears, because both Murder and Carter kept their weapons locked and loaded.

Miamor let off a shot in the air to get their attention, and then aimed her gun at them.

"Shoot this nigga, Miamor!" Murder ordered. "*He* did this to you. Kill him, Miamor!"

Miamor turned her gun toward Carter, tears in her eyes. Their eyes met. No words needed to be spoken between them for her to know that she couldn't pull the trigger. She sobbed uncontrollably as she changed her mind and turned the gun toward Murder.

"Miamor," Murder uttered, disappointment and hurt in his tone.

Miamor shifted her gun back and forth indecisively. *Who do I choose?* "I can't choose!" she said aloud.

Click-clack!

They heard the sounds of a fourth gun being cocked back. They looked around in confusion, wondering where it was coming from. It wasn't until Miamor turned her head that she saw Mecca Diamond, but by then it was too late.

Boom!

Mecca sent a bullet crashing through Miamor's skull, finally winning the game of life and death they were playing.

"Nooo!" Carter and Murder screamed as they watched in horror as Miamor's body dropped to the ground, and Mecca stepped out of the shadows with a smoking gun in his hand. On instinct, both men loaded Mecca up with bullets.

Mecca's body jerked, and he tried to squeeze off a few crazed shots before the bullets from Murder and Carter's guns robbed him of his life. He went out with a smile, because he had finally gotten his revenge. Now he was going to reunite with the rest of the Diamond dynasty.

Carter rushed to Miamor's side and held her in his arms. The crimson hole in her temple let him know that she was long gone, but he cradled her anyway, and cried as he kissed the top of her head. He was in shock and hysterical. All of the beef that he had been through, and all of the material things that he had gained seemed worthless to him now as he sat in a puddle of Miamor's blood. Her death had broken him down to his weakest state.

Murder fell to his knees and put his hands on the top of his head. His heart was broken and in complete anguish as tears also fell down his face. He pointed his gun at Carter. "You did this to her!" Murder screamed. He wanted to end Carter, but it would not bring Miamor back. Murder lowered his weapon and hit the floor with his bare hands as he cried and mourned over Miamor.

Carter didn't focus on anything but the woman in his arms. He tuned everything else out as he spoke in Miamor's ear. "I'm so sorry, ma! I love you, Miamor! Wake up for me, ma! You got to wake up!" Carter cried. "Wake up, ma . . . wake up! Wake up!"

"Wake up, bitch!" Miamor gasped and sucked in air as her eyes shot open and she looked around in confusion. Her vision was blurry, but she could see that her arms were still bound, and Fabian loomed over her, swinging the deadly chain in his hands. "It's about time you woke up, bitch! I thought you had died on me for a minute," he said with a devious smile. "You passed out, but don't worry, I'ma make sure the next time you black out it'll be for good." "Carter . . . Murder?" she mumbled frantically as she looked around the basement that she was trapped in. The hope that had filled her slowly fizzled away. *I passed out. None of it was real,* she thought as tears came to her eyes. *I'm dying. I just saw my entire life flash before my eyes. It was all a dream. I'm right back where I started . . . right back at the beginning. None of it ever really happened. Carter, Murder, Mecca, Breeze . . . I made it all up in my head.* It was at that moment that Miamor realized that she was not invincible. This was not a dream, and the lifestyle that she had lived was finally catching up to her. Her karma had come full circle. *I'm going to die down here,* she admitted to herself.

Miamor was truly terrified, and she began to weep as she realized there was no avoiding her fate. "It was all a dream!" she whispered in disbelief as she cried desperately. The mind is a powerful tool. It's the most powerful weapon that a human possesses, and when Miamor's body could no longer endure the physical pain, her mind had temporarily taken her to a different time and place . . . to a place of relief. But now that she was awake, her circumstance was still the same.

The putrid smell of human waste mixed with blood filled the air. This was truly hell on earth, and her torture had just begun. It wouldn't end until Fabian said so, and he had a whole lot planned for her before putting her out of her misery.

Her eyes widened as Fabian lifted the chain and brought it down across her naked body. "Aghhh!" Miamor screamed in agonizing pain. Just when she thought it was all over, the torture had just begun.

The entire story you just read was all a figment of Miamor's imagination. Not until you open the pages of The Cartel 3 *will you figure out her fate.*

The Cartel 3

(Commencement)

Prologue

"We are gathered here today to celebrate the lives of three of God's children."

The preacher stood before the many people who attended the funeral of street royalty. It was a sad day in Miami, and on this day, the streets were like a ghost town. It seemed as if the entire underworld had stopped to commemorate those they had lost. Everyone within the city limits felt this grief. The lives of three street legends had been destroyed, and grief overflowed in the ceremony as three silver-plated coffins sat side by side with an array of flower arrangements around them. It was a bright, sunny day, and it seemed as if God shone his light down from the heavens above to make that hard day seem a tad bit better for the mourning attendees. It was a triple funeral to bury the last of the Diamond family—Breeze, Carter, and Mecca.

The Cartel was no more, and it was the last chapter to what was to be named one of the biggest legacies in Miami's underworld history. Their story was legendary, ruthless . . . and most of all, classic.

Many people were in attendance, but the most important guests were not there to pay their final respects. They were there to confirm that the last of The Cartel was deceased and about to be buried into the ground.

Robin and Aries were in attendance, draped in all-black dresses with big shades on to keep a low profile. Murder also sat beside them. The demise of The Cartel was bittersweet for him, and he gritted his teeth tightly as he thought about Mecca and the missed opportunity to personally kill him on Miamor's behalf. Nevertheless, Mecca was dead, and that would have to be enough for him.

Emilio Estes, Leena, and Monroe Jr. were also in attendance, mourning the loss. They were the only people left alive who could sit in the front pew reserved for family. Although far removed from the Diamond legacy, they were the last of a dying bloodline.

There was an eerie feeling in the air, and everyone there could sense it. As the preacher held the Holy Bible tightly in his hand and read from the book of Psalms, a stretch limo with tinted windows rolled up slowly about fifty yards away from the service. Many people didn't notice it, but the trained eyes were glued to the approaching vehicle.

Emilio Estes looked back and saw the limo pull up, and he watched as it came to a slow stop. Estes knew exactly who it was; it was the crew responsible for the very funeral he was at. Emilio, being in his mid-sixties and not willing to step back into the streets, conceded defeat and pulled his white handkerchief from the top pocket of his suit.

To many, it looked as if Emilio was just removing a hanky, but veterans of the street game knew what that small gesture meant. Emilio wanted the bloodshed to stop, and signaled that he would not retaliate. The war was finally over and The Cartel was no more. Literally, he was waving a white flag. It was officially The Cartel's last chapter.

Chapter One

"Bad girls die slow."
—Fabian

The blood in Miamor's eyes blocked out the image of Fabian standing over her, and her shallow, desperate breaths drowned out all sounds in the room. Death loomed over her. She knew it was near. The chill in her lovely bones was every indication that her life was slipping away.

A breathless Fabian stood over her. Her tormentor, her grim reaper leered at her menacingly. The smug grin on his face sickened her as her heart filled with hate for him. It pleased him to watch her die. It was vindication for the hell that she had once put him through, and she knew that the lifestyle she led had ultimately determined the cruel way in which she was about to die. It was the law of nature. She had taken more lives than she could count, had destroyed too many families to remember, and her heart had turned cold so long ago that she did not even care. Now it was her turn. This was her fate, her karma, and because she had pushed away everyone who had ever cared for her, no one would even know that she had disappeared from the face of the earth.

Most people in her position would repent. They would beg for their lives, or feel regret for all of the events that had led up to this torturous moment, but Miamor was not most people. Her hard shell had not cracked, and even under the most gruesome pressure, she still had to maintain some form of control.

Fabian wanted to see her break down. He had done everything that was physically possible to get her to give in. Her face was badly disfigured, her fingernails pulled from their nail beds, and her bones crushed and broken, but still not one tear had fallen. She had passed out many times, but that was a physical response to the pain. Crying was controlled by her mental state, and that was one resolve that was too strong for anyone to conquer.

"Bitch, you're going to beg me for your life," he seethed as he circled her, sweaty from his ruthless assault on her. He lifted his hand and backhanded her with the butt of his gun, causing her neck to snap violently to the right.

Miamor bit her tongue to avoid screaming out in agony. She wouldn't give him the satisfaction of seeing her so weak. Blood poured from her mouth, but it only mixed in with the rest of the blood that soaked her battered body.

He had been in the basement for a full twenty-four hours, killing her slowly, but no matter how hard he tried, he couldn't feel the satisfaction of revenge that he sought. There was something about the look in her eyes that said "fuck you," and even in her most fragile state, her mentality never failed her.

Murder was bred deep within her. Fabian was committing the act of murder, but Miamor was a killer. She breathed murder. It was all she knew, the only thing that she had ever been good at. It was her profession. So, even as she sat in the damp basement, her soul slowly abandoning her, her dainty wrists tightly bound to a wooden chair, her eyes still told the story of the greatest bitch who had ever done it. She was merciless, and even death couldn't wipe her off the map.

There was no escaping this. Her time had come, and Miamor had no regrets. She was on her way to hell, but it was worth the legacy she was leaving behind. Yes, her lifestyle had led her to nothing but loneliness and misery. She had loved two men in her lifetime, but never truly had room in her world for either of them. They would have never understood how she lived or the things that she had been through, and because of this, she had never fully given her heart to another. She had given up so much in order to reign terror in the streets, and to her, it was worth it. If she had chosen to play wifey to men like Murder or Carter, people would have forgotten an ordinary young woman named Miamor; she would have been lost in their shadows. So, she had chosen something much greater. She had chosen the life of murder-for-hire, and now, even after her death, her name would resound loudly in the streets. Her small feet would leave huge shoes to fill in the game. Legend of her notorious wrecking crew, the Murder Mamas, would ring true for years to come. She had made sure that no one would ever forget. Every new hustler coming up in the game would eventually hear the story of Miamor, and now she would forever be notorious.

The sound of the basement door opening and the heavy thud of boots descending the staircase announced a new presence in the room, causing Miamor to lift her head weakly. Anxiety made her heart gallop as she watched a cool, calm, and freshly dressed Mecca saunter down the stairs. A machete hung from his hand.

"Damn, nigga, you ain't done killing this bitch yet? This shit make your dick hard?" Mecca cracked, knowing that an erection would never be possible for Fabian again, thanks to Miamor.

"I wanted this bitch to hurt like I hurt. Bad girls die slow," Fabian stated. "I just want to hear this bitch scream before I kill her."

Mecca's eyes opened wide in surprise as he looked around the room at the carnage that Fabian's torture had produced. "You done used every trick in the book and you still can't make the bitch holler?"

"Bitch ain't human, fam," Fabian replied.

Mecca chuckled mockingly as he shook his head. "You really are a bitch-ass nigga," he mumbled as he approached Miamor, the blade of the machete screeching across the floor as he dragged it.

Miamor knew that the time for games was over. Mecca had not come back for nothing. He was there to end this, and there was no doubt in her mind that he would. He was the only nigga she had ever met whose murder game matched her own. Mecca would not hesitate. He would kill her without second guessing it. She knew this because if the shoe were on the other foot, he would already be a distant memory.

The faces of everyone she had ever loved flashed before her eyes. She closed them and welcomed the images: Murder,

Anisa, Robyn, and Aries. They were all a part of her final fleeting thoughts, but the face the stuck out the most, the last person she thought of, was Carter Jones, the love of her life. He was the man who had showed her a love so strong, one that she knew she would have never been able to fully return. As much as she loved him, she did not deserve him, and he did not deserve the tyranny that she had brought into his life.

She had played a cat and mouse game with Mecca for too long; now it was time for the charade to end. The scent of Mecca's Issey Miyake cologne invaded her senses as he bent down near her ear.

Miamor's eyes remained closed as Mecca took in the image of her. Seeing her this way was poetic for him, a beautiful demise for an ugly situation. The two of them could never co-exist. Her day of reckoning had come.

"My man here feels like you owe him something. Now, I have a proposition for you. I think you've learned your lesson. I'm not usually a forgiving man, but if you apologize to Fabian here and you admit that you can't fuck with me, then I won't kill you. I'll let you go, as long as you leave Miami . . . my city," Mecca whispered in her ear. He wasn't a nice guy and didn't even imitate one well. He knew that he would never let Miamor live, but he wanted to hear her apologize, and he wanted to hear her admit that that she was beneath him . . . that he held the power . . . that only he could determine whether she lived or died.

Miamor bit into her inner jaw because she had never hated anyone more than she hated Mecca Diamond, and there were so many emotions pulsing through her body that she could not stop the hot tears from falling down her face.

"See, the bitch does cry," Mecca pointed out to Fabian, who stood baffled behind him. "Now, tell me I'm the best, bitch. Let me hear you say it."

Miamor's body shook with rage as Mecca waited impatiently for her response. Blood poured out of her mouth as she hung in the balance between life and death. She was barely strong enough to hold her head up. As she opened her mouth, she whispered, "Come closer so you can hear me." Barely audible, she waited until Mecca leaned close to her ear.

She didn't want him to miss a single word of what she was about to say.

"Say it, bitch. Give up your pride to save your life," Mecca proposed as she breathed in his ear.

"You'll never be the best, Mecca, because I'm the best. You can kill me, but it'll never change the fact that I took everybody you ever loved away from you. You made a mistake when you killed my sister. You take one from me, I take two from you, and the rest of my people are in the wind. They're untouchable. I did that. I made sure of that. If you were the best, you would have done the same. Every day for the rest of your life, you'll think of Miamor, nigga. I promise you," she whispered.

She kissed his cheek, instantly turning his skin cold and running shivers down his spine. It felt like the kiss of death, and Mecca stood to his feet with fire in his eyes. There was nothing he hated more than a slick-talking-ass bitch, but Miamor was like a pit bull; she never let go. Once she put her beam on somebody, nothing could stop her—nothing short of death.

Miamor closed her eyes as she allowed the last tear to fall, then she inhaled deeply before focusing on Mecca, staring him in the eyes. Although he hated her to his core, he knew that they were more alike than either of them had ever cared to admit, and he silently respected her and hated her all in the same moment. They both knew that she had just taken her last breath.

Miamor glared unflinchingly at him and waited for what she knew was to come. It was over, and in that instant, everything went black.

Candles laced the entire basement as the smooth sounds of Bob Marley's "Redemption Song" danced through the airwaves. Marley had a way of speaking to a person's soul and conveying his words on point and full of passion. Ma'tee felt this song more than ever as he closed his eyes and absorbed the powerful lyrics of the legend.

Plush velvet carpet, smells of relaxing lavender incense, and flickering candles all set the mood for what was to be Ma'tee's grand finale. He stared at Breeze, who was lying in the bed dressed in a red lingerie set that he had picked up for her for their special day. He smiled as he looked at Breeze, who was in a dazed-like state, trying to raise her head from the pillow.

It seemed as though a fog had fallen over her. It was as if she were in a hazy dream as she tried to fight the sedation. Ma'tee looked on and smiled at her. "Don't chu try to fight the drug, baby girl. Relax, me lady," he instructed softly as he ran his fingers through her long hair. Ma'tee had heavily drugged her, as he did every night just before he made twisted love to her. In Ma'tee's demented mind, Breeze Diamond was his woman, and he had fallen deeply in love with her over the time she had been in his clutches.

Breeze played the role to the tee as she pretended as if she were off point, but unbeknownst to Ma'tee, Breeze was as clear-headed as she had ever been. Uncharacteristically, Ma'tee had taken his eyes off of Breeze while giving her the drug. Breeze saw an opportunity, and took it by quickly spitting out the pill and pretending as if she had swallowed it. She was just waiting for the right time to make a dash for the stairs that led up to the main floor of Ma'tee's home. Ma'tee was completely naked and ready to lay down with Breeze for the final time, because he had planned for that night to be their last.

As soon as he turns his back, I'm going for it, Breeze thought as nervousness overwhelmed her and her hands began to tremble. Ma'tee turned his back and walked over to the table where the nickel-plated .45 was placed. He was going to shoot Breeze in the head just before he took his own life. In his mind, it was a sure way for them to be together forever. Nevertheless, Breeze had another plan in mind. She was going to break away from Ma'tee—or die trying.

Breeze waited patiently for the right time to make her move and dart for the steps. As soon as Ma'tee's back was totally turned, she took off running as fast as her petite legs could go.

She hurriedly skipped two steps at a time, trying to climb to the top.

"Breeze!" Ma'tee yelled as he heard the commotion and saw her take off. He quickly took off after her, remembering that he hadn't locked the door that led to the main floor. "Nooo!" he yelled as he gave chase up the stairs with the gun in his hand.

Breeze sprinted full speed and burst through the door. Her heart began to pound heavily as she was hit by the rays of sunlight shining through the blinds. It had been so long since she had seen sunlight that it was like a punch to the face. Breeze quickly shook off the initial shock and darted out of the basement door, desperately searching for a door to escape the spacious house.

As she frantically ran through the house, Ma'tee was right on her heels. Breeze knocked over lamps and chairs trying to evade his clutches and buy herself more time.

"Please! Let me go!" Breeze pleaded as she approached Ma'tee's front door. But it was to no avail. He had two deadbolts. She tried to unlock the door quickly, but by that time, Ma'tee had caught up with her and grabbed her from the back. Breeze kicked and screamed, but Ma'tee's strength was too much for her to match. He wrestled her to the floor, and that's when the tears began to pour from Breeze's eyes. She knew that she was about to die. At that very moment, she lost all hope, and her soul no longer belonged to her—it was Ma'tee's.

Ma'tee pointed the gun at Breeze's head and prepared to pull the trigger. "Chu will forever be me lady," he said as he pressed the barrel to Breeze's temple.

Breeze closed her eyes and tried to brace herself for the impact. "God, please have mercy on my soul," she whispered just before the boom. It wasn't a boom from the gun, but the sounds of items falling from Ma'tee's walls and cabinets. The earth began to shake at a magnitude that would be documented in history as one of the worst earthquakes the world had ever seen.

"What the—" Ma'tee tried to stand, but the violent vibrations from the ground knocked him off his feet.

Breeze didn't know what was going on as she looked around, frantically trying to figure out what was the cause of all the rumbling. The ground shook so intensely that Ma'tee's windows shattered and his floor began to crack. The sounds of trees crashing against the earth whistled through the air, and before long, Ma'tee's house began to crumble, as the earth seemed to swallow the house's foundation. Breeze screamed at the top of her lungs. She was in the middle of the pandemonium.

Ma'tee tried to run under his kitchen table for protection, but he never made it. The roof caved in and crushed him, burying him in debris. Breeze witnessed Ma'tee's death just before the roof crushed her also. Breeze was instantly knocked unconscious as the earth crashed down on top of her.

This natural disaster had made an imprint on Haiti's country that would be talked about for years to come.

Carter walked through the cellblock with a folded blanket and thin pillow in his hands. Two guards escorted him to his cell as the sounds of the rowdy inmates echoed through the corridor. Carter walked at his own pace with his head held high. The sound of someone yelling, "The Cartel is in the building!" sounded off, and Carter smirked, knowing that some of his soldiers were on his cellblock. The feds had come in and locked up most of his crew, and some of them were in the same penitentiary Carter was currently at, which meant Carter was still in a position of power.

"Stop right here," the guard said as they approached the last cell on the block.

"Open D-one!" he yelled down the corridor. Moments later, the door slid open, exposing a heavy set Latino man with a salt-and-pepper beard. He looked to be in his mid to late fifties.

"Garza, you have a new celly," the guard said, referring to him having a cellmate.

"You know the rules. My cell is not to be shared!" Garza objected as he sat up from his bunk and placed down the book that he was reading.

"The prison is full and there is no other place he can go. He has to come in here," the guard said as if he were explaining to Garza rather than telling him.

"I don't want a nigger in my cell," Garza said as he gave Carter a dirty look.

Carter nodded and gave Garza a small smirk just to piss him off more.

"It is what it is, Garza. He's your cellmate. Step in," the CO said as he stepped to the side, clearing the way for Carter.

Carter stepped in and placed his things on the top bunk. Moments later, the guard yelled for the cell to be closed and the door slid shut, leaving Garza and Carter alone in the small room.

"Don't get comfortable. You won't be in here for too long," Garza said as he sat back on his bed and focused on his book.

Carter hopped on his bunk and ignored Garza's comment, not wanting to make any enemies so soon. He smirked and shook his head, knowing that Garza didn't realize whom he was talking to, or the power that Carter had. But the truth was that Carter didn't realize the power and connections that Garza possessed.

Robyn walked into the crowded courthouse. Her expensive pencil skirt and matching cropped jacket with ruffle top gave her a professional appearance that allowed her to blend in with the lawyers and officials that filled the building. She smiled at the security guard at the entrance as she placed her briefcase on the conveyor belt and then stepped through the metal detector. With her Hermès briefcase in hand and a cardboard tray of Starbucks in the other, she seamlessly bypassed security. Her five-inch heels click clacked across the wooden floor, her step so precise that one would think she was on a runway. She slipped into courtroom A. She peeked at the schedule and noticed that the next trial would not take place for another hour. It was more than enough time to handle her business and disappear.

Just as she suspected, the stenographer was a light-skinned young woman with cute features. The presiding judge had a thing for young black girls. Robyn walked inside and smiled humbly at the girl.

"Hi, I'm Vanessa. I'm the new stenographer for Courtroom B. I'm supposed to be training underneath you today," Robyn stated. The lie came off of her lips so smoothly as she put down her things and extended her hand to the girl.

"Oh, no one told me that I was supposed to be training today. Um . . . well . . ." The girl seemed to be put on the spot and completely unprepared for the task at hand.

"I think that they said they were replacing girls because of them being ill prepared," Robyn added slyly as she watched the girl's eyes grow wide in concern.

"Right . . . of course. I remember now . . . the training session today. I'm Melissa," she said as if she had suddenly remembered.

Robyn smiled and grabbed one of the cups of coffee. "Well, Melissa, it's nice to meet you. I can't get through my day without my morning cup of coffee," Robyn said as she extended the cup to the girl. "Consider this as the student bringing the teacher an apple. It's my way of sucking up on the first day."

Melissa accepted the coffee and nodded toward the chamber doors. "You better go introduce yourself to Judge Marrell. That's who you should have purchased coffee for. He's the one to suck up to," Melissa stated playfully.

Robyn winked and replied, "So I've heard." She then made her way to the large wooden door and knocked lightly.

"Come in," she heard the judge say, and she slid inside the plush, prestigious office. The middle-aged white man looked up at her from his desk. "How can I help you?" he asked.

"I'm Vanessa Riley from the District Attorney's office. I'm here to drop off some motions from our office," Robin stated, making up another lie on the spot. She had been doing this for so long that it was nothing for her to switch personas. Lies were more familiar to her than the truth.

"Let's see them, Ms. Riley," he said as he gave her his undivided attention.

Robyn set her briefcase on his desk and unhinged the gold clasps.

"Why haven't I seen you before? I thought I knew everyone from the D.A.'s office," Judge Marrell said.

As Robyn pulled the papers from her briefcase, she replied, "You do know everyone from the D.A.'s office." She smiled and he looked at her curiously. Robyn removed the paperwork from her briefcase and set it in front of the judge.

As the judge looked over the papers, he stated, "What is this? These aren't from the D.A.'s office." He looked up at her in confusion.

"I have a message for you," she stated. She removed a ruler from her briefcase and leaned across the desk. Before he could even protest, she swiped the metal edge across his neck. The normal metal of the ruler had been replaced with a razor blade, and cut through his flesh effortlessly. Blood gushed from his wound as he grasped at his bleeding throat. His eyes widened in fear as he silently pleaded for her to help him.

"Frankie Biggs sends his regards," Robyn stated.

The judge couldn't believe his ears. A man that he had sentenced to life in prison just weeks before had reached out from behind the wall and ordered his execution. For the right price, the Murder Mamas would hit anyone, including a state judge.

As soon as the judge's head hit the wooden desk, Robyn stood up and walked out of his chambers. She bypassed the young girl, Melissa, whose head was face first on her typewriter. The cyanide-laced coffee had done its job to perfection.

Without looking back, Robyn exited the building unnoticed, with a satisfied smirk on her face. She waltzed down the stairs outside the front of the courthouse and slipped into the black Benz that was waiting for her curbside.

Aries pulled away discreetly, and without any words, they got ghost in the wind. Aries felt the engine purr beneath the hood of her Mercedes as she pushed the beautiful car along the California coastline. The wind whipped through Robyn's hair as she pulled off the honey blonde wig that was her disguise.

The mystery that lay behind their designer shades was more deadly than any onlooker could ever imagine. Business was good, as usual. After the tyranny that had taken place in Miami, they had started anew in the City of Angels. There was more money to be made on the West Coast than they had ever encountered before. Leaving bodies in their path, their murder game had soared to new heights.

Still, they couldn't help but feel like a fundamental piece to their puzzle was missing. What had started out as band of five ladies with murder as an agenda had quickly become four, but then four had turned to three, and now after all the bullshit, the last two were standing. Too many mistakes had caused their numbers to dwindle, and not knowing where Miamor was weighed heavily on both of their minds.

The West Coast had been the plan all along. It had all been Miamor's idea. They would take Miami by storm and stack their paper, until Murder was released from prison. That had all been tossed aside when Carter Jones entered the picture. Miamor had forgotten her own rules and gotten so caught up in her emotions that she had broken their cardinal rule: *Money over everything*.

Now Murder was out of prison, Miamor was nowhere to be found, and it was up to them to fill him in on everything that had gone down since the last time he had seen her.

"What are we going to tell him when he asks about her?" Aries asked as they pulled up to the Union Station bus terminal.

"We're going to tell him the truth: Miamor chose a nigga over him and over us," Aries replied uncertainly, knowing that Murder would not receive the news well. When they had contacted him to let him know their whereabouts, they never mentioned that Miamor had not relocated to L.A. They hoped to get him there first and inform him later, because they knew he could help them bring Miamor home and talk some sense into her.

Aries pulled into the parking lot of the station and put the car in park as both she and Robyn peered anxiously toward the door.

"Didn't his bus get here like an hour ago?" Robyn asked.

"He's here. He's watching us. Murder don't move until he's ready to. That's where Miamor got it from," Aries replied confidently as she recalled the many stories that Miamor had shared with her about the man.

Finally, Murder came sauntering out of the station, his pants low, fitted hat worn over his eyes, while his head sat on a swivel neck as he surveyed his surroundings. Even though no pistol dwelled on his hip, his hand was instinctively planted there.

Robyn smirked as she popped the locks for Murder to enter the car. "You're all the way in Cali. Who you looking for?"

Her tone was playful, but his was not when he replied, "I've popped niggas in Cali." With that, he ducked low in his seat and pulled down his hat as Aries put the car in drive.

"Where's Miamor?" he asked immediately. She was whom he had made the trip to see. After years of lockup, their reunion was inevitable.

"We have something to tell you." Robyn turned around so that she was facing Murder. "In the letter we sent you, we didn't tell you everything."

"Where's Miamor?" Murder asked again, almost impatiently.

Aries was silent as she drove. She didn't want to be the bearer of bad news. The hairs on the back of her neck stood up as Robyn spoke up.

"She's not here. She decided to stay in Miami. She's fucking with the same niggas that murdered Anisa," Robyn stated.

Murder's temperature went through the roof as his jaw tightened and his brown eyes turned black. "My li'l mama wouldn't do that," Murder replied assuredly as he stretched out across the backseat of the car.

"It's not exactly how Robyn is making it sound," Aries cut in. "When we went to Miami, we accepted a contract to hit a group called The Cartel. Anisa was murdered, and after that, everything spun out of control. Miamor met this nigga named Carter. She fell in love with him, but did not know that he was affiliated with The Cartel."

"Affiliated how?" Murder asked. His words were calm, but the blaze behind his stare revealed his true emotions.

"He's the brother of the nigga that killed Anisa," Robyn finished. "When we left, she stayed behind. She's not the same, Murder. That nigga Carter got her all fucked up in the head, and we need your help to get her back."

Murder was livid as he processed everything the Murder Mamas had told him. He had been gone for too long. He was out of touch with the streets, and even worse, out of touch with Miamor. Although he had never expected her to wait for him, hearing that she was so loyal to another man sparked a flame inside of him that he tried to snuff out long ago. He was ready to go retrieve Miamor, and anybody who stood between them could get it.

They rode in silence, until they reached the condo that Robyn and Aries shared. As they walked up their walkway, they immediately noticed that things were not as they left them. The curtains in the living room window had been shifted slightly, and the piece of clear tape that they had put at the top of their front door had been ripped in half, indicating that someone had come in or out of the condo.

Aries put her finger to her lips and pulled out her 9 mm pistol as she stepped into the condo first. Their place was untouched; nothing was out of place, but they knew that someone had crossed their threshold. They filtered through the place, going in separate directions, until every room had been checked.

"There's nobody here," Murder stated.

"But somebody's been here," Robyn stated as she finally noticed the medium-sized packing box that sat in the middle of their kitchen island. She picked it up, and Aries gasped as she noticed the blood-stained bottom.

"Robyn," she said as she pointed at the red color.

Murder walked over to her and removed the box from her hands.

He opened the box, and when he noticed what was inside, his stomach folded, causing him to bend over as if someone had punched him in the gut.

"What is it?" Aries asked in a panic as she watched Murder's reaction.

Tears filled Robyn's eyes as she shook her head back and forth in disbelief. She ran over to the kitchen sink as the contents of her stomach erupted from her mouth.

"What the fuck is it?" Aries asked again as she stormed over to the box, but Murder stopped her in her tracks as he wrapped one hand around her throat.

"Why did you leave her there?" he asked. "You should have never left her in Miami!" he stated, his eyes ablaze with anger.

The mixture of devastation and rage that twisted his features told Aries all that she needed to know. She violently slapped his hand away from her neck and rushed over to the box. Her heart felt as if it shattered into tiny pieces when she saw the severed hand that lay inside. The cursive *Murder Mama* on the wrist revealed her identity. It was Miamor. They knew that only one person could be this ruthless.

"She's dead," Aries whispered in disbelief.

Robyn stood from the sink and walked over to Aries as they wrapped their arms around each other. "We shouldn't have left her," Aries whispered regretfully.

There was an address written on the inside of Miamor's hand. It was a sign of respect that only someone in their profession would understand. It was Mecca's way of letting them know where they could find her body.

Without turning around, Murder stated, "I want to know everything you know about The Cartel." No more words needed to be spoken. They all knew what had to be done. It was time to go back to Miami.

Chapter Two

"Please, God, let somebody come for me."
—Breeze

Every inch of Breeze's body ached unbearably as the weight of Ma'tee's home rested on top of her. "Help me!" she screamed, her voice raspy and sore from strain. For two days, she had been trapped beneath the rubble. She was trapped next to Ma'tee's decaying body, and the smell was slowly driving her insane. His dead eyes haunted her as they stared in her direction. She could still hear his voice in her head, terrorizing her, telling her that she would never escape, and she felt nothing but utter hopelessness, because she knew that no one even knew where to begin looking for her.

Breeze's body wanted to give out on her. Without food she was weak, but she knew that she could not give into death. She had to make it out of this alive. She had come too far to die now. Ma'tee could no longer hold her captive.

All I have to do is hold on. Someone will come, she thought. *They have to.* She sucked on the wet dirt beneath her to provide herself with some type of water. It was all that her body was surviving on, but she knew that it would not be enough for her to make it much longer. Being trapped beneath the steel and concrete was like being buried alive.

Physically, she knew that she was injured, but she blocked out the pain as she tried to keep her mind strong. She knew that once her will disappeared she would die, so she tried her best to remain calm. Her father had always told her that panic sent logic right out the window, and she would need to think clearly in order to survive.

The excruciating heat made her feel as if she were roasting in a cement oven. The blocks resting on top of her baked beneath the sun all day, burning her so badly that it felt as if a hot iron were being placed to her skin.

She was grateful when the sun began to set, but the night brought on a completely different set of problems for Breeze. The sounds of the jungle terrified her, as the wildlife was attracted to the scent of Ma'tee's corpse. She wished that she could cover her ears, but her hands were smashed beneath the rock, and the only thing she could do was close her eyes.

Zyir's face popped into her mind as she tuned out the sounds of the night. He had always been her voice of reason when she needed him, and as she visualized him in her mind, she realized that she couldn't quite remember all of the details of his face. Too much time had passed, and she no longer held his exact features to memory. It was then that she grew more determined than ever to make it home. *Please, God, let somebody come for me,* she prayed.

She had very little faith that her prayers would be answered. Speaking to God had not saved her from Ma'tee's torture, so she was skeptical that He would spare her from this. She was tired of the hardship that had become her life, and a part of her wished that she had been the one to die when the earthquake first hit. It seemed that Ma'tee had been granted the easy way out, while she was left to suffer.

She could feel herself dying slowly. With every minute that passed, her heartbeat slowed down. It was only a matter of time before it gave out. Breeze suffered through the sounds of the night with her eyes closed, but sleep never came. Her nerves were too on edge for her to rest. The ground had not stopped shaking beneath her. Every few hours, another aftershock set off more destruction, shifting the house on top of her and causing her even more pain. The threat of it falling in on her completely was a constant threat. Any second she could be crushed to death, and the impending circumstance caused her body to tremble.

She began to talk to herself just to stay lucid, singing songs that she remembered to stop herself from giving in to the pain. Everything in her just wanted to let the earth swallow her. Exhaustion and fatigue caused her eyelids to become heavy.

Just as the daylight came creeping back across the horizon, she heard the sound of human voices. She strained to listen, thinking that her mind was playing an evil trick on her.

"Hello? Is anyone out there?" she called out at the top of her lungs. When she didn't hear a response, her heart dropped in disappointment, but the footsteps around her grew increasingly more audible. Straining her ears, she finally confirmed the voices. She could not make out what they were saying, but it didn't matter; she could not let them pass her by.

"Help! Help me!" she yelled desperately as she pushed against the rock, steel, and slate that imprisoned her. She screamed so loudly that her lungs hurt and she choked on the dust in the air, but she did not stop until she got the attention of the men. After locating her voice underneath the ominous pile, they rushed to her aid.

"Get me out! Get me out!" she cried frantically. "Please hurry!" She panicked as she felt the men lifting the concrete from her body. The closer they got to rescuing her, the more Breeze hyperventilated. Relief washed over her as she wept loudly. She had never been so glad to hear another human voice.

The men worked diligently to dig Breeze out as they spoke in a native Haitian dialect that she could not understand. They had no machines or forklifts, only their bare hands and the strength that God had given them, but that did not stop them from helping Breeze. Although a language barrier stopped them from communicating, they knew what the look in her eyes meant. They could see her pleading with them to get her out.

The more weight that was lifted off of Breeze, the more pain she felt. Her legs were completely useless. The blood flow had been cut off from them, and her light skin had turned a sickening blue.

Once they could maneuver her out, one of the men picked her up, while the others began to dig out Ma'tee.

"No!" she yelled. The men looked at her in confusion, but none of them stopped digging. They refused to leave a man behind. When they finally removed Ma'tee from the rubble, they realized that he was already dead. They debated whether they should carry his body down the mountain, but there was no point in wasting their energy on him. Even if they did take his body to the town, it would just lie out in the streets. No one who died in this tragedy would receive a proper burial, so they figured it best to just let him be.

Breeze let her head rest against the chest of one of the rescuers as they began their descent down the mountain. Not once did she look back. She was eager for help, and expected to be rescued as soon as they finished their descent down the mountain. She was unprepared for the chaos that awaited her in the city of Port-au-Prince. Everything had been destroyed, and there were too many people to help and not enough relief to make a difference.

The men dropped Breeze off at a safety site that had been set up, and went on their way. It was a free for all; everyone was out for self, and the lack of organization gave her no one to turn to. She was left to fend for herself.

The safety site looked more like a demolition site to Breeze. Makeshift tents had been made out of sheets and spare fabric to cover some of the injured people being treated by the doctors. The chaos was overwhelming as Breeze surveyed the aftermath of the quake. Trapped atop the mountain with Ma'tee, she had no idea how big the earthquake really was.

The magnitude of its destruction was unimaginable. Everyone was displaced, everyone was injured, everyone needed help. This natural disaster had destroyed an entire nation of people, so much so that even the organizations that had come to help did not know where to start.

Breeze had been one of the lucky ones. She had made it out of the rubble. She was cut badly, bruised beyond belief, and starving for nutrition, but she was alive, and as she looked around sadly at all of the dead bodies, she realized how grateful she was.

When the circulation finally came back to her legs, she walked aimlessly, trying not to stare at the lost children who walked the streets, many in search of parents they would never find. Their cries made her cringe because she knew exactly how it felt to be ripped from those you love.

American camera crews recorded the horrendous tragedy, and even CNN's Anderson Cooper reported live in an attempt to display what was happening to the world. Haiti had been impoverished for years, but the earthquake had put the international spotlight on the black nation.

Breeze was dumbfounded because although America was reporting on the situation, she never saw one reporter put down their microphones to assist or offer help. When the little red lights of their camera came on and the crew was filming, they were engaged and sympathetic, but when it came down to actually contributing to humanity, they all recoiled selfishly. As soon as the cameras stopped rolling, their concern for the earthquake victims dwindled, proving to Breeze that it was all for show. There were people dying around them, and all they cared about was the story.

She was in desperate need of medical attention, sustaining not only injuries from the quake, but also injuries from being raped by Ma'tee. She was physically, psychologically, and emotionally troubled, but as she looked around her, she realized that that was not only her story, but the story of so many others as well.

There was no food, no water, no relief whatsoever, and Haitian citizens were beginning to get restless. Breeze watched as gangs of individuals looted whatever places were still standing in attempts to find supplies and food. The scarcity of resources was making everyone desperate, and as Breeze noticed a fruit truck being looted, she could not stop herself from following suit. The hunger pangs shooting through her stomach justified her actions as she ran over to the truck and pushed her way to the front to grab her share. After filling her hands with four large oranges, she attempted to run, but was stopped by a woman who was fighting to snatch the fruit from Breeze.

"No," Breeze protested as she pushed the woman off of her violently. She ran away from the scene and found an empty cot near the safety site. She collapsed as she tore open the fruit and sucked the juices from the inside. She resembled an animal as she ate ravenously, keeping her eyes up as she guarded the only meal she had received in days.

Her heart tore in half when she saw a little girl eyeing her desperately. Breeze knew that her soul had disappeared when she shouted, "What the hell are you looking at? I don't have anything for you!"

It was then that she realized that Ma'tee really had turned her soul black. Before landing in his company, she had been selfless and giving. Even amongst the worst of predicaments Breeze had always maintained a good heart.

Guilt plagued her as she looked down at the three other pieces of fruit she had stolen. "Here," she said to the small child as she held out an orange for the girl. The little girl's eyes lit up as she thankfully took the fruit.

They sat eating the meager meal together as if it would be their last. Breeze did not know what her next move would be. Waiting would be like torture, but she had no other choice. She didn't know if she was waiting to live or waiting to die; she only hoped that a resolution would eventually come.

Chapter Three

"The connect ain't fucking with us because we got that federal eye in the sky on us." —Zyir

Mecca sat back in the large meeting room of the Diamond family mansion. Pretty soon it would belong to someone else. Mecca had put the beautiful property up for sale. It was too hot, and now it was time to rebuild the Diamond legacy somewhere else. Everything had been cleared out except for this one room.

He closed his eyes as his mind drifted back to the days when his father used to hold court for his head lieutenants in that very space. It seemed that his father had run things so smoothly. The Cartel of today was a far cry from the organized crime family his father had started. Now everything around them was chaos, and with Young Carter in jail, Mecca was unsure if he could fill the shoes of the leader and effectively run The Cartel.

It was no longer a family operation. Only one Diamond was left standing, and although Carter was his half-brother, it wasn't the same. They had suffered too many casualties, and loyalty was a rarity nowadays. His father had ruled with love, whereas now Carter, Mecca, and Zyir were holding down their spot in the streets with fear.

With the spotlight of the feds shining on them, nobody wanted to deal to closely with The Cartel. The streets were talking, and word was out that Carter just might lose his case. Niggas from the bottom to the top were shook, including their coke supplier.

The sound of the foyer door opening snapped him out of his reverie, and he stood to welcome Zyir.

"What's good, fam?" Zyir greeted as he embraced Mecca briefly.

"You tell me. How's that paper looking?" Mecca asked.

As The Cartel's most trusted lieutenant, Zyir's ear was glued to the street. There was nothing that got by him. Mecca had been forced to lay low because of his beef with Emilio Estes, so it was up to Zyir to ensure that their presence remained known in the streets.

"Shit is slow. Carter's case got everybody running scared. The connect ain't fucking with us because we got that federal eye in the sky on us, nah mean?"

"What about the niggas that owe us money?" Mecca asked irritably. It seemed as if everything they had built was now on the downfall.

"Oh, I got that cake . . . believe that. Ain't nobody skipping out on the bill, but nobody's re-upping. It's like niggas is cutting ties. Nobody wants to be associated with a sinking ship. Niggas only loyal when the getting is good. I mean, we still got a few men who standing tall, but I ain't gon' lie. Shit ain't sweet," Zyir informed. "With everything seized, that shoebox money running real low. Carter's lawyer expecting another payment today, and even my stash is hurting."

Mecca knew that things would get tight for everybody with Carter locked up. The government had frozen all of their legitimate accounts; even Diamond Realty profits could not be touched until a resolution to Carter's case was reached. Everyone, including Mecca, was living temporarily off of whatever money had flown under the radar; but random money that had been stashed in safes wasn't enough for men who spent it as if it grew on trees. Between the two of them, they had a little over a million dollars, but with Carter's case eating into their finances and a paranoid cocaine connection, that large sum of petty cash was dwindling by the day.

"What time do you have to meet the lawyers?" Mecca asked.

"In about an hour. After that, I plan on checking in with Carter. I need to let him know what's going on, and he's been asking me to check for his chick, Miamor," Zyir replied.

"Tell him to stop looking," Mecca stated coldly.

"What?" Zyir questioned. "You know he ain't gonna stop looking for her. That's his bitch."

Mecca removed the scowl from his face and replied, "I heard she left town, so tell him to stop worrying about a bitch. We gotta keep his mind right so he can beat this case."

Overwhelmed and worried about the state of his family's empire, Mecca sighed. "I'll drop that payment off to the lawyer. You holla at Carter. Let him know what's been going on. See what he want us to do to stay afloat."

As Mecca watched Zyir leave, he collapsed back into his father's chair. The throne that he had sat on for many years seemed too big for Mecca, the responsibilities of heading The Cartel too daunting for a hothead like Mecca. Mecca was built to be in the game. He was a goon, a killer, and his natural born hustle was innate, but being the leader had never been his forte. That role had better suited his twin brother, Money.

The thought of Monroe brought tears to his eyes. He had hardened himself to insanity after he had murdered his brother, but the extreme guilt that still plagued him over his actions always broke him down. On the rare moments when he was alone and had time to reflect, he remembered that fateful night, and he mourned the lost of his other half. Monroe was his only weakness—and his murder was a secret that Mecca would take to his grave.

Zyir sat across from Carter, six inches of glass separating them from one another, and Zyir felt a sense of despair on behalf of his mentor. Carter was his brother, and in a way, the only father figure that Zyir had ever had. It pained Zyir to see him confined, his usual designer threads replaced by an orange jumpsuit.

Carter had taught Zyir everything he knew about the game. Carter had groomed him for this exact moment because he understood that the game did not last forever, and once he met his downfall, he was confident that Zyir would be able to take his place.

"How you holding up?" Zyir asked as he gripped the telephone, obviously uncomfortable within the confines of the federal penitentiary. There was something about being behind those walls that terrified Zyir, despite the fact that his own freedom wasn't at risk.

"Wipe that sad look off your face, li'l nigga. You look like you're standing over my casket or something," Carter joked charismatically while smirking.

Zyir loosened up a little and chuckled a bit before replying, "Just don't feel right, nah mean? Looking at you through this glass. We working on that as we speak. Got your legal peoples working around the clock on your case."

Carter respected Zyir for his loyalty and support. Carter wasn't an optimist, however. He was a realist, and he wanted to prepare his little nigga for his potential conviction.

"Zy . . ." Carter cleared his throat and rubbed his growing goatee as he stared intently at his protégé. "You know there's a possibility that this could all end badly for me."

Zyir shook his head in denial and replied, "Nah, fam. Shit is going to work itself out. Before you know it, you'll be home."

Carter nodded his head and didn't press the issue further. He just wanted to put it out there. He knew Zyir like the back of his hand. He had planted the seed in Zyir's head, and knew that Zyir would make the necessary plans just in case.

"Why hasn't Miamor been to see me? I can't reach her by phone. Have you heard from her?" Carter inquired.

Zyir shook his head. He hated to be the one to tell him the news, but thought he deserved to know. "Mecca heard she skipped town right after your arrest," Zyir stated.

Carter frowned and replied, "Skipped town?" The news was disturbing to hear. Nothing about it resonated as true in his heart. His case had nothing to do with her, and he knew that the only time a bitch was leaving town was if she was running away with a bag full of money. Miamor never had access to his paper, and he had never involved her in his illegal dealings, so she had no reason to run. It didn't make sense to him, but he knew that he was in no position to worry about her whereabouts. If and when he got out of prison, he would handle the situation; until then, he stored the information in his mental Rolodex.

After Zyir informed him of the state of The Cartel, their visit was cut short. He had a lot to think about. He had played the game for many years, and now it seemed that it had finally caught up to him. His judgment day had arrived.

Mecca emerged from the family mansion cautiously as he looked around him in paranoia. He knew that his grandfather, Emilio Estes, would not stop until his head was on a platter, and that his power was far reaching. Mecca had no idea who Estes was going to send at him, so he watched his back wherever he went. He slid into his Lamborghini and left rubber in his path as he sped off toward the lawyer's office.

Alton Beckham was a defense attorney who had been on retainer from the very beginning. A friend to his father, Mecca knew that Beckham was Young Carter's best chance of getting off. His unscrupulous morals and greed for money were the main reasons why he was so beneficial to his clients.

Mecca walked into his office, where Beckham's receptionist greeted him. She stood to greet Mecca.

"Hello, Mr. Diamond. If you'll have a seat, Mr. Beckham has another client in his office, but—"

Before she could even finish her sentence, Mecca bypassed the secretary as if she were invisible and walked directly into Beckham's office.

"I'm sorry, Mr. Beckham," the secretary stated as she rushed inside behind Mecca. "I told him he had to wait."

"I don't wait," Mecca stated simply as he took a seat next to the client that was already sitting, with no regard for the meeting that he was interrupting.

Beckham stood up from behind his desk. "It's okay, Tracy. Mr. Diamond is always welcome." He then turned to his client and extended his hand. "I apologize, but I'm going to have to cut our meeting short. You can reschedule out front." Knowing exactly who Mecca Diamond was, the other client didn't protest before walking out of the room.

Once the office was clear, Beckham got down to business. He loosened his tie and sat back in his plush leather chair as he reached underneath his desk, pulling out a bottle of cognac. He poured two glasses and then held one out to Mecca.

Mecca smirked at the Jewish lawyer before him. "Every time I accept a drink from you, bad news follows." Mecca was only half joking. He knew that Beckham was a beast in the courtroom, but he was a snake outside of it. He offered his expertise, but it came at a hefty price.

"Carter's case requires more time than I previously anticipated. The federal prosecutor really has a hard-on for your brother. He's doing everything he can in order to send Carter away. They don't just want a conviction; they want a life sentence, and they want to make an example out of The Cartel. In order for me to prepare the best defense, I'm going to have to go up on my price."

"Don't beat around the bush, Beckham. The bottom line is money. How much do you want?" Mecca asked. "I brought a payment here for you today." Mecca placed a money-filled manila envelope in front of the lawyer. "Fifty thousand dollars."

Trusting his long working relationship with the Diamond family, Beckham did not feel the need to count it. He put it in his desk drawer and replied, "That's a start."

"What price will finish it?" Mecca questioned.

"Double," Beckham responded.

Mecca did not have a problem paying the fee. It was worth Carter's freedom, but he wanted to make it clear that if he was going to spare no expense, then Carter's freedom better be guaranteed.

"You know, with that type of paper, you'll have new responsibilities. I will personally expect more from you. You accepting that type of money tells me that my brother will walk. Things could turn out real bad for you if you don't live up to these expectations. You understand?" Mecca asked boldly.

Beckham was well aware of who he was dealing with, and he knew that by charging The Cartel double for their leader's defense, he was playing with his own life. If he lost, the consequences would be devastating for him, but greed outweighed his reason. "I understand," he replied as he extended his hand.

Once Mecca accepted it, the new deal was done. Getting Carter out of prison would not be cheap, but it was worth it, because only Carter had the foresight it took to get The Cartel out of its slump. He could re-establish their cocaine connection. Once Carter was out, everyone would eat again, and the balance of power would be restored.

Mecca emerged from the attorney's office and removed his car keys from his back pocket. When he was halfway across the street, he hit the remote starter on his keychain.

BOOM!

Glass and metal flew everywhere as Mecca's car exploded, knocking him from his feet and sending him flying backward onto the pavement.

"Oh shit!" he yelled out in panicked alarm as he scrambled to his feet and backpedaled away from the blaze. He looked around in bewilderment as flames engulfed his five-figure car and a crowd began to draw around him. "Fuck!" he yelled as he put his hands on the side of his head. He knew that only one person would have the balls to come after him—Emilio Estes—and as he looked on in pure rage, he knew that this was far from being over. His grandfather would not stop until he put Mecca in a grave—right next to his twin brother.

Leena sat in the opulence of the oceanside villa that was now her home. She could not believe that her life had come to this point. She had played a dangerous game by falling in love with two brothers, and the end result had proven deadly. She could still feel the ache where Mecca's bullet had penetrated her, but it didn't hurt nearly as much as the fact that she had sparked a beef between two brothers.

She had created a divide between two men who should have been inseparable . . . impenetrable . . . invincible, but because of her, everything had been torn apart.

She smiled as she looked at her child, Monroe's only son, as he sat playing quietly on the floor beneath her feet. The only living seed of the late Monroe Diamond sat so innocently, so unaware of his status. He was the heir to so much power and money. Her son was a Diamond, and it was that fact that kept her safe. It kept her alive. It had made her untouchable.

She had been whisked away from the hospital to this world of luxury. She had been there for over a year, and now she sat eating nervously, silently, across from Emilio Estes, the man who had made it all possible. Her child had given her access to the throne, a throne so much bigger than she had ever been appointed.

The Dominican born Estes was more powerful than anyone she had ever met, including the Diamond brothers. He was their grandfather, and now he was her provider.

As she picked at the chef-prepared meal before her, she kept her eyes on her plate. She could feel the power emanating from him all the way across the table. He intimidated her; there was a mysterious nature to him. He was a man of few words, and during the time that they had spent together, he asked more questions than he ever answered. He observed her, and although she felt sheltered around him, she still feared him.

What does he want from me? Why am I really here? she asked herself.

He insisted that she stay with him, but in spite of the time that she had been a guest in his house, she still did not know him. Estes spared her nothing and lavishly showered her with gifts. She was his unspoken possession, one that was well kept and polished. He had expressed his interests in her by giving her material things and security. He ensured that her every need was attended to, but for Leena, love was elusive. She knew that she could never give Estes what he sought.

He kept her around as the lady on his arm, but the only reason she allowed him to was because she had no other choice. How could she turn down the man who had taken her in after she had been shot? He had nursed her back to health and saw her through her entire pregnancy. He had treated her well, and because of this, she felt indebted to him.

"What is it that you want from me?" she asked as she finally mustered the courage to look up at him across the long dining room table.

He was reading the daily newspaper while sipping coffee, and he took his time before he acknowledged her question.

Her stomach was in knots as she watched him. He always moved in his own time, and his silence caused her heart to gallop in anxiety.

"I just want you to care for my great-grandson. That's all I require of you," he replied without looking up from his newspaper.

"That's my responsibility as a mother. I understand that you want your great-grandson to be here with you, but why am I here?" she asked.

"I hoped that you would allow me to share in his life with you. I told you that my lineage would always be taken care of. You are the mother to my grandson's first born. Monroe would have taken very good care of you if he could have. In his absence, I plan to ensure that you want for nothing; that my great-grandson wants for nothing. I have become very fond of you since you have been here. I know that you are reluctant to return my affections, but you are young, and your heart is still broken from losing Monroe. In time, I hope that your heart will warm to me."

Leena nodded, but could not find the words to respond. Her emotions were so mixed when it came to her situation. She was more appreciative than anything. He was so kind and so generous, but she could not help but to walk around on eggshells.

To be in the presence of a man so great would take some getting used to, but Estes had already established that he wanted her around, and she was silently relieved to have his support. In honesty, she was still afraid of Mecca. She knew that he had cared deeply for her, and her betrayal had pushed him over the edge. He did not know that she had survived, and she was afraid that if he ever found out, he would finish what he started. By choosing to be with Estes, she knew that Mecca couldn't touch her, and that alone was reason enough for her to stay, despite the fact that her heart was not fully invested.

Chapter Four

"It doesn't feel as good as the first time."
—Breeze

The chaos around her was overwhelming as the devastation of the earthquake displayed itself all around her. Escaping Ma'tee's imprisonment should have brought some type of relief, but being free was overshadowed by the catastrophe that had occurred. Her bruised and cut up body was nothing compared to the dead bodies that littered the streets, decomposing before her terrified eyes. The overwhelming heat mixed with the smell of death in the air caused her insides to erupt. She had thrown up so many times that she had lost count, and with no clean drinking water in sight, she had nothing to replace the energy that was leaving her body. She could barely breathe because the stench was so horrifying. She had never yearned for home more than she did at that moment.

Her heart raced every second because she did not know what to expect next. The unstable ground beneath her threatened to crack every time the earth shook. How had she come to be so far away from the safety of the Diamond mansion? Her life had been a living hell, and Mother Earth was taking no prisoners as it destroyed everything in its path. The people of Haiti had just had everything stripped from them, and Breeze was amongst them. The little bit of hope that she had left had been buried underneath the rubble. She was going to die in Haiti. What Ma'tee did not finish, Mother Earth surely would.

As Breeze lay on the blood-stained cot out in the open sun, it felt as if she were baking alive. Her light skin had burnt badly, causing her open wounds to crust over with infection. It was so hot that the vision before her eyes was hazy, as if steam was rising from the cracks in the ground. Circumstances had never been so dire. Breeze's survival was out of her hands, and as the bodies continued to drop like flies around her, she silently feared that she would be next.

Breeze could barely lift her head as she watched those around her. She noticed a white woman going around with water-filled canteens. Too weak to even call out, she silently prayed for the woman to come her way. She noticed how the woman picked some of the younger ladies to follow her as she made her way through the thick crowd. It was as if the woman was looking for someone in particular.

When the woman finally crossed Breeze's path, she reached out her arm and grabbed the woman's leg in desperation. The woman turned to Breeze and stared down at her in sympathy.

"Please. I need water," Breeze whispered, her eyes pleading.

"Of course," the woman replied as she knelt beside Breeze. She motioned for the young women who followed her to halt, and then she lifted the canteen to Breeze's lips.

Breeze greedily gulped the water, the coolness of the liquid soothing her dry insides. She closed her eyes. Nothing had ever been so satisfying.

The woman could not see Breeze's face through all of the dirt and ash that covered it. She smiled slightly as she wiped the dirt from Breeze's ashen features, trying to show her a friendly face amongst the debris and turmoil.

"I'm Ms. Beth," the woman stated. "What is your name?" she asked.

"Breeze," she responded as she continued to drink the water, hydrating her soul as much as her body.

"Breeze, where is your family?" Ms. Beth asked.

The thought of her loved ones brought tears of pain to her eyes. She had not seen them in so long. Her heart broke to pieces as she began to sob. "I don't know. I'm not even supposed to be here," she cried.

"Come on, sweetheart. I can take you somewhere safe," Ms. Beth stated as she helped Breeze to her feet. Feeling a sense of trust for the first time since she had been taken away from her family, Breeze stood on her shaky limbs and joined the small group of young women as they walked behind Ms. Beth.

"Where is she taking us?" Breeze asked one of the girls who walked beside her.

"She came through here yesterday and helped a lot of people. She gave them water and food, then she took them somewhere safe. I think she works for a charity in the States. I hope that she is taking us there. I've always wanted to go there," the young Haitian girl said whimsically.

"She's taking us to the Unites States?" Breeze repeated. Her heart fluttered as visions of home flooded her mind.

The girl nodded her head, and it was all the confirmation that Breeze needed to continue to follow Ms. Beth as if she were the shepherd leading her sheep. Breeze looked back at what was left of the city of Port-au-Prince, and she was just grateful that an opportunity to get out had arisen. She had thought that she would be forever lost in the buried city, but Ms. Beth had just come to her rescue.

They walked for miles before Breeze finally saw the boat. It looked like a large military ship. The massive piece of steel that sat in the water sent shivers down her spine, and as Breeze looked on at the group of girls she stood amongst, she recognized the same glimmer of hope in everyone's eyes. All they wanted to do was get to a better place, to feel safe. Even though the boat was daunting, it was their only way out, and none of them was going to deny it.

Breeze's eyes fell upon the side of the medium-sized vessel. The word MURDERVILLE had been graffiti-painted on the ship's starboard side.

Breeze wanted to call her family so badly to let them know that she was alive and that she was safe. They were the first people she wanted to see when she finally made it to the States.

There were about fifty other girls all around her who were just as eager as Breeze, but all of their fear originated from the quake. Breeze's torture had included so much more. The rape, the kidnapping, the degradation from Ma'tee was a precursor to this natural disaster, and if she did not speak to her family soon, she was sure that her sanity would crack. Overwhelmed and anxious, she pushed through the crowd to get to Ms. Beth.

"Ms. Beth!" Breeze called out to get her attention amongst the many young women. As Ms. Beth tried to organize the crowd, Breeze followed behind her. "Ms. Beth, do you have a cell phone that I can use? I haven't talked to my family in so long. I just want to let them know that I'm coming home. They don't even know I'm alive."

Ms. Beth was too busy to stop her stride, but Breeze followed behind her as she watched everyone begin to form a line.

"I'm sorry, Breeze. I don't have a phone that is available for you right now. There's no service on this side of the island. As soon as we reach the States, I will get you to a phone so that you can call your family," Ms. Beth stated. She could see the disappointment in Breeze's eyes, so she put one hand on her shoulder and added, "Don't worry. Everything will be fine now. You will be back with them before you know it."

Breeze nodded.

"Now, go ahead and get in line so that you can get your vaccination. We can't have you bringing any diseases back to the U.S. with you," Ms. Beth said reassuringly.

Breeze got into the line, and when it was her turn to receive the medicine, Ms. Beth tied a thick rubber band around her arm, causing a huge vein to emerge. Ms. Beth smiled at Breeze and said, "I promise all of your pain will go away, Breeze."

"I hope so," Breeze answered back through tear-filled eyes. Ms. Beth stuck the needle in Breeze's arm and injected it slowly. As the drug entered her system, a warm, euphoric feeling traveled up her arm and spread throughout her entire body.

"You'll be tired for a while, but this will keep you from getting sick. A disaster this big brings about a lot of infection," Ms. Beth stated. "There will be a cot for you to rest on once you're on board."

Breeze nodded, but really did not pay attention to anything that Ms. Beth said. The euphoric feeling that took over her body made all of her worries, all of her pain, and all of the horrible memories of Ma'tee's abuse go away instantly. Her eyelids felt so heavy that she could barely keep them from closing, and her mouth fell open slightly in satisfaction. Every spot on her body tingled, and her clitoris hardened as the drug surged through her veins. Breeze felt so good that she came to an orgasm where she stood, causing the place between her legs to become wet with her own juices. She obediently fell in line as she followed the rest of the girls onto the boat.

Breeze awoke to the prick of another needle being put into her arm. This time, it wasn't by Ms. Beth, but one of the men she had seen when she boarded the boat back in Haiti. As she looked around, she noticed that the other girls were being injected as well. She wanted to ask what they were giving her, but as quickly as the thought of protest popped into her mind, the drug took its effect and erased any objection that she had. A stupid grin spread across her face as her neck muscles weakened slightly, causing her head to dip onto her chest. Nothing had ever felt better, and she welcomed the sensations that traveled through her.

She had no idea that Ms. Beth and her team were forcing heroin into her system. All she knew was that the medicine made her feel good. It made everything feel like bliss, and numbed her emotions to the point where she forgot about all that had happened. She was almost drunk with ecstasy as her body began to warm. It did not feel as good as the first dose, and as the man stood to move to the next girl, Breeze grabbed his arm.

"Can you give me a little more? It doesn't feel as good as the first time," she whispered.

The man chuckled and shook his head. "It never does, sweetheart," he replied before moving on to his next victim.

Ms. Beth was in the business of human trafficking, and went from impoverished island to impoverished island in the Caribbean to lure young women and children with the hopes of a better life. The children that she abducted were usually trafficked into modern day slavery, but the young women were like budding flowers and were picked for the sex trade.

When she stumbled across Breeze, she knew that she had hit the jackpot. Her American clients would go crazy over the young beauty, and she would make a big profit off of her because of her fair skin tone.

The heroin made it easier to take advantage of her victims. The drug kept them under control and dependent. Breeze had just been introduced to the world of addiction, and she would always chase the potency of the first high that she had been given. Her ignorance would only last for so long, and by the time she realized that she was hooked, it would be too late for her to stop. Even though she was on her way back to the United States, she was now more far away from home than she had ever been. Now she was lost in a boy that was so strong that once he got a hold of you, he rarely ever let go.

After two days of traveling underneath the deck of the ship, Breeze was relieved when the boat finally docked. Breeze rushed up the stairs. The door leading to the main deck was always locked. The girls traveling below were not allowed on the main deck, and as they traveled, they had confined below, anxiously awaiting their arrival. For many of them, it was the start of a new life. For Breeze, it would be a return to her old one. Breeze beat the door with her fists as she anticipated the reunion she would have with her family.

The door opened, and Breeze rushed out only to be stopped by one of Ms. Beth's workers.

"What are you doing? Let me go. I just want to see where we are," Breeze shouted as she struggled against the man.

It wasn't until she felt the hard sting of his hand that her instincts told her something was horribly wrong. Now that her high had worn off, she was able to process the situation in a new light. She did not know what was going on, but now that they were back in the U.S., she wanted off of that boat. "Where's Ms. Beth? I need to speak to her!" she yelled persistently as she was pushed back beneath the deck. "She said I could make a call."

At that moment, the metal door opened and Ms. Beth walked down with five men following behind her.

"Ms. Beth!" Breeze shouted as she pushed past the man apprehending her. "Where are we? I felt the boat dock. You said I could call my family," she reminded desperately, but as Breeze spoke, she noticed that the disposition of the friendly woman she had met in Haiti had changed. Her eyes were cold and revealed sinister intentions as she stared unflinchingly back at Breeze.

Her father always told her she could see the character of a person by looking in their eyes, and as Breeze studied Ms. Beth, she finally saw the devil that dwelled inside of her. Her brow furrowed in confusion.

"You said you would help me get home!" Breeze shouted as she watched Ms. Beth's staff filter through the room and begin to blast heroin into the other girls' arms.

Breeze backed away from Ms. Beth as she looked down at her own arms. Non-stop needles had been put into her veins for the past forty-eight hours, and foolishly, Breeze had allowed them to do it.

"What have you been giving me?" she screamed hysterically. "Why are you doing this?" Breeze demanded.

"Restrain her," Ms. Beth said calmly to one of her workers.

"You bitch!" Breeze yelled as she charged Ms. Beth. She smacked fire from Ms. Beth before she was finally subdued, and she screamed like a mad woman as she watched the woman who she thought would be her savior approaching her with the needle.

"No! Please . . . I just want to go home. You have no idea what I've been through," Breeze reasoned.

Ms. Beth ignored the pleas and jammed the needle painfully deep into Breeze's vein.

"Aghh!" Breeze cried out as blood trickled from her arm. She could feel the tension leave her body as a tear of defeat slipped from her eyes.

"What are you doing to me? What have you been giving me?" Breeze whispered as the orgasmic high once again came over her.

Ms. Beth looked cruelly back at her and smirked before replying, "Heroin. By the time I'm done with you, you will be nothing but a junkie whore."

Breeze's soul cried out silently as she felt herself going into a nod. The last thing she heard was Ms. Beth's voice.

"Shoot her up twice. She's going to be a handful. The faster we get her hooked the better. She'll learn to go with the flow one way or another."

Chapter Five

"Everything is easier if you forget about your past."
—Liberty

It was pitch black when Breeze finally came to, but she could hear the cries and groans of the other girls around her. The air was so thick that she could barely breathe, and her stomach rumbled violently as the urge to defecate overwhelmed her. She could smell the stench of bodily waste around her, and she gagged from the horrendous odor. She was sick partly from the stench and partly from her body craving its new best friend, heroin.

Breeze did not know how long she had been out, but she knew that Ms. Beth was transporting her somewhere. As she reached out her hands, she felt the steel walls. The bumpy road beneath her let her know that she was in the back of an industrial truck. The wails of the young women around her told her that she had been there for a while.

Her situation had just gone from bad to worse. She took deep breaths to stop herself from panicking, but it was no use. Breaking down was the only thing left for her to do. *I should have never trusted her,* Breeze thought as she withdrew into herself, curling up with her knees to her chest. She cried so hard that her chest hurt, and each time she gulped in air, she felt like she was suffocating. Unable to hold it in any longer, she threw up all over herself.

"It's easier if you breathe out of your mouth," she heard a girl beside her say. "It won't smell as bad if you take it in through your mouth. Bring your face low near the seams of the wall. There's a little bit of fresh air down here. I have a small blanket you can breathe into."

Breeze huddled down near the girl and took a small piece of the fabric into her hands as she breathed into it. The girl's technique did not provide much relief, but it was better than nothing, and Breeze was grateful for it.

"Thanks," Breeze whispered.

"You're welcome. I'm Liberty," the girl stated.

"Breeze," she replied. No other words needed to spoken to establish a friendship. They took a liking to each other because they both realized that they were one and the same. Their fates were not their own, and their lives no longer theirs to live. As they clung to the blanket, they wrapped their arms around one another and prayed together. Neither of them knew what lay in store for them, but they were both terrified of the possibilities.

"How long have we been in this truck?" Breeze asked.

"I've seen the light come and go two times. Two full days have passed," Liberty replied, referring to the tiny bit of sunshine that crept through the crevice in the wall.

"Where are they taking us?" Breeze asked frightfully.

"They are taking us to Murderville," Liberty replied solemnly. "I am not new here. I've been there before, and it is worse than death."

Breeze did not respond, but her thoughts ran wild. She had seen the name MURDERVILLE scribbled in graffiti on Ms. Beth's boat, and now she hated herself for allowing the white woman to sell her a dream. She had been to a place that felt worse than death when she had been with Ma'tee, and now thanks to her naivety she was on her way right back to hell.

After seeing the sun rise and set one more day, Breeze felt the truck finally stop moving. Hungry and soiled, she peeled herself off of the floor when the back door was lifted. She felt like cattle marching to slaughter as she was herded off of the truck. They were placed in a line side by side, and because she had no one else to turn to, Breeze grabbed Liberty's hand tightly. They barely knew one another, but at that moment, a new friend was better than facing the unknown alone.

"Take off all your clothing," a black man stated as he walked up and down the rows of girls. Breeze was reluctant, but everyone around her obediently began to disrobe.

"Undress," Liberty whispered urgently.

"What?" Breeze exclaimed. "No."

"Everything is easier if you forget about your past. Your place is here now. Just do as they say," Liberty warned.

Feeling as if she could not sink any lower, Breeze pulled off her clothes. The life and times of being a Diamond heir, her father's princess, were so far removed that it almost felt like she had never lived it. She could not believe that her life had come to this. Her father had kept her closely for most of her life. He had protected her and guarded her, but instead of helping her, his overprotection hindered her. It had made her vulnerable, and that vulnerability had led her to this place.

She was nothing like her brothers. She was weak. As she stood in the line, tears flowed freely down her dirty face, and she helplessly watched as the man grabbed a high-pressure hose and aimed it at her line. She closed her eyes as she was blasted with cold water like an animal. Through it all, she cried. Liberty held her hand while the little bit of Breeze Diamond that was left was washed away.

"Hold out your arms," the man stated when he finally put the hose down. Breeze already knew what that meant, and although her mind told her to protest, her body urged her to give in. It had been three full days since Ms. Beth had injected her with her last fix, and already her body was hooked. It craved the drug against Breeze's will, and instead of fighting it, Breeze gave up. If she was going to have to live like this, she may as well be numb to the pain.

Breeze clung to Liberty as if her life depended on it. Day in and day out they kept each other sane, until one fateful afternoon, Ms. Beth came to the camp where they were being kept. Whenever she came around, an eerie aura swept over the girls. She was the one who had manipulated most of them into coming to Murderville in the first place, so everyone feared her. She was the perfect example of the blue-eyed, blonde-haired devil, and Breeze hated her.

As the girls stood to their feet and waited for Ms. Beth to deliver their daily fix, the room was silent. It had not taken long for Breeze to become a full-blown addict, and her eyes widened in anticipation as she watched each girl get their turn before her.

As Ms. Beth administered the deadly drug, she separated the girls into two different groups. Some of the girls would be taken and groomed for wealthy buyers, but the unfortunate young women would stay in Murderville and work in the brothels. They would be contracted out for private parties and have their bodies sold to those who could afford it. The girls in this group would be common whores, and once they were used up to the point of no return, they would be executed and replaced. This was the group Ms. Beth put Breeze in, while Liberty was one of the lucky ones. She was taken away to be groomed for a high-priced auction.

With no one left to depend on but herself, Breeze submitted to the world of drugs and sex. She was taken to a house with ten other girls and dressed up in sexy garments. She was so high that everything was a blur as the madame of the brothel put makeup on her face and sprayed perfume all over her body.

Lazily, Breeze lay sprawled across the satin sheets as her first client entered the room. Just looking at her, no one would have ever pegged her for a junkie. The only thing that gave her away were the track marks underneath the sheer fabric of the negligee.

The man that lingered over her lusted over Breeze's beautiful appearance. Under no other circumstance would he ever be able to be with a woman of her beauty.

Breeze was so out of it that all she could do was lie there as the man had his way with her. It was something that she had gotten used to. She had never chosen to give herself away to any man. She didn't know what it was like to feel a man's gentle touch. Her womanhood was always taken away, and she was never in a position to say no.

Chapter Six

"Forever Miamor would sleep with the fishes."
—Unknown

Murder arrived in Miami on a commercial flight with hatred in his heart. He soaked up all of the information from the Murder Mamas about The Cartel and Miamor's worst enemy, Mecca. With a thirst for revenge and pictures of the entire Diamond family, he was ready to find what was left of Miamor and get at The Cartel. Murder's hands never stopped shaking throughout the whole flight, not because of nervousness or fear, but because of the itch to get at whoever had brought pain to Miamor.

Murder demanded that Robyn and Aries stay in L.A., so that he could work the way he did best—alone, strategically, and uninterrupted. They all hoped desperately that Murder would find Miamor alive, but deep in all of their hearts, they knew what was to be found.

Murder got his bags and headed to the curb to catch a cab. He was headed to the exact address that was left inside the box with Miamor's severed hand. Murder's heart hurt every time he thought about the pain and agony that Mecca had brought upon his favorite girl, Miamor. He carefully studied the picture that Robyn and Aries had given him of the heads of The Cartel. He could pick Mecca's face out of a sea of people. Although Murder had never seen Mecca face to face, he knew his every facial feature, and it was a face that would be etched in his mind forever.

Every time Murder thought about Miamor's angelic smile, he had to fight back tears while wishing she was in his arms. It was a love that was unexplainable. Although Miamor looked at Murder as a big brother, Murder looked at Miamor as much more. He knew that she was the love of his life, and he would never be able to win her over, because deep in his heart, he knew she was dead.

He pulled out a picture of Mecca that Miamor had taken while she was preparing to hit him, and he studied it once more. Murder's hands began to shake as he clenched his teeth so tightly that it seemed as if he would chip a tooth. Just as a driver pulled up on him, he stuck the photo in his inner jacket pocket and caught a cab to his hotel.

Mecca cruised through the Miami streets unable to focus on the road because he kept checking his rearview mirror. He suspected that the tinted minivan was following him for the past few blocks. "What the hell?" Mecca whispered as he glanced in the mirror again and saw that the van had made the same right turn that he did. Mecca, tired of playing the game of cat and mouse, reached under his seat to retrieve his automatic handgun. He smoothly placed it on his lap as he approached the upcoming yellow traffic light.

"Niggas trying to catch me slipping? Not today," he stated as he eased up to the light and made a complete stop. The van pulled up behind him, and that was when Mecca clicked on. His street instincts took over, and he acted on impulse. He threw the car into park and quickly hopped out of the car, gun in hand.

"Why the fuck are you following me?" Mecca yelled. He had his gun gripped tightly, holding it like a professional marksmen, almost like a cop would do. Mecca quickly crept up to the car, not giving the driver time to make a move. When Mecca got a glimpse of the driver, he instantly felt silly.

A pregnant, blonde white woman was the only person in the car. She quickly threw both of her hands up and froze in utter terror as a pool of tears filled her eyes. She tried to scream, but Mecca was in her grill so quickly that she had no time to let out a sound. He waved the gun in her face through the open driver's side window.

Mecca saw the terrified look in the woman's face and instantly felt guilty. He knew that his nerves were making him reckless, and he made stupid choices when he was reckless. It was something that he was trying to change. His paranoia eased up. *Everybody's not out to get you,* Mecca thought as he regretted assaulting the soccer mom.

"Sorry, ma," Mecca said as he lowered his gun and took a deep breath. "You can go. I thought you were someone else," Mecca explained as he tried to give the woman a slight grin to ease the tension.

The woman still had her hands up and remained fearful as she stared into the eyes of a killer.

Mecca dropped his head and shook it from side to side as he lightly chuckled to himself. *I'm bugging the fuck out, spazzing on pregnant women and shit*, he thought to himself as he turned to head back to his car.

He began to think about the shadow of Estes that loomed over him. He knew that he would never be at peace until the beef with Estes was settled. He had to go to Estes and ask for his forgiveness. If he didn't, Mecca would always have to look over his shoulders, wondering when one of his grandfather's henchmen would kill him for what he had done to his twin brother.

Just as Mecca took the second step, he heard a familiar noise, which was that of a gun jamming. He quickly swung around and fired a bullet straight through the woman's neck. Mecca had underestimated Estes. He had killers on his team from all over, and the woman who he had thought was so innocent was really there to murder him.

She dropped the chrome .45 as her hands instinctively grabbed her neck. Blood gushed out of the hole like a faucet.

Mecca quickly stepped closer and let off another round, that time catching her in the forehead. Her head jerked back and she stared into space. Dead on impact.

Enraged, he lifted her shirt to reveal her bulging belly, only to find a pillow stuffed underneath. Estes was pulling out all the stops in the hunt for Mecca's head.

Mecca breathed hard as he held the gun tightly. He looked down and saw the gun in her lap. He knew that Estes' hired guns rarely missed, and if her gun had not jammed, he would be a dead man. Mecca gave her another shot to the chest for good measure as his temper flared from the rage he felt.

He was tired of running. He couldn't beef out with Estes. His grandfather's reach was too far, and Mecca knew that eventually he would lose. He paused, staring at her, knowing that he had almost been caught slipping.

"This shit has got to stop!" he yelled in frustration as he tucked his gun in his waistline and ran to his car, leaving the woman slumped in her seat.

Mecca sped off, filling the air with the sound of screeching tires. He knew exactly what he had to do in order to end the madness.

Murder stood at the front desk as he checked into the five-star hotel in Ft. Lauderdale. He wanted to observe from afar, and decided to stay in a suburban hotel instead of directly in the city, so that he could remain low key.

"Do I have a package waiting for me?" Murder asked as he gave the desk clerk a smile.

"Um, I don't know. Let me check," the young blonde said as she returned the smile to Murder. The desk clerk looked behind the counter and smiled as she saw the FedEx box addressed to the occupant of room 403, which was Murder's suite.

"Here we go, sir. It was dropped off this morning for a . . . Mr. M," she said as she glanced oddly at the box.

"Yeah, that's me. Thanks," he said as he slid his room key off the counter and grabbed the box. He headed for the elevators and hurried up to his suite.

Moments later, Murder ripped open the neatly packed box, retrieving two chrome 9 mm guns that Aries had sent to him. He loaded the clips and pulled out the piece of paper that had the address on it. He immediately placed the twin millies on his hip and headed out the door.

An hour later, a cab pulled outside of the brick house that sat on a small hill. Murder tipped the cabbie and watched as he left. Murder then looked at the house and took a deep breath. Murder began to second-guess his plan, and wondered if he was walking into a setup. He pulled out his guns and approached the house, going all out.

He approached the front door and turned the doorknob. It was unlocked, so he pushed the door open. He carefully stepped through the door with his gun drawn. The familiar smell of a rotting body overwhelmed him as he winced in displeasure. The horrendous stench was overbearing, and he instantly pulled his shirt over his nose.

Murder's heart began to thump as he got deeper into the empty house. The smell got heavier and heavier as he approached the door that led to the basement. He quickly snatched open the basement door and pointed his gun through the opening. The rotting smell had been magnified by ten when he opened the door. He held his breath as he began to walk down the stairs, preparing himself for what he was to find.

"Miamor, please don't let this be you," he whispered as his eyes got teary.

When Murder reached the bottom step, it felt as if his heart had dropped into the pit of his stomach. He saw a decomposing corpse sprawled on the floor, hog-tied. He looked at the arm and noticed there was no hand attached to it. It was then that he knew that it was really Miamor. He instantly dropped to his knees and turned his head away, not wanting to see Miamor that way. Although he had known that finding her alive was unlikely, seeing her tortured and dismembered in the tomblike basement ripped his insides to pieces. The confirmation of her death was the only pain he had ever felt in his entire life. Murder was a cold soul, and before meeting Miamor, he didn't even think he was capable of love. But she had always been his weakness. She was the woman who could penetrate him, and now she was gone.

"No, ma . . . no," he whispered as he put his hand to his ears to drown out the sound of his own internal misery.

Murder's heart had just been broken in two. He had just verified that the world lost one of the realest bitches who ever walked it. The ultimate sin had been committed against her. It was about to be murder season in Miami. He didn't care if he had to make the entire city bleed. Somebody had to pay, and he was determined to get vengeance.

***

Murder, Aries, and Robyn sat on the fifty-foot yacht as they stared out at the Atlantic Ocean, all of them with pain in their hearts and revenge on their minds. Murder had sent for Robyn and Aries right after he found Miamor's body. They all knew that she was dead before Murder came to Miami, but they had to make sure. The vase full of ashes in their hands confirmed it: they had lost. They both had looked to Miamor as their leader. Her confidence made them confident, and now that she had been touched, they felt extremely vulnerable. Even though the sun was shining, it was a very cold day for Murder and the Murder Mamas.

"I'ma make sure all them niggas pay for what they did to Miamor," Murder mumbled as he shook his head from side to side and kept visualizing Miamor's beautiful smile.

"I know Mecca did this. He is sick in the head, and the only person twisted enough to do something like this. That crazy mu'fucka is the only one who would go to this extreme to do this to her," Robyn said as she held her lips tight.

"Yeah, Mecca did this to she," Aries whispered in her heavy accent as she shook her head in sadness.

"I'ma avenge Miamor's death for sure. These south niggas don't know how I get down. They ain't seen a nigga like me before," Murder said through his clenched teeth.

Robyn shook her head in disagreement. "It's not that simple, Murder. This shit is real. We've been hitting niggas for years, and we have never encountered any organization like theirs. They killed Anisa and Miamor. That shit don't happen to us. We were untouchable until we faced them. They are not like regular niggas. We are fucking with The Cartel, and they're not like these ol' corny clique-naming-ass niggas. Their shit is legit. I'm talking the best security, crazy gun power, and not to mention the entire fucking city rocks with them.

"If they move like they used to, it's hard to catch them together all at once. We tried to kill them one at a time, and that plan only backfired on us. I know how you get down, but you're only one man. You'll be going against a thousand niggas just as grimy as you are.

"This time, don't even give them a chance to hit back. You can't kill one; you have to kill them all. If you want to get them and do it right, you have to infiltrate their organization. You have to get close and go from the inside out," Robyn said, thinking about how they failed at every attempt to take down The Cartel using other tactics.

"Fuck that! I'ma do this my way," Murder said as his trigger finger began to itch.

"No, Murder. Chu have to listen to Robyn. You are going to be next if you go in blazing. Me no want to see no more dying. If anybody is going to be put in the dirt, let it be someone from the other side. Trust us. Please just do it our way," Aries pleaded as she looked into Murder's bloodshot eyes.

Robyn placed her hand on Murder's shoulder and looked in his eyes. She noticed the burning desire for revenge, and she had to let Murder know that he was dealing with a different breed when it came to The Cartel. "Murder, these niggas not playing. If you kill one, they are going to come and kill ten of yours. That's how they operate, so you have to do this thing right. You have to get in good with them and find out a way to kill them all at once. That way, you can dismantle them from the top. Kill the head, and the body will fall. Trust me!" Robyn said as a tear dropped as she thought of Miamor.

Murder nodded his head, giving in to her. He was willing to do whatever it took to take down The Cartel.

"We are going to get these niggas back," Robyn said as she quickly wiped the tear away and looked into the waves bouncing on top of the massive body of water.

"I want to do this one alone. The best way to do something is to do it solo. That's how I work," Murder said as he dropped his head and shook it from side to side. He then looked over at Aries and said, "Let's get this over with."

Aries opened the urn that had Miamor's remains in it. They decided to have her cremated because there was no way that she could have a funeral. Mecca had cut her up in four different pieces to prevent any hopes of a traditional open casket ceremony. Aries took a deep breath, glancing at Robyn and then Murder before she dropped a tear and released the ashes into the ocean. Forever Miamor would sleep with the fishes.

Chapter Seven

"Even family will betray you."
—Garza

Carter may have been locked up, but he wasn't dead, and in any circumstance, his survival instincts always kicked in. He was a hustler and could sell whatever, whenever, wherever, and prison was no exception. He knew of the weakened state that The Cartel was in, and he did not want to depend on anyone to keep him afloat, so although they had trapped his body, the feds could not contain his hustle. They had taken him off of the streets, but he had brought the streets to him.

He easily brought his product into the prison, and now he was running a lucrative heroin operation while locked up. The one thing that the game had taught him was that everybody loved money, and as long as everyone ate, things ran smoothly. Using a bitch as a mule was a sure way to get caught, so instead, he put correctional officers on his payroll. They brought it into the prison for him, and Zyir ensured that they were compensated properly with an anonymous wire transfer into each of their personal bank accounts. The guards were making more money working for Carter than they did on their day jobs, which made them compliant with all of his requests.

Carter wasn't flashy, however. He got money low key, keeping just enough to keep his books full, and then had the rest delivered to Zyir, who was putting it toward his case. He kept to himself, and spent his time reading books. He knew that the only person who truly cared about his freedom was himself, so he educated himself on the law so that the system would not be able to jam him up. He refused to let the feds lock him up and throw away the key.

As he sat silently on his bed, he peeked up at his cellmate. He knew that the Mexican cat did not like him, and the feeling was mutual. Carter would much rather be in a cell alone, but the overcrowding issues of the prison made it nearly impossible. The two never spoke. They kept a respectable distance from one another, always keeping their interactions to the bare minimum. They were a part of two different worlds, and because they had respect for the game that they both played, they had established an unspoken truce. What Carter did not know was that Garza had been watching him, and he had the power to offer Carter what he desperately craved—his freedom.

Carter sat alone at his table in the cafeteria as he ate silently. Although other members of The Cartel were incarcerated with him, he felt no need to be friendly. They were there for his protection and only his protection. He didn't need another man to keep him company; his thoughts were enough. Miamor plagued his mind, as did the current state of The Cartel. They needed a plug and needed it bad. The low quality heroin he was running through the prison was not potent enough for his outside dealings. Scarcity made it acceptable inside the walls, but on the outside, it was a completely different game. Zyir and Mecca were grasping at straws trying to secure other connects, but nobody was willing to mess with them. Everyone was afraid of the repercussions of being associated with The Cartel. He was carrying huge burdens on his shoulders, and being locked up made him feel powerless. Detaching himself from the outside would be the only way that he would become accustomed to prison, but with Zyir, Mecca, and the responsibilities that came with being the leader of The Cartel it was hard to block it out.

As Carter ate, he watched an inmate approach his table. Carter continued to eat, unfazed as one of the members of The Cartel got up from the table next to him. His goons were never out of arm's reach.

"Hold up, homeboy," the loyal affiliate stated as he stopped the inmate in his tracks.

"Yo, I'm not on no beef shit. I know better than to beef with this man. I just came to rap with him for a second," the inmate stated as he pulled a carton of cigarettes out of the top of his jail jumpsuit. The cigarettes were a sign of respect. In prison, money did not come easy, so the fact that the little nigga had spent a nice chunk of his commissary on them bought him a moment of Carter's time.

Carter's goon looked at him for approval, and Carter nodded his head for him to let the boy pass. The goon patted the inmate down for good measure to ensure that the visit really was a friendly one.

"Carter, I've heard a lot about you, and I just wanted to personally introduce myself. I'm from Opa-Locka, and when I was on the outside, I was doing my thing thing, you know?" he stated as he clapped his hands together. "I know that's your territory and all, 'cause you sent the young goon Zyir through to shut my shit down. I wanted to let you know ain't no hard feelings or nothing on my end, but I am trying to get on board with your movement. I'm outta here in a few months, and I don't got nothing to go home to. Like, nothing, fam. So when I say I'm hungry, I mean it. I don't want to make the mistake of stepping on your toes again, so I wanted to know what I have to do to get down. I'll put in work any way you need me to," the guy finished.

Carter continued to eat and didn't even look up as he said, "What did you say your name was?"

"Ibrahim," the guy replied.

Carter took his time and gathered his thoughts before he spoke. The uncomfortable silence between the two men made the inmate shift nervously from side to side.

Finally, Carter looked up at the dude. "Sit down, my man. Everybody don't need to hear what I'm about to say."

Feeling as if Carter was about to put him on, the guy smiled as he took a seat across from the hood legend. Carter's name indeed rang bells in and out of prison. Anyone in the game knew exactly who he was.

"You said my li'l man Zyir shut your shit down?" Carter asked.

The dude nodded and replied, "Yeah, he told me I was out of bounds. That those blocks were already spoken for."

"And what did you do to handle that situation?" Carter asked.

"I didn't mean no disrespect, fam. I moved my operation to a different block," he replied.

"See, that's where my problem lies, Ibrahim. Do you think I got where I am by letting other niggas run me off the block?" Carter asked. "Now, if you had blazed on my li'l nigga, maybe then we would have something to talk about. That would have showed me you had heart, but you didn't. You let another man, who bleeds just like you bleed, stop you from getting money. I can't afford to have any weak links in my chain, Ibrahim."

With that said, Carter resumed his meal as he waited for Ibrahim to dismiss himself. The conversation was over, but Carter knew there would be more to come. Many men had approached him since he had been locked up, and it was always the same story. Everybody wanted to be put on, but Carter didn't rock with new niggas. He knew that if he let too many people into his circle, it would not seem exclusive. Everybody in the hood wanted to be a part of something, but unfortunately, not many fit the bill to be a member of The Cartel. Carter definitely had no use for a scary nigga. He only wanted the elite.

The inmate nodded his head, his ego slightly bruised as he stood to his feet. He slowly slid the cigarette carton over to Carter.

"For your time," he said respectfully.

Carter nodded his head and stood to his feet as he headed back to his cell. He handed the carton to Garza as soon as he entered. Carter didn't smoke cigarettes, and although he never spoke to his cellmate, he always passed the unwanted gifts along to him.

"How did you end up in here?" Garza asked. Carter looked up in surprise. They had never engaged one another before, so the question was completely unexpected.

"An associate of mine found himself on the wrong side of the law. It was a person who I thought I could trust, someone who I grew up with. He was like family."

"Even family will betray you," Garza interrupted as he lit a smoke.

"So I learned," Carter replied with a chuckle. The situation was comical to him. He had done nothing but show Ace love, but the first chance Ace got, he had stabbed him in the back—and plunged the blade deep. Carter knew that once Ace took the stand and testified against him, that it would be all the jury needed to hear to convict him.

"I've been watching you, observing how you move. I've seen how the men in here treat you," Garza replied. "Even the guards march to the beat of your drum. It would be a shame to see a man of your talents end up in here because of a snake. It seems that your problem could be handled if you knew who to ask for help."

"I don't ask for help. Anything that I can't do on my own is not worth doing. I've never owed anyone anything a day in my life," Carter stated surely. He did not know what Garza was getting at, but already he did not like the sound of it.

"That is the problem with your kind."

"There's not another man like me. I don't have a kind," Carter interrupted sternly.

"I do not mean any disrespect, but the Blacks don't know how to form alliances. Someone with your mentality could be very valuable. The way that you move product is a skill that not many people have. The power you have over others is rare as well. I've done my research on you and The Cartel. If you are willing to extend a hand of friendship, I know some people who can help you out of your predicament."

Carter's interest was piqued. "Nobody does anything for free."

"A partnership between the Diamond Cartel and the Garza Cartel would be payment enough. We have the product that you need, and you have the influence that we need in the South. Together we would be unstoppable."

"Until one party becomes envious of the other," Carter protested.

The old man shook his head as he continued to smoke. "That will never become a problem for us. I can guarantee that my people are not in it for the limelight, only the money. As long as the money is correct, there will not be a problem. This could be a beautiful thing if you are willing to expand your horizons."

"I don't work underneath others," Carter insisted.

"Not under others, Carter, *with* others. There is a difference. Working with my people, your reach will be limitless. Mexico is not like the United States. In my country, we are above the law," Garza explained.

"Why are you still in here? If it is so easy to make my case disappear, why not do the same for yourself?" Carter asked. Although the deal was appealing, he was skeptical to trust Garza's word too quickly. He wanted to cover all of his bases.

"I chose my own destiny. I'm an old man. An organization of my family's magnitude leaves a lot of bodies in its path. Someone has to be held accountable for those. I took responsibility because I saw the bigger picture. I'm in here for twenty different counts of confessed murder. I have lived my life and done my part so that my family's reign could go on. What I'm offering you is a deal too sweet for any man to refuse."

Garza extended his hand, and Carter reluctantly accepted. "Nothing will be set in stone until a face to face is held. I'll send my right hand, Zyir, to meet with your people," Carter stated.

"I will phone home tomorrow to let my brother Felipe know to expect him. This will be a beautiful thing for everyone involved."

"Only time will tell," Carter responded. He knew that getting in bed with the Mexican drug cartel could prove very wise. He just had to ensure that everyone understood the terms of the agreement, because if something went wrong, Carter was almost certain that The Cartel would not be able to withstand another war.

Mecca could not take it anymore. Watching his back every second of every day was becoming too much to bear. He knew that there was only one way to dead his beef with Estes. He had to go see his grandfather. The same man who had sent the killers to his front door was the only one who could call them off. He hoped that he could reason with Estes and that he would remember that Monroe was not his only grandson.

He had made a mistake by killing Monroe, and it was a regret that he would live with for the rest of his life. Estes' vengeance was not necessary. The burden was already heavy enough, sometimes too heavy for him to carry.

As Mecca ventured on his grandfather's side of town, his instincts sharpened. He kept his eyes in his rearview and one hand on his pistol. He never wanted to be caught slipping again, so he stayed ready, safety off. It would be the wrong day to run up on him unannounced. He knew that he would never make it through his grandfather's door with a gun, so he hoped that Estes did not have him killed on sight.

Mecca had love for no one besides family. He remembered the Christmas holidays and the many birthdays that had been spent in his grandfather's presence. How long ago that seemed now. How easily they both had forgotten.

It seemed to Mecca that Estes placed more value on his relationship with Monroe. The little boy that respected his grandfather simply wanted to be loved, but the grown, cold man that Mecca had come to be wanted to place his grandfather in the dirt.

As he finally neared Estes' home, he parked at the public beach and decided to walk along the sand behind his grandfather's house. The fact that Estes' house sat directly on the water helped Mecca go undetected. The many people that were enjoying the sun allowed him to blend in, and as he neared his grandfather's home, he noticed that Estes was outside sitting on his patio. A few feet away from him, a woman stood in a sundress and large sunhat, holding a child in her arms. Estes seemed to be distracted by the woman's presence as Mecca approached.

He wished that he had brought his pistol with him. It was the first time he had seen his grandfather so relaxed. There were no bodyguards in sight, and it would have been the perfect time to end their beef once and for all, but Mecca knew that he did not have time to go back to his car. He had to try to reason with Estes.

Mecca watched the woman go inside, and Estes' eyes were so focused on the woman that he never saw Mecca walk up.

"Hello, Grandfather," Mecca greeted in a low, steady tone.

Caught completely off guard, Estes turned around to find Mecca standing before him. He half expected to be shot instantly. Mecca lifted his arms and shirt and then said, "I'm not strapped."

"Why not? I would not have extended you the same courtesy," Estes replied as he pulled a .45 from underneath the table. It had been resting in his lap, but Estes immediately showed his cards to let Mecca know that he was constantly aware of the business he was in.

"You're still alive," Estes observed as his eyes roamed his grandson cautiously, surveying him to see if he was injured.

"Diamonds are forever," Mecca replied.

"Tell that to your brother," Estes shot back. He clicked off his safety as his finger gripped the trigger of his gun. "You're a snake, Mecca. You're a traitor. You killed my grandson."

"Am I not your grandson, Estes?" Mecca asked.

Estes fixed his mouth to respond, but was interrupted when Leena emerged from the house with her son in one arm and a bowl of fruit in her hands. She was so busy trying to balance everything without dropping it that she didn't look up. When she finally did, both she and Mecca got the surprise of their lives.

"Leena?"

Her name fell out of his mouth without him even knowing it, and the sound of his voice caused her to drop the glass bowl in her hands, causing tiny glass fragments to explode on the ground. Her heart beat in fear as she instinctively gripped her son in protection.

Mecca's eyes widened as if he were seeing a ghost. He had shot her himself. For all this time, he had thought that she was dead. Now here she was, standing before him, as beautiful as he remembered. His gaze went from her to the child in her arms. He looked like a tiny replica of Mecca, but deep in his heart, Mecca knew that the little boy was not his seed. Mecca was sterile, and the child in Leena's arm was his nephew. It was Money's son, and that fact brought the betrayal that he had felt rushing back to him.

Tears came to Leena's eyes as she saw Mecca's expression go from sad to angry. She knew him, and felt as if he would explode at any moment. Estes didn't hesitate to chamber a bullet in his gun. He, too, recognized the look in his grandson's eyes.

"It's that easy for you to shoot me, Estes? Your flesh and blood," Mecca stated as he looked back and forth between Lena and Estes. Seeing her reminded him of his sins, and his bottom lip began to quiver uncontrollably. He held his arms out at his sides as Estes' finger rested on the trigger. "Did Money mean that much more? Why is his life more valuable than mine? Huh, Estes? Why does everybody hate Mecca?"

Estes was silent but unflinching as he listened to Mecca break down. "Ever since we were little, everybody always favored Money. Mecca was the bad twin. I was the unwanted seed! My heart was cold before the streets ever got a hold of me. Everybody always loved Money . . . never me," Mecca shouted, getting years of pent-up emotion off of his chest.

His words brought tears to Leena's eyes, because even she had chosen Monroe over Mecca. She had contributed to his hurt, to his isolation.

"There is no excuse," Estes spoke up, unaffected by Mecca's outburst. "You murdered your brother. You knew what the consequences would be for your actions. Be a man and take what you deserve," Estes said without the theatrics. He was calm and sure of his decision as he raised his gun, aiming it at Mecca's heart. Just as he was about to pull the trigger, Leena stopped him.

"Emilio, please don't," Leena whispered. She couldn't take her eyes off of Mecca as her tears began to flow. "There has been enough bloodshed." Her voice was pleading, and even though she hated Mecca, she did not want to see him dead. He looked so much like Monroe, like her son, and as she read the hurt in his stare, she began to think about Mecca's pain for the first time since she had been shot.

"Leena?" Mecca repeated in disbelief as he stumbled backward a bit, completely in shock.

Estes stood to his feet and stepped close to Mecca. His gun hung threateningly in his palm. "She just saved your life, son.

You are no grandson of mine. You will keep your distance," Estes said. He did not raise his voice, but his tone was all the warning that Mecca needed.

"What do I have to do to get your forgiveness, Estes?" Mecca whispered so that only the two of them could hear his plea.

"Ask God for forgiveness. I have none to give," Estes replied.

Mecca stepped back and wiped his face with one hand. "You'll call off your dogs," Mecca countered.

Estes looked back at Leena, who nodded her head as she wiped the tears away while holding her son tightly.

Estes replied dryly, "I will."

Mecca extended his hand to his grandfather, but Estes walked away disgusted. He had no respect for Mecca, and did not want there to be any misunderstandings. Estes would never welcome Mecca back into his family.

Mecca walked away stunned. His mind was completely blown. The mixed emotions that Mecca felt threw him completely off balance. Seeing Leena alive and healthy, seeing her breathing, had taken his mind back to when everything was as it should be. She reminded him of the days that were so carefree, and the baby boy that mirrored him in image made him think of Monroe. He wanted to think that the fresh little man he had just seen was his own son, but he knew better. It wasn't even possible for Mecca to procreate. He was shooting blanks. It was as if God knew that nothing good could ever come from him.

Leena had given birth to his nephew and had been in hiding, living with Estes all this time. Now that he had seen her, he did not know if he could just walk away. Her affair with his flesh and blood had led Mecca to kill his own twin. Her survival enraged him, while at the same time, it pleased him. He had so many questions that only she could answer.

How long had she and Monroe been fucking? Why did she choose him over me? What the fuck is she doing with Estes? Mecca thought as he sauntered blankly down the sandy beach. These things burned in his mind, and he knew that he would not be satisfied until he got some answers. He got into his car and pulled away, knowing that he would not stay away for long.

***

Leena watched from the upstairs window as Mecca disappeared up the beach. Fear paralyzed her as she thought of what he might do now that he knew of her existence. Seeing him again terrified her, but when she had looked in his eyes, her heart felt like it would beat out of her chest.

Mecca symbolized so many things in her life. He looked as if he had been through so much anguish since the last time she saw him. He had aged, matured, changed, and she did not know if it was for the better. She saw misery in his stare, and his features were so identical to Monroe's that she could not help but fall in love at first sight.

She did not know how two brothers who were so physically alike could be so different on the inside. She hoped that Mecca would let her be. She had pieced her life back together seamlessly with the help of Estes, and the last thing she needed was another Diamond brother to come along and tear her world apart.

"Are you okay?"

Leena released Mecca from her gaze as she turned around at the sound of Estes' voice. She nodded unsurely as she put on a phony smile. "I'm fine," she replied.

Estes came over to her and removed baby Monroe from her arms. The one year old went to him happily. Estes was the only man that had ever been around her son. He was the only stability in her life, but seeing Mecca had been like a bad omen, and she felt it in her bones that a deadly storm was about to blow her way.

Chapter Eight

"A real live American boy."
—Illiana

When Zyir stepped off of the private plane, the overwhelming heat hit him instantly. His baggy khaki shorts and white button-down linen shirt seemed too heavy for the Mexican heat. He unbuttoned his shirt, revealing the crisp white wife beater underneath. His eyes were hidden behind the Homme shades he wore.

The hidden airstrip that they had used to fly in on was undetected by the Mexican government, so Zyir felt secure as he stepped off of the plane. Still, he knew that because his presence in Mexico was completely undetected, if something were to happen to him, no one would even know where to begin looking.

He had wanted to bring Mecca along, because that was the one person he knew would not be afraid to pop off if things got out of hand, but Mecca was a hot head, and could easily blow this deal for them. Because of this, Carter had insisted that Zyir go alone, and even though he went everywhere strapped, he felt that it would be of little use in the foreign country.

"*Buenas tardes, señor,*" the driver greeted as he held open the limousine door.

Zyir nodded his head to greet the man, and then stepped inside of the plush vehicle. A full liquor bar was set up for him inside, but he chose not to partake. He was there to handle business only. He could bullshit back home.

He attempted to keep his bearings as the limo took him to his destination, but he quickly realized that it was no use. He did not know where he was being escorted, and the fact that he was not in control pushed him out of his comfort zone.

Trust would be his only way of getting through this meeting. He would have to hope that the men he was about to meet with were men of honor. If not, he was about to walk into a situation where he was greatly outnumbered.

Zyir watched as the city turned into countryside as they drove along the coastline. An hour later, they pulled up to an estate much grander than anything he had ever seen. The beauty of it was magnificent. He admired the stone exterior. He was brought back to reality, however, when he noticed the armed guards standing post at the gates and aiming their automatic sniper rifles from their high towers. The property was guarded like a fort.

Zyir's palms began to sweat as he attempted to keep his composure. He removed his pistol and placed it underneath the seat of the limo. He knew that the sixteen bullets from his 9 mm would be no match for the artillery that the guards were equipped with. They would fill him with holes before he even let off a shot. So, he was making the first effort to establish a trusting alliance with the Mexicans by going in unarmed. It was his way of showing good faith.

The guards peered into the car, and once Zyir's identity was confirmed, he was admitted onto the property.

The atmosphere was not what he had assumed it would be. There were no bikini clad women and no sleazy lifestyle taking place. It reminded him of the Diamond estate. It was a family home, and he relaxed a bit when he stepped out of the car.

"Welcome to Mexico, Zyir," a man greeted as he emerged from the mansion.

"You must be Felipe," Zyir responded. "I appreciate the invitation. We have a lot to discuss."

"That we do, but my wife has prepared a beautiful lunch for you on the back terrace. Let's eat first. The time for business will come soon," Felipe stated. He led Zyir through the home and out onto the back terrace that faced the ocean.

"Zyir, this is my wife, Maria, and my sister Illiana," Felipe introduced.

"Very nice to meet you, Zyir," Maria greeted.

"A real live American boy," Illiana stated as she surveyed Zyir, her dark, mischievous eyes looking him up and down as she sipped on a cocktail.

Her dark hair and striking features immediately stood out to Zyir. He had never seen a woman so beautiful. As she stared him down, Zyir knew that there was nothing good about this girl. She was a temptress, and the deep pools that were her eyes were hypnotic. He quickly broke their stare to avoid becoming lost in them.

She was the most exotic young woman he had ever seen. She exuded a confidence and sexiness that he had never encountered before. Zyir was no fool, however. He knew that to do business with the Garza family meant that Illiana would be the forbidden fruit. Wars had been sparked over women, and no matter how exotic she appeared, no pussy was that good. He was always about his dollar.

Not wanting to appear too friendly, Zyir nodded his acknowledgements and took a seat. It was customary for a wife to welcome the guests of her husband, and Maria ensured that Zyir was comfortable. The four ate and spoke as if they were old acquaintances, but Zyir was simply being polite and going through the motions. He was itching to get to the money, but knew that he had to build a rapport before Felipe would even bring it up.

Although there were only four people at the table, Zyir was well aware that he was being evaluated by many more. After much unwanted banter, Zyir finally spoke up. His patience was running real low. *I'm not here on a social call,* he thought. *If we ain't talking money, then we're wasting time.*

He leaned into Felipe so that the women could not overhear and said, "I'm ready to get down to it. I appreciate your hospitality, but it really isn't necessary. Time is of the essence, nah mean?"

Felipe put his hand on Zyir's shoulder. "My man . . . in such a rush. Sometimes you have to do things slowly in order to do them efficiently, my friend," he replied. He stared tensely at Zyir, and then snapped his fingers, making one of his housekeepers rush quickly to his side.

"*¿Sí, señor?*" the elderly woman asked.

"Rosa, please take my friend's glass and get him a fresh drink," Felipe instructed.

Zyir never broke Felipe's stare, because there was not a man on this earth who could intimidate him. He was fearless as he sat, one man against what he was sure was an entire Mexican army lingering in the shadows of the massive estate. It was clear that Felipe held the power, and by making Zyir wait, he was sending a clear message that everyone on the southern side of the border moved at the pace of the Garza family, including Zyir.

Illiana watched Zyir's interaction with her brother and secretly admired him. In no form was Zyir bowing to Felipe, and his demeanor intrigued her. She was not used to opposition. No one ever had the balls to hold their ground against the Garza Cartel, but it was obvious that the reputation was not impressive to Zyir.

The housekeeper came back with a new drink for Zyir and then turned to Felipe and announced, "It has been done, señor. He is not in the database."

Felipe's mood immediately changed, and his callous expression transformed into a satisfied smile. "I apologize, Zyir. I had to make sure that you are who you say you are. I lifted your prints off of your cocktail glass and had one of my men run them through your country's national federal database. All federal agents must have their prints taken. A man in my position can never be too cautious," Felipe explained.

Not wanting to appear too impressed, Zyir held his cards, but he was inwardly pleased at how thorough Felipe was. "I understand," Zyir replied.

"Now, if you two will excuse us," Felipe stated as he stood to his feet. "I think I have wasted enough of this man's time."

"Surely lunch with me was not a waste of time," Illiana spoke up, seduction oozing off of her words.

Zyir smirked and then followed Felipe into the mansion.

By the time Zyir departed Mexico, he had secured a new connect and partnership with Felipe. The Cartel was back on, and with the pull that the Garza Cartel possessed, it was only a matter of time before Carter was free and money flowed again.

***

As Ace stared out of the hotel window, he could not believe his life had come to this. Hiding out in northern Pennsylvania with no contact to the outside world was not what he called a life. Foolishly, he had tried to backdoor The Cartel and sell bricks of cocaine on the side. He had gotten greedy. Tired of constantly working beneath Carter, he had tried to expand on his own, but there was a reason why Carter kept him in the background of the operation. Ace did not have the makings of a boss, and he proved that when he sold a kilo of coke to an undercover federal agent. The feds could almost smell the fear on Ace, and they took advantage of it from the very beginning. Once Ace revealed his connection to The Cartel, he became a pawn in their game to take down Carter, and like a true snitch-ass nigga, Ace obliged to save his own behind.

The life of a federal witness was not what he anticipated. He was forced to go into hiding until the end of the trial, and the detachment he felt knowing that he had turned on his former best friend ate at him. He was set to testify in court in two weeks, but the closer the date came, the more he wanted to change his story. He knew that things could never go back to the way they used to be, but he had come up from the gutter with Carter, and he knew that if the shoe was on the other foot, Carter would have never betrayed him.

Ostracized from everyone he loved and knew, Ace was living a lonely existence. At least in prison he would still have his family. If he had lived by the code of the streets and stayed true to the game, he would have been able to hold his head up high. He was a man, and no one had forced him to play the game the way he had. In his heart, he knew that he had no honor, and that he was causing the demise of another black man. He wanted to recant the statements that he had made to the feds, but he knew it was too late.

Even if he took everything back, the hood would know that he had flipped on Carter, and they would never forget. The streets had no love for snitches, and he was already a marked man. His only option was to testify and then disappear in the witness protection program. It was his only way to start over and begin a new life.

When we started in the game, neither of us ever thought it would turn out like this, he thought solemnly as he reminisced over his early days hustling with Young Carter.

A knock at the door interrupted his reverie as one of the federal agents entered the room. They were his protection, the only barrier between him and the ruthless team of killers that he was sure Carter had ordered to find him. Ace was sure that Mecca was among the wolves coming for his head. Ace only hoped that they never found him. This was how he would live the remainder of his days, looking over his shoulder every second of every hour as the paranoia ate away at his existence.

"Here's your food," the agent stated as he wheeled in a silver covered platter.

"Thanks," Ace stated as he sat down to eat his meal alone. Halfway through his meal, he grasped his throat in horror as he felt his airway become constricted. He attempted to yell out in distress as his eyes widened and he struggled to breathe. He stood frantically, knocking the table on its side as he flailed around the room, gasping for air. Sweat poured from his brow as his insides burned.

The federal agents burst into the room to find their key witness on the ground. His bloodshot eyes pleaded for them to call for help.

"Call a bus!" one of the agents shouted as he bent over to check Ace's pulse. He looked at the food on the floor and concluded. "Secure the cooking staff downstairs. It's the food! He's been poisoned!"

Ace felt himself slipping in and out of consciousness as the agents rushed into action around him. The paramedics finally arrived on the scene and lifted his convulsing body onto a gurney.

"Please . . . help," Ace managed to squeeze out.

"We are going to take care of you, sir," the paramedic stated. "Try to focus on me. Stay with me. You're going to be okay."

Ace focused on the sound of the paramedic's voice as he was loaded into the back of the ambulance. The man's words reassured him, but he knew that this would only be the first attempt of many on his life. The Cartel had failed this time— fortunately for him, the federal agents had gotten him help in just the nick of time— but they would not always be around to protect him, and now that his location was known, Ace was more fearful than ever before.

The ambulance sped recklessly through traffic as it rushed him to the hospital. Ace closed his eyes to conserve his energy. It wasn't until he felt the electric bolts pulsing through his body that he realized something was wrong.

"Aghhh!" He yelled as the paramedics shocked him. The voltage was up so high that the hair on his bare chest smoked. "Fuck is going on?"

Before he realized what was happening, he watched the Mexican man place a gun in the center of his forehead. He did not recognize the men, and the look of confusion was apparent on his face. The ambulance stopped moving, and the back doors were snatched open. He looked up and into the face of the devil—Mecca Diamond. Next to him stood a stoic Zyir.

Felipe's soldiers removed their paramedic disguises and hopped out as Mecca and Zyir climbed in.

Ace attempted to sit up, but was laid back down by the butt of Zyir's gun as it cracked the bridge of his nose.

"Zy, man . . . come on. We're family. I swear I won't say shit, fam. You don't have to do this," Ace begged as he reached out his hand toward Zyir.

Mecca scoffed in disgust. "This ol' pussy-ass nigga. Where the fuck Carter get this mu'fucka from?" he asked as he aimed his .357 and blew a hole through Ace's pleading hand.

"Aghh! Fuck!" Ace yelled in excruciating pain as blood spewed from his wound. He held his injured hand.

Ace knew that there would be no reasoning with Mecca, so he hoped that Zyir would show him sympathy. "Zyir, we came in this together."

"And you going out alone, my nigga," Zyir stated coldly. His loyalty was to Carter. Any love that he had for Ace had dissipated when Ace turned snitch. Zyir figured that if Ace was willing to turn Carter in, it would only be a matter of time before his own name turned up on a federal affidavit.

Tired of the "remember the times" love song that Ace was singing, Mecca emptied his clip into Ace, silencing him forever. Zyir then walked around to the driver's seat and put the vehicle in drive. He and Mecca stood as they watched the ambulance roll through the highway rails and plunge down into the mountainous valleys below.

They turned around and shook hands with Felipe's men. Their connection with the Garza Cartel was already proving to be valuable. It was Felipe who had located Ace, and because of him, at that very moment, the federal judge presiding over Carter's case was being paid off handsomely. Without Ace, the feds' case would be too weak to convict, and when Carter's lawyer requested a dismissal, the judge would oblige.

Chapter Nine

"Yeah, I know you're a Diamond, Mecca. Me and everybody else in Miami knows!"
—Leena

Making the trip to Mexico the second time was bittersweet for Zyir. He was eager to begin their business relationship with the Garza Cartel, but he was upset by the fact that he missed Carter's last day in trial. He would soon have his freedom, and Zyir wanted to be there to congratulate him when he walked out of the prison walls. He knew that his task in Mexico was more important, however. Carter had groomed him well, and he knew that above all else, the money was always first priority. They could celebrate later. Today, Zyir had three tons of cocaine to pick up. Nobody dealt in quantities that large, and with that much access to the product, it was only a matter of time before they were the largest drug cartel in the nation. Miami was only the beginning.

When Zyir pulled up to the Garza estate this time, there was no hesitation. He had already established a level of trust with Felipe, and was granted access with ease. He was greeted by Felipe, who stood waiting with open arms.

"Zyir, my friend," Felipe said as the two men embraced briefly. "I have something to show you."

Zyir followed Felipe around to the back of the estate, until they came upon two Mack trucks.

Felipe pulled up the back of one of the semi-trucks, and his eyes widened as he took in the beautiful sight before him: rows and rows of neatly packed kilos. There were so many bricks that they gave off a sparkle. Zyir had never seen so much work in his life, and the sight made his hands itch, because he knew that soon a lot of money was going to flow.

"There are three tons between the two trucks. I have the entire first shift of border patrol on payroll. You and your people will be able to drive straight through without being stopped," Felipe stated.

Zyir quickly added up the total worth of the cocaine in his head. Three tons equaled three thousand bricks. They would easily go for twenty-five a pop, and even after splitting the take with Felipe, The Cartel stood to profit almost $40 million. It was a big payday for everyone, and as long as everything went flawlessly, there were many more lucrative deals to come in the future.

"Cat got your tongue, Zyir?"

Zyir turned around and saw Illiana standing behind him. Her tanned skin glowed flawlessly, and she hid her mysterious eyes behind large Dior sunglasses. Her voluptuous body was displayed in the designer two-piece bikini and matching cover-up she wore. Every part of her appeared perfect as Zyir took a quick glance, admiring her top to bottom, taking in everything from her pedicured feet to the seductress red stain on her lips. "Illiana," he acknowledged. He kissed her cheek quickly before turning his attention back to the task at hand.

Felipe put his arm around Zyir. The gesture was too friendly for Zyir, and he had to bite his tongue quickly so that he did not react. He had never let another man "son" him in his life, and although he was young in age, he was wise in years, something that Felipe would learn in time.

"I am aware of The Cartel's recent financial troubles, so I am willing to extend these kilos on consignment. However, this is too large of an order for me to just entrust them to you. I'd like to send one of my people to Miami with you to watch over my investment," Felipe stated.

"That won't be a problem," Zyir replied. "We fully understand your position, and Carter extends his assurance that this partnership will be beneficial for all involved."

"I'll have to meet this Carter. My brother Garza speaks highly of him. After his legal affairs are handled, I would like to invite the two of you back down here. No business . . . just a meeting among men. I'll have to show the two of you a good time."

"I'll be sure to extend the invitation," Zyir answered. "Who will you be sending to Miami?"

"Illiana," Felipe replied.

Zyir stopped walking mid-stride, as if he had heard Felipe wrong. "Illiana?"

"She will not get in your way. She will simply be my eyes and ears. I hope that you will put her up temporarily," Felipe suggested.

Zyir looked back at the seductive Illiana. He knew that her presence would only mean trouble.

"Of course," he said as he turned back to Felipe. Illiana would be a beautiful distraction, and he would have to stay focused on his hustle to make sure that things remained professional between them.

Carter sat reserved behind the defense table, completely confident as he sat poised and attentive. It had not been a good day for the defense. After losing their key witness, they were grasping at straws to keep the case alive. Carter's defense was all over it. Beckham was definitely earning his keep as he demolished the federal prosecutor, making Carter look like he was a saint, while discrediting the federal agency that had made his arrest.

"Your Honor, it is clear that without the key witness, the federal prosecutor has no leg to stand on," Beckham stated.

"No, Your Honor, the only thing that is clear is the obvious witness tampering involved in this case. My witness was murdered in cold blood."

"The witness was in protective custody and was rushed to the hospital because of food poisoning," Beckham shot back. "It is on the official State of Pennsylvania police report that the ambulance transporting the witness lost control and crashed. That is how the witness died. My client, who was hundreds of miles away and locked in a prison cell, could not have orchestrated such events!"

"And the bullet holes in his body were just there for decoration!" the D.A. shouted sarcastically. "Your Honor, you can not let this man—this gangster—make a mockery of the law."

The prosecutor stood to argue more, but was interrupted by the impatient banging of the judge's gavel.

"Does the State have any other evidence to present besides the witness?" the judge asked.

"No, Your Honor, but—"

"I move for immediate dismissal of the case." Beckham was a shark. He did not even give his adversary a chance to finish his sentence.

All the while, Carter sat back unscathed as he watched the amusing charade go down. It did not matter how much protesting the prosecutor did; he was getting off. The amount of money that the Garza Cartel had put up to make it happen ensured it, and as the judge looked his way, they shared a knowing glance.

"Motion for immediate dismissal granted," the judge announced. The courtroom erupted in mayhem as Carter shook his attorney's hand.

Before Carter could celebrate too much, the prosecutor stood. "Your Honor, the defendant has a new charge pending. He was involved in a prison brawl that resulted in the injury of one of his fellow inmates. We ask that he be held on this new charge that we will be actively pursuing." Carter's eyes burned holes through the white man as the judge approved the request. The government was doing everything in its power to keep him locked up.

Before Carter could even express his displeasure, Beckham leaned into his ear. "Don't worry about it. That is just the desperate measures of a persistent D.A. You just made them look bad. Not many people are able to beat a federal conviction. They are pulling tricks out of their bag to delay your release from prison. I'll make sure that the technicalities are taken care of immediately. You will be out by this evening," Beckham assured.

"Ensure that I am," Carter instructed as he allowed the bailiff to escort him away. He told himself that it was the last time he would ever be placed in handcuffs. Prison was not for him. Although he had gained a valuable new connection behind the wall, he had also had a piece of his soul taken from him, and he would die first before he ever allowed anyone to drag him back to hell.

***

Mecca sat patiently on Estes' block as he monitored his home. Since he discovered that Leena was alive, she had been on his mind constantly. He was the last person that she wanted to see, but he only needed a moment of her time. She was the only person who could supply him with the answers to the questions he sought.

Her fear of him was evident, and it disturbed Mecca that a woman he had once loved was so terrified of him. Although his anger was still fresh, he had convinced himself that enough was enough. Murder was not the way to solve this problem.

Mecca was tired of killing. He resented his position as the bad seed of his family. Even he had to admit that his aggression and disregard for life had pushed him to the edge. It was one thing to murder because you had to, but Mecca actually enjoyed it. He looked forward to the powerful feeling that taking a life gave him, but it had become a problem when he had begun hurting those that he loved. His ruthless nature was once his best quality when he knew how to control it, but he had taken it too far. Now all he was seeking was redemption.

He had been stalking Estes' house for hours, patiently waiting for his chance to get Leena alone. Finally she emerged, and Mecca admired her closely as she secured his nephew in the backseat of one of Estes' luxury vehicles. He was curious about her relationship with his grandfather, and as she pulled away from the villa, he followed, keeping a comfortable distance so that she would not detect him.

He noticed that Estes had one of his men following Leena as well. It would not be easy for him to get her alone. As she moved in and out of the boutiques on Collins Avenue, Mecca kept a close eye. He was just waiting for the right opportunity to make his move. Estes' men were well trained, and there would be no getting to Leena undetected. The only way for Mecca to approach her would be to go through her protection.

He watched as Leena stopped at a small eatery. He knew that her brief lunch would buy him some time. He parked a block away and then went to the nearest pay phone. He usually hated the police, but today they would aid him in distracting Leena's bodyguard.

He placed a 911 call, giving the police the license plate number to the bodyguard's car, and accusing him of harassing shoppers. Knowing that they were in a prestigious part of town, he knew that the cops would respond almost immediately.

As soon as he saw the squad car flash its lights on the bodyguard, Mecca slipped into the store. Spotting Leena at a quaint table in the back, Mecca approached her.

It was as if her body sensed Mecca's presence. The hairs on the back of her neck stood up and her breath caught in her throat before she even knew he was there. Warning bells went off in her head, and when Leena looked up from her menu, she froze like a deer in headlights. Because of Mecca, she was that tuned in with danger. Mecca's presence made her body tense in trepidation.

"I'm not here to hurt you," Mecca stated peacefully as he stopped where he stood. "I just want to talk to you, that's all."

Leena looked around for her bodyguard, and when she did not see him, she immediately began to gather her things. The small caliber handgun she carried in her child's diaper bag gave her a small peace of mind, but she knew that her shot could not match Mecca's. If he wanted to kill her, he would. She had seen how he got down with her own eyes. She picked up her son. She knew that Mecca would not pop off on her in the crowded eatery. He didn't like witnesses.

As he watched her scramble with her things, his heart broke. At one time, he really had loved her, and he knew that only he was responsible for the fear that she felt toward him.

"Leena, you have my word," Mecca said sincerely. He peered outside of the café window and noticed that the guard was still being harassed by the cop. "Can we go somewhere? Leena, give me at least that."

Leena wanted to tell him no, but she would only be avoiding the inevitable. Mecca was persistent, and his arrogance did not allow for people to turn him down. If she told him no today, he would only come back tomorrow and the day after, until she eventually said yes.

"Lift your shirt," Leena stated, her tone serious.

Mecca lifted his shirt discreetly as he stepped close to Leena, so that the other patrons in the bistro could not see what was going on. She removed his pistol and pressed it against his back. If they were going to talk, it was going to be on her terms. “Walk to the back,” she instructed nervously, baby in one hand and gun in the other.

Mecca smiled as Leena took him for a walk out of the back entrance. She had most definitely changed for the better. She was a bit wiser, more cautious, and definitely more street savvy than he remembered. Her time around Estes had not gone by in vain.

When they were finally out in the alley, Leena asked, “What do you want?”

The gun was still pointed in Mecca’s back as he replied, “I’m going to turn around now.” He chuckled at the irony of the situation and continued. “Whatever you do, don’t shoot.”

Leena’s hand trembled, yet her eyes were determined and revealed to Mecca that she would protect herself if he gave her a reason to. When he was fully facing her, he said, “Is this Money’s son?” He already knew the answer to his question, but he needed to hear her confirm it.

He could see a sense of pride and also shame wash over her face as she answered, “Yes.”

Mecca smiled at the sight of his nephew. “What happened, Lee?” he asked, calling her by a nickname that only he used. “How did everything get so fucked up?”

Leena steadied her aim as she answered, “I was in love with two brothers. Money and I never meant to hurt you, Mecca.”

“He was my brother. How could you fuck with him, Leena? How could he fuck with you? He knew how I felt about you,” Mecca whispered.

Leena’s eyes widened in disbelief. “How you felt about me, Mecca?” she shrieked. “I didn’t even think you were capable of feeling. You wanted Money to see a love that didn’t exist.”

“You can really stand there and say you didn’t love me?” Mecca stated angrily.

“You know I loved you, Mecca . . . but you were the one who never showed it back. Why would Money, or Breeze, or anyone else for that matter know that you loved me? I didn’t even know! All you did was ho me, Mecca. You fucked around with this bitch and that bitch, all the while wanting me to stay faithful to you." Utter confusion spread over her face and she stared at him as if everything was his fault.

"Those other bitches didn't mean shit to me, Leena! You knew that! I'm a Diamond."

Leena rolled her eyes at his arrogance and lowered the gun as she dropped it on the ground in disgust, unable to let him finish his sentence. "Yeah, I know you're a Diamond, Mecca. Me and everybody else in Miami knows! That still doesn't give you the right to behave the way you do. It didn't make how you used to treat me hurt any less." She shook her head back and forth. "You know what? I don't even know why we're standing here doing this," she said as she began to turn away. Mecca grabbed her arm to stop her from leaving.

"Leena, I didn't always know how to show it, but I did love you. You were the one I broke bread with. You were the only woman I trusted. You knew everything . . . what I did, where I slept, the combination to the safe. It may have been a fucked up way to love. Shit wasn't sweet or on no lovey-dovey type shit, but it was the only way I knew how to show it," Mecca revealed. "I've never been like Monroe."

"I never asked you to be." Leena stopped him. "But when things got really bad, I began to notice how gentle Monroe was, how patient and loyal he was, and I got caught up. I fell for him. I know that it was wrong, and I knew all along that it would hurt you, but as much as you had hurt me, I did not care. I just wanted to be happy."

"All the bitches in Miami, and Money had to choose mine," Mecca stated callously.

"I think you should know that Money loved you. He loved you so much that he was going to cut everything off with me. The night you caught us, he told me that he would never be with me," Leena admitted.

Hearing this caused Mecca's eyes to become misty as he tried to control his emotions. "I killed him, Lee," Mecca said aloud for the first time as he broke down. There was no reason to lie to her. She had been there. She was the only person in the world who truly knew every aspect of the truth. He hit the concrete wall with his fist.

"You did," Leena replied. Although her heart ached for him, she held back. He did not deserve her sympathy. She could not allow Mecca to pull her back into his chaotic world. Her life was centered, healthy, safe, and nothing but danger dwelled around him.

"I'm sorry, ma. I'm sorry for everything," he finally said, conceding to the guilt that had been torturing him from the very beginning. He did not know what the hell was happening to him, but he did know that the lifestyle he led was slowly becoming harder to maintain. Everything had been so much easier when he had his family behind him. When his father, brother, mother, and sister were alive, he had something to go to war over. He had things to kill for. But now that they all were gone, Mecca felt empty.

"I'm not the person who can forgive you, Mecca. You have filled your life with so much bad that you have no room left for the good," Leena whispered. "God is the only one who can take the burden away, the guilt. You need to talk to Him."

Mecca nodded his head and gripped the bridge of his nose as he nodded toward his nephew. "Can I hold him?" he asked.

Reluctantly, Leena handed her son to his uncle. The Diamond familial connection was so strong that the little boy instantly took to Mecca. Her eyes filled as she watched her son wrap his arms around Mecca's neck.

"What's good, li'l man?" Mecca greeted as he hugged Monroe Jr. Everything about the little boy reminded him of his late twin. "I owe you the world," he said as he kissed the little boy on the forehead and handed him over to Leena.

Memories of his childhood years with his brother flooded him. It was as if he were staring directly at the past when he looked at Leena's son.

As he began to walk away, one more question nagged at him. He stopped and said, "One more thing. How long have you been living with Estes?"

"Since the day that you shot me," she responded.

Tension filled the space between them as they both recalled that fateful day, and although Mecca had no right to ask, he had to get one more thing off of his chest.

"Are you fucking him?" His tone was not demanding or angry. It was just something he needed to know.

Leena wanted to tell Mecca that it was none of his business, that he was no longer entitled to know who she chose to become intimate with, but she did not. A part of her—the part that felt guilty for sleeping with Monroe, the part that felt guilty for having his brother's child, the part of her that hated the sad look in Mecca's eyes—this part of her allowed her to answer.

"No, Mecca. I'm not sleeping with Estes. He says that he loves me, but I don't know if I can give it back," Leena replied.

Relief washed over Mecca, and he said, "I want to see you again, and I want to get to know Money's son. I know I have no right to ask, but—"

"Estes will kill you, Mecca. He isn't making idle threats. If he even thinks you are around Money's son . . ." Leena objected. Estes was not her only concern; simply the only one that she voiced.

"I don't care. I have a lot to make up for, Leena. I don't owe Estes shit, but I owe Monroe everything. If you don't want me around, then I'll leave without looking back, but nobody else will stop me from getting to know my brother's son. I'm trying to make things right," he stated sincerely.

"This is all too much for me right now. I love my son, Mecca, and I'm not going to lie; I don't trust you. " Leena opened the back door to the bistro. "I'll think about it. Just give me a little bit of time."

Chapter Ten

"I'm not one of God's children, because I'm too much like the devil."
—Mecca

Carter embraced Garza and patted the old man on the back as they said their final good-byes. It was the inevitable day that they both had orchestrated, and now Carter was leaving with his freedom, while Garza would be left behind.

"Enjoy those cigarettes, old man," Carter joked as he pointed to the boxes that Garza had stacked up in the corner, courtesy of Carter.

"Visit the priest for me. Make sure you give him what he has coming to him, and please ensure that my name is the last one he hears," Garza replied in a low tone.

Carter nodded, letting Garza know that no further words needed to be spoken.

The tier of prisoners erupted in loud, boisterous cheers as Carter made his last walk down their halls. They were giving him praise for beating his case. Carter took it all in stride, never appearing arrogant, and simply making his exit.

Carter emerged from the prison gates with a luxury Lincoln town car awaiting him. Mecca emerged from the back of the car, and the usual tension that dwelled between the half-brothers was non-existent in this moment. Mecca was genuinely happy to see Carter free, because he knew that Carter was the only one who could reorganize The Cartel. Things would be business as usual under Carter's reign.

"Good to see you, boy," Mecca stated.

Carter slapped hands with Mecca and then embraced him tightly. "It's good to see you too, fam. Real good," Carter replied as he stepped inside of the car.

Carter gave the driver Miamor's address. Now that his freedom had been reestablished, hers was the only company he wanted to keep upon his first night home. Her absence from his life had been slowly driving him insane.

He had sent Zyir by her place a few times, only to be told that she never answered the door and was nowhere to be found. He wanted to find out for himself, because he knew Miamor well. It was not in her character to leave him on stuck when he needed her most.

With the Garza Cartel connection being secured by Zyir, he knew that all of the pieces of his life were about to realign. She was the only thing missing. The center of his puzzle was lost and he had to find it, because without her, everything would be for nothing.

Mecca rode silently as he looked out of the window. *The sooner this ol' lovesick nigga get over this bitch, the easier it's gon' be on him. Ain't no coming back from the place I sent her,* he thought. A part of him just wanted to tell Carter the truth, but he knew that it would only complicate things. So, he allowed Carter to go on the dummy mission of searching for a girl he would never find.

"I had Zyir looking for Miamor while I was locked up. He said you told him she had skipped town," Carter said as they pulled up to Miamor's high-rise building.

"That's what I heard. The bitch is bad news, bro. The way you were wife'n her before you went in, she should have been the one by your side through it all. She didn't stand tall, my nigga. Before the ink on the indictment papers dried, she got ghost on you. Fuck her, fam. It ain't worth the headache. You're out, and it's time to move forward."

Mecca's advice would have resounded loud and clear if had been any other woman besides Miamor, but she was like an infection of the heart. Letting go would not be so easy.

Knowing that Mecca was too callous to understand the connection he shared with Miamor, he changed the subject. "When Zyir arrives, it's back to business. Until then, I'm going to lay low and get my mind right. I have a couple of loose ends to clip before the shipment arrives," he said.

Mecca nodded. "Your car will be delivered tomorrow morning."

Carter exited the car and made his way up to Miamor's condo. Although he had a key to her place, he knocked politely, not wanting to intrude. When he didn't get an answer, he opened the door anyway and stepped inside. He immediately knew that she had not been there lately. The smell of rotting food permeated through the condo, and she had twenty new messages on her answering machine. As he moved through the apartment, his suspicions arose.

Where are you, ma? he asked as he inventoried her bedroom. Her closets and dressers were still filled with clothes. He knew that she didn't leave town, because she would never leave her possessions behind. As he collapsed onto her bed, his gut twisted in premonition. He had a feeling that her disappearance was not coincidental, and he was determined to find out exactly where she had gone.

But first, he had a message to deliver. Josiah Garza was about to reach out from behind the prison walls and seek vengeance for an unspeakable crime committed against him many years ago.

Leena's words haunted Mecca: *God is the only one who can take the burden away, the guilt. You need to talk to Him.*

He knew that she was right. He had never been a religious man, but the crimes that he had committed against his own family were torturing him. *If there really is a God, I need Him to take the pain away,* Mecca thought.

Although he had no regrets about killing Miamor, he did hate himself because he knew that by doing so, he had taken away someone who had meant the world to his brother. Carter was all he had left, and he feared that if the truth were ever revealed, he would have no one. For the first time in his life, Mecca felt remorse for things that he had done that hurt other people.

Even he had to admit that if he had not murdered Miamor's sister, then she would have never come after his family. He had lived his life recklessly, without regard for others. Any way he tried to spin the situation, everything, all of the chaos and misery, led back to him. He had been the spark of it all. Mecca was the root of all evil. Bullets had been the answer to all of his problems, and now all of the lives he had taken were coming back to haunt him. He could barely sleep at night because he was afraid to close his eyes. If he could make amends, he would, but there was no reversing the things he had done.

As he sat in front of the Catholic Church, he knew that there was only one thing left to do: give his burdens to God and hope that his soul was capable of being cleansed. He wasn't a Catholic, but knew that he could never confess his wrongdoings to a black minister. His business would travel through Miami's gossip grapevine for sure. So, he chose a place where he could be low key. Confessing to a white man in a white church, he was confident that the conversation would go no further than the four walls of the cathedral.

As he stepped out of the car, he felt his gun on his hip. As many people as he had murdered, it would be foolish to leave it behind. But he removed it from his waistline anyway and placed it beneath his car seat. Despite the fact that his conscience screamed for him to stay strapped, he did not want to carry the weapon inside of the church. He took a deep breath as he headed for the entrance, feeling as though his judgment day had arrived.

Carter walked side by side with the priest of St. Jude Catholic Church as he explained the concept of forgiveness and redemption. Carter had spent the past hour speaking with the old man at the request of Garza. Garza wanted to know if the priest displayed any remorse for the children he had betrayed in his past, and Carter followed his directions precisely. He was given specific instructions: "If the priest shows remorse, kill him quickly. If not, then a slow death will be better suited," Garza had said.

"Have you ever done something that you are not proud of, Father?" Carter asked as they sat down near the front of the church.

"Son, no man is without sin. There are things that I have done in my past that God will hold me accountable for," the priest replied as he became slightly emotional. "Some things that I have done I can never take back."

"Father, I'm here to hold you accountable for those actions," Carter stated in a low, serious tone. "Josiah Garza sent me."

The old white man's eyes widened in paralyzing fear as he allowed the emotion in his eyes to fall down his wrinkled cheeks. He knew exactly who Carter spoke of, and his mind flashed back to the acts of molestation he had committed against Garza when he was only a small boy. It was then that he realized that today would be his last day on this earth. The priest began to weep as he leaned forward, resting his head on Carter's shoulder.

Carter didn't speak as he closed his eyes. He removed his .38 pistol from the jacket of his Brooks Brothers suit and placed the barrel directly against the priest's chest. He allowed the old man to weep on his shoulder as he pulled the trigger, sending a bullet piercing through his heart.

"Forgive me, Father," Carter whispered.

Even the dull sound of the silenced bullet echoed slightly against the walls of the cathedral. Carter caught the old man's body as gravity took it to the floor, and he laid him down to rest behind one of the church pews. The old man's eyes stared up into space, and Carter closed them. It wasn't a task that Carter had wanted to do, but he had given his word. The old man had it coming to him for all of the abuse he had inflicted on the young boys of his parish over the years.

The clanking sound of the doors opening startled Carter.

"Fuck," he whispered, knowing that he could never make it to the back door without being seen. He made sure that the priest's body was out of sight, and then slid into the confessional. He hoped that the intruder would come and go quickly, without throwing a wrench in his program. He had planned to execute the priest quietly, without interruption. Carter did not want to have to hurt an innocent bystander for being in the wrong place at the wrong time. The tension in his body was so high that he could hear his own heartbeat.

The other side of the confessional opened and Carter prepared himself to take another life. He saw the shadow of a man sit across from him on the other side of the lattice. Carter pointed the gun to the center of the shadow's face, but the voice that he heard come from the other side stopped him from shooting. He froze as he listened to a confession that he was never meant to hear.

"Forgive me, Father, for I have sinned," Mecca stated. "I don't know how this usually works, but I'm just gonna speak my piece. I feel like this is the only place where I can admit the truth without being judged. I know I'm not a good man. I've known it all along . . . ever since I was a kid. There was always something evil living inside of me, but I kept it dormant for a long time, until the day I killed my twin brother. I have a lot of blood on my hands, Father, but the blood of my brother I can't seem to wash away. It's like I see it on my hands all day." Mecca lowered his head into his hands. Even admitting his sins behind the protection of anonymity was hard.

"I murdered my brother out of rage, out of jealousy, and then I lied to my entire family to cover my tracks. It feels like I've been lying ever since. I murdered my older brother's girlfriend, and I look him in the face every day, watching the hurt in his eyes. I pretend like I don't know why it's there, when in actuality I caused it. When he asks about her, I plant seeds in his head to make him think she left town, when I know I left her in a basement in pieces.

"The sick part about it is that I enjoyed it. I know only God has the power to judge, but I was that bitch's judge, jury, and executioner. She took too much away from me to let her live.

"My father would be ashamed of me. He put family above all else, and all of his sons were built just like him—except for me. Money was a good nigga, Father." Mecca choked up and stopped speaking momentarily to get himself together. "He was my other half.

"My older brother is so much like our pops that it scares me. I know I'm not one of God's children, because I'm too much like the devil, but I'm tired, Father. I just want the demons in me to die. I want to be like my father—good."

***

Carter sat on the other side of the booth with his finger wrapped tightly around the trigger of his pistol. Disbelief clouded his brain as he pictured Miamor's face in his head. He pointed the gun directly at Mecca's face. All he had to do was let off one shot to make things right. With one bullet, the deaths of Miamor and Monroe could be avenged, but the fact that Mecca was his brother made him hesitate. They both came from the same bloodline. They were the last of a dying breed. Carter wasn't sure if he would be able to live with his decision if he chose to kill Mecca.

Carter put his hands to his face as he felt the hot tears threaten to fall. He was in utter turmoil just at the thought of Miamor's death. She had been his life, his everything, the woman that he had wanted to marry. He had planned to spend an eternity with her, and in the blink of an eye, she had been taken away. Mecca had robbed him of his only chance in life to be truly happy. Miamor was his happiness.

Carter already knew of the basement that Mecca spoke of. It was The Cartel's torture chamber, and he knew that Mecca had made her suffer a horrible death. He could hear Mecca crying as he poured out his sins, and Carter closed his eyes, allowing his own silent tears to fall. Both brothers sat on different sides of the booth in turmoil.

The nigga deserve to die. All of this, this entire war started because of the lies he told. Everybody would still be alive if it wasn't for Mecca. We broke the truce with the Haitians because we thought they were responsible for Money. All along it's been him, Carter thought. His rage was so prevalent that it burned his insides, making him feel as though he would explode at any moment. Hearing Mecca's confession and finally finding out the truth caused his stomach to turn violently. He was sick with grief. He had loved Mecca and trusted him.

How could he kill Money? He was our brother, Carter thought. *How did I miss what was right in front of my face for so long? Mecca murdered Miamor.*

Carter couldn't grasp the fact that two people he had cared dearly for had been ripped from underneath him. It was unfathomable, and even though he had heard the words come directly from Mecca's mouth, he still did not want to believe them. Carter remembered all of the lies that Mecca had told to cover his tracks as he watched Mecca rise and begin to walk away. It was up to him to end Mecca's reign of terror, but he could not do it. Sitting underneath's God's watchful eye, all he could do was mourn the deaths of those he had lost at the hands of his only remaining sibling.

When Mecca exited the church, Carter stood to his feet and stumbled out of the confession booth. He stepped over the priest's dead body and down the long aisle of the church. He palmed his gun tightly in his hand; the security of having it locked and loaded reassured him. He had no idea what his next move would be, but there was one thing that he was sure of: his brother, Mecca, could not be trusted.

The nigga has destroyed everything around him. It'll only be a matter of time before he comes for me.

"What's the matter, Zyir? You're not used to riding in things this big?" Illiana asked as she lit a cigarette and blew the smoke into the air. "You're going fifty-five miles per hour. The limit is seventy."

Zyir sighed as he reached over and pulled the cigarette from between her lips. She had been talking nonstop since they left Mexico, and he was more than tired of hearing her talk slick out of the side of her neck.

"Hey!" she objected as she turned in her seat and looked at Zyir in irritation.

"I said no cigarettes," Zyir replied as he kept his eyes fixed on the road in front of him. Driving from Mexico back to Miami was a four-day trip, and he was sure to go crazy with Illiana riding shotgun.

Illiana rolled her eyes and crossed her hands over her chest. She pointed at the highway sign and said, "Pull over at the next stop."

"What the fuck for?" Zyir asked. "I can't keep stopping every hour. We'll never make it back at this rate."

"I have to piss, so unless you want me to soak these fucking seats, pull over at the next stop," Illiana replied bossily.

Zyir glared over at her. He had to bite his tongue to stop himself from barking on her. It was obvious that she was used to men catering to her every whim. *This bitch is going to drive me crazy,* Zyir thought as he pulled over at the next rest stop. "Hurry up," he instructed.

Illiana purposefully took her time as she watched Zyir through the window of the truck stop. She enjoyed giving him a hard time. It was foreplay for her. Since the moment she had seen him, he held her attention. He was focused, powerful, and had a dominant personality that piqued her interest. It was she who had convinced Felipe to send her to Miami. It would be the perfect opportunity for her to get to know Zyir. She was a woman who did not understand the word *no*, and when she saw something she wanted, she went after it relentlessly. Zyir was in her line of sight and he did not even know it.

As she finally emerged from the rest stop, she noticed Zyir standing outside of the truck, waiting impatiently and looking around cautiously.

"Relax. Nobody's watching, Zyir. You American boys are so paranoid. You watch too many gangster movies. My brother has moved shipments like this for years and nothing has ever gone wrong," she stated as she stood directly in front of him. She was standing so closely that she could feel the imprint of his penis rubbing against her. The thin linen fabric of her sundress blew in the wind, and she made no effort to move.

Zyir smirked at her blatant attempts at flirtation. "Get in the car. We're not stopping again," Zyir stated in a firm tone as he pushed her gently away from him and hopped back into the truck.

Zyir got back onto the Interstate as Illiana reached for the radio to turn it up. Zyir immediately switched it back off.

"What, the radio isn't allowed either?" Illiana asked. "I'm supposed to ride for days without any entertainment?"

"I can't hear the sirens if the radio is blasting," Zyir answered simply. "Read one of your magazines or something."

"I guess I'll have to entertain myself then," she replied with a mischievous smile as she opened her legs and slipped her fingers up her dress. She played with her clit as one of her straps fell off her shoulder. Zyir peered over and almost slid off the road as he swerved in surprise.

"What are you doing?" he asked as he cleared his throat uncomfortably and regained control of the wheel.

"You told me to read or something. This is something," she whispered. The look in her eyes radiated lust as she put on a one-woman show for Zyir.

He couldn't help but to look over at the lovely sight as she closed her eyes and worked her fingers in and out of her wetness. He could see her juices flowing onto the seat.

"You can touch it, Zyir. I know you want to." Everything about Illiana was inviting; even her words teased his ears as he struggled to keep his attention focused on the road. His manhood hardened at the visual Illiana was providing him with.

Illiana was a seductress, and she laughed slightly because she knew that Zyir was trying to resist the inevitable. She crawled across the front seat of the cabin and climbed into Zyir's lap, straddling him.

"Yo, fuck is you doing, ma?" Zyir asked, his voice low with indecision as he continued to drive. "You gon' make me crash this big mu'fucka."

Illiana reached down and massaged his hard-on through his cargo shorts before removing it from its confinements. "Hmm," she moaned as she kissed his neck.

The scent of her invaded his nostrils as he gave in to the temptation. She was too beautiful to resist, too enticing to turn away, and although he knew that mixing business with pleasure was for the foolish, Illiana was too hard to turn away. Just like all of the other men she had encountered, he could not tell her no.

"Let me pull over," Zyir whispered as his breath caught in his throat when she slid down on his shaft. She was so tight that it felt as if his dick was in a glove specifically sized for him. "Damn, ma."

"No, keep driving. Don't stop," Illiana moaned as she worked her hips in circles, enjoying how he filled her up perfectly, taking up all the space in her pussy. The girth of him took her breath away as she rode him slowly.

The ecstasy was so great that Zyir could not stop his eyes from closing. He was high off of the feeling that Illiana was giving him, and the harder she rode down on him, the faster he pushed the large Mack truck. The mixture of speed and sex tickled his loins as his adrenaline rushed him. He removed one hand from the steering wheel to grip her voluptuous behind.

"Ooh, Zy, cum with me, papi," she urged as she felt the intensity building between her thighs. The sound of her voice in his ear as she rode him only heightened his lust for her. Zyir was ready to pull over and beat it up.

"Ride it faster, ma," he coached.

Illiana began to work her vaginal muscles, tensing them around his thickness until Zyir could no longer take it. He lifted her off of him with one hand just as he exploded. He closed his eyes, and his mouth fell open as he rode the powerful wave of the orgasm.

"Zyir!" Illiana yelled as the truck veered into the next lane. She grabbed the steering wheel, laughing hysterically, until Zyir regained his composure.

"Is it too much to ask for you to pull over again at the next stop so I can clean up?" she asked.

Zyir nodded and gave her a rare smile, turning his usual serious face into the most handsome one she had ever seen.

"Yeah, ma. Whatever you want. I got you," he replied.

Carter stood outside of the house where Mecca had murdered Miamor. It wasn't hard to find. The Cartel had used the dilapidated structure many times before. Things didn't make sense to him. He did not understand why Mecca had taken such extreme measures.

What did she do to deserve this? he thought as he stepped foot inside. The stench of death invaded his nose instantly. It was almost too much for him to stomach.

Making his way down the basement steps, he saw the remnants of Miamor's murder. The floor was painted with stains of her blood, and the entire room only gave him unwanted images of her death. He stood in the middle of the room as he absorbed it all. He could feel Miamor's ghost lingering over him. It pained him, because he would never even get to lay her to rest properly.

"I'm sorry," he whispered aloud as he turned to leave. As he looked back one last time, he noticed something on the floor. A necklace, one identical to the one that he wore, lay near the wooden chair. He walked over to it and picked up. His hands instinctively went to his own neck to touch the small cross that hung from it. It had been a gift from their father, and because they were the only two left, he knew that it was Mecca's.

The walls of the basement began to close in on him as his grief threatened to swallow him whole. Not only had he lost his woman, but his brother as well. No matter how he chose to resolve the situation, things would never be the same. With a new connect, things were supposed to be looking up, but deceit was threatening to tear The Cartel apart from the inside out.

His cell phone rang just as he made his exit. He answered it immediately, already knowing that it was Zyir.

"Zy, I got to talk to you about Mecca."

"I just got off the phone with him. We about to get this money, fam. Mecca's on his way to the warehouse. Meet me there."

"I'm on my way, but do me a favor, Zyir. Don't trust Mecca. Be careful around him. I'll explain later," Carter replied in a tone of warning.

"No explanation needed. It wasn't a day that I didn't move carefully around him anyway, fam. A nigga with a body count like that you gotta watch, nah mean?"

Carter walked into the warehouse to the most beautiful sight he had ever seen. Three thousand kilos of cocaine sat lined neatly side by side, one on top of the other, composing a wall of riches before him. The math was easy to do. Flipping that many birds meant that they were about to be stupid rich.

"Yeah, boy, you can crack a smile. No need to be the boss at all times," Zyir joked as he slapped hands with Carter and embraced him briefly. He missed Mecca with the introductions. He had no desire to show his brother love when all he was feeling in his heart was hate.

"We're back. I can put this work out a.s.a.p. Let niggas know the drought is over," Mecca stated.

Carter stared at Mecca for a long time and found it hard to conceal his rage. Fire burned in his eyes, and even the stature of his presence was stiff, cold, as if Mecca were the enemy.

"What's good, Carter? You a'ight?" Mecca asked. He had no idea that his secret was out, but as he looked in his older sibling's eyes, he felt that the times of treachery were headed his way.

"Everything's good. Just thinking about how niggas might want to steer clear of stepping on my toes. I made the mistake of trusting Ace too much. It's always the closest niggas to you that do the most harm," Carter replied while never averting Mecca's gaze.

"Nah, baby, you don't put in work. You just sit back and drive this ship. Take us to the money like only you can do. Me and Zy can handle the beef. All snake-ass niggas have been taken care of," Mecca replied.

"It's always one left hiding in the grass," Carter responded.

The tension in the room was high and put Mecca slightly on edge. He felt as if he were staring into the eyes of his father. It felt like Carter was looking straight through him, and the only other man who had ever been able to make him feel so transparent was their father.

Zyir was silent because he knew Carter well. He was speaking in codes, and Mecca didn't even have a clue that the beef Carter had was with him.

Larcenous-ass nigga, Carter thought.

Zyir pulled two keys from his pocket and handed one to both men. "I had the locks changed. Only the three of us have access to this building, so each and every bird should always be accounted for," Zyir stated. "Felipe sent his sister Illiana back to Miami with me. She's here to protect their investment . . . a set of eyes for the Garza Cartel."

"Where is she now?" Carter asked.

"I took her to my crib. I didn't know if you wanted her to know the location of the warehouse. Three thousand joints are too many to take any risks," Zyir stated.

"You can show her, and only her, where we keep 'em," Carter stated. "She doesn't need a key, however. If the Mexicans want her here to make sure everything is moving right, then we have nothing to hide from them. It'll show good faith."

Carter began to walk away, and Zyir stated, "I know we gon' celebrate tonight. This is a power move we're making."

Carter turned around and shook his head as he looked at Mecca. Disappointment, anger, sadness . . . it all consumed him simultaneously. Without responding, Carter made his exit. He had thought when he emerged from prison that all of his problems would be behind him, but now the dilemmas in his life seemed even more prevalent than before.

"Fuck is up with him?" Mecca stated.

Zyir feigned ignorance and replied, "I don't know, but I'd hate to be a problem of his. Just because he don't talk about it, don't mean he ain't about it, nah mean? Carter ain't about playing gangster. He don't got to be all extra in order to get his point across. That macho shit is for dumb niggas, and dumb mu'fuckas are the easiest to clip."

Zyir sat in the apartment like a seasoned chemist as he took it back to his humble roots, cooking dope with ten naked women around him. The titties and ass that were on display were of no interest to him. It only ensured that nobody got sticky fingers. Theft was impossible when you wore no clothes to stash the product. The Cartel took to the streets like never before, and in addition to selling the bricks wholesale, they had chosen to break down three hundred of them.

Zyir was a perfectionist when it came to stretching cocaine, and he was more than willing to put in the work to turn three hundred into six hundred, with the help of the lovely ladies around him. While Mecca thought he was above serving fiends, Zyir wasn't for turning away a single dollar. He loved money, and while Mecca had the wholesale market covered, Zyir was taking over the streets. He kept it hood and set up his operation on every inner city block in Dade County.

He wasn't about the gunplay, because he did not need any unnecessary attention from the boys in blue, so instead of forcing his competition out, he played fair and simply offered them an opportunity to work for him. His affiliation with The Cartel put stars in niggas' eyes and they instantly jumped at the chance just to be down by association. Zyir had so many hustlers working for him that he never personally saw the blocks. He simply organized the operation, supplied the dope, and sat back as the money piled in. Nobody caused conflicts because everybody was eating.

Miami had never seen a movement like The Cartel's. It was calculated carefully and executed with efficiency. It was all about the money, and the more they accumulated, the more the streets began to forget the troubles that had plagued them surrounding the law.

The Cartel was back and better than ever. They had learned from their mistakes, and this time what they were building was untouchable. The only thing that could tear down their empire was self-destruction.

Chapter Eleven

"Young Zyir is simply a protégé of yours. You both are men of little patience, always eager to get to the dinero."
—Felipe

Carter pulled up to Felipe's estate. He had moved through the bricks and it was re-up time. Carter made hustling look easy. Most men wouldn't know how to handle one brick, and within a month, he had burned through three thousand. Now he was back in Mexico to pay the piper.

He was eager to meet his connect face to face for the first time. He no longer needed Zyir to play middleman. Now that he was free, he could handle his own affairs.

He was unimpressed by the opulence around him as he entered Felipe Garza's estate. If anything, the flashiness of the place turned him off. It was obvious that Felipe was living the lavish life, and Carter only hoped that his new connect was smart enough to ensure his longevity. If Felipe's spotlight was too bright, then others would surely be watching. The estate was beautiful, but it was excessive and massive, too much for any one man.

Carter hoped that linking up with this new connect did not prove to be a costly mistake. He took a deep breath to calm himself before he exited the car. His recent stay in prison had caused him to be increasingly aware of every move he made. He viewed the streets as a chess game, and he wanted nothing more than to win.

"Carter Jones, my brother Josiah Garza speaks highly of you. It is good to finally meet with you," Felipe greeted, extending his hand as the two men shook.

"Likewise. I know this visit is unexpected. We were not scheduled to meet for another three months, but I like to move quickly . . . efficiently," Carter stated.

"I understand. I was under the impression that we would meet once you were done with the entire package. It does me no good to receive my money in pieces. I'd like the entire forty million back at one time," Felipe replied.

Before he responded, he walked over to the limo and knocked on the window. The driver emerged and popped the trunk where duffel bag after duffel bag filled the interior.

"Like I said, I move quickly. That's the entire forty with an extra five for you as repayment for the work you put in concerning my case," Carter stated. "You can have your men unload it. The first deal proved to be very lucrative. Let us waste no time in doing it again."

Although it was Carter who was the guest, he took charge as if he were on home turf. He held out his arm and motioned for Felipe to walk with him. He could see the displeasure in Felipe's eyes. The Mexican drug lord was used to other men following his lead, but it was clear that Carter Jones had no intentions of playing the back. He was a boss, and conducted himself as such.

Felipe had taken a keen interest in Zyir. He had liked the young fellow because he had displayed the proper etiquette in dealing with someone superior to him. Carter, however, had put a different taste in his mouth. In his presence, Felipe felt inadequate, and it was then that he realized that all of the things he had heard about The Cartel was true. He was staring into the eyes of their leader, a man even greater than himself. Carter had experienced a minor setback when he had fallen under a federal microscope, but now that things were back on track, he had the potential to overthrow any empire. Felipe knew that this was not the intention of Carter, but his demeanor indicated that it was always a possibility. Felipe would have to be careful with how much power he helped The Cartel re-attain.

"Now I see that young Zyir is simply a protégé of yours. You both are men of little patience, always eager to get to the dinero," Felipe stated. "Let us get to know each other as men first, and then we will discuss our arrangement. I own a few brothels and gentlemen's establishments that I'm sure you will enjoy."

Carter nodded and obliged with a discreet smirk because he knew that Felipe was trying to feel him out. He had sent Zyir to Mexico with specific instructions to go with the flow, because he did not know what he was getting his li'l man into. He, on the other hand, was there to establish boundaries and to ensure that both parties understood each other clearly. He wasn't there to party and bullshit, but this would give him a perfect opportunity to turn the tables and learn more about the Garza Cartel's operation.

Murder discreetly picked the lock to Miamor's old condo, the same place where Carter had recently taken residence, and slipped inside. The place still held Miamor's scent, and Carter had removed none of her old belongings, which made memories of his li'l mama come rushing back to Murder. It was as if she still lived there and could walk through the door at any moment.

Being so close to The Cartel was eating him alive. He was in the same city and had barely made a move on them yet. He didn't want to make the same mistakes that had cost Miamor her life. He wanted to study them from afar first, before moving in. Without a doubt, he knew that Mecca had been the one to end Miamor's life, but that did not relieve the blame from Carter's shoulders so easily. He wanted revenge on them all. Carter was the leader, and above all else, he had chosen to wife Miamor. He should have ensured her protection.

What type of nigga lets his chick be murdered in cold blood? Murder thought.

Murder would have never let anything happen to Miamor. She had been the only woman he had ever loved. He remembered how infectious her personality was, how easy it was to become consumed in her beauty, how he would have done anything for her. He concluded that any man who truly loved Miamor could have never let this happen.

Miamor was the type of woman that you kept shielded from the world because she could not be replaced. She had been a rare find, an unspoiled soul with a ruthless talent for killing. There was not another soul like hers in existence, and now that she was gone, Murder saw nothing but black. There was no white in his world, no silver lining around his dark cloud. She had been the best part of him, and even from afar and through the isolation of the prison walls, he had loved her. She wasn't simply the type of chick who would blow through your money and whisper sweet nothings in your ear. She was the type to blow a hole through a nigga and hit his safe right next to her man if need be. She was loyal.

Before Murder had ever gotten a chance to truly build a life with her, Carter had come along, snatching her heart from underneath him.

Murder moved quickly through the condominium. He wasn't exactly sure what he was looking for. He simply needed to know more, and with Carter out of town on business, this was the perfect opportunity for him to search for answers. He came across a photo of Miamor and Carter. The happy snapshot featured the couple vacationing on a beach. Jealousy burned through him as he placed the picture face down on the mantle.

Just as he was about to make his exit, he noticed a book that stuck out slightly from the collection on the bookshelf. He walked over to it and pulled it gently. As he suspected, a trap door opened, and Murder slipped inside. It looked like an army's arsenal closet. For a man of Murder's profession, it was like being a kid in a candy store as he admired all of the flawless guns. He knew the room had not been meant for anyone's eyes but Miamor's. It was where she kept all of the details of the jobs she accepted, and tacked to the wall was a huge picture of Mecca Diamond with a red circle around it.

As he stared at the extensive research that Miamor had done on the Diamond family, he was amazed. She had been so detailed, so precise. She had indeed become the best at what she did. Even Murder did not realize what she was capable of. She even had monitors that showed the inside of her own home, so that when she was inside of the room, she would know exactly who was inside her place and what room they were located in.

He froze when he heard the lock to the front door turn. Luckily, Murder had made his way through the condo in the dark, and his identity was hidden behind the ski mask he wore. He turned off his flashlight and pulled the trap door closed as he watched the monitor to see who was coming inside. His temple throbbed when he saw Mecca Diamond enter.

Mecca had noticed that Carter had been throwing him shade lately, and he had a feeling that it had something to do with Miamor. He wanted to know how much Carter actually knew. It would give him a better idea of how to play the situation. He left the lights off as he moved through the place.

As Murder watched Mecca disappear through the monitors, he crept out quietly, .45 in his hand. Killing Mecca would be sweet for him, and as he stood in the middle of the living room, he contemplated his options. The Murder Mamas had advised him to play his cards right. If he hit Mecca tonight, it would throw a red flag to the rest of the members of The Cartel. There would be a contract out for Mecca's murderer almost immediately, and with everybody on edge, it would make it even harder for Murder to get to Carter.

He silently headed for the door and was about to leave when an overwhelming hatred for Mecca overcame him. His murder game clicked on, and he turned on his heel and headed toward the bedroom.

Fuck hitting these niggas all at once. Another opportunity like this ain't gonna present itself, Murder thought as he preyed on Mecca, letting his gun lead the way down the pitch black hallway.

Mecca used the tiny flashlight as his only illumination as he went through Carter's possessions. When he found the small 14 karat gold cross that his father had given him, he froze. He hadn't seen it since the day he killed Miamor. He had beaten her so mercilessly that it had fallen from his neck. The fact that Carter now had it meant that Carter had been to Mecca's torture house. He had seen the tools that had been used to torture Miamor.

He knows, Mecca thought. He had hoped that it would not have to come to this. He had witnessed firsthand how much Carter cared for Miamor, and this would surely put them at odds.

He just couldn't let the bitch go. That's why he's been looking at me sideways. Fuck! Mecca thought. He knew what had to be done, but was no longer sure if he could do it. He did not want to murder another brother. He was trying to become a better man, and it was no longer in him to take the life of someone he loved.

As Mecca thought over his dilemma, an eerie feeling suddenly came over him. He was a breed of mankind that had not been reproduced yet, and he instantly knew that someone was behind him. He could almost smell the gunpowder from the weapon that was pointed at the back of his head.

Mecca bucked back violently. "Aghh!" He screamed as he pushed back with all his might, throwing Murder off balance as Mecca rammed him into the wall.

A fight between the two men was useless. They were both too skilled to get the best of the other. Every blow Mecca threw, Murder blocked, and each time Murder wrapped his finger around the trigger, Mecca averted his aim. Their battle was like a synchronized dance as they attacked each other with full force, each becoming increasingly frustrated because neither could gain the upper hand.

"Who the fuck sent you?" Mecca barked. He was not sure who was gunning for him now. It could easily be Estes, but with this new revelation, it could be Carter as well.

Murder finally managed to get his finger around the trigger, and he fired relentlessly as he wrestled with Mecca for control of the gun. Sparks erupted from the barrel of the gun like a fireworks display on the Fourth of July.

Murder's skinny build failed him in a fistfight. He would shoot the shit out of a nigga before he ever sparred with him, but Mecca, on the other hand, was good with his hands. Mecca's well-built, solid frame allowed him to finally overpower Murder, causing the gun to go flying across the room.

Murder knew that Mecca was strapped, and went for the only exit in the room, the bedroom balcony. He ran full force, breaking through the glass, and disappeared before Mecca could get off a shot. Mecca was far from a rookie, however. It was the same exact escape that he had used to get away from Estes' goons, and his hollow point bullets could swim. He knew to aim straight for the pool below.

He reached out and rushed to lean over the balcony, only to find the pool undisturbed below.

"Fucking nigga ain't Superman. Where the fuck did he—" Mecca stated in confusion, but before he could even finish his sentence, Murder's gun emerged from the balcony below. Without hesitation, he fired, hitting Mecca in the face.

Murder was grateful that he always carried a weapon on his ankle as he ran through the empty condo and out the front door, where he skirted off into the night.

The music in the club blared loudly as Carter sat back in the booth while a beautiful Mexican girl danced in front of him. His eyes graced the delicate curves of her body as she put on the best performance he had ever seen. Seeing her before him made him feel empty inside. Outwardly, no one would be able to tell that he was in turmoil, but in the privacy of his heart, he was broken from losing Miamor.

I should have been there for her. I could have stopped Mecca if she had just come to me. How did I not know what was going on right underneath my nose? A part of Carter felt like he did not even know Miamor. She had lived a lifestyle so closely linked to his that it was scary. His logic told him that he had been a target of hers along with the rest of The Cartel, but he could never bring himself to believe that she would ever bring him harm. The love that they had built was too deep, and although so many things she had told him had been lies, he knew that her feelings for him had been truth. He was in a daze as he thought of her, placing her face on the dancer in front of him.

"They don't make tits like these in Miami, eh?" Felipe asked, interrupting Carter's thoughts. "This is pure bred Mexicana pussy," he bragged as he tipped generously and sipped at his glass of cognac.

Carter chuckled as he raised his glass to acknowledge the beauty that surrounded him in the club.

"This is the business that you need to get into. The drug money is good, but this is where it's at," Felipe stated surely.

"Prostitution?" Carter said doubtfully.

Felipe shook his head and smiled coyly while pointing at Carter. "No, my friend. That's where you're wrong." He pointed to the girls around the club. "This right here, this is just one entity. Trafficking, that's what I'm into. I buy and sell girls. I put them to work in clubs, brothels, on the street. Sex is man's biggest addiction, Carter. I supply that demand, and it makes me filthy rich. Let me show you something."

Carter stood and followed Felipe through the club as he explained his operation. "This club is one of many of my establishments. I own every property on this street, and each one serves its purpose." Felipe led Carter out the front door and then pointed to the house next door. "That house right there is the brothel, and the one next to it is an auction house."

"An auction house, as in slave auctions," Carter stated condescendingly.

"Modern day slavery, if that is what you would like to call it. Human trafficking is big business. It is happening all over the world. I buy my girls from all over and I put them to work. Pump 'em up on heroin and they'll do anything I say."

"How do you keep them from running away?" Carter asked as they stepped into the brothel house.

"Where are they going to go? They have no one, no family. They come from many different places. Some from Africa, some from Asia, the Caribbean . . . you name it. All they have is me and the addiction that holds them hostage," Felipe replied.

The house was littered with drug paraphernalia. Dirty needles lay out on tables, and the smell of sex filled the air. Carter was almost too disgusted to continue the tour. He could only imagine the type of clientele that frequented the spot. Brothel was just a friendly name for a whorehouse, in his opinion, and he knew that this would never be a type of venture he would be interested in taking. He didn't believe in exploitation, and as Carter looked around the house he knew that the women trapped there were simply waiting to die.

"The money never touches the girls' hands. The men pay the madame on the way in," Felipe stated.

He expected Carter to be impressed, but his creased brow revealed his contempt. His moral compass allowed him to do many things. He had killed, robbed, and deceived, but to kill a person's soul and force them into prostitution was beyond Carter's ability. His moral compass would not allow him to ever become that lost.

"I know what you're thinking. You think I'm running a trashy establishment here," Felipe stated. "I only buy the best girls. Let me show you the grade-A pussy I'm selling here."

He led Carter up the stairs to one of the closed bedroom doors. Before Felipe opened it, he said, "All you need is a few like this one in here, and men will come from everywhere to sample her. She is my big moneymaker."

He opened the door, and when Carter stepped in, his heart broke in half. The sight before him almost brought him to his knees. It was as if he were seeing a ghost.

She's supposed to be dead. How long has she been here?

As the girl lifted her head, her eyes met Carter's. It had been a long time since they had seen one another. It was a reunion that neither of them ever thought would come. Before him was Breeze Diamond, on her knees in front of a john. She was so high out of her mind that she did not believe what was appearing before her very eyes. She had imagined her family too many times to get her hopes up. She was so high that she thought Carter was simply another customer waiting to be serviced. She shed a single tear as she lowered her head back into the man's crotch and went back to work.

Zyir sat back on his plush king-sized bed as he and Illiana counted the money he had just collected from the streets. The first flip had been good, and everybody was eating again. In fact, the streets had never seen a cocaine epidemic like the one that The Cartel was pushing. It was a new day, and although internal tensions were at an all-time high, everybody was putting their differences aside, because they all saw the bigger picture.

It was time to move on and let past beefs die. The Cartel was in a stage of rebuilding, and money was always the common denominator that put everyone on the same page.

"How much is that?" he asked as he threw a large stack at Illiana, causing her to drop the blunt that was hanging loosely from her lips. It fell onto the exposed skin of her thigh.

"Damn it, Zy!" she screamed as she frantically hopped up, wearing nothing but lace panties and one of his button-up shirts. "You burnt the shit out of me," she whined.

"You'll be a'ight. Finish counting that," Zyir instructed. He continued the count in his head as he began to flip through a new stack of money. He was a mathematician when it came to his paper. The sound of the bills flipping through the money machine was like a classic melody to him, but even he questioned its accuracy. After the machine counted it, he counted it—every dollar, one by one, until he was content with the amount.

He would usually do the task alone, but he knew that Illiana posed no threat. She wasn't your average woman. She did not need to steal, because she had her own, and her bank account was filled with endless zeroes. It was for this reason alone that he allowed her to be present.

After many lonely nights, Illiana's presence in Miami had become surprisingly welcomed. She was a distraction, someone he felt comfortable enough around because she understood his world. At first Zyir was hesitant to keep her too close, but after many lonely nights, the feelings of isolation and the ghosts that haunted his mind became too much. He needed companionship, and the time he spent with Illiana became convenient for Zyir.

Her warm body filled the empty space in his bed most nights, but unfortunately for Illiana, his heart remained ice cold. That was a void that only one woman could fill, and he had closed it off to the rest of the world the day that Breeze had been kidnapped. The day that she disappeared was the same day that Zyir gave up on love. Hustling was all that mattered, getting money his only concern. Even a woman as strikingly beautiful as Illiana could not soften his reserve. She had managed to squeeze into his bed, but he would never allow another woman to enter his life in the magnitude that Breeze Diamond had. Meeting her had changed the man that he was, and losing her had killed his spirit.

No, I can't afford to feel like that again. Loving a woman hurts too bad, he thought as he watched Illiana carefully.

"Why are you looking at me like that, papi?" Illiana asked, snapping Zyir out of his daze. "You see something you like?" Her flirtatious nature surfaced as she threw the money from her hands up into the air.

"What you doing, ma? You're fucking up the count," he objected with dismay.

Illiana shrugged her shoulders as she began to unbutton the shirt she was wearing, revealing her perky breasts and quarter-sized nipples.

"You're just going to count it again anyway," she said as she brought her face close to his and kissed his lips. Zyir turned his head, allowing her kisses to fall on his neck. Having a woman's lips on his own was too intimate for him. You kiss those that you love, and there was nothing but lust between them.

He flipped her over so that he was on top, and tapped her ass slightly. She already knew that he wanted to hit her from the back. He liked to see her derrière jiggle as he slid in and out of her.

Illiana was willing to give Zyir anything he desired. She was desperate to become his and to be affiliated with everything concerning him. She had never dealt with a man like him before. Everything about him attracted her, and she was pulling out all the stops in order to appeal to him. She wanted to be down, and the fact that he was a business associate of her brother's was even better. It meant that he was powerful because the Garza Cartel only dealt with the elite.

As he slid into her, she grimaced from his size, but with each stroke he put down on her, the pain slowly gave way to pleasure. She threw her pussy on him as if her life depended on it. There was no slow lovemaking going on. Zyir was beating it up. Illiana moaned loudly, unable to contain herself. He reached around her body and fingered her clit simultaneously, making her call out to him in Spanish. It didn't take her long to cum. Zyir was well versed in the female persuasion, and brought her to an orgasm better than any man before him ever could.

Money stuck to her sweat-covered body as she breathed in heavily from their intense escapade. She collapsed on the bed, exhausted as she watched Zyir stand before her.

"Come lay with me," she said as she rubbed the empty spot next to her. She saw the look in his eyes and knew that he was about to tell her no. She knew she had to turn up her game in order to get her way. He was constantly pulling away from her. Sex was her only weapon, the only thing that kept him near. "I'm not done with you yet," she said as she reached up and grabbed his penis. It came back alive instantly from her touch, and she smiled as she crawled to the edge of the bed and took him into her mouth. She was an expert at keeping a man interested in the bedroom. All she had to do was figure out how to keep Zyir focused on her once the sun came up. She wanted him for herself, and was willing to go to any extreme to ensure that he belonged to her.

Chapter Twelve

"I've killed niggas for less than what you've done."* *—Carter

The Cartel had buried Breeze's memory so long ago that Carter did not believe his eyes. *This can't be her,* he thought as he rushed over to the bed and pulled the girl off of her knees.

"Hey! Wait your turn," the john protested. Carter pulled his gun and trained his aim on the man, who bitched up quickly, raising his hands in defense. He scrambled to get his clothing before scurrying out of the room.

"Breeze?" Carter called out. Breeze heard her name being called, but her high had her in a nod too deep to come out of.

"Carter, what is this? This is my place of business, señor. You can't just . . ."

The girl before him was a mere shell of the vibrant young woman he had come to know. His mind told him that this girl couldn't be Breeze. They had left her for dead so long ago and he was skeptical, but the resemblance was too similar to miss. When he saw the small gold cross hanging from her neck, her identity was confirmed. Through all of the storms that life had thrown her way, the necklace was still there. It had been the only piece of home she had left.

Carter turned his attention on Felipe as he rushed him with his gun drawn. He wrapped his hand around Felipe's throat as he put his gun directly to his forehead, forcing him against the wall of the bedroom. "Where'd you get her?" he barked as spit flew from his mouth.

Felipe could see that Carter was irrational. "I can see that you're upset over this girl—"

"She's my sister!" Carter shouted as he pulled back the hammer on his gun. "Where did you get her?" It would be his last time asking.

Carter knew that his actions were irrational and stupid, but he was acting out of emotion alone, disregarding the voice in the back of his mind telling him to calm down.

"Carter, this is not going to end well for you. I understand your reaction, and I can assure you that I had no idea of her affiliation to your family. Now that I know, something can be worked out," Felipe stated calmly yet firmly.

Carter released Felipe and rushed back over to Breeze. She was delusional as she reached up and wrapped her arms around his neck.

"Come here, baby. Let me make you feel good," she whispered, thinking that Carter was a john.

Pure emotion pulsed through him as he scooped her into his arms. Seeing her like this was breaking down the very essence of his manhood, making him feel weaker than he ever had before. He had failed her, Mecca had failed her, every man in her life who was supposed to keep her safe had failed.

"This ain't for you, Breeze," he stated sadly. "None of this was ever supposed to happen to you." Carter carried her over to Felipe, her head resting upon his broad shoulders as she fell into a nod.

"I'll buy her," Carter said. "A half a million dollars." There was no negotiating this bargain, and Felipe could see that bartering was not an option. Carter was a man who was protecting his family. That connection had no boundaries. Felipe knew this, because he would go against a thousand armies to ensure the safety of his own loved ones.

Felipe nodded and placed a hand on Carter's shoulder. He was not willing to give her away. To him, Breeze was just property, an expensive piece of real estate, but to maintain the business he was establishing with The Cartel, he was willing to sell her back. "If I could give her back to you for free, I would, but I paid a high price for her. A half a million dollars is not necessary. Just replace the seventy-five thousand dollars I spent in acquiring her and you can take her home," Felipe said.

Felipe opened the bedroom door. As Carter stepped out, he was instantly surrounded by Mexican men who held automatic machine guns pointed his way. He had no idea that Felipe had so many soldiers throughout the brothel. They were his security, and every room was monitored.

Felipe knew that he had never been in danger. The only person whose life was at stake was Carter's. Felipe lifted his hand to halt his army of loyal shooters, and shook his head from side to side.

"Let them pass," he said. Felipe turned to Carter. "My driver will take you back to the airstrip. I know you are eager to get home. We will take care of the details later."

The men lowered their weapons obediently, and Carter carried Breeze out of the brothel as she clung to him. He kissed the top of her head as he stepped into Felipe's limousine. When he was inside of the tinted vehicle, he broke down over Breeze, cradling her closely and hugging her tightly as his tears fell relentlessly. There was no stopping them. This was his baby sister, the most innocent one of them all, and yet she had been through the worst hell imaginable. The rest of his family had played the game and accepted the risks, but it was Breeze who had been sucked in by association, only to be chewed up and spit out. He could only imagine the cold and lonely place that she had just come from.

As he looked down at her face, he noticed the change in her. Whatever she had been through, it had drained her spirit. Even through the high from the heroin, he could see the hopelessness in her eyes. He grimaced as he thought of all of the men who had invaded her body, and as she began to scratch herself in her sleep, he saw the tell-all signs of a junkie.

As they pulled up to the airstrip and boarded the private jet, Carter held onto her tightly, as if she would disappear.

Breeze opened her eyes slightly and looked drowsily up at her older brother. "I just want to go home. Please take me to my family. They don't even know I'm alive," she whispered, still disoriented and unaware of her surroundings.

"I'm taking you home, Breeze, and nobody will ever hurt you again."

***

Zyir awoke to the sound of his cell phone vibrating against his wooden nightstand. He sat up and wiped the sleep out of his eyes as he reached over Illiana to answer it. Carter's name appeared on the screen, and he answered it immediately.

"Yo, fam, it's like seven in the morning. You know the streets don't see me until noon," Zyir stated with fatigue.

"I'm outside of your building. Buzz me in. We need to talk," Carter stated. Zyir had known Carter long enough to know when something serious had gone down.

"I thought you weren't due back from Tijuana until—"

"Open the door, Zy. I'll explain when I see you," Carter replied. His tone was demanding, but Zyir knew Carter too well not to pick up on the anxiety that was in his voice.

Zyir hung up his phone and then slid out of the bed to avoid waking Illiana. It was obvious that Carter wanted to discuss business, and he wanted the conversation to remain private. He shut his bedroom door as he exited and buzzed Carter in.

When Zyir opened the door and saw the stress lines on Carter's forehead, he knew something had gone awry. His red, sorrow-filled eyes told a story all their own.

"I need to talk to you," Carter stated as he stepped inside. Carter knew how Zyir felt about Breeze, and although her return was a joyous event, he wanted to prepare Zyir for it. He knew that Zyir loved his younger sister, and he did not want her condition to be a surprise to him. Breeze was not the same girl she used to be.

"No doubt, fam. Come in," Zyir invited as he stepped to the side to allow Carter to enter.

"It's about Breeze," Carter started.

"Breeze?" Zyir repeated in confusion. "Breeze is dead. We said our good-byes to her a long time ago."

"She's alive, Zyir," Carter stated as he put his hand on Zyir's shoulder.

Zyir smacked his hand away. It was the first time that he had ever bossed up against his mentor. His face frowned in pain as he backed away from Carter, bumping into his end table and sending a lamp crashing to the floor. The mere mention of Breeze's name was a soft spot for Zyir.

"Fuck is you saying, fam? She's been gone for almost two years! She's dead. We held the service . . ."

Carter stood stoically as he nodded his head. He knew that Zyir would take Breeze's reemergence just as hard as he had taken her actual death. "I know. We were wrong. She was still alive."

Zyir began to tear up as he put his hands on his head. "Don't say that to me, man. That means I gave up on her, fam. If she's been out there all this time, then I failed her. I was supposed to bring her home," Zyir stated emotionally as he punched the wall in frustration, putting his fist through the plaster and causing his knuckles to bleed.

He put his balled fists to the sides of his head in utter turmoil as he closed his eyes in horror. This was the last thing he had expected to hear Carter say. Wars he was ready to fight, money he knew how to collect, beef he enjoyed to cook, but to hear that the only girl he had ever loved had come back from the dead had him shook. It was the only situation that he was unprepared to handle. It was a chapter that he had closed in his life, and now it was about to be rewritten.

Zyir's grief reminded Carter of his own. It was the same way he felt about Miamor. He wished that she would magically reappear the same way that Breeze had done, but there was no bringing her back. She was gone forever, and because of this, he hoped that Zyir appreciated the gift that he was being given.

"She was working in one of Felipe's brothels. He says he purchased her from a woman who runs a human trafficking camp called Murderville. I don't know what Breeze has been through, but I know that she needs you."

Zyir looked at Carter in utter astonishment as he collapsed onto the couch. He buried his face in his hands and shook his head from side to side. His brain could not process the information, but his heart had sped up dramatically and felt as if it would beat out of his chest.

"Take me to her," Zyir stated.

"Take you to who?" Illiana's voice broke through the conversation and was an unwelcomed intrusion. She wasn't shy, and she made no efforts to cover her scantily clad body as she stood in front of Carter and Zyir while smoking a freshly rolled blunt.

Zyir ignored her question and refocused on Carter. "I need to see her, fam."

Carter saw the look of displeasure that crossed Illiana's face. He hoped that Zyir could see the signs that Illiana was giving off. It was obvious that she wanted more than Zyir was willing to give. The jealous look on Illiana's face spoke volumes, and Carter made a note to put Zyir up on game later.

"Handle your business and wrap things up here. I'll be waiting downstairs. Breeze will be happy to see you," Carter replied.

As Zyir dressed, Illiana stood in the doorway of his bedroom while smoking the cush weed slowly. *I know he's not rushing out to see some bitch when he has me here. Ain't nothing better than this,* Illiana thought arrogantly.

"Who is this Breeze bitch you're so worked up over?" Illiana asked.

Zyir stopped dead in his tracks and approached her as he buttoned up his Armani cardigan. He stood two inches away from her face as he said, "Don't ask questions about things that don't concern you. You're here to keep track of your brother's money, so start counting," Zyir stated, referring to the money that they had sexed on the night before. Without another word, he walked out of the room. Illiana's feelings were not his concern. He had one thing and one thing only on his mind—getting to Breeze.

"Thank you for meeting me," Mecca stated as he sat down on the park bench next to Leena and his nephew. She looked up at him and noticed the graze wound on his face. She had known him long enough to be able to tell that it had come from a bullet, one that had barely missed him.

"What happened to your face?" she asked.

"I had a little run-in with someone. Nothing major. I appreciate you showing up, Lee," he said, changing the subject.

"You said you had something to say," she replied. Leena was so short with him. She could not let go of the tiny piece of anger she still held onto, and Mecca heard it in her voice.

"You still toting pistols in my nephew's diaper bag?" Mecca asked, trying to lighten the mood.

Leena ignored his question as she looked out at the children playing in front of her. "What do you want, Mecca?" she asked impatiently.

"I don't know," Mecca replied honestly. "I want us to become friends again if that's possible."

Leena raised her eyebrows skeptically. "Friends?" she repeated.

"I know that's a lot to ask for, but it's the truth. I did what you said. I asked God for forgiveness."

"That's good, Mecca. I'm glad you took that first step," she admitted. She looked into his troubled eyes and said, "I wish you had taken it a long time ago."

"How do I know if it worked?" Mecca asked sincerely.

Leena looked at him suspiciously. She had never seen this side of Mecca before. "You will start to feel better," she replied. As she looked down at her son, who had fallen asleep in her lap, she said, "He looks just like you."

Mecca nodded and replied, "Money was always the winner. He was a lucky man."

"You were too, Mecca. You just didn't appreciate me like you should have," Leena admitted. The crowded, public place put her at ease around Mecca. She had snuck out while Estes was out playing golf, but she didn't dare meet Mecca in private. She chose a place where there would be too many witnesses for Mecca to try anything stupid.

"I appreciate you now," Mecca replied. "I'm tired of living recklessly, Lee. I know I've made a lot of mistakes in the past, but I need your help to make my future better. I have no right to ask you this, but you're the only person who can make me better. I don't want this life no more, ma."

Leena hated the fact that her heart raced around Mecca, but she could not stop it.

Just as she was about to respond, Mecca's phone rang loudly. He answered it.

"Yo, Mecca, you need to come to my place right away. It's important," Carter stated.

"I'm kind of in the middle of something," Mecca protested.

"It can wait," Carter insisted before hanging up the phone.

Mecca sighed as he turned back toward Leena. "I have to go, but I want to finish this discussion. Can we meet again?" he asked.

Against her better judgment, Leena nodded. "Yeah, Mecca. I'll meet you whenever you call."

It was a small step, but Mecca was grateful because it meant that it was possible for him to close the gap between them.

When Zyir saw Breeze lying in the bed, his knees almost gave out. The dark circles around her eyes, the track marks on her arms, and the bruises and cuts on her body made him cringe as if he could feel her pain. He sat in the chair next to her bed as Carter stood near the doorway.

"They doped her up," Zyir whispered, grief stricken as he grabbed her limp hand and held onto it gently. He kissed it and noticed that she was ice cold. She was in such bad condition that he almost didn't believe she was alive, but the rise and fall of her chest, along with the weak pulse he felt, told him otherwise. "What did they do to you, B? I'm sorry," he whispered.

He felt her stir slightly in her sleep as she began to come to. Her eyes opened, and she began to panic at the sight of the unfamiliar setting. She sat up in bed and put her back against the wall as she prepared to defend herself, but when her eyes met Zyir's, a sense of safety fell over her.

"You're not real," she uttered.

"I'm real, ma," he assured her as he reached out to touch her cheek.

She looked around in bewilderment. "I'm home?" she asked. "This is real?"

"Yeah, you're home, Breeze. You're safe now," Zyir stated. Breeze fell into his embrace as she wept heavily on his shoulder.

"I should have been there," Zyir said.

Breeze was too hysterical to respond. She choked on her own tears as Zyir held her tightly. Words would only complicate the situation, because neither of them could express how they were feeling.

It was the first time in his adult life that Zyir had allowed himself to cry. The love of a woman had made him whole again. Just seeing her face uplifted him. "I'm not letting you go, ma . . . ever. You hear me?" he stated as he held onto her tightly. "Tell me you trust me, ma. I'm sorry. I'm so sorry," he repeated over and over again.

"I trust you, Zyir," she whispered, absorbing his presence. She sucked it all in, because she was sure that at any moment she would wake up and it would all be a dream.

Mecca knocked on Carter's door, and when he saw his brother's face, he immediately became concerned.

"What happened? What's so urgent?" he asked.

"I found Breeze," Carter revealed. Mecca's eyes opened wide with hope as he raced past Carter and went from room to room until he finally located her in the spare bedroom. He stopped in his tracks when he saw her weeping passionately in Zyir's arms. He noticed her track-ridden arms immediately and winced in internal pain.

"Breeze," he called out to her, causing her to look up.

"Mecca!" she yelled as she jumped up and leaped into his arms. She wrapped her legs around his entire midsection as if she were still a little girl. He rubbed her hair and rocked her back and forth. He held onto his sister so tightly that she could not breathe, but she did not protest.

This feeling of familiarity, of safety, felt too good to Breeze. She had been deprived of her family for too long, and now she was back. It was too much for her to handle as she sobbed into Mecca's shoulder.

"Shh, it's okay now, B," he whispered as he held back his own tears. His efforts to stay strong failed him as tears began to fall from his eyes. "I'm going to kill a nigga. Everybody who ever hurt you, Breeze, I promise," he pledged as he felt her heart beating through her chest. "I thought you were gone, Breeze. I thought you were lost forever."

"They hurt me, Mecca. Over and over again," she cried.

"They're dead, B. Don't even think about that," Mecca said soothingly. He wiped his eyes as he held onto her. She was so weak that he had to be her strength. There was no room for him to be fragile. Breeze needed him, and as he caressed her hair soothingly, he gritted his teeth from the very thought of the abuse she had suffered. He had never been as gentle with anyone as he was with his baby sister at that moment. The Diamond family had kept her the most sheltered. She was their world.

The excitement of being home overwhelmed her, and her stomach began to boil as she realized how long it had been since her last fix. A full twenty-four hours had gone by, and to an addicted Breeze, that felt like a lifetime. She was used to being high around the clock.

"I'm going to be sick," she gurgled as she released Mecca. Zyir grabbed a small trash bin that sat beside the bed and rushed to her side as she threw up. Violent fits of vomit spewed from her mouth as Mecca watched in agony.

He knew that her body was craving heroine. He had been in the streets for too long not to notice the symptoms. Breeze was a dope head. His beautiful baby sister had been turned out, and the dismay he felt was written in agony on his face.

"I got her," Zyir stated, knowing that Mecca was about to break down any second.

Zyir laid Breeze back down in the bed as Mecca nodded and walked out of the room. It was too much for him to bear to see Breeze in so much distress.

Carter stared callously at Mecca as he entered the living room, and an uncomfortable silence filled the space between the two. He walked over to his wet bar and poured two glasses of cognac. He handed one to Mecca.

Mecca hesitantly took the drink from his brother as he stared at him intently. "Is it safe to drink?" Mecca asked directly.

"Why wouldn't it be?" Carter shot back.

As the two men sat waiting for Zyir to finish his time with Breeze, they did not speak, but the silence spoke louder than any words ever could. This reunion was supposed to be joyous, but there was a great divide between the two brothers that put a thick fog over the mood.

"Fuck it, nigga, let's get everything out in the open and lay the cards on the table. I know you know I killed your bitch," Mecca stated bluntly as he put his hand conveniently on his waistline near his .45.

"You gon' shoot me like you shot Monroe?" Carter countered, unrattled by Mecca. Carter had never been afraid of another nigga a day in his life, and the loose cannon in front of him was no exception. The safety on Carter's pistol was already off, and by the time Mecca chambered a round he would already be circled in chalk, if he wanted to play it that way. As Carter stared at Mecca, his nostrils flared in anger, but he kept his composure.

"That was a mistake," Mecca stated.

"I should have killed you. I've killed niggas for less than what you've done, but you're my brother, Mecca. I'm not like you. Loyalty is everything to me. If you had been any other nigga, I would have blown your brains out of your fucking head," Carter stated, enunciating each word so that Mecca understood him clearly. He paused as he stared intently at Mecca.

"Then why didn't you?" Mecca asked as he removed his .45 and placed it on his lap, his finger wrapped around the trigger, just in case. He did not want to have to shoot Carter, but there was malice in the air, and he knew that if he gave Carter the chance to bust first, it was over.

"Because you're not any other nigga. You are my blood, and having Breeze back has brought some perspective into my life. Family is all there is. Our sister is in that room right now, suffering because of a war you started . . . because of a lie that you told. We are the last three standing, and because of that, I cannot kill you. My sister . . . our sister loves you and she needs you. It is because of her and because of her only that I am willing to leave the past in the past."

"Everybody wanna label Mecca the bad guy," Mecca stated as he hit his chest and put his gun away. "You think this family isn't everything to me?" he asked. "I was out of my mind when I shot Money. I never meant for him to die, but you can't point fingers, Carter, because if family was so important to you, then you would have watched the company you kept."

"I'm not in the mood to decipher riddles. If you got something to say, just say it," Carter replied.

"That bitch Miamor! Open your eyes! She was just like me. She poisoned my mother, and her fucking Murder Mamas tried to kill me."

"Don't put falsehoods on a ghost, Mecca. As a matter of fact, don't even speak her name," Carter stated harshly. It was too soon for Mecca to even try to justify his actions. Thinking of Miamor was like pouring alcohol on an open wound for Carter. It was excruciating.

"See, that's the shit I'm talking about! The truth has been in front of your face the entire time. You don't want to see it! You were fucking the enemy, and I wouldn't be surprised if you were just a mark to her all along. The bitch was a killer—a damned good one, too," Mecca stated with an ironic chuckle. "I did what you would have never been able to do! I protected this family, no matter the cost, so you can blame me all you want, but let me ask you this question: If I didn't kill her, who would she have killed next?"

Zyir came into the room and cleared his throat, interrupting the heated conversation. "She needs to be checked out by a doctor," Zyir said.

"I have a private physician coming here first thing in the morning," Carter informed. "She's out there bad. It's going to take a while for her to readjust and get the drugs out of her system. They were feeding her heroin three times a day, every day, in Mexico. We will all have to keep a very close watch over her."

"She's not staying here," Mecca spoke up. There was no way he was going to let anything happen to Breeze again. Anyplace where Miamor used to rest her head was not safe enough for his little sister. "She'll be safer at my place."

"She's not staying with you," Carter said with authority. There was no way he was entrusting her life to Mecca. "We both know what you're capable of."

"Fuck is that supposed to mean?" Mecca shouted defensively. He didn't appreciate the subtle jabs that Carter was taking at him. There was no way he would ever bring harm to Breeze.

"Means what it means, Mecca. She's not staying with you," Carter countered.

Just as an argument was about to break out, Zyir interjected. "She'll stay with me." The tone of his voice left no room for argument. Both Mecca and Carter respected Zyir. It was the best place for Breeze to recuperate safely.

Mecca grabbed his jacket and brushed past Carter as he headed for the door. "I'll be by to see Breeze tomorrow, Zyir. Keep her safe," he said sincerely.

Zyir nodded, and Mecca walked out without acknowledging Carter as he slammed the door forcefully behind him.

Zyir looked at Carter curiously. "Fuck was that all about?" he asked.

Carter shook his head as worry lines creased his forehead. He downed the rest of his drink before replying, "He killed Miamor."

Although Zyir had a million questions to ask, he knew that if Carter wanted him to know details, he would have elaborated. Without hesitation, Zyir answered, "You want me to handle that?"

Carter sighed, wishing that the solution could be so easy. He poured himself another drink. "There's nothing to handle. He's my brother. I can't give that order after everything that this family has been through. Just take care of Breeze, Zy. That's all I need from you right now. You're the only person who I can trust at the moment. Everybody else in this fucking city has been wearing a mask all along."

Chapter Thirteen

"The line between the two is so thin that I go back and forth every day."
—Leena

Zyir paced anxiously back and forth outside the closed bedroom door as the doctor examined Breeze inside. Worrying over her condition was heart wrenching. He had no idea what she had gone through, and he only hoped that the damage she had suffered could be repaired. The nervousness and gut-bubbling concern that he felt for her was almost unbearable. He felt an overwhelming responsibility to rehabilitate Breeze, to restore her to the beautiful, unscathed young woman she used to be. The love he had for her extended that of girlfriend/boyfriend. He felt obligated to her just as much as he was to himself. It was as if they were one and just by looking into her eyes, he had absorbed all of her pain; he shared it with her and knew that he had to help her heal. Finding her had only been half the battle. The other half was yet to come.

Illiana watched Zyir in silent disgust as she fumed on the inside. *All of a sudden this Breeze bitch comes home and he acts like I don't even exist,* she thought irritably. *The junkie bitch ain't even all that. What the hell does he see in her?*

She had no idea just how deeply Zyir's affection ran for Breeze, but seeing him completely absorbed in her was enough to make Illiana green with envy. It was the attention she craved from him. The love she was scheming to get. Rejection was something she had never learned to take, and Breeze being back in the picture only complicated things for her.

"Why don't you come to bed, Zyir? It's three o'clock in the morning, papi," she said as she walked up on him and wrapped her arms around his neck. Her blood red painted nails scratched him softly with every caress. Staring into his eyes, it seemed as if he had aged overnight. He was carrying the burdens of a man twice his age, and they were evident in the frown lines that creased his brow.

He shook his head and removed her arms from around him. "Go ahead and get your rest, ma. I'm going to wait to speak with the doctor. I have to find out what happened to her, and I need to make sure she's okay," Zyir replied.

Displeased with his lack of attention, Illiana rolled her eyes and sighed angrily as she retreated to Zyir's bedroom.

Zyir ignored the little show she was putting on. *She's not my chick, just someone to pass the time with. I've never given her a reason to think this is anything more than what it is,* he justified in his head.

He didn't want Illiana to become too attached because now that Breeze was back, he knew that one day he was going to have to let Illiana go. He would just have to use tact and be careful with the way he ended things. Illiana was more connected than an interstate highway, and he didn't want to cross those who she had ties to.

I'ma have to play that situation right. Can't have a scorned woman fucking up business, Zyir thought.

The doctor finally emerged from his guest bedroom, breaking Zyir from his thoughts.

"Yo, Doc, how is she?" Zyir asked in a low tone. Breeze's condition wasn't everyone's business. He did not want Illiana, or even Breeze herself, to overhear the prognosis.

"After a full physical and vaginal exam, I found that she is in overall good health considering where she was found. A lot of girls coming from her circumstances contract incurable diseases. She is one of the lucky ones. I did find a lot of tearing and bleeding, which leads me to believe that she's been raped repeatedly for some time now.

"I found antibiotics in her system. Wherever she was, they kept her clean so that she would not infect their clientele with any sexually transmitted diseases. That alone may have saved her life.

"She has a lot of contusions and bruised bones. I even found a hairline fracture on the back of her skull. Those things will heal with time and a lot of rest. There are high levels of heroin in her system, however. She needs to be admitted to a rehab facility immediately. I can recommend some if you would like," the doctor said.

The more the man spoke, the more dismayed Zyir became. It seemed that every part of Breeze was scarred. His chest tightened as he thought of the men who had violated her and of the abuse she had been forced to endure; all the while, the people who loved her, himself included, had moved on without her.

As Zyir walked the doctor to the door, he relived the moment that he had slipped up and she had been kidnapped. It had been the worst day of his life. The doctor could see the turmoil on his face.

"Thank you for coming and for all of your help," Zyir stated as he went into his pocket and handed the doctor a decent-sized knot of crisp hundred dollar bills. "We appreciate your professionalism and discretion."

The doctor knew that Zyir spoke on behalf of the greatest criminal enterprise in the state of Florida. He nodded his head in acknowledgement, but before he was all the way out the door, he said, "My greatest concern for Breeze is her mental stability. She won't talk about what she's seen or been through, which leads me to believe that it is too traumatic to relive. I strongly urge you to watch her closely, twenty-four hours a day if you have to."

"Suicide watch?" Zyir questioned.

The doctor nodded grimly and replied, "Unfortunately, yes. She is going to need a lot of support. She needs to regain her physical health as well as her mental health. No one but Breeze knows the things that she's been through, so handle her with extreme care."

Zyir watched the doctor leave and then made his way to Breeze's bedside. She slept restlessly. Sweat covered her body and she twitched involuntarily as the potency of her last high passed out of her. Zyir got on his knees and grabbed Breeze's hand as he put his head down. He didn't want to wake her, only to let her know that he was right beside her and he wasn't going anywhere.

Illiana awoke to the loneliness of an empty bed and frowned. The undisturbed sheets let her know that Zyir hadn't been beside her all night. She climbed out of bed and pulled one of his shirts over her head before she went searching for him. Tiptoeing through the house in the dark with ease, she crept to the door of the guest bedroom.

Zyir was so unaware of anything and everyone except Breeze that he did not notice Illiana standing behind him. The delicate way in which he touched her made Illiana sick. There was no misinterpreting his actions toward her.

He loves this girl, Illiana thought as she scoffed and crossed her arms. She walked back to the bedroom knowing that with Breeze Diamond in the picture, she would never secure a spot in Zyir's world.

I have to get rid of her, she thought as she climbed back into bed. It was the only solution.

Illiana's features were so striking that they appeared deadly. As the wheels of manipulation began to turn in her pretty little head, she smiled deviously. These were exactly the type of games she loved to play. There was only room for one woman in Zyir's life, and she was determined to make sure that she was it.

Leena lay in bed with the silky sheets wrapped around her gorgeous physique as if she were a Greek goddess. Her mind spun wildly as thoughts of Mecca filled her head. Her son lay beside her, and Estes rested on the other side of him. On the outside they looked like a happy family, but on the inside, she yearned for something more, something irresistible, something dangerous—and that something was a new life with Mecca Diamond.

Don't be stupid Leena! He shot you. Don't go there. Stop thinking with your heart and use your head, she told herself. She could not understand how she could still care for the man who had tried to end her life, but her heart was a puzzle that was too complicated to piece together. It wanted what it wanted, and the more she reacquainted herself with Mecca, the more she wanted him.

There was something about the Diamond mystique that always pulled her in. She had felt the same thing with Monroe, and now that Mecca seemed to be changing, he was magnetic to her as well.

She was so conflicted, so torn over him. Everything in her wanted to hate him. He deserved to be punished for the acts of sin he had committed against her, but seeing his transformation made it easier to forgive. He was slowly changing into a better man. She had known Mecca for a long time and knew that it would not be easy for him to give up the life he had been born into, but he was trying, and that alone impressed her.

The ticking of the antique grandfather clock in the corner of the room kept her awake as her heart raced in the midnight hour. *How can you still love him?* She asked herself, but she knew that she loved Mecca because it was the next best thing to loving Monroe. They were so much alike that she could not keep up her angry visage toward Mecca. Every time she saw his face she remembered Monroe. Identical in every way except demeanor, Mecca and Monroe were two halves that made up her whole heart. Those two halves equaled the one true love of her life.

Hesitantly, she sat up in bed and peeked over at Estes. His light snoring indicated that he was in a deep sleep. She took a deep breath as she leaned down to kiss her son's cheek before she slid out of bed. She knew that the decision she was about to make could be detrimental to her health.

I have to see him, she thought as she slipped on her clothes, moving silently through the dark as she dressed. She grabbed her Chanel bag and fished out her keys as she snuck out of the door, hoping that Estes would not awaken before she returned.

Fear, anxiety, and anticipation filled her as she pulled away from Estes' home. She pulled out her cell phone and dialed Mecca's number.

"Mecca, I need to see you," she said as soon as he answered.

Without hesitation, he gave her his address, and she sped through the city streets, her Benz making its way to Mecca's place in record speed. She sat in front of his building for an hour, listening to the pattern of the rain falling on the roof of her car. It was as if the sky were crying right along with her as her own tears flowed down her cheeks.

Confusion plagued her as she tried to make sense of her feelings. Knowing that Mecca was no good, she started to leave, but every time she went to put the car in drive, she froze. She needed to see Mecca, and although the consequences of her actions would be great, she decided to stay.

She got out of the car before she lost her nerve, and ran into the high-rise building. Her throat felt as if it would close as she took the elevator to the penthouse on the top floor, and nervous energy filled her.

She went to Mecca's door and lifted her hand to knock, but before she could, Mecca pulled it open. He stood before her, shirtless, with a blunt in one hand, as weed smoke danced in the space around him.

She took in everything about him. Mecca was a beautiful man. From his broad and well-sculpted chest to his strikingly handsome features, he was perfect. His only flaw was his dangerous temper. She had seen it firsthand. It had almost cost her everything, yet there she stood, intrigued and forgiving in front of him.

Overwhelmed by his presence, she stopped thinking and did what felt right to her: she kissed him passionately, catching Mecca off guard as she backed him into the penthouse. Their pace was feverish as desire filled the space between them.

Mecca fumbled to put out the blunt without breaking their connection. "I'm so sorry, Lee," he whispered over and over again in her ear, causing her tears to flow.

Hearing the sincerity in his words was like a punch to the gut as she pushed him away. "Why did you have to speak, Mecca? Why did you have to remind me of what you did? Every time you apologize, I remember that night!" she yelled as she put her hands to her face and turned toward the door.

"Leena—"

Before Mecca could get his words out, she stalked over to him in a rage and slapped him across the face. "I hate you, Mecca. I hate you for what you did!!" she yelled, her anger ablaze in her emotion-filled eyes.

"Then why are you here?" he asked as he touched the side of her face. The gentleness that he displayed was uncharacteristic for him. This new version of Mecca that stood before her was so much easier to love than the callous gangster she knew him to be.

She sobbed as if she were ashamed of herself. She replied, "Because I love you. The line between the two is so thin that I go back and forth every day."

Mecca embraced her, and she fought him as she tried to regain control of her heart.

"No, Mecca, I have to go. I shouldn't have come here. What the fuck was I thinking? I have to think of my son," she protested.

"Stop fighting me, ma," he whispered. He took her chin into his hand and lifted her face to his, kissing her gently. She melted as she kissed him back, indulging in the forbidden affection she felt for him.

"I'm trying, Leena. I'm trying to change. You don't know how much I wish I could take back—"

"Don't," she said as she looked up at him. "Don't keep making me relive it, Mecca. We can't take back the things we did in the past, and it's too painful for me to think about. I know that being here with you is a mistake, but please just let me make it."

"Okay," he replied simply as he picked her up, her long legs wrapping around his body as he placed his hands on her behind. He carried her to his bedroom as their tongues performed a delicate dance. He laid her down on his bed and then stood up as he admired her.

Seeing her in his bed, alive and breathing, caused him much distress as he felt his chest swell. Although he had hurt Leena, she had hurt him as well. She was a constant reminder of the monster he had become. At that moment, everything sexual about their interaction went out of his mind. His motive was different. What he sought from her was intimacy. He wanted to feel the unconditional love that she had for him.

As he looked down at her, his heart swelled, and for the first time in his life, he was selfless, thinking of her before himself. After everything he had done to her, Leena still came back to him. The hollow space inside his chest, where his heart should have dwelled, ached because he realized that he loved her too. He lay down beside her and pulled her close to his body.

"I just want to hold you, Lee. Just stay here with me. Forgive me, Leena," he whispered as he kissed the top of her head.

Leena closed her eyes as the heat from his body warmed her. She was reluctant in her decision, but knew that it was one she would still make, despite the warning bells ringing in her conscience. "I do, Mecca. I forgive you."

When Breeze opened her eyes, her entire body hurt. She had been asleep for three days straight, but now that she was awake and coherent, she felt the horrible effects of withdrawal. She reached for the IV that was in her arm and weakly pulled it out. As she stood to her feet, the weight of her body was unbearably heavy. Despite the fact that she had lost tremendous weight, it felt like her bones would break with every step that she took. Her body had been dependent on heroin for so long that it was no longer producing the endorphins she needed to resist pain. Every inch of her body hurt. The pressure of her feet hitting the floor felt as if she were walking on glass. It was no longer a matter of enjoying the high; she needed heroin to keep her functioning. Without it, she felt sick.

For so long she had convinced herself that she would never make it home. Now that she was back, she felt dirty and ashamed of where she had been. As she made her way out of the room, she gripped her churning stomach with one hand while keeping her balance against the wall with the other. When she stepped into the hallway, the smell of food cooking drew her to the kitchen.

She was caught off guard by the unfamiliar face that greeted her. Illiana stood in a Victoria's Secret negligee as she prepared breakfast. Breeze gasped at her beauty, and instantly began to smooth out her own hair from insecurity.

I used to look like that, she thought as she fumbled nervously, ashamed of her appearance.

When Illiana realized she had an audience, she smirked. "So, the famous Breeze Diamond does more than sleep," she said as she motioned her hand for Breeze to sit.

"W–where's Zyir?" Breeze asked as she sat down timidly, wincing from the pressure of her tailbone hitting the wooden chair. She looked around nervously as she shivered and rubbed the goose bumps on her bare arms. Being home felt odd, as if she no longer belonged, and the way Illiana was looking at her made her feel out of place.

"He's in the shower," Illiana replied as she looked Breeze up and down from head to toe. *I don't see what all the fuss is about,* she thought as she instantly judged Breeze.

"Who are you?" Breeze asked.

Illiana fixed herself a plate and began to walk past Breeze. She stopped right next to her and replied, "I'm the new bitch in Zyir's life that you don't want to fuck with." She placed the plate of food down in front of Breeze so hard that some of the food fell onto the table. "Here, you need this more than I do. You look like shit."

Feeling as if she hadn't eaten in days, she dug into the plate, as Illiana shook her head and walked away.

She's pathetic, she thought as she walked back into Zyir's bedroom.

"You cooking?" Zyir asked in surprise as soon as she came into the room. Water dripped from his rock hard abs, and the white towel that was hanging from his hips barely covered his family jewels as she eyed him hungrily.

"Don't act so surprised, Zyir. Our houseguest woke up, so I just thought I would make her something to eat. She looks so unhealthy," Illiana replied with fake innocence. "Your plate is on the stove."

Zyir nodded his head, but looked at her skeptically. "Play nice, Illiana. Now is not the time for bullshit," he warned.

"What?" she feigned. "Can't a girl do something nice?" she asked.

"Not a girl like you. Every move you make is calculated," Zyir answered as he finished dressing.

He bypassed Illiana as he went to join Breeze in the kitchen. He noticed that when he approached her, she wouldn't look him in the eyes. He walked right up on her and kneeled in front of her. Reaching up to touch her face, he felt his heart speed up. No matter how much she had changed, he was grateful to have her back. He had never thought he would see her alive again.

"You should be in bed, B," he whispered as he brushed a piece of food from the side of her delicate mouth.

"Where is everyone, Zyir? I just want my mother. Has she been to see me? Why am I not at home with her?" Breeze asked.

Zyir became silent. A lot had happened in Breeze's absence, and it had slipped his mind that she was unaware of her mother's death.

I can't tell her that, he thought. *She should hear it from Carter or Mecca.*

Breeze noticed the look of uncertainty in Zyir's eyes. "Where is she, Zyir? Where is my mother? I need her," she said in a pleading tone.

"She's gone. She died after you disappeared," he said, giving her the news as gently as possible.

Breeze reached out and gripped Zyir's shirt tightly as her head fell onto his chest. Her vision was so blurry with tears that she couldn't see as she cried silently. She could not even form the words to express the sharp pain that radiated through her heart.

"I know, B . . . I know," Zyir soothed as he rubbed her back.

"It just hurts so bad. I wasn't even here. I missed everything," Breeze cried.

"Nah, ma, everything missed you. Nothing has been the same since you've been gone. You're home now, and I'm gonna take care of you," Zyir assured. Zyir picked her up and carried her back into the guestroom.

"Aghh!" she whimpered as he lay her down. Even the thousand thread count sheets felt painful to her. She gripped his hand as he watched over her sympathetically. "Zyir, please . . . this hurts too bad. I need you to help me. Please just give me a little bit to make me feel better."

Hearing her beg him for dope broke his heart. He would do anything to take her pain away—anything except what she was requesting of him.

"I can't do that, Breeze. You don't need that, ma. I'm going to help you through this, but you've got to be strong," he said.

Breeze began to shake as a chill set into her bones, and she squirmed uncomfortably.

Tears of rage rushed Zyir, but he held them back, refusing to let even one fall. He dipped the sponge on the nightstand into a bowl of cold water and wiped it across her forehead. "What happened to you, ma?" he asked. "Tell me who did this to you. Who took you, Breeze?"

Breeze closed her eyes, because she knew that once she admitted what had occurred, Zyir and her family would never look at her the same.

"Talk to me, Breeze. You can tell me," Zyir urged. He was ready to pop off on anyone who had played a role in kidnapping Breeze.

"It was Ma'tee. I was trapped in Haiti with Ma'tee," she replied. Images of the constant rape raced through her mind as she shook her head from side to side, her eyes still closed from fear of the look that Zyir was giving her. "He raped me every day Zyir, and no matter how hard I try, I can't stop feeling his hands on my body."

Her revelation would not allow him to remain strong. He cried at her bedside as he gripped her hand and kissed her face repeatedly. "I'm going to murder that nigga, Breeze. You hear me? I'm going to—"

"He's already dead," she whispered. "The earthquake killed him. It was how I got away from him, but I only went from one hell to another."

It took everything in Zyir not to explode, and he turned away from Breeze so that she could not witness his grief.

"That's why I didn't want to tell you. You don't want me anymore," Breeze said.

Zyir cleared the tears from his face and gained his composure before turning around. "I'll always want you, Breeze, and you never have to talk about it again. You are home now, and that is all that matters. I'ma stick with you through it all,

B, and I'll body anyone who ever hurts you again. All you have to do is promise me you'll try . . . try to kick this shit, Breeze. That's the one thing that I can't do for you. You have to want that for yourself."

Breeze nodded and replied, "I will, Zyir. I promise you I'll get clean."

As Illiana's prying ears eavesdropped on the conversation, she felt reassured. She had seen the effects that heroin could have over a person. Breeze was hooked, and Illiana was going to make sure that she stayed that way. Illiana's infatuation with Zyir was so strong that she never even considered how evil her actions toward Breeze would be. She was out for self; nobody else mattered.

Dawn came too early for Leena as the rising sun shone brightly through the floor to ceiling windows of Mecca's penthouse. She knew that she had stayed too long, but being wrapped up in Mecca's arms felt so good that she did not want to let him go.

She slid from beneath him and walked out onto the large balcony. She wished that she could stay there forever and just move forward without ever looking back, but her son kept her rooted with Estes. Estes was security, and although she did not love him, she knew that he had the means to provide her child with everything.

The purple and orange hues that blended in the sky relaxed her, and she sighed as she thought of how complicated her life had just become.

"Why did I come here?" she asked herself, knowing that she had just opened Pandora's box.

She felt Mecca walk up behind her, and her shoulders tensed as the hairs on the back of her neck rose in fear.

"Don't fear me, Lee. I'm trying to show you that I'm not a monster," he whispered into the back of her neck with his eyes closed as he inhaled her natural scent. He wrapped his arms around her waist and she relaxed.

"I know, Mecca. I'm trying. I just have to get used to this new you. You have to be patient with me. My trust in you isn't something that can be restored overnight."

The feeling of Mecca's lips on the nape of her neck caused her love box to throb in anticipation. It had been so long since she had been pleased. She wanted to slow things down, but the spot between her thighs had a different agenda. She gasped as Mecca's hands caressed her thighs, moving higher and higher until his fingers found her clit.

Without speaking, he moved with expertise as he spread her legs and removed his manhood. She felt the girth of him as he rubbed his thick head against her voluptuous behind. She dripped in anticipation. Nothing had ever felt so forbidden, yet she still craved it. She wanted him to put his thing down. The bedroom was the one place where his aggression never scared her.

Bending her over the thirty-five-story balcony, he parted her glistening southern lips and entered her from behind.

"You want me to stop?" he asked as he paused inside of her. He wanted her to be completely comfortable with what was about to go down.

"No," she replied. "Psst," she sighed as she felt every inch of him dig into her from behind.

Mecca's hand gripped the sides of her ass. Her wetness was like heaven to him. Her juicy peach fit snugly around his shaft as her muscles pulled him tighter and deeper with every stroke.

"Oooh, Mecca," she moaned as she bucked back on his dick, loving the mixture of pain and pleasure that he was giving her. Her head spun from orgasmic intoxication as she took in the scenery below. She could feel herself being sucked back into Mecca's world, but at that exact moment, she did not care.

If this is what it feels like, I wanna be here forever, she thought as her eyes closed in pleasure.

The morning air caused her nipples to harden as Mecca turned her around. She mounted him as he held her up with one hand and palmed her perky breasts with the other, all the while their tongues intertwined. It had been so long since a man had been inside of her. Estes had expressed his interest, but she could never bring herself to sleep with him, and now all of the sexual tension that she had built up was about to come down.

"I'm cumming," she whispered feverishly. "Ooh, Mecca, right there."

Mecca increased his pace as the tip of his dick swelled, and a tingle ran down his spine. "Me too, Lee. Shit, ma."

Mecca cried out in pleasure as he shot his load into her, but he did not stop pleasing her until she creamed all over him.

Exhausted, she fell into his chest. Her labored breathing filled the air. She didn't know what her next move would be, and she hid her face to avoid reality.

"Lee," he said as he lifted her chin. "I want you to leave him."

"I don't know if I can," she admitted honestly. "I owe him so much. He has been nothing but generous and kind to me."

"Are you happy?" he asked.

"Will I be happy with you?" she countered with raised eyebrows. She wanted him to reassure her, to convince her that she would be, but it was something that Mecca could not guarantee.

He lowered his gaze.

"Exactly. I didn't think so," she said sadly as she walked back into his penthouse.

Mecca listened as the shower ran in his master bathroom, and he sat down on his bed with his face in his hands. He was trying. He was doing all that he could to redeem himself, but he wasn't completely sure that he could purge himself of all the evil that lived inside of him. He wanted Leena. She held the key to his future, but he did not want to hurt her again.

As she emerged from his bathroom fully dressed, he knew that she was ready to walk out of his life.

She's better off with Estes, he thought as she headed directly to the door. The selfishness in him caused him to stop her.

"Leena . . ."

She paused mid-step and turned to him, revealing a tear-streaked face.

"Leave him. Come away with me," he said.

"My son," she protested.

"He has my blood in his veins, Leena. Let me raise him. I'll take care of you," he replied.

Leena wanted to say no because she knew that it was the right answer, but her heart would not listen to reason. She ran toward Mecca and kissed him passionately.

"Okay . . . okay, Mecca. Just let me do this on my own terms. I'll leave him, I swear."

"Leena, I'm leaving with or without you, but you would make my life so much better if you come," he admitted.

"Just tell me when and where to be. I'll be there. I'll leave with you," she said as she walked out the door.

Mecca watched her leave, but he was confident that she would soon be back. The game was getting old for him, and at that moment, all he wanted was to leave his old life behind so that he could start anew with Leena. She was slowly becoming his only priority—and even Estes could not keep him away from her.

Emilio Estes sat behind the dark tint of the Lincoln truck and held his great grandson in his arms as he watched Leena leave Mecca's building. Disappointment filled him as he kissed Monroe Jr.'s chubby cheeks. "I can't let your mother make this mistake," Estes said, more to himself than to the baby in his arms. "I told him to stay away."

He shook his head in disgust as he thought of how he would have to press the button on Mecca. He was a liability. As long as he was around, Leena would be drawn to him, and Estes was not giving her up, especially to his crooked grandson. Mecca was a ticking time bomb, and before he could explode again, Estes would kill him. This time, there would be no mercy. Mecca had to go.

Chapter Fourteen

"I stay strapped."
—Murder

Murder had been patiently waiting to see Mecca again. Murder had staked out Monroe's grave all Sunday morning, hoping to see Mecca there again, just as he had done one week before.

This nigga is bound to show up here sometime, he thought as he sat back. He thought about what the Murder Mamas had said about him taking a different approach in killing the remaining leaders of The Cartel. He knew that to do it, he would have to get in close with them so he could kill Zyir, Mecca, and Carter with ease. He didn't have the luxury of just killing one of them and being satisfied. In Miamor's honor, all of them had to go.

He looked across the cemetery and saw a tinted truck and knew that Robyn and Aries were waiting inside, strapped. He had a plan, and if everything went as expected, he would be in a better position by the end of the day.

Just as expected, Mecca's car rolled up slowly and parked. Mecca stepped out of the car, scanned the area, and checked his surroundings. Once he felt comfortable, he closed the door and headed toward Monroe's grave.

Murder hopped out of his car also and tried to look as casual as he could as he headed to the grave. Murder patted his hip to make sure his .40 caliber pistol was in place.

Mecca was on the path to the tombstone and didn't notice Murder walking a couple of feet behind him. Murder looked across the site and nodded, knowing the girls were watching closely and waiting for his signal to go through with the plan and get it popping.

On cue, tires began to screech and the sounds of gunfire erupted. The Murder Mamas had on ski masks, and Robyn had an assault rifle. She was hanging out of the window. Aries drove by while shooting her own handgun out of the window.

Murder quickly dove on Mecca, knocking him out of the way as he was taken by total surprise. Murder began to fire back, but he aimed high purposely, so he wouldn't hit Robyn and Aries.

The whole scenario was planned to a tee. It was done and over within fifteen seconds, but those fifteen seconds were instrumental in Murder's plans.

Mecca was taken off guard, and he had left his guns in the car, not thinking anything would pop off at a cemetery. He breathed hard as he saw Murder send bullets at the tinted car that was speeding out of the cemetery. Murder ran after the car, firing bullet after bullet until his clip was empty, showing Mecca that he wasn't scared.

"You good?" Murder asked as he looked back at Mecca, who was still on the ground.

"Yeah, I'm good," Mecca said as his heart beat rapidly. "Damn!" Mecca yelled as he thought about how his life had almost ended. "You saved my ass," Mecca added.

"Don't trip. I saw that shit coming from a mile away. I'm just glad that I had my strap on me. You must have an enemy somewhere, huh?" Murder said as he extended his hand to help Mecca up.

"Yeah, something like that. Thanks, fam," Mecca said as he stood up and dusted off his pants.

"Don't mention it," Murder said as he walked toward the tombstone as if the conversation was over.

"Yo, hold up," Mecca said as he followed Murder. "That was some real shit. What, you a cop or something?" Mecca asked, wondering why he would just be carrying a gun on him.

"Hell nah. I hate cops," Murder answered as he put his gun inside his holster. "I stay strapped, that's all."

"Yo, I'm Mecca," Mecca said as he extended his hand for a shake.

"I'm Leon, but my people call me Murder."

"Okay, Murder. Nice to meet you. Let me bless you for doing what you did." Mecca said as he reached into his pocket and pulled out a stack full of money.

"Nah, I'm good. You keep that. I just acted on impulse. It was nothing," Murder said.

"Well, at least let me buy you a drink," Mecca asked with a small smirk. He liked Murder's style and quick thinking. He knew that he could always use a live nigga around him. Murder impressed him just that quick.

"No doubt," Murder responded, accepting the invitation. Mecca had just fallen right into Murder's trap, and although Murder had a stone cold expression on his face, on the inside he was smiling, because he knew that the countdown to the end of The Cartel had just begun.

"And that's how I ended up in Miami," Murder said, just finishing a made-up story to Mecca. He told Mecca that he came from Atlanta searching for a coke connect, and had only been in town for a couple of months. Murder also told him that his father moved to Florida and had recently passed, which was something Mecca could relate to. Needless to say, they hit it off quickly.

Murder took a shot of Patrón and slammed the glass on the table. Mecca signaled the waiter to bring them another shot as they sat in the rear of a low-key bar that Mecca frequented. Murder's trigger finger was itching, and he wanted so badly to pull of his .40 and blow Mecca's head clean off, but he knew that he couldn't show his card this early in the game. Murder's hand began to sweat and he gritted his teeth, all while keeping on a smile in front of his enemy.

How can I be having a drink with the coward that killed my baby? Miamor was my mu'fuckin' heart. I should blow his head off right now, Murder thought as he casually slipped his hand down to his waist where his gun rested, locked and loaded. He quickly snapped back and thought about the bigger picture, and that was taking them all out.

"You say you looking for a coke connect, right?" Mecca said as he leaned in closer to Murder so that no one could overhear him.

"Yeah, that shit in Atlanta is so stepped on, and when we do get a good batch in, they taxing up the ass," Murder said.

"How about . . ." Mecca started, but stopped when the waitress came and set the two shots of Patrón on the table. He continued when she left. "How about I show you how to make some real money?" Mecca said as he leaned back and took the shot with no chaser.

"How can I do that?" Murder asked as he sat back looking very interested, knowing that Mecca was playing into his little trap.

"I saw the way you reacted out there today. I need a nigga like that on my team. You feel me?"

"I'm listening," Murder stated.

"I want you to be my enforcer, my bodyguard for a couple of months. I will also plug you in on some bricks when you go back to Atlanta. Unstepped on, raw," Mecca offered.

"Word?" Murder asked as he took his shot and looked Mecca in the eyes.

"Word!" Mecca said as he extended his hand, waiting for Murder to seal the deal.

Murder shook Mecca's hand, and thoughts of Miamor's horrific murder scene popped in his head. Murder's trigger finger began to itch again, and he gritted his teeth, feeling disgusted that he was shaking his own enemy's hand. Nevertheless, Murder stayed calm and didn't show his cards so soon. He knew that in due time, he would get his revenge in a major way.

Murder left that meeting feeling like in some way he had betrayed Miamor; however, he knew that to take down The Cartel correctly, he would have to play a role. Murder had just ordered the Murder Mamas to head back to L.A., and even though they were against leaving him there alone, Murder insisted. Murder had taught Miamor everything she knew about her profession, and off the strength of that, Robyn and Aries listened to him.

At that moment, Murder was on his way to meet Mecca at a warehouse, and the Murder Mamas were in the air headed home. On that day, Murder was supposed to meet Zyir and Carter for the first time. Murder questioned his willpower. He was not sure that he would be able to handle seeing Carter without reaching for his gun and going all out. Only time would tell.

Murder took a deep breath and whispered, "I love you, Miamor," as if she were in the car with him. Deep in his heart, he was confident that she could hear him.

As Murder pulled into the warehouse where Mecca had directed him to meet them, he took a deep breath to prepare himself. It was an old steel factory on the outskirts of Miami. The Diamond family owned the property, so it looked as if it was a shut down establishment, but it was where the bricks were stored and shipments were dropped off.

Murder stepped out of the car, and moments later, a Lamborghini pulled up behind him, shining its lights on him. Murder blocked his eyes and tried to see who the driver was. It wasn't until Mecca killed the lights and the butterfly-style door arose that Murder saw who it was.

"What's up, fam?" Mecca asked as he approached Murder.

Murder instinctively clenched his jaws as his hatred for Mecca surfaced once again. Murder caught himself and calmed down before Mecca got close enough to read the expression on his face. Niggas like Mecca could sense larceny, so Murder had to be sure to keep his temper in check at all times.

"What's good?" Murder said between clenched teeth. He shook Mecca's hand and put on a fake smile just before Mecca led him into the warehouse.

Carter and Zyir were already there, counting money and loading duffel bags with the bricks so that they could be distributed to their blocks. They had been there for over an hour and had parked in the back out of sight.

As Murder walked in, he had to stop his mouth from hitting the floor. He had never seen so many kilos of cocaine in his life. It was then that he knew that The Cartel was much more than street legend. They were the real deal.

Having Carter, Zyir, and Mecca in one place at the same time, he thought about taking them out right there. But he quickly changed his tune when he saw the arsenal of automatic weapons sitting on the table near the money.

"What took you so long?"Carter asked as he thumbed through the hundred dollar bills without looking up.

Zyir frowned when he saw the man following Mecca. "Fuck is this new nigga?" Zyir asked, not one to hold his tongue.

"I had to make a stop, but check it. This is my man I was telling you about. This nigga is on some Jet Li type shit with the pistols. He's nice," Mecca bragged.

"Word?" Carter said as he stood from the table to shake Murder's hand. Mecca had told Carter and Zyir about Murder, and they needed an enforcer, so they had wanted to meet him. But when Carter shook Murder's hand, he felt that something was off. Call it a hustler's intuition; the handshake wasn't right, the eye contact was too stiff, and Murder's body language didn't match his facial expression.

"Murder, this is Carter. Carter, Murder," Mecca said, introducing the two men that both loved Miamor to the bone.

"What's up?" Carter said.

"'Sup family?" Murder returned.

"And this is Zyir. He handles everything on the street level," Mecca said. Zyir was so busy counting the money that he didn't even properly greet Murder. Zyir just glanced at him briefly and nodded his head.

Carter didn't say anything then, but he made a mental note to tell Mecca to ditch the new nigga. He didn't get a good vibe from him, and rightfully so, because Murder wanted all of them dead.

"Yo, let's wrap this up. I got to make a move," Carter said, trying to cut the night short. He didn't feel comfortable around Murder and wanted him gone.

Zyir picked up on Carter's vibe and agreed. Mecca was slipping, and Carter was going to tell him about himself later.

***

The next day, Mecca had a talk with Carter, and he instantly cut off Murder. They also shut down that location as a drop-off and pick-up spot. Carter didn't know if Murder was a fed or an enemy, but he knew one thing: he could never be a part of The Cartel.

Chapter Fifteen

"The Cartel runs this city,
not y'all. You work for us!"
—Zyir

Breeze paced the spacious room back and forth, trying not to think about the subject that overwhelmed her thoughts. She was battling her conscience, and also the pain that was in the pit of her stomach. Heroin was calling for her, and she was on the brink of answering.

No, Breeze, you can't. I can fight this shit, she thought as she clutched her stomach and fell to her knees in pain. The pain that shot through her stomach was almost unbearable as she collapsed to all fours and began to cry.

Breeze couldn't understand what was going on with her body. She had never had an itch so bad, and whether she knew it or not, she was going through withdrawal. She was so used to getting dope shot into her veins on a daily basis that the first time her body went without it, it became excruciating. She kept thinking about what her father would say if he saw her in the state that she was in at that moment.

Breeze stood to her feet and took a deep breath while still clenching her stomach. She was ashamed of what she was about to do, but she couldn't help it. She had to shoot the magic into her veins immediately. She had to. She craved the warm sensation that the dope had when it crawled up her veins after injecting it. She kept thinking about how good it would make her feel, and that thought alone was almost orgasmic. She had spent the last fifteen minutes going back and forth, hoping that she would have enough willpower to fight the urge. However, when that monkey is on a person's back, all logic goes out the window.

Breeze quickly rushed to Zyir's room and began to search through his drawers, trying to find any money she could. She ran across a rubber band full of hundreds, and immediately clipped two of the crisp bills. She then rushed to the front room and grabbed Zyir's car keys. She was out the door and on her way to the trap to cop a fix.

Breeze cruised the streets, searching for a dope boy to serve her a fix. She had on a jogging suit with house shoes on her feet as she pushed the new model Benz down the street. Before, she would never have been caught looking anything less than glamorous, but now it was a different story. She was no longer street royalty. She was just a junkie looking for a fix. She was a completely different person than she once was, and life had taken a toll on her.

She pulled onto a side street that was known for drug trafficking and parked her car. She noticed a group of young thugs posted on a stoop and waved one of them over. All eyes were on Breeze as she posted on the block and waited for the young hustler to approach her car. Breeze was fidgety and anxious as she tapped her wheel repeatedly, waiting for the guy to approach. "What's up, ma?" the hustler asked as he bent his head down and licked his lips.

"What's up? You got some 'boy'?" Breeze asked, cutting straight to the point while clenching her stomach.

The young thug squinted his eyes and recognized Breeze when he looked closer. He couldn't believe what she was asking him for. Here she was, the daughter of Carter Diamond, sister of the most ruthless gangster, and the dream girl for any dope boy that ever laid eyes on her, and she was looking to cop some dope from him. He instantly knew that she was craving dope from her body language.

"What?" he asked, thinking he had heard her wrong.

"You heard me. Do you got some or not?" she demanded again, but this time she pulled out a hundred dollar bill from her bra. The hustler couldn't believe what she was asking, and he knew that her brother would not appreciate him serving Breeze, so he stepped back and shook his head.

Breeze smacked her lips and put up her middle finger as she began to look past him, searching for a willing hustler.

"You know I can't do that. This is Mecca and Zyir's territory, ma. You can't do that," he said, trying to put her up on game without getting disrespectful. He knew that the dope he had in his pocket came from The Cartel, and to give it to Breeze would be straight up violating.

"Nigga, fuck what you talking about? You just scared, that's all," Breeze said as she waved him off, dismissing him like a flunky. At that point, she bruised the young hustler's ego, and it noticeably got to him.

"I'm not scared of yo' peoples, believe that. I just ain't for the bullshit that comes along with this," he responded.

"Like I said, you scared," Breeze said as she realized that her words were getting him upset. Breeze was smart enough to know that when a man's ego is bruised, it'll make him do things he usually would not do. In this case, he played right into Breeze's hand.

"Look, ma, I ain't scared of no damn body. I just—"

"You just a pussy," Breeze interrupted as she waved the hundred dollar bill in the air. The hustler looked around and then reached into the car, snatching the money out of Breeze's hand. He then dug into his pocket and pulled out two packs of dope and tossed it on her lap.

"There you go. Fuck it," he said as he stood back up, feeling like a big man.

Breeze's eyes went directly to her lap and on the packs. Her eyes lit up and her anxiety went into overdrive as she anticipated what was to happen next. She couldn't wait to get back to Zyir's house. She wanted to shoot up immediately.

"Yo, is it somewhere I can take my medicine?" Breeze asked as she turned off the car and looked at the hustler.

"Yeah, up there," he said as he threw his head in the direction of the house behind him. "Just go through the back and then you can do your thing in there," he said, feeling like a big man now that he had served her.

Before he could complete his sentence, Breeze was out of the car and headed to the back of the house. All of the hustlers looked at her as she passed as if she were crazy. They looked at her nice body and the jogging pants that hugged her petite behind.

Breeze went to the back of the house and entered. The foul smell of blood and body odor filled the air as Breeze made her way through the shooting gallery, a nickname junkies gave a residence where users went to shoot their dope. Breeze walked through the house and saw different people scattered throughout the studio-style place, all using their preferred drug.

She stepped over a man that was laid out on the floor in a deep nod and found a table that was in the far corner. She quickly sat down and pulled out her two packs. She reached into her purse and got a shooter, also known as a syringe, and began to set up. Once she melted down the drug and got everything in order, she was ready to take the mystical train to cloud nine. As she filled the syringe with the smack, she felt her vagina get wet as if she were about to have sex with her dream man; however, the only thing that was about to go into her was a needle filled with heroin.

She pulled off the jacket to her jogging suit and grabbed a belt that someone had left on the table. She tied the belt around her arm and fastened it as tightly as she could. She put the end of the belt in between her teeth to keep the tension. She slowly pushed up the syringe to eject the water that was at the tip, and prepared to put it into the big green vein that had formed on her forearm. She slid the syringe into her vein and slowly ejected herself with the dope.

She instantly became relaxed, and a small smile formed on her face as her eyes closed. Drool began to creep out of the left side of her mouth as she slumped into the chair. Within seconds, she had slipped into a deep nod, and all her pain was temporarily taken away from her.

Unbeknownst to Breeze, another hustler by the name of Scoot had known about the relationship Zyir and Breeze once shared, and he immediately called his mentor to tell him that Breeze was inside of the dope house shooting up. Scoot knew that once Zyir or Mecca found out that Breeze had been served on one of The Cartel's blocks, it would be hell to pay. That's exactly why Scoot called Zyir to notify him, hoping he would be saving his own ass.

***

Zyir sped down the street with Illiana in the passenger's seat. Their lunch date was cut short by a phone call Zyir had received moments ago. "Can't believe this shit," Zyir whispered as he maneuvered through traffic, trying to get to Breeze. Illiana sat in the passenger's seat with her hands crossed over her chest tightly. She had a major attitude, and the way that Zyir cared for Breeze had her jealous.

"Just let her be," Illiana said as she rolled her eyes at Zyir. He shot a look over to Illiana that said much more than words could describe. Basically, if looks could kill, Illiana would have been dead right then and there.

Zyir pulled onto the block, turning the corner almost on two wheels. He stepped out of the car and began yelling. "Where she at?" he asked no one in particular.

Everyone pointed to the house, and Zyir quickly entered his dope house and scanned the room. What he saw in the corner broke his heart. Breeze was nodding, with a syringe stuck in her arm.

"No, Breeze . . . no," Zyir whispered as he slowly walked over to Breeze. She was so high she didn't even know that he was there. Zyir reached Breeze and dropped to his knees so he could be eye level with her. He slowly took the syringe out of her arm and forcefully threw it across the room in anger. He then grabbed Breeze by the face and lightly smacked her, trying to wake her up.

"Wake up, beautiful. It's time to go," he said as his heart ached. Seeing Breeze high was one of the worst things he could ever endure. He loved Breeze, and he refused to let her continue down the path of destruction.

"Breeze!" he called again.

"Hey, Zyir," she said in a slurred voice, barely opening her eyes. She smiled goofily because the drug had her in a total daze, and her body was completely relaxed.

"Come on, baby," he said as he picked her up and headed out the door. Zyir kissed Breeze on the forehead gently as she kept nodding uncontrollably.

"Open the door," he ordered to Illiana. She rolled her eyes and got out to do as he requested.

Zyir slid Breeze into the back seat and then closed the door. Zyir immediately pulled out his gun and made his way to the stoop where the hustlers were posted.

"Who served her?" Zyir asked with an ice-grill expression on his face. He was extremely upset, and was about to show the youngsters how The Cartel got down. "Who?" he asked again after not getting an immediate response. The hustlers on the stoop knew that Zyir meant business, so it did not take long for the finger pointing to begin. Zyir saw that everyone, including Scoot, pointed out the guy who had sold the dope to Breeze. Zyir instantly grabbed the dude by the neck and put the gun in his mouth.

"I want everybody to listen and listen close," Zyir yelled, trying to get everyone's attention. Everyone on the block looked at Zyir as he dragged the young hustler to the middle of the street. "Nobody serves Breeze. Do you fuckin' hear me? The Cartel runs this city, not y'all. You work for us!" he yelled, something that he rarely did. "If I hear about anybody giving her dope, this is what's going to happen."

Boom! A single shot rang through the air as the young hustler's brains were blown all over the pavement. His body instantly went limp and dropped. Zyir released his grip and let him fall.

The entire block was stunned. It was so quiet, you could hear a pin drop. Zyir had just shut down the whole block with a single shot. Zyir wiped the blood off of his face and looked around, giving every single hustler direct eye contact. He sent a message that would be embedded in each one of their hearts forever.

Zyir sat with Breeze twenty-four hours a day for weeks as she kicked her habit cold turkey. It was so painful for him to watch her body go through withdrawal, but he knew that it was for the best. By giving her tough love, he was saving her from herself. She had not asked to be introduced to addiction, but she was allowing it to eat her alive. He knew that she was strong enough to overcome the monkey on her back; all he had to do was convince her of that. He had never thought he would see the day that she would be so strung out, and he had to remind himself daily that she did not choose this lifestyle; it had been forced upon her.

The more time he put in with Breeze, the more irritated Illiana became. Zyir didn't have time to babysit her, however. His only focus was helping Breeze get better. He even missed out on money to be with her. Everything in his life was put on hold. Nothing mattered more than she did. This was not a battle that she could fight on her own, so he was going to walk with her and fight it for her every step of the way.

Nobody really understood the connection that he felt for her. All they saw was a black girl who had been lost to the game, but in her, Zyir saw so much more. He knew that the girl he loved was still somewhere inside of her. All he had to do was love her through her pain and help her get back to the beautiful young girl she used to be.

Breeze's body went through hell and back. Zyir saw things come out of her that no man ever wanted to see, but he never turned his back on her. There were even days when she degraded herself. She had been so used to being used and abused that she offered to trade sex for drugs with Zyir. She had no clue how her words tore his heart out of his chest. All she knew was that she wanted her fix.

Zyir attributed everything to the heroin and took it all in, absorbing the pain every day in order to help her get better. Zyir did not care for many people, but for Breeze he would go to the end of the world and back. She had captured his heart and loyalty forever. He knew that she would never be the perfect girl. She was too jaded, too scarred to revert back completely, but as long as she was able to get clean, she would be perfect for him. That's all that he could ask of her, and he was doing all in his power to ensure that she made it through.

Chapter Sixteen

***"I'm the only fucking professional out of the bunch."*
*—Robyn***

Carter sat at his dining table as he stared in disbelief at the information in front of him. After hiring a private investigator, he had found out Miamor's true profession. The truth was staring him in the face, and he finally understood why Mecca's hatred for Miamor ran so deep. A part of him wondered if what they had was even real.

He refused to believe that she was playing him just to get to The Cartel. He had gotten inside her head, he had explored the space between her legs, and had learned to control her heart. The way he had loved her was rare. He had never given himself to a woman the way he had with Miamor. To think that it was all a lie was unfathomable.

Before him were pictures of the Murder Mamas, newspaper clippings from the crimes they committed, and an address where they could be found now. Carter's P.I. had tracked them down in California. As the evidence of Miamor's ruthlessness haunted him, he felt an overwhelming urge to speak with the members of her crew who were still standing. He remembered meeting them once at the club, but had no idea how dangerous the ladies were at the time. As he found out about Miamor's life as a murderer for hire, he developed a newfound attraction to her. She was the best at what she did.

She could've trusted me with this secret, he thought.

The Murder Mamas' track record was so brutal that he knew he was lucky to be alive. Even none of his own young gunners had the body count that Miamor and her crew had attained.

If I had known, I would have put her down with The Cartel, he thought, impressed and intrigued all at the same time. Miamor had truly been one of a kind, and he did not know how much so until now.

Through all the anger and confusion he felt, the love he had for her was still present. Despite the fact that she had played a vital part in the demise of his family, the spell she had cast on him was still too potent for him to shake her loose. Her spirit was with him. He was in love with a killer—a Murder Mama.

They could have been the power couple sitting at the top if she had just been honest with him. Her hatred for his family could have been resolved, her ongoing beef with Mecca settled, if only she had told him the truth.

She was ruthless, but she had bitten off more than she could chew when she became Mecca's opposition, and as much as he wanted to, he could not blame Mecca for the decision he had made to put her down.

Carter finally understood that he was not the only one involved in a love affair with Miamor. Mecca had had his own relationship with her as well, but instead of exchanging whispers and kisses in the night, Mecca and Miamor exchanged hollow points and warfare. They had been enemies of the worst kind.

Mecca was right. Would she have killed me next? He had to know the answer, and the only way to find out was to talk to the people who had known her best.

He looked at the California address once more and hopped up. He had to see Robyn and Aries. They were the ones who could give him the answers he so desperately sought.

Carter cocked his gun to load a single bullet in his semi-automatic and removed the safety as he placed it on his hip before getting out of the car. He carefully approached the front door to Robyn and Aries' place. Their good looks concealed their malicious intent, but now that Carter knew how they got down, he would not be caught slipping. He didn't come to play games; he simply wanted answers. A conversation was all he wanted, and he hoped that they could put aside their hatred for him for the moment.

He placed his hand near his waistline as he knocked on the door. When Aries pulled it open, she gasped in surprise. A mix of emotions filled her as she pulled her baby .380 without hesitation and pointed it directly in Carter's face.

"Aries, who is it?" Robyn shouted from the kitchen.

As tears filled Aries' eyes, she couldn't move her mouth to answer.

Carter didn't flinch as he stared at Aries sincerely. "I'm not here for all that. I come in peace. I just want to talk."

Aries' lip quivered as she thought of pulling the trigger on the man that Miamor had loved. "You let she die," Aries whispered.

"Aries! Who is it?" Robyn asked as she walked up and pulled the door open fully. She stopped and stared Carter in the eyes. "Shoot him," she said.

"Me friend is dead because of you," Aries said again.

"I know. Please, I just need to know more. I know about everything, about her affiliation with the Murder Mamas, and I just really need to speak with the two of you. I have to know if anything she said to me was ever real. Was I just a target?" Carter asked.

Both Aries and Robyn could see the pain in his eyes. Aries lowered her gun and stepped to the side as Robyn relieved him of his weapon.

"Are you alone?" Robyn asked reluctantly.

"Nobody knows that I'm here," he replied.

"Come in," she said as she led him to the kitchen table, while Aries walked behind him with her gun still in her hand.

Carter took a seat across from Aries as Robyn went back into the kitchen.

She emerged with two plates of food. "We were about to eat. You might as well join us." She placed the food in front of Aries and Carter before going to fix her own.

Once they were all comfortable at the table, Aries asked, "How did you find us?"

"If your money is long enough, anybody can be found," he replied.

"Well, you didn't come all the way out here for nothing, so what do you want to know?" Robyn asked.

"Was I just another target to Miamor?" Carter asked.

"Miamor wasn't a dumb girl. She stayed in Miami to be with you, not get at you. She loved you even though we told her she was crossing the line," Robyn admitted.

"Our target was The Cartel. Mia did not know chu were a part of it until she saw you at your brother's funeral. We came to shoot up the entire front row, but she called it off when she saw chu. We tried to get she to stop seeing you, Carter, but she wouldn't," Aries revealed.

His relief could be felt around the table as he sighed deeply. He had flown three thousand miles just to hear those words.

"She's dead because of you. If she had come here with us, she would still be alive. Her death is on you. I hope you know that," Robyn stated sadly.

"I think about it every day," he admitted.

"Thinking about it don't bring she back, Carter. What are chu going to do about it?" Aries asked. "We know who did this to she. Chu didn't know before, but now you can't play dumb. Chu know everything. Something has to be done."

Carter sat back in his chair. "He's my brother," Carter whispered in turmoil.

"Well, he isn't ours," Robyn stated harshly.

"No matter what happens from this point, she isn't coming back," Carter stated, heartbroken. "I loved Miamor. I had plans to have her in my life for a long time. I just want the two of you to know that. Nothing about what I felt for her was fake." Carter stood and Robyn handed him his gun back. "Thank you for telling me what I needed to know," he said.

"Chu are welcome," Aries stated.

Robyn walked him to the door and came back to find Aries reaching for Carter's plate of food.

Out of nowhere, she slapped the fork out of her hand, sending it flying clear across the room.

"Ow, bitch! What the fuck did chu do that for?" Aries asked, looking at Robyn as if she had lost her mind.

"Okay, go ahead and eat it. You know how I get down. I don't give a fuck if the nigga came over here to pour out his love for Miamor. You know what I put in that. The nigga was just too smart for his own damn good. He didn't even touch his plate," Robyn replied with a smirk.

Aries burst out laughing as she pushed the plate away. “Thanks for the heads up.”

Robyn cracked up too and playfully answered, “With your friendly ass. I don’t know what it is about that pretty-ass nigga. All my girls turn to mush around his ass. First Mia, now you! I swear I’m the only fucking professional out of the bunch.”

Chapter Seventeen

"When the Mexicans come, they'll come with the army of an entire country behind them."
—Carter

Breeze was finally adjusting to being back home, and although weaning her body off of heroin was an everyday struggle, with the help of Zyir, she finally felt a sense of belonging again.

He was great for her in so many ways. Despite the time that had passed between them, they were able to pick up right where they left off. They were so close that it seemed as if they lived in a world by themselves. They rocked with one another and no one else. He was her best friend, and she loved him for not judging her.

She was still very rough around the edges. The glamour and prestige of the young, spoiled Breeze Diamond no longer existed. Now she was simple, timid, and trying to find her new identity as a young woman who had lived a rough life. She had seen too many bad things to go back to the naïve princess she had once been. Life had grown her up, and now Zyir was helping to stabilize her.

Most of her family was dead. The only people that she had left were her two brothers and Zyir. Those relationships meant everything to her. They were the only normalcy she knew, and everyone else was considered an outsider.

As she lay in bed, Zyir knocked on the door and peeked his head inside.

"You awake, ma?" he asked.

Breeze sat up against the headboard and smiled as she fixed her frazzled ponytail. She patted the bed beside her, motioning for him to sit next to her.

"Yeah, I'm up," she replied as he crawled into her bed. He kissed her cheek.

"You good?" he asked. "You need anything?"

Breeze shook her head and replied, "Just you, Zyir. You're so good to me. I don't know what I would do without you."

"You don't have to think about that, Breeze. You will never have to be without me. I'ma always be here for you," he whispered.

Breeze shook her head and replied, "How long do you think your little girlfriend is going to let me stick around? She don't want me here, Zyir. You say you will be here now, but when she makes you choose . . ."

"I'ma choose you," he replied. "You know me, ma. I'm not into knockoffs. I need the real thing, and now that you're back, it's a wrap for everyone else."

Breeze blushed as she lowered her chin to her chest. "Compared to Illiana I'm the knockoff. She's beautiful, Zyir. I can't compete with that . . . not anymore."

Zyir could hear the insecurity in her voice, and it bruised him deeply because no other woman could hold a candle to Breeze. She was in a league all her own. She used to know this, but her self-esteem had been beaten into the ground, and now she felt threatened.

He had already stopped sleeping with Illiana. Out of respect for Breeze, he slept on the couch, but he could see that the better Breeze's health became, the more she felt second rate to Illiana. Balancing the personalities of the two women was hard for Zyir, and although he wanted to cut Illiana off completely, he knew that he would have to do it slowly. The last thing he wanted to do was create a riff between the Garza Cartel and Carter's operation, because he had made the mistake of becoming sexual with Illiana.

"You don't have to compete, Breeze. She doesn't mean anything to me. I'm only worried about you right now," he said. "Okay?"

She nodded her head. "Okay."

"I know what you need, ma. You need to get out of the house. Is shopping still your favorite pastime?" he asked playfully.

"I haven't been in so long I might not remember how to do it," she replied with a laugh.

Zyir reached into his pocket and began to pull out a knot of cash, but he stopped himself. He didn't want to put any money in Breeze's hand. Although she had shaken off her addiction, her sobriety was important to Zyir, and he did not think she was ready to have cash in her hands.

It might be too much temptation for her, he thought.

"I'm going to arrange for a driver to take you and Illiana shopping today. I'll leave some money with her, and you can go relax. Enjoy a day out on me. The sky is the limit, so get whatever you want," he said.

Breeze nodded and closed her eyes as Zyir kissed her forehead before walking out of the room.

The limousine was silent as Illiana and Breeze were escorted to Bal Harbour's elite shopping boutiques. It was obvious that the girls did not care for one another. Their only connection was Zyir, and each felt like her position in his life was threatened as long as the other was around.

Illiana sipped on champagne as she looked Breeze up and down from behind the tint of her Chanel shades. As the limo pulled curbside, Illiana stepped out of the car and did not wait for Breeze before she strutted into the boutique. Expecting to be catered to, she was taken aback when the salespeople bypassed her to service Breeze. The Diamond family's legacy was known throughout the city, and as much as Breeze used to frequent the shops, her face had not been forgotten. The salespeople waited on her hand and foot, while Illiana shopped alone, heated.

Breeze was overwhelmed by all of the attention, but it felt good to knock Illiana off of her high horse. For the first time since her return, she was receiving the type of respect that her last name demanded, and it felt good. She could feel Illiana's envy all the way across the room. Soon Breeze was back in her element, and she found herself buying up everything in sight as she went from designer shop to designer shop. Before she knew it, the day had passed by and they were back in the limousine headed home.

Illiana was steaming, and she was determined to knock Breeze off of her high horse. She rolled down the window that separated them from the driver and said, "I need to make a detour to Sixty-third Street." She was about to take Breeze to the infamous Pork 'n Beans Projects in Liberty City. Tired of playing nice, Illiana had something sinister in store for Breeze that would be sure to banish her from Zyir's life forever.

The luxury Chrysler limousine seemed out of place in the dilapidated housing community, and the weary corner boys looked on curiously as it rolled to a stop.

"What are we doing here?" Breeze asked Illiana as she peered out of the tinted windows.

"I just need to cop a little something to take the edge off," Illiana replied devilishly as she saw a familiar spark go off inside of Breeze. "You need anything, or you good?"

Breeze shook her head as she felt the familiar tingle of anticipation fill her loins. All of a sudden, her craving came back full force. "No, I . . . I'm good," she replied.

Illiana shrugged her shoulders and got out of the car, taking only a hundred dollar bill with her. She quickly copped Breeze's drug of choice and hurried back to the limo.

"I got you a little something just in case," Illiana said as soon as she stepped back inside. She opened her hand to reveal the tiny packs of dope that she had inside. Breeze's eyes widened eagerly as she reached out her hand to grab them, but she resisted and snatched her hand back as if it were on fire.

"I can't. I promised him," Breeze said as she tried to convince herself to do the right thing.

"Who said anybody besides you and me has to know?" Illiana replied. Breeze didn't respond, but Illiana already knew that Breeze was going to indulge.

Once a junkie, always a junkie, Illiana thought. She placed the packs on the seat beside Breeze and watched in amusement as Breeze slowly but surely picked them up and tucked them inside her jean pocket.

She could not wait to get back to Zyir's place and get high. She was so anxious that she began to fidget in her seat.

Illiana had just sent Breeze spiraling back down into the abyss, hindering her recovery. There was no remorse to be felt by her, however. Life was a game of chess, not checkers, and Illiana didn't care how many queens she had to destroy in order to win.

Zyir walked into his place, exhausted from a long day of hustling. His home was unusually quiet, and an eerie feeling passed over him as he entered. It was two a.m., and he knew that Breeze and Illiana were probably asleep. He knocked on the guest bedroom door. He didn't want to disturb her, but he had to see her face before he went to bed. Ever since Breeze had been back, seeing her face had been like a blessing to him. Her smile made him smile, and he wanted to see how her day had gone before he retired for the night.

When she didn't respond, he opened the door and eased inside. Her bed was perfectly made, and he frowned when he saw her sitting on the floor in the dark with her back leaned lazily against the bed.

"B, you a'ight in here?" he asked as he stepped inside.

He turned on the light, and what he saw enraged him. Breeze was on the floor, in a deep nod, as drool ran out of the side of her lip. The belt she had used to produce a vein was still tied around her arm, and the empty packs of heroin littered the bedroom floor.

Zyir bit into his bottom lip to stop himself from screaming out loud as he rushed over to her side. "I told them niggas. I told 'em," he mumbled as he saw red. The burner on his hip was calling his name. There was no doubt that he was going to murder a nigga tonight.

"Breeze, wake up, ma. Wake up," he said as he picked up her frail body from the floor. "Breeze!" he shouted as he slapped her face gently to stir her from the nod.

He carried her wildly into the adjoining bathroom as he placed her in the bathtub and turned on the shower. The shock of the cold water woke her up.

"You promised me, ma," he said in defeat as he got on his knees to stare her in the eyes. He gripped the sides of her head tightly. He was so angry with her, so disappointed in her. "You were doing so good. Fuck was you thinking, Breeze?" he shouted.

"I'm sorry," she replied, her eyelids still low. "I can't stop."

"Who gave you this shit?" Zyir screamed like a maniac. He was so livid that he thought about striking her, but he could not bring himself to do it.

She can't help it. It's not her fault, he kept telling himself.

"Who served you?" he asked.

A slight smile spread across her lips as Breeze whispered, "Your fucking girlfriend did, okay! I was trying, but I'm not strong enough to kick this, Zyir. Illiana gave it to me. I could have said no, but I took it. I wanted it."

Before Breeze could finish her sentence, Zyir was up and out of the room with a flash. He was so out of his mind that he didn't stop to think before he burst into his bedroom. A sleeping Illiana was caught by surprise when Zyir pulled her out of his bed by her legs.

"Bitch, you gave that shit to her?" he asked. Not waiting for an answer, he smacked fire from Illiana.

"No! Zyir, she's lying!" Illiana screamed as Zyir's open hand closed and came barreling across her face. She saw stars as he attacked her relentlessly. "No! Please stop!" she hollered, but the soundproof walls intercepted all of her pleas. She had no choice but to take this ass-whooping.

Zyir went bananas on Illiana. Beating a woman was so out of his character, but he had snapped. All he could see was an addicted Breeze as he punished Illiana.

She curled up in a fetal position and tried to cover her face as Zyir loomed over her, raining punches down over her.

"You dirty bitch," Zyir raged. He straddled her and wrapped his hands around her neck as he squeezed the life out of her. Zyir didn't come back to reality until he felt someone's hands pulling him off of her. He heard Breeze sobbing by the doorway.

"Zyir!" Carter yelled as he hemmed him up. "Chill out!"

Sweating profusely and breathing erratically, Zyir was an emotional mess.

"Is she dead?" he asked as his rage subsided. He noticed that Illiana wasn't moving. "Fuck!" he yelled.

Carter kneeled over her still body to check her pulse and answered, "She's alive, but I've got to get her to a doctor. This is bad, Zyir. You know who she's connected to. Fuck was you thinking?" Carter knew that if Breeze had not called him, then Zyir probably would have killed Illiana.

"I wasn't. She gave Breeze dope and I lost it!" he whispered as he looked back at a fearful Breeze. He quickly turned his head. He couldn't even look at her right now.

"You know what this means, right?" Carter asked.

Zyir nodded. "I'm sorry, bro. I spazzed." Wearing his heart on his sleeve was so uncharacteristic for Zyir, but Breeze was his weak spot. Ever since she came home, he had been a loose cannon, acting without thinking about the repercussions.

"As long as you're prepared to deal with the consequences. This is the beginning of another war, and this time, we can't afford to lose."

"What about her? What are we going to do about her?" Zyir asked.

"I'm going to get her admitted into the hospital. When she wakes up, she'll call for her family without a doubt. We just have to be prepared, because when the Mexicans come, they'll come with the army of an entire country behind them.

Chapter Eighteen

"Don't know, but I'm ready for whatever."
—Zyir

Murder forcefully flipped down his phone after he got a disconnection message when he tried to call Mecca. He knew something was up because Mecca had gotten his number changed and hadn't called him back. Murder kept regretting the fact that he had Carter, Zyir, and Mecca in a room all together and didn't pop off.

"Damn it!" Murder yelled as he began to pace the room. He was determined to kill The Cartel. He was done playing around and trying to sneak his way in. He was about to blow heads off and play it how it went.

Murder loaded up some explosives that he had purchased from one of Aries and Robyn's weapons connect. He gently placed them in a duffel bag and prepared to take them to the warehouse that Mecca had taken him to. He knew eventually that they would meet there again, and when that time came, he was going to light that warehouse up like the Fourth of July. Murder loaded up and headed out, seeking blood.

Carter and Zyir made it to the hotel where Breeze and Mecca were staying. They were about to have a small meeting and decide on what to do about the new problem with the Garza Cartel.

Carter had switched cars, and his paranoia was at an all-time high. He knew that his team was no match for Felipe and his organization. Felipe had a whole country behind him, so no matter how many goons Carter killed, Felipe would just keep sending crews until The Cartel was completely dead.

Carter tried to call Mecca, but his phone kept going straight to voice mail. Carter noticed when he was pulling up to the hotel's entrance that the door was blocked off and an UNDER CONSTRUCTION sign was put up.

"We probably have to go through the back," Zyir said as he took a look at the blocked off door.

It was something like no other. Twenty-two bodies lay sprawled out on the block at ten o'clock in the morning. The same block where Zyir had blown off the hustler's head now looked like a battleground after combat. All of the hustlers and some of the drug users were dead at the hands of automatic assault rifles. More than five hundred shell casings were scattered over the block, and the Garza Cartel was the cause of this melee.

Felipe had declared war and sent his hoodlums to kill anything moving. Anyone who had anything to do with The Cartel was a target. It was something that Miami had never seen before, and it was only the beginning.

Illiana failed to mention to Felipe that she had slipped Breeze dope, and only told her family about the beating Zyir had put on her. Needless to say, they were infuriated. The sad part was that this was only the beginning.

Zyir and Carter pulled onto the block to witness the scene. Carter shook his head from side to side as he thought about what Zyir had gotten them into. Carter couldn't get too mad, because he knew that he would have reacted the same way if he had caught Illiana giving Breeze the dope.

"This isn't good," Carter said in a low tone as he slowly drove by the scene, not wanting to stop. Zyir looked at the bodies and saw his li'l man Scoot lying awkwardly on the pavement with blooding leaking from his body.

"Damn, the kid was only sixteen years old," Zyir said as he quickly turned his head, trying to look at the kid's lifeless eyes.

Police had begun to rope off the area, and ambulances were at the scene, but it was all for nothing, because there was no one to save. Everyone was dead.

Just as Carter reached the end of the block, they were taken by surprise. Two white vans without windows blocked Carter's car, boxing him in so he couldn't escape.

"What the fuck?" Carter said under his breath as he watched the scene unfold. He didn't realize what was going on, but he would soon find out. A third van quickly pulled up in front of Carter's car, and the sliding doors on all the vans seemed to open at the same time.

Three men jumped out of each van, all of them carrying military assault rifles. They began to riddle the car with bullets. The Garza Cartel had orchestrated a perfect hit. They knew that Carter, Zyir, or Mecca would visit the crime scene, and preyed in anticipation until they eventually showed up.

Carter quickly ducked down, and Zyir did also. The thuds of the bullets hitting the car sounded like a hailstorm, as the gunmen spared no ammunition and lit the car up in broad daylight.

Luckily, Carter was driving his bulletproof Benz, and no bullets penetrated the interior of his car.

The Miami police ducked for cover and began to call for backup on their walkie-talkies as the block underwent pandemonium. Some of the officers began to run toward the gunmen with their guns drawn, demanding them to drop their weapons. The Mexicans didn't care if they were uniformed cops. They shot at them also. In their country, there was no authority above their cartel. The Mexican gunplay was too much for the officers, and the Miami Police Department had to back down and wait for help.

After noticing that Carter's car was bulletproof, one of the gunmen said something in Spanish, and the Mexicans hopped in their vans and peeled off, leaving black tire marks on the pavement and smoking tires. Carter and Zyir grabbed their guns from under the seat and watched as the vans disappeared off the block. Both of their hearts were pounding rapidly as they escaped the deadly ambush by the skin of their teeth.

"You good?" Carter asked as he looked Zyir's body up and down to see if he was hit.

"Yeah, I'm good. You?" Zyir asked as he breathed heavily.

"Yeah," Carter responded as his phone began to ring. He looked at the caller ID and noticed that the incoming call was blocked. Carter picked up the phone and heard the operator's voice. The call was from a federal penitentiary.

"I accept," Carter spoke into the phone.

"My dear friend, I am hurt that you crossed the line . . . and for that, you will suffer," Garza said calmly and confidently. "I have no control over what happens after this point. My only advice to you is to flee as far away as you can. There is nowhere in the country where Felipe can't find you and your family. With that, I'll say good-bye," Garza said just before hanging up the phone.

Carter didn't know what to say, so he didn't say anything. He just closed his phone and shook his head from side to side.

"We have to get out of here," Carter said as he steered the bullet-riddled car off the block. The tires were flattened, but Carter wanted to leave before the cops approached them, asking questions.

Zyir and Carter were silent because they knew that they had just started a war with one of the deadliest cartels in North America.

In the meantime, Breeze was asleep in a hotel room, with Mecca present with her. Mecca was up looking out of the window with a gun in his hand. After giving him the news of the melee on their block, Carter had told him to check into a hotel downtown just to be safe. He knew that Illiana knew about their personal residences, and he didn't want to take any chances.

Mecca looked at the gun in his hand and shook his head. He didn't feel the same adrenaline rush that he once did when feeling the cold steel in his palms. Actually, it started to disgust him. Mecca was tired of selling drugs, tired of murders, and tired of The Cartel. He knew that if his family wasn't a part of The Cartel, they would all be there with him and not dead.

He looked over at his sleeping beauty, his baby sister, and wanted more for her. He refused to lose her again.

Mecca's mind ran wild as he began to think about religion, and it seemed as if every time he closed his eyes, he saw a person's face that he had once murdered. Throughout his killing career, it never bothered him to look into the eyes of a person he killed, but now, it was crashing down on him like a ton of bricks.

Since Mecca was a young boy, he'd always wanted to be a gangster—nothing more, nothing less. But now he wanted to be just a regular man, a family man. His mind was clear since he hadn't been using drugs or drinking, and he really wanted a change.

This new beef with the Mexicans was one that Mecca didn't want to see. He knew the ramifications of a war, and he wasn't willing to lose any more family over it. Mecca glanced at Breeze once again and then walked over to her and knelt beside the bed next to her. He did something that he had not done since he was a little boy. He began to pray.

Carter and Zyir entered the hotel from the back entrance, using the keycard that was provided for the guests. They stepped in and saw three Mexican men run by them with guns in their hands. Carter and Zyir quickly ducked back and out of sight as the men whizzed by them, not even noticing them.

"What the fuck?" Zyir whispered as he and Carter pulled out their guns. Carter had underestimated the Garza Cartel. He knew that they had come for blood.

"Breeze and Mecca are up there!" Carter said as he looked around the corner and saw that the three Mexicans were headed up the stairs.

"Let's use the elevator," Carter suggested as he cocked back his gun and flipped it off safety. Zyir and Carter flew to the elevator, hoping that they would reach the fifth floor before the Mexican goons did.

Carter hurriedly tapped the button in the elevator, trying to make the doors close faster, and Zyir immediately hit the camera that was in the top corner of the elevator, knowing that they were about to get into some shit. The door finally closed and they began to go up.

"Come on, come on, come on," Zyir repeated as he stared at the numbers indicating what floor they were passing. They knew that they only had a small window of time to make it to the room before the Mexicans did.

"I wonder how many are here," Carter said, believing that Felipe had sent more than three men to do the job.

"Don't know, but I'm ready for whatever," Zyir said bravely as he thought about his love, Breeze, who was in the room with Mecca.

They finally reached the fifth floor and—

"Where is the food?" Mecca asked, flicking through the channels as Breeze sat next to him in the bed.

"Just call Carter and tell him to bring us something on his way here," Breeze said, not wanting to eat the nasty hotel food anyway.

"Cool," Mecca agreed as he picked up his phone. "Damn, I don't have any service."

As soon as the words escaped his mouth, a knock on the door sounded.

"Room service," a maid announced with a heavy Spanish accent.

"Thank God! Finally some food," Breeze said as she sat upright and looked at the door.

Mecca got up and grabbed his pistol off of the bed, wanting to be cautious as he approached the door. He peeked through the peephole and was at ease when he saw that it was a maid with a platter in her hand. Mecca tucked his gun in his waistline and removed the chain lock that was on the door. He reached into his pocket and grabbed some money and opened the door.

As soon as the door opened, a Mexican man stepped into view with a sawed-off shotgun aimed directly at Mecca's chest. Before Mecca could even react, the loud sound of the shotgun rang through the air. The blast struck Mecca in his sternum, causing him to fly back viciously.

Breeze was startled by the blast, and she screamed at the top of her lungs as she saw her brother get blown off of his feet.

Breeze screamed at the top of her lungs as she tried to scramble off of the bed and run for cover. The man ran in and grabbed Breeze by the hair and flung her violently across the room. He was speaking Spanish, so Breeze couldn't understand him, but his body language and facial expression clearly stated that he hated her and wanted her dead.

He grabbed her by the throat, still speaking Spanish, and he sinisterly smirked as he put the gun to Breeze's face. Boom! A loud shot rang throughout the hotel room, and blood and guts splattered all over Breeze's face—but not blood of her own. It was the blood of the gunman.

She screamed hysterically as the man lay slumped on her with his face blown off. Mecca stood behind him with a smoking gun. He ripped open his shirt, revealing his bulletproof vest, something he never left home without.

He pushed the man off of Breeze and helped her up.

"Are you okay?" he asked as he held his chest. It was tender, sore, and felt like it had been hit with a bat swung by Barry Bonds.

"Yeah, I'm good," Breeze answered as she hugged her brother tightly.

Mecca heard commotion in the hall and knew that there were more goons coming. He thought quickly and looked toward the window for an escape route.

"Come on," he said as he pulled Breeze toward the window, knowing that his one gun couldn't go up against whatever was about to come his way. Mecca, all of a sudden, heard shots ringing out and three bodies dropped, tumbling over one another. Mecca quickly pointed his gun at the door, ready to bust at whatever came through. He breathed heavily and stood in front of Breeze, willing to be her shield.

Carter and Zyir had just dropped the three Mexicans with their accurate shots, and they made their way to the room where they knew Mecca and Breeze were.

"Mecca!" Carter yelled as he ran down the hall with his gun in a firing position.

"In here!" he heard Mecca yell from the suite.

Zyir and Carter ran to the door, but looked back and noticed about ten more Mexicans coming from the staircase. Zyir and Carter quickly dipped into the room and closed the door, knowing that they only had seconds to think of something.

"Is Breeze okay?" Zyir asked as he ran to her and she hugged him tightly while still crying hysterically. "I got you, ma," Zyir whispered in her ear as he rubbed her hair. That moment was short-lived because Zyir knew that they would be busting in at any moment.

"How many?" Mecca yelled as he pointed his gun at the door along with Carter, waiting for them to come in.

"Too many," Zyir said as he shook his head.

"He's right. We can't win," Carter said as he thought about how many goons he saw at the far end of the hall, heading their way.

"We have to jump. It's the only way to make it out alive," Zyir said as he slid the patio door open and looked down at the pool five stories below.

"Fuck we waiting for?" Mecca asked frantically while still aiming at the door.

The sounds of bullets trying to shoot the lock off erupted, and they had to make their decision quick. The old Mecca would have never thought twice about shooting it out with the Mexicans and dying in the blaze of glory, but the new Mecca wanted to live. He thought about Leena and his nephew and the fact that he hadn't gotten his redemption yet. That reason alone was enough for him to concede defeat and try to escape.

"Fuck it!" Mecca said as he hurried to the balcony and looked over. Without hesitation, he jumped feet first into the deep pool. Breeze, then Zyir, followed suit and jumped also. Carter was the last to jump. Just before Carter jumped, the door flew open and the sounds of the drums letting loose and releasing numerous bullets sounded. Bullets whizzed by Carter's head and body, forcing him to jump prematurely. He landed into the water and they barely got away.

The Garza Cartel was too much for them to handle. Ruthless would have been an understatement.

Carter and Breeze were stationed outside of the warehouse, waiting for Zyir and Mecca to return. The plan was for them to retrieve all of their owed money out of the streets and flee the state. The long arm of the Garza Cartel was too much for Carter and The Cartel. Carter made an executive decision to leave town; he chose not to fight another war. He was smart enough to know when he could not win. The Cartel was not as strong as it once was, and this was the proof. The Mexicans had pushed them into a corner, and this was the last resort.

"Is everything going to be okay?" Breeze asked her big brother in her most innocent voice. Carter could sense the fear in her tone, and he calmly looked over at her and smiled.

"I got you, Breeze. Everything is going to be all right. Tonight is the last night we ever will step foot in Miami. This drug game has tore this family apart. I'm going to make sure that I put this family back together and start a new type of legacy, one built on love and not power. I got you, baby girl," he said as he leaned over and kissed her forehead.

Breeze felt warm inside, and for a brief second, she thought she was listening to her father. Young Carter resembled him so much, and he also had a way of letting her know that everything would be okay, just as her deceased father did when he was still alive. Breeze smiled and sat back in the seat, confident in his words.

"We just have to go in here, count the money, and wait for the sun to rise so we can head out to the airport," Carter said. He felt safe at the warehouse, knowing it was a spot that the Mexicans would not think to look for them. His plans were to end The Cartel's legacy that night and leave the drug game behind.

Mecca and Zyir pulled up with three duffel bags full of money. They had collected all of their funds out of the streets, and if blocks were short, they just took what they had and called it even. They needed cold, hard cash to relocate and start over.

Carter and Breeze saw Mecca's car pull behind them, and they got out of the car to enter the warehouse. Soon, they would all be on a private jet to an unknown location. Well, at least that was their plan.

Members of the Garza Cartel were parked about a half-mile away from the warehouse, waiting for The Cartel to arrive, and just as they thought, they were there. They were waiting for them to enter so they could go in and ambush them and leave them all dead. They looked through binoculars, watching the whole scenario unfold. Little did they know, they weren't the only eyes watching The Cartel on that night.

Murder waited patiently on the side of the building watching The Cartel walk in. He smiled as he thought about what was about to happen. He held a detonator in his lap. He was about to send all of them to hell, first class. Murder was doing this for Miamor, and it made him feel good inside.

He watched closely as they all entered the building just before he pulled away. He waited until he got far enough to be clear of the upcoming explosion.

"Fuck The Cartel," he mumbled as he pushed the button and heard the loud boom of the explosives go off. He began to drive away as the debris flew into the air and a massive fireball formed fifty feet into the air. His mission was done and The Cartel was officially over.

"May they all burn in hell," he said as he chuckled to himself, disappearing into the night.

The Last Chapter

"She probably is in hell, smoking a blunt. That's a real bitch."
—Unknown

"We are gathered here today to celebrate the lives of three of God's children."

The preacher stood before the many people who attended the funeral of street royalty. It was a sad day in Miami, and on this day, the streets were like a ghost town. It seemed as if the entire underworld had stopped to commemorate those they had lost. Everyone within the city limits felt this grief. The lives of three street legends had been destroyed, and grief overflowed in the ceremony as three silver-plated coffins sat side by side with an array of flower arrangements around them. It was a bright, sunny day, and it seemed as if God shone his light down from the heavens above to make that hard day seem a tad bit better for the mourning attendees. It was a triple funeral to bury the last of the Diamond family—Breeze, Carter, and Mecca.

The Cartel was no more, and it was the last chapter to what was to be named one of the biggest legacies in Miami's underworld history. Their story was legendary, ruthless . . . and most of all, classic.

Many people were in attendance, but the most important guests were not there to pay their final respects, but to confirm that the last of The Cartel was deceased and about to be buried into the ground.

Robin and Aries were in attendance, draped in all black dresses with big shades on to keep a low profile. Murder also sat beside them. The demise of The Cartel was bittersweet for him, and he gritted his teeth tightly as he thought about

Mecca and the missed opportunity to personally kill him on Miamor's behalf. Nevertheless, Mecca was dead, and that would have to be enough for him.

Emilio Estes, Leena, and Monroe Jr. were also in attendance, mourning the loss. They were the only people left alive who could sit in the front pew reserved for family. Although far removed from the Diamond legacy, they were the last of a dying bloodline.

There was an eerie feeling in the air and everyone there could sense it. As the preacher held the Holy Bible tightly in his hand and read from the book of Psalms, a stretch limo with tinted windows rolled up slowly about fifty yards away from the service. Many people didn't notice it, but the trained eyes were glued to the approaching vehicle.

Emilio Estes looked back and saw the limo pull up, and he watched as it came to a slow stop. Estes knew exactly who it was; it was the crew responsible for the very funeral he was at. Emilio, being in his mid-sixties and not willing to step back into the streets, conceded defeat and pulled his white handkerchief from the top pocket of his suit.

To many, it looked as if Emilio was just removing a hanky, but veterans of the street game knew what that small gesture meant. Emilio wanted the bloodshed to stop, and signaled that he would not retaliate. The war was finally over and The Cartel was no more. Literally, he was waving a white flag. It was officially The Cartel's last chapter.

Breeze, Zyir, Mecca, and Carter were behind the tint of the stretch limo, watching their own funeral service. They had faked their own deaths, knowing that the Garza Cartel was too much for them. Carter knew that his suspicions about Murder were correct, and he had one of his goons trail Murder. He eventually found out that Murder had placed bombs at the warehouse. Carter then used that to his advantage. It was a risky plan, but it worked. As far as the Mexican beef, it was a war that they could never win so they outsmarted their enemy, rather than outshooting them. Carter came up with the plan to fake their deaths, and it worked like a charm.

Carter knew that the Garza Cartel would be watching them when they went to the warehouse, so he orchestrated a plan to sneak out of the back just before he blew the place up. He paid a coroner for four dead bodies that matched closely to himself, Zyir, Mecca, and Breeze, and placed them at the scene to be found by the authorities.

His plan had worked perfectly. They all sat in the limo with champagne glasses, celebrating their victory.

"This is to new beginnings. The Cartel is no more," Breeze said as she raised her glass. Everyone joined her as she began her toast. With the support of her family, she was doing so much better. She had vowed to never touch another drug in her life, and so far, she was beating her addiction. She was more than ready to leave everything behind.

"To The Car—" Mecca started. He forgot that The Cartel was news of the past. "My fault. That gangster shit still in me," he said while smiling. "To family," he said as he raised his glass a tad bit higher.

"To family," everyone said in unison, repeating what Mecca had just said. Another limo pulled up behind them, and they all knew that it was Felipe and his people. They had come to confirm their deaths.

Carter laughed and signaled for the driver to pull off. They had to catch a flight to Brazil. The Cartel was officially dead to the world.

2 Weeks Later in Brazil

Zyir looked at Breeze as she approached him with a flowing white dress and a veil over her face. Breeze had never looked more beautiful to him than she did on that very day.

Mecca walked on her right side, where their father should have been, and he gripped her hand for support. It was her wedding day, a day that their mother and father had looked forward to since Breeze was a young girl. Although they could not be present, Mecca felt their spirits in the air.

"They're looking down on you today, Breeze. They're here," Mecca whispered.

Breeze knew that he was speaking of their parents, and smiled as her eyes lifted to the sky to acknowledge them.

Carter was next to Zyir, acting as his best man for the ceremony. The only witness present outside of The Cartel family was the Catholic priest of the church they used.

Zyir smiled from ear to ear as he patiently waited to be joined by his bride. As they approached, Zyir looked at Breeze and promised himself that he would take care of her forever and a day. She made him happy, and he was determined to return that favor for a lifetime.

Zyir asked Breeze to marry him while they were on the jet coming to Brazil, and she graciously accepted. It didn't take long for them to start planning for the small ceremony and make it happen.

Breeze approached Zyir ,and they stood face to face, looking into each other's eyes.

Breeze was full of tears because not only was she overwhelmed with happiness, but also great sadness. She wanted to share this special day with her family, but she only had a few people left. This day had brought about mixed emotions for her. She had never missed her parents and Monroe more than she had today, but the man who stood before her gave her strength. In his eyes, she saw her future, and it was filled with love. Her newfound joy with Zyir allowed her to push the sadness out of her mind, and she smiled from ear to ear.

The priest began the ceremony, and it was nothing but love in the room. They were a match made in heaven.

“I now pronounce you man and wife. You may kiss the bride,” the priest said as he smiled and nodded his head at Zyir.

Zyir then slowly raised the veil that covered Breeze’s face and exposed her magnificence. He put both of his hands under her chin and kissed her.

Carter and Mecca clapped as Zyir kissed his wife. They both turned toward the door and started to walk down the aisle, but before Zyir took two steps, he turned back to Carter and whispered something that was one of the hardest things he ever had to ask him.

“Do you want me to take care of it?” Zyir asked.

Carter watched as Breeze hugged Mecca and looked at Zyir. “Nah, I got it. Enjoy your wedding day. I will see you when you get back,” he said calmly and smoothly, all with a small smile on his face. “I love you, Zy, Carter said to his protégé that was now a man.

“I love you too, big homie,” Zyir replied.

Breeze approached Mecca as he held his arms out. He had tears in his eyes. Crying was something Breeze never saw Mecca do.

The tears in Mecca’s eyes were ones of joy rather than pain. It felt good to see his sister smiling for a change. He saw that Zyir made her happy, and that was what was important to him.

He glanced at Zyir, who was talking to Carter, and smirked, knowing that Zyir would take good care of his sister. Mecca then focused back on the approaching Breeze.

"I love you, sis," Mecca said as she slid into his arms and into his warm embrace. Mecca was so happy to see his sister in the pretty white dress, and he knew that his mother and father would have been proud of her if they were still alive.

Their family had been through war and rain, but now it was time for sunshine. He was her only remaining full-blooded relative, and he knew that he symbolized more than himself. He was there on the behalf of Monroe, Taryn, and their father, Big Carter.

"I love you too, Mecca," Breeze said as she rested her head on his chest and hugged him tightly. Her eyes were closed, but a tear managed to slip down her cheek. She enjoyed that moment like it would be her last. The drama and turmoil that she had been through over the years with the ills of the drug game and the family business had her jaded.

She thought about being in the basement of Ma'tee's home and being hopeless and ready to die. She thought she would never escape his grasp, but to be married and starting a new chapter in her life brought joy to her heart.

Mecca wanted to confess to his sister and tell her all of the wrong he had done, just as he had done with the priest, but he could not bring himself to let Breeze know that he had betrayed the family in such a heinous way. How was he supposed to tell her that he had murdered his own twin brother and reignited the beef with the Haitians? All of Mecca's betrayals eventually led to the death of Taryn and Breeze's own kidnapping. How could he tell her this? He couldn't, because he feared that she would never forgive him, and he needed his sister to look at him with admiration as she had always done.

He needed her love like he needed the air in his lungs, so as he stood before her, the only words he could let slip out of his quivering lips were, "Sorry. I'm so sorry." He gently grabbed her shoulders and looked into her beautiful eyes. He saw his father's features in Breeze, and also their mother's, and it tore Mecca's insides apart.

Breeze looked into Mecca's eyes and felt his pain through the windows to his soul. She didn't understand fully what Mecca was sorry for, but something told her not to ask. Breeze just smiled and nodded her head.

"It's okay, Mecca. I forgive you," she whispered as she wiped the single tear that streamed down his clenched jawbone. She didn't know what she was forgiving Mecca for, but she understood that he needed to experience forgiveness. She felt obligated to let him know that whatever he had done, it was in the past.

Zyir finished his brief conversation with Carter and headed over to Mecca and Breeze. He approached Mecca as Breeze stepped back and gave them room to converse.

"Congratulations," Mecca whispered as he looked at his comrade, Zyir.

"Thanks, fam," Zyir said with a smirk on his face. He embraced Mecca and hugged him tightly as he cherished the moment. He knew Mecca was a gangster, and real always recognized real. Needless to say, Zyir respected Mecca and vice versa.

Mecca noticed that Zyir hugged him tightly, and Mecca felt the genuine love coming from his new brother-in-law. The moment was almost enough to make Mecca cry again, but he held his composure and respected the authenticity of Zyir.

Zyir hugged Mecca like it would be the last time he would see him. "I love you bro," Zyir said as he released his embrace.

"I love you too. Take care of my sister, a'ight," Mecca said as he winked at Breeze.

"I got you," Zyir said as he held out his arm for Breeze to latch on. Breeze did so, and they strolled down the aisle and out of the doors, where a cocaine white limo was waiting for them at the foot of the steps. The newlyweds were off to board a private jet to Rome for a weeklong honeymoon.

Carter and Mecca watched as they disappeared behind the large double doors of the sanctuary, both of them with smiles on their faces. Mecca looked to Carter and rested his hand on Carter's shoulder.

"That's our baby sister right there. I'm glad to see her happy," Mecca said with deep sincerity.

"Yeah, Zyir's a good dude. I raised that kid. I know that he's one hundred percent . . . no cut. He is going to take care of his family no matter what," Carter stated with a blank expression on his face.

Carter's words were like a dagger straight to Mecca's heart, as Mecca thought about his ultimate betrayal of his own family. He knew at that very moment that he wasn't cut from the same cloth as Zyir or Carter. It was the hurtful truth that he would have to live with for the rest of his life.

"We all we got," Mecca said as he looked into Carter's eyes.

Carter noticed that Mecca's eyes didn't reflect that of a killer's. Mecca looked as vulnerable as a lost young boy, and his words were heartfelt and without prejudice. Mecca truly meant what he had just said. He had made the transformation. Mecca was ready to leave the gangster life alone and live life without regrets. He hoped that the new country of Brazil could give him peace of mind and rinse him of the blood that seemed to stain his hands back in Miami.

The priest walked up to them and prepared to exit the church. He shook Mecca's hand and then Carter's.

"Thank you, Father," Carter said as he gripped the priest's hand. The priest exited the church, leaving Mecca and Carter alone.

Mecca put both of his hands in his pockets and turned on his heels.

"Excuse me for a second, bro. I have to make a quick phone call," Mecca said.

Carter nodded his head and watched as Mecca faded into the back of the church where the dressing room was located. Carter thought back to the day that he was in the confessional booth and Mecca told on himself. He thought about how Mecca had killed the only love of his life, Miamor. He also thought about how Mecca cold-bloodedly killed Monroe.

Carter shook his head, not believing the disloyal acts of his only remaining brother. Images of Miamor smiling and in his arms popped into his thoughts, instantly making Carter chuckle while remembering the bond that they once had shared. He remembered how gangster she was, yet she was so soft, so ladylike. Miamor was built for a gangster like him, and Mecca had taken that away from him.

"I love you, Miamor," Carter whispered as he looked to the head of the church and stared at the cross with a statue of Jesus Christ hanging on it. He hoped Miamor heard him from the depths of the heavens. Little did he know, with Miamor's resume, she was probably in hell smoking a blunt. That's a real bitch.

Mecca held his cell phone up to his ear, waiting for the person he was calling to answer.

"I'm on my way to the airport now," Leena said as she smiled and made her way through the airport with her son by her side. She wore oversized sunglasses and a wrap over her head to try to disguise herself from any of Estes' goons. Her son had on a baseball cap and heavy clothing, making him chunkier than usual. She was in a rush, trying to get to Mecca, the man she loved, the man who had once almost taken her life. She had snuck away from Estes and was on her way to Brazil to raise her son with Mecca.

Mecca smiled when he heard her voice, and the thought of sharing a life with Leena was inspirational. "Hurry up and get to me, baby," Mecca said, filled with joy.

"I can't wait to see you," Leena said as she gave the flight attendant her boarding passes.

"I can't wait to see you either, beautiful. I am going to make this right, and we are going to be a family. I am going to raise that boy like he is mine and teach him how to be a man . . . a good man. Just like his father was," Mecca said, meaning every word of what he was saying.

"I know you are, Mecca. I know. We are on our way. Mecca Diamond, I love you," Leena said as she boarded the plane.

"I love you more," Mecca said just before he flipped down his cell phone and smiled. "Thank you, Lord," Mecca whispered. He was beginning to believe that there was a God. He was determined to get a better relationship with his Savior and live his life right. He couldn't wait until the rest of his family arrived in Brazil so that his new life could begin. Nevertheless, he would never get to see them.

Mecca heard the sound of a gun being cocked behind him, but he didn't seem startled or even turn around, for that matter. He just took a deep breath and placed his hands together in a praying gesture.

"Our Father, which art in heaven, hallowed be thy name . . ." Mecca said as tears slid down his face. He already knew who was behind him, and it came as no surprise to him.

Carter began to recite the prayer along with his brother as he pointed the gun to the back of Mecca's head.

Mecca had always known that Carter would eventually seek revenge for Miamor's death. He had loved her way too much not to come after him. Mecca's only dilemma had been to figure out when and where Carter would take his life. Mecca was a seasoned street veteran, and the one thing that he knew for sure was that "the eyes don't lie" and on that day, Carter could not hide the hatred he had inside.

Carter knew that if he let Mecca live, Mecca would possibly turn on him one day, just as he did to Monroe. He also felt obligated to avenge Miamor's death, so killing Mecca was inevitable.

Mecca also knew the game. Mecca realized that if he were in Carter's shoes, he would have done the same, so he wasn't mad at Carter for what he was about to do. Once the prayer was over, Mecca stood unflinchingly, with his heart pounding through his chest. There was no malice in his heart, only regret, but he knew that his oldest brother was about to deliver his retribution.

"I love you, Carter," Mecca said as he straightened up his tie and prepared for his death.

"I love you too," Carter replied sincerely as he wrapped his finger around the trigger. "I always will, bro."

Boom!

A single slug went through the back of Mecca's head and clear through his forehead, rocking him to sleep forever at the hands of his own flesh and blood. Karma is real, and The Cartel was no more.

Epilogue

"Diamonds are forever."
—Carter Diamond

Leena covered her ears and took deep breaths as the plane flew through the turbulent skies. She hated to fly, but she hated being apart from Mecca even more. She knew that Estes would be hurt when he read the letter she had written. A single note was all that she had left behind. She knew that he would never understand why she had chosen Mecca over him, but it was something that she had to do. It was a decision that only she would understand.

Her heart jumped out of her chest as the plane dipped violently, almost as if it would fall from the sky. She snuggled her son tightly to her chest and whispered, "Please, God, keep this thing in the air."

The captain turned the seatbelt sign on, only scaring Leena even more. She instinctively reached out to grip the arm of the gentleman sitting next to her.

"Oh, I'm sorry. This flying thing has me kind of shook," she explained in embarrassment.

"It's okay. You're good. The turbulence is really only potholes in the sky. They won't do any real damage. They're just good at causing uneasy passengers a nice scare," he said.

Leena nodded and inhaled deeply to calm her nerves.

"Besides, if you ever want to know if something is wrong, all you got to do is look at the flight attendants. When they panic, you panic, but until then you're good," he said.

Leena snuck a glance at the stewardess and noticed that she was calm as ever and joking with one of her colleagues. Leena smiled and shook her head in amazement. "Thanks. That actually just gave me peace of mind," she said to the guy beside her.

"No problem. Let me know if you need my arm again, though. I'll be happy to lend it to you," he replied with a smirk and the wink of an eye.

"I'm Leena," she introduced.

"Murder," he replied.

"Wow, that's quite a name," she stated.

Murder smiled, but he didn't reply as he glanced at her sleeping son. The young boy looked like a tiny replica of the very man he wanted to kill. He was definitely a member of the Diamond lineage, a bloodline that Murder planned on destroying.

The funeral service may have been convincing to everyone else, but in the back of Murder's mind, he had known that it was all for show. It was no coincidence that he was on the same plane as Leena. He knew that if he followed her, sooner or later she would lead him to The Cartel, and as he sat next to her his trigger finger began to itch.

"What brings you all the way to Brazil?" Leena asked.

"I have a score to settle with an old friend. Unfinished business."

Breeze boarded the private jet with Zyir behind her. He tapped her lightly on her backside, and she giggled like a schoolgirl as she swatted his hand away.

"I don't know what you acting shy for. I'm about to induct you into this mile high club," he said jokingly. He was completely at ease for the first time in years. There was no business to tend to, no reason to watch his back every second, and no street code to uphold. It was just him and Breeze. Nothing had ever felt so right, and happiness surged through him as he sat next to his wife.

"You're so silly," Breeze said as she leaned into his shoulder and rested her forehead against his. "I can't believe we did it. I can't believe I'm married."

"Do I make you happy?" he asked as he gripped her chin gently.

She nodded. "You know you do," she replied as their tongues met. Finally they were together, and all of the horrible things that had kept them apart for so long no longer mattered. They were soul mates and had weathered the storms that life had thrown their way. Now it was time for their new lives to begin.

"I'm going to go get a few blankets from the flight attendant before we take off," Breeze said. She stood, still dressed in her beautiful white dress, and walked past Zyir.

"Yo, B?" he called after her.

She turned around and was so radiant that his breath caught in his chest. "I love you."

"I know you do, Zyir. You know everything there is to know about me and you still love me. That's why I love you so much," she said. She blew him a quick kiss before walking to the front of the plane.

Zyir closed his eyes in relaxation, but it was soon interrupted when he heard Breeze's blood curdling scream. He jumped from his seat and ran to the front just as Breeze came staggering back down the aisle. A knife was imbedded deeply inside her chest, causing her white dress to slowly turn bloody red as the wound in her chest bled out. Her eyes were open wide in bewilderment, and her hand reached out to Zyir.

"Breeze!" he cried. "No, ma. Not now. Not like this."

She opened her mouth to speak, but choked on her own blood as she fell into his arms.

"Help me! Somebody please!" Zyir gripped the knife and tried to pull it from Breeze's body, but the more he tugged on it, the more blood seeped out.

"No, ma. No. You've got to live," he whispered.

Breeze's eyes spoke to him, telling him all the things that she could not physically say.

"I love you too, ma . . . forever, baby girl," he said to her. "Don't die on me, Breeze. I'ma get you some help." He was too heartbroken to even worry about who had harmed her. He just wanted to get her help and keep the love of his life alive.

He picked her up, scooping her into his arms as she struggled to hold on, but it was no use. His wife died in his arms before he could even step off of the plane. He buried his head in her long hair as he let out a scream of agony.

It wasn't until he heard footsteps in front of him that he looked up.

"Hello, Zyir," Illiana stated with a devious leer as she pointed a gun directly at him.

He instantly regretted leaving his pistol behind. While reveling in his newfound love with Breeze, he had gotten too comfortable, and that mistake had cost him dearly.

As she pulled back the hammer of the pistol and wrapped her finger around the trigger, he didn't even look at her. He focused his attention back on Breeze and hugged her dead body tightly. They had been so close to escaping it all. They had almost had their happy ending, but almost doesn't count. Zyir closed his eyes as he waited for the inevitable shot that would end his life.

Carter Diamond, the man who had started it all, sat at the head of the rectangular dining table and smiled as he looked around at his children. His beautiful wife, Taryn, sat directly across from him at the other end. Finally, they were all together again. Heaven had opened its gates for the entire Diamond family, and they all sat amongst a feast fit for kings as they enjoyed this fateful reunion.

Monroe hugged Mecca tightly in forgiveness, as Taryn looked in amazement at Breeze in her beautiful wedding dress. All the while, Carter Diamond presided over them all. He was as distinguished in the afterlife as he had been on Earth, and his heart swelled at the sight of his family. They had been reunited at last. Death had come for them all, and only had one last member to claim.

Young Carter's seat was the only one that sat empty, and although Carter Diamond was proud of his oldest son for surviving in a game where so many had fallen, a part of him still wished that he could be there at this moment. He belonged with his family.

Taryn walked over to her husband's side and kissed his cheek. "He'll be here soon enough," Taryn whispered in his ear. "Let him live his life, and when it is his time, he will fill that seat and our family will be complete."

Carter Diamond nodded and kissed his wife's cheek as he raised his pure gold wine goblet. "To my beautiful wife, twin sons, my dearest Breeze, and to my son who isn't among us just yet. I love you all," he toasted.

They all raised their glasses and drank together as they watched over Young Carter. Through him, the legacy of The Cartel lived on, and it would not end until he had joined them in heaven, where Diamonds lived forever . . .

To the dedicated readers, we love you all.

Thanks for helping us make history.
—*New York Times* bestselling authors,
Ashley & JaQuavis